TRANSCENDENT LOYALTIES

A NOVEL OF THE AMERICAN REVOLUTION

S. D. BANKS

This book is a work of fiction. The characters, incidents, and dialogues are products of the author's imagination and are not to be construed as real. Any resemblance to actual events or persons, living or dead, is entirely coincidental.

Library of Congress Control Number: 2016910963
CreateSpace Independent Publishing Platform, North Charleston, SC

To my husband
Lee

And

In memory of our son
Travis

TRANSCENDENT LOYALTIES

CONTENTS

PROLOGUE

The handful of years prior to 1770 had been plagued with unrest among American colonial factions who felt abused by the king's many new trade and taxation policies. For many Bostonians, that discontent reached a watershed moment on the evening of March 5, 1770.

The city, simmering with irritation for weeks now over its occupation by British Regulars, had been particularly unsettled most of that day. In and of itself, the fact that troops were there to police Boston's citizens was inflammatory. But soldiers looking to supplement their meager army pay were competing for local jobs and, given that the soldiers had another source of income, they were willing to work for lower wages. The uneven competition for jobs only served to add fuel to the smoldering disgruntlement. Townsfolk murmured in small groups on street corners and in shops, the talk in taverns grew brazen and full of bold threats, and every slight or insult was cause for exaggerated reaction from both sides.

Earlier in the day, an altercation between one of the Regulars and a local boy over some small insult had fomented a spike in the building tension. Tightly knotted gangs began to roam the streets, shouting angry protests against the presence of the troops and against the king's policies in general. For the most part, the small clusters of protesters tended to dissipate of their own accord. Encouraged by a handful of loud, opinionated men, others would quickly fill the void, however. In time, some of the gangs melded into larger mobs that took on lives and energy of their own. Anticipating an eruption of violence, many merchants shuttered their shops early, and cautious citizens retreated to the safety of home.

But not all.

1770

CHAPTER ONE

Stealing through her uncle's back gate into the dark, narrow alley, Anna shifted her shoulders in a feeble attempt to improve the fit of the ragged clothes that were her disguise. At age thirteen, her ability to pass herself off as a boy should have been an annoyance. In Anna's mind, however, such things were of little importance.

She shivered. Boston was a mere five days into March, with spring seeming a distant prospect and, though a good disguise, her grubby, ill-used coat and breeches were no match for the biting cold. The frigid night air was pungent with the smoke that rose from the city's many chimneys where it languished, doggedly hovering above the rooftops to conjure images of the warm hearth waiting back in her bedroom. More than once she considered abandoning her quest to return home to clean clothes and a warm bed. The lure of adventure and pull of curiosity won out, however, exhorting her forward through snow already well-trampled by a multitude of footprints. The mobs were out in force, it seemed.

The hour was well after nine-o'clock when Anna scurried down the hill from her uncle's prosperous neighborhood. She slowed as she skirted the Common and turned east onto Tremont Street. Its darkness punctuated by guttering light from oil lamps placed at the occasional gatepost, the street was deserted now, a marked contrast to how it had been only minutes before. A palpable sense of tension hung in the air, and she heard troubled voices raised in anger somewhere in the distance. The sound of conflict, unmistakable in its timbre, echoed through the otherwise quiet streets and alleys, bouncing off cold brick walls and muffled by snow drifts in such a way that made its point of origin unclear.

Anna's breath quickened and heart raced as she brashly continued on her course, wary of every shadow, alert to every sound. So cold was her nose that she was forced to breathe through her mouth, and she could see puffs of steam in front of her face each time she exhaled. She turned onto King Street and found herself closer to the shouts and commotion. It seemed likely that the trail would take her to the Custom House. The regimental pay chests were housed there, and she'd heard whispered fears that the dissidents had designs upon the place. Her steps faltered momentarily. What would she do if she arrived to find a mob plundering the Custom House?

A great clamor of rattling muskets, boots pounding out a quick march on the ground, and shouted commands rumbled up the street behind her.

She ducked into the shadows just in time to allow a file of red-coated troops hurry past. Wishing she could become invisible, she pulled her battered hat lower on her head and sank as far as she could manage into the feeble concealment of the shadow. She counted seven British Regulars hurrying past without so much as a glance in her direction, and flinched when the eighth man, their more alert commander, caught sight of her. He jerked his head back in the direction from which they had come in a gesture meant to send her away.

"Move along there, lad," he ordered. "There's trouble brewing here that you've no need to be part of."

She nodded, but did not look up, afraid of revealing her identity. The man's face was a familiar one, for Captain Thomas Preston was well known in Boston. She hung back for a few seconds before, in careless disregard of the captain's order, ducking into an alley she knew would take her more directly toward King Street than the route the Regulars followed. Keeping to the shadows, she scuttled along, her heartbeat pounding in her ears, the cold now all but forgotten. Whatever was happening, to have drawn the troops from their billets, it had to hold excitement.

Suddenly, the bells of a nearby church erupted into the alarm for fire, startling her. Summoned by the alarm, people began to stream into the street and she found herself swept up into a prodigious, roiling crowd. The crowd poured into King Street, whereupon they became part of an even larger mob, tense, and milling uncertainly, all of their venomous energy focused on the lone sentry standing guard in front of the Custom House.

The mob screamed at the sentry, yelling taunts and insults, hurling snowballs, and pressing ever closer to the solitary young man. He pointed his bayonet-spiked musket at his tormentors with all the assuredness drilled into him during his time in the king's army, but his eyes revealed an inexperienced youth on the verge of panic. And not without reason, Anna thought, for the mood of the crowd was ugly and apparently bent on harm.

"Fire, damn you, fire!" someone yelled. "Bloody lobster-back. You dare not fire!"

"He cannot fire," a man near her said to no one in particular. "Not without orders, and such orders won't come." He was sneering, sure of the peculiar vulnerability of the young soldier. "Damned musket isn't even loaded."

To Anna, whether or not the musket could fire seemed rather irrelevant in the face of the lethal bayonet fixed to its barrel. Making her way through the crowd, she heard snatches of comments here and there offered as explanation for the outraged assemblage.

"Bastard bloodied young Garrick," one man told another. He jerked his head in the direction of the sentry. "Took offense over some harmless jest and hit the poor lad on the side of the head with the butt of his musket, he did. Just like that! Hurt 'im bad." The outraged man spat in the snow to emphasize his point, barely missing Anna. "Ah! Sorry," he said, genially slapping her on the back. "Didn't see you there, lad."

Anna pulled her hat down and moved on, listening. "Knocked a boy down and beat him something terrible," she heard another man say. "Just like all these Regulars; thinks he can abuse us because he wears the king's uniform!" The last words were said more loudly, and were obliquely directed at the young sentry. "Bloody lobster-back coward!" the angry man called. "Afraid now? Afraid now that you be facing grown men instead of helpless boys?"

Anna had no doubt that the sentry was afraid. Her uncle had told her more than once that fear often made a man dangerous, and so she began to retreat, edging her way toward the back of a crowd that had grown noticeably thicker in the passage of only a few minutes. Townsfolk who had arrived full of tension at the expectation that they would be fighting a fire swelled the ranks of the crowd until, Anna guessed, there had to be at least four-hundred overly-agitated people assembled in the street. Though tense, most of them seemed peaceful. A handful was not, however, and that handful was determined to drive events. More snowballs and chunks of ice flew toward the young sentry who was clearly struggling not to flinch, not to give in to his fear.

Finally, the sentry's reinforcements arrived and overwhelming relief suffused his face. Six privates, led by a corporal and followed closely by Captain Preston, filed decisively through the crowd. Momentarily quieted by the arrival of the troops, the crowd gaped as the Regulars formed a defensive line in front of the Custom House. The soldiers' movements were precise and practiced, a machine-like reflection of their hours of drill. At a sharp command from their corporal, the Regulars loaded their muskets with two lead balls each. Then, at another command, the muskets were leveled at the crowd, which collectively took one cautious step back. Captain Preston took up position with his men, quietly speaking words designed to calm them, steady them, help them hold to their discipline.

The heartbeat of silence was broken by the advance of a huge mulatto man. Anna had seen him about and knew his name was Crispus Attucks, but that was all she knew about the man. Brandishing a club, Attucks took a step toward the Regulars, daring them to fire at him. "Come on you rascals, you bloody scoundrels, you lobster-backs!"

Others followed his lead, waving clubs and even a cutlass or two. "Fire if you dare. We know you dare not!" More snowballs sailed through the air, along with chunks of ice and rocks. Wide-eyed, Anna took another step backward. Her sensible inner voice urged her away, but she could not quite compel herself to leave, for the scene unfolding before her was too enthralling, too incredible to abandon. A wave of unease rippled through the mob but, perhaps for the same reason that Anna remained rooted in place, few heeded the sense of danger.

A group of merchant seamen arrived. Full of loud exhortations, they pummeled the Regulars with sharp-edged oyster shells and threatened them with firewood brandished like clubs. "Kill them! Knock them down!" the rowdy, ill-humored seamen urged.

"Fire!" someone on the far side of the crowd shouted.

"No!" another man called. Anna recognized the rumbling voice of Henry Knox. His bookshop was a favorite of hers, and knowing that the level-headed merchant was present calmed her. "Captain Preston," Knox begged, "you must not give the order to fire! I implore you!" He turned to urge the crowd to disperse but was forestalled by yet more shouts of "fire!" erupting here and there across the crowd.

Anna watched Captain Preston. He stood firm, as did his men, impassive in the face of the onslaught. There was no suggestion of any intent to order his men to fire. Instead, his lips were pressed into a tight, thin line of determination.

"Fire, damn you! Fire if you dare!" The taunt was repeated over and again. "Fire!"

Someone — and, not surprisingly, no one could later say who exactly had done it — clubbed one of the Regulars on the head, knocking him to the ground. Bleeding from the scalp wound, the infuriated young private regained his feet just as someone was shouting "fire." The private fired his musket directly at Attucks.

The single shot triggered an entire volley that slashed the night with fire and a thunderous roar, and engulfed the scene in a pall of smoke.

"Cease fire!" Captain Preston ordered, "Stop firing!" But his voice was drowned by the musket fire. "Cease fire!" he demanded again as his troops began to reload. He stepped forward, bellowing the order again and again. The Regulars finished reloading their muskets and brought them up to firing position but did not fire. Preston had finally made himself heard.

A blanket of smoke enveloped all but the farthest reaches of the crowd, and the overpowering, sulphurous stench of spent gunpowder fouled the air. Like most of the spectators, Anna stood frozen in place, momentarily stunned by what had happened. A few seconds, then a few more, and the smoke began to waft away, unveiling a scene horrible beyond Anna's imagination. Eleven men, Attucks among them, were sprawled on the snow in dark, spreading pools of their own blood. Some were moving, writhing in agony. At least four men were lying in the motionless, unnatural awkwardness of violent death. Paralyzed by shock, Anna gaped at them, unable to move to offer aid to the fallen, nor to turn and flee.

It all seemed to happen with eerie, uncanny slowness, and yet she knew only a few moments had passed since that first musket shot had shattered the night. Cries and screams began to penetrate Anna's consciousness, and she was buffeted by people suddenly frantic to be away from the scene. The confused, retreating mob flowed past, making her feel disoriented and filling her with a rising sense of panic. Seemingly from nowhere, a child appeared before her, crying and alone, and at risk of being trampled. Anna scooped the toddler up and out of harm's way, only to have her immediately snatched away again by a woman who was apparently the child's mother.

As the woman seized the child from Anna's arms, Anna stumbled and fell. In vain, she tried time and again to get to her feet. Too small to be noticed by men in panicked flight, she was repeatedly knocked back to the ground where she was in certain danger of being kicked and trodden upon by the frenzied mob. After several more futile attempts to get to her feet, she curled her small body into a ball and covered her head with her arms, hoping to ride out the crushing wave.

She wailed with pain when a boot struck her hard on the back and again when someone stepped brutally upon her ankle. Then, with a suddenness that robbed her of breath, a hand reached down and grabbed a fistful of her jacket, wrenching her to her feet. "Come along," a male voice ordered, and she was dragged toward the safer fringes of the fleeing crowd.

With the tall, strong man pulling her along, they were able to get clear of the crowd. But, even when they'd reached relative safety, he did not stop or release her. Alarmed, she tried with steadily increasing determination to resist his pull until, all else having failed, she simply picked up her feet. The unexpectedness of the action and the sudden shift of her weight toppled them both to the ground. Quickly, Anna scrambled up and managed one step toward freedom before the man's iron grip caught at her ankle. With an angry cry, she swung her free leg around and kicked him in the groin with as much force as she could manage. The man groaned and doubled up, but did not release her. She was prepared to repeat the blow when a familiar, albeit pain-tinged voice halted her.

"Hello to you, too, Mouse."

Anna froze in place, and then bent to look at the man's face. "Daniel?" Though contorted with pain, the lean face with its halo of black hair was startling in its unexpected familiarity.

"Is that the way you thank a friend for saving your troublesome little hide?" he asked through gritted teeth.

"*Daniel?*" she repeated, her tone more an accusation than a question.

"Yes." His voice was strained as he labored to his feet. He wiped his hands together to remove the ice and grit. "You little brat. Why did you kick me?"

"How was I supposed to know it was you?" she demanded, angrily planting her hands on her hips. "Why didn't you let go of me? What in heaven's name are you doing here, anyway? Oh, wait." She folded her arms across her small chest and narrowed her eyes. "There was trouble. Of *course* you're here."

Blinking in disbelief, he stared at her. She was wearing a hat, jacket, and breeches apparently obtained from some street urchin who was likely better off without them. "I think the question should be what are *you* doing here? And, what in blazes are you wearing?" He brushed disgustedly at the faded wool of her tattered jacket. "Does your uncle know you're here?"

"Of course not," she snapped. "I—"

Her words were cut off when a small band of men stumbled past, full of angry oaths as they staggered under the weight of the wounded compatriot they were attempting to help to safety. In the distance, Daniel and Anna heard orders being barked out and the unmistakable sounds of troops on the move.

"Come along," Daniel demanded, tugging at her jacket and drawing her with him before she could protest. "We can't be here if the Regulars come. The devil knows what other damage they might do tonight."

They ran, stumbling often, Daniel pulling at her arm to the point of occasionally lifting her off the ground in an effort to help her keep up with his longer stride. It seemed to Anna that their course was in the general direction of her uncle's house. The route was not wholly familiar to her, however, interwoven as it was by shortcuts through narrow lanes and back alleys. Shouts and shadows followed close on their heels, though how much of a threat they represented was unclear. Neither of them wanted to linger to find out.

On they ran until Anna was breathless. A sharp pain in her side begged her to stop and double over to soothe it, but she did not give in to the urge. Her childhood memories were punctuated by failed attempts to tag along after Daniel and his friends, trying desperately to be included in their fun and mischief, constantly excluded because she was too young, too small, or simply because she was a girl. Even now, childish pride filled her with a fierce determination to keep pace with him. Constantly steering a course that took them away from sounds of other people, they skidded along slick alleys and jumped across ice-crusted puddles

Just as she hopped over the tiny rivulet of filthy water that streamed out of one alley, Anna's attention was caught by the sound of a man calling out in distress from somewhere in the dark space between the buildings. Pulling back against Daniel, she paused to squint into the darkness. Slowly, her eyes adjusted to the dim light until she could just make out the shapes of three men standing in a group over a fourth, who was on the ground. It took a moment for her mind to comprehend that the man on the ground was being attacked.

Daniel, having witnessed the same scene, hesitated as though he might intervene. A glance down at Anna changed his mind, however, and he drew her onward. But another cry for help stopped him. Anna heard him swear under his breath. "Stay here," he ordered, unceremoniously shoving her into the shelter of a door stoop. "Do not move from here, and keep out of sight. Do you understand?" His tone was urgent, too insistent to be debated.

Wide-eyed, she nodded, and watched in astonishment as he made to return to the alley. "Daniel!" she hissed. "There are three of them. You can't go in there alone! I should—"

"You will remain here as I instructed," he barked, pushing her back against the door. Then, before she could say more, he disappeared down the alley.

Anna flattened herself against the wall, afraid of being seen, and edged along until she could peer around the corner of the building. She could make out Daniel's tall silhouette, boldly striding toward the group of men, none of whom had noticed his approach.

Without breaking stride, Daniel snatched up a stray board from a pile of rubbish, and brandishing it like a club, launched himself at the first of the unsuspecting men. Entirely without preamble, Daniel struck the man on the head with his improvised weapon, astonishing Anna. The single blow knocked the man flat on his back where he lay, motionless, in a stream of filthy slush. The victim of the gang's assault, an older man, struggled to his feet. He wavered a moment as though he wanted to assist in his own defense, but Daniel urged him away. Anna watched the poor man stagger off down the alley.

Now, the second of the three thugs rounded angrily upon Daniel, assailing him with a string of expletives. Undaunted, Daniel grabbed a handful of the man's coat and violently shoved him back against the brick wall, pinning him there with an uncompromisingly firm grip. Heated words were exchanged, punctuated more than once by Daniel thumping the man's head back against the bricks.

Finally, the third man, who was larger than all the rest, intervened. To Anna's surprise, he did not attack Daniel. Instead, muttering something that made Daniel relax his grip, the big man reached around and took hold of his companion, forcefully dragging him from the alley. Daniel watched them go before bending to rouse the man he had knocked to the ground and roughly sending him on his groggy way.

Anna ducked back around the corner just as Daniel turned to leave the scene of the altercation. He emerged from the alley and, without even a glance in her direction, grasped her elbow and began again to lead her down the street.

He said not a word for the several long minutes it took to reach the back gate at her uncle's house. Daniel lifted the latch and pulled the high, heavy gate open wide enough to admit them. The hinges creaked softly, and the two remained motionless for a moment until assured there would be no response from within the darkened house. He led Anna to the foot of the porch steps and swung her around to face him. The moon had emerged, and he could just make out her features. Though she had done a good job of disguising her appearance, the wide, amber-tinged brown eyes were unmistakably Anna's. He'd always been amused by her — challenged by her, if he had to admit it. She was far too outspoken and too much the tomboy, yet she was full of intelligence and a sense of adventure.

But, for now, all he had for her was anger. "You still don't listen, Mouse."

"Stop calling me that."

"I told you to stay out of sight and, there you were, lurking at the corner like some gawking child at the carnival."

"I was doing no such thing!" She shook off his grip on her arm and drew herself up defensively. "What if you'd needed help?"

"A little thing like you? Help?" He snorted in derision. "Far more likely that you'd have become yet another victim for me to protect."

"Who was that man?"

"I have no idea."

"And yet, you risked a great deal to defend him?" She cocked her head, brows drawn together as if she were trying to solve a puzzle.

He hesitated a beat and his eyes sparked. "Of course I helped him. Why should that surprise you?"

She shrugged, but said nothing.

Twisting his mouth with distaste, Daniel flicked his fingers at her battered hat. "What's all this about, then? What are you doing gadding about dressed as a boy? And what business do you have being out so late at night?"

"I needed to go out," she huffed. "Under the circumstances, it seemed much safer for people to think I was a boy. And, even were that not the case, I certainly couldn't go out in a fashion where I'd be recognized. My uncle would surely hear of it, and I think he'd not be amused."

"No doubt."

She responded to his sarcastic tone with a mincing look and folded her arms across her chest. Daniel had always been able to intimidate others merely by looking down the knife-edge of his nose at them, his blue eyes frigid in their stare, but Anna refused to be cowed. She glared up at him just as hard as he was glaring down at her and felt a small triumph when he looked away first.

"Explain," he insisted again. "Why did you need to go out? Why were you at the Custom House?"

"I intended to go to Faneuil Hall. I understood there was going to be a speech by that man — Samuel Adams. I wanted to hear what was said."

"There was no meeting and no speeches tonight."

She snorted. "No. Obviously Mr. Adams was too busy stirring up trouble. And don't try to deny that he was behind that horror."

"As far as I know, Mr. Adams wasn't even there."

"Even so, he was there in spirit. My uncle says Samuel Adams is a middle-aged man who has never grown up and has never quite succeeded at anything worthwhile. He seems to be making a roaring success of rabble-rousing, however. In that pursuit, I'd say he has found his calling! I've no doubt that he is somehow to blame for the whole thing."

"I'd say that the troops who occupy our streets and take our jobs and abuse our citizenry carry more of the blame."

"The Regulars wouldn't be here if it weren't for the mischief you and your friends get up to. And stop treating me as though I've done something wrong," she added indignantly. "I have as much right as anyone to be out — to know what is happening in Boston."

"Read the broadsheets." One corner of his mouth lifted in a smirk but, after a moment's consideration, the flicker of amusement was replaced by skepticism. "So, you wanted to hear Mr. Adams speak? Do you mean to tell me that you're considering becoming a Patriot?"

"Don't be ridiculous," she snapped. "And don't use such a noble-sounding word to describe that rabble. They're not patriots. They're a bunch of malcontents at best, and a pack of treasonous criminals at worst."

He chuckled. "Or so says your uncle, anyway, I'm guessing."

"Of course that's what my uncle says. My uncle is loyal to his king and country, as am I." She jutted her chin forward, full of pride and self-assurance, as though she truly believed that her small chin could withstand any attack.

"And yet, you want to hear what Mr. Adams has to say? Or, did you merely want to see if he has a tail and horns?"

"Of course not, you ninny. I want to know for myself what is being said and done. I'm tired of relying on crumbs of information dropped by my uncle and his friends." She drew herself up into a defiant posture. "I want to see for myself."

"Yes, well, that way of thinking got you into trouble when you were six-years-old, and it's going to get you into bigger trouble now that you're, what? Ten?"

She narrowed her eyes at him. "You know perfectly well that I am thirteen. I'm only four years younger than you, Daniel Garrett," she retorted hotly. "So, I think you have no call to treat me like a child."

Now he laughed outright. "You are a child, Mouse." He skimmed her hat from her head and ruffled her dark, ginger-infused hair.

"I told you to stop calling me that." She snatched the hat back from him and reached up to smooth her hair. "I'm not a mouse. You've always called me that, and I've always hated it, so stop!"

"A little brown mouse of a child who should be safely abed in her uncle's house, not out at night wandering the Boston streets," he said, ignoring her infuriation. "Now, inside with you, and no more of this foolishness."

"I'll go inside when I'm ready," she insisted tersely. "Tell me what you were doing at the Custom House."

"The same thing as you, apparently."

She huffed. "More likely, you were there to abuse that poor soldier. I know well enough the things you and your friends have been up to."

"Do you, now?" Seriousness replaced his cavalier manner, and he leaned down so that his face was close to hers. "If you know so much," he said quietly, "then you know that the protests are serious business, and you know that you should be nowhere near any of it. Now, get inside, and promise me you'll not be larking about like this again. Otherwise, I'll ensure that your uncle finds out what you've been about tonight."

She opened her mouth, and then closed it again, something in his mien quelling the rejoinder she had planned. "Very well," she chirped amiably. "I promise. On one condition."

Exasperation rumbled up from his chest into his voice. "I should not be surprised," he grumbled. "But, no. I'll hear of no *conditions*."

"If my uncle finds out I've been out tonight, he'll be cross with me, and he'll forbid me from such adventures in the future. His anger will pass, though, and little will be any different than it would if I simply made the promise you seek. However, I would prefer to avoid the unpleasantness, if possible."

"Your uncle should have taken a rod to you more often," he growled.

"My uncle never took a rod to me." Indignation filled her voice and inflated her posture.

"Exactly. And look where that neglect of his duty has led."

"Save your poor wit for someone dull enough to appreciate it. Do you want to hear the bargain I'm proposing, or not?"

He considered a moment, reluctantly curious to learn what condition she might try to impose. "I do not, but I suspect I've little choice if I'm to get the assurance I want. So, under what condition will you promise no further escapades?"

"You must promise that, if your new friends plan any violence against my uncle or his property, you will warn me ahead of time so that I can conspire to keep him out of harm's way."

He laughed. "Are you a spy for the redcoats, now?"

"Don't be ridiculous," she huffed. "I won't do or say anything that would cause the authorities to become involved. It's not my intent to set up an ambush. I merely want to be able to ensure my uncle's personal safety. He's convinced that he's safe simply because he's not one of the king's officials."

"And he is probably correct."

"Can you guarantee that the protests will only be directed at the king's officials? Are you absolutely certain that these mobs will not decide to turn their attention to the property of a Loyalist merchant?"

He shook his head. "No, I can't guarantee that. There are too many disparate elements involved. Nor can I guarantee I'll know in advance what any one of them will do."

"Where there is trouble, Daniel, particularly of the violent kind, you always seem to be close by."

It was a painful barb that hit its mark. "You are sometimes excruciatingly direct, Mouse." He wiped one hand down his face in irritation. "Alright," he said after some consideration. "I agree. I think it's an unrealistic request but, if it will elicit your promise that you'll go on no further adventures like tonight, then I'll agree."

"Very good." She nodded curtly and stuck out her hand. "I promise then, also. No more adventures like tonight."

Skeptical, he stared at the proffered hand for a long moment before reluctantly extending his own. They sealed their agreement with a hand shake, then he shooed her up the steps toward her uncle's back door. "Inside with you, Mouse."

He watched her climb the steps. She was right, he knew, about his being only three years her senior; and yet, to look at her, one would have guessed the gap in their ages to be far wider. She'd been quite convincing in her disguise. He knew of no other girls, even among those as young as Anna, who could pass themselves off as a boy, and he thought that it probably did not even occur to her to be chagrined at her own ability to do so. He liked that about her, the lack of self-conscious vanity.

"Daniel." She paused on the top step and turned to look down at him curiously. "Why did you ask me to make the promise? Why do you care what I do?"

"My mother raised me to look after the weak and foolish," he said, shrugging dismissively.

She ignored the insult. "There are a good many things your mother tried to teach you, Daniel Garrett, most of which you pointedly ignored."

"I never ignored the lessons that suited me." He flashed a roguish grin. "Now, inside with you." He watched her until she had disappeared into the house then, silently letting himself back out through the gate, went off in search of three ruffians with whom he intended to finish an inharmonious discussion.

*   *   *

Making his way back across Boston — from the respectable street on which Anna and her uncle lived to the seamier streets near the waterfront — Daniel reached the docks. Hat pulled low to hide his face from the clusters of men who gathered here and there, he passed men playing games of chance on the damp pavement, and others huddled about glowing braziers for warmth. All of them seemed uneasy and restless. He moved among them without greeting or acknowledgement and, with caution, approached a squalid, tumbledown building at the far end of the waterfront.

The evening's events, and particularly his encounter with Anna, had replayed in his mind as he crossed Boston. Now, he pushed all of it into a closet and shut the door. That clearing of his mind, the elimination of all extraneous thought, was necessary to survival. It was a lesson he had learned when only a young boy, and it had become instinctive with him. Boston's wharves tended to attract the toughest sort, many of them predatory in nature. These men were not afraid of violence, and were ever-vigilant for an opportunity to enrich themselves. The public house he sought was something of a refuge in this wilderness, kept as respectable as a waterfront public house could be by the diligent effort of its wizened proprietor.

The building stood stoically facing the harbor, its wood planks weathered and decayed by the sea air. It looked, as it had for longer than anyone could recall, as though it might collapse at any moment. But Daniel knew that was an illusion. Like many of the salty, gnarled denizens of Boston's docks and warehouses, it was deceptively sturdy and resilient, reflective of a hard life of challenges met and overcome. The tavern on the ground floor had served two generations of seamen and fishermen, and the rooms upstairs were rented to those same men, some of them less reputable than others. It was in one of those rooms that Daniel expected to find Teague Bradley and Drummond Fisackerly, for his two friends had long made the place home.

Inside the tavern, the stifling air reeked of stale alcohol and pungent, unwashed men. Daniel paused to allow his eyes a moment to adjust to the pale light given off by hissing oil lamps. The usual crowd of men huddled at the tables or warmed themselves at the fire, mugs cradled protectively in work-worn hands, their conversations kept unusually low. He suspected that the subdued atmosphere had something to do with the evening's events at the Custom House. These men, like others all over Boston, felt themselves increasingly under threat and were, therefore, mistrustful of any unknown ears around them. Catching snatches of conversation along the way, he crossed the room toward the owner of the establishment. The man, whom everyone called "Withers" as though it was the only name he possessed, looked up from the dented mug he was wiping and smiled crookedly in greeting.

"Are they here?" Daniel leaned close to the old man and kept his voice low.

Withers nodded and jerked his head toward the stairs. "Been here only a few minutes," he said quietly. "No doubt, they were part of that trouble tonight." He gave Daniel a weighted look.

"No doubt," Daniel replied. He knew the old man wanted more details, gossip, or any bit of the sort of information that was the stuff of his stock and trade. But on this night, Daniel felt disinclined to conversation. With a quick parting smile, he climbed the sharply-angled wooden stairs that led to the rooms above.

He approached the door slowly, knowing his two friends would be waiting for him and that their welcome was not likely to be warm. Pausing at the door to knock only once, he did not wait for a response but let himself in as had always been his habit. Though he did not live here, he had spent enough time in this room with Teague and Drum to feel he was more than a mere visitor. Teague, his back to the door, stood staring out the small, discolored window, one arm braced against the frame. It was a pose, deliberate in its attempt to appear relaxed, but radiating desperate unhappiness instead. Teague did not speak, nor did he turn to face Daniel.

Drum sat on a chair that seemed fragile under his enormous frame. Drummond Fisackerly, Drum to his friends, was not fat, but his proportions were massive. He easily stood more than a head taller than just about any other man, and his strong, broad shoulders and arms dwarfed them all. If not for the fact that he unendingly exuded a kind of innocent openness, he would have been a fearsome sight. But with his fair hair, pale, china blue eyes, and freckle-dusted face, his countenance bordered on angelic. He looked up now, his eager face full of a mixture of anticipation and dread, like a child who fears he is about to be reprimanded and is eager to please. It made Daniel's heart ache, and he felt even angrier at Teague as a result.

Daniel allowed the door to slam shut behind him, and took a bit of pleasure in the fact that it visibly startled Teague. "What the hell do you think you were doing out there tonight?" Daniel's voice, harsh and accusatory, cut across the room like an arrow leveled directly at Teague.

But Teague had prepared for this fight. He whirled to face Daniel, his eyes dark, glittering black holes in his face. "You sorry bit of hog slurry," he spat. "What gives you the right to barge in here like this or to talk to me that way? Just who do you think you are?" His dark hair stood out around his head as though he'd been raking his hands through it.

"I'm your friend," Daniel snapped. "A friend who does not want to see you in trouble. Now, I shall ask again. Why were you assaulting that man in the alley?"

"You have no right to say anything about it, and you had no business stopping us."

Daniel gaped incredulously. "As a citizen of Boston, it is most definitely my business to stop an assault on a helpless man. And when the thugs are people I consider friends, it becomes even more my business."

"A 'citizen of Boston.' Listen to you! Mr. Citizen of Boston." Sneering, he scoured Daniel with cold eyes. "That man was a Tory," Teague snapped. "A bloody, king-loving Tory! You should be thanking us for attacking him."

"And when did it become acceptable for us to physically attack and rob a man simply because his politics differ from ours?"

Now it was Teague's turn to register incredulity. "Oh, and aren't you the fine one now! It was you who dragged us into this in the first place. You were the one who was so enthralled with Sam Adams and his lot."

"I got us involved in the cause they stand for," Daniel corrected. "Beating a man and stealing his purse are not part of it. And do not try to tell me that you attacked that man because he's a Tory. You do these things for your own personal gain. What you're doing is wrong, and you know it. If you can't understand the morality of it, I'd at least think you would acknowledge that it's illegal."

Teague laughed. "You are such a bloody hypocrite! Everything Adams and the rest of you do is illegal! You'd best not be judging me."

"And you cannot see the difference between what we do and the things you do?"

"No," Teague insisted, still laughing derisively, "I cannot. And I'm certainly no hypocrite. I don't pick and choose the laws I obey like you and your new friends do. I don't follow whatever authority appeals to me at the moment. I've no use for any of it, equally!"

Dejection sank like a stone into Daniel's stomach. "I thought better of you. I thought you could understand the difference between the actions of the Sons of Liberty and the actions of a common thief."

"Oh, for Chrissake! Do you hear yourself? I need money, Daniel," he snarled angrily. "Drum and I need something to live on. We can't run home to mummy when we get tired or hungry."

"I work for my living, Teague." Daniel narrowed his eyes. The notion that, no matter what, Daniel had a mother and home to which he could return had long been a sore point for Teague, and Daniel was weary of it. "And I thought we agreed that you would work for yours as well."

"No. You decided. Like you always do, you expected us to fall into line without question. You seem to think that, just because you issue an order, we'll follow it. We're not yours to order about."

"It was not an order," Daniel said, his voice frayed and impatient. "It was . . .," he swept his hand in a gesture meant to demonstrate something he could not put into words. There was some truth to Teague's accusation that Daniel had changed paths without consulting either of them regarding their feelings on the matter. The two of them had for many years followed his lead, and it had not occurred to him that they might do otherwise in this. Now that Teague seemed reluctant to do so, Daniel was not quite sure what to think or how to cope with it.

Watching Teague and Daniel, Drum fidgeted uncomfortably. He did not like it when they were angry with each other, when they quarreled. They were the two people he cared most for in the world, and he was pretty sure they were the only two who cared for him, and he could not bear for them to be at odds with each other. Lately, they seemed to be angry with each other more often than not. It seemed to Drum that it had started when Daniel began to insist that Teague limit himself to honest work and when he had begun attending his very secretive meetings. Drum had gone with him to one such meeting and had not understood a thing about it except that everyone seemed to be unhappy with a man named George.

"I do not take orders from you," Teague repeated through gritted teeth. "I'll do as I please and you can go to hell."

"Very well." Daniel was tired — far too tired to deal with Teague's obstinacy. "Do as you please," he said resignedly. "But you'll not drag Drum along with you. You'll not drag him along with you to the stocks, or whipping post, or worse."

"Drum can decide for himself what he wants to do."

"He follows whatever you do, Teague. He has no idea—" He cut short his own words as he looked at Drum's face. He could not say aloud what was going through his mind, that Drum had no notion of the consequences of their actions. It wasn't that he was stupid. Certainly he was capable of learning. But he was slow, and it seemed as though the part of his mind that dealt in abstracts did not exist. For Drum, everything was concrete and literal. Drum did not understand everything that happened in the world, but he did understand when his deficiencies were being remarked upon, and he was always deeply wounded by those remarks. "You are correct," Daniel said, fixing his simple, trusting friend in his gaze. "Drum can decide for himself what he wants to do."

Drum looked from one young man to the other. He liked Teague, but he loved and respected Daniel. Teague could be cruel at times, teasing Drum in ways he did not fully understand but felt hurt by, nonetheless. Daniel was always patient with Drum's slowness and was never cruel.

Drum frowned with the effort of sorting out his thoughts. "I don't want to do anything that's wrong." He spoke slowly, more distinctly than most people, as though he stopped to consider each word before he said it. "I want to be good." Eyes full of despair, face questioning, he looked up at Daniel. He had made the same statement so many times to his father in what seemed like another lifetime, but it had made no difference. His father had discarded him. He was desperate that Daniel and Teague not do the same thing.

"I know you want to be good." Daniel's manner became gentle. "Do you think it was a good thing to beat that man? Do you think it's a good thing to steal from people?"

"But Teague said th—"

"Don't think about what Teague said." The words sounded sharper than he had intended and caused Drum to recoil. Daniel stepped back and paused for two beats before continuing. "Is that how you'd want to be treated?"

Drum shook his head. "No." He hung his head and seemed suddenly to be overly-interested in the fraying hem of his coat. His face had reddened all the way up to the top of his scalp.

"Then, no more of this, all right?"

Drum nodded his agreement.

"That's very well and fine," Teague scoffed. "How's he to pay his share of our rent? How's he to pay for his share of our food?"

"He can stay with me," Daniel declared.

"I can work." Drum's voice was full of pride. "The men down at the warehouses. They pay me to help them move crates and things off the ships."

Teague rolled his eyes. "Well, you go right ahead, then, you gull. Work until your back breaks for a few small coins."

Drum frowned and looked up at Daniel. "Will my back break?"

"No, Drum." Daniel tried not to laugh. "Not really. Teague just means that you'll have to work very hard. It may make you tired and sore."

That made Drum laugh. "I never get tired and sore," he boasted. "And I like to work hard. I like moving the crates. It's something I'm good at."

"You're good at many things," Daniel assured him with a chuckle.

Watching Daniel draw Drum away from him, Teague began to regret his intransigency. His hot-headed tendency to act without thinking had kept him in trouble most of his life, and it seemed that Daniel had always been there to get him out again. Now, as he sensed his friend drifting away, he felt anxious. Alone was not something Teague Bradley wanted to be.

"You make too much of this," he told Daniel, brushing aside their disagreement with a wave of his hand. "I thought the idea was to harass the Tories any way we could. How could I know you'd object to me fattening my purse a bit in the process? That's all it was. If it matters so much to you, I'll stop."

Daniel eyed him narrowly, not completely convinced. "The idea is to put pressure on the king and the Parliament to hear our concerns," he corrected. "Not to commit assault and robbery."

Teague snorted with derision. "Tell that to the officials whose offices have been closed or who've had their persons threatened by the Sons of Liberty."

"I never said I condone everything they do. All I can do is try to be part of the rational element, not the more radical."

Teague shrugged. Daniel had begun talking that way more often lately, and he did not care for it. It made him feel as left behind by Daniel's thoughts as he did by Daniel's actions. "It makes no difference to me either way. If you want us to walk the straight-and-narrow, so be it. There's no need for you to be so high-handed about it."

"Then, I apologize for my high-handedness."

"And, I apologize for my harsh words." Teague bowed dramatically, inadvertently undermining his attempt to appear sincere. "We've been friends too long, Daniel, to quarrel over something so trivial."

Daniel was not sure he considered the matter trivial but nodded his assent anyway. It was far easier to allow himself to be mollified than it would be to walk away from their years of friendship. And, though he had doubts about the sincerity of Teague's promise to stop his illicit behavior, he knew that the promise was far more likely to be honored if he kept Teague close.

"Good." Teague grinned in the disarming manner that was his specialty. "And now, I think you should buy us a mug or two downstairs. Withers has missed us, I'm sure." He swaggered toward the door as though enormously pleased with himself. "I'll just say," he added as he opened the door, "that you picked a damned inconvenient time to grow a conscience. There's a lot of profit to be made from discord." He shrugged off the censorious look Daniel leveled upon him and sauntered out the door.

*   *   *

A little over a week had passed since Anna's brush with disaster at the Custom House and, to her annoyance, she had heard little discussion on the matter from her uncle, John Wilton. She wanted to know of the aftermath and what was being said about the cause of the incident, and was frustrated that her uncle remained steadfastly tight-lipped on the subject. The newspapers were of some help, but she suspected that the talk in the taverns and coffee houses would be far more interesting and revealing, and it was those conversations she was eager to hear repeated.

Wilton's friend, William Sprague, with whom he frequently argued over political matters, had not visited in his habitual way since that night, and her uncle seemed disinclined to discuss the event with anyone else. She had watched her uncle read the newspapers and broadsheets, then pace and fidget as he digested all that he had read. Many of Boston's printers were in league with the Sons of Liberty, meaning that the Loyalist viewpoint was only carried by a precious few. The disparity made it difficult for men like John Wilton who would have preferred that at least some fair representation of the Loyalist viewpoint be heard. He felt overwhelmed by the vitriolic opposition propaganda that was flooding Boston.

Anna watched her uncle worriedly. John Wilton was a small man with a timid appearance that belied the inner strength and vitality that had helped him achieve success in Boston. Despite his advanced years, his posture was firmly upright and his eyes bright. A short bristle of grey hair covered his round head — a head that only rarely sported a wig. He was a thoughtful man with a quiet, gentle nature. His face was furrowed by time and toils but, from behind the round lenses of his spectacles, his eyes usually sparkled as though he anticipated something new and exciting at any moment. Now, under the burden of recent events, that sparkle was much diminished. It battered Anna's heart to see him so deflated in spirit, for she loved him dearly.

Days later, Mr. Sprague finally did come to call. Latching onto the first opportunity she could find to attend the two men, Anna intercepted the maid on her way to serve their tea, offering to carry the tray in for her. She knew it for what it was — a shameless bid for the chance to eavesdrop — but she straightened her shoulders and went forward, nonetheless. As was often the case when they were together, the two men were arguing in the controlled way of old friends, their voices audible before even she opened the parlor door.

Sprague was speaking as she entered the room, his voice low and solemn, and she paused to listen.

"If you think about it, John, this is not so new. Not too long ago, you may recall, the Crown and Parliament decided that our cheap labor and the trade imbalance created by our rather impressive productivity was injuring England's economy. They were quick to imposed regulations and, like frogs in a pot of boiling water, we were content to keep swimming until it finally dawned upon us that we were being cooked alive. At that point, we were certainly passionate in our protest, and you did not stay out of the fray, if memory serves." He cocked one eyebrow, challenging Wilton to deny the good natured charge.

"That was different. This quarrelling over representation and the rest of it — this is self-indulgent nattering about points of principle." Her uncle's voice sounded unusually gruff. "They make too much of it and it begins to threaten our livelihoods!"

"You may recall that a civil war was once fought on English soil over what were largely matters of principle."

"Are you suggesting that this could escalate into a civil war?"

"If events continue on their present course, I think it is possible."

Wilton harrumphed and shrugged off Sprague's statement.

"It's a different world, John," Sprague persisted. "And it's changing rapidly. Especially here in these colonies." Sprague worked to compose his words into a gentle dance around his friend's strained emotions. "Ever since the Stamp Act, there has been something stirring here, something just under the surface that bubbles along and keeps things perpetually unsettled."

"Yes! These mobs of malcontents! They keep things perpetually unsettled!"

Sprague frowned at the deliberate misconstruction of his words.

"England is a rock that will stand forever," Wilton insisted, grudgingly returning to Sprague's point. "She will weather this storm as she has so many other storms over the years."

"Perhaps," Sprague agreed. "But she may have to bend a little if she is not to be broken by this particular storm."

"Bah."

Anna crossed the room, her feet silent on the carpet, holding the tray carefully before her so as not to rattle the china. Fragile spring sunlight found its way into the room through the rippled window glass, casting a soft illumination where it fell. The warmth of the room was welcoming, as was the rich fragrance of pipe tobacco and leather that hung softly in the air. Her uncle and Mr. Sprague sat in matching chairs facing the fire, a small tea table between them. Both men stretched their legs toward the hearth, but Sprague's feet were deriving more benefit than those of Anna's uncle for Sprague had several inches in height on Wilton. Sprague sported a horsehair wig complete with two stylishly requisite rolls over each ear and a short queue at the back. Anna guessed that the wig was uncomfortably prickly because it was slightly askew from Sprague's frequent efforts to scratch his scalp.

The two men continued their conversation without pause, for neither had heard her enter the room. Their attention and their conversation seemed to center on the crumpled copy of the *Boston Gazette and Country Journal* William Sprague held in his hand. "This younger generation does not see things as we once did," Sprague said with a thump of the *Gazette* for emphasis. "For us, it was all hard work and trying to survive; trying to carve out our place in the world. Now, our children are building on the foundation we laid. They enjoy the luxury of not having to spend their every waking moment working just to remain solvent. They have time to read the philosophers and to discuss what they consider enlightened ideas."

"And they reward us for that bequest by spending their time fomenting dissent, trying to turn it all on its head and destroy what we built," Wilton asserted. He started slightly when he realized it was his niece who carried in the tray. "Why, Anna! You came in so quietly. I apologize for not noticing you."

She smiled and set the tray on the table between the two men. "I didn't want to interrupt your conversation." That was true enough, she thought, though it had not been manners, but curiosity that had softened her step. She held her hand over the teapot, one eyebrow arched in silent question as to whether or not she should pour.

Reacting to Anna's sudden presence, Mr. Sprague grinned broadly and, putting aside the *Gazette*, jumped to his feet to execute a small bow. "Miss Somerset." He adopted an exaggerated formality that made her giggle. "Good day to you."

Sprague radiated an energetic joviality that made him seem far younger than his years. Friends and acquaintances chuckled behind their hands about the paradox of his sunny disposition, for they knew him to be a man much put upon by his domineering wife and spoiled daughters, a man who would have been fully justified had he chosen to adopt a perpetually cloudy outlook. In fact, because of the lack of domestic tranquility, Sprague spent as many of his waking hours as possible away from his house. He had an elaborate and extensive circuit of friends, business interests, and taverns, all of which he visited routinely in his quest for absence from home and hearth. John Wilton's parlor was his destination two afternoons each week. It was an arrangement Anna's uncle encouraged, for Sprague was a particular friend.

"And good day to you, Mr. Sprague," she replied as she bobbed her best curtsey. William Sprague had played this game with her for as long as she could remember, greeting her as he might the finest of ladies. It had made her giggle when she was a precocious five-year-old and continued to do so even now. Only when he had regained his seat and his face was once again illuminated by the fire did she realize that there was a sizeable bruised lump on his forehead and several scratches on his cheek. She gawked at the sight.

"It's nothing," he insisted, brushing aside her apparent concern. "An unpleasant encounter with some young hooligans Monday evening before last, that's all."

Her face reddened as she remembered the assault Daniel had interrupted. "But, you are quite recovered now?" She busied herself with pouring the tea and would not meet his gaze.

"Oh, yes. Fortunately, I was rescued by an anonymous good Samaritan." He gingerly touched two fingers to the lump on his forehead. It looked like a pigeon's egg had lodged under his skin, which was turning a peculiar shade of greenish purple. "Young fools apparently thought I had silver on me," he chuckled. "Had they known how my wife and daughters customarily empty my pockets before I ever leave the house, the foolish ruffians would not have bothered!"

Anna, smiling weakly, handed him his cup of tea, then retreated to the window seat and picked up her needlework. Her uncle watched her and, not fooled by her attention to the needlework. He knew she was all ears when she sat quietly off to the side like that, hoping she would not be noticed. She had from an early age been mature beyond her years and so bright that it astounded him, and he had always vacillated between feeding that intellect and trying to protect her from the world.

Wilton returned his attention to this friend. "I still say it was foolish of you to be out alone so late in the evening. The streets are rife with troublemakers and thugs of late."

"I was responding to the fire alarm," Sprague sighed. "Did you not hear the bell?"

"I heard it," Wilton replied, nodding. "And I was walking down the steps to respond when two sentries hurrying toward the Custom House told me to return home, that there was no fire."

Anna's heart skipped a beat. It had never occurred to her that her uncle was out on the streets where he might easily have discovered her clandestine adventure. She missed a stitch and stabbed her finger with her needle. Sucking at the tiny drop of blood on her fingertip, she ruefully observed that there was more than one spot of blood on the piece, for her skill with a needle, as the housekeeper often told her, was considerably less than proficient.

Sprague grunted. "Not sure I would have believed a couple of lobster-backs," he said. "They would as soon see Boston burned to ashes, I suspect."

"I sincerely doubt that," Wilton replied in a weary tone. He removed his spectacles and rubbed his eyes.

"True," Sprague grinned. "If for no other reason than that they, like us, would have no roofs over their heads if the town burned." He winked and shot a glance over his shoulder to see if Anna appreciated his wit more than her uncle did, but she did not look up.

"It seems to me," Wilton responded sternly, "that we should not make light of the events of last week. Whether we are discussing your near escape from acute harm or the tragedy that unfolded in front of the Custom House, it was all a serious business." He took a sip of tea, noticeably wincing at the bitterness. With the nonimportation and non-consumption practices being urged on Bostonians, good English tea was becoming difficult to obtain. He had forbidden his housekeeper from purchasing tea known to have been smuggled in, and so she had begun adulterating her supply with other ingredients, some less palatable than others.

"I agree that it is serious business." Sprague nodded and guiltily erased the smile from his face. "I did not mean to imply otherwise. In fact, that is what I've been trying to tell you, John. The events of that evening are not merely serious business but are full of foreboding. I fear that what happened at the Custom House is a prelude to more unrest and tragedy. The soldiers involved in the incident have been arrested and will stand trial, but for many townsfolk, that will not be enough."

Wilton grunted. "I cannot believe the things that are being said about that horrid business. And, Revere's outrageous engraving and the article!" He looked distastefully at the *Gazette* Sprague had laid on the table between them and tapped the folded pages for emphasis. "I worry that these things will so slant public opinion that there can be no fair trials for Captain Preston and his men; that there can be no true justice done. I cannot bring myself to believe that Preston ordered his men to fire on that crowd."

Anna pursed her lips, checking the impulse to tell her uncle that he was correct, that the captain had not issued the order to fire. She could hardly tell him she was there, however — that she was looking directly at Preston when the firing began and saw with her own eyes that no such command had come from his lips.

"Even if Preston gave the order, however," her uncle continued, "would he not have been within his rights? Is it not the right of a soldier to defend himself?"

"Defend himself from legitimate threat of attack, perhaps, but it appears that this was merely an unruly crowd, merely a rabble of mischief-makers full of taunts and vinegar. There seems to have been no real threat." Sprague frowned down at his teacup as he attempted to retrieve what might or might not have been a loose tea leaf floating there. "If the troops had simply marched away or, better yet, not have been there at all, the whole situation would have been defused, and no lives or property would have been lost on either side. It is folly to have the troops occupying Boston. It was only a matter of time before something like this occurred, and it will not likely be the last."

"It's a sad situation," Wilton agreed, nodding his head. His voice was weary and his shoulders seemed to slump as he stared into the fire. A sad situation from which there appeared no easy extrication, he thought.

"Sad, indeed," Sprague nodded. "More than that, it is tragic. Several are dead, at least one of them a child. The disposition of the town is, understandably, at a boil. On the one hand, Governor Hutchinson is pleading for the rule of law; on the other, loud voices are demanding that the troops be removed from Boston."

"Hutchinson will maintain order," Wilton insisted with more assurance than he felt. "And John Adams has agreed to defend Captain Preston and his men. That will help."

Sprague nodded. "That was a good development, I agree. People see John Adams as a fair, level-headed man. Pedantic," he chuckled, "but fair. The man believes in the rule of law almost to a fault."

"And," Wilton interjected hopefully, "London will see that we are a people governed by law, not by mob rule. They can only respond positively to that."

"Perhaps." Sprague drew a small flask of his favorite brandy from his pocket and held it up questioningly. At Wilton's assenting nod, he dashed the dregs of his and Wilton's tea into the fire. From the flask, he poured a healthy tot of brandy into each cup and settled back into his chair. In afterthought, he glanced over his shoulder to assure himself that Anna had not witnessed his subterfuge. Her head was convincingly bent to her sewing, and he could not see the little knowing smile on her face.

Sprague fortified himself with a sip of the brandy, and then another, cleared his throat, and leaned forward in his chair. He waited for Wilton to meet his eye before saying in a lowered voice, "John, I have been as loyal to the king as you are. And, like you, I have hoped that this dispute would sort itself out given time and the predominance of cooler heads. I tell you now; I'm filled with certainty that such will not be the case."

"This will settle, William." John Wilton lightly pounded his fist on the arm of his chair for emphasis. "How many times in the history of our nation have such disputes arisen? We have a proud tradition of settling our differences within the framework of our legal system. I am confident that such will be the case this time as well."

"That sounds very optimistic, and it certainly is what we want to believe of ourselves. But how can you be so certain that events will follow the peaceful path?" The timbre of Sprague's voice went up a notch in his frustration with what he saw as his friend's naiveté. "In approaching those numbskulls in London, Dr. Franklin has encountered only dismissal and scorn. The king shows little inclination to listen, and understands nothing of what he actually hears."

"But, the Parliament—"

Sprague leaned forward in his chair, and his tone became more urgent. "Parliament is the very root of the problem, John. We are not represented there. That is the whole point of all of this." He waved his hand in a gesture meant to include every protest raised over the many past months across the whole of the colonies.

"That is ludicrous." Wilton sat his cup down a bit too hard, rattling the other china on the table. "Parliament has our interests at heart if for no other reason than because the well-being of colonial merchants and industry is critical to the nation's treasury."

"In a sense, that is my point. They are not representative of *us*, of our interests or wishes." Sprague's voice was low, but his words were spoken with feverish intensity. "They are representative of their own pockets. They see us as a source of revenue, John, nothing more. We are not viewed as citizens on an equal footing with the people of London or Southampton or any town or hamlet within England's borders. You can hear it in the tone they take when they speak of colonials. They imbue the very word with disdain. They have our interests at heart only in so much as those interests overlap their own."

It was a point with which Wilton could not argue. He stared into the fire for several long moments, wishing for a helpful revelation, but none came.

Sprague, regretting that he had distressed his friend, settled back into his chair and adopted a gentler tone. "I'm afraid that, in my view, this business at the Custom House underscores that disdain. The military occupation of Boston must end. It's true that the Regulars have withdrawn to Castle William, but that is not enough. They are still on our doorstep. Surely London will see that no good can come of keeping troops in our midst."

"The king is within his rights to protect his property. You have seen what these self-styled Sons of Liberty have done. Property destroyed, lives destroyed. No, William. I, for one, rest better at night knowing that the Regulars are here to protect us from those mobs of ruffians. Sometimes I think we would all be better served if the whole rotten bunch of them were rounded up, sailed to the middle of the Atlantic, and tossed overboard!"

Hearing her uncle's atypically harsh words, Anna almost fell off the window seat. Should she be concerned for Daniel's safety? Or, furious with him for being part of the thing that was driving her uncle to such uncharacteristic causticness?

"I agree that some have taken things too far on occasion," Sprague allowed. "And yet, without the ear of the king or Parliament, what is a man to do to make his grievances known?" He raised his hand to preempt the argument that was forming on Wilton's lips. "Yes, I know there are political avenues for such grievances, but increasingly it appears that those avenues are, for those of us here in the American colonies, a chimera. And now, this disaster on King Street. What could they have been thinking, John? To deploy armed Regulars against Boston's citizens? To actually fire on unarmed civilians?"

"The men in that mob were not what I would consider 'unarmed.'"

"A few sticks and oyster shells against muskets? Hardly a level battlefield in my view."

Wilton snapped up the copy of the *Gazette* and waved it in the air. "These inflated accounts in the papers will only make things worse." He smacked his hand against the paper as though chastising the editors. "This is political propaganda at its worst."

"I agree." Sprague's voice reflected his effort to rein in his agitation. "But the fact remains that there are few other avenues for making London aware of the situation here."

"We are talking in circles. And you sound as if you side with these criminals!"

"I side with Boston, John. The atmosphere here becomes more volatile at every turn and there is little to indicate that the king or Parliament will respond in any way but one that will further fan the smoldering flames. That is what I fear. That is why I believe we are headed for something far beyond anything that could have been foreseen." He paused, giving his friend a moment to digest what he had said. "You called them criminals. Are they, though? These are our friends and neighbors. We know many of these men, and we know they are not criminals. Can you not bring yourself to consider what must be in their hearts to have driven them to this point?"

When Sprague had departed, John Wilton sat staring thoughtfully into the fire. Watching in silence, Anna's heart ached for him. She crossed the room and perched on the arm of his chair, slipped her arm about his shoulder and leaned down to rest her cheek against her uncle's head. "Dear uncle." Her softened voice was full of affection and sympathy. "I wish this would all end, for your sake, if for no other reason. I'm not accustomed to seeing you so irritable as you've been lately, and it breaks my heart to see you so grieved."

Wilton took hold of her hand and patted it reassuringly. He smiled up at her. "Now, my darling girl, I'll hear of no broken hearts on my account. Everything will come right sooner or later — of that I'm certain. If I seem troubled by it all from time to time, please take no account of it. I grow old and crotchety."

Anna laughed. "That will never happen," she protested.

"I fear your confidence may be misplaced."

She shook her head. "You will never be anything but wonderful in my eyes," she assured him as she got to her feet. "I shall take the tea tray away. Are you going over the accounts before supper?"

"No," he sighed. "I think I shall just read for a bit."

She scooped the paper off the tea table, and replaced it with a leather-bound book from his desk. "Then read something more worthwhile than the *Gazette*," she demanded crisply.

He narrowed his eyes at her but chuckled. "You are far too much like your mother," he asserted good-naturedly as she walked toward the door. "Your mother – my sister – was a bossy bee, if ever there was one."

"Hush now, uncle," she replied over her shoulder. "You could be saddled with the likes of Mrs. Sprague."

Wilton so comically contorted his face in mock horror as to send her out of the room laughing.

CHAPTER TWO

April brought somewhat warmer temperatures to Boston — but only just. It also brought a new irritant in the form of a persistent and increasingly notorious chicken thief. Many households kept a few laying-hens, which were easy pickings for the licentious scalawag. The constable had investigated and, because some victims reported seeing what looked like a red-coated Regular fleeing the scene, he had turned the matter over to the regimental authorities. In turn, those authorities launched their own investigation and, to no one's surprise, quickly ruled that none of their men were guilty. The thefts continued, compounding the town's hostility toward the presence of the Regulars in their midst. For the propaganda value, if not a desire to see justice done, there was among the Committee of Safety a determination to prove unequivocally that the redcoats were responsible for the thefts and, in consideration of his particular knowledge of Boston's seamier side, Daniel was charged with obtaining such proof.

Daniel took only grudging comfort in the fact that the unique set of skills he had learned in some of Boston's meanest streets and alleys was now useful to a good and just cause, wishing instead that everyone, including himself, could forget what he had once been, what he was trying so hard to leave behind. Nevertheless, most nights found Daniel skulking alone through alleys, hiding in trees, and occasionally skimming along the odd rooftop, following every out-of-place sound or hint of movement in search of his quarry. There was a time when Teague would have gladly accompanied him on such a mission. Lately, however, Teague was more interested in pursuing his own interests, the nature of which Daniel knew little.

Pondering all of this, Daniel crouched on the roof of a shed overlooking a particularly large chicken coop. Assuming that the thief would eventually find his way to such a tempting target, Daniel had watched the spot for several consecutive nights. The cold nights kept the hens huddled in their boxes, still and quiet, ready targets for a thief. From his perch, Daniel could clearly make out the shapes of the yard's outbuildings, their silent darkness washed grey by the bright moonlight. Over and again, he blew into his cupped hands trying to warm them, but dared not make any other movement. Lying flat and motionless, uncomfortable against the wooden shingles, he did all he could to become a part of the shadows. One frustrating night after another had been spent in this fashion, and Daniel dearly hoped this would be the last.

Time passed until he judged that he'd been waiting for over an hour without seeing or hearing anything amiss. The monotony was broken only occasionally when one of the resident cats prowled by, its only interest the odd bit of discarded food or the myriad rats that scuttled among the piled detritus in the alley. Thankful that his nose was too cold to smell the unpleasant odors intrinsic to alleys, poultry pens, and pigsties, Daniel watched and waited while his limbs stiffened in the chilly night air.

He was beginning to fight off drowsiness when he was brought to attention by a sound so slight he wondered for a moment if he had truly heard it at all. He waited, senses alert and fired by a sudden surge of adrenaline. Then a figure came into view, moving in the erratic fits and starts characteristic of those engaged in dishonest work. The man picked his way between casts of shadow and light toward the chicken enclosure. Daniel smiled in satisfaction when a dash of moonlight momentarily caught and illuminated a red coat slashed across the breast with a white cross-belt. A British Regular, he thought. Capture him, and they would have their proof.

Daniel watched the thief let himself into the coop and cross the small enclosure toward the hen house, lingering in the shadow of the low, wooden structure for a moment to assure himself that he was as yet undetected. Once satisfied, he slipped through the flimsy wooden door, leaving it slightly ajar. Without a sound, Daniel lowered himself to the ground and crept toward the coop, keeping carefully to the shadows. He made his way to the corner of the garden wall and peeked around, assuring himself that the location afforded him a good view of the thief's exit path. Daniel slipped a flintlock pistol from where he had carried it under his cloak and ensured its readiness to fire.

After several long minutes, a faint squeak of door hinges warned him that the thief had emerged. Daniel stole a cautious look around the corner. The thief had let himself out of the pen and was walking toward him, a chicken dangling from each hand, their necks already having been broken. Daniel drew his head back and made himself flat against the shadowed wall, held his breath, and waited the several seconds it took for the thief to round the wall. The instant the thief had passed by his hiding place, Daniel stepped out and coolly pressed the flintlock into the back of the man's head.

"That's a pistol, loaded and ready to fire," he told the now motionless man. "And I *shall* fire it if you move." He gouged the pistol's barrel deeper into the man's scalp. "Now, then. Arms straight out away from your body, please. Don't drop the birds."

The man did as he was told and Daniel, putting a few paces safe distance between himself and the thief, urged him forward into the alley. Moonlight illuminated the thief as he stepped away from the wall, allowing Daniel to see that he was a particularly short man, reed-thin, with wispy, straw-colored hair that stood out in a frizzed cloud around his collar.

Daniel also noticed something peculiar about the man's coat. Puzzled, he ordered the thief to stop and turn around to face him.

"You one of them militia men?" the thief asked as he complied.

"More or less." In fact, Daniel was not officially a member of the militia, but there seemed little point in explaining his situation. Now that Daniel had a clearer view of the thief's attire, he had to work at not letting the surprise show on his face. The thief was no redcoat. The illusion was created by a coat painted red with white stripes crisscrossing the front and on the facings in feeble imitation of a Regular's uniform. "Cunning ruse," Daniel said, pointing toward the ersatz uniform.

The thief grinned. He seemed to be missing more of his teeth than not, and his face and hands were caked with grime. "No need for this," Toothless argued genially. "You can have the chickens and we can go our separate ways."

Daniel shook his head. "Not interested." He was preparing to direct the thief to precede him down the alley when, suddenly, he saw white-hot pinpricks erupting behind his eyes. He staggered forward, barely able to keep his balance as he grappled to understand that he'd been hit on the head.

"You should have taken the offer." The husky voice came from behind him, along with strong hands that grabbed the back of his collar and used it to sling Daniel against a wall.

Daniel, silently cursing himself for not considering that there might be more than one thief, groaned and strained around to get a look at his attacker. All he could make out was a dark shape looming behind him.

"'Bout time you showed up, Dodd," Toothless whined. Juggling the two dead chickens, he retrieved the pistol from where Daniel had dropped it and tucked it under his belt. "Bugger could've killed me!"

"Nah," Dodd assured him. "This one ain't interested in killing no one. More likely, he's lookin' to be a hero." His voice had a dull, stubbed quality. "More likely, he's lookin' to turn you in for some sort of reward. Ain't that right, hero?" Dodd punctuated the question with a wave of his pistol.

Daniel, gingerly touching his fingers to the back of his head, said nothing. He studied Dodd through squinted eyes. It did not take clear vision to see that this man was much larger than Toothless. Almost, Daniel thought, as large as Drum. The big man's head was completely bald, his fearsome face full of scars likely acquired during a lifetime of fighting. Certainly, his knobbed and crooked nose appeared to have been broken on more than one occasion.

Dodd jerked his head at Toothless. "Get over there and pick up my sack," he growled. "I left it by that woodpile down a ways when I had to come save your bunglin' arse."

"I didn't bungle nothin'," Toothless protested touchily.

"No? You let this bastard nab you. I'd call that bunglin'."

Indignant, Toothless gaped at him. "I watched a good long while before I moved in, I did," he insisted. "Didn't see nothin'. I don't know where the bastard come from. Come from thin air, seemed like. He be a right sneaky one. Not like them other militia boys what've been lookin' for us."

"Would you shut your mouth," Dodd snapped. "Go get my sack like I told you. I did better'n a couple of scrawny chickens, and I'm of no mind to leave it here."

Daniel watched as Toothless scurried down the alley, arms ludicrously akimbo, a chicken in each hand. He stopped at the location Dodd had indicated and turned in circles, searching for the sack. "I don't see it," he called.

Dodd swore heartily. "Quiet!" He waved his pistol at Daniel. "Move," he growled. "That way." They joined Toothless, and Dodd used the toe of one boot to poke at a small bundle hidden behind a roughly-stacked woodpile. "There, you idiot. Can you see it now?"

Scowling, Toothless shifted his burden of chickens to one hand and picked up the sack with the other. His rustling about disturbed a sow in the adjacent yard, and, grunting her threats, she bumped against the wooden fence, startling Toothless. Discomfited that Dodd had noticed, he quickly composed himself and hefted the sack. The weight surprised him. "What you got in here?"

"I'll show you later," Dodd snapped. "Right now, we need to deal with hero, here."

"What're we gonna do with him?" Toothless asked.

"Well, shite-for-brains," Dodd said, his voice full of disdain, "seein' as how you told him my name, and seein' as how he has seen both our faces, I'd say we're goin' to cut his throat and dump him in the harbor." Once again, he waved the pistol at Daniel. "Move," he ordered. "I ain't carryin' your sorry sack of bones all the way down to the harbor. You can walk there yourself, then we'll see to your throat."

Toothless, one hand clasped around the necks of the dead chickens, the other grasping Dodd's sack of stolen goods, did as he was told. But Daniel did not move.

"I told you to walk," Dodd snarled, jabbing Daniel with the pistol.

"Or, what?" Daniel asked. "You've already said you're going to kill me. Actually, I'd prefer that you just pull that trigger now. The gunshot will likely rouse every household within hearing, meaning that you'll be caught. So, not only will you be punished for stealing, but you'll also hang for murdering me. At this juncture, I'd say that is about the happiest outcome for which I can hope."

While this exchange was taking place, Toothless decided to see for himself what was in Dodd's bag. "There's silver in here!" he exclaimed gaping at the contents of the bag. He frowned at Dodd. "There's candlesticks and a couple of silver dishes in here. You never said nothin' about stealin' anything like this! Where'd you get this?"

"Close the sack," Dodd barked. "An opportunity presented itself, and I took it."

"How many times have opportunities like that presented themselves?" Daniel asked, further stirring the discord. "And have you always given Toothless his share?"

"I told you to keep quiet." Dodd struck Daniel on the side of the head with the pistol. "And you, too." He waved the pistol in Toothless' direction.

"I still want to know what you been up to," Toothless insisted. "You never told me nothin' about stealin' things like this." He shook the bag, rattling its contents.

"Close that bag and pick up the birds," Dodd ordered through gritted teeth. "We'll work this out after we get rid of hero, here. Unless you want me to shoot you and dump you in the harbor with him?"

Toothless frowned and shook his head.

"I didn't think so. Now, pick up the birds and keep your damned mouth shut."

Watching Toothless sullenly bend to pick up the chickens, Dodd was caught off guard when Daniel abruptly flung himself backwards into him, knocking the pistol from his hand. The pistol discharged when it hit the ground, and Daniel heard Toothless wail in pain as he was grazed by the errant shot. Riding on the momentum his turn had created, Daniel's fist flew up and slammed like a mallet into one of Dodd's ears. The blow propelled Dodd backward several stumbling paces, and Daniel increased that effect by punching Dodd's midsection so hard that it launched the big man into a nearby wall with a crash.

Daniel immediately returned his attention to Toothless. In a tableau that would have been pathetically funny under other circumstances, Toothless, still standing, had dropped his chickens and the sack, and was focused on the pistol wound in his leg to the exclusion of all else. He was surprised, then, when Daniel struck a fist into his windpipe. The blow sent him reeling, clutching his throat and gasping for air. Before Daniel could finish his plan to incapacitate Toothless, however, he heard Dodd's labored breath closing in on him from behind.

Daniel turned to see that the oversized thief, who had regained his equilibrium amazingly well, was lumbering toward him, methodically setting up his attack, thinking as most big men did that their superior size and strength would always win. Dodd scythed one mammoth fist in the direction of Daniel's head, but he had taken so much time to launch his swing that Daniel saw it coming and easily dodged the blow. Dodd tried again with the other fist, this one no more nimble than the first, and Daniel blocked it with his left forearm. There was an instant in which Dodd seemed baffled by the fact that Daniel had confounded him, and Daniel used that moment to drive the heel of his hand viciously upwards into Dodd's nose. He heard bone crunch and felt it grind under his hand. Roaring with pain and staggering backwards, Dodd's hands flew protectively to his face. Blood was streaming down onto his hands and forearms, and he huddled against the wall moaning and cursing Daniel.

Shaking off the discomfort in his hand, Daniel turned on Toothless who, bleeding, breathless, and afraid, was reviewing his options. He wanted to flee, but Dodd's words came back to him. If Daniel survived, he would be able to identify Toothless to the constable. Daniel was moving toward him, forcing him to a decision. But Toothless had waited a beat too long. By the time he shifted his hand toward the pistol stuffed in his belt, Daniel was there. Without bothering to tug the pistol free, Daniel grasped it and pulled the trigger. The blast and blinding flash of the pistol firing were quickly followed by screams of agony from Toothless, who dropped straight to the ground as though his legs had been cut from under him. Dark blood stains spread across his breeches, and small flames spluttered to life where the powder had ignited his painted jacket.

Daniel, momentarily transfixed by the sight, failed to see Dodd roaring toward him, infuriated and thundering with rage. Dodd collided into him from behind, the strength of his impetus carrying both men forward to splinter through a low wooden fence and into the pigsty. Their abrupt arrival startled the sow into a hasty retreat toward the far end of the pen where she stood bellowing her anger at the intruders. Both men scrambled to their feet, slipping in the muck and paying little attention to the angry sow.

Hoping to take advantage of Daniel's momentary unsteadiness, Dodd attacked first. Fighting to keep his footing, the big man leaned forward into the effort of moving across the pen toward Daniel. He slogged through the mire, his velocity increasing with each deliberate step. Daniel held his ground, and watched Dodd come. Within a few feet of Daniel, Dodd launched himself through the air. The full force of his weight and momentum hit Daniel, knocking both men to the sludge-thick ground.

Too late, Dodd realized his error. He had not seen Daniel slip his dirk from its sheath and he rolled back now, staring with amazed incomprehension at the knife handle protruding from his own chest. Unerringly, Daniel had guided the blade up under Dodd's breastbone and into his heart. Dodd would live only seconds more, long enough to know the fear of approaching death. His stupefied eyes rolled from the knife to

Daniel and back again as he tried to solve the puzzle of how his life had ended so unexpectedly.

Winded and spent, Daniel got to his feet. He pulled the dirk from Dodd's body and wiped the blade clean on the dying man's jacket. He was still standing over Dodd's body, watching as the thug's blood flowed out to mingle with the filth of the pigsty when, roused by the commotion, neighbors began to arrive. Daniel kept silent for a long while, leaving the gawking men to wonder at the two blood-soaked corpses in their midst. The flames that had flickered on Toothless' clothing had died, leaving a peculiar charred area that stretched from his stomach to his knees. The smell was bitter, rivaling even the pigsty. Some men covered their faces with scarves or their hands, and all of them gaped as they looked first at the bodies, then at Daniel.

Once he had regained himself, Daniel approached the group of men. "These are your chicken thieves," he told them. He pointed to the two dead chickens, and then to the sack of Dodd's stolen loot lying near Toothless. "I'll leave it to you gentlemen to sort out ownership of all that." He walked to where Toothless lay. "I'm taking his coat," Daniel said as he leaned down to the body. "I'm taking it to the captain of the militia."

"It's painted to look like a Regular's uniform," one of the bystanders observed, puzzled.

Daniel nodded again. "That's why I need the coat. We may have plenty of reason to dislike the redcoats, but this episode of chicken stealing isn't one of them." He sensed a wave of disappointment moving through the gathered neighbors and suspected that the men who had sent him on this mission would be likewise disappointed. So be it, he thought.

He looked from the body at his feet to the pig enclosure. The sow was taking an interest in Dodd's body, and the pig's owner was rallying assistance to move the corpse out of the pen. Though Daniel had fought many a fierce fight, this was the first time it had been to the death. That it was a matter of self-defense was of little comfort. He hated the killing; hated that he had turned out to be good at it. It seemed one more thing to add to his list of dubious skills. And, for the moment, he hated the Committee of Safety for putting him in this position. Angrily, Daniel pulled the charred coat free from Toothless' body. "Let them be disappointed," he said to no one in particular.

*   *   *

Selah Garrett's millinery establishment stood in the middle of a neat row of shops on Kilby Street, just off King Street and a stone's throw from the Custom House. The sign over the door read "Healey's Millinery," but everyone knew it was Selah Garrett's shop now, and had been for some time. The shop was sturdily built and neatly painted, and the door was well-fitted with three small windows set in a row toward the top. The brass bell, which jingled whenever someone opened the door, had hung there for years, having been put there by the shop's previous owner, Mr. Alden Healey. The front of the store boasted an unusually large mullioned window, an extravagance on Mr. Healey's part, but one that gave the shop a particularly elegant and unique look from the street as well as allowing in an abundance of natural light.

The morning after Daniel's encounter with the chicken thieves, Selah stood at the large window, watching and worrying. Worry seemed to be a constant for her of late — but then, she thought, when had her life not been burdened with worry? There had been a time, she knew, but it was so far removed from the present as to be almost non-existent. Absently wringing her hands, she leaned closer to the glass so she could see farther up the street. Her raven-black hair escaped in wisps from under her frilled cap, and her brilliant blue eyes were slightly red-rimmed. Aside from the dark circles under her eyes, there was little color in her face.

Over a month had passed since the incident at the Custom House and, despite the fact that the troops had withdrawn to Castle William, the atmosphere in Boston remained tense. The trials of Captain Preston and his men were not scheduled to begin for several months, and she hoped the delay would give folks time to shift their attention to other matters. Instead, it seemed that each day brought only more impetus for the antagonism on all sides.

None of that worried her as much as did her son, however. Daniel had gone out again the previous night to hunt the chicken thief who had plagued Boston neighborhoods, and he had not yet returned. Everyone was convinced that the thief was a redcoat, and Selah wondered what would happen if that turned out to be true. If Daniel caught a redcoat in the act of stealing, what might be the unintended consequences?

Sooner or later, she believed, Daniel's involvement with Sam Adams and his troublemaking cronies was going to lead to an unhappy outcome. At the very least, these men were guilty of an array of violations against persons and property, and she had no desire to see her son imprisoned. But if things continued to escalate, became more outright treasonous, she could even find herself watching her son hang. She had worked so hard, with old Mr. Healey's help, to steer Daniel away from the corrupt influences to which he'd been attracted when, following the death of Daniel's father, she and Daniel moved to the city so that she could take up employment with Mr. Healey. Lately, it seemed that effort had been all for naught.

For herself, she wanted only peace. She knew Daniel was disappointed that her blood did not rise to a boil every time the king, or Parliament or whoever happened to be handing out that day's insults acted. To Selah, it did not matter who was dictating public policy, the result was always the same — the people were dealt a new discomfort, generally in the pocketbook. Shaking herself out of her morbid and wholly unproductive frame of mind, she moved away from the window and busied herself about the shop.

In less than an hour, everything that could be swept, dusted, or straightened had been. Selah surveyed her work, pleased at the result of her efforts. She was proud of her establishment. Under Alden Healey's proprietorship, the shop had been a hodgepodge of notions and sundry items, anything a seamstress might need side-by-side with household items of every sort. It had simply been known as "Healey's Sundries" in those days. With all the necessary materials ready to hand, however, Selah had begun to indulge a new-found fondness for making all sorts of ladies' headdress. It started with the occasional creation of a hat or bonnet as time allowed. The lovely hats, carefully crafted to mimic drawings of London and Paris fashions, were quickly snapped up, and orders for more came in so steadily that, over time, the shop became "Healey's Millinery."

It was still Healey's Millinery, though Alden Healey was no more. Three years earlier, the old man had passed away and surprised everyone by settling his entire estate on Selah. His solicitor and those who knew him knew he had done so because he was genuinely fond of Selah and Daniel, and because it was Selah who had cared for him during his last, feebly helpless months of life. The less charitable speculated that there was more to the relationship than friendship, but they continued to frequent the shop nonetheless. It was a touch of irony that the gossip had given a caché to the shop that it would not have otherwise enjoyed.

Selah stood, hands on hips, mulling possibilities for improvements to the shop when the bell over the door jingled. She looked up, and inwardly groaned. As much as she wanted customers this morning, she would have preferred that her first one not be this particular young woman.

Charlotte Ainsworth entered the shop much as she made her entry into any room — with a regal flourish that demanded attention. She was a striking girl, tall and possessed of an elegant bearing that gave one the impression that her social standing must surely be significantly higher than it actually was. A gust of uncomfortably cool air came through the door with her, stirring the ribbons and feathers on the hats Selah had on display and filling the shop with the tang of sea air.

Selah sighed. Charlotte occasionally purchased expensive items, it was true, but Selah knew that the girl's ulterior reason for frequenting the shop was Daniel. Charlotte made some effort to hide her interest in him, but it was all too apparent to Selah. And Charlotte Ainsworth was not a girl Selah would have wholeheartedly welcomed as a daughter-in-law. Selah pasted a smile on her face and greeted Charlotte with a show of far more enthusiasm than she felt.

She watched patiently while Charlotte ran her lithe fingers over some beautiful silk evening gloves Selah kept on display more for the color and elegance they added to the shop than anything. Such items were not in high demand in Boston, especially in these harder times. "I have some kid gloves that are quite lovely and which would be much warmer if that's what you need," Selah said. She waited, one hand resting lightly on the handle of the drawer in which the more practical gloves were stored, knowing all the while that it was most likely that the girl was not interested in gloves at all. Probably, she would take up the better part of an hour of Selah's time, stalling in the hope that Daniel might appear, and then leave empty-handed.

Charlotte's eyes, the pale green-flecked grey of sea water, skimmed from the gloves to Selah, then beyond her to the back of the shop. Finally, with a sigh of resignation, she produced a small bundle from where she had discreetly carried it under her cape. "Actually," Charlotte said demurely, "I've come across something I thought you might be interested in purchasing." With an affected flourish, she placed upon the counter a roll of very fine brown velvet.

Selah's eyebrows shot up in surprise. Charlotte had come into the shop from time to time with bits of lace, fancy buttons, and other unique bits of trim a milliner would find useful, but never anything so large. "Surely, you didn't find this in a trunk in your father's attic!" It was as much a question as a statement of surprise. Trunks of clothing and other personal articles that had belonged to Charlotte's mother and grandparents were stored in the Ainsworth attic and, judging by the items Charlotte brought in to sell, each trunk was crammed full of pieces of clothing embellished with expensive laces, exquisite buttons, unusual feathers, and even the odd bit of gemstone or jewelry. Charlotte sold the pieces whenever she needed money, which was increasingly often of late.

"No," Charlotte said, a bittersweet smile flickering across her face as she tenderly stroked her hand across the velvet. "This was a gift from which I was expected to have a gown made. But the color would not suit me." She lightly caressed her fingertips along one pearl-white cheek.

"Are you certain? It's such beautiful fabric."

Charlotte shook her head. "No," she insisted. "I would prefer to sell it."

Selah was lifting the folds of the material, examining it for flaws and attempting to gauge its value. She suspected that Charlotte's recent need for money was linked to her father's declining health, for Martin Ainsworth was ill more often than not. "How is your father?" Selah asked without looking up. "I've not seen him in a very long time. Has he taken to his bed again?"

Charlotte smiled wanly. "Thank you. Yes, he has. It has been quite difficult." She turned her face toward the window, allowing the watery light to illuminate her equally pale skin. Her hair, so blonde that it seemed white, curled from under her bonnet here and there, a softly shining frame around a porcelain face. She turned a stiff smile upon Selah. "But, I'm managing," she chimed brightly, her eyes glimmering. "The doctor says father suffers from dropsy, but his condition doesn't seem to be following the common course. He has terrible periods where his limbs are so swollen and painful that he cannot get out of bed. But then he recovers and seems little worse for it." She frowned slightly, thinking. "Though I do believe each occurrence weakens him."

"I'm certain that you must be a great comfort to him," Selah allowed sweetly, though she did not quite believe the words. Judging by what she knew of Charlotte, Selah guessed that Martin Ainsworth's daughter was more of a trial for him than any such man deserved. But she forged ahead. "And so helpful. You've always been such a clever, resourceful girl. I know that your father adores you, and that he must be wondrously proud of you."

"Ah, well," Charlotte waved away the disagreeable subject. "It is not a happy topic for me."

Nodding her understanding, Selah returned her attention to the velvet, unrolling it just enough to guess at its dimensions. There was an ample amount of fabric, and she envisioned the many uses to which it could be put. With some regret, Selah remembered the limited funds she had available at the time. "I'm afraid I could not give you an amount approaching its value. I do know someone who might be able to make you a better offer than can I, however. Would you like for me to ask him about it?"

Charlotte brightened visibly. "I think I'd prefer to deal with him directly — if you wouldn't mind giving me his name," she added quickly.

Selah nodded. Before she could supply the information, however, they were interrupted by the jingling of the bell over the shop door. A young girl hesitated in the doorway as though uncertain of her next step. Little more than a silhouette was visible as she stood with her back to the sunlight, an outline of feminine clothing the only clue to her gender. Charlotte turned away from Selah and, head cocked to one side, watched curiously as the girl hung there, wavering between entering the shop and retreating back to the street.

"May I help you?" Selah asked in a tone she hoped would be encouraging.

Visibly drawing a deep breath to fortify her resolve, the child carefully closed the shop door and advanced to where Charlotte and Selah stood at the counter. With only an evanescent glance at Charlotte, she bobbed a tiny curtsy to Selah.

"Good day to you, Mrs. Garrett."

"Good day." Selah's brow creased in a puzzled frown. Now that she could see the girl more clearly, Selah realized that she was older than she had first appeared, certainly older than her diminutive stature implied and, more than that, realized that she knew her. "Why, Miss Somerset! I've not seen you in such a long while; I almost didn't recognize you!"

Anna smiled, and opened her mouth to respond, but her words were cut off by an outburst from Charlotte. "Well, my goodness!" Charlotte exclaimed. "Anna Somerset! Just look at how much you have grown up." She raked Anna with an appraising look and seemed to be amused by what she saw. Clearly, she did not think Anna had grown up much at all. "Dear little Anna."

Anna glared daggers at her. Charlotte, like Daniel, was only a few years older than herself, and yet she insisted on addressing Anna as though she was not only an inferior, but a much younger inferior to boot.

Selah's gaze was equally appraising, but she liked what she saw. Anna's tawny eyes, full of mischief, intelligence, and feeling, the ginger-kissed brown hair that swept to one side from a cowlick at the hairline above her left brow, and the dimples that formed near the corners of her mouth at the slightest suggestion of a smile — all of these things combined to form a most charming picture. Anna's parents had died of one of the myriad fevers that struck so inexplicably and often, she knew, and then the infant Anna had been taken in by her uncle, John Wilton. But Selah knew little else about Anna Somerset beyond the fact that the little girl could sometimes be seen doggedly tagging along in the wake of Daniel and his friends. Selah rummaged her memory in search of the last time she'd seen Anna and came up with no answer. "How have you been?"

"I've been very well, thank you." Anna would have liked to add some caustic qualifier regarding the fact that her well-being was despite the misdeeds of Daniel and his cronies, but she held her tongue.

"And your uncle? Is Mr. Wilton well?"

Accustomed to being the center of attention at any gathering, Charlotte was growing impatient with the exchange of pleasantries and Selah's attention to the scraggly girl. There was very little about her that would make anyone consider her pretty, Charlotte thought. She was tiny and lacked a single feminine curve. Large brown calf-eyes dominated her unremarkable face, and her hair was straight and barely contained in a childish braid that fell down her back, flopping about like a horse's tail. She wore sturdy, practical boots, and her too-short, unfashionably cut skirts were dashed here and there with dirty smudges as though she'd been gamboling in the woods.

"I've just remembered the last time I saw you!" Charlotte cried triumphantly. "You were a tiny thing — well, I suppose you're still tiny, aren't you?" She tittered lightly, excusing any offense the remark might give. "You were dressed in a scruffy little skirt and apron you'd kirtled so you could climb a fence. And you'd got caught." She laughed heartily. "Stuck right on the top rail of the fence. Oh, Mrs. Garrett! I wish I could describe the scene to you! It truly was quite comical. I'm certain she would be stuck there still had not Mr. Garrett helped her out of her ridiculous predicament." Her eyes narrowed slightly, and her scrutiny became more focused. "That seemed to happen to you a great deal, as I recall — Mr. Garrett having to rescue you, I mean." She turned to Selah affecting compassion and commiseration. "Poor Mr. Garrett. Between this little one's antics and Drummond Fisackerly's need for constant supervision, I'm certain he felt as though he had his hands over-full."

Selah noticed that Anna had blushed scarlet with embarrassment but had not flinched. The girl stood firmly rooted, back ramrod straight, refusing to be cowed by Charlotte's callous trouncing. "Knowing my son as I do," she assured Charlotte, "I submit that caring for his friends is not something he considers a burden."

Anna swallowed hard. So many biting retorts had welled up in her as she endured Charlotte's anecdote, lodging themselves in her throat, constricting it and making it difficult to get her words out. "Mrs. Garrett," she said tightly, turning her back on Charlotte. "I've come for two purposes. First, I am in need of new gloves. My uncle is sending me to London, and it seems that I have no gloves he regards as adequate to either the sea voyage or London society."

The explanation drew a gasp of excitement from Charlotte. "You're traveling to London? How thrilled you must be!" She was almost breathless, but her smile was tight. Anna Somerset was going to London. How could it be that this girl was to achieve the dream Charlotte herself had harbored for as long as she could remember?

Anna took a step back, overwhelmed by Charlotte's sudden change in demeanor. "Unfortunately, yes. I'm traveling to London. Though, I can't say that I count a sense of being thrilled among my feelings on the subject. To be thrilled implies that there's some element of pleasure involved. For me, there is no pleasure in my contemplation of this journey."

"But then, why are you going?" Selah asked. "Are you accompanying your uncle while he attends to some business?"

Anna shook her head. "No. I'm going alone, which makes the whole thing all the more unappealing in my view. My uncle worries about the violence that has erupted here in recent weeks." She dared a meaningful look in Selah's direction. "He is convinced that I'll be safer in the care of his friend and business partner in London. He'll not go with me because he feels that he should remain here to look after his interests. I argued with him until I could argue no longer, and his mind would not be changed.

S.D. BANKS

Unhappily, he managed to arrange passage for me on the very next suitable ship, which leaves two weeks from today."

"But, how could you not want to go to London?" Charlotte pressed. "I'm certain it is the most wonderful of cities!" In full loathing of fates so unfair that they would send unworthy Anna to that Elysian city while keeping her, Charlotte, a prisoner in lowly, backwards Boston, Charlotte looked at Anna with a mixture of envy and disbelief.

Anna frowned. "And, *I'm* sure that I am quite content with Boston. Certainly I'd prefer to stay with my uncle."

"Let us discuss your need for gloves, shall we?" Selah interjected. "I am understanding that you'll need a warm pair that will serve you against the challenges of the voyage, and another pair or two that are more refined — for when you reach London?"

"That sounds right. I thought two pair would suffice, but Mrs. Sprague insists that I shall need at least two for the voyage and four for London. She says that it will not credit my uncle for me to arrive without a complete wardrobe."

"And, of course she is correct," Charlotte concurred gravely.

Selah and Anna put their heads together over Selah's stock of gloves and, despite Charlotte's frequent interruptions to express her own opinions on the choices, quickly came up with something that seemed in Anna's estimation to be more than satisfactory.

"You said you had two reasons for visiting me today." Selah reminded her as she wrapped the gloves. "What was the second?"

Anna flushed again, and shyly produced a letter from her pocket. "I also wanted to leave a message for Dan— er, Mr. Garrett." She handed over the letter, which was folded and sealed, and had Daniel's name written on the front in neat, careful script. "I know this is most unseemly, but I don't know that I will see him before the ship is to sail. I hoped it would not be an imposition to ask you to pass this along to him?"

"No imposition at all," Selah declared. Plainly curious, she accepted the letter.

Charlotte watched the letter pass from Anna's hand to Selah's, and felt an instant's irritation that Anna considered herself in a position to be sending notes to Daniel.

"I shall be happy to deliver your message, Miss Somerset." Selah smoothed the letter where it lay upon the counter, looking from it to Anna, still hoping for an explanation.

Anna did not disappoint. "The letter concerns a promise Mr. Garrett made to me some time ago." She shifted uncertainly under the resultant pair of astonished gazes. "The terms of our agreement need to be altered somewhat."

40

Charlotte almost choked on her surprise. "But, what sort of agreement could you and Mr. Garrett possibly have?"

"Not *that* sort of agreement," Anna replied, impatient with Charlotte's implication. "It's more of a business agreement, or . . . er, something of a political nature." Nervously, she shifted from foot to foot.

Selah thought Anna might turn and bolt from the shop at any moment. "Surely," she hazarded slowly, "you are not mixed up with Daniel's new friends, are you?"

"Oh, no!" Anna replied with an emphatic shake of her head. "Absolutely not! I abhor the things these people do." She reminded herself that she was talking about Mrs. Garrett's son, and softened her tone. "I worry for my uncle's safety, you understand. I think he is at far more risk than am I, and yet he sends me to London while he remains here. He refuses to acknowledge how easily he could become a target. I think he is being horribly pig-headed about it."

"Indeed." Selah's tone matched the wry twist to her mouth and, in that moment, her son's likeness to her was all the more apparent. She drummed her fingers lightly on the letter. "I would agree with your uncle that there's far too much violence in Boston of late. It's the very reason I prevailed upon Daniel to give up the rooms he had rented and move back here with me for a time. I feel safer with him here. I must say that I understand your uncle's impulse to send you away until these differences are all settled."

"Oh, but Mrs. Garrett," Charlotte protested, "Surely you're not concerned for your own safety! You're well regarded here, and you have a connection to the Committee of Safety through your son. I cannot imagine that anyone would direct any maliciousness your way."

"Many of the people who have been driven out of business, or tarred and feathered and driven out of the colonies altogether, were esteemed right up until the moment someone decided otherwise. And a mob has little regard for one's social or filial connections, I fear."

Selah's concerns echoed Anna's own. For so many weeks, as she had become aware of the violent episodes flaring up here and there in the colonies, concern for her uncle's safety had weighed heavily upon her. The epithet of "Tory" had been hurled at him more than once as he walked along the streets, making the fact that most of the violence was directed at crown officials of little comfort. Unrest was growing, and the consequential mobs were dangerous, unpredictable things that often heedlessly destroyed anyone who was not of like mind. Fear of this strengthening current was a significant part of her compulsion to know and understand all that was happening for it seemed the only way to judge how much danger there was for her uncle.

All of this was on Anna's mind when she left Selah's shop and, so, she did not see Daniel until he stepped directly in front of her, blocking her path. Blinking, she looked from him into the alley from whence he had come. "Daniel?" She turned her quizzical gaze from him back across the street to Selah's shop. "I was just in your mother's shop leaving a message for you."

Keeping one eye on Selah's shop, he took Anna's arm and maneuvered her around the corner into the alley. "Well, Mouse," he said with a grin, "you've found me. What's the message?"

She sighed, and decided against telling him once again how much she hated his nickname for her. "What are you doing?" she asked, slapping at his hand where it grasped her arm. "Why are you skulking here in this alley? And, why is Drum acting like his clothing is infested with ants?" She gestured to where Daniel's friend stood, his immense frame half-hidden by a wood pile. He was fidgeting about, red-faced and apparently anxious. "Hello, Drum," she called gently.

Drum, shyly returning her friendly smile, emerged from his ostensible hiding place. "Hello, Miss Anna." Though his bashfulness was more acute when in the company of girls, he had always been comfortable with Anna. "How did you see me?"

Anna laughed. "You were never very good at hide-and-seek, Drum. There are not too many places someone of your stature can hide."

Drum liked the way Anna used the word "stature," making his size sound like something of which he should be proud, and he laughed. "I wasn't trying to hide." His smile changed to a frown. "Not exactly." Daniel had told him to stay out of sight, and it occurred to him that this was the same thing as hiding. He thought perhaps he should further amend his claim, and was thinking on how exactly it needed to be changed.

Anna had not lingered on the point, however. Her expression became less friendly as she returned her attention to Daniel. "What are you two doing hiding in an alley?" she demanded. "Are you in trouble again?"

"What?" He had not been listening and jerked his head back from where he'd been peering around the corner.

"I asked if you're in trouble again," she repeated.

"No," he retorted with a combination of irritation and self-consciousness. "I simply don't wish to be seen at the moment."

She followed his gaze to Selah's shop. "Charlotte Ainsworth is in your mother's shop," she informed him. "Hoping to speak with you, I'd guess."

"As I said, I don't wish to be seen at the moment." When Anna closed her eyes and shook her head in exasperation, he decided to go on the defensive. "Why were you visiting my mother?"

"Perhaps I was looking to purchase lace for a ball gown."

"Not likely," he scoffed. "What are you up to, Mouse? You said you had a message for me. Why leave it there?"

"Because, I didn't want to have to hunt you down. You've been absent a great deal lately — no doubt in hiding because of some mischief or the other you've committed."

"I haven't been hiding, just occupied." He sincerely did not want to tell her exactly what had occupied him, and especially not about his encounter with the chicken thieves the previous night. "What was the message?"

"I wanted to tell you that my uncle is sending me to London." Her tone was full of bad temper. "He's concerned that there will be more violence like that which occurred at the Custom House, and so he's sending me to London."

Daniel puzzled over the clipped, curtness of her words. The expression on her face stated plainly enough that she considered this turn of events his responsibility. "Is that what you've come to tell me?" he asked, confused. "That you're angry about having to go to London?"

"No. What I wanted was to remind you of your promise, and to leave a London address to which you can post correspondence. Though I'm being sent into exile, I shall expect you to keep me informed of happenings here."

"I can hardly warn you in advance of plans involving your uncle if you're in London," he pointed out. "It'll take weeks for any correspondence to reach you."

"I know that, you thimble-head. What I want is for you to tell me what is happening here in general and, specifically, to tell me if anything happens to my uncle. Regarding the general aspect, I would prefer a first-hand account of events I'm likely to read about in the London papers. Everyone who writes for the papers seems to do so with their own special interest at the core. At least I know your leanings, so I can compensate for any slant you apply."

"Can you." His tone made it a statement, not a question, and he folded his arms and waited for whatever was going to spring from her mouth next.

"Regarding the specific, I don't trust my uncle to tell me anything he thinks will worry or upset me. So, I'll rely on you for accurate information."

"Indeed. You're very imperious. I remember nothing regarding the writing of letters or serving as a conduit for general news being part of our discussion when you forced that absurd promise from me."

"Stop being contrary, Daniel. My request is still within the framework of your original promise. When one makes a promise to a friend, one does not attach caveats and exceptions." Before he could argue, and with head-spinning abruptness, she turned her attention back to Drum. Drum was still dancing about, shifting his weight from foot to foot, and was now flapping his arms like a deranged seagull.

"Drum," she demanded, understanding of his predicament finally dawning upon her, "why are you in shirtsleeves? It's too cold for you to be out without a coat."

"I had one," Drum replied sulkily. "But Daniel took it away from me."

Daniel swore under his breath when Anna turned on him with a hard glare. "I did not take it away from him," he insisted. "Not in the way he implies, at any rate." He fumbled for an explanation that would skirt the truth, which was that Teague had stolen the coat from a corpse and given it to Drum. It was infested with lice and other vermin, suspicious stains, and possessed of myriad offensive odors. "Teague obtained a coat for him, but it smelled bad."

"You could have tried washing it," she pointed out. "You didn't have to take it away from him when he has nothing else to wear."

"We tried that. And we tried boiling it."

"We tried putting it in smoke first," Drum added helpfully.

"Yes, we did. We tried smoking it, but that didn't help matters. Then we tried boiling it, but the boiling caused it to fall apart."

"I can help you get him a coat," she offered.

"No, thank you. I've seen the sort of male attire you choose to acquire. I believe I can do better."

She leveled a look of pure acid upon him. "Those clothes were meant to be a temporary disguise, you thimble-head. And, I thought you were not going to mention that episode again?"

"Nevertheless, I think we can manage without your help. We were on our way in to see what my mother might have for him when we were . . . distracted."

"When you saw Miss Ainsworth enter the shop, you mean. Why are you hiding from her? I thought you were somewhat smitten with her."

Drum snorted with laughter, and Daniel glowered at him. "Then you thought wrong," he snapped.

"Still, why are you avoiding her? You act as if you're afraid of her."

"Why do you ask so many questions? Come along. Drum and I should escort you home."

"I do not need an escort. I walked here without one, and I'm perfectly capable of finding my way home, thank you. Besides, you were on your way to find Drum a coat, remember?"

"I'm only cold when I stand still. We can walk with you, then go get the coat," Drum volunteered helpfully.

"Well, then," Daniel grinned, "we'll walk with you as far as our common path takes us."

"Our common path? I thought you were going to your mother's shop?"

"The plan has changed. Come along now. Stop being difficult."

They walked in silence for some way, Anna and Daniel side-by-side, Drum following behind. His eyes darted between Anna and Daniel. He could sense the tension between the two but could not comprehend it. "Where's London?" he asked. Given that London seemed to have something to do with the discord, he thought it would be good to know more about it.

"Across the ocean," Daniel told him. "In England."

"A very *long* way across the ocean," Anna amended. "Very far from here."

"You're certainly in high dudgeon this afternoon. Why do I get the feeling that you're cross with me?"

She stopped in her tracks and turned on him. "Perhaps because I *am* cross with you."

"I've not seen you for over two weeks. How could I possibly have done anything to annoy you?"

"I'm cross with you because I'm being sent away to London and it's your fault."

"Granting that being sent off to London is not a happy circumstance, I hardly see how you can blame me for this turn of events," Daniel replied indignantly.

"I blame you and your *friends*. If you would all stop behaving like louts — if you would all cease constantly stirring up trouble — the rest of us could get back to our lives and I would not have to go to London. You've delighted in making Boston a dodgy place to be these days, and *I'm* paying the price!"

He opened his mouth to respond but then, doubting that anything he might say would improve her mood, closed it again.

She shrugged and sighed. "Ah, well. Perhaps I shall like London. Miss Ainsworth seems to think it's the next thing to Eden." She turned on her heel and started walking again.

"Considering that Miss Ainsworth has never been outside of Boston, I don't know how you could credit her opinion," he scoffed.

"You've not been there either. And yet you seem to have very strong opinions on the subject."

"One has only to look at the things that come out of the place to form an opinion."

"Then your quarrel is with Parliament, not the city of London, surely."

"Parliament is in London. The king is in London. I need not say more."

"Very logical of you," she replied scornfully. "But then, you've ever been such a *rational* being."

"Mock me all you like, Mouse. You'll see. It's a crowded, dirty city full of priggish people who will look down their noses at you. Believe me when

I say, you have my full sympathy. Believe me, too, when I say that you should take care while you're there. Trust no one."

"I cannot imagine that I'll need to spend my days looking over my shoulder. I'm not the one running about harassing those who are loyal to the Crown," she pointed out. "Nothing I've ever done could be considered treasonous."

"Even innocent actions can be misconstrued by those intent on turning over rocks. Consider again whether it's wise for you to accept correspondence from me."

His words gave her pause, and she stopped in mid-stride to consider them. "I think your suspicious mind is the result of guilt. Or, perhaps it's meanness that drives you to try to worry me." She narrowed her eyes at him. "More likely, you simply want to wriggle free of your promise. But I'm having none of that." She wagged a warning finger at him. "Keep your promise, Daniel. I would know what is happening here."

He laughed. "Meanness? No. Guilty mind? Perhaps. However, I'll take the warnings of a suspicious mind over the blind folly of a naïve one any day."

"I am not naïve," she insisted, setting off once again. "There's a difference between naïveté and lack of information. That's my point. That's why I want you to keep me informed." She stalked on in silent protest of what she saw as typically imperious behavior on Daniel's part, hardly noticing when they arrived at her uncle's gate.

"Here you are, Mouse; home without falling into a wit of trouble."

"As though you had anything to do with it. I'm certain I'd have fared well enough. Given that I've never before needed an escort, it's telling that you think I now do. Before you and your hooligan companions took control of the streets, Boston's citizens had little to fear."

"Before Parliament decided to tax Boston's citizens without their consent, the Sons of Liberty did not exist."

She ignored the point. "You know," she leaned toward him and sniffed distastefully, "the two of you positively reek. I thought it was the alley, but the smell seems to have followed us. You smell of . . .," she sniffed again, "a pigsty."

Daniel shifted uncomfortably. "Yes, well, as we told you, Drum had an unfortunate encounter with an equally unfortunate coat."

"And what is your excuse? The offensive smell is stronger on your clothes than on his."

"It's a very long and tedious story," Daniel replied curtly, "for which we do not at present have time."

"A long and tedious story that involves some considerable waywardness on your part, no doubt. You both need a bath."

Drum screwed up his face. "I don't like baths," he declared with pronounced conviction.

Daniel groaned. It was an ongoing battle between the two of them, one of the few that Daniel consistently lost. When confronted with the prospect of immersing himself in water, Drum balked like a mule.

"But, Drum," Anna argued, "if you go about smelling as you do, no one will want to come near you."

"Baths are not good for you," Drum insisted doggedly. "Everyone says so."

"Baths are, perhaps, not healthy in excess, and one should exercise care," Anna allowed. "And yet, they are advisable from time to time. I believe in your case, now is such a time."

Drum shrugged. Anna looked to Daniel for support, but he merely mirrored Drum's ambivalence. If she thought she could do better in this contest of wills, he was willing enough to let her try. Rising to the challenge, Anna took Drum by the hand and led him to a bench just inside the gate. There, she sat beside him, talking in a voice so quiet that Daniel could not hear what was being said. Drum sat in silence, head hanging, staring at Anna's hand in his. Listening intently, he wriggled uncomfortably a few times and then nodded solemnly before Anna, smiling in triumph, patted him on the hand and sent him back to Daniel. She waved at them as she turned toward her uncle's house.

Daniel called after her, "Be careful among all those priggers in London, Mouse." He watched her walk away, rigid with the effort of snubbing him, until she had entered the house and closed the door.

"Why do you call her that?" Drum was frowning down at him. "Why do you always call her 'mouse'?"

"Because, she is like a mouse. She's always there, and always troublesome."

"I don't think you mean that," Drum contended soberly. "Miss Anna is nice."

Daniel shrugged. "She looks like a mouse, then. Small and never still."

"No, she doesn't," Drum insisted. He stared at the palm of his hand. It still felt warm from where Anna's hand had rested in it. "She's more like a little bird. Like a hummingbird, I think. Or, maybe a wren. A wren sat in my hand once, did you know that?" He held his hand out toward Daniel, palm up, a broad smile taking hold of him along with the memory.

"No, I didn't know that Drum." As happened occasionally during conversations with Drum, Daniel felt that he had wandered momentarily into some strange otherworld.

"You shouldn't call Miss Anna 'mouse,'" Drum repeated, doggedly returning to his original topic. "She doesn't like it."

Daniel laughed. "Did she ask you to tell me that?"

"No." Drum shook his head. "But I know she doesn't like it. You and Teague think I'm stupid, and maybe I am about some things. But I can tell when someone doesn't like something, and Miss Anna doesn't like for you to call her 'mouse.'"

Daniel sighed. "I don't think you're stupid, Drum. I do think that it's cold out here, though, and we should get on with the job of finding you a coat."

"Later," Drum said. "After."

"After what?" Perplexed, Daniel watched Drum march resolutely past him without so much as a sideways glance. "Where are you going?"

"I have to go take a bath."

"What?" The pitch of Daniel's voice arced up in surprise. "Now? You want to take a bath *now*? I thought we were going to get you a coat."

"After. I promised Miss Anna I would take a bath."

Daniel lengthened his stride to match Drum's determined pace. "I'm certain she didn't intend you to take a bath this moment. We have other things to do. You can bathe later."

But Drum just shook his head and marched onward, leaving Daniel to sigh and wonder what Anna could possibly have said to convince him to cast aside a long-held and unwavering conviction.

"Hummingbird or wren, my arse," he muttered as he followed in Drum's wake.

CHAPTER THREE

Charlotte had taken the long path home. She was in high spirits, pleased with the money yielded by the few items she had sold to various merchants that day, and was in no hurry to return to her father's house. She would sell the velvet later when she had time to contact the man Selah had recommended but, in the meantime, the day's transactions had proved more fruitful than expected. The list of items represented an odd assortment of things — an ivory comb, pearl-studded hat pins, a silver watch chain, and a ring. It had caused her some unhappiness to sell the ring, for it was quite pretty, but the money it would fetch held far more value for her than its aesthetics.

She wondered briefly where Teague had obtained the ring. Though his attention to her had been a nuisance in the beginning, she soon recognized his value lay in the fact that he liked to please her, and that he knew expensive gifts went a long way in that regard. Furthermore, unlike Daniel, who was not in the least malleable, Teague was easily bent to her will.

A well-heeled future on a far grander stage than Boston was paramount in Charlotte's mind and, given that the influx of troops into Boston had brought with it an officer corps that talked incessantly and in paradisiacal terms about London and its many glories, she decided that London was to be that grand stage. Teague's proclivity for obtaining valuable, saleable items was going to help her achieve that goal. Not that he knew what she was doing with his gifts. In fact, she suspected he would have been quite hurt had he known. But her own plans and dreams took primacy over Teague's feelings.

When she reached the house, Charlotte took the path around to the back and entered through the kitchen door. The maid had gone for the day and her father was in his study reviewing ledgers. She closed the door quietly and, shedding her shoes, crept softly through the house and up the stairs. From the upper landing, she hurried into her bedroom, shutting the door behind her and turning the key in the lock. She leaned against the door to catch her breath, listening until she was certain her father had not followed her up the stairs and then began the little ritual she had repeated on numerous occasions over the past year.

She tilted the washstand to one side so that she could slip a rag rug underneath, and used the rug to make it easier to slide the washstand out of the way without leaving tell-tale scratches on the floor. This was done with great care to keep her father from hearing, which meant she could not work as quickly as she would have liked. She knelt on the floor in front of the wall. There was a small door set in the wall, its edges hidden in the ribs of painted paneling so that it was not readily apparent. Even Charlotte, who had opened the door many times, had to feel her way until she found the latch that would release the secret door. Once opened, it revealed a compartment, to which she added the precious bundle of money from her pocket. She smiled in satisfaction at the level to which the pile of little bundles had risen. Though she had a rough idea of how much was there, she hoped an opportunity would soon present itself for her to take it all out and count it.

Charlotte loved counting the money and wished she could do so more often without risk of discovery. She always waited until the maid was not in the house and, more importantly, until her father was away for the day. He had what was, in Charlotte's view, an unfortunate habit of appearing at inopportune moments, and he was far too inquisitive regarding her activities. Fathers really should confine themselves to earning a living, she thought, and leave their daughters untroubled by their interference.

She reclosed the secret compartment, running her hands over the smooth wall as she did so. Finding a good carpenter with no ties to Boston and who would agree to do the work on a schedule prescribed by her father's absences had been no easy matter, but the end result was worth the effort. Once the compartment was resealed and the washstand replaced, she rinsed her hands in the basin, used the small dressing mirror to check the arrangement of her hair, and made a fuss of securing her favorite shawl around her shoulders. She leaned close to the mirror and lightly touched her fingertips to the pale, flawless skin on her cheek.

So perfect, she thought, smiling. *What a miracle it is! And, how I must have been favored by God to be left unblemished when my own mother was so ravaged and lost her life.* As a child, Charlotte had contracted smallpox at the same time as her mother. But in Charlotte's case, the disease had not taken her life, and had not left a mark on her perfect skin. Her father often said what a miracle he considered the fact that she had endured such a high fever for so many days without succumbing. Charlotte believed it to be a sign that she was destined for something special in life.

Quietly, she opened her door and stepped into the hallway, only to be brought up short by the sight of her father standing at the top of the landing. "I thought I heard you come in. It seemed peculiar that you came straight up here with nary a word. I wanted to see that everything was well."

"I am quite well," she insisted a little too sharply. "You've no need to spy on me."

Martin Ainsworth's shoulders sagged. He was short, and round as a child's ball, and allowing his shoulders to droop emphasized his unfortunate build. "Charlotte, my dear," he insisted wearily, "I was not spying on you. I was merely concerned."

"Well, you needn't be. My hair and dress were mussed from being out on the street, and I took some time to repair them. That's all." She brushed past him so closely that her skirts threatened to unbalance him.

He grasped the newel to steady himself. "You should have had Henry drive you. It's not necessary for you to trudge along the dirty streets, especially when it is so cold and damp out."

"I don't like your coachman. He looks like a common laborer. I prefer to walk." Especially, she thought, when she did not want to risk that the coachman would report her itinerary back to her father. "Go back to your ledgers, father. I'll see what cook has left for our supper and will bring it in shortly."

Watching Charlotte descend the stairs, Ainsworth stared hard at the back of her head as though he thought he might somehow be able to read her thoughts. He suspected that, were he suddenly endowed with such capability, he would be sorely disappointed. At least, he hoped disappointment would be the worst he would experience. In his more honest moments, he admitted to himself that he would likely be shocked or, worse, horrified by whatever drifted around inside Charlotte's pretty head. Martin Ainsworth loved his daughter to a fault, he knew. As a weak, ineffectual father, he'd been too indulgent, too afraid of upsetting her and triggering one of her frightening tantrums, but he had not known what else to do. Her mother's death left him alone and emotionally ill-equipped to deal with their spoiled, self-absorbed child.

Charlotte reached the bottom step and turned her placid, cool grey gaze up to him. "Come down, father," she said sweetly, "and wait in your study. I shall call you when supper is served." She watched him descend, smiling like an approving school master at his obedience.

He sat patiently waiting in his study, listening to her rattle around in the kitchen, knowing she was inwardly cursing the fact that the maid's absence forced her to perform the task herself. It took little time and soon they were seated at their meal. Charlotte afforded him not even a glance.

"I saw Anna Somerset today," she informed him as she settled her napkin.

A crease formed in his brow as he tried to place the name. "Am I acquainted with her?"

"Perhaps not," Charlotte's tone and shrug of one shoulder conveyed her opinion that Anna was without consequence. "But I believe you know her uncle — John Wilton?"

"Oh, yes. Well, I know *of* him. We are only slightly acquainted. He is a good businessman, I believe."

Charlotte nodded. It was just the sort of thought she hoped her father would have regarding Wilton. "Mr. Wilton is sending Miss Somerset to

London," she told him. "He is concerned for her safety, what with all the violence and unrest lately."

"Seems a bit of an overreaction. I daresay she is at greater risk of encountering trouble on the streets of London than here in Boston!"

"I think it is most commendable that her uncle shows such concern for her well-being. Likely it's not just a matter of her safety, but he doubtless feels she also will find better marriage prospects there."

"Then he is bound to be disappointed. She is a product of the merchant class and a colonist. Two things that will not set her in good stead with the better sort in London." He eyed his daughter from across the table. "I suppose you think I should send you to London, too?"

"Of course I do."

Ainsworth sighed. "My dear, as I've told you on more than one occasion, the life you envision having in London is simply not realistic. Since you were a child, you have entertained pictures in your head of being among London society — perhaps even being presented at court. That would not happen. Not only would we not move in the social circles you envision, but our whole standard of living would be lower there. And that assumes I could make a living there as I do here."

She fluttered her hand dismissively. "Of course you could. Furthermore, I cannot imagine that our standard of living would be lower. Why, Boston is a positive backwater compared with London!"

"And you know this how? You cannot make this judgment based upon what you hear some red-coated officer say. Many of them are from noble families. They associate with us here because they have few options. You can be assured that they would not be so friendly if we were in London."

It startled her to learn that he was aware of her discourse with officers. She had believed herself safe in the cloak of his ignorance. "You have said all of this before, and I do not accept it."

"Then we are at an impasse, and I am forced to simply say that we will remain in Boston."

You will remain in Boston, she thought, *but I will go to London*. It was her mantra, the thought that fueled her determination.

*   *   *

Boston
August 1770

Mouse,

Though I have nothing to report to you, I did not want you to think I was failing in my promise, so have decided to post these few lines to you. There have been small upheavals, and unrest lurks always beneath the surface here but, happily, the more reasonable among us argue for calm while they search for solutions that will please all parties. It seems an impossible task, and I am often glad that I am a mere player in the drama – not the playwright.

My mother sends her regards. Apparently, you made a Memorable Impression on her and, knowing you as I do, I asked if you'd done so by standing on your head while juggling apples on your toes. I am assured that such was not the case, but am given no explanation for her interest.

Something concerning your uncle has come to my attention and, though it seems likely that the matter was to be a confidence between yourself and Mr. Wilton, I feel nonetheless compelled to ask for confirmation of my suspicions. During recent casual conversation among some of those associates of mine for whom you hold so little regard, Mr. Wilton's name was mentioned. (I hasten to add here that there was nothing attached to this mention that should arouse your concern.)

On hearing your uncle's name, one of the other gentlemen present spoke out in most favorable terms, and recounted the fact that when, some years past, his watch and coin purse were stolen by what he termed "a Heathen little Ragamuffin," Mr. Wilton appeared to him within days of the event and recompensed him for his loss. Apparently, your uncle told him that "Extenuating Circumstances" were involved, and required of the gentleman that he allow the matter to drop without involving the magistrate. The gentleman understood that, though Mr. Wilton did not wish to embroil the authorities, he did feel it his Christian obligation to see that there was a level of justice done.

What I suspect, and what I wish you to confirm, is that the "heathen little ragamuffin" of the tale was, in fact, a dear friend of mine? I know that the friend has harbored ill will toward you these many years, and that the reason for his ill will was partly due to the fact that you heartily castigated him (no surprise there) and threatened to reveal him to the authorities if he repeated an offense to which you were witness. Given the unlikelihood of your having witnessed multiple such crimes, I must assume that they are one and the same and that you told your uncle what you'd witnessed, compelling him to make the victim whole.

If it is indeed the case that my good friend was the cause for your uncle's intervention, I feel indebted to you and to Mr. Wilton.

As I write this, your birthday will have been two months past, and by the time you read this my good wishes on the occasion will be all the more belated. Please accept them, nonetheless.

Your servant,
Daniel Garrett

* * *

London
December 1770

Dear Mr. Garrett,

I received your letter and appreciate your conscientious adherence to our agreement. I shall tell you that you are essentially correct in your assumptions regarding my uncle's largesse. I shall also say that you incurred no debt. If anyone is beholden, it would be your friend. However, given that no obligation can be expected of a man who has not asked for the favor, I absolve him as well. My uncle's part in the matter was enacted out of a desire to settle his own mind and to ease my discomfort with the situation. Rest assured that he has no knowledge of your friend's identity and is unlikely to have given the matter further thought once it was settled.

On another topic, I must report to you that London is the most amazing of cities. Contrary to your warning, I do not find that, as compared with Boston, it is any more – nor any less – populated with "priggers," or any other unpleasant sort of person, for that matter. Indeed, I have become rather fond of the city. I make this admission grudgingly, and hastily add that it is a fondness that has been slow in developing.

My initial welcome here was a stench that hit me before even I had disembarked from the ship. The smells of sewage and animals and too many people crowded into too little space assailed my nostrils and turned my stomach, and I was sorely tempted to have my baggage moved from the ship directly onto the next return ship to Boston. I have, however, learned that the smell is not so offensive every day and not in all parts of the city, and one does become adept at coping.

Beyond the stench and the appalling poverty that is too easily encountered, there is an energy to London that speaks to my soul and a treasure trove of intellectual stimulation that feeds my spirit. A cosmopolitan mixture of people throng the streets, and an equally fantastic array of goods fill the shops, all of it beyond anything I could have imagined. If there is any criticism to be made, it is that shameful hovels stand in strange counterpoint to the fabulous royal buildings and homes of the social elite, and large portions of the city, having been hurriedly rebuilt after being laid waste by a horrendous fire many generations past, seem slightly off-kilter. It is a combination that can make one feel uncomfortable and unsettled.

Nonetheless, theatre, art, and literature are available at every turn, and I would consider myself happily situated – if only this were the home of my heart. I long to return to my uncle's house – which IS home – and was hard-pressed not to say so in my last letter to *him. Instead, I wrote all of the above, save for the comment on wishing to return home. That last I omitted because I do not want to create unhappiness or guilt in him when I know that it is only my safety and best interest that spurred him to send me here in the first place. I tell you, however, that I shall rejoice when the DESPICABLE SCOUNDRELS who insist on creating such discord in Boston decide to get on with their lives and businesses so that we may all return to normalcy.*

A tutor, who constantly astounds me with the breadth of his knowledge, has been hired for me. In addition to his admirable intellect, he is blessed with a sympathetic and gentle nature, so we get on well. Before this time, his pupils have all been male, and he has not yet realized that Lady Eugenie's expectation was that he would temper the scope of my curriculum owing to the fact of my femininity. I am happy in that oversight on his part.

The highlight of my every week, however, is when Lady Eugenie takes me along to visit her very elderly aunt, Lady Sylvia Gordon-Hewes, whose residence is an EXTRAORDINARY estate on the outskirts of London. The estate, which she calls her "country house" despite the fact that it is essentially adjacent to the city, has a garden in which one could happily lose oneself when the weather is mild, and a beautiful orangery that is the most pleasant of places when the weather is disagreeable. I am not being immodest to say that Lady Sylvia has taken to me — mostly, I suspect, because I am willing to sit and read to her, or because I am willing to simply keep her company. She bids me visit even when Lady Eugenie is not able to join us, and it is always a pleasant experience.

You mentioned my birthday — which I greatly appreciate and certainly do accept your good wishes — and I assure you that I spent it most pleasantly. I shall follow your example and wish you a happy Christmas, though I know you will not read this until well after the day has passed. The Yule season is celebrated here, as is done in our southern colonies, I believe. Though I feel quite the pagan to feel so, I have come to quite enjoy the celebrations.

Give my regards to your mother. I am pleased that I managed to make a favorable impression on her, though I cannot imagine how I did so. Perhaps she was merely happy to meet someone who has no illusions about her son's character and, yet, still calls him friend?

Your sincere friend,
Anna Somerset

*   *   *

On the same December afternoon that Anna posted her letter to Daniel, her uncle, accompanied by William Sprague, walked out of the overheated confines of the packed Queen Street Courthouse into the bitter cold of a cloudy December afternoon. Each man was deep in thought, mulling the final act in the great drama the March 5 incident on King Street had become, and which had unfolded over so many weeks. Each man felt some satisfaction in the outcome, but each had quite different reasons to feel so.

Of all the British Regulars who had stood trial for the Custom House incident, only two were found guilty. Today, Wilton and Sprague had watched as those two, having invoked benefit of clergy and thus had their punishment commuted, had received their alternative punishment – that of having their thumbs branded. It had not been pleasant to witness, and yet, they suspected that the two young men considered it a small thing compared with the alternative.

"I hope," Anna's uncle commented, "that by these verdicts and punishments, Massachusetts will have shown itself to be a colony ruled by law and capable of mercy. Surely that message will not be lost on London."

Pulling his cloak more tightly about him, Sprague grunted. "My hope is that London will see Boston as a community capable of governing itself. Certainly they will have to admit the folly of this occupation. To keep troops here, policing civilians and behaving as though we are a foreign, conquered people, cannot stand."

"They seem to agree with you." Wilton gestured to the crowd that, despite the frigid temperatures, kept vigil outside the building as the punishment was imposed. Most merely grumbled about the occupation by British troops while others shouted their protests aloud. "And yet, they were not so unhappy about the presence of the Regulars during the war against the French and Indians."

"No one was happy about being forced to quarter troops in their houses and barns, you may recall."

"Perhaps not, but no one objected to the Regulars being here to protect us from the Indians and to drive the French out of these colonies. That they now object to paying for that protection irks me beyond words."

Sprague sighed. "How many times have we had this argument now?"

"I lose count. But we shall go on having it as long as this foolishness persists." Wilton indicated the protestors, most of whom had begun to disperse as word circulated that the punishments were concluded.

Sprague found it difficult to control his temper. "You do try my patience, John," he grumbled. "Can you truly not see it? Sharing the cost of that war is not the issue. Every colonist understands the obligation to pay taxes. Few do so without at least some complaint, but they understand the need. They understood, that is, until the taxes became unfair — before they became unreasonably burdensome — and before the decision to levy them was made without our agreement."

"Bah," Wilton waved his hand dismissively and assumed a sour expression.

Sprague caught at his sleeve, forcing his friend to face him. "I have the persistence to say this yet another time, John. They have restricted our trade and levied taxes without our consent. That is a violation of our charter with our sovereign. They dip into our pockets with one hand, and use the other to choke off our sources of revenue. You can argue about whether it is the fault of the king or of Parliament but, regardless of where you lay blame, that is what has been done. That is what I am against. We must regain our long-cherished rights as Englishmen. If Parliament will not be budged, and if the king will not hear our plea, then what are we to do?"

"Parliament will come 'round," Wilton insisted. "If we keep ourselves to reason and peaceful petition, I know all will be made right. But we cannot push them into a corner. When our unruly mobs are allowed to speak for us, threatening violence and recrimination, behaving in a way that is openly treasonous, then the king and Parliament have no choice but to stand firm. No government can allow itself to be threatened and bullied into action."

"And no government can afford to turn a deaf ear to its citizens. Certainly, an English king cannot afford to do so." He sighed in exasperation when Wilton's only response was to give a dismissive wave of his hand. "As I've said before, you must take heed of this, John. There will be more trouble. It has been coming for a long while now, and we've ignored the signs. The feeling is growing that Americans are a different set of men from those in England. London has certainly seen us that way, but now Americans see themselves as such — and they think it's a good thing. It's as if there is something in the soil here that has made us different in nature. As each year passes, the differences become more pronounced. That is not going to change. Where can it lead?"

The two friends, in silent agreement that this was a point on which they could not reconcile their opinions, took their leave and Wilton continued on alone. Absorbed in his own thoughts, he made his way through the streets without actually seeing anything he passed. He entered his house and went directly to his study, silently closing the door behind him. The maid had kept the fire at a smolder, and he poked the embers into flames before collapsing with a heavy sigh into his favorite chair. She would soon bring in tea to warm him, and he resisted the temptation to avail himself of stronger spirits. He hoped that what he had witnessed earlier that day would be the closing chapter on the long ordeal precipitated by the event certain elements in Boston had come to refer to as the "horrid massacre." Instead, precisely because of that element's insistence on referring to the

Custom House incident as a "massacre," he had little faith that such would be the case.

He thought hopefully on the speeches John Adams had made during the trials. Adams' heart may lie with his cousin and the rest of the rebellious crowd, but his undeniable command of the law, and his ability to inspire men to the just path were masterful and spoke to Wilton's heart. For, did not Englishmen believe in the rule of law above all else? For hundreds of years, had not a covenant existed between the Crown and its subjects that was based on that very premise? Had that not been the bedrock of their political structure, the thing that, in Wilton's view, separated the English monarchs from the despots of Europe?

It weighed heavily upon his heart that the king had not fully honored that covenant in regards to his American colonies, but Wilton believed that things could be made right if only the radically bent were not allowed to prevail. No doubt, the king was receiving bad advice and rational, humble appeals must be made to his reason. Threats of violence would only beget more violence. Was that not one of the lessons to be learned from the Custom House incident?

To all of the questions floating about in Wilton's burdened mind, he believed would come answers shaped by the time-tested traditions and institutions he held dear. England would not let him down. His king would not disappoint him. On that happy thought, John Wilton fell asleep.

1771

CHAPTER FOUR

For the months following the enactment of the sentence upon the soldiers, the city remained relatively quiet. Winter's harsh cold kept everyone cloistered wherever a warm hearth could be found. For men like Daniel and Drum, however, warm hearths were infrequently scattered between periods of paid employment interrupted by less-lucrative errands and activities on behalf of the Patriots. In Drum's opinion, these things kept them out of doors far too often. They went about their business bundled to the point that they could hardly move, while fighting the harsh effects of cold on noses, fingers, and toes. Worse still, the discomfort of being interminably cold brought dark, hurtful memories to the forefront of Drum's mind.

Winter also reduced shipping to a crawl, which meant letters from London were as few and far between as those warm hearths. Daniel pretended not to care, but Drum knew differently. It seemed plain to him that Daniel had come to look forward to Anna's letters as he looked forward to little else, that her correspondence had utterly captivated him. They desperately needed a break from the dull grey cold and isolation, so Drum was particularly happy when spring finally made its first appearance and then, after fits and starts, settled in to stay.

Drum tried to focus on that happiness now, but it was proving difficult. It was as fine a Sunday morning as Boston could wish for, and yet, the clear, sunny sky and crisp May air were momentarily wasted on Drum. As he had on many Sunday mornings for as long as he could remember, Drum stood half-hidden in an alley, peering around the corner at a house across the street. It was the large, fine house in which Drum's family lived, though he did not – and never had.

He had once lived with them in another house, very far away in a place with a name he could not recall. He remembered the short time he had spent living in the shed behind that distant house, though, and the memory was so full of pain and bitterness as to be almost tangible. The shed was a frightening place and, because it was winter, so cold he could not sleep for shivering. Sometime after what those around him referred to as "his accident," after the terrible thing happened to his sister, Nan, his father had told him that was where he was to live and, because he had always been an obedient child, he tried to do as he was told. But he hated it. He hated the cold, and the dark, and the horrible rank odors. Most of all, he hated the being alone.

He'd overheard talk between his parents about moving to a place where no one would know them, where no one would know what had happened to Nan, but he understood little of it. And then, abruptly, his family had packed everything they owned and left the old house. They said nothing to Drum, made no provision for him. Not knowing what else to do, he followed them. His family settled in Boston and seemed to forget about Drum. He was living on the streets, occasionally standing across from where his family lived as he wondered what he should do. Into that loneliness Daniel and Teague had come, befriending him and pulling him into their lives until they became his family. Fatherless and trying hard to keep from being an additional burden on his hard-working mother, Daniel had learned to survive on his own under the dubious tutelage of the orphaned Teague. They now took Drum under their wing, protecting him and helping him survive — if, at times, that survival was by the thinnest of lines.

The first Sunday that Drum had returned to watch his family depart for church, he had stood in plain sight. But they never looked his way. For a time, Drum wondered if he had become invisible. Daniel and Teague assured him that such was not the case, so he had taken to watching his family from a discreet hiding place. He told himself that it was so they would not see him and make him return to the shed but, in his heart, he knew it was because he did not want to feel again the way he had the day they looked through him. He did not want to feel invisible.

Drum could not remember how long he had lived in the far-away house or how long it was before he was relegated to the shed, nor could he remember exactly why. Neither did he remember the thing everyone called "his accident." The more insignificant details, he could recall in great detail. The bits that seemed to matter, however, were only fragments of images, too brief to make much sense, flashing by like images viewed through the spokes of a moving carriage wheel. Taken together, it all represented the only clues Drum retained as to why his life had become what it had. Sometimes a particular smell would cause one of the fragments to come into his head, sometimes a sound. Occasionally, they would come in the dark silence of the night, conjured by nothing more than the sound of his own heartbeat thrumming in his ears. It was at those times that the fragments were most clear and most likely to bear some thread of reason, blurred scenes playing out to a distressing conclusion that startled him awake, sweating and gasping for breath.

He watched now as the Fisackerly family — *his* family, though they would not have known or acknowledged him — emerged and walked toward their waiting carriage. He always watched until Mr. Fisackerly had helped his daughter safely into the carriage. Drum thought of Nan still as his little sister, though she was no longer a little girl. The image of her as a child was one of the fragments he most often saw, and one of the few that made him smile. She was such a little thing then, sweet and fragile. He was fairly sure that he'd been six years-old at the time, and also fairly sure that Nan was two years younger.

The thing he remembered with great certainty was how fiercely he had loved her and how hard he had tried to look after her — to protect her. At her birth, the responsibility was assigned to him with great solemnity by his father, but that had not been necessary. Wanting to protect Nan was instinctive in Drum from the moment he first laid eyes on her in her cradle. That part of his fragmented memory was what made things difficult because he knew he had failed to protect her. He had tried so hard and failed.

The two of them were — what were they doing? Sometimes he thought they were picking berries, and other times he thought they were supposed to be walking somewhere. But where? No matter how hard he tried, he could not recall. There was a stream. That he knew. And, it was a hot summer day, the air heavy with damp haze. Perhaps they were chasing grasshoppers? The heat was an oppressive, tangibly heavy thing pressing on them from all sides so that, when they found a wide, bubbling stream in which to wade, they were delighted. In a rush of excitement and anticipation, he had pulled off his boots and stockings and waded in, picking each step carefully so as not to slip on the smooth stones lining the streambed. The cool water rushed around his ankles, his every step stirring up muddy sediment. He tried to stand very still so the sediment would settle, hoping to catch sight of a frog or some other interesting creature. Why could he remember those details? That question mystified him.

His attention was away from Nan for only a short time, too short of a time for anything to happen, he thought. And then she had screamed. The sound instantly terrified him and propelled him into response. He was out of the stream so quickly it was as if he had flown, frantically searching for his sister. In so little time, how could she have wandered out of sight? Following the sound of the next cry, he pushed his way through a mass of sumac hanging beard-like from the branches of a low tree beside the stream. Deep in the shadows of the copse, he found Nan in the grasp of a large man he had never seen before. Shrieking what was tantamount to a war cry, Drum rushed at the man, throwing his six-year-old self at the hulking form.

He landed hard on the man's back, wrapped one arm around his throat, and grasped a handful of the man's hair in his other hand. He was pulling and clawing and biting every way he could, and the man flailed wildly trying to dislodge his assailant. Finally, the man was able to get a firm enough hold on one of Drum's arms that he could tear the boy from his back. Holding him in the iron grip of one large hand, he began to strike Drum, hitting him with vicious blows that left the boy battered and bloodied almost beyond recognition. Finally, he forced Drum backwards, pounding him against a tree until Drum was gasping for air, and then throwing him to the ground. Drum landed violently, his head snapping back to loudly crack against a rocky protrusion. The blow sent a blinding, searing pain through his skull, and then all was blackness.

Drum's memory held only painful shards of what followed. He remembered waking in fits and starts, back in his own bed. He had trouble moving and what little he could move hurt terribly. Most painful was his head. It felt as though a blacksmith was using his skull for an anvil, and he could see only an excruciating, white-hot light that forced him to keep his eyes closed. He occasionally tried to open them, testing, but it was always the same. There were shapes looming over him, shapes that came and went, but he could make no sense of them, who they were, or what they were saying to him. He tried to ask about Nan but could not seem to form words. So, he slept.

Gradually, his body healed. His head still hurt terribly from time to time, and sometimes the world went momentarily out of focus. He had great difficulty understanding what people were telling him, and then they stopped talking to him altogether. Instead, they talked over him, as though he was not there — as though he was invisible. Snatches of what was said made him anxious, for they implied that Nan was not well. When he finally managed to see her she looked well enough, which made him feel slightly better. But everyone around him seemed so troubled. Though he could not understand the scraps of conversation he heard, he sensed that something was terribly wrong, that the hurt that had been done to Nan was considered unspeakable.

In time, Drum began to realize that something else was terribly wrong, and that the thing was himself. Nan was growing and learning. She was the happy focus of adoring parents. Drum knew he was none of those things. No matter how hard he tried, he felt like he could never quite get his mind around things he knew he was expected to understand. Most pointedly, they became uneasy when he spoke of the bits and pieces he recalled from the day of the accident. They forbade him to speak of that day, or even think about it.

And then, his family had moved to Boston.

Now, as he had on so many other occasions, Drum watched his family drive away in the carriage, a lovely family on their way to church. Nan had looked very happy, he thought. She seemed safe. That pleased Drum, as it always did. It was what he had come to see, that look of happiness upon her face.

Content, he turned and walked away. He was so deep in thought that he did not see Teague rounding a corner from the opposite direction. The collision had little effect on Drum but sent Teague sprawling onto the pavement.

"I've been looking for you everywhere," Teague irritably informed him as he picked himself up from the pavement. "Where have you been?"

Drum shrugged and scuffed the toe of his boot in the dirt. "Somewhere," he mumbled vaguely. Drum did not know why he wanted what he considered his visits with his family kept secret, but he did.

"Well, never mind. I've found you now. Come along with me to see Miss Ainsworth, will you?"

Drum balked. Though he was as mesmerized by her looks as any of the other young men who found themselves in the pretty girl's orbit, he felt uncomfortable around Charlotte Ainsworth. Part of the reason was that, despite the fact that he towered over her, he felt as though she were looking down on him, disdain flowing from her like cold waves off the sea. "Why? Miss Ainsworth doesn't like me."

"Yes, she does, Drum. Everyone likes you. And, she specifically asked me to fetch you to visit her."

On the one hand, this seemed highly unlikely to Drum, but on the other hand, he could not think of a reason Teague would say it if it were not so. "But, why would she want me to visit?" he asked.

"She wants to ask you about doing some work for her father," Teague explained with forced patience. "Because he has been ailing, she has had to hire more help, especially for the heavier work. Miss Ainsworth mentioned that she hasn't been happy with the men she has found so far, and I told her that you are always interested in picking up the odd bit of work. She feels that you'd be ideal."

"I don't think so," Drum said glumly. The thought of having to spend much time with Charlotte Ainsworth scowling at him held little appeal. "There's usually work for me at the ropewalks. I was going to see the rope makers tomorrow morning."

"But, Drum, she'll be disappointed. I like Miss Ainsworth, and I want to make her happy. Won't you do it to help me?"

Drum desperately wanted to refuse, but the idea of disappointing Teague outweighed his reluctance. With a somber nod of agreement, he unenthusiastically trundled along behind Teague to the Ainsworth house.

*   *   *

Anna lowered Daniel's most recent letter to her lap and looked out across Lady Sylvia's luxuriant garden. He had written his letter in March, but it was now almost June. It was a letter without news, for Boston had settled into a stasis of relative peace. The uneventful state of affairs she considered good news in of itself, however. His closing paragraph, though, she found somewhat perplexing.

> *Drum thanks you for the gift you sent to him in my mother's care. He opened it in our presence, and we were both rather astonished to see that the little parcel contained several remarkably colored glass marbles. Such a trifle hardly seems worth all that went into transporting them across an ocean, but had you seen for yourself Drum's delight in the gift, I know that you would have considered your efforts worthwhile. Before this, I had not known that Drum maintained a collection of marbles, which he (for reasons that are beyond my comprehension) prizes quite highly. In this regard, I feel remiss in my friendship with him, and I am ashamed that you – who spend far less time in his company than I – knew of the collection while I did not. I should not be surprised, however. I believe it is a mark of your inherent kindness of heart and the singular thoughtfulness with which you invest your relationships, characteristics that make your absence from Boston all the more lamentable.*

She reread those closing lines of the letter several times, and felt astonishment each time. In the whole of their friendship, she could recall few times when he had spoken to her with anything approaching favorable regard. And now, here was that one sentence, jumping out to confound her. Finally, she decided that he must be mocking her and, newly annoyed with him, she brusquely returned the pages to the envelope and thrust it into her pocket.

She'd been in London for a little over a year, and an agonizingly long year it had been. Only a small part of the difficulties had she shared with Daniel, and none at all with her uncle. It all began with her arrival at the London townhouse of Sir Gregory and Lady Eugenie Etheridge. Lady Eugenie had welcomed her with all of the politeness and courtesy demanded by the circumstances, but Anna was painfully aware that Eugenie's subtle scrutiny found her lacking. Anna, wanting to do credit to her uncle, had changed into her best dress before leaving the ship. Her hands and face were clean, her hair neatly combed. But despite all her pains, standing in the elegant foyer of the Etheridge's townhouse made her feel small and shabby and insignificant. Her pride had not failed her, however, and she had returned Lady Eugenie's greeting with a bright smile and ramrod-straight spine.

Lady Eugenie Etheridge was a lady in her own right owing to the fact that her father was an earl. He was, relative to the rest of England's peerage, an impoverished and insignificant earl, and Eugenie was the youngest of his six daughters, all of which meant that the resources necessary to arrange a marriage to someone of her own class were almost nonexistent. Therefore, despite that fact that she was marrying beneath her, Eugenie's marriage to the well-heeled Mr. Gregory Etheridge had not been as frowned upon as it might otherwise have been. Nonetheless, a son-in-law bearing the title of "Sir" being preferable to a mere "mister," her father had quickly arranged for Mr. Etheridge to be knighted.

This convoluted history was explained by the young maid assigned to Anna upon her arrival at the Etheridge's London townhouse. The explanation was delivered with considerable gravity, as though it all mattered greatly. To Anna's mind, it mattered not at all. What mattered was that her uncle and Sir Gregory were old friends who had started out in life together, combining their assets, talents, and hard work in a loose partnership that had made them both wealthy men. Seeing the abundant opportunities the colonies offered, John Wilton had transplanted himself from England to Boston where he established the colonial end of a lucrative partnership that, until recent political events had interfered, seemed full of endless potential.

Anna reflected on all of this as she sat comfortably in Lady Gordon-Hewes' garden. The garden was an oasis of tranquility and bliss, and one of the few places she thought she would miss whenever she returned home. Everything was in full flower, creating a richly-textured mosaic of soft colors that filled the sun-warmed air with their wonderful fragrance. Honeybees went about the business of visiting each blossom in turn, and dragonflies bobbed and dipped over the decorative pool. She was sitting in her favorite spot, a bench near a fountain that featured alluringly-posed mermaids lolling among arches of water. A peacock, surveying a trio of peahens, fanned his tail and issued a raucous cry, but the hens continued their busy pecking at the ground, seemingly insusceptible to his charms.

"Poor fellow. All that effort, and the ladies seem quite indifferent." The voice, which came from behind, startled her so that she visibly jumped. "I do apologize." A sandy-haired man of middle age and trim build presented himself with a polite bow. "Christopher Hinton, Esquire, your servant."

Unsettled by the man's sudden appearance, Anna gaped at him as though nothing could be so extraordinary. He was of approximately the same age as her uncle, quiet and dignified, and possessed of a courtly demeanor. In contrast to all that dignity, the spark in his eyes suggested that he might harbor a joyful irreverence. His smile was warm, his manner pleasant and, had she not been so unbalanced by his sudden appearance, Anna might have been favorably inclined toward him.

"You are Miss Somerset, I believe? Lady Sylvia's new friend by way of her niece?"

She nodded wordlessly before recovering her manners. "Yes, Sir. I am. That is, I am Miss Somerset. I cannot vouch for whether or not Lady Sylvia regards me in the company of her friends."

"She does, or you would not be here," he chuckled. "It is a pleasure to make your acquaintance. I apologize for startling you. I did not realize you hadn't heard my approach."

"No, I didn't." Rising from the bench, she looked up the path toward the house, uncomfortable to find herself alone with a stranger. "Er— from where did you come?"

"I assume you are asking for an explanation of my appearance here and not for my place of birth?" He chortled in appreciation of his own wit.

Quickly composing herself, Anna put an additional step of distance between them and coolly folded her hands. "As you seem already to know these things about me, perhaps you should tell me both."

He quirked one pale eyebrow. "Point taken. I was born near Whitby in Yorkshire. I've come, just now, from Lady Sylvia's parlor, sent by said lady to fetch you for a cup of tea."

"Is it so late already?" Hurriedly, she gathered her belongings from the bench. "I understood that the footman was to fetch me as soon as Lady Sylvia awakened from her nap."

"I'm afraid my arrival altered the plan a bit. We had a small matter to discuss before you joined us." He gestured for her to precede him on the path.

"Are you her solicitor, then?" Anna paused, allowing him to come alongside her as they walked. "She told me her solicitor was to arrive this afternoon, but I understood it would be much later."

"And he will indeed be arriving later. I am a barrister," he explained. "Lady Sylvia is a friend, and likes to consult with me on certain matters before she meets with her solicitor."

"Seems a rather inefficient use of everyone's time."

"Ah, well," he chuckled, "I suppose it might be viewed as such. But I'm very fond of Lady Sylvia and do not mind humoring her." He walked with a relaxed step, hands firmly clasped behind his back.

"It's easy to be fond of Lady Sylvia," she agreed, smiling. A host of yellow butterflies erupted from a stand of larkspur, dancing about the two of them before continuing on to their next destination. Coming to a halt, Anna turned in a circle. "I fear we've taken a wrong turn. This isn't the path to the house," she observed, turning about as she attempted to get her bearings.

"We are to join Lady Sylvia in the rose arbor. She felt the weather sufficiently fine to have tea *alfresco*."

"And that sort of thinking," she laughed, "is one of the reasons I like her so much."

Lady Sylvia, cocooned in a pink froth of summer silk and gauze, had arranged herself among an assortment of plump cushions on a small wicker divan. The tea service was already laid out on the table before her, and she seemed to be waiting quite patiently for their arrival. A small dog of French breeding was ensconced on a cushion beside Lady Sylvia, eagerly enjoying the tidbits of food its mistress occasionally offered. The charming scene was attractively framed by a mature rose arbor that formed a thick canopy of pink and white climbers to shade them while they enjoyed their refreshment.

"How excellent! I see that you have found our Miss Somerset," Lady Sylvia chirped brightly as they took their seats. Lady Sylvia had aged the way all women hoped to age — with grace and dignity, her charm and the shadow of her youthful beauty intact. Her hair, now almost completely grey, still showed traces of the delicate strawberry blonde it had once been. Unlike many of her age, her face displayed few lines and wrinkles, and her eyes and lips seemed always to be in some stage of forming a smile. "And, Anna dear, now you have met our Mr. Hinton. I hope he has not been too dreary?"

"Not at all. He has been most pleasant." Anna was trying not to giggle.

"I find that those of the legal profession can often be tedious. But Mr. Hinton generally rises above the affliction of his profession."

Anna was prepared to be mortified on poor Mr. Hinton's account, but he responded quickly and with a smile. "Rising above the affliction of my profession requires a heroic effort, but I do try," he intoned drily with a sly wink at Anna.

Clearly, this sort of banter was characteristic of their relationship, enjoyed by both parties, which much relieved Anna for she did not like to think that Lady Sylvia's heretofore pleasant demeanor was but a cover for a hidden harridan. Lady Sylvia, her fingers graceful, her hand steady, went about the ritual of preparing the tea. A footman delivered a tiered tray of biscuits and scones, and Lady Sylvia smiled and thanked him without missing a beat.

"Miss Somerset is from the American colonies," Lady Sylvia told Hinton. "The Massachusetts colony, if I'm not mistaken. Is that correct, dear?" When Anna nodded, Lady Sylvia continued, her hands busily pouring tea into delicate china cups as she talked. Without consulting either of them, she added cream and sugar according to her precise knowledge of her guests' preference. "Miss Somerset is the niece of Sir Gregory Etheridge's business associate, Mr. John Wilton of Boston. They are in trade," she added in an aside as she handed cups of tea to Anna and Mr. Hinton, "but having met this young lady, I'm inclined to amend my former disdain for the sort."

"Very egalitarian of you," Hinton replied over the rim of his cup.

"Absolutely not!" She seemed horrified. "Just as you are doomed by your profession to a tendency toward insipidness, those of my class are, by nature, incapable of egalitarianism, republicanism, or any of the other 'isms' being so recklessly bandied about these days. It is simply unthinkable, and you will refrain from accusing me of such." She picked up a pair of delicate silver tongs and held them at the ready over the tiered tray. "Scone?"

"I offer my sincerest apology," Hinton said, holding out his plate to accept the proffered pastry. "It was a careless mistake, of course, and I beg your forgiveness."

"And so you should." She offered him a small tray of honeyed fruit.

"I did not expect to be treated to a plowman's supper, Lady Sylvia! You have assembled a veritable feast, and will surely cause too much strain on my weskit if you persist."

"Nonsense. I think it is lovely to break one's afternoon in this fashion, and it certainly helps to assuage the hunger pangs until the evening meal. I predict everyone will be routinely enjoying a small repast and afternoon tea before too long. It will surely become quite the *vogue*, and a most sensible trend it would be. The future of civilized conduct, in my view."

Anna had given up the attempt to stifle her giggles, and she earned a surreptitious look from Lady Sylvia, who punctuated her complicit smile with arched eyebrows. Anna accepted a proffered scone, which she knew from experience would surpass any she had enjoyed elsewhere, and took her first sip of tea. The appreciation of London's prime, unadulterated tea always inclined her to close her eyes while relishing the first sip of each cup. She had quickly schooled herself against that developing habit, however, for it often elicited irritatingly smug expressions from those around her. The colonial "tea situation" was but one more thing that set the colonists out as being apart from and inferior to England.

"But, to my earlier point, Mr. Hinton. I give little truck to all these dissident men, endeavoring to sound so enlightened, tossing about their pea-brained thoughts on representative government as though it is an entirely new concept just conceived by them. How long have we had a Parliament? And more, they imply that even the most witless of men should be heard, while women should continue to be pushed aside. It rankles. It rankles dreadfully."

"You consider that the Parliament should have less regard for the lower classes, favoring only the nobility? How very French of you."

"Do not be absurd, Mr. Hinton. I said no such thing. You twist my meaning." She looked at Anna. "Why do lawyers always do that — twist one's words? Is it a characteristic that is born in them? Or are they instructed in the skill by some reprehensible legal tutor?" She nodded in satisfaction when Anna could offer no explanation. "There, you see! There is no rational explanation." Satisfied that her point had been made and seconded, she returned her attention to Hinton. "And, furthermore, there is nothing French about me. I consider myself quite insulted."

"So says the woman who sits spoiling a French lap dog."

Lady Sylvia sniffed and pointedly fed the little dog a small morsel of biscuit. "Part of her lineage may be French," she corrected, "but her sire was decidedly English. She is symptomatic of what we English so often do — take the best others have to offer, refine it, and make it our own." She gave Anna a long, studied look. "Though, I dare say, we may have erred with this one." She registered Anna's blinking, dumbfounded expression, but continued unchecked. "Doubtless, she is representative of the best the colonies have to offer, and my niece has done all she can to bring out her Englishness. I cannot help but think that a disservice is being done."

Anna's face and neck blushed scarlet. "Lady Eugenie has been very kind and generous in all she has done to help me since I arrived here."

"That, I do not doubt, and I know that everything has been done with the best of intentions. But, because she is constrained by the expectations and convictions of our class, her vision of your future is limited to seeing you either appropriately, and unimaginatively, married, or respectably situated as a governess."

Anna's blush deepened, as did her chagrin at being so baldly discussed in such personal fashion. "As I'm still a few weeks shy of my fifteenth birthday, I think I have time yet for such worries," she said meekly.

"Lady Sylvia, you are distressing Miss Somerset, and making me almost equally uncomfortable." Hinton turned to Anna. "You must forgive Lady Sylvia's manners, Miss Somerset." His eyes twinkled. "Because she is so often alone, she forgets how to behave in company; and, because she so often forgets how to behave in company, she is often alone. It is a paradox of unending convolutions."

Lady Sylvia pursed her lips and affected a sour look. "Then I shall tell you directly, Anna, my dear. You are not to allow yourself to be stuffed into one of Eugenie's little social boxes. It is a bad habit of hers." She shot a pointed look at Hinton. "And Eugenie is my niece, so I can say so, and I'll have no more rebukes from you."

"I shall try quite hard to resist any machinations on Lady Eugenie's part," Anna promised earnestly. "You have my solemn word." She covered her mouth to stifle another urge to giggle, for Hinton was contorting his face most humorously.

"Tell me about your uncle, Miss Somerset. Lady Sylvia indicated that he is in trade?" Hinton took too big a bite of scone and sent crumbs tumbling down the front of his jacket.

Anna nodded. "Yes. He was born here in London but immigrated to Boston when he was a young man. His business has become quite successful, though he had to work very hard to make it so. He is the kindest, gentlest of men, and I miss him terribly. I know he believes he's doing the right thing to send me here, but I'd rather it were otherwise."

Hinton brushed the tumble of crumbs from his lap. "I'm surprised that he would send you here alone."

"He felt he needed to stay there to watch over his business interests. He said that, had it been merely a matter of his own choosing, he'd have sold everything and come away with me. But he feels he'd be letting Sir Gregory down if he did that." She recalled that he had also expressed concern about protecting Anna's inheritance, but she decided against mentioning that bit.

"Is your uncle in sympathy with the tax protests?" Hinton was not looking at her as he asked the question, but there was about him an air of marked interest, nonetheless.

Anna smiled slyly. "I've yet to meet a man who does not grumble about taxes," she quipped. "But my uncle is loyal to the king, of course, if that's what you're asking."

"As are all Englishmen, I suspect," Lady Sylvia retorted, "so long as they view their king and their nation as one and the same. One wonders how that might change once the two things no longer seem to be synonymous."

Hinton raised an eyebrow. "Are you suggesting that the colonies are somehow a nation separate and apart from Britain?"

"I'm suggesting that, if the colonies continue to be treated as a subordinate appendage of England, they well may begin to see themselves as something separate and apart."

"Oh," Anna quickly assured them, "I know that the two things are quite inseparable in my uncle's mind."

"Then, we must hope that those hooligans who are causing all the fuss will not make his life difficult." Lady Sylvia gave her head an emphatic nod, ending talk on the subject.

Anna unconsciously touched the letter tucked away in her pocket. Without intending to do so, Lady Sylvia had pricked a tender place in Anna's thoughts. It was a place dominated by fear that, no matter how much she tried, would not be assuaged.

*   *   *

Days later, in a world apart from Lady Sylvia's garden in more ways than simple geography, Daniel made his way across the taproom at Withers' tavern to where Teague waited for him. The place was not overcrowded, but many of the tables were full of men engaged in loud, semi-inebriated conversation. It was coming on to sunset, and Daniel's stomach was protesting the fact that he had not yet eaten supper. He and Teague were waiting for Drum to arrive, however, and were passing the time by sampling the good ale Withers kept back for favored customers. Daniel signaled Withers to send another round of drinks his way. The old man had hired a new serving girl, who smiled suggestively when she set the mugs in front of Daniel and Teague. "She likes you," Teague chuckled.

"She likes anyone who'll leave a few extra coins on the table for her." Daniel scrubbed his hand across his face wearily. He'd been to the Virginia Colony and back on an errand for Hancock, and weeks in the saddle on the rugged roads and hazardous trails between Williamsburg and Boston had taken their toll. "Where's Drum? I thought he was coming with you?"

Teague shrugged. "He was working at the Ainsworth house this afternoon. Probably just didn't finish up as early as expected."

"The Ainsworth's? Charlotte Ainsworth's?"

"Yes. He's doing odd jobs for them." Teague took a deep swallow of his ale, girding himself for the objection he suspected he was about to hear.

"I'm not sure that's such a good idea," Daniel submitted, frowning.

"Why? Because you don't care for Miss Ainsworth?" It had come out more angrily — more defensively — than he'd intended, and he quickly checked his tone. "Mr. Ainsworth has been ill. You know that. They need help keeping things up around the house and haven't been able to find anyone satisfactory. They like Drum. He does a good job and he's trustworthy. And, Ainsworth pays well."

Daniel looked doubtful. "Just so Drum isn't being taken advantage of."

"Mr. Ainsworth isn't the type of man to take advantage."

"No, but his daughter is. She'll ask far more of Drum than he bargained for. And, I wouldn't put it past her to try to cheat him on his wages."

"That's a hell of a thing to say! Just because you got crossways with her somewhere along the line doesn't make her dishonest!"

"And just because you've taken a shine to her doesn't make her better than she is. I know her, Teague. You don't."

"I know her well enough."

"Oh?"

Teague shrugged and hid his guilty expression in his mug. "I've been spending a lot of time with her lately. I think I know her pretty well." When Daniel didn't respond, he went on. "I do like her. I like her very much. And, I think I've a real chance with her. I think she likes me, too. In fact, I know she does."

Daniel was on the verge of telling Teague what he thought of that notion when Drum arrived, clearly unhappy and more than a little disheveled. "Where have you been?" Daniel asked.

"I've been trying to get here," Drum touchily informed them as he settled into the chair between Daniel and Teague, his back to the wall. "I'm hungry. Does Withers have stew tonight?"

"Yes," Daniel said. "We already ordered three bowls. The girl will bring them over now you're here. But, why are you so late? And what happened to you? You look as though you fell off a moving horse."

"I was coming here," Drum huffed, "and some men stopped me. They were telling me about a friend who was hurt, and asked if I could help carry him. Then, they took me to an alley but the man who was there wasn't hurt at all. He had a club and he was going to hit me over the head, I think." The serving girl set bowls of steaming stew in front of them, and Drum immediately dug into his.

Daniel and Teague waited, but it didn't seem that Drum intended to continue his story any time soon. "And?" Daniel prompted. "What happened next? Did the man hit you with the club."

Drum shook his head. "No, because I punched him in the stomach. He dropped the club then."

Teague looked from Drum to Daniel. "Press gang?"

"Sounds like it," Daniel concurred, nodding. Press gangs weren't too common in the area, but they did pop up from time to time.

"Navy?"

"Not likely." He frowned speculatively. "They have enough problems here without adding impressment to the list. Probably a gang off one of the merchantmen that found itself shorthanded after the last crossing."

Teague nodded his agreement.

"More than likely, though, they're shorthanded because the merchantman was waylaid by a warship looking to take on men," Daniel added. "One way or the other, the navy is responsible. Drum was lucky. If the press gang had managed to get him onto their ship, sooner or later they'd have been boarded again and the navy would almost certainly take him off their hands. Big and strong as he is, they wouldn't be able to pass on such a prize."

"Why, you could've ended up in His Majesty's navy, Drum!" Teague slapped him on the back to emphasize the jest.

Drum's spoon paused half-way to his mouth. "I don't want to be in anyone's navy," he said evenly. "I don't like boats."

Daniel looked up to see four men come slowly through the tavern door. They were moving warily, looking for someone it seemed. One was carrying a club, one had the beginnings of an impressive black eye, and one had an excessive amount of blood smeared on his face and down the front of his shirt. "Drum? Were there four men in that alley?"

Drum nodded without looking up.

"I thought you said you hit one of them in the stomach?"

"I did."

"If you hit him in the stomach, how did he get a broken nose?"

Drum looked up at Daniel, surprised by the question. "The one I hit in the stomach didn't get a broken nose. After I hit the man with the club, one of his friends got mad and tried to hit me. I raised my arm to stop him, but he was too close and my elbow hit him in the nose."

"Uh huh." Daniel watched the men come closer. They had spotted Drum and his friends, and were approaching with as much affected menace as they could manage. Considering that three of them looked like the walking wounded after a battle, their effort wasn't as effective as they might have hoped. "And, the man with the black eye?" Daniel asked. "How did that happen?"

Drum stared at him. "How do you know he has a black eye?"

Teague, following Daniel's gaze, had similarly deduced that the four men coming toward them were Drum's assailants. "I suppose we could just ask them about it and let Drum finish his stew," Teague suggested.

The four men had arrived at the table where they stood, towering over the seated men. The man with the club stood nearest to Daniel, with Broken Nose, Black Eye, and the fourth man lined up so that the fourth man was closest to Teague. They glowered at Drum, and the man with the club proclaimed, "You broke my friend's nose."

Drum frowned at Broken Nose. "It was an accident," he grumbled. "I just wanted to keep him from hitting me."

The man with the club was swinging his weapon in half-arcs, down by his knee, and then back up to smack against the palm of his hand. "I don't think it was no accident," he growled. "And, it don't matter anyway. We're here to even the score."

Drum stared at them blankly, which seemed to further inflame Club Carrier against him. Daniel would have laughed had the situation not been so precarious. "If my friend says it was an accident," he maintained, rising to his feet, "then it was an accident." He sensed Teague getting to his feet as well. "There's no score to even, so you fellows had best be on your way."

Club Carrier grinned and swung his club more emphatically. "We don't see it that way. No one gets away with that." He jerked his head to indicate his unfortunate friend with the broken nose and bloodied face.

Daniel glanced quickly around the taproom. There were clusters of patrons here and there, all pretty much minding their own business for the moment. He decided it might be time to change that. He turned the one empty chair around and rested his hands on the top rail of its back, seemingly relaxed as he spoke.

"If no one gets away with resisting you, it's most likely because everyone you deal with wakes up to find themselves miles offshore and part of a ship's crew they had no interest in joining. You're an impressment gang, aren't you?" He raised his voice enough so it would carry to the ears of other patrons. "Folks around here don't think much of press gangs." Many of the other patrons turned in their chairs, suddenly interested in the conversation at the back of the tavern.

Club Carrier was a hulking brute of a man whose mental capacity apparently did not fit his size. Thick-headed as he was, he failed to understand the warning. "Our business was with your friend. I think you need to keep out of it."

"My friend has no interest in becoming part of a ship's crew." He turned to Drum. "That's right, isn't it? You don't want to go to work on a ship, do you?"

Drum shook his head and repeated his earlier declaration. "I don't like boats."

"There," Daniel told Club Carrier. "You see? He doesn't like boats. So, I think you have no business with him."

Club Carrier looked from man to man, weighing his options, and chose the wrong one. Drum would have been a fine catch, but all three of them together would yield an even greater reward. Daniel watched Club Carrier's eyes and felt he could almost see the wheels turning in his tiny brain as he landed upon the fact that his men numbered four while Daniel and his friends were only three. To Club Carrier, it seemed an equation with an easy, uncomplicated answer. But Daniel saw it differently.

Club Carrier would have to be taken out first. Of that much, Daniel was certain. If the others were armed, their weapons had not yet been drawn, whereas Club Carrier was brandishing his with zeal. Furthermore, he was clearly the leader. Eliminate the leader of any gang and the others were easier to deal with. Broken Nose would doubtless hang back, not wanting to risk further pain to his face. Black Eye had been glancing about the room uncertainly ever since the gang had entered, so Daniel thought there was a chance he would fade the moment punches started being thrown. The uninjured fourth man was the unknown element, but Daniel had confidence in Teague's ability to deal with whatever that man decided to do.

To Daniel's way of thinking, there was some advantage to getting it all over with here and now as opposed to waiting for the men to jump them from a dark alley somewhere. In the tavern, there were witnesses who were hostile to press gangs and who might even be counted on for assistance if it became necessary. Daniel doubted it would be necessary.

Deciding that it would be advantageous to get out ahead of whatever Club Carrier planned to do, Daniel tightened his grip on the chair, swung it up, and drove it legs-first into Club Carrier's chest. He could hear enough commotion behind him to know that Teague had done something equally preemptive on his end, though he had no idea what. Daniel used the full force of his weight to push Club Carrier backwards. One leg of the chair was jabbing into Club Carrier's windpipe, restricting his breathing, and the struggling man dropped the club in favor of using both hands to try to remove the improvised weapon. But Daniel was pressing relentlessly, driving Club Carrier backwards until he collided with the bar. Without even a change of expression, Withers obliged Daniel by striking Club Carrier over the head with a truncheon he kept hidden behind the counter for dealing with unruly patrons. It took three good whacks to render Club Carrier unconscious and send him melting to the floor.

Daniel whirled about to see how Teague was faring. It seemed that he had managed to disable the fourth man but, to Daniel's surprise, Black Eye had decided to put up quite a fight of his own. He had pulled a knife, which he was swinging wildly at Teague. Teague was dodging the blade with ease, but was having difficulty getting close enough to Black Eye to incapacitate him. Daniel started toward them, intending to assist Teague, but Drum seized the opportunity before he could get there. Taking a page from Daniels' book, Drum swung his chair up into his hands and shoved into Black Eye from the side, knocking him to the floor. Black Eye dropped the knife as he fell, and it skittered across the floor to be retrieved by one of the watching patrons. Drum followed-through with the chair, pushing until it was positioned across Black Eye's prostrate form, then sat upon it, effectively pinning Black Eye to the floor.

Broken Nose fled.

Breathing hard with exertion, Daniel and Teague crossed the room to congratulate Drum on his success. Teague knelt to bind the trapped mans' hands. "Good job, Drum!" he said.

"He was going to cut you with his knife," Drum stated, unnecessarily explaining the cause of his bold action.

"He was going to try," Teague corrected.

"You did the right thing, Drum." Daniel peered down at Black Eye's furious face. "So, how did he get the black eye? You never got around to telling us that part."

"Oh," Drum said, taking a good look at Black Eye's face for himself. "I didn't do that. When I was walking away from them — after I broke the other man's nose — the man with the club tried to swing at me again. His aim wasn't so good and I ducked, but this man didn't duck and the club hit him in the eye."

Daniel and Teague laughed harder than they had laughed in a very long time.

"You lads best be on your way," Withers told them. He knelt to take over the task of tying Black Eye's wrists. "Someone's already gone to fetch the authorities."

"I hope we didn't make trouble for you here," Daniel said.

"No trouble. You know how folks feel about press gangs. There's a room full of witnesses here to say that these men were tryin' to take you all against your will. The four of 'em'll be locked up or shipped out. Either way, they won't be botherin' any of us again, I'd say. And, as far as the authorities, I don't think anyone here will be able to identify you three. As far as we're concerned, you're strangers. We never saw you before." He winked and grinned.

Daniel and Teague were still laughing as they left the tavern. Drum, on the other hand, was complaining that he had not been allowed to finish his stew.

CHAPTER FIVE

Charlotte was incensed. She had encountered Daniel earlier in the day and, despite the fact that the streets were simmering in unbearable August heat, had stopped him to converse. What started as flirtation on her part, ended with an unpleasant lecture from Daniel on the topic of his objections to her relationship with Teague. That Daniel thought he had the right to interfere and, more to the point, had threatened to endanger her schemes angered her beyond words. The encounter served to convince her that she needed to move quickly to secure Teague's loyalty before Daniel could sour him.

It amazed Charlotte that Daniel actually believed his friend capable of change. Considering that Daniel knew him better than anyone, it seemed that he'd have known Teague was far too grasping to settle for what he could earn with honest work and, moreover, that he needed the edgy excitement that came with danger. Daniel should also have known, she thought, that Teague felt he was being supplanted by Daniel's new associates and their undertakings. Busy with the effort of making his own living and distracted by his involvement in the ongoing political turmoil, Daniel had less time for Teague than Teague would have liked, and Charlotte was astute enough to see it and use Teague's jealousy to her own purpose. She had watched the restlessness build in Teague until, with impeccable timing, she set a hook that was all the more secure because Teague wanted it to be.

She sent a note asking Teague to call on her the following day, and she carefully staged his reception. Dressed in unusually sober attire and looking worn and fatigued, Charlotte greeted him with a wan smile, ushering him into the front parlor as she would a valued guest. She indicated a place for him to sit, and then perched near him on the edge of the divan. She made the requisite small talk while preparing the tea, ignoring his lack of enthusiasm for discussing the weather or other trivial matters. It was plain, also, that the tea had much less interest for him than did the crystal decanter of her father's best port sitting on the sideboard. But port did not figure into the performance she had planned and so she continued the ritual of pouring and serving.

She passed him his cup and saucer, which vibrated ever so slightly in her hand. Teague accepted the tea but quickly set it aside so he could take her trembling hand in both of his. It was a bold move, he knew, but he dared it in the hope that her apparent state of mind would permit the familiarity. He leaned forward and studied her face, taking in the red-rimmed eyes that, uncharacteristically, would not meet his in direct gaze.

"I apologize," she murmured, quickly withdrawing her hand. "I made a bad job of that, didn't I?" She manufactured a show of trying to smile but ended up biting her quivering lower lip while seemingly fighting tears.

"No," he responded quickly. "It's fine. You're obviously not yourself, though. Please tell me what has happened to upset you."

"I believe I am merely tired." Her tone lacked conviction. "Things have been a bit too much for me lately. My father suffers from dropsy, you know, and he has taken a bad turn. I've barely slept for attending to him. He will allow no one else to care for him and is quite demanding." This was far from the truth, but she knew Teague had no way of knowing otherwise. "I love him, of course," she added quickly, "and I want to take care of him, but there has been so much to do." Tears welled up in her eyes and her chin quivered. "He asks so much of me, and I try so hard, but," her voice broke on a tiny sob, "I find myself overwhelmed with trying to keep everything going. There's the house to manage and his business to oversee....." Her words trailed off and she waved her hands in a way meant to conjure a variety of mostly-fictional tasks for consumption by Teague's imagination.

"I understand." Teague took her hands in his, firmly this time so that she could not easily pull away. "You carry too great a burden and expect too much of yourself. You must allow your friends to help. I want very much to help you; you do know that?"

"Yes, and I'm so very grateful for you, Teague." She looked at him with wide, dewy eyes, and squeezed his hand gently. "I'm so very fond of you."

Teague cocked his head, frowning. "I sense that you meant to say 'but' at the end of that statement."

The expressive lashes fell again, a veil over enigmatic sea-grey eyes. "My father is ... difficult." The words were said with feigned prudence, punctuated by a slight biting of her lower lip. She raised her eyes, and wished that she could fabricate a blush. Tears were easy but, despite a good deal of trying to develop the skill, she had never been able to produce a blush at will. "He knows you have been calling on me," she blurted out as though it was something painful that she needed to say quickly. "He is most unhappy with me. I'm afraid he considers you ... unsuitable." Her lashes lowered once more like a theatre curtain dropping after a performance.

Hearing the words did not make Teague happy, but he could not say that he was surprised by them. He had hoped to be able to win Mr. Ainsworth over in time, but it was difficult to change the mind of a man one was never allowed to see or speak with. "Perhaps, when he has recovered some, he can be made to warm to me?"

She shook her head forcefully. "I don't think that is likely. I ... he ... well, it is complicated."

"No, it's not at all complicated. I understand. But I'm not willing to give up the fight. You're too dear to me, Charlotte."

"Oh, I'm so happy to hear you say that!" She was gushing now, energized by an apparent sense of relief. "You're the world to me, Teague, and it would break my heart to be parted from you. I've been turning the thing over and over in my mind, trying to see how I can be free — how we can be together — and the only solution that has presented itself is for me to be free of his control. If I had my own money, I could do as I pleased. We could go somewhere else — Philadelphia, perhaps, or London!" She had no intention of settling for less than London but sought to ease him into that choice.

"Yes," he agreed, slowly nodding his head. London? He was not so certain about that.

"Your tea has gone cold." She reached for his cup in a way that brought her body into close proximity with his. "Let me warm it."

"Oh," he interrupted quickly, "you really needn't bother."

She saw his eyes flick again, almost involuntarily, to the decanter of port. "Of course not," she said with an understanding smile. "You are a man who likes something more spirited in his cup. I admire that." She poured the cold tea from his cup. "But we will preserve the niceties." With a conspiratorial smile, she took his cup to the sideboard and filled it with a generous amount of the port. "There." Dotingly, she handed the cup back to him. "I believe that will be much more to your liking."

Teague took a small, testing sip of the port, and then a much larger swallow. "That *is* good." He had never tasted anything quite so smooth, quite so *comforting*. It imparted a wonderful warmth without any burn. "What is it?"

"Port. From Portugal." She sat beside him, smoothing her skirts with a nonchalant air. "My father says it's the best in the world, though I cannot claim to know whether or not he's correct in that assertion."

He closed his eyes as he enjoyed the next swallow. "Having tasted this, I believe he must be correct, indeed."

"I'm glad you like it." She was beaming at him, as though it pleased her enormously to find something so enjoyable to him.

And Teague was beaming back. He'd never had anyone go to so much trouble to please him — and certainly no one like Charlotte. When she had mentioned her thoughts regarding running away to Philadelphia or London, he'd been on the verge of saying that he did not see how the plan could be managed. The port had improved his outlook considerably, however, so that he said instead, "We'll go away just as you wish, Charlotte. I'm not picturing how the financial side of it can be managed, but some solution will no doubt present itself."

Charlotte clapped her hands delightedly. "I've been putting money aside for some time now, and have a tidy sum saved. It was to be my emergency fund in case my father passed away and left me with no option but to marry someone for whom I did not care," she explained hastily. In fact, she knew her father had no intention of doing any such thing. "I thought, perhaps, working together, we might amass enough to make it possible?" She did not wait for an answer. "Oh, Teague! Do you really think it could be? Have I been desolate for no reason?" She grasped his hand and clutched it to her heart, imploring him to not disappoint her.

Teague's head was swimming. For Charlotte to submit to him, to commit herself solely to him, was what he had wanted — had dreamed of. But he had envisioned it happening with her father's approval and financial backing. This newly suggested scenario caught him unprepared. Without her father's business, he doubted there was any honest pursuit that would enable him to realize Charlotte's design, and certainly nothing he could do to sustain her lifestyle once she had broken with her father. And yet, she was beseeching him, begging him to rescue her. He wanted so much to be her rescuer; he wanted so much for her to belong to him.

Charlotte saw the uncertainty shadowing his face. She had expected it, prepared for it. Becoming once more demure, she released his hand and lowered her head as though acutely embarrassed. "But I have been too forward."

"No!" He saw her begin to withdraw into herself and reached out, desperate to stop her retreat. "You haven't. Your words gladden my heart more than you can imagine."

She smiled, becoming the perfect blend of coy and innocent. "Before we go any further, I must confess something, Teague. May I? Will you promise not to be angry or think me horrid?" When he nodded vacantly, she drew a deep, resigned breath. "What I need to tell you now causes me great shame." Nervously, she fidgeted with the lace trim on her sleeve where it fell across her lap.

"Go on," he encouraged, unable to conceive that she could have anything to confess that would shame her in his eyes. He was perched on the edge of his seat, practically trembling with anticipation, signaling that ill thoughts of her were an impossibility.

"As I told you, I've been putting money aside — as I'm able — for quite some time now. The total was building slowly — until you started bringing me gifts." She looked up at him, carefully gauging his reaction. "Oh, Teague," she gushed, "I know it was horrid of me to do it, but I sold some of the lovely things you've given me. Not all of them, just the less personal things. Please don't be angry with me, and please don't be hurt. It's just that they fetched so much money, and I have become so desperate!"

Teague was taken aback, but could hardly complain considering that almost all of the items were stolen rather than purchased. Nor could he find fault; desperation was a state with which he was all too familiar. "No," he assured her. "I'm not angry. I understand, of course, and I'm just happy that my gifts were of good use." A part of him was not happy at all, but he did understand, and could not stir himself to annoyance against her.

"You are so dear." Once again, she clasped his hand in both of hers and pressed it against her bosom, her face glowing with adoration. "You have filled my heart."

Teague could not speak, could hardly breathe, for fear of bursting the golden bubble that surrounded them. Charlotte's words had never been more honeyed nor her touch so warmly intimate, and a part of him feared that it was all a dream from which the slightest motion would awaken him. He felt he could move mountains if that was what it would take for them to be together — and her father be damned. Slowly, carefully, he reached out with his free hand and touched one of the many ringlets that haloed her face, then lightly traced his finger along her porcelain cheek. It seemed a miracle to him when she did not flinch, did not move, did not brush his hand away.

"You've made me so happy," she breathed, trembling. "I feared that you would think ill of me. Worse, I feared that you'd not want me without my father's money behind us." She lowered her voice almost to a whisper. "I feared that you did not feel as I do."

He shook his head and swallowed the enormous lump lodged like a fist in his throat. When he tried to speak, his voice croaked a little, making them both smile. "We'll do whatever it takes," he assured her.

"I shall be ever so frugal, Teague. You'll see. Within only a few years, we'll have enough money to go away together."

He felt that, if he had to wait so long to be with her, he would explode. "You said the items I brought to you fetched a generous price?"

She nodded.

"Then there shall be more. I'll be vigilant for opportunities to obtain things that we can resell at a profit."

It was exactly what she'd been waiting to hear. "Of course, if it is not too much trouble for you." Her face puckered in a little frown. "You're certain this is what you want to do?"

"Quite certain."

"Well, then, whatever small things you find, you must bring to me to sell. You can best deal with the larger items. But you should not have to shoulder the entire burden. Besides, I've developed such good contacts for certain types of things."

"Very well, if you think that would be best."

"I do. Oh!" She hid a dainty giggle behind her hand. "Won't it be lovely when I can say that to you while we're standing in front of the vicar?"

He grinned idiotically and nodded his head. His mind was already spinning ideas and making plans. If Charlotte intended to sell items he procured illicitly, then he would have to obtain things from outside Boston — or, at least, things that would not be easily identified. It would be complicated but doable. Perhaps he could even renew old smuggling associations. He just wondered if he could manage to keep Daniel from discovering what he was about. That concern was shaken off easily enough, however, when he looked at Charlotte's happy face.

Teague immediately threw himself into the business of thievery with a dedication he had seldom exhibited in any undertaking. So engaged was he in his single-minded purpose that he hardly noticed the passage of time and was surprised when the heat and humidity of August gave way to autumn's chill. The smugglers had become a tight-knit cabal that did not welcome competition. That hurdle aside, he did not relish the idea of sharing profits with an entire gang of associates. Robbing houses in areas near Boston was a straightforward endeavor involving a minimum of planning. It had the advantage of being something he could accomplish without help but the disadvantage of yielding only small items that had to be sold carefully.

Much more lucrative were the wagonloads of merchandise being transported from Boston's harbor to inland towns and communities. Finding wagons on their own with little in the way of protection, or parked unattended while the driver and escort were enjoying themselves at some wayside public house, took time and effort, and the process of securing them carried significant risk. But the reward was great.

These profitable targets carried the inconvenience of not being something he could manage alone. Apart from Daniel, Teague had never trusted another person enough to form any sort of partnership, and finding a suitable collaborator for this endeavor taxed him greatly. He began his search upriver from Boston and, without revealing too much regarding his plans, was finally able to locate a suitable candidate. The man called himself "Joe," which Teague knew was no more the man's real name than the fictitious name Teague had supplied for himself. Joe's best asset was his skill at handling a boat and knowledge of the river, which would be valuable when it came time to move their stolen goods. So, Joe became part of the two-man team. He was reliable, closed-mouthed, did as he was told, and was more than happy with the pay Teague offered. For once, Teague thought, fate had smiled on him.

*   *   *

Lady Sylvia's coach was of the latest design and the most comfortable of its class. But it was not completely impervious to the December cold, nor did it offer a perfectly smooth ride. Every rut and hole jostled its three passengers, and the part of London into which they were venturing had more than its share of poorly maintained roads. Anna, swaddled in her warmest cloak, a blanket across her lap and a warm brick beneath her feet, nonetheless felt the tenacious January cold seep into the coach. On the other hand, Lady Sylvia, who was bundled to her eyebrows in layered furs and velvet, chatted away with Mr. Hinton, her excitement seeming to banish any suggestion that the cold was touching her.

Not that Anna particularly minded the cold or the occasional jarring to which her bones were being subjected because, incredibly, they were on their way to witness an exhibition of swordsmanship. Not only had Anna never witnessed such an event, she had never expected to do so, and her imagination was running wild with anticipation. Like so many of Lady Sylvia's adventures, this one was tinged with a rim of guilt. Anna had no doubt that her uncle would consider it a most unsuitable outing and that Lady Eugenie would be appalled to learn that her aunt had engaged in something so déclassé. This was simply not something done by well-bred young ladies — and certainly not those of the high-born type.

The outing was Mr. Hinton's suggestion. It was yet another in the constant stream of diversions he found for Lady Sylvia, many of which were questionable at the very least. But in his defense, those were exactly the diversions Lady Sylvia tended to favor, so he could hardly be blamed. This particular occasion had turned on the fact that his nephew, an officer in the king's army, was to participate in the exhibition. Worldly Lady Sylvia had blanched slightly when the excursion was first proposed for she had heard that establishments such as the one they would be visiting included disreputable females, scantily clad and scant of morals, who served food, drink, and themselves to gentlemen patrons. Mr. Hinton, blushing noticeably to be discussing such things with a lady, quickly assured her that he would never consider taking her or any lady to a place such as she described, would not himself set foot in that sort of establishment, and that his nephew would certainly never demean himself by patronizing anything less than the most respectable of enterprises. And so, fortified with those assurances, they had set off.

Their destination was a large, warehouse-like building positioned like the Colossus of Rhodes in the middle of an odd, socially-bisected street. When approached from one direction, the building seemed to be located in a derelict neighborhood, but when approached from the opposite direction, it seemed to be located among the emerging, respectable middle-class. Carefully sequestered behind the draperies that hung over the coach windows, Anna had not seen either view. She was merely confronted, on stepping from the carriage, with an imposingly large façade devoid of any decoration save for the neatly lettered sign over the door that read "Atkinson's Academy of Fencing and Pugilism." Atkinson's was among the more respectable of such establishments springing up all about London to serve the desire of the rising middle-class and the leisured upper classes to learn various arts involving swords and fists. It was also one of the few respectable venues of gentlemanly sports that allowed female spectators.

The air inside the building was blessedly warm but was permeated with the odors Anna associated with men — sweat, tobacco, and leather. The center of the building was an enormous hall that was open all the way up to the high ceiling and well-lit by tall clerestory windows. A second-floor gallery ran along three sides of the hall allowing spectators to watch the participants on the main floor below. Looking down into the hall, Anna decided that it was much like a large church gutted of its pew boxes, altar, and pulpit, leaving behind only an expanse of scuffed wooden floor. Racks of swords and various weapons, surprising in their variety, lined the walls.

Mr. Hinton guided Anna and Lady Sylvia to seats in the gallery and began to explain what they were seeing. The air was ringing with the sound of metal on metal, for numerous pairs of swordsmen were arrayed about the rectangle of open floor below, sparring lightly as they warmed their muscles and honed techniques for the competitive duels ahead. Anna felt a frisson of excitement pulse from her heart all the way out to her fingertips.

A few of the competitors, many of them men who carried the aura of experience on the battlefield, wielded basket-handled broadswords. A more complex weapon than the smallsword favored by fashionable gentlemen, the broadsword required a stronger arm and higher skill level than its more compact cousin. The men practicing with broadswords were given a wide berth by the other competitors, most of whom were clearly gentlemen who, beyond a strong sense of adventure, had no compelling reason for taking up a sword. All were armed with smallswords, which they referred to as "sabers." Mr. Hinton explained that these popular weapons had little resemblance to cavalry sabers, or even to the "hangers" officers wore. Being much smaller and lighter, they had become the favored accessory for gentlemen attempting to project a certain image, and the preferred weapon for personal defense and dueling. He made them sound quite harmless as compared to the military weapons, but to Anna, they looked sufficiently sinister.

In time, the Master-at-Arms called for the floor to be vacated. Swordsmen faded into the shadows under the gallery and, without announcement or preamble, the first two competitors walked to the center of the rectangular wooden floor. The two young men, who Anna guessed to be scarcely older than herself, saluted each other with their sabers, and the Master-at-Arms signaled the start of the match. Even to Anna's inexperienced eye, it was plain that the young men were raw novices, perhaps even experiencing their first formal competition. There was a good deal of dodging punctuated by the occasional wildly overenthusiastic thrust. The heels of their slippers squeaked and thumped noisily on the chalk-strewn floor, and both men quickly showed signs of fatigue. The audience occasionally rewarded the men with a smattering of polite applause, though there was an atmosphere of mild distraction as spectators expectantly studied the competitors who were waiting in the wings.

Mr. Hinton took the opportunity, in a voice lowered so that only she and Lady Sylvia could hear, to provide a quick primer on fencing. He explained the hours of practice required before one could truly master the basic saber defenses, and outlined the fundamental necessity for speed and endurance. He enumerated the advantages strength, precision, and flexibility afforded the swordsman, and the imperative of a well-disciplined mind. By the end of the second duel, Anna did not need Mr. Hinton to tell her that cat-like reflexes would be a fencer's ally, an easily distracted mind his enemy.

The second pair of competitors was hardly an improvement on the first, but the third pair brought the spectators, full of anticipation, to the edges of their seats. These were the broadsword competitors. Both men were taller than most and carried themselves with an assurance that was quietly confident without crossing the line into arrogance. One of the two particularly caught Anna's eye, for he was strikingly attired in a dark blue and green tartan plaid. She had seen kilted soldiers on occasion, however, so it was not so much his attire as his own appearance that had caught her eye. His impressive height and build, sharply-contoured face, and mane of raven-black hair gave him an uncanny resemblance to Daniel — albeit an older version. The Scot seemed cloaked in an invisible but weighty mantle, hinting at a vein of darkness in his nature. That, too, she had seen in Daniel.

Once their bout had begun, the men fought with an economy of motion and a dancer's grace. That such big men, wielding such heavy weapons could demonstrate fluidity and lightness amazed her. She was entranced, absolutely fascinated by the exciting art. Unlike the smallsword, which was a stabbing weapon, the broadsword had a multitude of uses that ranged from stabbing to slashing, and a good deal in between. The larger, basket-handled swords swung in controlled arcs, playing out a pattern of thrusts and cuts and parries. Once, the Scot struck a hard blow into his opponent's shoulder. The man stepped back, evincing both a pained reaction to the blow and anger at himself for the error he had made that allowed it to strike him. Anna reacted as well, leaning forward anxiously and clutching the rail before her, fearful that the man was seriously injured.

"The swords are blunt-edged," Mr. Hinton assured her. "The man will likely have a generous bruise to show for his error, but no real harm is done."

Anna responded with a doubtful look but forced herself to relax back into her chair. She glanced about the gallery surveying the faces of other spectators, all of whom were more knowledgeable than herself. No one else seemed to share her alarm, and yet, all were riveted by the action on the floor. There were appreciative smiles and brief outbursts of applause from time to time, but not a single face showed any concern that blood might flow.

Below, the pace of the match had increased dramatically. The Scot had taken advantage of a moment of unbalance on his opponent's part and was driving into him with powerful, fast-paced blows. His blade struck again and again, each blow so quickly followed by another that all the opponent could do was parry desperately, backing up a step as he deflected each blow, completely unable to mount any sort of counter-attack. Everyone in the hall knew the man was doomed to defeat, and yet he would not yield. It was remarkable, Anna thought, the determination to keep fighting even when the cost of losing was but a matter of pride.

Finally, the end came. The Scot drove his opponent backwards until he was against one of the columns supporting the gallery. In a smooth sweep of his sword, he disarmed the opponent, sending his sword clattering loudly to the floor. Then, with one fluid motion, the Scot completed the maneuver by touching the tip of his own sword to his defeated opponent's chest.

"End of match," the Master-at-arms called. "Victory to Captain Grant."

The two opponents saluted each other, and the spectators applauded the demonstration of good sportsmanship. There were two more rounds of opponents armed with sabers. In each case the men were well matched, experienced swordsmen who put on a display every bit as engaging as the broadsword competition, if less overwhelming in power. Anna felt them an anticlimax to what she had just witnessed.

Those matches complete, the final pair took the floor. Anna felt Mr. Hinton shift in his seat, sitting forward a bit, and was aware that a small ripple passed through the audience. Apparently there were others in the gallery Aside from Mr. Hinton who had come to see this particular match.

"Ah," Mr. Hinton announced. "Here is my nephew." For Anna's benefit, he nodded toward one of the men. "There. The fair-haired young man. His name is Edward Hinton."

Anna looked down to see two men taking the floor, sabers in hand. One was tall, brown-haired, and carried himself with a haughty insouciance. The other, the man Hinton had indicated, was young — in his early twenties, Anna guessed — of middle-height, with a slender build and bright, wheat-colored hair. His posture was erect, and if he was experiencing any reticence regarding the match, there was no indication of it in his demeanor. Edward Hinton's opponent was considerably taller, which seemed to Anna a dangerous portent. The little she had learned thus far indicated to her that being shorter, and thus having a shorter reach than one's opponent could be a significant, though not insurmountable, disadvantage.

"Edward's opponent is Warren Caulfield," Mr. Hinton told them. "He is known to be a superior swordsman. Mr. Caulfield is a member of the academy here, and Edward is competing as the guest of Captain Grant, whom you saw earlier in the broadsword match. This match is to settle some point of personal importance to Edward."

Before he could offer further explanation, the opponents saluted each other and took positions to wait for their signal from the Master-at-Arms. When the signal came, Hinton jumped quickly to the offensive. Caulfield, perhaps expecting a bit more caution on the part of his younger, less experienced opponent, was caught by surprise and forced back a step or two. He recovered quickly, however, and was soon driving Hinton backward with a dazzling array of thrusts and lunges. At one point, Hinton was thrown dangerously off-balance when his right foot slid in the chalk. Caulfield moved to capitalize on the moment, but Hinton was able to dart out of harm's way.

The spectators gasped and leaned in for a closer look. It seemed to Anna that crowd sentiment favored Hinton despite Caulfield's status with the academy. She glanced quickly to the side, wondering how Mr. Hinton was reacting to his nephew's plight. Taciturn as ever, he maintained a calm, almost detached mien, the only clue that he might be experiencing any nervousness an absentminded stroking of his finger along his upper lip.

Below them, Edward Hinton had successfully skirted disaster, only to find himself in yet another vulnerable position. Caulfield's barrage of attacking maneuvers was wearing Hinton down, and his energy flagged noticeably. Pushed to the edge of the floor, the young man parried each blow with hurried, thoughtless ripostes that demonstrated far more desperation than skill. Caulfield pressed his advantage, lunging in with a thrust that might have left Hinton with a cracked rib if the blow had connected. Instead, Hinton managed once more to dance away from Caulfield's saber.

Beside her, Anna felt the elder Mr. Hinton shift in his seat. He leaned forward, eyes narrowed in keen focus. Still, he did not seem concerned, merely engrossed. Anna realized her own palms were perspiring. Though she knew nothing of Edward Hinton, she wholeheartedly did not want his uncle to have to watch him fall to defeat. From somewhere nearby, she heard one of the spectators comment on Edward Hinton's weak performance, and she felt indignation on the young man's behalf.

The blades were ringing upon each other again, and it was a surprised Caulfield who found that each of his thrusts was met with a resounding parry, his young opponent stubbornly refusing to retreat or yield. Caulfield, himself beginning to experience some physical fatigue, not to mention a creeping frustration with the proceedings, decided the time had come to end it. He had not expected much of this young man who, as far as he knew, had no particular standing as a swordsman, but he had hoped at least for a quick end to the match. It should have been one more speedy victory to further burnish his already gilded reputation as a swordsman, but that had not happened. This prolonged confrontation was unacceptable. His eyes narrowed, and his jaw was set in a rigid, angry line.

And Edward Hinton saw it. If he had not, like his uncle, possessed an uncannily disciplined face that revealed not the slightest inner thought or emotion, he would have smiled in satisfaction. He allowed Caulfield one anger-driven thrust simply so that he could neatly sidestep the attempt and, with a speed that left everyone open-mouthed in amazement, drove the tip of his blade into Caulfield's shoulder. The Master-at-Arms called an end to the match.

Caulfield was stunned and furious. He raised his saber as if to threaten the young man who had dared to trick him into defeat. The Master-at-Arms rushed forward as Hinton knocked Caulfield's sword out of his hand, then nicked the man's right ear with the tip of his own blade. Despite the fact that it was dull, he managed to catch the ear in such a way as to draw blood. The Master-at-Arms intervened, angrily demanding a stop to the match.

Caulfield touched his fingertips to his damaged ear and, when they came away bloody, he turned angrily upon Hinton. "You filthy little cur," he spat, drawing a gasp from many in the gallery. "The match had been called."

"And yet," Hinton calmly retorted, "you were not surrendering your blade. You raised it to counter yet again."

"He is correct," the Master-at-Arms agreed. He planted a restraining hand in the middle of Caulfield's chest. "Mr. Hinton has the match. You will retire, gentlemen."

"Actually," Captain Grant interrupted, "It is Lieutenant Edward Hinton of the king's Own, the Fourth Regiment of Foot." He was carrying Edward's jacket, which he handed to the young man. It was scarlet wool with dark blue facings, unmistakably the uniform of one of the king's officers. Watching Hinton accept the coat from Grant, Caulfield's face turned as red as the wool of the jacket. He glowered at Hinton, then at Grant, before turning on his heel and marching out of the room.

Anna felt she was the only person in the gallery who did not know what had just occurred. She looked to Mr. Hinton for explanation.

Mr. Hinton was chuckling. "As I understand it, Mr. Caulfield bears an intense animosity toward officers of his majesty's army. Some say it is because he was bested by an officer in a contest for a young lady's affections. That hardly seems enough to account for the calculated ways in which he has embarrassed or even caused greater injury to young officers over the years but, whatever the reason, he has gone out of his way to damage lives, reputations, and careers. It seems that he crossed one of Edward's friends in a particularly malicious fashion, and Edward decided to take the opportunity to strike at the thing of which Caulfield is most proud — his reputation as a swordsman. It must be quite galling to the man to suffer such defeat at the hands of an unheard of young man, but to learn that he is an officer seems to have completely undone him." He chuckled again, enjoying a replay of the moment in his mind.

"But what did Mr. Caulfield do to your nephew's friend?"

Hinton practically blushed. "I should prefer to leave it unsaid, particularly to a young lady of such tender years and experience."

"Oh, pshaw," Lady Sylvia interjected. "If you think young ladies of tender years and experience don't whisper about these things among themselves, then you are a bigger fool than I would ever have believed!" She leaned conspiratorially close to Anna's ear. "Lieutenant Hinton's friend was to be married. It was a socially advantageous match, which happened also to involve great affection on the part of both parties. The young lady's father learned, however, that Lieutenant Hinton's friend was afflicted with a loathsome infirmity of the sort contracted in brothels, and put an end to the engagement."

Nonplussed, Anna blinked owlishly as she looked from Lady Sylvia to Mr. Hinton's suffused face. She felt quite certain she had never heard such a sentence spoken aloud in her presence, and wanted to prevent that fact from manifesting itself upon her face.

"It was untrue, of course," Hinton quickly added. "But by the time it could be satisfactorily disproved, Edward's friend had sustained considerable embarrassment and the young lady's father had begun entertaining alternative arrangements for the disposition of her hand."

"But what a terrible thing to come out of something that was nothing more than a horrendous rumor!"

"True," Mr. Hinton agreed. "But I would have thought you've spent enough time in London to know that reputation and an unsullied veneer are everything."

"She would not have had to spend a moment in London to know that, Mr. Hinton. I dare say it is the same everywhere, even in the colonies." Lady Sylvia lowered her voice and became secretive once more. "But do not despair for the young lovers, my dear Anna," she chortled. "I have heard things which suggest to me that all will come right for them in the end." She gave Anna's hand a reassuring pat, and then immediately turned her attention to an acquaintance who had made her way to Lady Sylvia's side for a chat.

Anna looked down to where Lieutenant Hinton had just finished shaking hands with Captain Grant. They parted and the lieutenant stopped to look up, searching the gallery for someone, it seemed. Anna assumed he was looking for his uncle, but once he had flashed a quick smile of recognition at Mr. Hinton, he continued his search. In that instant, Anna had seen beneath the golden hair a sharply-hewn face, strong-jawed, and possessed of the same frank expression she was accustomed to seeing on his uncle's face. His lips formed neither smile nor frown and somehow managed to be exceedingly appealing despite the projection of impassivity. Though he lacked the excessive height and bulkiness associated with ancient Viking raiders, everything else about him evoked his Saxon lineage. The clear north light flooding in through the clerestory windows seemed to sparkle like light on water in his crystalline blue eyes, causing Anna to catch her breath. She thought him the embodiment of all the tales she'd heard regarding the denizens of Valhalla — Thor come to life. Quite simply, he was the most handsome, god-like man she had ever seen.

And then he smiled, and Anna felt her normally even-keeled heart flutter like a butterfly drunk on nectar. The smile was not for her, however, but for a young woman, unrecognizable beneath her cloak, who was seated not far from Anna. For an instant, Anna wanted to hate that young woman, but then Lady Sylvia was requiring her attention, and she had to put that momentary bit of irrationality behind her. Chastising herself for having such an idiotic reaction to a handsome face, she collected her thoughts and calmed her racing pulse.

Lady Sylvia introduced her to the acquaintance who had joined them. The woman, who was bedecked in far too many frills for one of her advanced years and portly figure, tittered and fluttered over Anna as though she was something quite foreign and exotic. She then proceeded to regale Lady Sylvia with a litany of everything she had ever heard about the colonies, most of it completely erroneous but stated with all the authority of the sublimely ignorant. Anna pasted a smile on her face and stopped listening.

After what seemed an interminable amount of time, she felt a presence behind her and, thinking Mr. Hinton had stepped in to rescue her and Lady Sylvia, executed a quick pirouette to face him. A grateful smile had replaced the wooden one she had manufactured for Lady Sylvia's chatty acquaintance, but even that froze when she unexpectedly found herself directly confronted by Lieutenant Hinton's steady blue gaze. She felt herself begin to blush and, mortified, she railed inwardly at her reddening cheeks for their show of disloyalty.

"Ah, who have we here?" Lady Sylvia, having politely excused herself from the chatty woman, stepped close to Anna's side.

"Ladies," Mr. Hinton said, "Allow me to name to you my nephew, Lieutenant Edward Hinton. Edward, I present Lady Sylvia Gordon-Hewes, and her friend, Miss Anna Somerset of Boston."

Lieutenant Hinton bowed and said something in greeting that Anna could not hear over the sound of her own pulse rushing in her ears. Lady Sylvia, who was beyond being tongue-tied by a handsome face, showed more aplomb and sailed smoothly into a compliment on his victory, followed by a question or two just to show she had actually been paying attention to the match. Anna realized she was standing there dumbly, having not heard the questions. *This is absurd,* Anna told herself in her most authoritarian inner voice. *You are acting like a ninny. Stop it at once!*

"Yes, he is a rather formidable man," the lieutenant was saying. "I'm afraid I have only the honor of a brief acquaintance, however. Though I knew his reputation, I had never met the man before I approached him about helping me obtain an invitation to compete here today. It turned out that he has little use for men of Caulfield's ilk, and he was most willing to use his member's prerogative to sponsor a guest."

It took Anna a moment to catch up, but she soon realized that they were speaking about Captain Grant.

"You played Caulfield with aplomb." The senior Hinton was full of pride and admiration. "There was a moment when I was not certain you were feigning weakness."

The lieutenant laughed. "There was a moment when I was not certain myself. He has a skilled arm. Captain Grant had warned me about that, but I'm afraid I did not fully appreciate the level of skill involved. Grant had also told me that Caulfield's greatest weakness was his temper. I was beginning to despair of my ability to provoke that temper to my advantage."

Mr. Hinton chuckled. "Men of that sort generally require little provocation. But still, you took a risk, and have now made an enemy. Are you certain a soupçon of revenge is worth that?"

"Yes, it is," the lieutenant replied with a confident smile. He glanced past them to where the girl in the hooded cape was waiting. "It has been my pleasure to meet you, ladies." He fixed Anna with his steady regard. "If you will excuse me, however, I am required elsewhere." And with a small bow of courtesy and a flash of smile, he was gone.

S . D . B A N K S

1772

CHAPTER SIX

By January, Teague and Charlotte had accumulated such an impressive stockpile of stolen goods that a hiatus was in order. Unpredictable winter weather and the reduced overland flow of goods made both highway brigandry and the transport of their stolen goods out of the Boston area all the more difficult. Furthermore, Joe had begun to argue that it might be a good idea for them to take some time off and let anyone who might have been tracking them turn their attention to someone else.

And so it was that, because he suddenly had time on his hands, Teague found himself with Drum one frigid January morning, sitting astride horses loaned to them by John Hancock, waiting for Daniel to take delivery of some correspondence he was to deliver outside the colony. The cold was seeping through the soles of Teague's boots, and he was beginning to regret having agreed to join Daniel for this little adventure.

Daniel had made a number of these ridiculous trips, traveling across country to deliver messages from Adams and Hancock to key personages in other colonies. The correspondence was considered too time-sensitive and contained information too private to be sent via customary conveyance, so couriers such as Daniel were pressed into service. To Teague, it seemed like a lot of nonsense, nothing more than a reflection of the inflated opinion these men had of themselves and their purpose. He'd been honest in telling Daniel his view of the whole thing, for it gave him a plausible reason for rejecting Daniel's many invitations to join him. Teague certainly could not have told Daniel that he was too busy chasing down wagons loaded with bolts of silk, ivory chess sets, and silver tableware. But this time, he had accepted and was already regretting having done so.

Some distance up the street, Daniel waved to Teague and Drum, trying to reassure them that the wait would not be much longer. Like his two friends, he was feeling the cold, and constantly stamped his feet and rubbed his hands together in an unsuccessful effort to warm them. He wondered why it always seemed that he was called upon to make these journeys when the weather was at its worst, and then settled on the idea that fine weather was such a rare thing in Massachusetts, the odds were greatly stacked against him.

He had considered refusing to carry any more messages between Massachusetts and her neighboring colonies, in part because he was weary of the lengthy, treacherous journeys. Mostly, however, his reluctance was born out of his growing disenchantment with the tactics and hyperbolic

S. D. BANKS

bombast employed by Sam Adams and Revere. It was only because men like Joseph Warren and John Adams argued that good communications with the other colonies was their best hope for organizing peaceful opposition to the king's actions that Daniel continued to serve as courier.

Daniel felt drawn to the things John Adams said. Less popular than his gregarious cousin, John Adams was reputed to be a difficult man, impatient with foolishness, intolerant of inefficiency, and sorely lacking in the areas of tact and humility. Nonetheless, he was well-regarded for his intelligence and legal mind, and judicious men were increasingly inclined to his influence. To Daniel, how well the man could get along with others seemed of less importance than the thoughts that came out of his head.

Finally, the man for whom Daniel waited arrived. He carried a quantity of letters separated into bundles by the towns to which they were destined. Daniel quickly flipped through them before shoving them into his saddlebags. He had once been told that he would be carrying something down to Rhode Island only to find himself entrusted with letters that had to be carried almost to Canada. Today, he was expecting bundles for Rhode Island and Connecticut, and was pleased to see that the plan had not been altered.

"Josiah drew the straw for the northern route." The messenger grinned. He knew Daniel did not like to travel farther north in the dead of winter. No one did.

Daniel nodded and thanked the man, then swung up into the saddle. He settled himself, and then nudged his horse into a walk toward where Teague and Drum waited at the far end of the street. With only a nodded greeting, they fell in with him, just as they always had. A mile or so outside of Boston, their path narrowed so that three could not ride abreast. Drum dropped behind, which he did not mind because it meant he could be alone with his own thoughts and fancies instead of struggling to follow the conversation between Daniel and Teague. He was just happy to see them getting along as they had before Daniel had begun to change. For the moment, they were close, side-by-side, talking or gently ribbing each other, and Drum felt content.

The three friends rode through the dim, pre-dawn light, hunched in their saddles against the bitter chill. Drum's nose was so cold that it kept dripping, forcing him to continually wipe it on his sleeve. As dawn approached, pale light began its subtle spread across the sky, and a few hardy creatures took up the day's business. With no leaves on the trees to absorb the sound, every call and rustle cut through the air with sharp clarity. Drum, tired of the cold, wished the sun would rise more quickly, and he kept squinting off toward the horizon as though watching for it would make the first warm, golden rays appear more quickly.

Once the sun did emerge, it seemed to rise swiftly in the cloudless sky, making them feel warmer despite the frigid temperature. Their breath turned to steam, and steam rose from the horses — and their droppings. Drum found the sight of steam rising from the fresh piles of manure particularly funny, and made an inane joke about being able to see the stink rising from the shit every time one of the horses raised its tail. He kept it up until Teague turned in his saddle to glare at him. Drum quickly shut his mouth and settled back into silence.

"Leave him be," Daniel chuckled as he watched Teague right himself in his saddle, cursing under his breath. "He isn't hurting anyone."

"I'm going to hurt *him* if he doesn't stop," Teague growled.

"You don't mean that."

"No, I don't. But there are times when he grates on me."

"You're very irritable today. I think something besides Drum is grating on you."

Teague shrugged but did not reply. He had managed for several months to hide from Daniel the fact that he had reverted to a life of thievery, and he had said nothing regarding the commitment he had made to Charlotte.

"Are you still calling on Charlotte Ainsworth?"

Teague flinched in surprise, feeling Daniel had somehow sensed his thoughts, and did not respond immediately. "What if I am?" he said finally, his tone markedly defensive.

Daniel shifted his weight in the saddle and looked off into the distance, reluctant to meet his friend's eye, knowing that he needed to tread carefully. "It's simply that I feel she isn't right for you."

"Because you think she's too good for me? I know she is, Daniel. I never in my wildest dreams thought someone like me could have a chance with someone like her."

"A chance? A chance for what, exactly?"

"Well, you know. A *chance*. A future."

It was the very thing Daniel was hoping not to hear. "It isn't that I think she's too good for you. I think she's not good enough for you."

Teague barked with laughter. "You're having me on, now!"

"No, I'm not. I'm quite serious. I don't think she's right for you."

"How can you say that? Aside from the fact that I'm over fond of her, she's my opportunity to move up in life. Of course, I don't know how I'm going to get around her father when he returns to health, but I'll work something out." The last statement was in essence a lie, but he felt it might be a good idea to ease Daniel into the notion of the actual plan. "I know you'll find this hard to believe, my friend," he insisted cavalierly, "but you don't always know what's best for everyone else."

Daniel stared at him. How could he, without angering him, tell Teague that he did not trust Charlotte? To tell him of Charlotte's pursuit of himself and other men, her suggestive advances, or her scheming ways would only hurt Teague and possibly push him into blaming the messenger. Better to let things run their course, he thought. Teague had been infatuated on previous occasions only to lose interest when the chase was over. Even if he stayed the course with Charlotte, Mr. Ainsworth would never allow a match between his daughter and someone like Teague. Pushing the matter now could needlessly damage their friendship. "Just be careful," Daniel advised simply. "I don't want to see you hurt." He hoped it was prudence, not cowardice, that made him let the subject drop.

They rode for a while in silence, but of the companionable sort rather than the silence of enmity, and Daniel felt relief that the conversation regarding Charlotte had skirted so near disaster without going over the edge. He squinted up into the friendly winter sun, gauging its height. His plan was that they would reach a familiar lodging place before nightfall, and they were making good progress in that regard.

"I need to piss," Drum suddenly announced. Without waiting for them to respond, he curbed his horse, slid out of his saddle, and walked into the tall, dry grass at the side of the road.

"Well, hell," Teague said, watching him. "Might as well." He slung his leg over the pommel and jumped to the ground in one smooth, easy motion that Daniel admired. Teague had always been the best horseman among them.

Shrugging in assent, Daniel followed suit. The three of them stood, side-by-side, emptying their bladders into the dry grass. Their urine steamed in the frigid air, and Daniel hoped it would not set Drum off on another round of absurd jokes. Prickly as Teague seemed to be, Daniel did not want to find out what might be his reaction to further vexation from Drum. Thankfully, if the steaming urine had struck Drum as amusing, he refrained from saying so.

Soon, they were once more on their way, keeping their horses to a steady gait. In less than an hour, Daniel noticed the wind picking up.

"Look over there," he told Teague, pointing to the northern sky. A band of ominous darkness was roiling up from the horizon, full of low, threatening clouds.

"Looks like a storm's coming."

"Sure does, and it's moving fast. I don't want to get caught out in it."

They kicked their heels back and increased their pace, but the improved progress did not last long. Around one bend, they could see ahead of them a farm wagon standing at the edge of the road where its two right-side wheels had left the beaten track and become mired in the softer ground. The farmer was inciting his team of mules to pull the wagon forward, but the stubborn wheels would not budge.

"I think he's stuck," Drum observed as they neared the farmer and his wagon.

"Thanks for the information, Drum," Teague responded flatly. "I don't think we'd have figured it out if you hadn't told us."

Drum glowered at Teague's back in response to the sarcasm. "I think we should stop and help him," he answered curtly. "That's all I meant."

Teague darted a quick, questioning glance at Daniel, who responded with a shrug. Almost in unison, both men touched the dirks hidden at their backs as though to ensure their readiness. The time Daniel had spent traveling the roads and byways between the colonies over the past months had involved enough encounters with highwaymen and trouble to teach him to be cautious of every stranger he met along the way. They warily scrutinized the wagon as they approached, one eye always on the driver. The wagon was loaded to overflowing with straw, and with what appeared to be barrels of apples. There was no one around except for the farmer, who was swearing a multitude of oaths at his mules, the wagon, the ground, and anything else he could find to blame for his predicament.

"Hello there, neighbor," Daniel called as they curbed their horses near the wagon. "Looks like you've got yourself into a bit of difficulty."

The farmer shoved his hat back on his head and looked up at the three young men. He seemed to study them with a good deal more suspicion than Daniel would have expected from a farmer in need of a helping hand. The farmer's gaze moved quickly from Daniel to Teague to Drum, lingering a bit longer on Drum's imposing frame. A stiff smile forced its way onto his face and, without taking his eyes off Drum, he said, "I dozed off and the mules wandered too near the side of the road." Now he directed his attention to Daniel, gesturing with one hand to the wayward wheels. "These two wheels here are stuck good. I've tried putting down some straw but, as you can see, it did no good."

"I can help," Drum proclaimed cheerily. He slid down from his horse.

The smile disappeared from the farmer's face as he watched Drum move toward the back of the wagon. "I don't want to put you men out," he insisted. "I sure could use some help, though." It was apparent that the farmer would prefer not to need their help but knew he had little choice but to accept it. His only other options were to remain stranded or to abandon his wagon while he rode one of the mules ahead in search of a familiar face who could aid him. With a winter storm looming, neither of those was attractive. Nonetheless, he kept a distrustful eye on Drum until he was satisfied that the big man's intentions were all directed at the problem of freeing the wagon.

Attributing the farmer's reticence to Drum's intimidating size, Daniel relaxed his guard and slid from his saddle. Leading his own horse, he grasped the reins of Drum's mount and walked the two animals toward the wagon. "We don't mind," he assured the farmer in the friendliest tone he could muster. In fact, he did mind because there was no guessing how much delay this would represent, but his conscience would not allow him to abandon the man. "Daniel Garrett." He bowed slightly. "Your servant."

"Henry Califf." The farmer doffed his hat and stuck out his hand for Daniel to shake. Califf's grip on Daniel's hand was strong and sure, his palms rough with calluses. He was in his middle years, lean, and weathered as most every farmer Daniel had ever met.

Daniel looped the two sets of reins through eyelets in the wagon boards. "Let's get to it," he told Teague, nodding his head toward the troublesome wheels. "Sooner we get started, sooner we finish."

Teague, who was never in much of a mood to play the Good Samaritan, glowered at him and hesitated a moment before reluctantly swinging down from the saddle. He muttered under his breath as he tethered his horse to the wagon, making no effort to hide his displeasure. "All right," he snarled, "let's find something to use as a lever under the wheels."

Drum stopped them. "It would be easier to do if we unload the wagon. If it's not so heavy, it'll be easier to get it unstuck." Teague and Daniel stared at Drum, surprised by his sudden flash of authority, but quickly agreed with the astuteness of his observation. Owing to his strength and size, Drum was often called upon to help in similar situations and, so, had far more experience in the matter than either of his two friends.

"Oh, no," Califf protested quickly. "We'll never get all that straw loaded again, and it took a winch and pulley to load the barrels."

"I can—"

"No. Let's try the levers, first. With four of us, I think we can lift both wheels at once. That should do the trick." When Califf's statement was met with three dubious gazes, he insisted again. "Let's just give it a try. I don't want to lose most of my straw if I can help it, and lose it I will if we have to unload it. Please?"

"I say we leave him and his precious straw here and offer to send back help when we reach lodgings," Teague suggested crossly as they set about scouting for suitable levers.

Daniel was tempted by the suggestion but felt the tug of his conscience again. "It'll take a long time for us to send help back. He'll be out on the road, alone, after dark."

"So?"

"So, there's a storm coming. And, that aside, you know as well as I do that there are gangs of thieves roaming the roads — particularly at night. I can't in good conscience leave him to fend for himself."

Teague, who knew about thieves along the roads even better than Daniel realized, growled at him nonetheless. "I can. I'd leave him without injury to *my* conscience."

"Let's just try it his way." Daniel did not know what was more irritating, the farmer's obstinacy or Teague's surliness.

It took several minutes, during which Teague complained without pause, but eventually they found some long, sturdy tree branches that seemed suitable for their purpose. They returned to the wagon, and soon worked themselves into a sweat doing all that was necessary to force the branches under the wheels. Drum manned the branch at one wheel, while Teague and Daniel put their weight to the other, calling out a signal to Califf when they were in position. The farmer gave the mules a slap, which sent the animals lurching forward against their traces. When leverage was applied under the wheels, the wagon edged slightly forward. Faces contorted with the effort, Drum, Teague, and Daniel strained to put the full force of their weight into the task, and the wagon seemed to inch forward but not enough to roll free. They tried several more times until Teague, sweating and breathing hard, gave up.

Daniel was on the threshold of conceding that either the wagon must be unloaded or they would have to abandon Henry Califf until help could be directed his way, and Teague was already headed for his horse. The wind had increased considerably, driving ruthlessly into their faces, and the dark clouds had spread southward toward them. But Drum, annoyed that he might be facing his first defeat in such matters, circled the wagon, frowning as he studied the situation.

"Wait!" he cried just as Teague raised his foot to the stirrup. "Let's try again. I think I know what'll make it work." Ignoring Teague's protest, he began issuing instructions to Daniel and Califf, positioning them to his liking. "And you stand here," he told Teague, indicating the lever he himself had previously been manning.

Teague was taken aback by the fact that, in his enthusiasm for solving the problem, Drum had abandoned his customary deference. "And what exactly will you be doing?" He listened to the first few words of Drum's explanation, then waved him off and stalked back to his appointed place at the wagon. Whatever scheme Drum had in mind, it would take longer to talk Drum out of it than it would to simply allow him to try and fail.

"I'll be here." Drum bent at the waist and stooped slightly so that he could fit under the back end of the wagon.

Teague stared at him. "You cannot be serious," he exclaimed, realizing that Drum intended to try to lift the back of the wagon. "Do you have any idea how heavy this thing must be?"

"Just push hard on that branch," he assured Teague. "I think this'll work. I don't really need to lift it, just make it a tad lighter on its wheels."

They began the whole process again, this time with Drum adding lift to the tail of the wagon. His back was braced against the underside of the wagon bed, and his knees were bent. When Califf started the mule team pulling forward, Drum tried to straighten his legs, pushing up against the underside of the wagon as he did so. It tested Drum's strength considerably, but he was able to get enough lift to raise the wagon an almost imperceptible amount. At the same time, Daniel and Teague leaned all of their weight onto the branches they were using as levers under the wheels. The wagon slowly rocked forward and then back before suddenly lurching free of the deep furrows and leaving Drum sprawled in the dirt.

"Are you hurt?" Daniel scrambled around to the back of the wagon and held out his hand to help Drum to his feet.

Drum shook his head and then collected his shabby hat from where it had been knocked to the ground. He looked with satisfaction at the wagon, which now stood squarely on the road. "It worked," he declared, beaming with pride when Daniel congratulated him and told him he had done well.

They wasted no time in getting back on their horses, and Teague could not refrain from directing a pointed look in the direction of the advancing winter storm. "I see it," Daniel said. "We'll be riding in the dark before we get to the layover. We'll just have to make the best of it."

Califf had climbed up to the wagon seat and waited for them to come along side. "There's a farmhouse not far off the road about two hours ahead. That's where I was headed with all of this." He jerked a thumb toward the load in his wagon. "I know the people there well, and they won't mind putting you up in their barn for the night, especially when I tell them how you men helped me out."

Daniel could not see that they had much choice, so the three of them fell in behind the overloaded wagon to follow Henry Califf toward the promised shelter. The sun was on the downward side of its daily arc, and the temperature was dropping fast. The storm would be on them soon. Daniel hoped Califf was right about the prospect of sheltering in a relatively warm barn for the night.

As they rode, Teague considered the awkwardly ambling wagon. "Something's not right about this," he told Daniel, his voice low enough to keep his words from Califf's ears. "Why would one farmer be taking apples and hay to another? Everyone around here has apple trees. Why would any farmer need apples and hay from someone else's farm?"

"Not sure," Daniel shrugged. "Maybe the second farmer had a bad crop. I agree it seems odd, but there must be a good reason." He was watching the wagon lumber along in front of them. It was a substantial, sturdily-built wagon, but it seemed to sag beneath the weight of its load. "I agree that something doesn't seem right, though. I'm wondering," Daniel mused, his eyes never leaving the wagon, "why that thing seems so heavy. Look at how it wallows. And, the way it sank in the soft dirt back there — doesn't seem like a few barrels of apples and a bunch of straw should weigh that much."

"Do we want to follow him when we don't know what he's up to?"

"I'd rather not, but I'm not of a mind to spend the night out in that storm. I say we stay with him but keep our eyes open. Besides, as I said, we may be overly suspicious. We're likely letting our own fears and fancies run away with us."

By the time the group reached the farm, sleet had begun to fall. Driven by the wind, it pricked their cold faces with icy needles, and what little daylight remained was fast being consumed by the low, dark clouds. The approach to the farm was a narrow road running between two gentle slopes. Up the slope to their right, a solid, serviceable farmhouse stood, smoke lazily curling from its chimney. An orchard, its trees stark in their winter bleakness, flanked the house on one side, and stubble-covered fields stretched behind. In perfect symmetry with the house, a large barn loomed up to the left of the road.

Califf led them toward the house, pulling the mules to a halt directly in front of the long, covered porch. A man and woman, followed by two children, emerged from the house as the wagon drew up. The woman, hugging herself against the chill, waited near the door, her two children close to her side, but the man stepped down off the porch and walked toward the wagon. He greeted Califf warmly but expressed concern that he had arrived much later than expected. Gesturing to where his wife waited on the porch, the farmer remarked, "Lydia made your favorite apple tart, Henry, and she was afraid you might not get here to help us eat it."

"Fool that I am," Califf explained, "I managed to get the wagon stuck in soft ground by the side of the road. These three young men helped me out." He gestured toward Drum, Teague, and Daniel, who politely tipped their hats to the farmer and then to his wife on the porch. Daniel felt a few pellets of sleet make their way down his neck before he got his hat back on his head.

"Well, I thank you for helping my friend," the farmer said. "Name's Thessalonius Johnson." Daniel, Teague, and Drum replied with their own names, and Daniel explained that they were travelling from Boston.

"I told them I thought you'd be willing to put them up in your barn for the night, Thess," Califf explained. "This storm's going to be a fierce one."

Johnson nodded and pointed toward the barn. "Go on and bed your horses down," he told them. "Then come up to the house for some supper."

They turned their horses toward the barn, expecting Califf to follow. Instead, he slapped the reins on the mules' backs and guided the wagon around toward the back of the house. The three friends had finished rubbing down their horses and were climbing down from stowing their blankets and haversacks in the loft when Henry Califf entered the barn with the mules. A rush of cold air and sleet followed him through the big doors as he entered, and Drum had to strain against the powerful north wind to push the doors closed behind him. Because they were hungry and particularly eager to be inside the warm farmhouse, even if for only a while, all three helped Califf bed the mules down, which made quick work of the task.

Supper was biscuits with a hearty stew so delicious that Daniel and Teague, knowing the farmer's wife had not anticipated feeding three additional men, were hard pressed to eat sparingly. Hiding the fact that she had hoped the pot of stew would feed her family through the next day's noon meal, Lydia Johnson politely offered them second helpings. Calling on all of their willpower, they both declined. Drum, who had no idea that he might be creating a hardship for the family, gladly accepted not only the offer of more stew, but multiple helpings of the mouth-watering apple tart she put on the table when the stew was cleared. Lydia was clearly taken with Drum's enthusiasm and openness, and it occurred to Daniel that she minded the disappearance of tomorrow's meal less and less as she basked in his appreciation.

The two little girls, Esther and Beatrice — whom everyone called "Bee" — were close together in age, both less than ten. Their round cheeks were burnished pink by cold wind and good health. Like their mother, they were tow-headed and blue-eyed and, though they exhibited happy dispositions, they were overwhelmingly shy. Also like their mother, they seemed drawn to Drum, who was every bit as shy as the girls. And he was drawn to them. While everyone around them talked of the weather, the outlook for next spring's planting, and a good many other things that held no interest for him, Drum exchanged cautious smiles with the girls and thought his heart would break when Bee, seeing how much he liked the apple tart, pushed her serving toward him. She was so like Nan that he found himself having to duck his head to hide tears.

Daniel saw, though he pretended otherwise. He wished with all his heart that he could conjure a family like the Johnsons for Drum. Drum would flourish in a home like this and, if anyone deserved such a place, Drum did. These people were nothing more than simple farmers, he thought, quiet and good-mannered — fiercely devoted to each other, their land, and their faith — and he felt guilty for having suspected Henry Califf of being otherwise.

When the meal was finished, the three young men returned to the much chillier barn, leaving the farmers to smoke their pipes, feet warming at the hearth. After being in the pleasant, cozy farmhouse, the cold was a shock to their bodies, and they were shivering visibly by the time they fastened the man door behind them and climbed into the loft. The barn cat, which had made a place for herself and her kittens in a corner of the loft, watched them with wide, unblinking eyes as they carved out make-shift beds in the hay. The hay was fragrant, and the loft was surprisingly warm. Daniel was beginning to thank whatever fate had placed Henry Califf in their path.

No sooner had they settled when the wind managed to blow open one of the hay doors. It clapped against the side of the barn with a loud bang, letting in a gust of cold, damp air, and demanding that Teague, who was closest, get up to rectify the situation. Cursing under his breath, Teague scrambled through the hay toward the open door. He had to lean out to reach the rope handle that would allow him to pull the door shut, and he looked down toward the house as he did so. "What the hell?" He pulled the door closed but did not latch it. "Come take a look at this," he urged Daniel.

"What is it? What's the matter?" Daniel reluctantly abandoned his blanket and joined Teague at the door.

"What do you think that's all about?" he asked, opening the door a slit and pointing toward the farmhouse. Daniel peeked out and, in the light spilling from the farmhouse windows, could just make out the shapes of Henry Califf, along with Thess and Lydia Johnson, bundled against the cold and carrying lanterns as they moved around outside the house. "It seems unlikely that Mrs. Johnson needs apples to make another tart."

"No," Daniel agreed. "Something's odd about it." He pulled the door closed and looked at Teague, considering. "Think we ought to check it out?"

"No." Teague was emphatic. "It probably doesn't concern us, and it's damn cold out there."

They sat on their haunches, looking at each other for several long seconds while they weighed the matter. Whatever the two farmers were doing out in the storm, Daniel doubted that he, Teague, and Drum needed to be in any way involved. But curiosity is a powerful thing, and Daniel's curiosity was more powerful than most. "I'm going to have a look." He rose abruptly and, snatching up his hat, made for the ladder to climb down from the loft.

"Then I guess I'm coming with you." Teague glared at him. "I don't see any way that this concerns us, but damned if I'll let you go alone."

"Me, too." Drum was getting to his feet somewhat reluctantly for he had no desire to go back out into the winter storm.

Daniel and Teague paused, looking at each other, then at Drum. "No, Drum." Daniel put his hand on Drum's shoulder. "Stay here. If we're gone too long, you'll need to come find us because we're probably half-frozen to death somewhere."

Feeling himself charged with something important, Drum nodded and settled in to wait. He watched them climb down the ladder and let themselves out through the door, and then opened the hay door a crack to watch them cross the yard toward the house.

They took a route that skirted through the bare trees in the orchard, which was on the opposite side of the house from where they'd seen the farmers. Once clear of the orchard, they ran half-crouched through the dry stubble of a field behind the house. A hostile wind screamed across the open field, driving sleet down their collars despite the scarves they had wrapped around their necks and faces. Pulling their hats down more securely, they continued on until reaching a place where they could see the wagon. It stood in the lee of a grape arbor that, owing to its midwinter nakedness, allowed glimpses of movement around the wagon.

They dashed across the open space between the field and the house, slipped around the corner, then dropped to the ground, inching along until they came to a woodpile that stood between them and the wagon. They paused a moment to ensure that they had not been noticed before carefully peering over the woodpile to where Califf and the Johnsons were unloading the wagon. The arbor protected a small animal enclosure in which a goat was penned. The goat had been moved to one side and tethered to the fence, and the floor of the pen cleared to reveal a hidden door that led to an underground dugout.

Straw was removed from the wagon bed to expose several long wooden boxes. They were unmistakably the sort of crates in which muskets were shipped. These were guns likely intended for the troops occupying Boston, which helped to explain the urgency in getting them hidden. Once the crates had all been lowered into the dugout, they rolled the barrels off the wagon and stored them with the muskets. Finally, everything having been safely hidden away, the farmers closed the large wooden trapdoor. Lydia Johnson returned to the house, leaving Califf and Thess to take up pitchforks and spread straw over the door until it was well disguised. Thess released the goat so that she once again had the run of her cozy enclosure, and he and Califf tromped toward the back door of the house, passing directly by the place where Teague and Daniel were hidden.

"They're stealing muskets!" Teague was incredulous. They had waited until returning to the relative comfort of the barn before discussing what they had seen. "They're stealing muskets! I don't bloody believe it!" he repeated, his voice pitched with astonishment. "And, judging by those barrels, probably black powder and shot as well!"

"It appears so," Daniel agreed. He was rubbing his arms and blowing on his hands, trying to get feeling back in his frozen fingers.

"Why? What the hell do farmers need with so many muskets?"

"Selling them, I suppose. Probably a big demand for them among the settlers on the frontier. And the Indians will buy them, too, no doubt."

"Well, I'll be damned. I'd sure never have taken these folks for illicit munitions dealers!"

"Well, at least we know why Califf was so skittish back on the road. He had something to hide, and must have feared we'd discover it." Daniel sounded disappointed.

"I suppose everyone does what they can to get by." Teague laughed. "I must say, I'm impressed. I would not have guessed they had it in them."

Daniel scowled at him. "Let's get some sleep." He moved about crossly, snatching up his bedding and kicking at the hay to create a place to lie down. "If the weather lets up, I want to get out of here before dawn tomorrow."

"But Mrs. Johnson said we could stay for breakfast," Drum protested.

"We're leaving as soon as possible." Daniel jerked the corners of his blanket about him and turned his back on his two friends.

Teague and Drum, sensing it was best to keep further comments to themselves, settled into the hay. Both were snoring away long before Daniel managed to fall asleep.

Though he knew he had dreamed — a cavalcade of incomprehensible images involving wagons and mules and muskets and apple tarts — it seemed to Daniel that he had slept only minutes before Teague kicked at the sole of his boot and hissed for him to wake up. He blinked at the soft glow that was just visible through the cracks in the barn walls and realized he had slept longer than he thought. Dawn's first light was already pale in the sky. He had hoped to be gone before this.

"We've got company," Teague whispered and, by his tone, Daniel guessed that he was not referring to either of the farmers. "Come take a look." He led Daniel toward the hay door, talking softly as they went. "I stepped outside to take a piss and saw them moving up." He had opened the door a crack, and was looking in the direction of the orchard. Daniel was surprised to see that, at some point during the night, sleet had given way to snow, which had thickly blanketed the ground. Looking where Teague directed, Daniel could see five men moving furtively through the trees, their shapes dark against the snow as they approached the farmhouse. "Who do you think they are?"

"Don't know." Daniel narrowed his eyes as he tried to focus in the dim light. "Whoever they are, though, I'm thinking they're not friendly."

"Maybe the Regulars, come to take back their muskets?"

Daniel shook his head. "Not their style. Regulars would be marching down the middle of the road with a fife and drum playing and some peacock of an officer leading the way. These men aren't in any kind of uniform."

"Maybe not, but they're well-armed. Every one of them has a musket."

Daniel nodded. He had already recognized the familiar silhouette of a man carrying a musket at the ready. "Yes, and some of them have bayonets fixed." Cursing softly, he carefully closed the door. "Let's go." He turned and moved quickly across the loft to where their packs and blankets were still scattered in the hay.

Startled by the sudden urgency, Teague hesitated. "Why? What's wrong?"

"Two of them broke off from the rest and they're headed straight for the barn." He was hastily gathering up his belongings as he spoke and directing Drum to do the same.

"There's not time for us to get out of here," Teague argued, his voice an urgent whisper.

The moment the words left Teague's mouth, they heard the man door open on its squeaking hinges. Reflexively and in unison, all three of them dropped to the hay-covered floor and lay, silent and motionless, on their stomachs. They could hear the two men shuffling about in the darkness below as they tried to locate lanterns and get them lit.

Teague leaned close and whispered, "Whatever they're after, they'll look up here. There's no place for us to go."

Daniel nodded, understanding that Teague was suggesting that they reveal themselves to the armed men, give them what they had come for, and then be on their way. But his every instinct argued that it would not be that simple. Furthermore, he worried about the correspondence he was carrying in his haversack. What would happen if these men decided to rifle through their belongings and discovered that correspondence? Daniel felt unwilling to chance that these men would not be smart enough to recognize that the letters might be valuable — or useful — to someone. Teague was pushing up on his arms, ready to get to his feet, and Daniel knew he had to come up with something quickly. He grasped Teague's wrist, forestalling him, and motioned for him to wait a bit longer.

In the barn below, the two men were making a good deal of noise fumbling about, cursing as they bumped into things, and complaining to each other about the cold and the fact that they had been sent on this errand. Daniel slid silently on his belly until he could just peek over the edge of the loft. Teague and Drum joined him and the three peered down to where the two armed men were moving about the barn, lanterns held aloft as they searched every possible hiding place. Each man carried a musket and wore a heavy-bladed sword at his waist. One of the two had a pistol slung in a holster across his back.

Made uneasy by the disturbance, the horses nickered and huffed as they shifted about in their stalls. The lone cow stamped her hooves and tossed her head threateningly while the two men searched her manger, but they ignored her. Casting about with their lanterns, the men moved in small puddles of light, beyond which there was only darkness. Daniel realized the armed men could clearly see only that which was illuminated by their lanterns, meaning that a great deal of the barn was beyond their field of vision at any one time, and he began to turn his attention to the darkness in the rafters above them.

"Would you stop following me about, Murphy?" one of the men barked, breaking the quiet and startling the three watchers in the loft. "I'm tired of you breathing down my neck. Go search the stalls on the other side."

One of the puddles of light broke off as Murphy did as he was told, cursing when he stepped in some mule dung. "I think we're wasting our time," he complained petulantly.

"I agree, but Bartlett told us to search, so we'd better search."

"If I was hiding muskets I'd stolen from the redcoats, this barn's the last place I'd put them because it's the first place the redcoats would look if they came after them."

"Maybe so," the first man conceded, his tone markedly impatient. "But, like I said, Bartlett told us to search here, so we're going to search here. Besides, these folks are farmers. They're new to this business, and probably not as smart as us."

"True," Murphy conceded. He turned out a tack box, strewing its contents across the floor. "Bartlett says as soon as we get the muskets, he's going to kill the farmers to teach them a lesson. If they're dead, how can they learn a lesson?" Murphy seemed to have given the matter considerable thought.

"Not to teach *them* a lesson, you mule's arse. To teach the others a lesson. Bartlett don't want these farmers getting the idea that they can elbow in on his business, that's all. He figures to make an example out of these two old clodders."

"Then he should've said he was going to make an example of them, not that he was going to teach them a lesson."

"Just hunt for the damned muskets and stop your yammering!" He turned in a circle, searching for another possible hiding place. "Climb up there and check the loft."

Murphy stood at the base of the ladder, lantern held high as he tried to see into the loft. There was nothing but darkness, which unnerved him. "I don't want to climb up there," he huffed. "I'm telling you, it's a waste of time."

"Just do it, Murph."

Murphy raised the lantern again, with no better result than the first time. "I think I heard noises up there earlier." It was an uneasy, self-conscious admission of his real reason for not wanting to make the climb.

"Probably just a cat. Or an owl. Or rats."

Murphy swallowed hard. "That's exactly what I was afraid of," he admitted. "I hate rats."

"Shut your mouth and get up there. You're stinkin' unbelievable, you sniveling little girl."

Murphy slung his musket strap over his shoulder and, holding the lantern aloft in one hand, began to climb. It was an awkward business because he had only one free hand, and he complained all the while, but he finally made his way almost to the top of the ladder. He raised the lantern and waved it about, more to scare any rats back into their hiding places than as an attempt to actually see anything. One more step up the ladder, and he could just peer over the edge of the loft. Nothing moved within the small arc of his lantern's light, and he could not hear anything moving beyond it, so he gathered the courage to set the lantern at the top of the ladder and pulled himself up over the edge.

The moment he gained his footing, Murphy snatched up the lantern and, holding it high over his head, spun about as he anxiously searched the floor for signs of scurrying undesirables. He almost dropped the lantern when the light caught in the barn cat's eyes, startling him with their chatoyant glow. Making as much noise as he could manage, his guard up in case any rats emerged, Murphy began to search the loft. He rifled through the hay with little enthusiasm, in part because of his fear that some angry rodent would suddenly leap out at him, and in part because he was convinced that he would not find anything. There were places where the hay was quite packed down as though something heavy had rested on it recently, but there was no evidence of anything freshly turned. Murphy picked up a pitchfork and stabbed it at random intervals throughout the piled hay, and peered down into the small space where the roof rafters met the wall at the eaves.

"Find anything?" his associate called from below.

"No," Murphy replied. "There's nothing up here but hay and a cat with a bunch of kittens."

"Come on down, then. Let's go find the others."

From their hiding place among the roof trusses high above the barn floor, Daniel, Teague, and Drum watched Murphy climb down from the loft. It had been no small feat for them to inch out along the beams without being detected, especially given the fact that Drum was horribly afraid of heights. They perched there, clinging to the cross-supports that were their only concealment, hoping that a flash of light from Murphy's lantern did not catch on one of their faces or hands in such a way as to betray their presence. In fact, the light had briefly washed across them at least twice as Murphy had spun about but, because his focus was entirely on the floor, he had not seen them.

Simultaneously, they released breath they were unaware they had been holding, though they dared not move until Murphy and the other man had left the barn. Drum's knuckles were white with the strain of clasping the beam and he was visibly quaking with fear. Daniel wanted to reach out and touch him encouragingly but was afraid it would startle Drum and cause him to cry out or fall. Daniel looked down to assure himself that the men had left the barn.

As Murphy prepared to step through the man door, his voice drifted up to where they waited, still and quiet as stones, in the dark rafters. Murphy was holding his lantern out, looking from it to the hay-strewn floor. Hoping to replace the cowardly image he knew he had created in his companion's mind when he expressed his fear about climbing into the loft, Murphy decided to do something bold and ruthless. He cast the lantern down in the hay. The glass globe shattered, allowing the flame to catch on the dry hay.

"What'd you do that for?" his companion cried. "Bartlett never told us to burn the place down!"

Murphy shrugged. "Farmer won't be needing it any more. Besides, if Bartlett wants to get the attention of others looking to edge in on his business, this can only help."

His companion was not so certain. "Maybe," he granted. "But Bartlett don't like it when we do things without his orders."

Irritated by the fact that his attempt to impress his crony had fallen short, Murphy seized the lantern from his hand and tossed it to the floor beside his own. "Let's get out of here." He shoved his companion through the man door.

Daniel watched as the armed men closed the door behind them, and heard the latch slide into place. "Let's go," he said. "That fire will spread fast."

Smoke was already beginning to rise up to their hiding place, which distracted Drum enough from his fear that he was able to move more quickly than when they had climbed out into the rafters. Once they had alighted back in the loft, they snatched up their hidden belongings and tossed them down to the barn floor, then moved urgently toward the ladder. Teague descended first, his aim being to get something to smother the fire before it grew beyond that possibility. Daniel intended that Drum follow Teague down the ladder, but Drum confounded him by heading, instead, to the far end of the loft. With Daniel nagging at him the whole time, Drum threw his blanket over the cat and her kittens, then unceremoniously bundled the whole lot onto his back for the climb down from the loft.

As they reached the barn floor, the flames were steadily spreading through the dry straw, generating a thickening cloud of choking smoke. Teague was doing all he could to contain and smother the fire, but it appeared that he might lose the battle. Acutely aware of the danger, the horses tossed their heads and whinnied frantically. Daniel considered getting the animals to safety and leaving the barn to the fire, but the intrinsic fear of uncontrolled fire took hold. He shoved Drum in the direction of the stalls, directing him to get the animals out of the barn. Grabbing up a horse blanket, he quickly soaked it in a water trough and joined Teague in his effort to beat out the fire.

Drum first led the mule closest to the danger from its stall, talking to the frightened animal as he tugged it toward the paddock door at the far end of the barn. Once he reached the door, however, he was frustrated to find that it was latched from the outside, as was the man door. Putting all his weight into it, he butted the smaller door with his shoulder. The wood was old and the latch insubstantial, so the door gave way more easily than he had expected and he toppled through to the other side, dropping his bundle on the ground and sending the cat and her kittens tumbling. She hissed angrily at Drum before scampering off, her kittens in her wake. Drum unlatched the big paddock doors and swatted the mule's rump to send it out into the pen. Then, he swung one of the doors wide and propped it open before returning to the barn for the horses and second mule.

The horses were kicking at their stalls, and needed no coaxing to get them to evacuate the barn. They bolted through the open door and, eager to put as much distance between themselves and the fire inside the barn, ran circles in the paddock looking for a way out. The second mule, its eyes rolled back so that the whites showed, at first balked and danced away when Drum entered its stall, but was soon convinced to leave the barn.

The cow was more of a challenge. Frightened and confused, her faulty instincts told her to stay put. She stood, bellowing and refusing to budge despite all of Drum's coaxing and pulling on her lead. Drum's eyes were burning, and he was choking on the smoke, making him disinclined to humor the stubborn cow. He braced her stall open and worked his way in behind her where, abandoning the gentleness he characteristically employed when dealing with animals, he gave her tail a sharp twist that sent her lurching forward and out the paddock door.

Without turning to look, Daniel and Teague had known the moment Drum opened the paddock door, for the sudden rush of air helped clear some of the smoke — but it also invigorated the fire. They had made some headway against the fire with their wet blankets. Now, given the new influx of air, small flames began to flicker here and there among the straw, too spread out for the blankets to tackle effectively. Returning to the trough to soak his blanket again, Daniel was struck with an idea. "Teague!" he called. "Come give me a hand."

Teague wheeled about and, immediately understanding what Daniel had in mind, abandoned his blanket. In an instant, he was at Daniel's side and helping him push with all his might against the water trough. The trough was large and completely full of water, and was designed specifically to make it difficult to overturn, so they were having little success until Drum arrived. He lent his considerable strength to the effort and, slowly, the trough began to tip. The water sloshed, and then the trough went over, pouring its contents onto the barn floor. The water spread quickly, soaking the floor and all of the straw in its path, and extinguishing most of the fire. The few flames that remained were relatively easy to smother with their wet blankets.

The three friends stood, panting hard, surveying the damage done by the fire. Their faces were smudged, their nostrils stinging with the remnants of the acrid smoke. Daniel recovered himself first. Moving purposefully, he retrieved his haversack from where he had dropped it and stood, casting about him for a place in which to hide it.

"What are you doing?" Teague asked as he watched Daniel stow the pack behind a manger. "We need to get out of here before those buggers come back."

"No," Daniel corrected. "We need to get up to the house before they kill those people."

"You cannot be serious. There are five armed men up there!"

"Exactly why we need to help." Hurriedly, he put his dirk in its place behind his back, and began to load his pistol.

Teague stepped up and grabbed him by the arm. "This is not our fight, Daniel. We need to leave. We saved their barn for them. That's enough."

"We can't leave those people alone. They're farmers. They are no match for these men."

"You don't know that. Besides, they're the ones who stole the muskets in the first place. They had to know they were buying trouble."

"Maybe," Daniel stowed the pistol at his waist. "But I can't just walk away."

"It isn't our fight," Teague repeated through gritted teeth.

Ignoring him, Daniel continued his preparations.

"You are going to get us all killed."

"You don't have to stay. Take Drum and get out of here."

Teague ran his hands through his hair in exasperation. "Oh, for Christ's sake! Why are you doing this?"

"There's a woman and two children in that house, Teague. I cannot just leave them without trying to help."

Teague picked up a pair of gelding tongs and angrily hurled them against the wall while, at the same time, hurling a string of verbal epithets at Daniel. "You are going to get us bloody killed!"

"You already said that, and I told you, you don't have to stay." He turned on his heel and walked toward the paddock door.

"But Daniel!" Drum, confused and frightened by Teague's anger, followed him.

"No, Drum. Go with Teague," Daniel told him. "Go with him and keep him out of trouble. I'll see you back in Boston."

"No you won't," Teague growled. "Not without our help."

Daniel gave him a long look but did not reply, then turned and walked out the door. He made for the orchard, planning to take roughly the same route toward the back of the house that they had followed the previous evening. The sun was just emerging from its hiding place behind the eastern horizon, sending bright light streaking between the trees in long, golden fingers that sparkled on the new snow. All sign of the previous day's storm had left the sky, and it promised to be a crisp, brilliant day. Daniel hoped he would live long enough to enjoy it.

Weaving through the leafless trees, he worked his way toward the house, keenly aware that his dark clothing must stand out like a stain against the pristine white ground. Footsteps crunched in the snow behind him. He spun quickly, landing in a crouch, pistol at the ready in one hand, dirk in the other. It was Teague and Drum.

"I thought I told you to go," Daniel said crossly as he relaxed out of his defensive stance.

"Drum wouldn't leave you," Teague responded, just as crossly. "And, I wasn't inclined to sit in that barn waiting for your corpses to get tossed out the door." He crouched beside Daniel and surveyed the farmhouse. Everything seemed still and quiet despite the fact that the tracks leading toward the house suggested that the armed men were already inside. "What's the plan?"

"Not sure." Daniel's eyes roamed the scene in search of a logical strategy. "I thought I'd try to get close enough to take a look inside and work out what to do from there."

Teague nodded, but glowered at him through narrowed eyes. "Can I just say," he hissed, "that you picked a damned inconvenient time to grow a conscience?"

"You told me that once before."

"Yes, well, it's still true."

Daniel was studying the approach to the house and checking for any sign of movement at the door or windows. "You and Drum wait here," he instructed. "I'm going to try to make it to the porch. If I keep low, I might be able to peek in the windows without them seeing me. If I can find out what's happening, then maybe we'll be able to figure out what to do."

Teague shook his head. "No. Drum and I should skirt around through the orchard and make for the back of the house. After you get a look inside, you can meet us there. You're not as likely to be seen as you would be if you came all the way back out here. And, if something goes awry, Drum and I will be in a better position to help you."

"If something goes awry, you take Drum and get away."

"I've come this far, I'll see it through." Teague scowled, but a part of him was enjoying the risk, and it showed. "Besides," he added quickly, "even if I could get Drum to agree to abandon you, I don't want to have to take care of him by myself for the rest of my life."

Unamused, Daniel narrowed his eyes at Teague. "Let's go," he said succinctly. Keeping low to the ground and availing himself of every possible opportunity for concealment, he darted toward the house.

Hiram Bartlett sat in the Johnson's kitchen trying to decide on his next course of action. The kitchen was blissfully warm, and he had forced Mrs. Johnson to serve him breakfast, so he was in no particular hurry. He languished in his chair, dabbing at a pool of honey with one of Mrs. Johnson's biscuits while he considered his situation. The two farmers, Lydia Johnson, and the two young girls stood in a row, watching him eat, trembling with fright — in part because his men were pointing pistols at them, but also simply because Bartlett's appearance had that effect on people. It was a fact that had served him well in his former career of piracy, then highwayman, and was proving to be advantageous in his current attempt to become a prosperous gunrunner.

At no point in Bartlett's life had he been considered even remotely attractive. He was short and stocky in a particularly unflattering way that made him seem stunted. Most men of comparable build were viewed as somehow comical, but there was nothing comical about Hiram Bartlett. The only smiles that ever tugged at his thin lips were full of cruelty, and his forehead was thick, adorned with bristling black brows and creased in a perpetual frown. Most striking was the red, puckered scar that curved from the middle of one eyelid all the way up and over the top of his bald head as though someone had at some point tried to cleave his skull. The damaged eye punctuating one end of this prominent scar was milky white. Most men would have concealed the scar under a wig or hat, and the grotesque eye under a patch. But Bartlett enjoyed the effect his disfigurement had on people and so disguised none of it.

He wanted to find out where the farmers had hidden the muskets, but the men had obstinately chosen to claim no knowledge of any stolen armaments, so he needed to make some decisions. Though he had sent Murphy and Dewhurst to search the barn, it was without expectation that they would find anything. Farmers, he was learning, were amazingly creative at hiding things. Long experience had taught him that the quickest route to finding something a man had hidden was not to search for it himself, but by the strategic use of a pistol pointed at a head, or knife pressed to a throat. The trick was in determining whose head or throat should be threatened. That was what Hiram Bartlett was now considering as he sopped up the pool of honey on his plate.

All of these people were going to die; that he had decided before ever entering the house, for the great lesson learned during his pirate days was that a reputation for brutal ruthlessness was the best deterrent to resistance or competition. He was considering allowing the girls to live, however. Being young, reasonably attractive females, they could prove valuable. But the two men and the woman would not see nightfall. He just needed to decide which should die first in order to achieve his ultimate goal.

Murphy, as was characteristic of the man, was proving to be an unwelcome distraction, however. He was supposed to be keeping an eye on farmer Johnson but seemed instead to be preoccupied with looking out the front window of the house toward the barn. Bartlett picked up his empty plate and slung it across the room toward his recalcitrant henchman. Everyone in the room jumped, startled by the sudden action. "What the hell's the matter with you, Murph?" he bellowed, springing from his chair.

Mouth agape, Murphy looked from where Bartlett's chair had loudly toppled backwards, to Bartlett's outraged face. All of Hiram Bartlett's men were profoundly aware of their boss' hair-trigger temper — how he could go from relaxed bonhomie to a murderous rage in the snap of a finger — but every wild swing of his disposition astonished them, nonetheless. "I was — er, I just—"

"You was just what? You're not supposed to be doing anything but keeping watch over him!" He jabbed his finger into Thess Johnson's chest. "*That* is your job. That one thing! What is so damned interesting about that barn?"

"Uh, I just thought it would be burning by now, is all." Murphy's voice was barely audible in the otherwise silent room.

"You what?" Bartlett leaned close and made him repeat what he had said. "Why would it be burning?"

"Uh, because we—," a sharp look from Dewhurst made him correct himself. "I—, because *I* started a fire when we finished searching it," he stammered.

"And who told you to do that?"

"No one." Murphy's voice was so soft now that they were all straining to hear him.

"No one. Exactly. So, why the hell'd you do it?" Bartlett screamed at him. Spittle flew from his mouth into Murphy's face, but the cowed man dared not move to wipe it away. Nor did he dare to offer any explanation. What had seemed like such a good idea as they were leaving the barn, now seemed like the worst mistake of his life. Murphy shrugged uncertainly.

Bartlett let loose a string of invective and violently overturned the kitchen table. Mrs. Johnson watched as the remnants of food, her crockery, and the cutlery scattered across her clean wooden floor. Without thinking, she took one step toward cleaning up the mess but recoiled back to her place at the sight of Bartlett, red-faced with fury, storming toward the window. He stood there, his back to them, breathing hard, fists clenched, staring at the barn, momentarily uniting everyone else in the room in their anxiety over what would come next.

"You say you set a fire in the barn before you left it?" Bartlett asked the question without turning around, and Murphy responded with a nod as though he thought Bartlett had eyes in the back of his head. "And you say no one was in the barn?" Bartlett, his rage replaced by concentration on the new puzzle before him, turned and stared at them. "There's smoke coming from the barn," he stated, "but not much. Apparently your fire didn't last long or do much damage."

Murphy and Dewhurst looked at each other, not quite believing that the fire hadn't spread as expected through the dry straw. Murphy swallowed hard, fearful that he was now to be berated for not doing the job well enough.

But Bartlett had moved on to the next piece of the puzzle. "Did you let the animals out of the barn first?"

"No." Murphy's response was almost a whisper.

"There are horses in the paddock now," Bartlett told them. "And a cow. And two mules. There was no livestock there when we arrived." He looked at each of his men, curious to see if any of them were picking up his line of thought. "How'd the animals get out of the barn?" It disgusted him that not one of his men seemed to have even a hint of intelligence.

"The latch on the paddock door is weak," Mr. Johnson suggested. "If they were frightened by the fire, the horses probably kicked at it until it opened."

It was a feeble explanation, made too quickly, that also failed to account for the fact that the animals would have had to get themselves out of their stalls, and Bartlett pounced on it. Like metal to a magnet, he was across the room and standing nose-to-nose with Thess Johnson.

"Who else is here?" Bartlett demanded.

"No one," Johnson stammered. "There's just my family here, and Califf stayed the night on account of the storm. That's all."

"Someone let those animals out," Bartlett posed, "and someone probably put out the fire. Now, who else is here?"

"No one."

Had he not been convinced that he needed Johnson alive for a bit longer, Bartlett would have taken out his knife and gutted the stubborn man right there. Instead, he grabbed a fistful of Mrs. Johnson's hair and used it to twist her, wincing with pain, to her knees. He jerked her head back, exposing the delicate skin on her throat, and pressed the knife against it hard enough to cause a thin red line of blood to well up.

It was all the persuasion Thess Johnson needed. "Three lads," he said quickly. "Three young men came in with Califf. They stayed the night in the barn." His eyes, silently pleading for her release, darted from his wife's face to Bartlett. "I thought they left before dawn," he added as though he deemed it necessary to cover his earlier lie.

Bartlett released Mrs. Johnson and whirled on Dewhurst and Murphy. "You two," he growled, gesturing at them with his knife, "said there wasn't anyone in the barn."

"There weren't anybody, captain," Dewhurst protested. He knew Bartlett liked to be called "captain," and used the word whenever he felt the particular need to curry favor. "We searched every inch, and there weren't nobody."

"Well, obviously, you didn't search as well as you thought. Now get out there and correct your mistake. Go find those three. And, not that way, you fools," he added as Murphy and Dewhurst started toward the front door. "Go out the back way. If there's someone out there, they'll be waiting for us to come out the front." It amazed him that he was the only one who could think of these things. Muttering about his men's mental deficiencies, he returned to the window to watch for the two to come around from the back of the house. It was to be a much longer wait than he had anticipated.

Dewhurst and Murphy exited through a back door located in a small mud room off the kitchen and, as they stepped out the door, literally collided with Drum and Teague. Always quick to recognize a threat, Teague intercepted Murphy's advance by driving his dirk straight through the startled man's windpipe. Murphy, his expression frozen in surprise, buckled to the ground, clutching his throat and gasping for air. Blood bubbled up from beneath his Adam's apple, and his mouth was flapping open and closed like that of a landed fish. Dewhurst had barely registered this scene before Drum knocked him unconscious with a shovel he had acquired in his trek around the house. It all happened so quickly that neither downed man had managed to cry out a warning to their comrades inside the house.

Without preamble, Teague crossed to Dewhurst's inert form and dispatched him with the same precision he had demonstrated on Murphy. He stood over the body, surveying his handiwork and wiping his dirk clean on Dewhurst's shirt.

"Why'd you do that?" Drum asked, tossing the shovel aside. "He wasn't going to bother us for a while."

"He would have *bothered* us eventually, though," Teague growled. "He would have killed us if he could, Drum. He would have waked up, and he would have come after us."

Drum was not wholly convinced, but decided not to argue about it until he'd had time to consider the matter further. He cast a guiltily uncomfortable glance in the direction of the two dead men, then followed Teague's lead toward the back door. "What are you doing?" he asked as Teague, taking great care not to make a sound, opened the door.

"The others will wonder what happened to those two," Teague explained nodding toward the bodies. "I'd like to catch them before they have time to become suspicious and get their guard up."

"Daniel told us to wait here," Drum insisted.

"Daniel was looking for an opportunity," Teague pointed out. "I'd say we just found an opportunity. Now, keep quiet and let's go." Dirk at the ready, he edged through the door, pausing with each step to listen for trouble.

Daniel considered it a small miracle that he had made it to the porch without being seen. Stooping down below the window, he crossed the length of the porch to the door, expecting someone to step out at any moment. But his luck had held. Crouched there on his heels, he felt the cold invading his limbs and his muscles began to cramp as he had listened at the door to the angry conversation. When he dared, he would peek up through the bottom of the window to get a better idea of what was happening inside. His every instinct told him that Bartlett would not hesitate to kill his prisoners, and the fact that the highwayman now realized Daniel and his companions were there made it all the more imperative that they act soon.

When Bartlett's two men went out the back door of the house, Daniel feared for Teague and Drum. Hurriedly, he slipped around the house, making it to the back just in time to see his friends entering the house through the back door. It was an unexpected development, and one he was not certain he welcomed. He took several steps toward following them into the house, wondering as he went what had happened to Murphy and Dewhurst — until he practically stumbled over one of the bodies. With only a glance at the dead men, Daniel continued toward the back door. His hand was poised over the door handle when it occurred to him that, if he went back and entered the house through the front, they would have Bartlett and his remaining men more or less surrounded.

Berating himself for not thinking of it sooner, and fearing that he might not make it back to his position at the front door before Teague decided to do something rash, he hurriedly retraced his steps. His dirk clasped in one hand, his pistol in the other, Daniel edged around the house, ducked under the front window and, heart pounding in his chest, stood flat against the wall while he caught his breath. Carefully, he peered around the edge of the window in an effort to glimpse what was happening inside.

117

Bartlett was standing closest to the window, his back to the door. To his left, one of his men was guarding the two farmers. This second man was inordinately tall with a thick black beard that almost entirely obscured his face. Thess and Califf were standing in front of him, and he held his pistols jabbed into their spines. On the far side of the room, directly facing Bartlett, another of his men was keeping watch on Lydia Johnson and her two daughters. He was wearing a knit toque on his head and held a pistol in one hand and a sinister-looking cutlass in the other. He was amusing himself by repeatedly using the cutlass blade to raise the hem of Lydia's skirt, peek underneath, and then giggle childishly when she slapped her skirt back into place.

Between the farmers and Lydia, there was a gap through which Daniel could just see across the kitchen area to the blanket-draped opening he knew led into the mud room. He guessed that, whenever Drum and Teague decided to make their entrance, it would be through there, and his mind quickly whirred through an array of possible plans of action. And then, everything fell apart and all plans became irrelevant.

Bartlett swore again. Murphy and Dewhurst had never appeared from the back of the house, and none of the possible explanations for their absence appealed to him. The veins in his neck were bulging, and he was casting about for something to throw. "Enough." He spit his words. "I've had enough of this." His eyes landed on Mrs. Johnson, filling her with a cold dread. "One of you is going to tell me where those muskets are hidden," he darkly informed Califf and Thess.

Watching as Bartlett stalked across the room to where she stood, Lydia pushed Esther and Beatrice behind her. Her heart pounded in her chest, and she set her jaw in grim determination against showing her fear. Bartlett snatched the pistol from the man with the toque and held it directly in front of her face. She could see its every detail, smell the gunpowder and oil, and feel the unbearable grief that these might be the last sights and smells of her life. Her daughters were clinging to her, and the sound of their sobs tore at her heart.

"No!" Thess Johnson cried. "I'll tell you where they are! Please, don't hurt her!" He had taken a step forward, but Bartlett's associate grasped his collar and jerked him back. "They're buried under the goat pen. It's on the side of the house. I can show you!"

"Yes," Bartlett sneered, grinning malevolently. "You will show me." And he cocked the pistol.

When Bartlett cocked the pistol, it set into motion a sequence of events that occurred in such quick succession that they seemed to be happening all at once. Recognizing the threat, Bee began to scream and, before her mother could stop her, lunged for Bartlett, her fists flailing wildly. Bartlett, taken aback by the sudden assault, defended himself without hesitation by striking the furious girl on the side of her head with his pistol. The blow sent her flying against the wall behind her, where she slid to the floor, unconscious.

The moment Bartlett raised his pistol to strike Bee, Daniel knew how Drum would react. And he knew that he had to react as well, or all would be lost. Without hesitating to think, Daniel burst through the front door into the room while, simultaneously, Drum came roaring from the mudroom. From his hiding place, Drum had seen Bartlett hit the girl and, as Daniel expected, the act had sent him into a rage. He made straight for Bartlett, who just managed to fire his pistol before Drum landed on him with the full force of his substantial weight. The shot had grazed Drum's head, and he was bleeding from the wound, but he took no notice. Upon downing Bartlett, Drum struck him twice squarely on his nose, leaving Bartlett's face red with freely-flowing blood. Blood dripped from Drum's brow and mingled with Bartlett's own blood while, his hands on Bartlett's throat, Drum repeatedly slammed the man's head against the wood floor.

Toque man stood over them, blinking and stupefied with surprise. It took him precious seconds to gather his wits and remember the cutlass in his hand and those seconds were all Teague needed. He had come into the room directly behind Drum, just in time to see toque man shift his grip on his cutlass. Teague fired the pistol he had recovered from Murphy's body, hitting toque man squarely in the chest as he raised his arm to strike Drum with the cutlass, thus putting an expedient end to the outlaw's participation in the proceedings.

Daniel heard the shot Teague fired at toque man but could not see who had been hit for, once through the door, he had immediately fired his own pistol at the man with the black beard. The bullet tore through black beard's upper arm, surprising but not disabling him. Daniel rushed him and, taking advantage of his own momentum and black beard's confusion at having been shot, managed to knock the much larger man to the floor. Black beard's pistol fired as he fell, managing through pure chance to hit Henry Califf. The farmer dropped to the floor, writhing and crying out in pain, but Daniel had no time even to glance in his direction. Despite black beard's wound, it was taking all of Daniel's weight pressed against both arms to keep the big man pinned down.

Desperately, Daniel feigned a shift to one side while, using his weight against black beard's arms as a fulcrum, he slung his legs upwards. As his legs came back down, he pulled one knee up and landed with that knee directly on black beard's groin. Daniel heard a sickening crunch, and felt black beard spasm under him. The blow had momentarily taken black beard's strength. Daniel rolled free, swinging out with his newly-freed dirk, and drove the weapon point-first through black beard's throat. The knife slid from black beard's hand as he clutched at his throat, gurgling and fighting for his last few breaths. Winded, Daniel struggled to his feet.

Teague, who had been on the verge of helping Daniel out of his predicament when Daniel landed the crippling blow, grinned at him. "You always did fight dirty," he observed.

"Whatever it takes," Daniel said. He was breathing hard and wiping sweat from his face with his sleeve. "I believe you taught me that." He recovered his dirk from black beard's throat and carefully wiped the blade clean as he turned to survey the room. Black beard and toque man were already dead, and Bartlett would soon join them. Drum stood over him, seemingly unaware of the blood pouring down the side of his head. Anger visibly drained from him much as Bartlett's life was draining away. Henry Califf lay groaning, but alive. Aside from a sizeable lump on Bee's head, all of the Johnsons had escaped harm. The room was in disarray, and blood was splattered across the floor in broad, dark patches. An unnatural, stunned quiet descended, somber and relieved. Daniel knew a tinge of guilt would creep in before long to mingle with the thankfulness each would feel that it was not their own blood seeping across Mrs. Johnson's kitchen floor.

Lydia was the first to break the sudden peace. Taking charge of the situation as though there was nothing novel in it, she grabbed a pan and sent Esther for water and clean linen to tear into bandages. Gently, she took a befuddled Drum by the arm and steered him to the closest chair. "Here, now." She spoke as though soothing a wounded horse. "Come sit here and let me look at your head."

"Is she hurt?" Drum asked. "Little Miss Bee. Is she hurt bad?"

"No," Lydia replied. "A bump on the head and bruises that will heal. That's all."

"Califf isn't as bad as I thought," Thess informed them. He was kneeling beside his friend, probing the wound with his fingers. "We should be able to patch him up fine."

"You're all damned lucky," Daniel growled angrily. "What are a bunch of farmers doing stealing munitions, anyway? You have no business getting mixed up with this sort." He used his dirk to indicate the dead men on the floor.

Thess Johnson frowned up at him. "But we didn't steal them. We bought them."

"Bought them?" Teague was dubious.

"The army's not in the habit of selling perfectly good muskets and powder to local citizens," Daniel said. "They don't want us any more armed than we already are. Besides, those muskets are too precious to them. Replacements are months away across the Atlantic."

"Well, it's possible that the army doesn't know they're being sold," Johnson admitted sheepishly. He bent to the task of tending to Califf. "We found an enterprising supply officer who apparently has plans that involve a need for a great deal of money. He managed to put a few things aside for us in exchange for a hefty sum."

"It was a considerable sacrifice for us to accumulate enough to buy them," Califf added defensively. He was gritting his teeth and struggling to sit up. "We did not steal them."

Daniel sighed in exasperation at the fine line they were drawing between an honest and an illicit transaction. "But why?" he asked. "Why do you need all those muskets?"

Johnson frowned at them. "I thought you boys said you were from Boston?"

"We are," Teague confirmed. "What has that to do with it?"

"Well, I'd have thought you of all people would understand the need. We can see how this conflict is going, and it's not going to be decided peacefully. More Regulars land here every month." He shook his head sadly. "No, it will not be decided peacefully. There'll be a fight, and the colonial militias will need muskets. As it is, we've barely a gun for every two men, and most of those are no better than old fowling pieces folks use for hunting. We need to arm ourselves, and we need those good muskets to do it."

Daniel and Teague gaped at him, then at each other. "Do you mean," Daniel asked as though he wanted to be sure he understood correctly, "that you think the local militias can stand up against an army of Regulars? That all the militia needs is muskets and it's an even fight? A bunch of farmers are going to face down the most powerful army in the world — is that what you're telling me?"

"Well, of course it won't be an even fight," Johnson snapped indignantly. "But at least it'll be a fight. Whatever they force on us, we won't give in without a fight."

"I am not believing this." Teague looked from face to face, stunned by what they suggested, mystified by their determination.

"There are men," Daniel told them, his voice steady and full of reason, "far smarter than any of us who are working every minute of every day to make the Parliament see reason. I cannot believe that they will fail."

"Well, lad," Johnson said, "I hope your belief is the clear-sighted faith of reason, not the naïve faith of youth. I do hope you are right. But while I'm hoping for peace, I'm going to prepare for a fight."

"Well, perhaps you should prepare for another kind of fight as well," Teague observed. "If you're going to involve yourselves in the business of stolen guns, you can expect to encounter men like Bartlett from time to time."

Califf nodded his head in agreement. "You're right about that, son. We should never have let them sneak up on us like they did. We have to be more watchful."

Daniel looked at Lydia Johnson and her daughters. If she was worried by the dangers inherent to the path her husband had chosen, it did not show on her face. Though her left hand absentmindedly stroked her daughter's hair — a tender, soothing gesture — her face was all steely resolve. "We need to be on our way," he insisted gruffly. "Are you going to be able to ride, Drum?"

Drum nodded. He was grinning unreservedly; his happiness that Bee had not been more injured transcending any discomfort his own wounds caused him.

The farmers, who could not seem to thank them enough for all they had done, refused to let them help bury the bodies, and helped them saddle their horses. Mrs. Johnson packed small bundles of food, which they tucked away in their saddle bags, and Esther and Bee rushed to say goodbye to them as they rode away. Daniel looked back over his shoulder and thought it would have been an idyllic scene had he not been aware of what the innocent-looking farmers were up to.

Unlike Daniel, Teague had not harbored any illusions or ideals to be tarnished. Though he too rode in silence, his was the silence of concentrated thought because he could see in the idea of stealing munitions an intriguing and potentially lucrative opportunity. He'd been thinking about it ever since they learned what the farmers were about and, after evaluating all of the angles and eventualities, he was convinced that he could improve on the farmers' scheme. If all went as he thought it might, the time before he and Charlotte could go away together would be substantially shortened. Teague felt himself smiling. It was all he could do to not burst into song.

CHAPTER SEVEN

True to the adage, March had come in like a lion and, mercifully, was promising to leave like a lamb. There were fewer days of low, woolen clouds to dust the city with snow and more days of crisp, clear blue skies. Frigid winds continued to nip at faces and fingers, but the promise of the warmth to come gave everyone and everything a happier outlook. William Sprague stood outside the chocolate shop, anxiously looking up and down the street. For the third time in fifteen minutes, he consulted his watch and then returned it to his pocket before looking down the street once again. John Wilton was, uncharacteristically for the man, very late. As of twenty minutes ago, they should have been sitting together in the shop, enjoying a nice cup of chocolate while they watched the ongoing parade of interesting and assorted characters who populated Boston's streets. Sprague considered going into the shop and having a chocolate alone, but the prospect seemed less inviting without the company of his friend, so he continued to wait.

There was a shop directly across the street, a milliner's, which stood out among its neighbors on account of its elegance. He squinted at the sign until he could make out the words "Healey's Millinery." The name seemed familiar, but it took a few moments for him to recall that his wife had mentioned the shop as being one of her favorites and had recently talked at length of a lace-trimmed fichu that had caught her eye there. She had spent too many words to suit Sprague lamenting the cost of the item, dithering over whether or not to purchase it as though Sprague could possibly care one way or the other.

He crossed the street and reached to open the door when a young man emerged from within the shop. The young man paused long enough to hold the door open so that Sprague could enter, allowing Sprague an opportunity to get a good look at him. He was a handsome young man, lithe and robust in the way of youth, and possessed of dark hair and brilliant blue eyes. Sprague thanked him for his courtesy and proceeded into the shop but then paused to look out the window, watching the young man proceed up the street. Something about the man was familiar, though he could not quite say what.

"May I help you?"

Sprague heard the woman's voice and turned to see Selah Garrett emerging from a curtained passage from the back of the shop. "Good day, ma'am." He removed his hat and bowed. "Do you know the identity of that young man?" he asked, waving his hand in the direction of Daniel's departure. "The one who was just here; are you acquainted with him?"

"Yes," she admitted cautiously. She was wary of conversations that began with a question regarding Daniel because they so often did not go in directions that she liked. "He's my son."

Sprague crossed the room toward her, a smile spreading across his face. "Ah, yes. I see the resemblance."

Selah did not drop her guard. "Why do you ask?"

"Because, he did me a great service two or so years ago. It was the night of that horrible business in front of the Custom House. Do you remember?"

She nodded her head. How could she forget? But the wary frown remained on her face. It seemed unlikely to her that anything Daniel might have done that evening could have been of service to this man.

"I was set upon by three young hooligans intent on robbery. They were being unnecessarily zealous in their treatment of me — for I would gladly have surrendered my purse if it would have sent them on their way — when your son happened along. He stopped the attack, saving me from what would have undoubtedly been a severe beating. As it was, I escaped with only the inconvenience of a few bumps and bruises. He was quite brave, I thought, to wade in as he did. I saw his face clearly but did not know his identity until this moment. May I ask his name?"

"Daniel. His name is Daniel. Daniel Garrett." Despite the man's apparent sincerity, she remained uneasy. "Did you also see the faces of your attackers?"

"No," he sighed. "I did not. They wore scarves over their faces. I owe your son a great debt, ma'am," Sprague insisted. He fished one of his calling cards out of his waistcoat pocket. "Please tell him I would appreciate the opportunity to repay that debt at some point in the future."

"I doubt that Daniel considers there to be any obligation on your part, Mr. . . . .," she consulted the card he had handed to her, "Sprague."

"All the more reason that I hope I may be of service to him one day," Sprague chuckled. He turned his attention to the shop's interior, gazing around with no hint on his face that he noticed Selah's dwindling stock. Most Boston shops were suffering the effects of the various boycotts and embargoes, so she was not unique in that regard. "But encountering your son as I entered the shop was a matter of happenstance. I actually came here in search of a gift for my wife's birthday. She has made frequent mention — a fact I take to be a hint on her part — of a particular fichu she has seen in your shop. It is, according to her, made of linen so evenly textured that even the angels would admire it, and trimmed with lace of such delicacy it is difficult to believe that it was achieved by human hands."

Selah laughed, shedding her wariness to reveal the attractive sparkle that had won her more than one admirer. "I believe I know the item to which she refers; though I cannot say even I would describe it in such glowing terms." She moved to a bank of shelves on one wall of the shop and removed a thin white box. "It was on display for several weeks, but as no one purchased it, I thought to let it rest a while." She opened the box and withdrew the fichu, spreading it carefully across a felt-covered table. "As you can see, the linen is indeed quite fine, and the lace is of the best workmanship."

Sprague, who could hardly tell fine linen and expertly crafted lace from whip-stitched sailcloth, scrutinized the fichu with a manufactured air of expertise. He lightly skimmed his fingers across the linen and was surprised to be able to feel that the texture was indeed superior to most. "It is lovely," he agreed. Still, he wondered if the gift would be enough to please his wife. The fichu seemed an insubstantial thing, and the price Selah had named was reasonable.

Sensing his indecision, Selah showed him a pair of delicate glovelettes constructed of the same lace that trimmed the fichu and, with no haggling, Sprague agreed to purchase the combination. While she wrapped the fichu and glovelettes, he wandered to the front of the store and peered out the window just in time to see John Wilton striding toward the chocolate shop. Sprague popped his head out of the shop door and whistled like a seaman to attract his friend's attention. Wilton raised one hand in acknowledgement and crossed the road to join Sprague.

John Wilton entered Selah's shop with a good deal of uncertainty. He knew nothing about the establishment except that it was the sort of place frequented by fashionable ladies, which made it an unlikely place for him to find his friend. But sensing his perplexity, Sprague hastily explained the circumstances the moment Wilton had stepped inside and removed his hat.

"You're late," Sprague admonished.

"I am not," Wilton replied with curt indignation. "We were to meet at half-past three o'clock, and," he tapped the watch he had already removed from his pocket, "it is precisely that time."

"We agreed to meet at three o'clock," Sprague argued. "I remember it quite well because we wanted to be there a full hour before they close."

"The shop closes at four-thirty, William."

"Does it?" Sprague looked to Selah for confirmation and was crestfallen when she nodded her head. "Oh, dear," he said. "It appears that I muddled the appointment." Easily dismissing the error, he brightened. "Well, never mind. Come and let me introduce you to this lovely lady who has been of great assistance to me in my quest for a suitable gift for Dorcas."

Selah had listened to their exchange as she tied up Sprague's parcel. It was difficult to hide her amusement, and the trace of a smile lingered on her lips as she handed the package over to Sprague.

"Allow me, Mrs. Garrett, to name to you Mr. John Wilton. Not always the most agreeable of friends, but certainly the most prompt, and possessed of the best memory for detail."

Wilton greeted her and immediately flushed under the scrutiny of her blue eyes. Aside from his niece and the servants, he was unaccustomed to feminine company and was momentarily tongue-tied by this striking woman. But Selah's quiet graciousness helped put him at ease.

It had been Selah's plan just before Sprague entered her shop to sit down and enjoy a pot of genuine, unadulterated China tea brewed from a small supply of leaves sent to her by Anna. She found the two men so entertaining that it was difficult to let them go, so she ventured an unconventional invitation. "I'm afraid I've no chocolate to offer you. But I had just put the kettle on to boil and was preparing to brew a pot of real tea from leaves sent to me by a friend in London. Would you gentlemen care to join me?"

In the view of both gentlemen, a cup of tea in the company of this handsome woman held far more appeal than anything the chocolate shop could offer, so they accepted the invitation with only a perfunctory expression of their desire not to intrude. Selah led them through the curtained passageway, through her little storage room, and into a tiny kitchen facing onto the back of the building. There was a well-worn, sturdy table in the middle of the room and a hearth that was small for a kitchen hearth, though ample enough for Selah's needs. The room was warm, functional, and surprisingly comfortable, Wilton thought.

"You are fortunate to have a friend in London to provide you with good English tea," Sprague remarked, indicating the little tin of tea leaves Selah had just opened. He watched her carefully spoon leaves into the infuser, then tightly close the lid on the tin before replacing it on a high shelf.

"Very fortunate," she agreed. "Though, in truth, she is my son's friend. I've known her from a distance for many years, but met her more formally before she left Boston. She made an entirely favorable impression on me. Happily, I must have made an equally favorable impression on her, because she has sent these little gifts from time to time during her stay there."

"Or, perhaps she hopes to curry your son's favor?" Sprague's eyes twinkled as he made the suggestion.

Selah laughed. "She already has his favor, though not in the way you imply. They have, since childhood, been friends of a sort. I believe he looks upon her as one might a younger sister who is at once a nuisance and a pet." She set the porcelain teapot on the table and added a bit of the scalding water, swirling it to warm the pot and then pouring it out.

"It's an interesting coincidence," Wilton commented as he watched her fill the pot once more with hot water and add the infuser, "that my niece is currently staying in London. She sends me small supplies of tea as well. It

must be the talk of London that we here suffer from a dearth of Bohea."
He chuckled, and did not at first notice that Selah was staring at him.

"Wilton?" His name had only just registered with her. "You are John
Wilton?"

"Well, yes." Wilton looked from her to Sprague, uncertain of what he
might have done to cause this sudden change in her demeanor. "I am."

"And, is Anna Somerset your niece?"

Now Wilton was all the more perplexed. "Yes, ma'am, that's correct.
But I fail to under—"

"Oh, my." She covered her laughter with her hand and sank into a
chair. "I cannot imagine how I failed at first to make the connection.
Perhaps it's because of the different surnames."

Sprague, seeing the confusion on his friend's face, came to the rescue.
"I believe, John, that our Anna is Mrs. Garrett's friend in London."

Selah nodded, confirming the suggestion, and Wilton settled back into
his chair. "Well, I'll be," he murmured. "I had no idea she was
corresponding with anyone else." Thoughts were tumbling around in his
head, quickly arranging themselves into a cohesive picture. "Though, I
suppose I should not be surprised. Anna has always been so very
independent."

Sprague and Selah were both laughing now, though Selah's laughter was
more guarded. What might Anna have told her uncle regarding Daniel?
Her son was working so hard to put his life onto a better tack, and she
desperately wanted people to see him for the person he was now trying to
be — not the person he had once been. Anna had known Daniel through
all of those troubled years. It seemed reasonable that she might have
mentioned him to her uncle. Sprague had a good opinion of Daniel, and it
was a good opinion that was worth having. Could Wilton destroy that?

"You say she and your son have been friends since childhood?" Wilton
was remembering some of the ill-chosen acquaintances Anna had made
over the years — particularly the young friend whom Wilton had gone to
such great lengths, on Anna's behalf, to protect from the punishment he
likely deserved. Anna had never told him the boy's name, and he wondered
if it might have been Selah's son.

"Yes." The shield was falling back into place, her wariness plain in her
bearing. "They have." Concentrating on keeping her hands steady, she
busied herself with pouring out the tea.

"I suspect master Garrett was a good friend for Anna to have," Sprague
told him as he accepted his cup. "It turns out that he is the young man
who came to my rescue the night I was set upon by robbers. It was the
night of that bloody business on King Street. Do you recall it?"

Wilton nodded his head. He doubted he would ever forget the sight of the bumps and bruises that adorned his friend's face after the incident, and certainly no one could forget the violence of that night.

"I passed young Mr. Garrett as I was entering the shop," Sprague continued. "He was departing as I arrived. I knew at once that I'd seen him before, but it took me a few moments to recall just where. Imagine my pleasure at being able to extend my thanks to him, if only through his mother." He sat back, beaming with satisfaction.

Wilton began to relax. Though he was not altogether pleased to know that Anna had male acquaintances who were unknown to him, he could hardly fault her. He had never been as watchful as he should have been, and the price was that Anna had frequently pushed the boundaries of wisdom and propriety. But in the final analysis, he trusted her judgment, and if this young man had come to Sprague's aid at such a terrible moment, then Anna's friendship with him could not be entirely ill-advised.

Their first sips of tea were accompanied by silent appreciation and eyes closed in the bliss of the moment. "Blessings on our Anna!" Sprague broke the silence and made them all laugh with his zeal. "We have missed her sorely." He drew a nod of agreement from Wilton. "But I suppose that is somewhat ameliorated by her gift." He hoisted the cup in salute to the absent girl, and then sipped again at the perfect brew.

"I have, indeed, missed her dreadfully," Wilton agreed. He was staring into his cup as though he could see Anna's face reflected in the dark liquid. "I long to have her back here in Boston with me, but at the same time, I feel wholeheartedly that I did the right thing in sending her away. It's not merely a matter of her safety. Life here grows more difficult and incommodious with each passing month, it seems. I like knowing that she is in a place that is without deprivations and that is full of opportunities."

"Perhaps Boston will be such a place again before too long," Selah gently suggested.

"Perhaps," Wilton said, nodding thoughtfully. "Just perhaps."

*   *   *

Daniel returned Anna's most recent letter to his weskit pocket. He and Drum were traveling to New Hampshire on an errand for Sam Adams and had made camp for the evening. Anna had written her letter in March, and it had taken six weeks to find its way into his hands. She wrote of attending a séance – of all things – at the home of the woman she so often mentioned, Lady Sylvia Gordon-Hewes. The thought of Anna attending a séance was almost unfathomable to him, though he found much humor in her cynicism regarding the whole affair.

This made the third or fourth reading of her letter, and he felt foolish for carrying it with him so that he could read it again and again, but could not seem to help himself. Drum watched him from across their small fire, but Daniel pretended not to notice. Drum had received a letter from Anna as well but had needed Daniel to read it to him. The letter was the first Drum had ever received, and though he could not actually read the words, it made him feel special to see his name so boldly printed on the envelope. He was fascinated by the notion that Anna could deposit the letter with a carrier on the far side of the ocean, and in mere weeks, it would make its way to him in care of Selah Garrett's shop. Daniel had admitted to Drum a similar wonder not just at the speed with which the correspondence had reached him, but with the fact that it had found him at all.

He had not expected to receive responses from her when he, true to his word, had sent brief missives regarding developments in Boston. But she had written letters that, like her, were bright and witty, and full of mockery and reproach when she felt he had acted with less rectitude than she thought him capable. Because he so looked forward to them, he had begun to find the smallest excuse to post a note to her, knowing it would prompt a response. He knew that loneliness was the true motivation behind her correspondence, but felt in no way slighted by the fact.

Even from across a wide ocean, Anna could fill his heart with laughter as no one else had ever done. Her letters were very much like her — adult thoughts wrapped up in a childlike package — and, also like her, they simultaneously provoked and amused him. Words tumbled across the page in her flowing script, replete with flourishes and curlicues and the occasional drawing in the margins. He heard Anna's voice and felt her exuberance and energy in every line. But he also sensed her fascination with London and worried that she would become completely captivated by its allure.

He would feel buoyed by her letters until he recalled his encounter with the chicken thieves, or the men at the Johnson's farm, and then a weighty melancholy would set in. Even if she returned to Boston, her easy way with him would undoubtedly suffer when she learned of the things he had done. The thought sat as a painful lump in his chest and, despite all effort, could not be dismissed.

*   *   *

Teague spent months carefully considering from every angle what he had seen at the Johnson's farm. By May, he arrived at the conclusion that, one way or another, having a stockpile of munitions on hand and ready to sell when the opportunity presented itself could turn out to be far more lucrative than anything in which he had so far dabbled. He was reluctant to purchase weapons from a bent supply officer as the farmers had done, but knew there may be no way around such an arrangement, however, given that stealing from the army was not an easy matter.

He felt unsure of Charlotte's reaction to the idea but thought she could be convinced when all of the details — including, most importantly, the potential profit — were laid before her. As it turned out, he could not have gauged the situation more accurately. Teague's suggestion that he and Charlotte avail themselves of the profit to be had by dealing in stolen munitions had delighted Charlotte. She demurred at first, managing a good show of possessing an innocent, delicate nature to which such an idea would never have occurred, and she evinced just the right amount of concern for the risks Teague would be taking. But once those pretended niceties were out of the way, she let loose her enthusiasm.

She did not mention to him how timely his suggestion truly was. It would have surprised him to know that she, having grown impatient with her situation, had strongly considered dodging off to London, taking with her what cash they had accumulated. But presented now with the possibility of greatly increasing her fortune in such a short time, it was an easy decision to bide a bit longer. It was her plan to abandon her home, her father, and all the other unwelcome encumbrances in her life, slip away to one of the southern colonies and, from there, take ship for London. The plan could be enacted with a good deal more style and comfort if Teague did his part.

Teague's chief concern was finding a suitable place to hide the stolen goods until a buyer could be found for them. He told her about the farmers' misadventure and their ingenious solution regarding the hiding of their munitions, and he explained his concern that either Regulars could come looking for their missing property or that competitors might attempt to appropriate his hoard in lieu of doing their own work. They needed, therefore, a place that would be secure and that would be perceived as the most unlikely of hiding places. She was somewhat irritated that Teague could not think of the obvious solution without her hinting and prodding. Even then, he'd been resistant to what struck her as a brilliant idea. But as was always the case when she managed him properly, he came around to her viewpoint.

He was staring out of the parlor window, downing his second glass of her father's port while he pondered their discussion. "We must take care that Daniel doesn't learn of this. Heaven help us if he finds out where we've decided to hide the guns and powder until they can be sold."

A small frown creased her brow. Daniel would indeed be livid if he learned of their endeavor, and she had no doubt that most of his anger would be directed at her. Momentarily uncertain, she looked at Teague. He was resolved, she could see, and would carry this through with unwavering determination. Furthermore, he would deflect Daniel's anger, should it come to that. There was no danger that she would suffer any consequences.

"Yes," she agreed, her face relaxing into a smile. "We will have to take care that Daniel does not find out."

*   *   *

Freshly returned from his trek to New Hampshire, Daniel decided to seek out Dr. Warren. The doctor was particularly adept at helping him sort out his thoughts and, lately, his thoughts needed a good deal of sorting. Though Warren was a master of lofty contemplation, he was equally at ease in his chair before a fire, freshly-filled tankard in hand, engaging in easy, friendly conversation; never above listening to a man's smallest troubles and dispensing advice when it was asked of him. At age thirty-one, he was somewhat closer to Daniel's age than Sam Adams and, thus, seemed more approachable.

Daniel found Warren at the Bunch of Grapes tavern, long legs stretched in front of him as he lounged in his chair and listened to the conversation of others at the table. Sam Adams was there, his paunchy body rocking with animated outrage over something the Governor had said. There was a third man, whom Daniel did not recognize. The man was built like a barrel, Daniel thought; short and stocky, but plainly as strong and sturdy as a man could wish to be. Warren spotted Daniel the moment he entered the tavern and waved him over to join his table. Before any protest could be made, Warren called up and paid for a pint for Daniel. Though Daniel did not recognize the third man, he knew within seconds of sitting down that the stranger was an Irishman and, judging by the heaviness of his brogue, not long removed from that country, an impression that was confirmed by Warren's introduction.

"Daniel Garrett, please meet Michael O'Keefe, lately of Clonakilty in County Cork, Ireland."

They exchanged courtesies and O'Keefe picked up the trail of what he had been saying as Daniel arrived. "I tell you, I see it clear as day, I do. All the things we suffered in Ireland — those things will happen in the American colonies if folks here don't wake up!" He was trying to keep his voice down, but his passion for the topic was making it a struggle. "Those bleedin' lobster-backs. King Georgie and all the bloody English kings before him sent more and more of 'em until they crushed us. Bloody English buggers! Crushed us! If they want something, they take it. The more valuable the colonies become to London, the more grasping, and greedy, and bloody tyrannical they'll become! And I watch folks here go about their business like they think the buggers will just up and go away and let the colonies alone."

It was no surprise to Daniel that Sam Adams was quick to agree with O'Keefe's assessment. "He's right, you know," Adams concurred. "People here think the threat has gone. They take the peace and prosperity for granted, like they think it will go on, unhindered, forever — as though it's God's blessing on us as a righteous people or some such rubbish. They don't see that our success is one of the very things that fuels London's desire to put us on a tight leash."

Warren nodded as he considered his response. "I agree with you. But beyond what we're already doing, I don't know what can be done to rouse people from their complacency. We continue our arguments in the newspapers, taverns and coffee houses, even from many pulpits. There's nothing else to be done. Boston's citizens are, understandably, weary of discord. They've had their fill of mobs and violence and costly damage to property."

"Somehow, we must continue to stir the fire," Adams insisted. "A way must be found before it's too late — before we are become like the Irish." He slapped his hand on O'Keefe's shoulder, a reminder to Warren of the horrific tales the Irishman had been telling them earlier; tales of confiscated land and property, arable land given over to money crops so that there was not enough food, disenfranchisement, discrimination, and unshackled abuse at every turn. "The king and Parliament are the *English* government, their first concern being England's best interests. And, as far as they're concerned, we are not fully English. That fundamental principle lies at the heart of every issue, and it will not go away, will not change."

Warren shifted his tankard, playing his finger along the ring of moisture it had left on the table. He studied the spilled ale so intently that Daniel wondered if he could divine some solution like a gypsy reading tea leaves. When he spoke at last, it was with deliberation. "Taking care of England, considering what is best for her before all else is Parliament's primary responsibility. If we lived in London, we would think it right and proper for them to put our interests first. But you are correct. The king and Parliament have demonstrated on more than one occasion that they do not consider us to be part of that exclusive circle they feel compelled to serve."

He leaned in and lowered his voice. "I believe that, if we continue to ply the message with diligence, and if we are patient for a while longer, the king — in his fathomless ability to misread a situation — will do the rest for us. The pressure on his coffers is too great right now and Parliament becomes increasingly divided. Something will have to be done to ameliorate the situation, and I believe we can count on the king to do the wrong thing — at least, wrong from the perspective of the colonies. He will come at us again, and I wager it will be soon and it will be in a more egregious fashion than we have yet seen. When that happens, I believe we will see no more complacency in these colonies. We can, and must, continue to beat the drum loudly, but I think it will be King George himself who will make people get up and march to that drum."

"You have more faith in your countrymen than do I," Adams groused sourly.

Warren's face erupted into a broad grin. "That has ever been apparent, Samuel," he laughed. "That has ever been apparent."

Daniel lingered after Adams and O'Keefe had left. He and Warren talked about myriad topics but nothing of consequence. Daniel wondered if Warren had many such opportunities to think and talk about trivialities. Given the man's numerous activities, it seemed unlikely.

Warren, who was devoted to his family, shared an amusing anecdote about one of his children. "You are of an age to be thinking of taking a wife, Daniel. Have you any plans in that regard? I highly recommend the state of marriage, I must say." His eyes twinkled, and he gave Daniel a wink.

Daniel shrugged and stared at the tankard he was gripping between his two hands as though his life depended on holding on to the pewter. "I doubt the sort of lady I'd be interested in would be interested in me."

"Why not?" Warren laughed and clapped him on the back. "You're not so bad looking, you've more brains than most, and you're industrious!"

Daniel tried to laugh along with him. "I've no steady employment, no roof of my own, and what little money I have would not go far in supporting a family."

"Most young men share your condition," Warren pointed out. "It's a condition that deciding to settle oneself generally cures. And, in your case, the potential to rise above your current state is greater than most."

"Perhaps." He took a long swallow of ale and still would not meet Warren's eye.

"Daniel," Warren's tone gentled, "I believe I've been callously flippant. I sense this is a painful subject for you. Why?"

This was what he had come to discuss with Warren but, now the moment was upon him, he found that it was difficult. "I have killed men." He left the statement out on the table, waiting for a response. When none came, he continued. "You know about the chicken thieves two years ago? And I told you about what happened at that farm this past winter?"

"Yes. I remember both of those. One instance was in defense of your own life and the other was in defense of the lives of others. I don't understand why this troubles you, or why you think it makes you undesirable husband material?"

"I've always known I was good at fighting. Turns out, I'm good at killing, too."

"We all have gifts and skills that could be used for either good or bad. The important thing, is which one you choose. Your skill is tempered with a conscience, a sense of right and wrong. That makes a world of difference. Not everyone is capable of defending themselves. If there were not people like you, the world would belong to the most violent bullies."

"But what if those are the only things I'm good at? What does that make me?"

"A soldier."

"We're not at war."

"There is more than one kind of war, more than one kind of soldier needed in this world."

"In my experience, soldiers don't make good husbands, and they sure don't make good fathers." He swallowed hard. Had his father not been more soldier than farmer, how different might life have been for his mother? "Not unless they're British officers, maybe, and that's something I'll certainly never be!"

"Listen." Warren drew his chair nearer to the table and leaned closer to Daniel. "It seems to me that America is to be a nation not of nobility, but a nation of ordinary folks. To be a great nation, those ordinary folks will have to be willing to step up and do the extraordinary from time to time. Look around you. The men who work toward our common goal are honest, industrious men. They are farmers and fishermen and merchants. They go to the polls as religiously as they go to church; argue political philosophy as readily as they argue over the merits of livestock breeds or the best approach to catching fish. During the Indian wars and every sort of trouble, they have not hesitated to put down their plows and pick up the sword or musket, and they won't hesitate to do it again should it become necessary. There is nobility in that. But those farmers and fishermen will need men like you, men who know how to fight to win. Do not underestimate the value of your skills. You belong among the men who will shape these colonies, Daniel. You will take your place among them, I have no doubt. And that will be a noble thing."

Daniel thanked him for his kind words, and for the pint. Bidding his friend a good day, he then stepped out into the bright May afternoon. He tilted his head back, enjoying the sun on his face, before putting his hat on his head and starting off up the street. The street was a maze of carts and street vendors of all sorts, and a bedraggled girl selling cut flowers caught his attention. The flowers had likely been snatched from the Hancock's garden, and Daniel found amusement in that. He exchanged a hard-earned coin for one of her small bouquets. His mother would like them. She would say he had thrown his money away, but she would like them.

He tucked the flowers under one arm and felt the lump where Anna's last letter sat tucked away in his weskit pocket. He rested his hand over it, quieting the sound of the crackling paper. He had thought, at first, to discard it. But, no. He would take it back to his room and hide it away in the box where he kept all the others. He was not the best man for her, of that he was convinced beyond anything Dr. Warren might argue. But he at least felt easier in his mind regarding his worthiness of her friendship, and that was a balm to his spirit.

*   *   *

Daniel was able to enjoy only a short respite from travel. In little over two weeks, he was on the road again, this time to Rhode Island. Rhode Island, Daniel thought, was so very different from Massachusetts, and he wondered how that could be when they were such close neighbors and part-and-parcel of the same land. In fact, each of the colonies he had visited had its own unique flavor, its own unique way of thinking and doing. Sometimes, it seemed even the language was different. Adams, Warren, and Hancock said time and again that the only way the colonies could stand up to the king would be for all of them to stand together. Daniel did not see how such disparate people could ever be brought together — could ever agree on what they would stand for, or how they would go about doing so. It was one more thing he was glad to have in the hands of wiser men than himself.

He removed his hat and wiped the sweat from his forehead. The June sun, unrelenting in its torturous beating, was directly overhead in a cloudless, brilliantly blue sky. Drum and Teague had both declined to join him on this trek, and he was beginning to think they were the sensible ones. He stood on the wharf, looking out over the water. Sun glinted on its surface, breaking into sparkling bursts across the waves and swells rolling off Providence Bay. He had hoped to enjoy a cool wind coming off the water, but there was not enough breeze to make it worth standing in the sun, so he returned to the inn.

On leaving Boston, his plan had been to stop at the small tavern anchoring a crossroads just outside Providence. Bess, a pretty girl with a lackadaisical attitude about morality, worked there serving food and drink to travelers, and could generally be counted on to serve a bit of entertainment to Daniel if he stayed the night. Instead, he had bypassed the tavern and ridden on to Providence and, having delivered his last packet of letters, found near the wharf an inn that offered hearty, palatable meals and reasonably clean beds for a decent price. The name of the place was Sabin's, and it featured a fine taproom that looked out across the wharf. There he sat, pretty Bess far from his mind, as he re-read Anna's latest letter for the third time.

He continued in his steadfast refusal to analyze his reasons for carrying with him whichever of her letters was most recent, or why he read them so often. Nor did he want to admit to the fact that Bess was no longer of interest; he told himself that these things simply *were*, and that they were not matters for reflection. He convinced himself that he re-read Anna's letters because he found them so entertaining. He smoothed the letter before him and his eyes went straight to his favorite paragraph.

> *Though I cannot be in sympathy with the cause to which you have aligned yourself, I acknowledge and admire the fact that you are acting on principles as you perceive them and not solely out of self-interest. It is in keeping with the best part of you, I think, that you are willing to sacrifice your personal safety and comfort for something that is bigger than yourself. But because I cannot see how all of this can come to a happy outcome for you and your associates, I urge you to take care and not completely abandon common sense and caution, as you so often accuse me of doing.*

It made him laugh aloud each time he read it, though he doubted laughter was what she had hoped to inspire. Anna was one of the few people he knew for whom friendship transcended personal philosophies or opinions. She was also one of the few people he knew who could so seamlessly weave censure into a compliment. As he did after reading each of her letters, he reminded himself that a girl hardly beyond childhood had penned the letters for, as when she spoke, Anna's thoughts found expression in a manner considerably beyond her years. But he checked the impulse, suddenly realizing that she would turn sixteen before the month was out. He thought of her still as the young girl she'd been upon departing for London and wondered what changes the ensuing years might have wrought in her.

He folded the letter, tucked it away in a pocket, and turned his attention to the other denizens haunting the tavern. Small clusters of men sat and talked in low voices, their tone serious, their deportment radiating tension and intensity. It occurred to Daniel that he had witnessed this same scene frequently since arriving in Providence. In his experience, men ignoring their work in favor of spending a good deal of time with their heads together in grave and guarded conversation represented a prelude to trouble. Certainly, it was a scene that was played out on an almost weekly basis in Boston of late, and he had not known the outcome of such deliberations to be without unpleasant consequences for someone.

It took some time, but Daniel finally ingratiated himself to a disgruntled merchant who was willing to share his table and some conversation. His name was Emerson Sackett, and his acquaintanceship came at the cost of several tankards, but Daniel considered it worth the price when the man began to talk. According to Sackett, the folks of Providence had developed a considerable grudge against one Lieutenant William Dudingston, commander of HMS *Gaspee*, a schooner that was part of the king's naval contingent sent to patrol the waters off Rhode Island. The schooner sailed out of Newport and, like most naval vessels in colonial waters, the *Gaspee* was primarily charged with the enforcement of maritime trade laws. As various trade restrictions and levies were imposed on the colonies, that role had expanded to include the search for smugglers. Locals complained that the lieutenant had taken his orders as a license to harass and abuse Rhode Island's honest fishermen and seamen, but their grievance, when voiced to appropriate authorities, had fallen on deaf ears.

Daniel chuckled, shaking his head. "It seems that the king treats Rhode Island with the same tact that he has employed in Massachusetts. I believe many Bostonians thought we were being given special favor in that regard. Apparently it was a mistaken impression."

"Oh, I believe it's the king's doing, all right. Some folks argue that it's just that corroded piss-pot Dudingston acting on his own, abusing his power. But if that were the case, why won't the naval authorities do anything about it? Why is he allowed to keep up his pestering? I tell you, it has become too much." He set his empty tankard down and wiped his mouth on his sleeve, clearly hoping that Daniel would offer to buy another round. "The *Gaspee* carries eight guns, and she's fast. She can run down just about anything we have on the water. Dudingston doesn't need cause. He's even stopped ships that have cleared customs in Newport, and he's confiscated cargoes. Owners never see their cargoes again, and no point complaining about it."

Daniel waved the barmaid over and gave her enough coins for two more drinks. "But what's happening today?" Daniel asked. He gestured to a group of men in one corner of the taproom and another outside the window on the street. "I notice that it has been like that all afternoon. People seem particularly concerned about something."

Sackett waited until their drinks had arrived before explaining, his voice low, "Ben Lindsey's packet sloop, the *Hannah*, was to sail out of Newport for Providence earlier today. She should have put in by now, but no one has seen her. Talk is, Dudingston may have waylaid the sloop."

"If that turns out to be the case, will there be trouble here?" Daniel thought of Anna's charge that, where there was violence, he seemed always to be nearby. He was beginning to wonder whether he was following the violence or it was following him.

"I'm afraid there will be. Captain Lindsey's a good man who runs an honest sloop. There's no smuggling going on there. If he is stopped, I fear it just might be the final straw for many around here. Especially if his cargo is confiscated for 'further inspection,' as Dudingston likes to say."

Daniel now understood the atmosphere of anxiety-laced tension and was more than a little curious to see how things would play out. The two men talked through the afternoon, though Daniel did most of the talking, as Sackett was keen to hear a first-hand account of events in Boston, and to hear news from the other colonies to which Daniel had traveled. Sackett lamented the haphazard sharing of information between colonies, a complaint Daniel had heard often enough. Most of what Emerson Sackett and men like him learned came from correspondence similar to that which Daniel was carrying — letters that represented limited exchanges between friends and acquaintances, each man writing from his own individual perspective. There was no uniformity in the messages, and the messages went only to the particular friends of the writer. Given the increasingly serious nature of events, it was becoming an unsatisfactory arrangement for quickly circulating information.

There were those among Daniel's Boston friends who wished to establish in each colony a committee of select men who, utilizing frequent correspondence, would be responsible for an organized and systematic gathering and disseminating of information between colonies — and, Daniel suspected, for shaping the message to suit their purpose. He saw the potential value in establishing such correspondence committees but suspected such a scheme would mean far more traveling for him — something he did not relish.

As the sun dropped lower in the sky and began to cast the long shadows of late afternoon, a man entered the taproom in such a way as to draw the attention of all present. He was of advancing middle-age, lean and neatly groomed, and fairly unremarkable in every way except for the air of authority he carried. Sackett, who seemed surprised by the man's sudden appearance, told Daniel that he was John Brown, a leading citizen of Providence. "He's not generally an excitable man," Sackett said, "so his agitated state alarms me, I must say."

John Brown stood at the center of the room and, once assured that he had everyone's attention, addressed them in an abrupt, straight-to-the point style. "The *Hannah* has just put in," he announced, his voice easily carrying across the room, "and Ben Lindsey tells me that they were set upon by the *Gaspee* shortly after leaving Newport."

A wave of angry murmuring swept around the room, and Brown held his hands up to bring it to a halt. "The story of their encounter is worth hearing, but it's critical that we move quickly right now. Suffice it to say that, in the course of the chase, Lindsey managed to lure the *Gaspee* across the shallows off Namquid Point where she ran aground on a sandbar." The cheer that echoed around the taproom was quickly stifled by Brown. "Now is not the time to celebrate," he argued. "Now is the time to act. The *Gaspee* is hard aground and will be as helpless as a beached whale until the tide comes in tomorrow."

Daniel looked around the taproom at the faces of men who, presented with an unexpected opportunity, were just beginning to realize its full potential.

"Tide comes in around three o'clock tomorrow morning," one of the men observed. "That gives us plenty of time to take action."

"What sort of action?" another man asked.

It was Brown, plainly having considered the matter, who replied. "I say we destroy the *Gaspee*."

Daniel was taken aback by the suggestion and waited for someone to point out the unpleasant consequences they would likely face if they destroyed one of the king's ships. But no such concerns were voiced. Instead, someone from the back of the room called, "What about Dudingston and the crew?"

Brown shrugged. "We set them ashore and let them walk back to Newport. We'll not harm them. I simply want to be rid of the *Gaspee*."

Everyone seemed to agree with this loosely formed plan, though a handful would have preferred harsher treatment for Dudingston. It seemed to Daniel that it was a risky plan, both for its likelihood of success, and for the probable response from the navy if it did succeed, but in a roomful of strangers, he kept his doubts and opinions to himself.

Daniel downed a hasty meal of cheese and bread, and watched as men, aroused by a town crier sent out by Brown, began arriving at Sabin's, armed with whatever they had to hand and full of vengeful spirit. Some of the men commandeered the kitchen and set about the task of making musket balls, while others hammered out a plan and arranged longboats to ferry the slapdash little militia out to the stranded *Gaspee*. An almost suffocating tang of molten lead mingled with the smell of agitated, unwashed men driving Daniel closer to the door in search of fresh air. The atmosphere was heavy with tension and excitement, the men's talk full of bravado.

Word came that it was time to depart, and despite Daniel's reservations, his curiosity and taste for adventure compelled him to join in the endeavor. Settling his pistol firmly at his waist, he followed Sackett and the rest of the men across the road to Fenner's wharf. Eight longboats were assembled there, gunwales and oarlocks wrapped with cloth to help muffle the sound of their approach across the dark water. Captains from various ships each took command of a longboat and acted as steersmen, a man named Abraham Whipple being in charge of the longboat in which Daniel and Sackett found themselves. The boats pushed off from the wharf and formed up into a tight line across, with Captains Whipple and Hopkins, as the most experienced, on each wing.

After the heat and closeness of Sabin's taproom, the fresh sea air was welcome and invigorating. Daniel looked about the boat at the men's faces, barely visible in the darkness, and saw only grim determination. A pale sliver of moon provided some light, but to Daniel, they seemed to be rowing into a black abyss. The muffled oars made insignificant noise against the constant of lapping water and ocean breeze, and the captains communicated with only shielded lanterns and low calls to each other. The men themselves were silent.

After what seemed to Daniel an eternity, a murmur spread along the length of the boat — the *Gaspee* was in sight, her deck lanterns giving her dim illumination. Daniel guessed they were about sixty yards off when they heard the *Gaspee's* sentry hail them. No one from the longboats responded, and they continued their approach. Men began to check their weapons and shift nervously on the benches, anticipating the action to come.

"Steady, men," Whipple urged. "I believe she's too canted to use her big guns. Row on."

As the longboats closed on the *Gaspee*, her sentry continued to hail them, but they staunchly sustained their silence.

Finally, out of patience with the lack of response, Dudingston himself mounted the starboard gunwale, angrily calling, "Who comes there? Make yourselves known!"

The oarsmen in the longboats rested their oars, maintaining a controlled drift toward the *Gaspee*. Captain Whipple, his declaration salted with the sorts of expletives favored by seamen, announced himself as the sheriff of Kent county and that he carried a warrant. Finally, he demanded Dudingston's surrender.

Dudingston, who seemed of no mind to do any such thing, began to shout back. But even before his words could reach the longboats, a young man standing ahead of Daniel on the main thwart in Whipple's longboat leveled his musket and fired at Dudingston. To everyone's surprise, the shot hit its mark, and Dudingston fell back onto the *Gaspee's* deck. "Well done, Bucklin!" another man exclaimed. "I believe you've killed him!"

Daniel was stunned. With that shot, they had intentionally fired upon a British naval officer. It would, he did not doubt, be considered by London as a clear act of treason. If this fact concerned any of his fellows in the longboat, however, it was not apparent. Instead of the astonished silence he felt, they were all rejoicing and calling once again for the *Gaspee's* surrender. Daniel watched the schooner's gunports warily. He was not certain he shared Whipple's estimation regarding the uselessness of the *Gaspee's* cannon, and fully expected that the gunports would any moment explode in a line of fire and smoke as they unleashed their retaliatory fury upon the longboats.

But the retaliation did not come. To the contrary, the *Gaspee's* sentry called out that their captain was gravely injured and had instructed them to surrender the vessel. The longboats were quickly brought alongside the *Gaspee*, and the Providence men encountered no opposition as they scrambled up onto her canted deck. Whipple and Brown asked to see Dudingston, though they hardly needed direction for they could easily follow the trail of blood to the captain's cabin. The other captains instructed the *Gaspee's* crew to gather their belongings and prepare to be taken ashore in the *Gaspee's* longboats. Most of the Providence men stood sentinel to ensure that no mischief ensued during this process, while a few milled about taking note of the schooner's construction, outfitting, and furnishings. She was a fine little ship, they all agreed, and it was a shame she was to be destroyed.

Emerson Sackett and Daniel were standing nearby when Brown popped his head up above decks again, his expression grave, and called out to a young lad. "Ephraim! Find John Mawney and make it quick. Dudingston is in a bad way, and Mawney is the only one among us who knows anything about tending such wounds." He started to return to Dudingston's cabin, then stopped and turned to Sackett. "You and that lad there," he directed, indicating Daniel, "see what you can find in the way of bandages and anything else you can think of useful for dressing a wound."

As he'd been directed, Daniel scavenged about until he had located a quantity of suitable bandaging material. Hands full of what he had found, he entered Dudingston's cabin only seconds behind Mawney and young Ephraim Bowen. Dudingston was laid out on the sturdy wooden galley table that sat in the center of his cabin, with two men trying to keep him still. Bucklin, the lad who had shot Dudingston, stood over his victim, his face somber and almost as pale as Dudingston's. Seeing up close the effect of his fine marksmanship had somehow robbed the event of its luster. He visibly flinched when Mawney pulled back Dudingston's clothing to reveal a nasty wound at the top of his thigh in the groin area.

"Here," Mawney directed, waving Bucklin in to assist him. "Help me with this." He was pressing the ball of his hand hard against the wound to staunch the flow of blood. "Slide your hand underneath mine and keep pressure here, just as I'm doing," Mawney instructed. Dudingston was writhing under the pain the pressure on his wound was causing, but Mawney told Bucklin to ignore it. "Keep that pressure on, or he'll bleed out for sure." He jerked his head in a silent bid for Daniel and Bowen to help keep Dudingston still, nodding approvingly when they took firm, effective hold of Dudingston's shoulders and ankles.

"I've nothing here to take the ball out," Mawney told them. "We need to stop him bleeding and get him to shore. I'll be able to remove the ball, then." When no one made any sort of response, Mawney looked up and, seeing their faces, realized that none of the lads thought it likely that Dudingston would survive long enough to be carried to shore. "He's not as bad off as it looks," Mawney assured them. "As long as we get the bleeding stopped, the rest is manageable."

The three young men had their doubts but put their faith in Mawney's superior knowledge and training in such matters. They held Dudingston firmly to the table while Mawney successfully applied a compress to the wound and strapped it down by pulling a bandage around Dudingston's thigh. He drew the bandage so tight that it made Dudingston cry out at the discomfort.

"Stop your bleating there, you bilge-swigging nanny goat. If I loosen that bandage, you'll bleed to death. Or, would you prefer that?" He leaned over to look down into Dudingston's face. "No? Then we won't let you die." Mawney stepped back, wiping his bloody hands on one of Dudingston's clean shirts that hung nearby. "All right, lads. I think you can help Lieutenant Dudingston up on deck now."

Brown, who had come below during the treating of Dundingston's wound, was searching the lieutenant's documents. Anything he considered useful, he bundled up to be carried away. Now, he stood aside and watched as Daniel and the other two young men hoisted Dudingston off the table and onto a blanket that was doubled and folded as a make-shift stretcher. Lifting the edges, they carried him out of the cabin and, after some awkward negotiation of the ship's ladder, up onto deck. Several of the *Gaspee's* crew took over then, managing with seamans' skill the task of getting their captain into a longboat. Mawney joined them, and they immediately departed for shore and the availability of equipment to minister to the injured lieutenant's wound. All of the rest of the boats, save one, pushed off from the *Gaspee*, leaving the last boat for Brown, Captain Whipple, and a handful of other men who remained behind.

The pre-dawn sky was beginning to lighten now, which made navigation back toward Providence considerably easier. On the way, they stopped at Pawtuxet to deposit the *Gaspee's* crew. It was an inconvenient location at which to be abandoned, but not one completely devoid of shelter for the crewmen. As the longboats pushed away from the Pawtuxet wharf to continue their journey toward Providence, they saw thick, dark smoke rising from the stranded *Gaspee*. The men who had remained behind had looted the abandoned schooner and then set her afire before departing. The rowers rested on their oars for several minutes, watching as the flames took over the ship. Suddenly, her powder magazine having caught fire, the *Gaspee* exploded with a thunderous roar that sent flames, smoke, and debris shooting in all directions. It was a spectacular sight, and it elicited a great cheer from the Providence men.

Daniel watched in silence as the debris settled and flames consumed the remaining portion of the ship's hull. It would take some time, but the *Gaspee* would burn to the waterline, he expected. A jumble of thoughts fought for attention in his mind, but the one that kept coming to the forefront was the question of what, exactly, he was going to tell Anna about this event. Given that it had not occurred in Boston, he felt that, strictly speaking, it did not fall within the parameters of their agreement. But he knew that to omit the telling of it was a cowardly stand not worthy of her friendship. It was going to be a difficult letter to write.

1773

CHAPTER EIGHT

September 1773

My Dear Uncle,

Despite the fact that yet another scandal has occurred which should have supplanted it, London continues to be abuzz over the investigation into that dreadful business with the <u>Gaspee</u>. *The incident occurred over a year ago, and it seems amazing to me that deliberations continue. The fact that the Rhode Island courts chose to prosecute the ship's captain for illegally seizing goods while failing to prosecute his attackers has, understandably, outraged many here. And, for the commission appointed by Parliament to return to London empty-handed because not one person in Providence would give up the names of the culprits seems beyond comprehension.*

I fear that Londoners do not distinguish between the enactors of such behavior and those of us who are loyal to the King and strive to be ever law-abiding. They are increasingly convinced that we colonists are, on the whole, a lawless, reprobate people. It is a fact that weighs heavily on my own heart, so I know that it must be almost unbearable to you, and I long to be able to take your hand and offer solace.

In my mind, it is all a dreadful, ever-escalating conundrum. The Parliament behaves with less tact than would be prudent, which incites the seemingly increasing number of malcontents to lawlessness. In turn, that provokes more aggressive tactics by Parliament and the King's colonial officials, countered with more outrages on the part of the aforesaid malcontents. My concern grows that we are spiraling into a chasm from which there is no easy extrication.

I watch with trepidation to see the response to the Tea Act that Parliament enacted in May. While I can fully-understand Parliament's desire to undermine the colonial market in smuggled Dutch tea, I find myself a bit skeptical of Parliament's claims that the plan should be greeted with gladness in the colonies for it will lower the prices paid there on tea. In the first place, to ascribe no payment of duty to the East India Company, but to tax the tea, instead, at the port of entry, cannot fail to strike one as a singular effort to shore up that struggling company. Then, to appoint consignees at the specific entry ports there who will receive and sell the

tea, seems nothing more than another opportunity for a select few to
control a commodity and to reap the rewards of that control. I fear
that the Act will not be greeted in Boston with the enthusiasm
anticipated by Parliament, and I shudder to think what the response
will be.

    I hope you can tell me I am mistaken in my fears, and that hope
is not merely a desire for my own peace of mind. My greatest concern
is for your happiness and safety, and each new chapter in this
unbelievable sequence of events seems to threaten both.

    I am as always —

                Your affectionate niece,
                Anna

    Anna would grudgingly admit that three years in London had taught her many things and had given her deportment a fine polish far beyond that of her seventeen-year-old contemporaries at home. Had she been given to such vanity, she would also have admitted that her outward appearance had changed dramatically during that time and that the changes were positive in nature. To others, these would have been viewed as benefits to what she considered her exile. What mattered to Anna was the fact that she had rarely felt happy during the almost three years she had lived in London. While she would readily admit that nothing in the colonies could compare with the finery and sophistication of London, the city, for all its glories, was not home. Her uncle's relatively humble house in Boston was home, and with each passing month, the tug of that place upon her heart grew more acutely painful.

    All of this was going through Anna's mind as she rode seated beside Lady Eugenie in the Etheridge's carriage. Sir Gregory sat opposite them looking as though he were being dragged before a magistrate. Lady Eugenie had fussed over him, making certain that everything about his attire was just so, until he would have no more of it. Now he sat, silent, with a storm cloud on his brow and nary a glance at his wife. Anna imagined how she would describe the scene in her next letter to her uncle, and the thought forced her to turn her face toward the window to hide her smile. They were on their way to a dinner party over which Lady Eugenie had been euphoric for weeks. Sir Gregory and Anna, being less enthusiastic, had endured Lady Eugenie's nervous energy with good grace, though not without some resentment, especially on the part of Sir Gregory.

    The party was being hosted by an earl and his countess wife who were long-time friends of Lady Eugenie's family. Eugenie knew her inclusion on the guest list was merely a matter of courtesy to her familial connections, but that fact made her no less inclined to attend. It would be a glittering affair, graced by numerous personages more notable than the Etheridges;

an evening spent in the same rarified air Eugenie had grown up breathing and felt starved of since her marriage.

Their arrival was cause for some trepidation on Anna's part. After being presented to the hosts, making the requisite curtsies, and completing one obligatory turn of the ballroom in the company of Sir Gregory and Lady Eugenie, however, Anna found herself free to stroll the room catching bits of conversation and admiring the earl's impressive art collection. Finally, the dinner gong sounded and pocket doors opened wide to reveal several rooms adjacent to the ballroom in which the guests were assembled. There were tables in each, the most impressive of which was in the main dining room.

The exceptionally long, rectangular table in the main dining room was larger than any Anna had ever seen. It was set for twenty-two of the most illustrious guests, with the overflow being seated at smaller tables in other rooms. Anna was separated from Sir Gregory and Lady Eugenie and escorted to one of the smallest tables where she was confronted with a feast for the senses. That table, which seated a mere twelve guests, was situated in a lovely conservatory surrounded by potted orange trees and long, low planters of boxwood. The table, which did not at all fit Anna's definition of "smaller," suffered under an overwhelming burden of fine china, glittering crystal, and dazzling silver. A tremendous silver candelabrum woven with leaves, flowers, and fruit loomed up in the center like a great fountain of color and light, and the buttery aroma of beeswax candles melded with the fragrance of orange blossom and myrrh.

"They do know how to put on a show, do they not?"

It took a moment for Anna to realize she was being spoken to, and that the gentleman who was doing the speaking was Christopher Hinton. He nodded meaningfully toward the footman, who stood patiently holding her chair for her. Embarrassed to have been seen gawking, she smiled and hastily sat down.

"It's all a bit overpowering, I believe," Hinton declared, understanding her amazement.

"This is a pleasant surprise, Mr. Hinton. You'd not mentioned you would attend this evening." She tried to steady her nervous hands as she fumbled with her napkin.

"I had not planned to do so, but Lady Sylvia prevailed upon me to attend so that she could hear about the evening's high points without having herself to actually endure the event." He omitted that Lady Sylvia's main purpose in sending him was so that he could look after Anna who, she knew, would be uncomfortably alone. Indeed, it was Lady Sylvia's influence that had resulted in their seating arrangement.

Anna hid her smile and did a quick survey of their fellow diners. Because they considered it a reflection on the hostess' opinion of their status, several of Anna's fellow diners were grumbling about being seated in the farthest hinterlands. To Anna's mind, there could have been no better location in the whole of the palatial house.   In a discreet and well-orchestrated dance, footmen began circulating the various dishes among the guests. Quiet, polite conversations commenced around the table as dinner partners took the measure of one another, and Anna, seated between Mr. Hinton and a man she knew not at all, hoped the two men would be up to the challenge of carrying the conversation for her.

"Are you finding London to your liking, Miss Somerset?" the gentleman she did not know asked.

Nonplussed, Anna stared at him.   His English was quite heavily accented, and the fact that he knew her name further compounded her sense of being off-kilter. "I'm sorry," she stammered, "I've met so many people since I've been here, I do not recall—"

"I apologize." He bowed as best a man could when seated. "We have not been introduced.

Hinton quickly, and to the relief of both parties, intervened. "Miss Somerset, allow me to present Senhor Eduardo Luís Correia Ramos. Senhor Ramos is Portuguese, in case you did not guess. Senhor Ramos, this is Miss Anna Somerset."

"Please forgive my abruptness. I must explain that I knew your name only because I overheard your introduction to our hosts when you arrived. I understand that you are visiting from the American colonies?"

"Yes. From the Massachusetts Colony."

"Massachusetts? Boston, no?"

"Yes, Boston."

"The massacre," Ramos clucked his tongue. "Such a *tragédia*."

Anna was dreading the comments she knew would be unleashed by his remark. She had often enough heard the matter recounted and debated, for the Custom House incident had become inextricably linked with Boston in the minds of most Londoners. Though accounts of the event, whether favoring the Regulars or the colonists, were terribly inaccurate, she held her tongue rather than reveal that she had witnessed the event first-hand. Discussion of the incident was forestalled, however, by a statement that made Anna wish minds had stayed on the massacre.

"A colonial and a Portuguese." The woman seated directly across from Anna was speaking, her voice carrying with icy clarity to everyone at the table. "What a fine pair the countess has deigned to put in our midst." She hid the words behind a thin veil of humor, but the acidity was apparent nonetheless.

Anna, feeling embarrassed for Senhor Ramos and indignant for herself, put down her fork and, blinking, gaped at the woman. The ill-tempered woman was middle-aged, thin and angular, and adorned with every humanly possible artifice and enhancement. Her person was so laden with jewels that Anna suspected she had left nothing behind in the box. Pearl and gem-studded pins jutted here and there from her extravagantly piled hair, amethyst and diamond drops swayed at her earlobes, rope upon rope of pearls wrapped around her neck and formed graceful loops across her ample cleavage and down the front of her bodice. Ornate rings winked on her fingers and multi-jeweled bracelets at her wrists. Even her fan was jeweled.

"Do not mind Lady Brittlesey," a rakish man seated at the lady's left hand told Anna. "She is peevish because there was not enough dill in her soup." He was a handsome man, charming and affable, and the sort of man who made every female he met, regardless of age, feel like she was his Venus. He'd been caressing Lady Brittlesey's ego with his charisma since they first sat down, so his remark now struck the lady as a betrayal.

"You are an impertinent little man, Sir Edmond." Lady Brittlesey glared daggers at him. She unfolded a heavily-ornamented lorgnette and peered across the table at Anna. "Ah, well." She fluttered her fan contemptuously. "At least this little one seems to have acquired some fashion sense during her time here. I've yet to see a colonist who does not look as though he chose his clothing from a rag heap."

Many responses bubbled in Anna's brain, not one of them civil. She picked out her favorite and was preparing to lob it across the table when prudent judgment intervened. Escalating the situation could not possibly lead to a good outcome for herself and would certainly lead to embarrassment for Sir Gregory, Lady Eugenie, and her uncle. The goodwill of those three people was worth far more to her than the personal satisfaction she would get from lashing out at Lady Brittlesey.

"Senhor Ramos is a wine merchant who represents some of the best vineyards in Portugal. He is responsible for the excellent wine we are enjoying this evening." Mr. Hinton lifted his crystal wine glass and tipped it toward Ramos. "I salute you for your contribution to this excellent meal, Senhor."

The wine merchant grinned. "It is a happy consequence of the quarrel between your country and the French that English tables currently favor Portuguese wines. The vintners of my country owe the French a debt, I think." He laughed, as did everyone at the table except Lady Brittlesey. Ramos raised his glass in salute and then sipped his wine appreciatively. "Our hostess has excellent taste," he decreed, swirling the wine in his glass, admiring its rich color. "It is always a pleasure to assist her in procuring the vintage she desires." He returned his attention to Anna, apparently eager to ask a question that had been on his mind. "Are you acquainted with Dr. Franklin? He is from the American colonies, no?"

S . D . B A N K S

It seemed odd to Anna that people so often assumed that everyone in the American colonies knew everyone else. And, because he was the most well-known among them, it was generally Dr. Franklin they asked about. "Yes, he is from the American colonies," Anna replied. "But from Philadelphia. I'm afraid I've never met the eminent doctor."

Lady Brittlesey harrumphed. "Eminent, indeed. I understand that he is to be publicly reprimanded for his part in that shameful affair regarding Governor Hutchinson's correspondence."

Anna winced. The scandal over the publication in the *Boston Gazette* of some of Governor Hutchinson's old correspondence, and Hutchinson's subsequent expulsion from the colony, had outraged many in London. The government was determined to discover who had purloined the letters and provided them to the colonists, and the publicity was proving damaging to Dr. Franklin's reputation and impairing his ability to serve as colonial emissary to London. Furthermore, the incident was further arousing English antipathy toward the colonists, threatening the already precarious balance between those who sought a peaceful solution to the American problem and those who felt the colonists needed a firmer hand to bring them into line.

She knew, also, that a similarly delicate balance existed within the colonies. Even her uncle had expressed dismay over the revelation that the Governor had appealed to London to send more troops to Boston. If John Wilton, Loyalist that he was, felt betrayed by the revelation, how must those who harbored long lists of grievances feel?

"At this point," Mr. Hinton said levelly, "there is no evidence that Dr. Franklin is responsible for the publication of the letters."

"I believe that, in many countries, Dr. Franklin is highly esteemed for his many scientific investigations and his keen intellect," Ramos interjected. "Surely, such a great man would not have deliberately done anything to embarrass his government."

"He is well regarded in France," Lady Brittlesey said dryly. "In that country, heads are turned by the smallest distractions. But one wonders, Senhor Ramos, if the man would be so highly regarded in France if it was the French government he had betrayed?"

"To suggest that our government has been betrayed is surely too strong a charge," Mr. Hinton argued. "In my opinion, it is an embarrassment, nothing more. I do think it a shame that Dr. Franklin's reputation and credibility are being damaged. He seems particularly blessed with those skills requisite to an emissary."

"I must agree." Ramos waved his hand so that the lace at his wrists fluttered. "Too much is being made of it. Doubtless it will — what do you English say — 'blow over'?"

148

"I would never use such a vulgar expression," Lady Brittlesey sniffed. She was continually fiddling with her demitasse spoon, turning it over and over as though she was entranced by the reflected candlelight that flashed on it with each turn.

"Of course you would, my dear," her husband corrected. It was the first time he had spoken throughout the entire dinner. Indeed, he had silently lolled in his chair, apparently indifferent to the meal and bored with the company. "I'm certain I've heard you use it on more than one occasion." His face was expressionless when he spoke, and Anna was hard pressed to deduce whether he was in earnest. Based on the searing look Lady Brittlesey fixed upon him, Anna decided it did not matter — he would, at some point, be made to regret the comment.

Lady Brittlesey quit turning the spoon over and, instead, began to spin it on the linen table cloth like the hand on a clock.

"Well, now, Brittlesey," Sir Edmond intoned, taken aback by Lord Brittlesey's unexpected entrance into the conversation. "What's your opinion on all of this?"

"My opinion," the aloof man slurred, "is that I have no opinion. I work at not having opinions. In fact," he managed what Anna took to be a chuckle, "it is the *only* thing I do work at." He belched softly.

It finally dawned on Anna that Lord Brittlesey was extremely inebriated. Lady Brittlesey, on the other hand, appeared to be oblivious to her husband's embarrassing behavior as she continued to be engrossed in her game with the spoon. With the tip of her index finger, she scooted the spoon back and forth until she finally pushed it with such vigor that it slipped off the table and into her lap. She hunted for it among the folds of her skirt before triumphantly returning it to the table where she began the whole process over again.

Lord Brittlesey seemed to be warming to the fact that he had the attention of everyone at the table. "There's little point to me muddling about managing our estates. I have a very competent man for that, so it would be a waste of my time. And there is little point to attending Parliament. I've no interest, and they seem to manage quite well without me, so that would also be a waste of my time. No," he pronounced, gesturing for the footman to refill his wine glass, "none of that for me. It's all unbearably tedious. In my opinion, my time is much better spent with a good cigar, a really fine brandy, and several hands of whist. Everything else is just too taxing on a man."

Anna felt Mr. Hinton shift uncomfortably beside her. In truth, she sensed that everyone at the table was ashamed for Lord Brittlesey. Everyone except his wife. Lady Brittlesey had never missed a beat in her little game with the spoon. She was so engaged that she did not even seem to hear what her husband was saying.

Lord Brittlesey's homily continued, further appalling Anna as he gave a detailed accounting of his many titles and honorifics. This recitation of his pedigree was meant to impress, but it missed the mark with Anna. She found it difficult to be impressed by a man who filled his days with idle pursuits, and who could not even be bothered to take seriously the social and political responsibilities incumbent on him as a member of his class. Lord Brittlesey was, in her estimation, nothing short of disgraceful.

"Well, I must say, it is all becoming too much," Sir Edmond pronounced, returning to the earlier point and effectively stealing the conversation from Lord Brittlesey's control. "This Hutchinson affair follows too closely upon that horrid *Gaspee* business."

At the word *Gaspee*, Anna's fork paused momentarily in the process of putting a morsel of roasted venison in her mouth. Daniel had written to her with an account of the incident — an incident in which he had played too great a role for her comfort. Their comments overlapping one another, various guests around the table began to recount what they had heard about the grounding and subsequent burning of the ship. Most of what they knew was based on newspaper accounts, rumors, and sensationalized gossip, and differed considerably from Daniel's account, especially regarding the treatment of the schooner's crew. The one thing that unified all of the guests was their indignation over the fact that none of the colonists involved had been presented for prosecution.

"Are we supposed to believe that none could be identified?" Sir Edmond asked. "Clearly, the entire town should be held responsible."

"It is an intriguing situation," Ramos observed. "Had another nation committed such a deed, it would doubtless have been viewed as an act of war. I think your government responds with great restraint."

"True," Sir Edmond muttered. "Unlike the unfortunate French, *our* king is not a reckless despot."

"But the colonies are not a sovereign nation," Hinton pointed out. "I believe the government is prudent to regard this as an act of malicious mischief by a few individuals."

"Or, open rebellion," Sir Edmond posed.

Anna's fork paused again in midair.

"My father believes," Lady Brittlesey intoned, "and I agree, that the navy should have razed the town. The citizenry might, perhaps, have been afforded warning of what would happen if they did not remand the culprits for justice, but, failing their cooperation, the navy should have destroyed the entire town. Not only would justice have been served, but it would have set an example that would surely have brought those colonists who are of a rebellious mind to heel."

Anna's fork clattered loudly on her plate.

Mr. Hinton, seeing her distress, quickly steered the conversation away from colonial matters. But regardless of the topic, Anna hardly took her eyes off of Lady Brittlesey. The outrageous woman contributed little more to the conversation, absorbed by the fact that she had made her game more challenging by adding another spoon, which she had procured from Sir Edmond's place without his being aware she had taken it. The jewels on her rings and bracelets glinted as she deftly maneuvered the small silver spoons between her fingers, spinning them until they eventually dropped off the table into her lap. Unlike all the previous instances, however, this time the spoons did not reappear. Lady Brittlesey looked down and riffled among the folds of her skirt as though she would retrieve the spoons. Her eyes darted about the table to see if anyone watched her. She missed Anna's surreptitious scrutiny and, satisfied that she was not being observed, reached out and picked up her glass, took a long sip, and set it back down. Her attention was all for Sir Edmond, the spoons apparently forgotten.

Anna was flabbergasted. She had no doubt that the spoons had found their way into Lady Brittlesey's pocket. Had they fallen onto the floor out of reach, Lady Brittlesey would have demanded that the footman retrieve them for her. The poor footman, who found himself on the receiving end of Lady Brittlesey's sharp temper all evening, would most likely be blamed when the spoons were discovered to be missing, Anna thought, and that potential injustice was more than she could bear. She considered saying something to Mr. Hinton but did not want to put the kind man in the awkward position of having to confront Lady Brittlesey. For that matter, Anna supposed that not even the countess would be entirely grateful if she aired the matter. That left Sir Gregory or Lady Eugenie, and it seemed likely that they would not thank her for dumping the problem into their laps. The Etheridges would be her fallback plan, but she felt determined to devise a way to facilitate the return of the spoons.

She contrived to be pushed into Lady Brittlesey as they left the conservatory, and then again as the guests jostled for seats in the ballroom. On the second try, she had felt her hand press against what could easily be the outline of the spoons secreted in a pocket. As the guests enjoyed a brief recital by a well-known soprano and her accompanist, Anna considered several plans and then discarded each for various reasons. By the time the recital was over and the guests began to rise and mill about, Anna still had no concrete notion of what she would do. She worked her way through the mingling guests, watching and thinking as she moved closer to Lady Brittlesey.

She approached Lady Brittlesey, who was to her right and completely unaware of Anna's presence because she was so focused on Sir Edmond approaching from Anna's left. Lady Brittlesey was smiling broadly as Sir Edmond narrowed the gap between them, while Lord Brittlesey watched from the side, frowning and leaning on his cane. Anna, Sir Edmond, and Lord and Lady Brittlesey made up four compass points moving together from just beyond the edge of an Aubusson rug. The picture seemed to slow and become focused in the manner of a puzzle as the last pieces fall into place. Impulsively, Anna decided on a plan. And then, once her course was set, everything happened so quickly there was no opportunity for a change of mind.

As the four people converged from their opposing positions, Anna quickened her pace and, just as she reached Lady Brittlesey, carefully hooked the toe of her slipper under the edge of the rug, lifting it slightly. Lady Brittlesey, her eyes on Sir Edmond, did not see the hazard and tripped. As she toppled forward, Anna reached with her left arm to break the lady's fall while reaching with her right hand across Lady Brittlesey's shoulders to hook her finger under the strands of pearls looped about the lady's neck. She held tight to the pearls as Lady Brittlesey tipped forward, creating enough strain to break the strands. Between them, Anna and Sir Edmond caught Lady Brittlesey before she fell completely, but pearls were tumbling everywhere.

Watching her pearls cascade about her like hailstones bouncing on the polished wood floor or rolling across the Aubusson, Lady Brittlesey began to shriek at her husband. Guests scrambled to retrieve the pearls as they rolled about under their feet, which alarmed Lady Brittlesey all the more for she was certain she would never get them all back. Screeching at everyone to stay away while, in alternate breaths, crying for help, she dropped to her knees and began scooping up the scattered pearls. Anna got to her knees to help, carefully positioning herself in the pooled fabric of Lady Brittlesey's skirts. Moving quickly and with nimble hands, she picked up pearls and handed them to Lady Brittlesey, constantly shifting the folds of their mingled skirts as she hunted for more.

The room was chaos. It was as though Lady Brittlesey had unwittingly invented a wonderful new parlor game. People were clambering about on their knees searching for pearls and crying out in triumph when they found one. Small competitions developed as people began to keep score. Who had found the most pearls? Who had found the largest pearls? Sir Edmond commandeered a small porcelain cache pot and was walking about holding it so that guests could deposit their collected pearls inside. With the exception of Lady Brittlesey, they were all enjoying themselves immensely.

When they had found all they could, Anna helped a tearful Lady Brittlesey to her feet and handed her over to her husband. He escorted her to another room so that she could collect herself, Sir Edmond and his pot full of pearls following close behind. The guests, quite enlivened by the excitement, created a sudden demand for more champagne. Laughter bubbled around the room. And Anna was happier than all the rest, for she had in her possession the spoons she had managed to filch from Lady Brittlesey's pocket.

Anna wasted no time in slipping away to an adjoining salon to return the spoons to one of the footmen. She gave no explanation other than that she had come across them. The footman, whose expression suggested that a mystery was solved, looked relieved and thanked her before quickly disappearing toward the stairs leading down to the kitchen and butler's pantry. Anna took a long, deep breath and exhaled it slowly before turning to return to the other guests. She was startled to find Mr. Hinton standing in the doorway, watching her.

"Lady Brittlesey will not be happy when she discovers that her hard-earned plunder has gone missing." His tone was ironic, and the hint of a smile tugged at one corner of his mouth.

"You saw her take the spoons, too?"

"No, but I was watching you help her pick up the pearls. I saw you take something from her pocket. When I observed you returning the spoons to the footman just now, I inferred what had happened. That was a clever bit of work, by the way, picking her pocket. Do you have a great deal of experience?"

"Oh, no!" She was mortified to have him think picking pockets was a habit with her. "I've seen it done." She shrugged and said no more, hoping this would satisfy his curiosity. When he stood, silent, clearly unwilling to accept the vague explanation, she huffily insisted, "I am not a pickpocket. Or any kind of thief, for that matter." To her annoyance, Mr. Hinton raised one eyebrow and, folding his arms across his chest, leaned against the door frame. "Very well," she sighed. "I'm acquainted with someone who is very adept in that regard, and have seen him work."

"Indeed? And, I gather that you have never turned him over to the authorities?"

Things were getting complicated, and Anna wrung her hands as she searched for a way out. It was Teague whose skill had fascinated her as a little girl — until she realized that what he was doing was not magic, but the commission of a crime. Later, for her amusement, Daniel had taught her how to accomplish the little trick. "It wasn't necessary. I threatened to turn him in if I saw or heard that he had been at it again."

"And, he believed you would make good on the threat?"

She nodded. "He knew I would. I am to this day one of his least favorite people."

"It sounds as if that is not something you should regret." When she did not respond, he sighed and, straightening himself, moved several steps closer to her. "You took a terrible risk dealing with Lady Brittlesey's folly as you did."

"Her *folly*? Do you not mean her *crime*? It was stealing, after all."

"Nonetheless," he persevered, "your course of action was foolhardy. Audaciously brave, but foolhardy."

She became indignant. "In my view, a thing is only foolhardy if it fails."

He laughed. "Dangerously close to the view that the end always justifies the means. We do know how very perilous a philosophy that can be."

"If I had not acted," she retorted impatiently, "one of the poor footmen or some other servant would have been blamed. I could not allow that to happen. I thought if I told someone what I had seen, there would be a good deal of embarrassment all 'round, and I would not have been looked upon kindly for my pains."

"And yet, the better course would have been to tell someone," he insisted. "Or, perhaps, you should have let the matter go unremarked and let things fall as they may."

"Perhaps."

"Your instinct to prevent an injustice does you credit, Miss Somerset. But I fear that such instincts can become inconvenient at best and, at worst, can even prove dangerous. Take care."

"I appreciate your advice, Mr. Hinton."

"But you do not intend to heed it?"

Anna smiled. "I can try. I've been told on more than one occasion, however, that I have an unfortunate knack for getting into trouble, so I hold out no great hope that I'll be successful."

Hinton laughed heartily at that. "Are all Americans like you?" he asked.

Frowning, Anna cocked her head. "Of course not. No more than all Englishwomen are like Lady Brittlesey. What an odd thing to ask."

"Yes, I suppose it was odd. Forgive me. However, you mistake my line of thought. I meant to suggest a compliment to your countrymen."

"But you are one of my countrymen, Mr. Hinton. Do you forget that we are all British citizens?"

"I do not forget, Miss Somerset. But I sometimes think there is more than an ocean between your part of Britain and mine."

She nodded. "My uncle insisted that he was sending me to England because he wanted me to be safe. In retrospect, I have to believe that some part of him sent me here to reinforce my Englishness."

"But it has accomplished the opposite, has it not?"

She frowned. "I cannot say for certain. I, like my uncle, am still a Loyalist. But, unlike my uncle, there is a bittersweet quality to it because I've seen how I am different — how *we* are different — and I wonder if that difference is something the king can appreciate."

"It will be a very great shame if he cannot. But I fear he has little choice. And, I fear that we are headed toward a great cataclysm. As I said, take care, Miss Somerset." He bowed solemnly and watched in silence as she left the room. There was an air of finality to the parting, as though they both knew they were not likely to meet again.

One way or another, Anna decided, it was time to go home.

CHAPTER NINE

John Wilton stood, hands clasped behind his back, staring out of Selah Garrett's shop window. Aside from the entertainment to be had by watching passers-by negotiate the cold December wind as they struggled down the street, there was nothing of particular interest to see. He rocked forward and back, heel to toe, waiting for Mrs. Garrett to open the package he had delivered. There was no reason for him to wait, though he had told her he wanted to ensure that the contents of the package were undamaged. But he was loath to leave the warm, comfortable shop or the pleasure of Mrs. Garrett's company. He could hear her behind him, wrestling with the oiled paper outer wrapping, and then the sturdy paper inner wrapping that had to be removed to get to the box.

"I cannot imagine what this could be," she was saying as she removed the last of the wrapping paper. "Such an oddly shaped package." She ran her fingers across the top of the long, thin box.

"Anna's note indicated that she had considered for some time the best way to send the contents. Apparently the boxes used by swordsmiths suited the purpose. I am left to wonder how she obtained one, though."

Selah smiled and hefted the box, demonstrating its lightness. "Well, I doubt that this is a sword!"

Wilton crossed the shop toward her. She was inspecting the seal on the box, preparing to open it, apologizing again for the time he had taken to deliver it to her. He waved his hand dismissively. "It was not the merest trifle of trouble. I had other business in this street. Anna was wise to ask my business associate in London to send it along with a consignment addressed to me. There was no cost to her, and it ensured that the package would arrive in good order."

"Nevertheless," she demurred, hesitating over the last bit of seal to look up at him, "I'm in your debt for the delivery, and in Anna's for sending—," she frowned in puzzlement at the box, "whatever she has sent. She has been very dear to send the little fripperies she finds in London markets, and I've been able to make good use of them."

"I'd not realized that the two of you were such friends."

"I believe we have become friends through our correspondence," she laughed, "if one can truly build a friendship in such fashion. She is a lovely girl. Initially, I assumed her attempts to reach out to me were simply due to her friendship with Daniel. I've become disabused of that notion, however."

"I suspect it is more a matter of reaching for a female viewpoint. Perhaps even for a mentor," he said. Momentarily unwilling to meet her gaze, he addressed the handle of his walking stick. "I've been a poor substitute for her father, I'm afraid, and could not even begin to fill the void left by her mother's death."

Many comforting and reassuring words sprang to Selah's mind but, for fear of embarrassing him, she said none of them. "Oh!" She had finally opened the box and showed delight in its contents. "How lovely!"

Wilton leaned in, his head close to hers, and peered into the box. "What on earth . . .?" The box seemed to contain nothing but fantastic colors, lustrous, gemstone hues of blue and green. But these were not emeralds and sapphires. And there were others, larger and more billowing, patterned in black and white. "Are those *feathers*?" he asked.

Selah laughed and nodded. "Peacock and ostrich feathers, to be precise. I understand they are all the rage in London for decorating everything from hats to homes. I've found them difficult to come by. In fact, I can't say that I've ever seen quite so many in one place!"

Wilton lightly stroked the downy plumes of a large ostrich feather, and then picked up one of the more colorful peacock feathers and held it aloft. He frowned with the effort of imagining how such a thing might be employed. "How extraordinary," he responded simply. Carrying one of the feathers to the window that he might examine it better in the light flooding through the glass, he held the feather up allowing the winter light to play across the iridescent colors. "I must say, it's a sight prettier than turkey feathers," he allowed. Selah's laughter startled him, coming as it did from directly behind him. He had not realized that she had followed him to the window.

Their admiration of the feather was interrupted by a boisterous crowd moving down the street, shouting their outrage over the Tea Act. Selah sighed as she watched the crowd pass the window of her shop. "How much longer can these protests go on?"

Having no answer to her question, Wilton shook his head. "Anna suspected this would be the reaction when folks here learned of the Act. I was certain she was wrong. As much as the people of Boston love their tea, I could not imagine that they would protest the introduction of a less expensive supply."

"They love their tea, but they do not like the tax. And, more than that, they do not like the manner in which that tax is being imposed."

"And so," Wilton observed, his face twisting into an expression of distaste, "those few who are unhappy have saddled all of us with the consequences of their protests — high prices, scarcity, and an undesirable trade in smuggled, equally undesirable Dutch tea. I believe it might be termed 'cutting off one's nose to spite one's face.'"

"I'm not sure I'd agree that the numbers of the unhappy could be considered only a few," Selah ventured.

"Bah!" Wilton waved the feather dismissively and strode across the shop to place it back in the box with its colorful companions. "These people have become an unreasoning pack of malcontents who will not be satisfied until they've brought us all to ruin."

"Do you truly believe that?"

Wilton stared at the box of feathers for several long seconds before he replied. "No," he sighed. "I do not. In my heart, I know that the men stirring these protests with their impassioned rhetoric have reasons that, for them, are as solid as my reasons for holding steadfast in my loyalty to the king." He looked up at her with weary eyes. "And that is what makes me the most fearful of where it all will lead."

Selah considered her response as she returned the feathers to the box. She carefully replaced the lid and let her hands linger there for a thoughtful moment. "Disagreeable though it may be," she said with a sideways look and conspiratorial smile, "I happen to have some of that Dutch tea. Would you like to join me for a cup?"

Wilton nodded and followed her to the workroom at the back of the shop. He settled himself on a chair near the hearth where he watched her as she assembled the tea things. She was a handsome woman, he thought, graceful in her every gesture and dignified in her bearing. It was impossible to reconcile the woman he was coming to know with gossip he recalled hearing many years past. She hummed softly as she worked, a little tune that made him smile with recognition.

"That's one of Anna's favorites," he told her. When she hesitated over what she'd been about to do and looked at him blankly, he hastily added, "That tune you are humming; it's one of her favorites. I hear her hum it when she works." He had to look away quickly then, because his eyes had quite inexplicably filled with tears. "I hear her hum it every day, in fact, even now — even now when she is not present."

"I know you miss her terribly."

Wilton lowered his head and stared at his hands. "More than you can imagine. I long to ask her to return home and, yet, cannot bring myself to do so because I feel London is the better place for her."

"I'm not certain she would agree with that view." She took the seat opposite him, setting the tea tray on the table between them.

"No, I know she wouldn't. As I write every letter to her, I struggle against asking her to come home."

"But don't give in to the struggle?"

He shook his head. "No. I feel it's the right thing to do, the best thing for her well-being and for her future. Before she left for London, she argued against being sent away more than she has ever argued anything, and I would not be swayed. As much as I miss her, I still feel I did the right thing to send her away — though it is, perhaps, the most painful thing I've ever had to do."

Smiling, she handed him his cup, encouraging him to keep talking. Intuition told her that Wilton was putting his feelings into words for the first time.

"When Anna's parents – my sister and her husband — died, I was overwhelmed by the prospect of having to care for a little girl. I had no concept of how to go about being a parent, no idea where even to begin. Sometimes, I feel as though I never had a childhood myself; I could not imagine what a child's world should be like."

"And yet, the person that Anna has become would indicate that you managed very well."

"Thank you for that," Wilton said. "And I hope it's true." He took a sip of his tea and grudgingly admitted that, Dutch though it may be, it was very good. "In the beginning, I was unhappy to be burdened with the responsibility of raising her and, to my shame, explored many options for passing that responsibility off to someone else."

"But, in the end, you didn't do so."

"I did not, and thank the good Lord for that. It's an amazing thing, really, that something so unwanted could become the absolute core of my universe. She has been the light of my life." He hastily wiped the tears from his eyes before looking at Selah. "And now, the light of my life is in London. I fear that leaves me in darkness."

Selah placed her cup on its saucer and loosely wrapped her fingers around it, enjoying the warmth on her hands. "It's difficult to be parted from someone you love." She spoke softly, lowering her eyes.

Wilton followed her gaze and realized that she was focused on her wedding ring. He blushed visibly. "I do apologize, Mrs. Garrett. Of course, you must miss your late husband very much. It was thoughtless of me to carry on so. I have Anna's letters, and the knowledge that I will see her again. I should not be so self-pitying."

Selah smiled. "There's no need to apologize, Mr. Wilton. I understand your sadness. You certainly have a right to it though, as you observed, it might be helpful to focus more on the things you still have, and less on those you do not."

"Indeed, I should." He drained his cup and set it on the saucer, hoping she would offer to refill it, and she did not disappoint. "If it's not too painful, would you tell me about your husband?" He watched her pour the tea, noting that her hand did not waver at the mention of her late husband.

"It's not too painful. I much prefer to remember him alive than to focus on his absence. I'm glad to be able to speak of him, and I seldom have the opportunity."

"He was a farmer, was he not?"

"He was." She laughed softly. "Not a very good farmer, I'm afraid, but it was how he chose to make a living. I believe he would have made a very good soldier, and that's probably what he should have been. Before we were married, he considered enlisting in the king's army — something that seems quite incredible to contemplate right now, I must say. But then he met me, and chose farming instead. He served with the militia in the French and Indian war, and it was injuries sustained in that war that shortened his life. He came away crippled and ill, and never fully recovered himself."

"I am sorry." Wilton hated that the only words he could think of seemed so inadequate to express his sympathy. "It must have been a difficult decision for him to leave you behind to go away to war."

She nodded. "It was. I know it was. But I also know that a part of him reveled in it. James had a soldier's instincts and courage, and the skills requisite to being a good fighter. His skill with a sword far outshone his skill with a plow, I must say." Her eyes twinkled, and her face betrayed far more pride than embarrassment. "He had an uncommon taste for adventure as well, I believe."

"He would not be the first man who relished the thrill of battle, I suspect. I believe you have every right to be proud of him."

"Oh, I am. Daniel is so much like him, though. I worry about him, about the path he will be drawn to, if the dispute with the king continues to intensify."

"I would not worry, Mrs. Garrett. When one reviews the history of our great nation, there were many occasions when such rifts have developed between the Crown and the people. They have always been mended."

"But how much blood was spilled in the mending?"

That, Wilton did not want to answer. Their conversation became less personal, and went on far longer than he had intended. The clock chimed the hour, surprising him with the number of times it sounded. "I fear I've stayed over-long." He got to his feet and, claiming his hat and cloak, made for the door.

Selah watched him and, as his hand touched the door handle, she suddenly said, "The rumors were not true, you know." When he turned to face her, she realized by his expression that he did not understand. "The rumors about myself and Mr. Healey. They were not true. He was an employer, and then a friend. That was all there ever was between us." Her voice trailed off, regretful of the outburst. She had no idea what had made her blurt out the words, without thought, mortifying herself in the process.

Wilton smiled wistfully. "I believe you, Mrs. Garrett. And, may I be so bold as to add that I've no doubt Mr. Healey would have liked to have been young enough for it to have been otherwise." He tipped his hat to her, then turned and went out into the cold afternoon.

*   *   *

Teague, watching the passage of the same group of protestors Anna's uncle and Selah Garrett had observed earlier, was filled with joy at the sight. Having very successfully insinuated himself into one of the pipelines for smuggled Dutch tea, he had benefitted mightily from the peculiar situation created by the smuggling that resulted from the prohibitive Townshend Act, as had many reputable businessmen like Hancock and Sam Adams. Now, in an effort to regain the market the smugglers had commandeered, Parliament had granted the East India Company a monopoly on tea trade in the American colonies. It allowed the company to undercut local prices, which angered the Boston merchants whose economic interests were being threatened. A duty, which was simply another way to levy taxes, was to be collected on the tea before it landed, and it was that duty payment that Sam Adams latched onto as an excuse to oppose the Act. Screaming about taxation without representation, Adams swung his propaganda machine into full-tilt. Teague had to admit that he liked the man's style.

The opposition had begun in the autumn when editorialists peppered newspapers with heated arguments, condemnations of the newly-appointed tea agents, and outright threats. The tea agents in Boston had countered with the unfortunate claim that they — not the self-styled Patriots — were the true sons of liberty. In the course of the resulting furor, the agents were called upon to publicly resign their commissions. To no one's surprise, the agents refused, prompting an outbreak of mob violence and, given that the Regulars continued to be restricted to Castle William, there was little to stop the formation or progress of angry mobs.

Toward the end of November, the *Dartmouth* arrived in Boston Harbor loaded with a large shipment of tea, closely followed by the arrival of two more tea ships. The tea remained on the ships awaiting payment of the customs duty demanded by the new law as Bostonians conspired to prevent the tea from being landed. There seemed to remain only the option of returning the tea to England, which the governor, the merchantman's owners, and the tea consignees determinedly rejected. The tension seemed to ratchet up a notch each day as the stand-off between Patriots and the tea interests continued.

On December 16, Teague's patient vigilance was rewarded when an assembly of Patriots formulated their own solution. A meeting was convened, attracting an enormous crowd to listen to a string of impassioned, inflammatory speeches. Teague watched as the crowd swelled beyond the capacity of the meeting house, forcing the assembly to be moved to a larger location. The militant atmosphere was thickening along with the crowd, and speaker after speaker fed that militancy. Finally, the talk was done and action called for.

As the meeting adjourned, Teague, Daniel, and another sixty-or-so men, faces blackened with soot and blankets wrapped about their bodies in what onlookers took as a ludicrously thin Indian disguise, found themselves being followed by a burgeoning crowd down the street toward Griffin's Wharf. Earlier, during the astonishing assembly, John Adams had referred to their planned course of action as the "intrepid exertion of popular power," a statement heartily embraced by his listeners. Now the mob was riding the wave of that consensus toward the wharf, and toward a point from which any thinking man realized there could likely be no retreat.

It surprised Teague to find Daniel at his side as they made their way along the street, for Daniel had not participated in many of the tea protests. But he was here now and the part of Teague that longed to cling to their old camaraderie was happy to have Daniel beside him. But the person Teague had become in Charlotte's company knew that his friend's presence could interfere with his carefully-laid plans for the evening. And so, he deliberately allowed increasing numbers of counterfeit Indians to come between himself and Daniel as they advanced on the wharf.

For his part, Daniel moved with the crowd, so focused on what they were about that he was unaware of Teague's having distanced himself. The size of the crowd made Daniel feel as if every one of Boston's citizens, along with all the citizens of the surrounding counties, must surely be there. The overwhelming mass of people filled streets and lanes with a rumbling of feet and voices as they progressed, and almost every one of them carried a torch. Daniel knew that the merchantmen's captains must surely be able to see the approach of the torch-bearing crowd, and imagined the greeting the mob could expect from crews who feared their ships were about to be burned. Anticipating the worst sort of violence, he steeled himself as he resolutely marched onward, but could not help looking for Teague, eager for the comfort of knowing that he and his friend would cover each other's backs in the fight. To his disappointment, Teague was nowhere to be seen.

Daniel felt relief when no musket fire greeted their first steps out onto the wharf. Indeed, though the *Dartmouth*'s crew seemed prepared for a fight as they nervously surveyed the approaching mob, there were no muskets in evidence. A man emerged from the mob's ranks and walked toward the ship's captain, arms extended so as to appear non-threatening. The emissary's identity was carefully concealed under his hat and cloak, and that fact seemed to give the *Dartmouth*'s captain pause. The two men met at the top of the gangplank and Daniel, who was only paces away, heard the cloaked man offer reassurances that there was no intent to damage either the *Dartmouth* or its crew. This assurance being received, the captain wisely chose to stand aside, ordering his crew to do the same.

The Patriots poured onto the merchantman quickly and with little conversation. There was more noise coming from the crowd of spectators along the docks than from the marauders, Daniel thought, for these men were all about the business at hand. Who knew whether or not any troops would be sent from Castle William to fend off this attack, or how long they might take to arrive? With focused efficiency, the Patriots swarmed down the gangway into the merchantman's hold. Lamps were lit, and the strongest men brought their muscle to bear on the large, rough wooden crates that housed and protected the elaborately carved and painted Chinese tea chests inside. They shifted the crates into position and looked up through the hatch, waiting. On deck, a group of men undertook the task of swinging the block and tackle that would enable them to raise the large crates up from the merchantman's hold. They lowered slings to the men waiting in the hold and, once a crate was secured, went to work raising it to the deck.

Daniel was helping to shift the crates into position. The work was back-breaking, and he began to wish he had not been so adamant that Drum not take part in the night's dangerous adventure. One man, a merchant unaccustomed to this sort of work, cursed when his hand was painfully caught between two of the crates. Farther back in the hold, the pained oath of another man was immediately followed by a loud crash. The distinctive aroma of tea filled the hold, telling them all that one of the crates had broken open.

Though it was a frigid winter night, the ship's hold was oppressively warm, the air lifeless and stifling. Daniel frequently wiped at his sweating brow with his sleeve, leaving a dark, sooty smear from shoulder to elbow. The *Dartmouth* rocked almost imperceptibly on the calm harbor water, and he could hear timbers creaking all around him as though the ship protested this disturbance in its hold.

Before long, the inexperienced crew of marauders managed to foul the pulley and drop another chest. The men below jumped back, cursing those up on deck. They struggled to get another crate into position and stood well back as it began to rise from the floor. Daniel could hear the squeak of the pulley, and the creak of the massive ropes that worked to haul the heavy crate up to the deck. The men were surprised to see the crate rise swiftly and smoothly, and even more surprised when they looked up and saw that some of the *Dartmouth*'s crew had decided to assist the bungling Patriot marauders. Daniel and the other men looked at each other, not certain what to think or say. One of the men shrugged. "Guess they were afraid those botchers up there'd damage their ship if they didn't help out."

On deck, Teague watched as crate after crate was raised out of the hold. He was part of the group of men tasked with opening the crates and then transporting the smaller tea chests to the merchantman's sides where, to cheers from those watching from shore and exclamations of astonishment from the *Dartmouth*'s crew, the chests were unceremoniously dumped over the rails into the water. Dimly illuminated by the torch-carrying crowd assembled on shore, the wooden tea chests bobbed on the water, bumping against the *Dartmouth*'s black hull and waiting for the tide to pull them out of the harbor. There were so many that it looked as if a man could walk across the water by using them as stepping stones.

Teague helped, but mostly he watched and waited for the right moment to launch his own plan. The chests were beginning to stack up, and the deck was a swarm of activity with men moving in every direction, desperate to empty the *Dartmouth*'s hold before troops began to arrive. Once assured that everyone was fully engaged in the process so that his own actions would be overlooked, he took up one of the tea chests and, struggling slightly under the weight, made his way to the farthest point of the stern on the opposite side of the ship from where all other activity was occurring. Balancing the chest on the rail, he glanced over before toppling the chest into the water. Then, he retraced his steps and repeated the process several times over.

Unseen by Teague, Daniel had climbed from below deck just in time to witness his final trip to the stern. Something about Teague's actions raised his suspicions, so he waited until Teague had returned to the main deck, then darted directly to the spot where he had seen Teague dispose of the last chest. He leaned over, searching the water below. Ripples in the dark water were only barely visible where they picked up a glimmer of reflected light. He stared, searching, until he thought he could just make out an irregular shape, obscure against the darkness, moving away from the ship. In short order, a thin sliver of light appeared, the pattern of a shielded lantern throwing light into the path of a rowboat pulling away from the ship. Anger welled in his chest, and he pushed off the rail to return to the main deck.

It did not take him long to spot Teague, alone, heading down the gangplank toward the wharf. Daniel broke into a run, dodging men and crates as he made to follow. He scurried down the gangplank, skidding onto the damp dock when he reached the bottom. His first inclination was to catch Teague and confront him. Thinking as he ran, however, he decided instead to shadow Teague and learn the full-measure of his scheme. Teague was uncharacteristically incautious, making the following an easy matter.

The trail took him first to a public stable Daniel knew well for he used it as a place to board the horse Hancock had loaned him. Teague had a small dray of the type favored for use at the warehouses ready and waiting there for him. The wagon bore markings indicating that it belonged to Martin Ainsworth. Once Teague cleared out of the shed, Daniel roused his dozing horse, hastily fitted the mare with a hackamore and, not bothering with a saddle, slung himself up onto the bare back and nudged the animal out into the night.

Guessing at Teague's likely path was easy enough, and Daniel soon drew within sight of him following the shoreline north and inland along the river. The shore was dotted with myriad points at which a small boat could surreptitiously land, and Daniel had little doubt that one of those was Teague's destination.

Snow had fallen earlier in the day, and the clouds threatened more. The wind, which came in frosty gusts, lifted the snow from drifts along the road and carried it in wispy tendrils across his path. Snow that had accumulated in barren tree branches sometimes sifted down onto him, dusting his dark hat and shoulders like sugar. The road was crossed in places by tiny streams, trickles of melted run-off with frost-limned edges that suggested it would not be long before they were frozen solid.

He trailed Teague into the night until, finally, Teague steered the dray off the main road and onto a narrow track through a spinney of trees toward the water. Daniel could now guess exactly where he was headed. It was a spot the two of them had used often over the years for various purposes, with a gentle, easy slope to the water and good shallows for beaching a small boat. Daniel sharply reined his horse away from the oyster shell road and cut a diagonal path toward that point, moving steadily until he judged himself to be within a hundred yards or less. There, he left his horse and continued on foot, following a deer trail that cut through the trees and opened onto a rocky grade leading down to the gravel beach.

He could smell and hear the water before he saw it, the gentle waves coming off the river to lap at the shore. Keeping to the low scrub, crouching, he moved forward. Overhead in the night sky, the clouds were thinning, allowing the dimmest glow of moonlight to wash over the scene. It was not much light, but it was enough to show the outline of the wagon bumping and swaying toward the water's edge.

Daniel looked out across the river and had little trouble locating the boat for which Teague was waiting. A shielded lantern sat in the bow, its light cutting starkly across the rippling water toward the shore. Teague lit his own lantern and directed its light out as a beacon to guide the boatman. As the boat neared the shore, Teague waded out to help the boatman beach his small craft, and the two of them exchanged greetings and conversation, the tone of which reached Daniel, but not the words. The boatman hopped ashore and began to help Teague move their cargo from the boat to the dray.

Soon enough, the two men were parting company, the boatman returning to his small boat, and Teague climbing up onto the seat of the wagon. He shook out the reins and the dray stuttered and lurched until its wheels were clear of the depressions they had made in the soft sand.

Fighting his way up the slope and along the overgrown deer path, Daniel scrambled through the woods and back to his horse. He swung up into the saddle just in time to hear the dray roll past his hiding place and waited to emerge from the woods until he was certain Teague would not be able to see him if he looked back. He kept to the verge until he was beyond the oyster shell paving, then angled back onto the road. His horse, appreciating the firmer footing and clear path offered by hard-packed dirt, tossed its head in eagerness to pick up the pace, but Daniel kept a restraining grip on the reins. As long as he could hear the wagon rolling along on the road ahead of him, he had no need to follow closely enough to be detected.

With Daniel following at a discreet distance, the dray lumbered on until it reached a fork in the road. Teague took the inland fork, a narrow road that cut between fields Daniel knew were there but could not see. He caught the sound of an owl hooting from time to time and occasionally heard the shrill cry of rodents that had fallen prey to the night hunters, but he saw none of it. There was only empty darkness all around.

And yet, the road was familiar to him. Though he could not see through the darkness, he knew what every field looked like, knew where every farmhouse stood. He knew when they would pass the enormous rogue apple tree that loomed over a bend in the road, probably planted two generations earlier by a squirrel or bird, and left to its own devices these many years until it had become a landmark. He knew all of this because he had spent the earliest years of his life in the area and had visited from time to time since. With a sinking feeling, he suspected he knew as well exactly where Teague was going, and the realization fueled his anger all the more. He turned his horse off the road and cut a path across a wide, fallow field, moving slowly until he was within sight of the abandoned farmhouse, ghost-grey in the moonlight. He dismounted and tethered his horse, and then closed the last fifty yards on foot.

Every time he came here, he expected the house to be gone. He thought it would have burned, or succumbed to a storm, or, derelict that it was, might simply have collapsed of its own accord. It was the house in which he'd been born, the house in which his father had died, and he wondered if he would miss it when it was no more. Following Mr. Healey's advice, his mother had used money she could ill afford to hold onto ownership of the property. Her reasons for doing so baffled him, especially when she stated that one of those reasons was that he might one day want to take up the property for himself. The picture of himself as a farmer was beyond his mind's ability to imagine, however.

The house was small and square, sturdily built by a man who understood little about aesthetics, but a great deal about practicality and endurance. Originally, a covered porch spanned the front of the house, though that had long since collapsed. A door, which surprised Daniel by still being in place, bisected the front façade and was flanked on either side by perfectly balanced windows. There had been glass in them at one time, but that was long ago. Now, they were boarded up — something his mother had insisted he do some years earlier — giving the house a blind look. The wall on the right-hand side of the house was taller than that on the left so that the roof slanted instead of forming a peak. It made the house look like an oversized shed, but it was easier for a man possessing only limited carpentry skills to manage, and it did effectively shed rain and snow.

Initially, the house was painted yellow with white shutters. It had stood out, eye-catching against the surrounding fields, boldly proclaiming the love of the man who had built it for his new wife, and daring anyone to challenge their right to build a life together. Now, paint faded to a somber, weathered gray, it seemed to Daniel that the house was in mourning for the man who had put so much love into its building.

Daniel approached the house with particular stealth but soon realized that the extra care had not been necessary. Teague, who had hung a lantern on a hook mounted to the wall just outside the back door, was so absorbed in the process of unloading his plunder that he would not have noticed Daniel if he had ridden up on his horse. The back door to the small house stood open, and the wagon was backed up flush against its frame. Teague had ingeniously fashioned a small loading dock that stood just inside the door, its platform on a level with the wagon bed. From the platform, a ramp extended downward into the interior of the house. The arrangement enabled Teague to unload even large crates without help because he would never have to actually lift them. He could slide them out of the wagon bed onto the platform, and then slide them down the ramp into the house.

Daniel circled the house and slipped in through the front door. Every time he returned there, he was amazed that the house was so much smaller than he remembered. There were essentially only two rooms. One half of the house was a long, combined living and kitchen space that ran in an unbroken line from the front door to the back. The other half of the house was a small bedroom that his parents had used, with a tiny loft space above. That was where he had slept, directly under the eaves where, had it not been for the pains to which his father had gone to turn the space into a cozy cocoon for his son, Daniel would have felt the chill of every draft.

It was especially chilly now. Though he entered and quickly closed the door behind him, the draft of air flowing from the front to the open back door was enough to make the lamps Teague had lit gutter. Daniel froze in place, expecting the flickering light to get Teague's attention, but it did not. He was in the middle of maneuvering the last tea chest down the ramp, and that endeavor had his full attention. Quietly, Daniel took several steps into the room, looking about him as he went. There were assorted crates and boxes scattered everywhere, some of them opened to reveal their contents. He spotted a china tea set, a few bolts of silk, two swords with inlaid scabbards of the type British officers carried, every manner of silver toilet article, and six meerschaum pipes arranged in a velvet-lined case. One corner of the room was stacked with wooden crates and barrels that he recognized as containing munitions. He was staring at the cache of weapons when Teague finally noticed him.

"Your parents' old house turned out to be useful after all," Teague said, grinning and looking about him proudly. He seemed to think that insouciance would forestall Daniel's anger. "I couldn't dig a pit like farmer Johnson has, but this is even better."

"Have you lost your mind? It's bad enough that you have apparently been stealing on a quite grand scale — but, to hide it all *here*! How could you do this?"

"What's wrong with hiding it here? No one ever comes here; no one's going to find it."

"You don't know that. If the Regulars start searching, which they may well do if many more of their supplies go missing, do you think they'll pass this place by because no one lives here?"

Teague shrugged. "Even if they do find it, there's naught to link it to me."

"There is a great deal to link it to me, though!" Full of exasperation, Daniel's voice went up in pitch. "And to my mother!"

"But you don't live here, Daniel," Teague pointed out reassuringly. "Anyone could have put this here."

Ready to tear at his hair, Daniel turned about, surveying the amassed plunder. "You told me you weren't going to steal anymore. You said you were through with all of that."

Teague shrugged. "I changed my mind." When Daniel stared at him in wordless fury, he sauntered over and perched on the edge of a barrel of musket balls. "There's money to be made out of all this unrest, and you're a fool if you don't take advantage of it."

"All of this unrest, as you call it, is not about making money, Teague."

"Isn't it? Do you really think all those men you're so fond of listening to now don't care about making money? At the end of the day, that's what they're really after. Hancock and the rest of them, all of their high-sounding talk just comes down to protecting their own self-interest and increasing their own wealth. They don't care about people like you and me. They care about how much gold is in their pockets. Wherever all of this leads, the bottom line for people like you and me is that the rich will get richer and our lot will be the same as it has always been, if not worse."

"You're wrong. It isn't just about the money. That's part of it, but there's more. It's about demanding our due. It's about defending our rights as Englishmen."

Teague snorted derisively. "Our rights? Our due? The only rights we have are those the king and Parliament choose to give us."

"And we should have a voice in that."

"The only men with rights are the men with money, Daniel. You know that. The notion that the rest of us have any say in the matter is an illusion." His statement was met with only a hard look, which angered him. "The king and his English nobles will always have us dancing to their tune because they have money and power. Now I see an opportunity to at least get some of that money for myself and, from where I stand, I'd be a fool not to grab that opportunity."

"Dumping that tea in the harbor was supposed to be a protest, Teague. It wasn't about personal gain."

"Do you think all of those crates are going to be allowed to just float out to sea?" he scoffed. "At their first opportunity, every man in Boston who can manage it will be out on the water trying to capture one or two for themselves! I just made sure I got my share, that's all."

"And you used those of us who were there on principle for cover. If anyone else had seen you, it would have made a sham of the whole thing."

"Principles my arse. I'm tired of hearing about your principles! You can't eat principles, and you can't wear them to keep warm."

"Don't you ever get tired of the smallness of our lives? Don't you ever want your life to count for more? Don't you want your life to be about more than just survival?"

"Of course I do," Teague laughed. "That's what I've been trying to tell you. I see a chance to buy myself a better life, and I intend to take it."

Daniel shook his head. "I don't want to sneak in through the back door, Teague. I want to go in with my head held up, knowing I worked as hard to get there and have as much right to be there as everyone else in the room."

"Well, friend, if that's what you want out of all of this, I'd say you have changed boats in mid-ocean. That's a few steps beyond wanting fair representation in Parliament."

"I haven't changed anything. It's what I've always felt. It's what most men feel. We should be able to achieve that if our voices are heard."

"When did you become such a gullible fool? Maybe in heaven a man is rewarded for his hard work, but there's no place on earth where a man's destiny isn't decided by what family he's born into. Dumping a bunch of tea into a harbor sure as hell isn't going to change that."

"Dumping tea in the harbor gets the attention of those who have us under their thumb. Once we have their attention, maybe we can get them to see that the old ways don't work for us anymore."

"Getting their attention is more likely to get you hung."

"And stealing from them will most certainly get you shot. What do you think the redcoats will do with you if they find these muskets?"

Teague shrugged. "They won't find them."

Daniel raised his hands in the air, exasperated. "I don't know how to talk to you anymore. You're not capable of meeting me on rational ground."

"*Rational ground?*" Teague sneered at him. "From where I stand, your position looks about as irrational as it gets! Wake up Daniel. You're so caught up in those high-sounding speeches Adams and Hancock and the rest make that you can't see straight. They will push and push until the king has enough, and then they'll all hang. That's where they're headed, and they're dragging you with them."

"And where are you headed, Teague?" Daniel's anger was bubbling to the surface. "With all this money you're trying to accumulate, where do you think it will take you? Do you think Charlotte Ainsworth's father will suddenly find you acceptable because you have money in your pocket? Is that what this is about? Or maybe you think Charlotte will run away with you and pretend with you that you aren't buying your new life with stolen money." He was startled by the expression on Teague's face. "Oh, dear God," he murmured, taking a step back. "That is what you are thinking, isn't it? You think she will run away with you?"

Teague's jaw was flexing, and his eyes narrowed with building anger. "Leave her out of this, Daniel. You've told me often enough what you think of Charlotte, and I don't want to hear it again."

Daniel turned his back for a moment and paced about the room, sorting through the myriad thoughts that were suddenly tangling his mind. Abruptly, and full of focus, he stepped toward Teague. "Has she actually told you that she will go away with you?" His gaze was penetrating, as though he thought that if he looked carefully, he could see into his friend's mind, could see just how deep he had gotten himself into this nightmare.

"As a matter of fact, she has." Teague tried to sound offhand, but the defensiveness shone through, nonetheless.

"She won't go through with it." Daniel made the statement flatly, without any suggestion of doubt. "Or, if she does, it will be for her own purpose. She's using you, Teague. Can you not see that? She has some purpose in mind, and she is using you to obtain it. And once she has achieved that purpose, she will discard you."

"You're wrong. We love each other."

Daniel's laugh was sharp. "Love? Charlotte Ainsworth loves things, and she loves places. She does not love people. She doesn't know how."

"I won't stand here and let you talk about her that way."

"Why? Because you think she actually has some honor worth defending? I can tell you for a fact that she does not. And whatever sweet words she has said to you, whatever intimacies she has allowed you, I can assure you she has shared the same with others."

"Stop, Daniel. I'm warning you. Stop now."

"Shall I tell you the things she has whispered in my ear, Teague? Shall we compare to see if she sings the same song every time, or if she changes her tune to suit each new audience?"

Teague erupted. Launching himself forward, he took a swing at Daniel that would have knocked him to the floor had Daniel not managed to dodge the blow. Daniel turned quickly, guard up, but making no move toward Teague. "I do not want to fight you," he maintained.

"Why not?" Teague's expression was full of contempt. "Because you know I can beat you? Because you're afraid I'll show that I'm the better man?"

"Because we're friends."

"No longer." He swung again, only to find himself off balance when his swing connected with nothing but air, for Daniel had ducked again and darted to one side. Teague's frustration and anger were mounting, and his chest heaved with the effort of containing it.

"Stop it, Teague," Daniel said levelly. "I am not going to fight you."

When Teague turned on him again, Daniel was stunned to see a pistol in his hand. Carefully, he brought it to bead on Daniel. So overwhelming was his anger, however, that he could not manage to hold it steady.

"What?" Daniel asked, trying to look calmer than he felt. "Have you truly lost all reason? Are you going to shoot me? Are you going to *kill* me because I insulted Charlotte?" He managed an incredulous tone and forced himself to not look at the pistol.

"You high-handed pile of hog slurry. I'm going to kill you because I'm sick of you. I'm sick of the way you treat me, sick of your superior attitude. You have no right to govern my life, but you always manage to have everything your way, and I'm sick of it!"

"Do you hear yourself? Where did all of this come from? Did Charlotte put it into your head?"

"She didn't put anything in my head! I've felt this way for a long time. I've finally decided to do something about it, that's all."

"Do you hear how absurd that sounds? You think I'm too imperious, so you are going to *kill* me?"

"It isn't absurd to me."

"What do you want from me, Teague?" He waved his arms in vexation. "Do you want me to say it's all right with me if you go on stealing? I won't, because I care about you and I don't want to see you suffer when you get caught. Do you want me to say I think it's wonderful that you have fallen in love with Charlotte? I won't, because I don't want to see you hurt and I know that's the only thing that can come of it."

"I want you out of my life. That's what I want."

"Then, you shall have it." Daniel held up his hands in a gesture of surrender. "I'll walk away and let you be. But you will find another place to hide your stolen goods. I'll not have you use this house."

"I suppose you'll leave here and go straight to your new friends to tell them where they can find a cache of muskets and powder?"

"No. I have no desire to do that." He turned his back and had taken one step toward the door when he heard the click of the pistol hammer. Whether because he heeded the warning and fell to the ground, or because Teague's aim was shaky, the musket ball whizzed harmlessly past him. The ball struck the corner of a wooden crate, showering Daniel with splinters. Before the smoke had cleared, he was on his feet.

He flew at Teague, putting his full weight and momentum behind his charge toward Teague's body. Driving his shoulder into Teague's abdomen, he shoved him to the ground, knocking the wind out of him and momentarily dazing him. Taking advantage of the small opportunity, Daniel sat straddling Teague and pounded his face three times before Teague regained his senses enough to fend off the blows. He blocked one fist, then the other, then shot his own fist up, jabbing at Daniel's windpipe with as much force as he could manage. Gasping for air, Daniel reflexively relaxed his pressure on Teague, allowing him enough of a margin to shove free and spring to his feet.

Teague's face was bloodied and every bone hurt from the force of being thrown to the floor. Just about any other man would have given up, but he was stoked with pent up rage. Daniel was still on his knees before him, an easy target for Teague's furious kick straight to the center of his back. The blow sent Daniel sprawling and Teague immediately set upon him, relentlessly pounding every vulnerable spot until his own fists were on fire with pain. When Daniel stopped trying to shake him off and lay unmoving, Teague got to his feet and stumbled about looking for something to use as a weapon.

Daniel rolled onto his back and, through the bright pricks of light dotting his vision, saw Teague pick up a broken staff. He watched his friend move toward him, testing the weight of the shaft in his hand, swinging it like a club. Daniel could barely focus and every breath hurt. Teague stood over him and swung down with his club, aiming for Daniel's head, but Daniel rolled to the side, leaving the staff to strike the floor with a jarring thud. Daniel reached out and grasped the end of the staff, jerking it toward him and out of Teague's hands. The unexpected action pulled Teague slightly off balance, and he stumbled forward.

To Teague's astonishment, Daniel was quickly on his feet and swinging the staff toward his head. Teague dodged the first swing, but was caught by surprise by the quickness with which Daniel immediately brought the staff up again to smash into Teague's face. The blow broke Teague's nose, turned his lips to pulp, and sent him staggering backwards against a crate of muskets. Daniel finished him with a strike of the staff to his midsection. Teague doubled-over, retching and gasping for breath, and could do nothing to defend himself as Daniel advanced on him.

But Daniel did not strike again. Instead, he leaned his face close to Teague's and, his words ragged with pain and emotion, said, "You will clear everything out of this house. I am quit of you." Daniel used what little strength he still possessed to toss the staff across to the far side of the room. It crashed against the wall and clattered to the ground. Teague heard it, and watched through swollen eyelids as his friend walked out the door.

1774

CHAPTER TEN

Teague would have liked to crawl to Charlotte for comfort, but he was in so much pain that he could only slink into his own cot where he lay, unaided, for almost two days. Drum had not returned to their rented room, and Teague could only surmise that Daniel had taken Drum to live with him. He was alone for the first time since Daniel had come into his life, and that thought was far more painful than any of his physical injuries. That it was a matter of his own doing escaped him.

As soon as he could be on his feet long enough to tackle the job, he cleared the contents out of Daniel's old house and moved all of it to an abandoned shack a mile or so farther west of the Garrett property. The part of him that festered with resentment would have liked to thumb his nose at Daniel and leave everything exactly where it was. But he knew Daniel's retaliation would be steel-toothed, so he did as Daniel had ordered, rankling all the while over the fact that he could not shake his habit of doing as Daniel bid.

By the time Teague went to see Charlotte, his bruises had healed to some extent, and the version of the story that was told cast Daniel as an unreasonable villain who had provoked the fight. Charlotte had said nothing when Teague strode across the parlor to avail himself of a glass of her father's port. He had, for some time, taken the liberty of helping himself to the decanter without waiting for an invitation. In silence, she watched him drain one glass, then pour another. Teague had been pacing back and forth for several long minutes, railing against Daniel for his high-handedness, ranting about how he would repay him for the affront, and still Charlotte watched in silence, waiting for the worst of the storm to pass.

She had seen these tantrums before, and knew it would do her no good to try to speak with him before he had spent some of his furious energy. Despite his volatility, Teague was easy enough to master and manipulate. In her head, she was already formulating the soothing words she would say to calm him, the righteous indignation she would express, and the verbal salve she would apply to his wounded ego until, pumped up with her carefully placed words and affections, he would be malleable to even her most extreme suggestion.

It was critical, she knew, that she take firm control of the situation. He was hurt and angry now, but eventually he would regret his rift with Daniel. If she did not step firmly and completely into the vacuum left by his argument with Daniel, she knew that Teague would eventually swing back to the strong wind of Daniel's influence. That, she could not have. For the moment, Teague was her most viable means to a more desirable life, and she had no intention of allowing Daniel Garrett's principles to derail that. As she watched Teague pace, she carefully gauged the situation, deciding how best to reel him in and secure him to her cause once and for all. She was grateful that her father would be in Cambridge and would not return until after dinner, allowing her to take her time over the course she envisioned.

"My poor, darling Teague." Her cooing was full of warmth and understanding. "Come and sit beside me." Smiling her most munificent smile, she patted the place on the divan where she wanted him to sit. "I am sorry he has treated you so badly. The two of you have been friends for such a long time; I know it hurts you deeply for him to behave this way." She packed into her tone all the gentle sympathy she could muster and delicately laid her hand over his. Sighing as though a great disillusionment had been visited upon her, she sat in silence, ostensibly weighing some difficult notion, before continuing. "It seems apparent that he did not value your friendship as much as you valued his."

The words pierced Teague's heart with cold jaggedness, for the very thought had occurred to him as well. Unable to conceive of any wrong-doing on his own part, Teague looked at what had passed between himself and Daniel through a narrow, distorted lens. Daniel, it seemed, had used their friendship until he had no more need, then cast it all aside with stunning ease. If any part of him argued against this interpretation, Charlotte's words quashed the notion.

"I believe it was just a matter of time before this happened." Charlotte was speaking gently, but a slight firmness had come into her tone, a conveyance of the world's harsh realities and inevitabilities, as though she'd been burdened with explaining to a child why his puppy had died. "You have lived so long in his shadow. But you are your own man. I believe it was unavoidable that, when your moment came to claim the respect and equality in your relationship that is your right, Daniel would fight it."

Teague liked her words, felt heartened by them. He enjoyed the idea that she saw him in such a light, and particularly liked the slight to Daniel. Even now, the impression that she had once been far more interested in Daniel than in himself haunted him, stoking his uncertainties and jealousies with a generous measure of bitterness. Her next words were further balm for that festering jealousy, and on hearing them, his heart picked up a beat.

"Daniel's vanity and childish self-centeredness won't allow him to accept anyone else sharing his place in the sun," she sniffed. "To my mind, it explains his attachment to Drum. With Drum, he can always be in charge. But you are not Drum. I've watched the two of you for so long, and I was always amazed that you allowed yourself to be ground down under Daniel's boot. You've been a very patient and good friend, my darling Teague. Far more so than he has deserved."

He stared at her hand where it rested, watched her thumb slowly, lightly stroking the back of his knuckles. Against his own rough, nut-brown skin, her pale coloring seemed even more polished and marble-like. Her fingers, where they touched his, felt cool, but the stroking motion of her thumb was creating in him a subtle warmth, the smallest flame, like the tiny first flickers at the base of a pile of kindling.

"You are as much a man as he is — far more so, in fact — with just as much right to make your own choices and decisions." Her tone had shifted from compassion to indignation, carrying him along with it. "I cannot blame you for wanting to shed his authority. Why, it's rather ironic when you think on it! Daniel and his new friends complain about their treatment at the hands of the king, and yet he treats you much the way they complain of being treated!"

"I tried to tell him that very thing," Teague agreed, "but he wouldn't listen."

"No, I don't suppose he did." She resettled herself slightly closer to him. "Now you have as much reason to want to leave Boston as I do. You can start over fresh without his shadow looming over you, without him disapproving and criticizing everything you do. I admit that I'm somewhat relieved. I've been so afraid you would abandon me and would choose to stay here with him. Now my mind and my heart can be so much more at ease."

She seemed to consider the matter settled, though Teague felt far less certain. His head agreed with her assertion that he had no real ties to Boston; his heart was another matter. However angry Teague might be with him, Daniel represented the only family he had ever known. He raised his eyes to meet Charlotte's watery gaze.

"We will build a new family together," she vowed softly, her hands enveloping his as she spoke, her tone soothing him into ductility. "You and me. Two people who can count on each other always!"

Teague stared at her, momentarily overcome by the irrational notion that she had read his mind. But then, her words made their way to their target, and he could have cried with the emotion of their impact. "Yes," he said hoarsely. "Yes. I'll take you wherever you want to go. I'll do whatever it takes, and we will leave here. Together."

*   *   *

Anna was going to hell. She believed that with great conviction. Or, if not hell, then most assuredly not heaven. She wished she had paid more attention in church so that she might have an inkling of her likely destination and whether or not there was something she could do to

ameliorate her punishment. All she knew for certain was that she had told a
lie — or had told the same lie twice, to be more specific, which probably
carried an even greater penalty. Knowing that Sir Gregory and Lady
Eugenie would never allow her to travel back to Boston without her uncle's
consent, Anna had shown them a fabricated letter from an imaginary friend
indicating that her uncle was very ill, and asserting that it would be a good
idea for Anna to return as soon as possible. It was a terrible, but effective,
deception.

Then, after obtaining names of passengers who had already booked
places on suitable ships to Boston, Anna further compounded her sin by
telling the same story to the Reverend and Mrs. Mosely, a Methodist
minister and his wife, in order to persuade them to allow her to travel in
their company. The lies were necessary, she told herself, that she might
provide a chaperone sufficient to Lady Eugenie's standards. Lady Eugenie
did not approve of Methodists, but a clergyman of any sort being preferable
to no chaperone at all, she had relented. Thinking on Mr. Hinton's
admonition regarding "ends" and "means," it did not escape her that she
was off to a very poor start in terms of heeding his advice.

It was early March, six long months since she had first hatched her bold
plan to return home, and she stood aboard the merchantman *Sheridan*
contemplating the future of her soul. The *Sheridan* had limited
accommodation for passengers, and would be sailing for Boston in the
company of two other merchantmen. Without the westerly winds filling
their sails, the trip was likely to be interminably long, but the captain
seemed confident that they would be in Boston by June.

Space for personal belongings was scant, so she had arranged for several
trunks to be transported on a later ship. The moment she had learned what
ship she would sail on, she had posted a letter to Daniel asking that he
collect her at the dock, and asking that he say nothing to her uncle. It was a
sketchy plan, hastily cobbled together and full of potential for disaster, but
Anna did not care. She was going home.

There was one more wrinkle that made her prompt departure
imperative. When the captains of the ships whose tea had been dumped
into Boston harbor in December returned to London, they had been
summoned to appear before the Privy Counsel. Their testimony created a
furor. Demands were issued that the city of Boston make restitution to the
East India Company and, to everyone's astonishment, those demands were
rebuffed. Just before Anna departed for Boston, a decree was issued that
Boston's harbor would be closed until Bostonians compensated the East
India Company for its losses. The *Sheridan* and ships like it would be
allowed into port only because it carried supplies for the army at Castle
William.

Anna was frantic with worry. Closing the harbor meant food supplies would be cut off. There would be no trade, no fishing, no movement of goods whatsoever through the harbor, and Anna could not imagine how the city could endure. She also knew enough about the agitators to know that their pride, stubbornness, and unwavering devotion to their principles would not let them back down. Closing the port could, she feared, only lead to more violence.

Eager to be on her way home, Anna had boarded well before any of the other passengers. Despite her efforts to keep her baggage to a minimum, her equipage included an enormous trunk, courtesy of Lady Sylvia who, judging by the many gifts packed in the trunk, apparently thought Anna would suffer considerable deprivation once away from London. Upon stepping aboard, she was surprised to find herself standing in front of the ship's Captain, who was taking a very dim view of the large trunk.

Ezra Stone was an old Royal Navy captain with a marked lack of taste for the devastating yardarm-to-yardarm fighting that characterized so many naval battles, and to whom the greater rewards and autonomy of private enterprise had appealed. A man with abundant skill at navigating the oceans but little at charting the treacherous shoals of naval politics, Stone was comfortable with his cumbrous merchantman and absence of oversight. His employer cared that the cargoes were delivered on time, and how Stone went about achieving that was his own affair.

This was not to say that the captain had left behind all of the discipline and exactitude of his naval days. When it came to sailing, the ship's crew was able and efficient, and it was made clear to all hands that any sort of failure at one's duty would be met with harsh retribution. Everything on the *Sheridan* was flawlessly maintained, every detail checked and re-checked, and nothing escaped the captain's eye.

He greeted Anna with a sardonic expression, quickly turning her over to the cabin boy with the order that the youngster show her to her cabin. To Stone's way of thinking, female passengers were emphatically undesirable and the fact that he would have two on this crossing was not setting well with him. The cabin boy, who went by the mundane name of George Smith, touched his forelock in quick deference to Anna before taking off down the main deck toward a narrow companionway and disappearing before her eyes like a rabbit down its hole.

The boy was cursed with a spindly, misshapen body, but it seemed to hinder his mobility about the ship not a whit. They made their way through the dark, crowded passage to the stern cabins, which were arranged across the breadth of what had once been the gun deck. Anna was assigned the cabin on the starboard side, the Reverend and Mrs. Mosely would be in the center cabin, and the captain berthed in the larboard cabin.

The *Sheridan*, a three-masted barque, had begun its life under another name in the French navy. On only its first foray into open sea, the ship was captured by a British privateer with the intent of selling it to the Royal Navy. To his surprise, however, a better offer came from a private investor who needed a quick replacement for one of his merchant ships. And so, renamed *Sheridan*, the ship's gun ports were sealed and its lower decks reconfigured to offer a grudging bit of passenger accommodation and generous space for more profitable cargo.

None of this seemed as important to Anna as the fact that the ship was considerably larger than the tea ship on which she had made the crossing from Boston. The larger ship would, she hoped, handle rough seas a bit better, and her compartment, tiny though it was, seemed capacious when compared with her accommodations on the tea ship. Though she had developed a certain fondness for the gentle sway of the rope hammock in which she slept on the tea ship, the cot in her compartment aboard the *Sheridan* was an improvement if for no other reason than it doubled as a place to sit.

Having been told that passengers were not allowed back on the main deck until the *Sheridan* was underway, Anna remained in her closet-like cabin, arranging her belongings as best she could manage. The large trunk and two hatboxes, which were a gift from Lady Sylvia, took up a good deal of space and were promising to be a constant obstacle in the small cabin. The trunk and boxes had unexpectedly arrived at the door just as she was departing for the ship, along with a note from Lady Sylvia stating that Anna was to take the gifts with her, and no more to be said about it. Lady Eugenie had stared at the trunk as though Pandora's box had suddenly landed in her marble foyer. Overwhelmed with curiosity and more than a little jealousy that Anna had garnered such a gift, Lady Eugenie clearly wanted Anna to open the mysterious trunk so they could all view the contents. But showing a pertinacious streak that would have heartily amused Lady Sylvia, Anna had not done so.

Now, alone in her cabin, Anna started with the hat boxes. One contained just what it appeared to contain — a pretty summer hat that had probably cost Lady Sylvia a significant amount. The second box contained not a hat, but a beautiful china tea set, carefully packed in straw. *"I doubt,"* Lady Sylvia had written on the enclosed note, *"that the ship on which you leave us will be equipped with a single cup or teapot worthy of the name, so I send these along."* It was signed "Lady S.," and carried the post script that a supply of good English tea could be found in the trunk.

Anna held her breath as she opened the trunk, and then could only stand and gape at the contents. Layer upon layer of treasures and delicacies were packed inside with an admirable level of efficiency and precision, wasting not an iota of space, each item carefully wrapped in waxed papers or oiled cloth, presumably as protection against the sea air. In addition to the promised supply of tea, the top layers contained numerous tins of biscuits and hard candies, waxed packages of dried fruits, an array of olives and pickled vegetables, and comfit in carefully sealed packets. There were a dozen deliciously fragranced soaps, and several boxes of perfectly-formed beeswax candles.

Without actually removing anything, for she knew she would never be able to repack it all so proficiently, she burrowed down and discovered a blanket and a shawl of the finest, softest wool, and a pair of needlepoint slippers. Peering into the small gaps created by her rooting, she spotted a roll of lace, and another of colorful velvet ribbons, an entire box of elegant stationery engraved with Anna's initials, and a silver-backed mirror, hairbrush, and comb. Her fingers found several small boxes, the contents of which she decided to explore later, and a number of expensively-bound books.

At the very bottom of the trunk, she could feel two flat bolts of cloth, one silk and one velvet, and a small velvet purse, which she fished out of the trunk. To her utter astonishment, the drawstring bag held one-hundred gold sovereigns. She could not recall ever having seen so many of the precious gold coins at one time and knew for certain that she had never possessed such a large sum of money. Her breath was taken away by Lady Sylvia's inexplicable generosity and replaced by anxiety over the responsibility engendered by possession of the large amount of money.

Hastily, she returned the coins to the bag, pulled the drawstrings tight and knotted them, then buried the little treasure back in the depths of the trunk, snaking her arm down through the layers until she reached the bottom. She removed a tin of biscuits and a tin of hard candy, closed the trunk and refastened the straps, then sat on her cot, tins of treats clutched to her bosom, and stared at the trunk as though she thought it might sprout legs and dance a jig at any moment.

Once she had recovered from the shock of seeing the trunk's contents, her mind moved on to the question of what she was to do next. Aside from being told to stay in her cabin until the ship was underway, there was no information regarding what Captain Stone expected of his passengers, which was a quite different state of affairs from when Anna had sailed from Boston. On that crossing, she had been greeted the moment she stepped aboard with a recitation of the list of ship's rules for passengers. She tried to remember the rules now, assuming that they would be the same for the *Sheridan*, but could only recall a few including prohibitions against gambling (which everyone on that earlier voyage had seemed to ignore), cursing (likewise), and open flames forbidden. Due to the fear of fire, this rule was observed unfailingly. Indeed, she had noted as she was escorted to her cabin that the *Sheridan* seemed to have a bucket of water or sand standing ready at every turn.

Having settled herself in, she listened to the sounds vibrating through the ship as it lolled gently in port, the thuds of cargo being loaded and shifted into place, and shouted orders and footsteps on the deck over her head. There came a knock at her door and she opened it to find the Reverend Mosely, who was eager to assure himself that she had arrived safely. He and his wife had been alarmed by her announcement that she would make her own way to the ship, correctly deducing that their role as chaperones was already being undermined.

"Is Mrs. Mosely managing without too much difficulty?" she asked.

The reverend nodded. He was round as a cannonball, with a bald orb of a head and plump, rosy cheeks, and a jollity that was unlike anything she had experienced in any clergyman. "She is already suffering a touch of the *mal de mer*," he chuckled. "Considering we've not yet cast-off, I fear that does not bode well."

"I'm sorry for her. I understand that this is her first voyage. Is she anxious? Do you think it would help if I spoke with her? My crossing to London was without incident and it might perhaps help her to know that."

"Yes, I believe it would if I could trouble you."

And so, she sat with the reverend and his wife in their cabin, chatting away the time as she attempted to assuage Mrs. Mosely's many apprehensions. Seated side-by-side, the couple put Anna in mind of a pair of apples, for Mrs. Mosely was in every aspect as round as her husband. Anna would not have dreamed that it was possible for a grown woman to have so many unreasonable fears and misconceptions, some of which would have made her erupt with laughter had she not striven for tact.

It was an interminably long time for someone of Anna's nature to keep up the flow of mostly meaningless conversation, but she managed valiantly until, at last, they felt the ship rock gently as it was guided out into the middle of the Thames. Mrs. Mosely assumed a white-knuckled grip on the edge of her cot, and the three passengers simultaneously raised their eyes to the ceiling as they listened to the thud of footsteps and orderly cadence of shouted commands playing out up on the main deck.

Once the *Sheridan* had begun its careful progress down the river, little George Smith scurried down to tell them they could come up on deck. Mrs. Mosely agreed that fresher air might be desirable, and she and the Reverend followed Anna up the companionway into the chilly grey day. The ship slid silently on the receding tide, passing out of London and then through the countryside as they moved toward open water. The stench that clung to London's shoreline gradually gave way to the fresher air downriver until, at last, the quickening salt-tinged breeze told them that the open water was near. Seabirds carved tight arcs in the sky, screeching like a multitude of out-of-tune violins. Face turned up toward the pale, almost non-existent sun, she drew a deep breath of the fresh sea air and pushed back her hood to allow the wind to tousle her hair. The sense of freedom sent a quiver of joy racing through her body.

Reverend Mosely, his wife on his arm, joined her at the rail, marveling with the enthusiasm of a school boy at all he observed. He was most fascinated by the agility of the men who climbed into the rigging and prepared the sails to be unfurled. They were a fearless lot, as at home on lines and yardarms as they were on solid ground. In contrast to her husband, Mrs. Mosely seemed to find that looking up into the rigging made her dizzy, while looking out over the water unsettled her stomach. Reverend Mosely suggested returning to their cabin, but she insisted that she found the fresh air preferable.

"What do you think they are doing here?" Anna was looking toward a small group of redcoats standing together on the quarterdeck. She'd been told that there were four young army officers on board, uncomfortably billeted in hammocks with the crew. Only three men stood at the rail, however, huddled in close conversation, their attention all for two naval vessels sitting at anchor some distance away. "I wonder why they aren't crossing with their regiments?"

"I believe I heard someone say that those ships will not leave for another two weeks," Mosely replied. "General Gage has already sailed, and these men are following now to make arrangements for the arrival of their regiments in a few weeks." The officers were all cloaked against the chill, but there was an occasional flash of red or glint of gold braid where cuffs or collars poked out from beneath the more somber wool.

"Four regiments. Such a lot of men." She studied the young officers for a few seconds as though looking for some telling gesture or revealing expression. If reason and sensible men would but take the reins, she doubted it would be necessary for several thousand men and all of their kit to be deployed an ocean away from their home. "You said their general has already sailed for Boston?"

He stared at her, surprised that she did not know the identity of the eminent general. "Why, yes," he affirmed. "Thomas Gage. He has been sent to replace Governor Hutchinson. I'm surprised you've not heard of him. He was in New York for a time as commander of all the armies in North America. He has been home in England these past few years, but the king has charged him with returning order in the colonies."

"Yes, I know who he is." Anna stared toward the distant ship. She felt as though an iron weight had settled in the pit of her stomach. "The Massachusetts colony is to be governed by the military, then?"

"Essentially, yes."

The fourth officer emerged from below decks. His back was to Anna and Reverend Mosely and, the moment his head popped out of the hatch, he spotted his compatriots. Without looking back, he strode across the deck toward the other officers. The young men exchanged murmured greetings before returning their attention to the distant war ships. They watched for several minutes until, by some unspoken agreement, they seemed to feel their duty done. Tugging cloaks more tightly about them, they turned away from the distant ships and moved into the lee of the mizzen mast. Everything about them radiated a sense of desired apartness from the ship's civilian crew and passengers.

Anna was studying them, wondering if they would keep to themselves for the entire voyage, when one of the young men shifted his position so that, for the first time, she had a clear view of the officer who had been the latecomer. Not quite as tall as the others, but equally proud and erect in his bearing, Lieutenant Edward Hinton stood, his fair hair lifting lightly in the breeze, looking across the deck at Anna. Flustered by knowing that she'd been caught staring at him, she looked away. It was doubtful that he would recall their having met, she thought, with a tad of disappointment.

And yet, he was now striding toward her, smiling in a fashion that indicated he did remember. She turned her face ever so slightly into the chilly breeze hoping to extinguish the heat she felt rising in her cheeks. In only a few strides, he closed the distance between them, his eyes fixed on her face the whole while.

"Miss Somerset, is it not?" he asked when he reached her, inclining his head courteously. "We met briefly at Atkinson's Academy?"

Flustered, Anna found herself stammering. "Yes, er—. Yes, we did." She wanted to slap herself. It was not her nature to be unsettled by a handsome face, nor was it common for her to find herself tongue-tied. And yet, that was exactly her condition. She introduced Reverend Mosely and his wife, making as bad a job of it as if she had no idea of the proper manner in which to make an introduction.

"I was told you would be aboard," the lieutenant informed her. "It surprised me that a young Boston lady would make the crossing in the company of the likes of us." He gestured first to himself, then toward his fellow officers who seemed to be watching them with interest.

"In all honesty," she assured him, "I was not aware that there would be soldiers on board. But, given that this 'young Boston lady' is eager to be home, I doubt it would have made any difference." His smile had not faded, blue gaze had not wavered, and he was making her terribly uncomfortable. She cast about her suddenly addled brain for something astute to say.

Reverend Mosely unwittingly came to her aid. "You say you met at Atkinson's Academy?" His head was cocked to one side, brows knit together, as he tried to think of some academic circumstance in which these disparate people would both find themselves. "What sort of academy would that be? The name is not familiar to me."

She opened her mouth to respond, and then snapped it shut. Too late, Anna realized she was now in the position of revealing something about her London adventures that the Reverend would likely not approve.

"It is a fencing school," the lieutenant supplied, his tone clearly stating that he would brook no censure. "One of the finest and most respectable in London, patronized by only gentlemen and officers of the royal regiments," he added, apparently deducing Anna's predicament. "Miss Somerset was there in the company of my uncle and . . . I believe it was Lady Sylvia Gordon-Hewes, was it not?" This last he addressed to Anna.

"It was. And we thoroughly enjoyed the demonstrations."

"I'm glad to hear it."

"We were particularly taken with Captain Grant. Do you recall — the Scotsman who was part of the events that day? He was most impressive."

"A Scotsman?" Mrs. Mosely asked, sniffing. "Such a reputable establishment would allow entrance to a *Scotsman*? They are a brutish breed. Hardly suitable company for gentlemen."

"Captain Grant returned to his regiment," Lieutenant Hinton replied with sharp-edged politeness. Then, he seemed to ponder for a brief second. "I believe the word "impressive" does not begin to describe him, however. I have seldom encountered a man for whom I felt more respect. His rise through the ranks from common foot soldier to Captain is a rarity and speaks volumes about his performance. He's a Highlander, and warrior to the bone. They say that, as a lad, he fought beside his father at Culloden, though he could not have been more than a knee-high child at the time. I don't know whether the story is true or not. As an English officer, it seemed indelicate for me to ask. As so many did, Grant took the oath of loyalty and joined the Royal Forty-Second, the Black Watch, to prevent his family being deported or displaced from their land. You knew, did you not, that he is with the Black Watch regiment?"

She shook her head.

"I don't believe there is another regiment that can boast a more stellar history on the battlefield. It seems as if the greater the odds are piled against them, the more brilliantly they perform."

"What was he doing in London away from his regiment?"

"He was summoned by Horse Guards. They wanted him to take up a training command, but he refused. He's the sort of man who has little use for London or military politics. He would prefer to stay with his regiment, slugging it out with them in the worst of campaigns, than grow fat in the safety of a training ground."

"I think it must be difficult for men accustomed to a life filled with adventure to face the idea of a less-challenging or more sedentary existence."

"I agree. But in this case, I believe it is much more than that. The men of the Black Watch are fiercely loyal to each other and the regiment — more so than to just about anything else in their lives save for family. And, I believe they see the regiment as part-and-parcel of their family. There is unalloyed pride in the regiment's accomplishments. Each man feels that the regiment is only as strong as its weakest member, and no man wants to be *that* man. They believe everything they do as an individual reflects back on their regiment, their families, and the place from which they came, and woe be to the man who casts a poor reflection!"

"Admirable, but a difficult standard to maintain, I'd think."

"It is. But they do it. Year after year without fail. To be part of something like that — to feel such a connection of loyalty — must be an extraordinary thing. I envy them that."

"A man should reserve that level of loyalty for God and the church," Mrs. Mosely stated firmly. "A man's Christian duty, his faith, should command his unswerving allegiance, not a band of his fellow men."

The lieutenant gave her a long look but did not reply.

"Look there!" Reverend Mosely cried out so abruptly that they all flinched with surprise. "Are those dolphins?"

"Where?" Mrs. Mosely anxiously tried to follow her husband's gaze. "Where are they?" At the mention of dolphins, her entire aspect had changed. No longer the stern, disapproving woman, she was childlike with excitement instead.

"There." Reverend Mosely pointed vaguely toward the bow of the ship. "Let us go forward. I believe we'll have a better view from there." He politely bowed to Anna and the lieutenant, then took his wife's elbow and firmly steered her toward the ship's bow.

Anna hid a smile as she watched them leave. Reverend Mosely's attempt to extricate them all from what was soon to become an awkward situation had no more finesse than a barrel rolling unimpeded down a hill. Completely taken with the excitement of seeing her first dolphins, his wife had not noticed the ploy, however. "I'm afraid that Mrs. Mosely has very strong opinions," Anna told the lieutenant, "which she does not hesitate to share. And every single one of them is resolutely grounded in Scripture. Or, so she says."

Lieutenant Hinton laughed. "In the circumstances, I suppose it's understandable." He was watching the couple move along the rail, pausing occasionally to look out over the water in search of dolphins. "Do you think she'll realize that she has been hoodwinked?"

Anna shook her head. "I doubt she thinks Reverend Mosely is capable of deceit. Besides, there are always dolphins sooner or later. Whenever they appear, she will assume they are her husband's dolphins."

They watched the Moselys a bit longer in silence. Anna was uncomfortably aware of the lieutenant's nearness to herself and of the silence. "You indicated that you were told that I'd be on board. Who told you?" She had no idea why the question had suddenly come into her head, but it had at least given her something to say.

"My uncle, of course. I understand that he was dispatched to bring the full weight of Lady Sylvia's influence to bear in order to get you on this ship. He mentioned that he'd been successful. He seemed to feel that you might need looking after."

Anna snorted with derision. "I cannot imagine that he would have suggested any such thing. Mr. Hinton knows full well that I am perfectly capable of taking care of myself."

"Ah. I believe there was something said about your having an unhealthy attraction to adventure and inflated view of your invincibility."

"Oh. Well then." Anna's cheeks reddened as the myriad stories that could have been told flashed through her mind. She straightened her spine, drawing herself up to her full — if unimpressive — height, standing as though unimpeachable posture could somehow compensate for a less-than unimpeachable character. "Mr. Hinton is a barrister. Of course he looks at things through a rather more rigid lens than the rest of us might."

The lieutenant chuckled. "'Rigid' is not a word I would think to apply to my uncle. In fact, my father would tell you that quite the opposite is true. My uncle is quite the black sheep of our family, as you may know."

"No, I was not aware. Why ever so? He seemed to me to be forthright and respectable; a complete gentleman. And Lady Sylvia claims he is exceedingly intelligent and a very fine barrister."

"He is all of those things, plus more. I'm extremely fond of my Uncle Christopher. My grandfather intended him for the clergy, however, and I'm told that he became quite apoplectic when Uncle Christopher announced his intention to read for the law instead."

"I don't understand. Why should that upset your grandfather? It isn't as though your uncle had announced he intended to become a tonic salesman. Surely his choice of profession should have been his own?"

The lieutenant shook his head. "My father was born first, so he inherited the estates. My Uncle George came second and was thus groomed to take the king's commission. The third son, my Uncle Christopher, was destined for the clergy. That is the way it has always been in my family, as it is in many families like ours, and my grandfather did not like having tradition turned on its ear. He cut off Uncle Christopher's income and hardly spoke a kind word to him for the rest of his days. Not that my uncle minded, I think. Grandfather was a spiteful, unpleasant man, and Uncle Christopher has managed to support himself quite handsomely without his patronage."

Anna, nonplussed by the lieutenant's frank words, was not certain how to reply. She gestured toward his uniform. "You're the second son, then?"

"I am." He nodded, and reached up to steady his hat, which was suddenly unsettled by a gust of wind. "Second of two sons."

"I cannot imagine being anything but an only child. I think it would add something to one's life to have siblings."

"It adds many things," he chuckled. "Not all of them welcome."

"Do you get on well with your brother?"

"We fought like tiger cubs when we were boys. When I think on it, I pity our poor nurse. Now, I'd say we mostly get along with one another, but I cannot say we are close." He waited for her to nod in understanding. "And, you said you have no siblings?"

"That is correct. I assume it's because my parents did not have time to produce another child. They died of a fever when I was hardly out of the cradle."

"I am sorry."

"Thank you," she replied, smiling in a way intended to show him that the thought had not brought on any awkwardness. "Though I feel sorrow on their behalf, of course, and would prefer that they had lived — that I had known them — I've never felt the need or the right to be sorry for myself. My uncle has raised me with a great deal of love and consideration so that I've never felt deprived because I didn't have a mother and father." She cocked her head. "It's an odd thing to say — odder still for you to hear, no doubt. I hope you won't think me callous."

"No," he laughed. "I think you are unusually realistic and honest."

Thought of the dishonesty that had led to her being on the *Sheridan* made her shrink with guilt, and she looked for a way to change the topic. Once again, Reverend Mosely unknowingly came to her aid. He was standing near the bow, calling out and gesturing wildly for Anna to join them. "Oh, my," she said, indicating Mosely's excitement. "Apparently, the dolphins have been spotted. Please excuse me?"

Lieutenant Hinton bowed and watched her go. She was a pretty girl, he thought; diminutive in stature, but sufficiently shapely and attractive nonetheless. That much he had noticed the moment he laid eyes on her at Atkinson's. That first image had stayed with him, clear as the moment of a candle's being lit. On that day, the light streaming through the clerestory windows behind her seemed to catch in the fringes of her hair like a halo, golden flecks of sunlight caught among the mahogany brown and ginger strands.

Certainly, his uncle, who was not easily impressed, had spoken favorably of her, albeit with the caveat that he pitied any man who thought to domesticate her. It was his uncle's view that there would never be much that was conventional about Anna Somerset, that she would never be the sort of girl who could be happily confined to a drawing room or to the strictures of social minutiae. Edward wondered idly if his uncle's impression was too hastily formed. Doubtless, the character he perceived in Anna was a result of her colonial upbringing. It seemed a shame that she had not spent more time in London for it would surely have helped in that regard. But he could not wonder about any of this for long because his fellow officers were approaching, and they would doubtless want to know all he could tell them about the attractive young lady whose company they would enjoy for several long weeks to come.

*   *   *

The *Sheridan* was nearly five weeks into its voyage to Boston. As each day was ticked off the calendar, the weather grew more pleasant, promising that the chill of late spring would soon be altogether replaced by the more temperate weather of early summer. The passengers, adapting to both the rigors and tedium of ocean travel, had settled into a pattern of activities that was necessarily shaped and governed by the crew's routine. Anna had formed an easy friendship with Lieutenant Hinton and, to a lesser extent, with his friend, timid Lieutenant Lawrence Barringer, but she generally avoided the company of the other two officers whose dispositions she found less appealing.

It was Captain Stone's habit on two evenings a week to invite his passengers to join him for dinner in the compartment set aside for dining. For everyone except Captain Stone, these occasions were an awkward business, a farcical endeavor to achieve elegance and formality in an environment that did not lend itself to the affectation. The room's décor did reflect an admirable, if not completely satisfactory attempt at fulfilling its role in the pretense. It was lit by lamps that softened the atmosphere and muted the unfortunate shade of greyish-green that had been chosen for the walls. There was no tablecloth, but the table, polished to a warm patina, was set with fine china and silver. But no amount of paint and soft lighting could disguise the sounds, odors, and unsteadiness that were constant reminders that they were on a ship, not in a London dining salon.

Despite Stone's reservations regarding female passengers, he was a strict adherent to certain protocols. He insisted that Anna be seated to his left, opposite Mrs. Mosely to his right. Reverend Mosely sat to Anna's left, and the four officers were arranged according to rank in the remaining chairs. They were all lieutenants, and it amused Anna that they were so aware of the dates of one another's commissions that it was an easy matter for them to settle into the correct order. She watched the four lieutenants file in, solemn in their attempt to achieve the appropriate level of decorum. The most senior, Lieutenant Chastain of the Thirty-Eighth Regiment, seated himself beside Mrs. Mosely, followed by Lieutenant Barringer of the Fifth, and Lieutenant Bolton of the Forty-Third. That left Lieutenant Hinton, as the most junior, at the foot of the table.

As was generally the case, Captain Stone dominated the conversation, regaling them throughout the soup course with liberally embellished tales of his naval days. When tonight's main course — mutton with boiled potatoes and dried peas — was served, Anna ticked one of the sheep off the mental inventory she was keeping regarding the livestock she had seen brought on board. They were already down one pig, several chickens, one goat, and one lamb. By her calculation, that left two more sheep, one pig, one goat, and an estimated dozen chickens. She assumed some of the chickens would be kept for eggs, and the lone goat for milk, but could not be sure. Regardless, it was plain that the fresh meat-on-the-hoof would be depleted well before they arrived in Boston, at which time meals would become considerably less palatable.

"Yes, I can see how four regiments might seem excessive, but I believe His Majesty has made it clear to General Gage that he feels there has been far too much lenience shown the colonists and that he wants an expedient end to the dissention." Lieutenant Chastain's voice interrupted Anna's musings, and she realized that Stone must have asked him something. "You must remember that General Gage is not merely charged with closing the port," Chastain continued. "He has a full slate of orders, not the least of which mandates the remodeling of the Massachusetts government, doing away with the provinciality and the ad hoc councils that have given colonists the erroneous idea that they are not answerable to Parliament. It will be a significant undertaking, and I believe the king was prudent to give the general four regiments to back him up."

Chastain was sawing away at his meat as he talked. His voice, nasal and patrician, matched his demeanor. With his dark hair, noble features and bearing, he would have cut quite an elegant figure were it not for his unnaturally excessive height, which was lanky and ungainly to a point verging on comical.

"Almost certainly you are correct in your assessment, though," he continued with a sniff. "With the intimidation and force of the regiments in play, it will be a simple enough business. The rabble, and even the local militias are largely a body of farmers and merchants with neither the experience nor the stomach required to stand firm in the face of His Majesty's forces." He popped a piece of mutton into his mouth, and looked around the table with the air of a man who feels comfortably certain he will not be contradicted.

"The Coercive Acts are quite harsh." Lieutenant Barringer was speaking, quietly, diffidently, staring at his plate as he spoke. He was a reasonably attractive young man of medium height, with a stocky, muscular build that would have made him a good farmer. His blue eyes were bright, his nose small and puckishly turned up, and his smile was warmly engaging. "Even some in Parliament are denouncing the acts as tantamount to setting a flame to a stack of dry tinder. Given their history, it seems unlikely that the colonists will quietly accept having their port closed and their government refashioned. I fear, as many do, that we will be greeted with violence." Finally, he looked up, his eyes darting about the table for some sign of support.

"Ever the timid one, Barringer," Lieutenant Bolton replied with a sniff. He had wiry hair and pinched features and, though he was no more than average height, seemed to look down his beak-shaped nose at everyone and everything. Whether or not he came from a background that justified his haughtiness, Anna did not know, and she had no desire to learn.

Chastain waved his knife and fork disdainfully. "It makes no difference. Once the regiments arrive, that will be an end to it. The colonial rabble will wilt and run at the first sign of force. Then we can get back to business as usual."

Would that happen? Anna hoped so. She hoped there would be no bloodshed and that peace would return to her home. But when she thought of Daniel, of his compatriots and the courage and determination she knew they possessed, she had her doubts.

As though he read Anna's thoughts, Reverend Mosely questioned Chastain's position. "What if our show of force is not enough? What if they do not back down?" His eyes, desperate for some sign of reassurance, darted nervously between the officers. "Could this become a civil war?"

"Unthinkable," Stone stated. "Surely that is unthinkable."

Chastain shrugged. "It matters little. Though I've no personal experience with them, I've heard it reported by those who are in a position to judge such matters that the American militias are, on the whole, rather effeminate and entirely lacking in the stomach or patience needed for war." He chewed his food and his thought for a moment, chasing both down with an ample mouthful of wine.

Anna knew her cheeks were flaming angry scarlet but did not care. Her hands were in her lap, clinched in tight fists, and she glared so hard at Chastain that it made her eyes hurt. She would have liked to say that, certainly, none of the men of the colonial militias were dandy prats like Chastain, and she would unhesitatingly put her money on their ability to match him for courage and fortitude. She held her tongue, though it pained her to do so.

"Yes, I'd say it matters little what the dissenting rabble choose to do," Chastain pronounced. "The outcome will be the same. The Massachusetts colony — and all of her sister colonies, for that matter — will once again be firmly under His Majesty's thumb."

"One hopes that they will be more firmly under control than before. In my view, it is the lack of a firm hand that allowed things to deteriorate to this point." Stone had adopted his most stern aspect, as though the colonial discord had affronted him personally. "Once things are put to right, I hope there will be considerably more oversight in the future."

"What is your opinion, Miss Somerset? You have more knowledge of these people than any of us can claim." Reverend Mosely's tone was earnest and devoid of any suggestion of discourtesy.

Anna wanted to shrink in her chair when she felt everyone's eyes turn upon her, but Chastain's sneering comments and the disparaging tone Stone had used when speaking of her countrymen rankled. She drew herself up so that she sat as tall as she could manage. "I think you should not underestimate the dissenters," she averred quietly. "By and large, they are intelligent, courageous, and quite determined to defend their principles."

Chastain snorted and opened his mouth to retort, but Lieutenant Hinton cut him off. "I agree with her," he said.

"Of course you do," Bolton laughed. "Because you are intelligent, and an intelligent man knows always to agree with a pretty girl."

It was meant to provoke laughter but instead provoked a momentary, uncomfortable silence. Hinton considered apologizing to Anna but thought it might further embarrass her. Instead, he forged ahead with his argument as though Bolton had never spoken. "Look at the history. Many of the colonial militiamen fought in the war against the French. They reportedly fought well at the battles along the Allegheny and the Monongahela, and no doubt learned a good deal from experienced English officers in the process. What they may lack in organization, I fear they make up for in ability and knowledge of the land. Plus, that land is their *home*. No, gentlemen," he added with a shake of his head. "I do not think they will wilt. I think, if it comes to such a point, they will stand and fight."

"If that turns out to be the case, it will surely not be a very long fight." Captain Stone blustered. "Not with four regiments of fine British infantry stacked against them."

"It seems to me that the first order of business will be to disarm them." Chastain was staring at the ceiling, his face thoughtful. Clearly, he was mentally playing general, preparing to outline for them the brilliant plan he would, given the chance, adopt for suppressing the troublesome colonists.

Anna heard none of it. She was staring at the three peas that remained on her plate as though, by force of will, she could make them fly across the table and directly into Lieutenant Chastain's mouth. If she aimed them carefully enough to directly hit the back of his throat, might he choke? These men, like so many in London, spoke of the colonists as though they were recalcitrant children to be slapped back into obedience. Haughty and confident in their sense of superiority, the young officers expressed indignation at the gall of colonists who did not evidence respect for their betters, and found humor in the notion that those backward, ill-bred men thought themselves capable of controlling their own destiny.

Stone, Chastain, and Bolton spoke of the colonists as nameless, faceless, non-entities who occupied no more significance in the world than a swarm of gnats. But Anna knew the men and women of whom they spoke so contemptuously had names and faces, families and friends. She knew the work they did, and how they worshipped. Most importantly, she knew their hearts and minds, their dreams and aspirations, for she was one of them. Did these callous young men realize that?

Worst of all, the officers talked like backstreet bullies about to engage in a shoving match, heedless of the fact that enough shoving could ultimately result in a war. The idea of war seemed far-fetched to them, but Anna could envision the possibility quite well, and it filled her heart with a sharp-edged icy dread. All this coldly detached calculation was their job, she knew; it was how they were trained to look at things, to assess situations. But that did not make the hearing of it any easier — not when the assessments and strategies were applied to her home. The peas were beginning to swim, and she realized her eyes had filled with tears.

"Excuse me." Abruptly, she shot up out of her chair. "I do apologize, Captain Stone, but I fear something I've eaten did not agree with me." Without waiting for a response, she bolted for the door. Chairs scraped behind her as the gentlemen, caught off guard by her sudden action, tried to get to their feet. She burst onto the open deck, gulping one lungful of air after another as though she'd been suffocating.

Edward Hinton found her sometime later, huddled against the foremast to watch the last vestiges of the gloaming slip from the sky. "I feel I must apologize for the things that were said at dinner."

"Why?"

The question seemed to fluster him. "Well, because I am distressed that one of my fellow officers gave offense, of course. I'm certain he forgot that not everyone at the table was English."

"I doubt he forgot any such thing. You, as well as Lieutenant Chastain, or Captain Stone for that matter, seem to forget that I am as British as any of you. You are not alone in that, so I'll not hold it against you." Fighting the chill, she pulled her cloak more tightly about her.

He flushed and stumbled over his next words. "Well, I did not mean to imply—"

"I know what you meant to imply, Lieutenant Hinton." She sighed heavily, impatient and eager to be quit of him. "If it will make you feel better, I accept your apology and acknowledge that you are infinitely more the gentleman than either your fellow officers or Captain Stone. May I bid you good evening?" The last was more a statement than a question, leaving him red-faced and seemingly with little choice but to offer a polite bow and watch her walk away.

But he did not let her get far. "We are a supercilious, brutish lot," he called out. He waited for Anna to stop and turn, and she did not disappoint. She stood in an island of lamplight and looked back to where he stood in the shadow of the mast. "We English," he continued, "are usurping imperialists of the first order, full of our own self-importance and the conviction that we are singularly blessed by God."

She cocked one skeptical eyebrow.

Stepping into the spill of lamp light, he spread his arms out to his sides, as though opening himself up to whatever punishment she might choose to enact. "We would do the world a great favor if we would all return to our native soil, burn our ships, pull up the drawbridge, and never show our faces in the world again!"

"Now you're just being ridiculous," she scoffed.

"Am I?" He walked closer to her so that he would no longer have to speak in a raised voice.

"Yes," she said. "You are." He was standing very close — too close, she thought — and she backed one step away from him. "Somewhat accurate, but ridiculous, nonetheless."

He laughed but then quickly became serious again. "I do apologize, Miss Somerset." His voice was soft, as though he were sharing some intimacy with her, and she was once again aware of just how close he was standing. "Whatever you may think of me and my fellow officers, I assure you the remarks came out of thoughtlessness, not out of any desire to offer some slight. Please accept my apology."

"I already did."

"Did you?"

"Well, perhaps not." She felt her traitorous lips curl into a slight smile. "But I do now."

"Thank you."

Yet, he did not move but stood perfectly still, and so close that she could see the pupils expand within his china-blue eyes as he looked down into her face. "I should get to my cabin," she stammered awkwardly. "Captain Stone prefers that we keep to our cabins after sundown." She made an awkward, hasty escape, pretending that she did not hear his offer to escort her.

CHAPTER ELEVEN

Charlotte was finding the late May weather particularly agreeable, and considered that life in general was made all the more agreeable by the arrival of General Thomas Gage. That his arrival brought martial law to the Massachusetts Colony was, to Charlotte's mind, of less importance than the social opportunities his arrival engendered. Gage's first week in Boston had been a week filled with parties and celebrations, most of which even the most disaffected of Boston's leading citizens attended. Many clung still to the hope for some sort of compromise, a peaceful solution to the troubles with which all could live.

For Loyalists, there was jubilation in the promise of restored order under the general's command. Once and for all, they thought, the violent mobs would be quelled, the flow of vitriolic rhetoric stemmed. For Charlotte, to whom all of these things were unimportant, the general's arrival represented a different type of potentiality, however. A cadre of young officers traveled with the general, many of them unattached and eye-catching enough to warrant her notice, and all of them eager to socialize with the attractive young ladies of Boston. And with so many hostesses keen to ingratiate themselves with the illustrious general and his staff, there were plenty of occasions for socializing.

It had come as no surprise to Charlotte that her reclusive father wanted to decline all of the invitations that arrived at the Ainsworth door. But she saw in the invitations the opportunity to rub elbows with people who were freshly-arrived from London, the tantalizing prospect of socializing with the sort of people she felt Boston sorely lacked. Most of all, she saw the invitations as her chance to form a connection that could take her to London. Knowing it might not be favorably viewed by the people she wanted to impress if she arrived alone, Charlotte had wheedled, cajoled, thrown herself into tantrums, and cried until her pitiable father relented. They had attended several such fetes, and Charlotte was becoming discouraged. There was plenty to divert her, but no one she considered ripe · for her machinations.

At the fourth such event of the week, her father could take no more. His capacity for gossip, political maneuvering, and general excess having been reached, he cut the evening short. Sulky and bad-tempered, she plopped herself in the carriage and glowered at her father. She was wearing a silk gown with a low bodice and stays laced so tight she hardly dared to take a breath. The immoderate show of bare shoulder and emphasized cleavage was a further irritant to Martin Ainsworth, and he scowled at his daughter's dress.

"You might as well stop staring daggers at me, father." She made a show of arranging her skirts and plucked at the wilted lace drooping from one sleeve. "I absolutely adore this dress, and I sincerely do not care what you think."

"But I shall tell you anyway. I think it immodest in the extreme. I heard more than one whisper about it tonight."

"Oh? Did you? How delightful! I'm certain they are all green with envy!"

"That was not the sort of talk I was hearing," he corrected flatly. "It's almost impossible for me to believe that you would choose to give people such an . . . *impression* of yourself."

"Oh, la!" She fluttered her hand dismissively. "The little minds of Boston can think what they want. I'd not expect this unsophisticated lot to appreciate something like this." She waved her hand across her skirt. "The Londoners, however – they are a different matter. I daresay they were not engaged in boorish whispering. I have no doubt that they were suitably impressed."

"I *daresay* you are correct," he agreed drolly. "I *daresay* soldiers have quite an acute appreciation for ladies in revealing attire. I doubt, however, that it is the sort of appreciation you want."

"How would you know what kind of appreciation I want?" she snapped. "And it was not only the officers. Did you not see how kindly their wives treated me?"

"I saw a company of women with well-practiced political savvy who know how to paste smiles on their faces and put up convincing facades when the occasion calls for it. Those tight-lipped, pasted-on smiles may serve them well in London, but no one here is being fooled by them; except, I am sad to say, my daughter."

With a disgusted expulsion of breath, she leaned back and stared out the window as if she thought doing so would make her father disappear. "As always, you fail to understand the situation."

"No, my dear daughter. This time it is you who do not understand."

She snapped her head around and glared at him so sharply that it made him flinch. "I understand that my father is a narrow-minded, short-sighted, boorish little prig. Is that enough understanding for you? What I do not understand, however, is why my father tries at every turn to undermine my happiness."

"Undermine your happiness?" Ainsworth's genuine confusion filled his face. "Charlotte! I have given you everything it has been in my power to give! How can you say that I try to undermine your happiness?"

"The one thing that would make me happy, you deny me."

"Oh, Charlotte." He wiped his hand across his face in frustration. "Why will you not understand? I have explained this so many times. We have enough money to live well in Boston, but the same money would not get us so far in London. Furthermore, we would have no entrée into the sort of social circles you favor. I'll not throw away everything here to take you to a place where you would live a sub-standard life and where you would always be regarded as an inferior. I refuse to do that because it is not in your best interest and because it would not make you happy in the long term."

"You seem to underestimate my ability to catch a husband of better society."

"No. I do not doubt for a moment that you could *catch* such a man. And though he might be a man of the right class, he is unlikely to be the right sort of man for you — not likely to be a man of good family. At least, not the sort of family you envision."

"Because, otherwise, he would not marry a lowly little girl from the colonies?"

"Precisely."

"That is hogwash. One hears stories all the time. Why, even dancers and actresses occasionally make their way into London society!"

"But they generally do not make their way in through any sort of channel that would be regarded as respectable, and rarely do they find any measure of true acceptance." Ainsworth's face reddened with the discomfort of discussing, even in the most veiled language, the sort of scandalous behavior he knew was becoming acceptable in cities like Paris and London.

"Or, is it just that you would keep me from marrying at all?" Her eyes were shredding him. "I think that's your real hope, father; that I'll become one of those old spinsters who stay home and take care of their aged fathers. That is what you hope, is it not?"

Ainsworth gaped at her. "Of course it isn't what I hope! I've done everything a father can do to put you in the most marriageable position possible. I've invested money in you and put money at your disposal. God gave you beauty, and I've given you everything else to ensure that you would be sought after by the best young men in the colony!"

"I've no interest in the young men of this colony or any other! Not unless they will take me away from here! Not unless they will take me away from *you*! Do you have any understanding of how very much I loathe you? My mother must have loathed you as well. That's probably why she died! I survived because I was too young to know it would be better if I died. But she knew. She probably just gave up and died rather than face another day chained to such a pitiful little man!"

Martin Ainsworth was so taken aback, so entirely crushed by his daughter's words, that he could offer no response. Tears filled his eyes, and he receded into the shadows of the carriage so that she would not see them.

She had cracked his heart so many times and in so many places over the years, but now he felt she might succeed in breaking it completely. He placed his hand on his chest to muffle the sound of another, deeper fissure opening — one he suspected would never heal.

*   *   *

Teague's partner in crime, Joe, had disappeared. It was as though he had vanished into thin air, which, given the illicit activities in which he engaged, did not seem all that surprising to Teague. Whether it was by his own choice, or because someone else had wanted to be rid of him, such men did tend to vanish from time to time.

In the short-term, however, his more pressing concern was that he needed a new partner, and given his new focus on munitions, it seemed that it might be best to reconsider his earlier rejection of crooked soldiers. This decided, he found it unexpectedly easy to recruit men to help him realize his plans to increase the scale of his thievery. Soldiers were only paid a few pence a day, and — to the profound annoyance of the local population — were always keen to supplement that meager wage with civilian jobs.

As was ever the case with any large organization, there were plenty of dishonest men among the British Regulars who preferred the quick easy gain, or the lure of larger rewards than could be had by honest work. The men he found were not merely greedy, but possessed the additional qualifications of desperation, experience, and a lack of scruples to be got around. Privates Cudahy and Foster were tailor-made for Teague's purposes.

And best of all, they seemed unaware of the true value of the goods they were helping Teague steal. He could short their share, and they would be none the wiser. In his mind, he happily ticked off the number of weeks it would take to amass the kind of money Charlotte wanted.

*   *   *

June brought warm, pleasant weather to the *Sheridan*, along with calmer seas and a general lifting of spirits among the passengers who could pass sunny afternoons on deck playing at card games or engaging in the idyll of watching the sea pass by. Even the crew seemed more relaxed and there was often music played on some primitive instrument or boisterous competition involving climbing the masts or other activities calculated to impress the passengers.

As was the case with most of the ship's voyages, passengers aboard the *Sheridan* avoided the cabin boy, George, as much as possible. He knew it was because they were afraid of him. With the exception of Captain and Mrs. Stone, most people were afraid of him, but he did not mind. He had never known things to be any other way. George had a spindly body, with one arm shorter than the other, and a head that was far too large for such a frail-looking frame. Worse, his head was oddly shaped, like a melon with its face concave instead of convex, and his lower jaw did not quite line up as it should with his upper jaw. But he was not as frail as he looked, and his mind worked fine, and when he was at sea his physical appearance was of little consequence. The crew had become accustomed to him, were actually very fond of him, and any new crew members quickly learned that no abuse or harassment of George would be tolerated.

George could not remember where he had come from, who his parents were, or even how old he was. If he had ever known the name he'd been given at birth — assuming he'd been given one — that memory was gone as well. When Captain Stone found him, abandoned near the London docks, his best guess was that the boy was around two years old. The child was near to starving and the captain could not look the other way. He scooped the boy up and carried him home to Mrs. Stone, who took him in without hesitation. Because the boy was unable to furnish a name of his own, the Stones named him "George" in honor of the king, and "Smith" because it was a common enough surname that no trouble should arise from his becoming a sudden addition to their ranks.

So, little George Smith, aged three years old, had come into the world. Mrs. Stone, whose own children had mostly reached an age where they were off to lead their own lives, doted on him. George had adapted as readily as might be imagined to having a full belly and a warm, dry bed. The price of this comfortable situation was that he had to wash his face more regularly than he'd have liked, had to mind his manners, and had to learn his prayers, but the Stones neither abused nor neglected him, and he was quite happy for several years.

Dissatisfaction had set in once George was old enough to understand the nature of the captain's profession. For a small boy, the romance of life at sea was far more alluring than Mrs. Stone's domesticity, and he began to agitate for the chance of accompanying the captain on a voyage. The Captain was amenable enough to the idea, but Mrs. Stone would hear nothing of it until, after two years of listening to plaintiff pleas and convoluted arguments, she finally relented and agreed to one voyage.

George was about seven years of age when he first left home for the sea. (He liked to say it that way because it sounded so very dramatic.) He felt a pang of guilt when he recalled Mrs. Stone's tears and how the captain told her not to fret for he had little doubt that one voyage would be enough to quell George's fascination with the whole thing. George had looked back once to see Mrs. Stone snuffling into her apron as she waved them farewell, but he had never looked back again. Three years later, his love of life at sea had only grown. He liked serving as cabin boy to the captain, did not mind the hard work or privations involved in serving on a ship, and eagerly learned all he could of the art and science of sailing.

Most passengers shied away from him as though they thought his deformity might be catching, like the plague or smallpox. But Miss Somerset was different. Though George knew it was impossible that she had not done so, she seemed not to notice George's malformed features. She was pleasant — even friendly — towards him, showed interest in his conversation and acknowledged his superior knowledge regarding the intricacies of shipboard life. Occasionally, she would join in his games, or read to him from one of her books. Not least among her winning qualities was the fact that she seemed to have an endless supply of sweets, which she generously shared with George. He favored the hard, sugary lemon lozenges that came in small tins and that she invariably produced from her pocket whenever George came into view.

And, she would play at swords. Courtesy of the ship's carpenter, he had obtained several wooden dowels about as thick as a broomstick and cut to a length suitable for use as make-believe swords. Because he was constantly breaking his swords, he had a ready supply of them that he carried in an old canvas sack. George would gambol about the deck brandishing one of his wooden weapons, defending the *Sheridan* from a variety of imaginary enemies. He was delighted when Anna willingly joined his game, and impressed that she made such a worthy opponent. It elevated her far more in his esteem than even the candy or biscuits she shared with him.

One particularly fine day, when the sea was calm, the sky and winds fair, George and Anna were engaged in a dramatic duel for ostensible possession of the ship and the fictional treasure filling the cargo hold. They were on the poop deck, mostly out of the way of the crew and away from Mrs. Mosely's disapproving eyes. A light breeze came across the stern, stiffening the striped ensign out over their heads and swelling the sails, and the dazzling sun threatened their skin. In a fit of laughing abandon, Anna cast her bonnet aside and unrestrainedly gave herself over to the game.

George had declared Anna to be a "scurvy Frenchman," while he was a worthy pirate. Though she found his view on the world's ethical hierarchy to be somewhat dubious, she accepted her role without argument. They battled raucously, with George leaping about and hurling a good deal of what he imagined to be piratical taunts in her direction. Most of it was outrageously funny, and she laughed so hard it was difficult to keep up her end of the duel. She was unaware that they had gained an audience for, bored and in search of diversion, the four officers had heard George's whoops and cries and climbed the ladder to the rear deck. There, they gathered at the base of the mast to watch the little drama unfold.

Edward, employing the same sharpness of eye with which he appraised horses, marked Anna's agility, her energy, and the dancer's grace that seemed to imbue her every movement. She was no stranger to such activity, he guessed, nor was she completely ignorant of the rudiments of swordsmanship. Her stance, when George's shenanigans did not reduce her to laughter, would have earned high marks from any fencing master. There were flaws in the way she wielded her mock sword, but she had clearly learned the fundamentals somewhere.

Frustrated with the fact that she kept tripping on her hem, Anna called a momentary break in the action while she kirtled her skirts. The eyebrows on the faces of the four officers shot skyward as she revealed her ankles and a fair amount of her well-formed calves. "I say, now, Barringer," Chastain said, whistling softly through his teeth. "Splendid idea you had in dragging us up here. This is shaping up to be far more engaging than I anticipated." Edward glowered at him but, oblivious, Chastain licked his lips wolfishly.

George politely waited for Anna to complete her wardrobe adjustment and then launched a fevered attack that drove her backwards across the deck. Chastain separated himself from his comrades and moved forward a dozen or so paces, allowing Anna to collide with him. Startled, she turned and was about to apologize when she realized that Chastain was able to see her coming and had deliberately placed himself in her backward path. She narrowed her eyes. "I do apologize, Mr. Chastain." Her tone implied that the apology was not remotely sincere. She reached down and hastily returned her hem to its proper place.

"No need for apologies, Miss Somerset. It is completely my fault." He chuckled when she arched one acerbic eyebrow. No fool, this girl. "I simply thought that, if you wish to improve the young man's swordsmanship, you might suffer a suggestion or two regarding your own." He turned her about so that her back was to him and, standing far too close to her, guided the way she held the sword. Anna began to grind her teeth as she tried to decide the best way to rid herself of his unwelcome nuisance, and Edward had taken two steps forward with the intention of putting a stop to Chastain's conduct. They were both forestalled.

George, resenting the intrusion on his fun, had taken action of his own. With a loud thwack, he swung his wooden sword into Chastain's ribs, causing the startled officer to jump back with a cry of pain. George began dancing about, ready to dodge any retribution that might be coming his way, and calling out in his most convincing pirate voice, "Unhand her, you scurvy redcoat!" he cried. "She's the Pirate Queen!"

Completely taken aback, Chastain blinked in astonishment. Anna, who was pleased with her promotion from scurvy Frenchman to Pirate Queen, laughed and stepped to George's side. The boy was playing, but she sensed that Chastain would not suffer the blow to his ribs with good humor. Chastain's face had reddened and was now becoming purple with anger.

George extended his sword arm threateningly in Chastain's direction. "*En garde,*" he cried. "Attack at your peril!"

"You insolent little bastard." Chastain's demeanor implied that he intended to give George a smack across the face.

"He's just a child." Anna stepped quickly in between Chastain and little George. "He wants to play, that's all."

"I, Miss Somerset, am an officer in the king's army. I haven't the time or the inclination to engage in children's games." He turned and stalked away, disappearing down the ladder without looking back.

George, who had anticipated a great duel with a real soldier, was crestfallen, and Anna felt dreadful on his behalf. "I'm sorry, George. You'll have to be content with me, I'm afraid." She was resigning herself to returning to scurvy Frenchman status when Lieutenant Barringer stepped forward, a stick he had pulled from the canvas sack in hand.

"I heard there were pirates aboard," Barringer declared in his most soldierly voice. "But until seeing you, I did not believe them to be so fierce. Nevertheless, as one of His Majesty's own, I feel compelled to defend this ship even unto my last breath!" He leveled his wooden sword at George, ready to fend off whatever attack the boy might make.

Delighted, George's skewed mouth contorted into a wide grin as he hurled himself into the duel. Despite the fact that Barringer was making no serious effort in the matter, he occasionally whipped the stick under George's defenses, lightly touching a rib or backside in the interest of keeping George engaged. Watching them, Anna laughed heartily until she felt George was beginning to flag. Then she joined the fight, and the two of them beat poor Barringer back all the way to the taffrail.

A shrill whistle and call from the look-out interrupted them. Land had been sighted. Forgetting everything else, Anna rushed down the ladder and made her way to forward port. From there, she could just make out a thin, dark line running along the horizon, barely distinguishable from a low bank of clouds, and her heart raced with joy. The *Sheridan* was on a parallel course, riding the southerly wind toward Boston. It would be another day, at least, before they reached the harbor mouth, and then the interminable wait for the tides to be right for them to enter the harbor. After that, she would be home.

* * *

The flotilla of ships had arrayed themselves across the mouth of the harbor, effectively closing it but, also, suffering from distance to shore. Numerous longboats, small and white against the cold dark water, had to be dispatched to ferry passengers away from the ships. Most of the longboats carried supplies destined for the army, and those went directly to Castle William. But the few that carried passengers rowed toward the wharf where Daniel waited. Mainly, the boats carried merchant seamen eager to avail themselves of the long-anticipated recreation to be found on shore. But at least one of the boats carried a brilliant red cargo — officers of Gage's four new regiments. If one looked closely, a few civilians were visible among the red coats, earth tones among jewels. Daniel saw the longboats reach the wharf, and suspicion mingled with disgust as he watched the red-coated officers disembark. There were only four of them, but to Daniel, they represented the hordes of redcoats that would soon follow.

A group of seamen, a shore party from the *Sheridan* it appeared, walked down the wharf, their gait somewhat comical as they adjusted to the feel of solid land. Then a middle-aged couple followed by their daughter. The woman was clinging fearfully to her husband in a manner that made Daniel wonder if she was among those English who thought the colonies largely untamed and swarming with red Indians. He snorted, amused by the thought. Searching for Anna, he looked in vain toward the now-empty longboat. At the head of the wharf, the thin, straggling stream of passengers was beginning to form into small groups as they waited for their trunks to be ferried ashore in the trailing longboats. He surveyed the cluster of passengers and, when he could not find her, straightened and gave the effort more concentration.

Fifty yards or so from his perch, the middle-aged couple and their daughter stood with their backs to him. He was on the verge of dismissing them once more when something the girl did — some movement or gesture — caught his eye. Narrowing his focus, he watched her carefully. She was taller than he remembered Anna being but still shorter than most. Her posture was ramrod straight, her shoulders slim, and her waist narrow as a reed. All of that could be Anna, he knew, but the stillness and regality of her bearing could not. Furthermore, she was impeccably dressed with a care and style that even someone of Mrs. Hancock's ilk would admire. The girl's cloak was fine velvet, had not one visible smudge, and no frayed hem. She was wearing one of the fashionable flat straw hats that his mother called a "shepherdess hat," but which Daniel suspected no self-respecting shepherdess would ever deign to wear bedecked as it was with flowers and ribbon.

But the neatly coifed hair revealed by the forward tilt of that hat was like dark whisky, rich brown glowing in the sunlight with copper highlights, and it was that which made him watch more carefully. He walked slowly toward her, silently willing her to turn around so he could see her face. One of the officers approached her, smiling and obviously offering some form of assistance. The girl's head bobbed, setting him off on whatever mission she had entrusted to him. As he walked away, she turned slightly to watch his progress back down the wharf, and her profile was revealed. It was Anna, Daniel saw, though so changed that he felt as though he was looking on a stranger. He felt his heart plummet stone-like to his stomach.

"There." Daniel nudged Drum and indicated the direction with a small jerk of his head. "There she is."

Drum followed Daniel's leading gaze and, once he was pointed in the right direction, had little trouble recognizing her. A broad grin spread across his face. "She looks pretty, doesn't she?"

Daniel had to look again. "Yes, I suppose so." He shrugged. He'd not thought about it until that moment, but it seemed to him that Anna had always been pretty, after a fashion. It was just that her fashion was more akin to wildflowers growing willy-nilly in an untended field. Seeing what Drum now saw — the prettiness of a rose in a silver vase — he grumbled something incoherent, and then tugged at Drum's sleeve. "Let's go and fetch her, shall we?" Fixing on Anna as their compass point, they carved a path through the milling crowd, managing to approach undetected. He leaned close enough that he could just make out the suggestion of lavender water in her hair. "Hello, Mouse," he said quietly.

Anna felt him, felt his breath on the back of her neck as he spoke. She started, and turned abruptly to face him. The man standing before her made her blink for, though his voice was as familiar as any she knew, little else about him was so easily recognizable. She narrowed her eyes and cocked her head, studying him. His grin was as full of mischief as she remembered, but so much else was different. She knew that she had changed during the four years she'd been away, but she doubted that any change in her own appearance was a great as what those four years had done to him. He was taller, and the lankiness and knobbed joints of his youth had filled in and been given shape by sinewy muscle. Any childish roundness that had attended his face before was now gone, replaced by sharp planes and long angles. His skin was more weathered than it had ever been, and tiny lines radiated out from his eyes as though he'd been squinting into the sun a great deal. Some hasty calculating reminded her that, as she was shortly to turn eighteen, he was now — *oh, my,* she thought — twenty-two. The realization made her unaccountably shy.

"Do you not remember me?" he asked. He was scowling, but it was an obvious pretense. "For, if not, Drum and I shall be on our way and let someone else cart your troublesome little hide and your baggage."

She was laughing before he finished speaking. "Of course I remember you." His words had shattered her reserve, had brought her back to the easy comfort of his friendship. She wanted to throw her arms around him and tell him how happy she was to see him. "Hello, Daniel," she said instead, demurely folding her hands so that they would not, of their own accord, fling themselves about his neck.

"Welcome home." He doffed his hat and performed his most courtly bow, making her laugh again.

"I'm very glad to be here. I can't begin to—" she spied Drum a step or two behind Daniel. "Oh! Hello Drum!"

Drum was hanging back, hoping to be noticed, and he eagerly snatched his cap from his head and, wringing it in his hands, stepped forward awkwardly. "Hello, Miss Anna. You grew up."

Anna opened her mouth but, not knowing quite how to respond to the candid observation, closed it again.

"As you can see," Daniel told her, "some things have not changed. Drum, let's see if we can find Miss Anna's trunks, shall we?"

"Oh, that won't be necessary. A gentleman who was on the ship with us," she gestured toward Reverend and Mrs. Mosely, "has graciously offered to locate our baggage for us." The Moselys were regarding Daniel speculatively. "Oh! I'm so terribly sorry! I haven't introduced you." She made the introductions, pointedly adding for Daniel's benefit, "Reverend and Mrs. Mosely graciously agreed to serve as my chaperones aboard ship. I've explained to them about Uncle John's illness and how urgently I needed to return home." She smiled at the Moselys. "Mr. Garrett is an old family friend," she explained, "and kindly agreed to collect me and my baggage in my uncle's stead."

No sooner had these introductions and explanations been made when Lieutenant Hinton appeared. "I have located your trunks," he informed the three travelers, "and have arranged for those belonging to you, Reverend and Mrs. Mosely, to be carted to your hired carriage. Miss Somerset, as your uncle is not able, might I offer to arrange transportation for you to his house?"

"No, thank you, Lieutenant Hinton. My friends here have brought a wagon for my trunks and I'm quite happy to walk—"

"Miss Somerset's friends have brought a wagon for her baggage and a carriage to take her to Mr. Wilton's house," Daniel replied smartly. He'd been eyeing the lieutenant suspiciously and with a good deal of hostility, and was making no effort to hide the fact.

Hinton seemed taken aback by this man he had only now noticed. He arched one eyebrow at Anna, questioning the wisdom of sending her along in Daniel's company. "I apologize for my effrontery," he told Anna, though he clearly believed any effrontery to be on Daniel's part. "I did not know that your uncle was sending one of his servants to fetch you."

Anna started to laugh, but the heated look on Daniel's face choked back that impulse. "Mr. Garrett is not a servant," she responded, quickly correcting the misunderstanding. "He's a friend. Please allow me to introduce you. Mr. Daniel Garrett, this is Lieutenant Edward Hinton."

The men bowed curtly and exchanged the appropriate courtesies, but the frostiness in Daniel's demeanor could not have been more sharply edged. Dense as Drum could be, he had picked up on the simmer in Daniel that threatened to become a boil with little provocation. "If someone can tell me where to find the trunks," he suggested helpfully, "I'll see that they get loaded and taken to Mr. Wilton's house."

Anna smiled at him, grateful for the interruption. "Lieutenant Hinton, would you mind?" She could tell that Edward minded a great deal but, gentleman that he was, he could do nothing but agree to her request. With a bow to the ladies, he took his leave — but not before quickly telling Anna, "I look forward to accepting your invitation to take tea with you and your uncle." And then he was gone, Drum following in his wake.

Wishing Hinton had not made the statement in front of Daniel, Anna closed her eyes, waiting for the remark she knew would be forthcoming. She heard only silence. "What?" She looked up at him with exaggerated surprise. "No cutting remarks about Tories or taxes or redcoats? You surely have something smart to say, so be done with it."

Daniel's eyes were following Hinton, boring into his back so intensely that he knew the lieutenant had to be able to feel it. "I was just wondering," he told her without taking his eyes off Hinton, "do you think they wear those red coats to hide all the blood that must get spilled on them?" He turned his attention to Anna, ignoring her dark look. "It's just that, they seem determined to offend virtually everyone they encounter, so it makes one wonder—"

"Impossible man." She turned on her heel and marched away from him.

Chuckling, he watched her for a few steps. In contrast with the homelier colors around her, her clothes were a fetching combination of deep rose, pinks, and creams. Bright rose and cream-colored ribbons danced in the breeze as she walked, and she was turning more than one head. Daniel decided it might be unwise to let her put too much distance between them, and he loped after her. "I hope your uncle will be well enough to entertain the redcoat," he said, smirking, as he caught up with her. "I mean, Mr. Wilton being so mortally ill, and all."

She heard him laugh at his own jest and rounded on him. "I explained my reasons for that subterfuge, so do not remind me of it. I am mortified to have deceived so many people. Now, where is this carriage you claim to have?"

"There." He pointed to a fine open landau pulled by a team of matching bays and driven by a liveried coachman.

Her mouth fell open and then closed quickly as she narrowed her eyes at him. "Please tell me you didn't steal it."

"Miss Somerset, you offend me." He grasped her arm and led her toward the handsome equipage. "Of course it isn't stolen. It's quite legitimately borrowed from Mr. John Hancock, himself."

"Indeed." She struggled to look unimpressed. "And does Mr. John Hancock, *himself*, know that you are using it to transport the niece of a Loyalist?"

He snorted at that. In fact, he'd mentioned to Dr. Warren that he would be collecting Anna from the dock, and Warren had arranged the loan. "I missed you, Mouse." He brushed the coachman aside and helped her up into the landau himself.

"Did you?"

He nodded, then grinned broadly. "I like a good argument from time to time, and you're better at it than anyone I know."

She rewarded him with a mincing look. The breeze mischievously lifted the ribbons that trailed from her hat and tangled them on the folded armature of the landau's roof. Daniel reached around and easily freed the ribbons, but two came loose in the process. He started to return them to her but, on some impulse, tucked them away in his pocket instead as she was not looking.

Drum trundled into sight with an enormous hand-truck loaded almost beyond capacity with Anna's trunks. He set it down and approached the carriage. "Is all of this yours, Miss Anna? It's a lot. I don't want to get trunks belonging to other folks by accident."

"Yes, it's all mine." She heard Daniel snicker, and she shushed him. "Drum!" She called him back before he could walk away. "You look very dapper today. Is that a new suit of clothes?"

Beaming proudly, Drum nodded. "Mr. Sprague gave it to me," he said, fondly patting the front of his coat.

"Mr. Sprague?"

"Yes. He told me that I must look more presentable if I was to live there."

"If you were to live—" the meaning of what he had just said hit her somewhat slowly. "Do you mean to tell me you are living with the Spragues now?"

Drum nodded, but then hesitated, frowning. "I don't actually live with them. I have rooms over his carriage house, though. They are very nice, the Spragues. Now, I need to take these to the wagon. The driver and I will fetch your trunks up to Mr. Wilton's house, Miss Anna." He turned resolutely and made his way back through the crowd to where he had left the overburdened hand-truck sitting.

Anna cocked one questioning eyebrow in Daniel's direction. "He is living with the Spragues?"

"Yes." He reached up and grasped the side of the carriage, then hoisted himself into the cabin, closing the small door behind him.

"Did you not think that is something I might like to know?"

"It's a comparatively recent development," he shrugged. "And a story better told in person." He settled himself into the seat opposite hers, and the coachman shook out the reins. There was a lurch as they started forward, and the carriage rocked on its springs as they crossed from the wooden dock onto the road.

"So, tell me. How is it that Drum is living over Mr. Sprague's carriage house?"

Daniel shrugged again, and gazed out as though the scenery along the street was of far more interest to him than Anna's question. "Let us just say that Teague and I had a bit of a disagreement, and I didn't want Drum living in Teague's rooms any longer. I called in a favor that Mr. Sprague continued to insist he owed me — despite the fact that I saw no debt on his part — and arranged for Drum to live in their empty rooms." Now that it was told, he looked at her and saw, as expected, that she was well aware that there was a great deal more to the story.

"You and Teague had a falling out?"

He nodded.

"Over what?"

"Does it matter?"

"I'm curious."

"Don't be. It isn't worth your interest. Just enjoy the carriage ride, will you?"

"I do. Thank you for arranging it." She smiled and, closing her eyes, tipped her face up to the sun and listened, reacquainting herself with the sound of Boston's heartbeat. The streets were alive with throngs of people going about the day's business. Tradesmen's carts, children scurrying underfoot, and various stray animals darting here and there, filled the air with the sound of commerce and every variety of discourse. Church bells, each one having its own individual, recognizable voice, chimed the hour. A cool, fresh breeze was coming in off the water. Anna drew a deep breath, filling her lungs with all of the aromas — good and bad — that said Boston to her. She was home.

"Are you indeed glad to be back, then?" Daniel was watching her, appraising the changes and looking for signs that she was still the Anna he knew.

"Yes, very glad." Her cheeks dimpled at the corners of her smile, and her eyes shone bright with tears.

"It isn't London."

"It certainly is not, thank the Lord."

Daniel felt himself begin to relax. He realized that he'd been holding on to a concern that she would return to find her home lacking by the standards to which she'd been exposed. He gave some attention to the people they passed, noting the confused expressions on the faces of some observers. "I believe we are perplexing folks." He indicated a woman who unabashedly stared at them. "Likely they recognize the carriage, but not us."

She laughed. "I shall have to manage my best imitation of Lady Sylvia. Then, I shall at least look as though I belong here."

"You belong." He shifted his shoulders uncomfortably, keenly aware that he was the one who did not.

"You must thank Mr. Hancock for me. I'd have been perfectly happy to walk, you know."

"I know. This seemed a good way to welcome you home, however." He shrugged, dismissing the gesture, uneasy with the realization that some part of him had hoped to impress her. "I thought perhaps you might have grown accustomed to riding in carriages."

"Too accustomed, I'm afraid. I look forward to being able to walk wherever I choose again."

"Hopefully, not attired as a street urchin."

She grimaced. "I was hoping you'd forgotten that incident." Not wanting to meet his gaze, she looked at her skirt, fussily smoothing wrinkles that were not there.

"All things considered," he laughed, "it would be difficult to forget."

"I made a new friend in London, who, even before I'd had a chance to demonstrate the ability, seemed immediately to recognize my penchant for getting into trouble. If I had not known better, I'd have thought you'd been informing on me."

He laughed. "I never inform on friends. You know that."

"Yes, I do." She considered him for a long moment. "It's one of the things I like and respect about you."

"I'm glad — though surprised — to learn that there's at least one thing."

"That, and your willingness to get me out of trouble when necessary and with a minimum of complaint."

"Did your new London friend find himself — or herself — in the position of rescuing you?"

"Himself, and, no. He was merely an amused and somewhat disapproving spectator." She blushed slightly at the memory of the incident over the stolen spoons. "I was forced on one awkward occasion to give him a modicum of assurance that I would try to be more circumspect in the future."

"And how have you fared in that regard?"

"Not as well as I'd like," she admitted with a sigh. "Though I believe my judgment is much improved over what you may remember."

"Not too much, I hope," he chuckled. "I do believe I've missed the entertainment your many predicaments provided."

"Have you indeed?"

"I have." He shifted uneasily on the seat cushions and leaned forward slightly so that he could lower his voice. "In truth, I missed . . . you." He was fumbling now, unsteady on the slippery ice of a conversation headed in a direction he had not intended. "Because I value our friendship," he quickly amended.

She blinked, taken aback by the confession, and she took several beats to carefully choose the words for her response. "I'm glad to hear you say that. I value our friendship as well, and came to a realization while aboard the *Sheridan.*" He had leaned back, wary, cocking one eyebrow at her. It unnerved her, and she hesitated before continuing. She'd rehearsed the speech many times over the past several days but, now that the moment for delivery was upon her, she could remember none of the words with the fluidity in which they had flowed through her mind. "Yes, well," she forged on. "The way things are going here, I think it may be difficult for us to be friends, and I'm not quite certain what to do about it."

It was not what he had expected her to say, though he had not actually known *what* to expect. He sat back, blinking. "Why should it be more difficult now than it has ever been?"

"Because of . . . everything." She waved her hand as though to indicate the whole of Boston. "Because of all the things that are happening. Because—"

"Because I'm aligned with the rebels and you most decidedly are not?"

"In a nutshell."

He felt uncomfortable with the way this was going. "As I said, I fail to see how anything is different. Are you worried about the new friends you made in London? Do you feel such a strong loyalty to them that old friends are to be sacrificed?"

"Of course not. That isn't what I intend at all." She sighed in exasperation. "I can think of no way to say this, Daniel."

"Try."

"It's just that the situation has become more . . . *delicate.*"

"Delicate?"

"Oh, for heaven's sake, Daniel! Stop being so obtuse! You and your Sons of Liberty have pushed things beyond the point of mere protest. Can you not see the situations I have found, and may find myself in? Can you not see the conflicts of interest I may face?"

"Apparently not."

"Alright, then. If you require that a picture be drawn." She straightened her spine and squarely met his eyes. "During the crossing, I heard things from the officers that I thought could be useful to you and your friends. But to tell you those things would be a betrayal of the confidence placed upon me by those men, and of my friendship with some of them. On the other hand, to not tell you those things, or to not tell them what I know of you and your friends seems a betrayal as well. It is a dilemma."

He did not like hearing that she had formed such a friendship with any of the officers — especially considering that he felt it likely that Lieutenant Hinton was one of them. "What you are saying is that you don't want to be put in the position of spying for either side, correct?"

"If there must be 'sides,' then you are correct. I do not wish to be a spy. Mostly I don't want anyone to expect it of me."

"I wouldn't ask you to spy for us. And, I'd have thought you'd know me better than that."

"I do." She sighed. "I'm sorry. It's just . . .," she rubbed her fingers over her eyes. Suddenly, she felt very tired. "It's difficult to explain. It's just that . . . it has been so. . . .." Her words trailed off and she looked at him, pleading for him to understand what she could not explain.

"It's just that, you've been living among the English," he replied simply.

Somehow, he imbued it with a tone she had not intended, but it was close enough. "Yes," she agreed. "I've been living among the English."

"And, do your English friends expect you to spy for them?"

"Certainly not." She drew herself up indignantly.

Daniel studied her face. She may have said it was certain, but he suspected that she was not so sure. "I'm sorry I did not fully understand your dilemma. I had thought your interest was only in your uncle's safety and well-being. Beyond that, I thought you wanted to keep yourself apart from all of it."

"I wish that were possible. But I know now that keeping oneself apart — that remaining neutral, so to speak — is unlikely to be a possibility." She sighed and straightened her posture. "And, to be clear, my uncle may be my primary concern, but the safety and well-being of my friends — even those who have chosen to be rebels — is of great interest to me as well."

He relaxed back against the cushions. "Ah, well, Mouse," he said, grinning insouciantly, "you've no need to worry on my account. I can take care of myself."

"Oh, indeed." One corner of her mouth twisted with cynicism.

"So, if you'll not be spying for either side, then there is no dilemma. No doubt, we'll still find plenty of topics for disagreement, but that's nothing new."

"I'll not be spying for either side," she said smartly, and left unspoken the fact that she still considered the dilemma quite real.

The carriage drew up in front of her uncle's house and, waving the coachman back onto his box, Daniel quickly alighted and turned to help her down. The Anna of old, he thought, would have insisted on her ability to climb down without his help. But this Anna, the new Anna who seemed to have been shaped and polished and faceted like an exquisite gem, did not.

She extended one neatly gloved hand and descended the little fold-down steps with a graceful elegance entirely suited to the Hancock's fine carriage.

And then the elegance and sophistication dissolved. Her uncle, having seen the carriage approach, had stepped out the front door. The moment he saw that it was Anna come home, he froze in place, too happily stunned to move. She saw him and promptly forgot all the lessons regarding decorum and propriety that poor Lady Eugenie had worked so hard to instill in her. Gathering her skirts in one fist and clapping the other hand on her hat to keep it in place, she bolted up the path and into his arms. Her arms wrapped about his neck so tightly he could barely breathe, but he did not care. His Anna was home, and there were too many tears and too much joy to allow for the intrusion of even a question regarding how she had come to be there.

Wilton peered over his niece's shoulder to where Daniel remained beside the carriage. Good manners decreed that he should invite the young man into the house, but he was loath to share Anna just yet. He was relieved, then, when Daniel bowed respectfully, climbed back into the carriage, and rode away.

CHAPTER TWELVE

Charlotte's reflection stared back at her from the mirror, frowning over every curve of her face and curl of her hair. There must be some blemish here, she knew, something that had come off with less than perfection, something that had let her down. Otherwise, how to explain the fact that Daniel Garrett seemed to prefer the uninteresting little Somerset girl? Beside the beautiful swan that Charlotte was, Anna was a mere sparrow. Or a mouse. Charlotte liked that better. Why, Daniel himself had always referred to Anna Somerset as a "mouse!" Clearly, therefore, something was amiss regarding Charlotte's own appearance and it must be rooted out and rectified. Yet she could see nothing reflected in the mirror but the perfection she knew herself to be.

Charlotte had observed Daniel and Anna earlier — well, she thought with distaste, all of Boston had seen them — riding in the Hancock's open landau as though they belonged there. Daniel looked at Anna, smiled at her, in a way that he had never looked at or smiled at Charlotte, not even in her many dreams and fantasies of Daniel in the role of her imaginary lover. In that moment, that fragile bit of time in which she glimpsed such an intimate part of him, she began to hate. She hated Daniel for denying her that piece of himself that should have been hers. But more, she hated Anna.

How had Anna done it? How had Anna turned Daniel's head?

She turned from the small mirror over the washbasin to the tall cheval glass. It was a beautiful mirror, of a style and construction newly emerging into vogue, that her father had obtained at considerable trouble and expense merely because he thought she might like it. The piece had delighted her until now, until she saw in it only the image of her failure. She pirouetted slowly, watching how well the folds of her skirt moved with her, and smiled with satisfaction over how nicely the soft green velvet set off her eyes. As easily as it had appeared, the smile dissolved.

Eyes fixed on the pale, spring green velvet that was so flattering to her coloring, she did not see how her face had become a rictus of jealous hatred. With a seemingly perceptible throb and burn, the enmity flowed like venom through her veins, poisoning every cell out to her fingertips, into the very roots of her hair. Her body began to quiver from the rage that was overtaking her.

Charlotte reached out toward the reflection in the glass, placing her hands on the pale shoulders of the girl reflected there, and shoved with all her might. The mirror toppled backwards, crashed to the floor, and shattered into dozens of pieces. She watched the silvered glass shards fling themselves across the polished wood floor, diamond-bright bits that glittered prettily as they scattered. The sight drew a smile, and she picked up one of the shards of glass, pricking her finger in the process. A drop of blood welled up, ruby red against her pale skin. Carefully, she touched her finger to the surface of the piece of mirror in her hand, two times, two bloody smudges — one for Daniel, one for Anna. The crimson smudges were slightly transparent against the silvered glass, and she admired the effect of light playing on them as she turned the fragment this way and that. Finally, she dashed the shard to the floor and crushed it under her heel.

Several protracted seconds later, when she still had not moved, the handle on her bedroom door rattled and then came a timid tapping. "Charlotte?" It was her father's voice. "My dear, are you all right? I heard a disturbance. Are you injured?"

He sounded, Charlotte thought with annoyed exasperation, as anxious and obsequious as always. He'd been attempting to smooth things over with her ever since they had quarreled over her ball gown, and every conciliatory gesture he made only filled her with more loathing. "Yes. I'm fine." Her tone was sharp with impatience. "I broke some glass is all. Please leave me be."

The door handle jiggled again. "Please let me in. Perhaps I can help. You should not try to clean up broken glass — please be careful!"

"I am not a child," she snapped. "I can manage. Leave me alone."

"Charlotte!" He was pleading now. "I worry about you. I'm your father. Won't you please unlock this door?"

"You needn't worry," she assured him. *And, you are not my father. You cannot be.* It was a notion that had lived in the darkest places of her mind, something that had, like some mythical beast, shown itself to her consciousness only on rare occasions. Now it jumped out, fully realized, and boldly marched out into the bedazzling light of her reality. Martin Ainsworth was not her father, could not be her father. In Charlotte's view, no woman as beautiful as her own mother would bed with such an unattractive, simpering, ineffectual man. Marry him for his money, yes, but allow him to father a child on her — never. Charlotte knew that her true father had to be a dashing man, tall and robust, and possessed of the full spectrum of gentlemanly virtues. Probably, she thought, a man like some of the dashing young officers gracing Boston's streets these days. Possibly even, a man with wealth and a noble house standing behind him. To her mind, it would explain so much.

She flung open the door and stormed past her father without so much as a glance in his direction. Ainsworth peered into her room and was shocked by the scattering of broken mirror. "Charlotte! What on earth happened?" As though she had not heard, she continued down the stairs. "Charlotte! I demand that you answer me! Stop right now and answer me!"

His voice was pitched, so that she knew without looking that the veins in his neck would be beginning to bulge, his face growing beet-red. Still she did not turn, did not stop. Instead, she raised one delicately regal hand as though to silence him. "I'm going out for a bit," she called back over her shoulder. "I've business that needs tending."

Open-mouthed, he gaped from her to the broken glass on her bedroom floor. When she had gone, he sat down on the top step and buried his face in his hands. It had been over a month since their last quarrel, and there had been no improvement in the air between them. Now, another blow had been struck. Martin Ainsworth felt that there was nothing left for him to do but weep. He felt himself dissolving into an uncontrolled paroxysm of sobs that made it seem as though his heart might be physically ejected from his chest by the spasms. Hugging his arms tightly about him, he pounded his head against the stair rails as he raged against the grief. It must end, he knew, though he could see no way out of the darkness his life had become.

*   *   *

Dinner parties were not her favorite thing, and for this one, Anna was particularly jittery, her nerves so brittle she felt that the smallest thing might shatter them. She stood in her uncle's sitting room, fidgeting unconsciously and laughing vacantly at the witticisms of their guests. Her mind was out on the streets of Boston, however, and she routinely flicked her eyes toward the front window, watching for the arrival of the final two guests, wrestling with the mixture of dread, apprehension, and anticipation that roiled inside her.

Though she had been home for over two weeks and felt sufficiently welcomed already, her uncle was determined to hold the dinner to formally welcome her home. The guests were his choosing, and the Spragues, of course, were at the top of the list. He had also insisted on inviting Lieutenants Hinton and Barringer, asserting his desire to meet the young men who had watched over her during the crossing from England. As far as Anna was concerned, they had done nothing to warrant the invitation, but suspecting that her uncle merely wanted to meet them because they were now to be counted among her friends, she did not argue.

His wish to invite Mrs. Garrett — and Daniel, as her escort — stemmed as much from his fondness for the lady, Anna guessed, as anything. Thus she received with an air of dubiousness his explanation that Mrs. Garrett had enjoyed her correspondence with Anna over the preceding years and had lent Wilton a patient ear on the many occasions when he lapsed into long discourse regarding his beloved niece. Seeing the cheeky smile that darted across her lips when he expressed his desire to invite Selah, Wilton had quickly dispelled any fanciful ideas she might be entertaining. "None of that silliness, now. Mrs. Garrett has become a friend, nothing more."

S . D . B A N K S

"But do you perhaps wish it could be something more?"

"Pshaw." He dismissed the suggestion with a brush of his hand. "I'm far too old for such things and hardly the dashing figure to court someone like Mrs. Garrett." He crooked his mouth at Anna's expression, which said clearly that she remained unconvinced. "I'm many things, Anna, but none of them a fool. And a man would have to be a fool to think he could win that particular lady. Her heart still belongs to her late husband. I believe I admire that in her, although I think it a waste of fine womanhood."

Anna giggled. "I believe you intended it as a compliment, uncle. However, I doubt many women would swoon to hear themselves referred to as an example of 'fine womanhood.' It's rather lacking in romantic character; it sounds as if you're talking about a horse."

"As I said, niece, we are friends. Nothing more."

Her uncle's friendship with Selah Garrett was of far less concern to Anna than the inadvisability of having Daniel among a party that included two officers of the king's army. She thought the potential misadventure had been averted when Mrs. Garrett told her that Daniel was traveling and was unlikely to return in time for the party. But only two hours earlier, her uncle had expressed his delight in a message from Mrs. Garrett indicating that Daniel would be accompanying her, after all. The moment Anna spotted the two of them coming up the path, she dashed to the door in a manner that precluded her uncle from receiving them.

Stepping into the small foyer, Daniel watched Anna greet his mother. The warmth between the two women surprised him and set him wondering about the correspondence that had passed between them during Anna's time in London. Yet, what really gave him pause was Anna. The ginger in her hair, the pale peach silk of her dress – she was a glorious sunset, though no more so than when he had collected her at the docks after her return from London, he realized. No, he was seeing something far different and more subtle than colors and pleasant features. He watched while she briefly conversed with his mother before suggesting something to her about joining the other guests, but he did not truly hear a word that was exchanged between them. The tilt of Anna's head as she spoke to his mother, the curve of her cheek and smile, even the sound of her voice; these things were what held his attention and disturbed the long-uninterrupted regularity of his heartbeat. She was no longer the mouse, and the acknowledgement of that fact hit him with a numbing thud.

He shook his head to clear it of the fog that had settled there. Suddenly, he realized that Anna had stepped in front of him and was looking up at his face, all sternness and censure. He could not fathom what he had done to deserve such a hard look, and it took a moment for it to dawn on him that she was deliberately blocking him from entering the parlor. The sound of voices raised to greet his mother drifted out to him, and he peered over

216

Anna's head to see who had spoken. He stiffened at the sight of a red jacket decked with bright gold trim.

Anna clutched his arm, arresting his attempt to proceed beyond her. "Behave yourself," she hissed in a voice only he could hear. "I would not have invited them save that your mother told me you were away and would not likely return in time to join us." His eyes, she saw, were razor sharp, and did not leave the center of Hinton's back. "I could hardly rescind their invitation, could I?" She glanced over her shoulder. How was it possible that Edward did not feel the stab of Daniel's gaze between his shoulder blades?

"Of course you couldn't rescind the invitation." He visibly relaxed, though the strain of the effort was apparent in the lingering tightness of his features. "And, of course I'll mind my manners." He grinned down at her. "It's me, Mouse. How could you think I might not?"

She rolled her eyes and, pasting a smile on her face, walked with him into the sitting room. Anna first introduced Daniel to Mrs. Sprague, and then to her two daughters, Amity and Judith. The girls were the younger of the Sprague's three daughters — the elder having married the previous year — and were invited primarily to balance the preponderance of male guests. The two were quite busy eliciting the attentions of the officers and, confronted with Daniel's appearance, they could hardly decide which way to turn next. Their flushed faces and giggling, self-conscious responses to Daniel's polite greeting surprised Anna. She understood how dazzling an officer's uniform could be, but Daniel was . . . well, *Daniel*.

She tilted her head back, narrowed her eyes and, trying for a different perspective, gave him a long, sideways look. He was an unusually well-dressed Daniel, she had to admit, with his ever-present stubble of beard shaved to oblivion and his dark hair neatly tied, yet she could not see anything worthy of the Sprague girls' fixed attention. He was simply Daniel.

"What is it?" he whispered, self-conscious under her scrutiny. "You're looking at me as though I have horns."

"I know you have horns. I'm just wondering where you've put them is all."

The quip provoked a broad grin.

Shrugging off the Sprague girls' fawning reaction to Daniel, Anna moved to the more difficult task of introducing him to Barringer and reintroducing him to Hinton. The tension between the three men was palpable as they exchanged courtesies, to the point that Anna was tempted to chastise all of them as she might three boys jostling for control of their favorite corner of the school yard.

Mr. Sprague's intervention saved the moment. "Mr. Garrett!" Seemingly delighted to see Daniel, Sprague stuck out his hand. "Well, met, my friend. Well met! It's good to see you again." He placed his arm amiably about Daniel's shoulders. "If I could steal you away from the younger company, I would like a word."

Daniel accompanied Sprague without argument, though he was loath to leave Anna in the company of the two redcoats. Half listening to the conversation of those around her, Anna kept one eye on Daniel and Mr. Sprague who, it appeared to her, had their heads together a bit conspiratorially. She would far rather have been privy to their conversation than where she was — trapped between Sprague's daughters and the two officers.

Dinner was announced, and the guests discovered that their places at the table were marked with place cards. It surprised Mr. and Mrs. Sprague, who were not accustomed to such formality in John Wilton's home, but they attributed it to the influence of London upon Anna. In fact, it was something she had decided to do only that afternoon when she learned that Daniel would be among the guests. She seated him at her right hand, as far away from the two officers as possible, and within striking distance of a rebuking kick to the shin should one be required.

When the first of the wine was poured, Mr. Sprague raised his glass in a toast. "To our little Anna," he said. "Welcome home." Anna beamed at him as the toast was echoed.

The cook came gliding in, closely followed by her daughter and the Wilton's maid, both of whom were recruited to assist in serving the large dinner party. They paraded in bearing abundantly piled platters of food. The cook was a striking woman, tall and slender, with fine bones and an elegant bearing. She had a delicate smile for everyone at the table except the Sprague girls and the two officers, Anna noticed, though she thought no one else had.

When the cook and her two assistants had swept away into the kitchen, Wilton raised his glass, "Welcome to all of our friends, old and new." He nodded toward Hinton and Barringer. "I thank you for joining us this evening to help me celebrate the joy I feel at having my niece home again." His eyes filled with tears, which he hastily dashed away on his sleeve. "And to thank you gentlemen," he again indicated the two officers, "for watching over her during the voyage."

"I fear I do not warrant your appreciation on that score," Hinton demurred. "Though my uncle and, by extension, Lady Sylvia, bade me watch over her, Miss Somerset seemed quite capable of looking after herself." He did not hear Daniel's discreet derisive snort nor see the sharp kick to the shin with which Anna responded.

"True," Barringer agreed. He popped a bit of roasted beef into his mouth, then scythed his empty fork through the air like a saber. "On several occasions, she successfully defended the ship against pirates and other brigands."

"And," Hinton interjected, "as pirate queen, she once defeated the entire British army." His smile, which Anna returned, was conspiratorial and set Daniel's teeth on edge.

Wilton put down his knife and fork and stared across the table at his niece. "Pirates? You never mentioned anything about pirates!"

Anna laughed. "Nothing to alarm you, uncle. The cabin boy, really just a child, had a fondness for playing at swords. I'm afraid I allowed him to lure me into his adventures on a fairly routine basis."

"No surprise there," Daniel muttered under his breath so that only she could hear, and he chuckled when she pointedly ignored him, jutting her chin and fixing her gaze on her uncle.

"We were all rather impressed with her skill," Barringer told them, a tone of delight in his voice. "Imagine my surprise when I learned that she'd been instructed in the fundamentals by one of the same masters who taught me!"

"I suppose that explains your feeble swordsmanship, Barringer. You learned from a woman's tutor." Hinton immediately regretted the barb, and blushed.

"Good heavens!" Mrs. Sprague was gaping at Anna, scandalized. "Do you mean to tell me you learned how to *fight*? With a *sword*?" Her voice increased in pitch with each question.

"Yes. I did. Well . . . after a fashion." Anna had already explained the circumstances to her uncle, who was amused by it all, and she felt disinclined to pretend contrition for Mrs. Sprague's benefit. "It was one of Lady Sylvia's more outrageous larks, I must admit, yet I did quite enjoy it. We attended a tournament and, because of my keen interest, she later arranged for a tutor to come to her London home to instruct me. I'm not sure you could say I learned how to fight, however. It was more a matter of learning how to hold the blade properly so that it would not be knocked from my hand at first contact. And, I assure you, that is no small matter."

"You learned your footwork as well," Barringer added, momentarily studying the small potato he had stabbed onto the end of his fork. "It's her footwork that was most impressive." He popped the potato into his mouth and chewed thoughtfully. "I wonder if women have an advantage there, though, being smaller and generally more graceful?"

"I'm sure a lady's grace should only be demonstrated at dance," Amity sniffed haughtily. "Do you dance, Mr. Barringer? I understand all officers do. I hope there will be a dance soon."

"I believe something is being discussed," Mrs. Sprague advised them, invigorated by the thought of her daughters dancing with gallant, red-coated soldiers. "Some of the more prominent Loyalists are planning a fete to properly welcome the new regiments. No doubt there will be dancing."

Anna flashed Daniel a look, silently pleading with him to not respond. His thoughts were plain enough on his face. *We are to celebrate the arrival of troops who have come to either force us to submit to the yoke, or put us in shackles?*

"Talking of the cabin boy's swordplay puts me in mind of Lieutenant Chastain." It was the first straw Anna latched on to in her quick mental search for a way to steer the conversation in another direction. "How is he faring these days?"

Edward laughed. "Not well, I'm afraid. The ability to adjust to new surroundings is not among Mr. Chastain's gifts, I fear, and the many adjustments he has had to make here have challenged him exceedingly." The thought of Chastain's many trials and discomforts amused him. "My fondest hope is that his next posting will be to the Indies."

Barringer laughed at that. "He'd resign his commission, I've no doubt. But he has launched upon on a new quest that seems to have absorbed him to some extent. At least he does not spend quite so much time complaining about the accommodations."

"For it to make Lieutenant Chastain happy," Anna retorted dryly, "his new quest must involve something that will bring him attention from his superiors without any particular exertion or actual accomplishment on his part."

"Anna!" Wilton was shocked by his niece's ungracious remark.

"I do apologize, uncle, but the man in question is of a sort I'm sure you would consider disagreeable in the extreme. It seemed apparent to me that his goal in joining the army had little to do with service to the king and a great deal to do with serving his own need for power and prestige."

"Sadly, I fear Miss Somerset's assessment may be more accurate than even she knows," Barringer agreed.

Edward nodded. "And, you are correct about the nature of his quest as well. It seems that a convoy of supplies on its way from New York was waylaid by highwaymen. The shipment included a number of General Gage's personal effects, most of which were stolen. The General is quite unhappy about it, not least because some of his wife's belongings were stolen as well."

Anna looked at Daniel, an unspoken question, and he responded with a barely perceptible shake of his head. He had nothing to do with the theft and knew nothing about it.

Barringer picked up the thread of the story. "Most troublesome, apparently, is an item the general purchased as a gift for his wife some time ago. As I understand it, the item is an unusual music box in the shape of an egg. It's blue enamel and decorated in gold filigree."

"It sounds exquisite!" Mrs. Sprague, always acquisitive, glanced meaningfully at her husband.

"According to General Gage, it is quite superb," Edward assured them. "And is both monetarily and sentimentally valuable. He would dearly love to recover the item, and Chastain has taken it upon himself to investigate the theft. No doubt he feels that, were he to recover it, he would earn the unending gratitude of the general — and, by extension, considerable advancement for himself."

"Well, I hope he catches the highwaymen," Judith declared. She self-consciously touched her hair. "What beastly men to take such a lovely thing! Mrs. Gage must be heartbroken."

"She has not yet returned from London," Edward said. "I believe the general hopes to have recovered her valuables before she joins him here."

Barringer snorted. "Well, he can rest assured that Chastain will do all he can to accommodate that desire."

"Then the man is not without a certain value," Wilton offered hopefully. "We must wish him good fortune in his hunt."

"Indeed." Anna raised her glass along with the others but saw that Daniel had not. His expression had taken on a brooding quality and, deep within his own thoughts, he was lightly drumming his fingers on the table. She nudged her knee against his, jolting him into awareness, and he raised his glass though he had no idea what was being toasted.

All of the food was beautifully prepared and presented, yet it was plain food. Anna knew these dishes might have been served below-stairs in one of England's great houses but would never have made it to the family dining table. Nonetheless, she felt proud of the feast, particularly the quality and quantity of meats and shellfish that were superior to anything she had enjoyed in London. The crab and oysters were devoured with unbridled gusto, and the strip roast brought an end to all male conversation as the men gave their all over to enjoyment of the beef.

"Mrs. Cook," Sprague said, addressing the cook as she circled the table to see that all was in order, "your meal is, as always, superlative. Especially noteworthy in these times of increasing shortages. I shall manage to steal you from Wilton one of these days. I shall make it my *raison d'être*."

The woman laughed. "Not going to happen, Sir." She glided off into the kitchen. She would not leave the Wilton's employ for the king himself, but she enjoyed the flattery of having people like Mr. Sprague attempt to lure her away.

"Your cook's name is 'Mrs. Cook'?" Barringer asked.

"Yes. It has been the source of comment by every dinner guest for years."

"She is a treasure," Mrs. Sprague agreed. "Everything is perfectly and deliciously seasoned."

"Mrs. Cook does know her craft," Anna agreed. "Even the simplest fare becomes a divine culinary experience in her hands."

"Mrs. Cook's husband is a fisherman," Daniel told them. "Oh, but I suppose that's not quite true. Given that the king has closed the harbor and put fisherman out of work, I'm not sure how Mrs. Cook's husband is making his living these days."

Anna cringed. She knew well enough the truth of what Daniel was saying for there was a good deal of muttering, banging of pots, and slamming of cupboards on the part of the otherwise good-natured cook when she learned that the two officers would be among the guests. The extra enthusiasm with which she wielded the meat cleaver was a bit frightening as well. But the meal bore no evidence of the cook's ill-will. Despite the truth of Daniel's statement, Anna wished he had not said it. She threateningly pressed her foot down on top of his toe.

"Yes," Hinton replied carefully, his words clipped and precise. "It is a shame that the innocent must be made to suffer because a handful of malcontents refuse to be brought to heel."

"Brought to *heel?*" Before he could say more, Anna stomped so hard on Daniel's foot that he flinched in reaction. He glared at her, but refrained from further comment.

Anna had no such control over Hinton and, to her chagrin, he had opened his mouth to make further response. "Oh!" she cried, startling them all, and effectively cutting off whatever he'd been about to say. "Mrs. Sprague, I've been longing to hear the details of Miss Sprague's wedding. I was so sorry that I was away and not able to attend." In fact, missing Margaret Sprague's wedding was one of the rare things that had made her happy to be in London, and she had no interest in the details, but she knew Dorcas Sprague liked nothing better than to talk about it. Mr. Sprague, having no desire to hear the details recounted for the umpteenth time, gave Anna a caustic look. She smiled at him and cocked her head, seemingly intent on every one of Mrs. Sprague's overblown words.

Completely unaware that she was in danger of putting the company to sleep, Mrs. Sprague rambled on and on, allowing Anna enough breathing room to silently communicate to Daniel her wish that her homecoming celebration not be spoiled by battles over politics and public policy. He rewarded her facial machinations with a look of contrition and shrug of acquiescence, though not without getting in one final sharp look at Hinton. *He shares the blame*, the look conveyed eloquently.

Mrs. Sprague's enthusiastic discourse continued. Though she did not actually say the words, it plainly was a great relief to her that her eldest daughter had finally procured a husband. The fact that it was more likely Mr. Sprague's money that had landed him than Miss Sprague's dubious charms was ignored. All three of the Sprague girls were afflicted with overly inflated opinions of themselves, and were vain, self-centered, and spoiled in the extreme. They had not a whit of intelligence between them, and if any of them had a particular talent, it was yet to be discovered. Despite all of this, it seemed a mystery to their mother that they remained so devoid of suitors.

"Margaret was an absolute *vision!*" Anna wished she had kept a tally of how many times Mrs. Sprague had uttered those words. At least this time, it seemed to be part of a general wind-down of her recitation. In closing, she beamed across the table at Selah. "Oh, and I should add that we owe a debt to Mrs. Garrett for the success of Margaret's wedding gown and her trousseau. How you managed such a marvelous gown with all the shortages is quite beyond me. I'm sure you must have a treasure chest buried away somewhere!"

Selah laughed. "Actually, you owe it to Miss Somerset. Much of what I used came by her generosity from London. Her generosity," she amended, "and her cleverness. I was endlessly amazed at how she managed to send things to us when our suppliers were so constrained!"

"I for one," Sprague pronounced, "enjoyed every drop of tea we made from the genuine oolong leaves you slipped past the authorities!" He was brought up short in his enthusiasm by Anna's red cheeks and the warning look she darted in the direction of the two officers. "Oh, my," he mumbled, suddenly awkward. "Perhaps I should not have . . . oh, dear."

"I believe her creativity is what we might call 'smuggling,'" Edward observed with a chuckle. "Perhaps Lieutenant Barringer and I should have taken a keener interest in the contents of that enormous trunk you brought aboard the *Sheridan*, Miss Somerset." It was said with his tongue firmly thrust against his cheek, and made everyone relax into quiet laughter.

"What *was* in that trunk?" Daniel asked. "I heard more than one comment regarding its size and weight when we fetched you from the landing."

Daniel had hit on one of her uncle's favorite topics for teasing her — that being the number of trunks she had brought home from London, particularly the enormous gift from Lady Sylvia. "You heard comments, Mr. Garrett?" Wilton asked with a chuckle. "Or, was it complaints?"

"I fear that they were more in the nature of complaints," Daniel admitted to the amusement of the guests.

"I did not choose that trunk," Anna replied with exaggerated indignation. "It was a gift from Lady Sylvia Gordon-Hewes. She filled it with things to make the voyage more comfortable, and small luxuries she likely thought I could not find here. Lady Sylvia has a rather imperfect understanding of Boston's level of sophistication, I'm afraid." She enumerated the contents of the trunk, omitting those items that were too

S.D. BANKS

personal or which might raise eyebrows. "And, she included a number of nicely packaged herbs. I believe they are intended for medicinal purposes. I know the uses of most of them, but there are a few that are unfamiliar to me."

"Why don't you bring them by my shop one afternoon?" Selah suggested. "Perhaps I can help you identify them."

"I would like that."

"I've learned that Mrs. Garrett is of as much use — if not more — than a physician," Wilton decreed. "She seems to have a cure for every ill."

"You flatter me, Mr. Wilton. During the war against the French and Indians, I assisted a surgeon who had trained with the best physicians in Scotland. I could never hope to match his ability, but I did learn a great deal."

"The Scots are a fascinating breed," Barringer said. "And the best friends one can have in a fight."

"Perhaps their fondness for a fight is the reason they produce such fine physicians?" Sprague jested.

"The surgeon's name was MacTiernan," Selah recalled. "The men considered him a bit daft because he always doused his instruments with Scotch whisky. He claimed it was to bless them 'good Scotsmen' so that he could trust them." Everyone at the table laughed.

"Seems a waste of good spirits to me," Sprague chuckled. "Maybe the man *was* daft."

"Perhaps," Selah agreed.

Anna told them about Captain Grant's demonstration at the fencing academy. "I don't believe I could ever have imagined someone like him." Her tone was reflective and admiring. "I kept thinking, Mr. Garrett, that — had your grandfather not chosen to leave Scotland and come here — you would be much like the Captain. Surely, you are cut from similar cloth." Immediately the words had left her mouth, she wished she could take them back. It was a ridiculous thing to say aloud, and it had caused Daniel some embarrassment.

But then, Selah compounded it. "Daniel's grandfather and father were both far too stubborn and unyielding to have made the necessary compromise to remain in Scotland." She was looking directly at Daniel when she said it. *And, you are exactly like them, my son.*

Anna noticed that Edward was speculatively assessing Daniel. *No*, she thought. *Daniel is not a man who will yield, not a man who will bend when it comes to what he believes is right. He will fight you to the death if that is what it takes. And there are hundreds more like him.* As though he could hear her thoughts inside his head, Edward shifted his attention to Anna. She offered him a thin smile over the rim of her wine glass. *I wish you luck, my friend, but am not sure that I wish you success.*

* * *

Charlotte contemplated Richard Chastain and decided that, what the lieutenant lacked in physical appeal, which was a great deal, was more than adequately recompensed by his sophistication and refinement. In these things, she felt certain that he outshone virtually any man in Boston. The fact that he was a Londoner, and would likely return there at the first opportunity, only served to further burnish his appeal, as did his all too apparent ambition. In Charlotte's view, ambition was among the most supreme of personal qualities.

This was her fourth encounter with the promising young officer since his arrival in Boston. With each meeting, the time they spent together increased until, on this evening, she allowed Chastain to completely monopolize her time. They were meeting, yet again, at one of the endless string of fetes Boston Loyalists had arranged for the entertainment of General Gage and his staff. She considered it a happy circumstance that Teague was often traveling far afield for long periods of time as he endeavored to sell his stolen munitions. With Teague absent from the picture, she was free to attend as many parties as she liked without having to offer any explanation of justification to him.

Despite the unvarying ponderousness of these evenings, invitations to the parties were highly sought after. But after their unresolved disagreement the first week after General Gage's arrival, Martin Ainsworth had refused to accept further invitations. Undaunted, Charlotte attended the more select parties alone, always telling the hostess that her father had taken ill but had insisted that she attend without him. The reward for her tenaciousness and audacity was an introduction to Chastain, in whom she felt she had found a kindred spirit.

A cursory survey of the clusters of guests scattered about the room made it plain that the popularity of any given officer was in almost direct correlation to the amount of gold braid decorating his uniform. So far, Richard Chastain had only a modest amount of this desirable adornment, and that was a deficiency he seemed eager to remedy. Possessed of a finely tuned intuition, Charlotte quickly and accurately surmised that Chastain would be interested in any potential source of funds to buy his captaincy, and that was the thing that made him a suitable object to enable the fulfillment of her own ambitions. His need for money was her leverage and, thanks to Teague's efforts, she had the money to exploit that leverage. All she needed now was a way to convince Chastain that a partnership with her would help him as much as it would help her.

Chastain followed her gaze to the cluster of officers orbiting Gage. "Look at them, how they honor him." He snorted derisively. "You'd think he was their sun and their moon." He took a sip of wine and wrinkled his nose with distaste.

"And, isn't he?" Her tone was mildly mocking, and there was a coquettish tilt to her head. "Isn't that what all of you believe?"

"Hardly. And they will only pretend to that belief so long as their fortunes rise with him. The moment his sun begins to set, so will their fortunes, and they will turn their backs on him with head-spinning rapidity. They will move on in search of a new sun to orbit."

She laughed. "It's refreshing to hear someone speak with such candor. Most of you officers go on and on about duty and loyalty and all those tiresome things until one becomes quite bored with listening to you."

"I do believe I have been insulted."

"Don't posture, Lieutenant. You know very well that I meant it as a compliment — to you, at least."

"I thought ladies particularly admired duty and loyalty. Aren't things like that, all of the so-called gentlemanly virtues, highly regarded by discerning young ladies with the luxury of being able to choose?"

"With some naïve little simpletons, perhaps. None of it amounts to a pile of salt in my view. Especially considering, as you said, it's all a façade." She watched the group of scarlet-coated officers, how they hovered about the general, hung on his every word, and her antipathy gained momentum. "Duty and loyalty my eye! The only person I'm loyal to is myself because 'myself' is the only person who will be always loyal to me. Everyone talks of loyalty to the king. Pshaw! As long as I pay all of his irritating little taxes, the king doesn't give a hoot about me. All of you smart soldiers puff your chests out and talk about loyalty to the king, but what you're really loyal to is your careers. That, I can respect. As for governments, they're nothing more than men who want my money and the opportunity to hold onto their power. Family members die, and friends are only around so long as my friendship benefits them in some way. No, Lieutenant. None of that for me. I'm in this life for myself, and myself alone."

"Such cynicism surprises me."

"Does it? I'd have thought you would understand it."

"Oh, I do understand it. I am nevertheless surprised to hear such words come from such a pretty head."

The wife of a local merchant brushed past, tittering with tipsy laughter at something her companion had said to her, eliciting a disdainful sniff from Chastain. Understanding well his scorn, Charlotte laughed. "You find us an amusing lot, I'm sure."

Chastain regarded her carefully. She was spectacularly pretty, and he enjoyed her company, so he informed his words with as much tact as he was capable of producing. "On the contrary, Miss Ainsworth," he smiled weakly. "I was just thinking how these little gatherings remind me of the pleasant dances with which we amuse ourselves when the nobility retire to their country estates."

"Ah, country dances. Yes, I suppose we could be likened to a gaggle of country folk." She lowered her lashes and smiled in a way she knew to be most winning. "But I suspect you are a man far more suited to the London salon."

Chastain preened unconsciously. "I confess, Miss Ainsworth, you have the make of me."

Laughter bubbled in her throat. "I have ever been told that I have a good eye for quality."

"Indeed." With one thin eyebrow arched pointedly, Chastain's reptilian eyes glistened. This girl may have the make of him, but he saw through her as well. What exactly her ambition was, he had not yet decided, but her character was familiar enough; he saw it every time he looked at his own reflection. "And you, Miss Ainsworth? Where would you prefer to spend your leisure?" He knew the answer but was intrigued to see how forthright she would be in her response.

"Oh, a London salon, of course! You cannot imagine how I long to see London!" The moment the words left her mouth, she knew she had spoken too quickly and with too much eagerness, endangering any hope she might have had of achieving a subtle campaign against Mr. Chastain's defenses. *Ah, well,* she thought. *In for a penny, in for a pound. Perhaps a bolder approach would serve just as well given the circumstances.* She felt color rising in her cheeks. "You must think me very unworldly," she burbled, "to place such importance on something that, to you, is surely so commonplace as to warrant no exceptional interest."

"I think you charming," he assured her, a slow smile tightening his lips. "And given that London is anything but commonplace, I can certainly understand your desire to see it."

"Father has promised for years to take me," she lied airily. "And now, these tiresome troublemakers have caused such a stir, we never know what will happen from day to day. It's impossible to plan such a journey. I'm so happy you are here, Lieutenant Chastain. I have confidence that you'll soon put things to rights."

"Certainly not myself alone," he chuckled, "though your confidence is well placed. General Gage has assembled far more troops than will likely be necessary to subdue the rabble. I cannot imagine it will take long at all."

"Well," she prevaricated, a coy tilt to her head, "I confess to a small hope that it won't be over too quickly. I should hate to see some of you depart before we have had the chance to become good friends."

"You are a novelty, Miss Ainsworth. A Bostonian who wants to become good friends with one of His Majesty's officers!"

"In all modesty, I do agree that I'm a novelty, Mr. Chastain. But I must point out that I had only a select one or two of you in mind — not the entire army."

"One or two of us?"

He had drawn quite close, and she had to fight the impulse to pull back from him. "At least one of you," she breathlessly told him.

The bold flirtation continued for a while longer until, finally, Chastain asked for permission to call on her. A rendezvous over tea the following afternoon was arranged, and Charlotte went home happy, her head full of plots and plans.

*　　*　　*

Daniel found the August heat to be almost crushing as he stood, along with a good percentage of Boston's citizenry, to watch the Massachusetts delegates ride out for the first meeting of what was being called the "Continental Congress" in Philadelphia. Sam Adams and his cousin John, Thomas Cushing, and Robert Treat Paine made up a small parade that passed virtually under General Gage's nose, and Daniel had no doubt that Sam Adams was enjoying every moment of it. Gage's arrival in Boston may have been met with politeness, but this little demonstration made it clear that the Patriots were not going to be bullied by his presence.

Daniel did not envy the fifty-or-so men who would have to button themselves into the close confines of Carpenter's Hall while they hammered out a unified response to the Intolerable Acts. Representatives from the other colonies were expected to advocate for more boycotts and petitions, but Sam had told him that the Massachusetts delegates intended to insist on a firmer stand and to push for the expansion and heavier arming of the colonial militias. It would amount to carrying an olive branch in one hand, a musket in the other, and it would be a hard sell. Daniel knew the Massachusetts men would give the other delegates little peace until acquiescence was achieved. It would be a protracted, unpleasant process, and Daniel was happy to not be part of it, especially because he had something far more pressing on his mind.

Encountering Anna had not been part of his plan for the afternoon, but he rounded a corner and there she was, emerging from a silversmith's shop — in the company of Edward Hinton. The handsome lieutenant carried a small parcel under his arm and was engaged in animated — and, judging by Anna's laughter, amusing — conversation with her. Daniel's eyes narrowed as he watched the pair. He knew he should pass by, yet he simply could not do it.

"Miss Somerset," he said, greeting Anna with a bow and tip of his hat. His greeting for Hinton was considerably more perfunctory. She was flushed, as though she'd been caught at something untoward. "Shopping for silver ware, I see. You should have taken him to Mr. Revere's establishment. His craftsmanship is far superior to Baxter's."

"I did not think Mr. Revere's shop would suit the lieutenant," she replied crisply. Anna was fully aware of Revere's position with the Sons of Liberty. Daniel was mocking her, and the look in her eyes told him she did not appreciate it. "What are you doing here?"

"I'm on my way to visit a friend."

"Then, we should be on our way, Miss Somerset." Hinton clearly wanted to dismiss him. "We would not want to distract you from your errand."

"You're not. Actually, I'm glad I bumped into you. I have information that might interest you."

"Oh?"

"Yes. I thought you might want to spread among your compatriots word of a fine opportunity."

Unable to imagine that Daniel could be offering any sort of useful information, Hinton arched his eyebrows.

"I wanted to be sure you're aware of the offer the New Hampshire colony has made to any redcoat who chooses to leave the army and take up residence there. They are offering three-hundred acres of land to any aspiring farmers among you."

"I am well aware of the bribe that is being offered to our troops." Hinton's posture turned rigid. "The rebels seem to know they are doomed and hope to buy off the threat. It will not work."

"Hmm. I understood that some twenty-seven men from the Inniskilling regiment alone have accepted the offer."

"I doubt the Twenty-Seventh suffers their loss." It was a thin lie, and he knew it. It was no secret that, with replacements so far away, the loss of even one soldier was a significant blow to any regiment. "Those men are deserters and, when caught, will be dealt with accordingly."

Daniel laughed. "There's a lot of countryside out there, Hinton. Do you really think you have enough men to comb through all of it in search of a handful of men?"

"We will do what is necessary."

"Enlighten us, please. If you do manage to catch them, what will be their punishment? Oh, wait! I believe I know. That would be flogging, would it not? You redcoats are particularly fond of that one. And what will the lads get? Ten lashes? Fifty? One hundred?"

Hinton cast an uncomfortable glance at Anna. "I hardly think this a topic for polite conversation," he replied tightly.

"Yes, it is rather impolite, isn't it? But then, it's just one more example of the obscene way in which the English choose to exert their will."

"Mr. Garrett!" Anna's face was full of thunder.

"Don't you wonder about it, Miss Somerset? What is it, do you suppose, that makes the English so fond of flogging? What makes that brutal iron fist necessary?"

"Stop it." Her hands balled into tense fists at her side.

Daniel ignored her anger. "Those Inniskilling men were all Irishmen. I wonder, Lieutenant, if your heavy reliance on the cat o' nine tails has anything to do with the fact that fully a third of your troops are Scots, another third Irish? That puts you English in a distinct minority among armed men who have every reason to hate you. Could that have anything to do with it? Are you afraid of what might happen if you don't keep all those *others* fully under control?"

Hinton stepped forward, drawing to within inches of Daniel. "The reason for the strict discipline becomes evident to any enemy that has the misfortune to face us on a battlefield."

"Perhaps. Though, not all battles are fought on a battlefield, are they?" Daniel pasted a carefree grin on his face and walked away.

"It is incredible to me that you count that man among your friends," Hinton told her as they watched Daniel walk away.

"Not nearly as incredible as it is to me," she muttered.

The smile vanished from Daniel's face the moment he turned his back on Anna and Hinton. He was angry with himself for stooping to such petty childishness. If he had wanted to show himself a better man than Hinton, and he was loath to admit that as his motive, he'd made a bad job of it.

He'd been trying to track Teague down for several weeks now, ever since the Wilton's dinner party. He had a suspicion that Teague was involved in the theft of Gage's belongings, and he wondered if Teague was aware of the hornet's nest he had overturned. Despite Daniel's resolution to be quit of Teague, his conscience would not allow him to stand by while someone who had once been the closest of friends blindly stumbled into a situation he did not fully understand. Daniel's conscience and habit of fidelity to their past friendship demanded that he warn Teague and be sure he was aware of the danger with which he flirted. That was all.

But Teague apparently did not want to be found. It was one of his talents — the ability to disappear completely when it suited him. Daniel had watched all of Teague's former haunts, and had even enlisted Drum's help, but without success. So for the second time in a week, Daniel was on his way to keep watch at the Ainsworth house. Like a bee to honey, Teague would surely return there.

Daniel had watched the house on several occasions and, though Teague was absent, the vigil had yielded one interesting surprise. One afternoon, an elegant barouche had drawn up in front of the house. Its occupant was a tall, gangling red-coated officer whose disjointed gait as he sauntered to the front door made him recognizable even from a distance. Daniel had been in Anna's company the first time he laid eyes on the young officer and was surprised when she pointedly avoided the man. She gave no details beyond the officer's name — Chastain — but it was plain to Daniel that the lieutenant had managed to offend her at some point. And then, there was the mention of him at John Wilton's dinner party. Now the unpopular officer was apparently squiring Charlotte Ainsworth. The two of them had ridden away in a carriage, full of laughter and high spirits making Daniel wonder what Teague would have thought had he been there.

After that day, however, Drum had told him that Teague always approached the house from the back side, and so he had relocated to a new observation point. Daniel had watched the alley several times to no avail. Deciding that Teague might prefer the cover of darkness, he arrived at his chosen vantage point before sundown, perching on a sturdy branch in a leafy elm tree that overlooked the enclosed area behind the Ainsworth house and settled in to wait.

It was over a half-hour after sunset, and Daniel was near to giving up when Teague finally appeared. So stealthy was Teague's approach that Daniel might have missed him if not for a flash of moonlight on something Teague carried in his hand. He watched Teague slip across the yard and rap lightly on the door. Shadows hid the identity of the person who opened the door, but Daniel felt fairly certain that it had to be Charlotte. Martin Ainsworth would never countenance such a visit.

He dropped lightly from the tree and followed the path he had watched Teague take to the back door. There, he knocked and waited. It seemed he'd had to wait too long, and he was on the verge of knocking again more loudly when the door opened. Charlotte stood there looking down on him.

Dispensing with any sort of polite preamble, he gruffly informed her, "I need to speak with Teague."

"He isn't here."

"He *is* here, and I need to speak with him."

"And what if he does not need to speak with you?"

"Bloody hell." He stepped up and laid one hand on the door. "I haven't the patience for this," he snapped, pushing past her into the house.

Charlotte stamped her foot. "How dare you force your way in here! Leave this house at once!"

"No." He was checking all of the adjacent rooms. "Not until I've talked to Teague. Now, where is he?" He glanced up the stairs.

"You will not go up there. My father is ill, and I'll not have him disturbed." In fact, her father had complained of a headache earlier in the day, and Charlotte had dosed him with enough laudanum to keep him dead to the world for hours. "Teague does not wish to see you," she hissed. "Nor do I. Leave this house now, Mr. Garrett."

He leaned down to thrust his face menacingly close to hers. It intimidated her, and she backed away from him until she bumped up against the wall. "Tell me where he is."

"I'm here."

Daniel spun on his heel to find himself facing the man who had once been his closest friend standing only a few feet away, pointing a loaded musket at Daniel's chest.

"I'm here," Teague repeated. "What do you want?"

Daniel held his hands, palms turned outwards, slightly away from his body, but the wariness on his face and tension with which he held himself indicated that there was no lack of caution. "I've brought you a warning." It was said flatly, without emotion. "It's about the army's supply convoy you raided. The one out of New York."

Testimony to his guilt, Teague's eyes flicked quickly to Charlotte, whose face showed only the briefest spark of alarm before becoming once again serene. Taking his cue from her, Teague composed himself and covered his stance in belligerence. "What makes you think I know anything about it?"

Daniel stared at him but said nothing.

Teague squirmed, struggling to regain his self-possession. "What if I do know about it? What makes you think I want to hear anything you have to say on the matter?"

"Your excessive fondness for self-preservation."

"Oh? You're here to offer more threats, then? And, what are you going to threaten me with this time? Seems to me you have naught left."

"Not me. The army."

"Did you think I'd need you to tell me the army would be a bit miffed to find some of their supplies gone astray?" he scoffed. "Do you really think I'm a complete imbecile without you to think for me?" His words were tight with anger and resentment, his finger dangerously tense on the musket trigger. "I've been watching my back. I always have. I certainly never had anyone to watch it for me."

Daniel let the jibe go past. It should no longer matter, but it rankled nonetheless. "This is different. You never tweaked the tail of a sleeping dragon before."

"The British army? You and your friends have been tweaking their tail for some time now. Why should they particularly take notice of me?"

"Because some of the things you stole were Gage's personal property, and there's a career-minded officer who would like nothing more than to recover the property for him, along with the head of whoever stole it." When Teague merely shrugged, Daniel became impatient. "From what I hear, this man will do whatever it takes to find you. He will bribe, bully, and turn Boston upside down if that's what it takes, but he will find you."

"And, what do you suggest I do?"

"Lay low. Leave Boston. Maybe even see that the stolen items anonymously find their way back to Gage's possession. Certainly, don't go after any more plunder for a while. If even one other person knows you were involved, this man will track you down, Teague."

"Seems to me," Teague asserted, brandishing the musket more aggressively, "that you are a part of my danger. You seem so certain I've done this thing. Maybe removing you should be part of the caution you are urging on me?"

Daniel glanced at Charlotte. She was still pressed against the wall, her face even more colorless than normal. "I don't think you'll shoot me now, Teague. You and Charlotte obviously have plans for the evening that would be seriously fouled if you shoot me and arouse Mr. Ainsworth." Now, he noticed, some color crept into Charlotte's cheeks. Without another glance in Teague's direction, he turned on his heel and started for the door. He was almost there when he paused, seemingly arrested by some sudden memory. He turned back to Charlotte. "By the way," he told her. "The redcoat lieutenant you've been riding out with? Name of Chastain, I believe?" He smiled in satisfaction when the blush spread across her neck and shoulders. "It happens that he's the lieutenant who is so bent on returning the general's property to him. Very eager for advancement is your Lieutenant Chastain. Given that you've been keeping company with him, I assume you knew that. My guess is, his plans for advancement are the reason you've been allowing him to call on you. No doubt visions of prancing about London, the wife of an army captain, have been bouncing around that otherwise empty little head of yours ever since you met him."

Daniel anticipated the slap and intercepted it with a firm grip on her arm. "Be assured, Miss Ainsworth," he said with an intensity that made her flinch, "that I shall learn what you are plotting. I'll find out, and I'll thwart you." He started toward the door, pausing there to make one last attempt to reach his former friend. "She will make you the fool, Teague. I promise you, whatever she is scheming, it will end up stinging you."

"Leave, Daniel." He jerked the musket to emphasize the order. "Now."

Once Daniel had gone, Teague slowly allowed the musket relax in his hands, the breath he'd been holding escaping as the barrel drooped toward the floor. But, Charlotte noticed, the storm clouds did not leave his face.

"What was he talking about?" he demanded of her. "What is this about you and some redcoat officer?"

She drew herself up, imbuing her posture with haughtiness and indignation. "It's nothing. More of his slanderous lies and exaggerations meant to pull us apart is all."

"Have you been riding out with this Chastain?"

"Oh, really, Teague!" She threw her hands up in exasperation. "Yes, I have. Along with my father, I should point out. Daniel deliberately neglected to mention that part."

The lie was told without a second thought. When he did not look satisfied, she sighed with heavy implication of her regard for his considerable thick-headedness. "The redcoats are searching everywhere for guns," she explained with an air of forced patience.

"I know that," he snapped. "I, of all people, know that! What has it got to do with you keeping company with one of them?"

"Lieutenant Chastain was in charge of the search party dispatched to my father's warehouse. For reasons that escape me, my father befriended the man and has invited him to the house on several occasions. It has been most inconvenient." She felt pleased with herself for so quickly conjuring such a plausible story. "I have no idea what sort of business they are conducting as I've not been privy to their conversations."

"Then why were you riding out with him in his carriage?"

She shrugged, dismissing the question as inconsequential. "There have been occasions when the two of them had some destination or another in mind and I was compelled to join them to look after my father. To tell you that I was nearly bored to tears the entire time would not begin to express how I felt about it."

He seemed to struggle with her explanation. "Why would Daniel lie? Why would he say you were alone with Chastain?"

"I don't recall him saying we were alone. But I agree that he certainly implied it, and the reason for that implied lie should be perfectly clear to you. He is jealous, and he would say anything to drive us apart — especially if it hurts me. He hates me, Teague. I've rebuffed his advances so often over the years that he has come to hate me." It was an easy fabrication, born out of her desire for it to be the truth. "He will do anything to assault us with his overwhelming jealousy and hatred."

Teague stared at her, weighing all she had said. While Charlotte waited for him to convince himself that she told the truth, her thoughts moved on to the new problem of Daniel. She had no doubt that he would stop at nothing to ruin her plans. That, she could not allow. And, so, she set her mind against Daniel with renewed fierceness. He would have to be dealt with, and she suspected she could not trust Teague to handle the matter.

"You will stay away from this Chastain," Teague finally decreed.

The fury in him bordered on violence, so she wisely bit back the retort she would have liked to make.

"You will stay away from him, or I'll take steps to keep him away from you." He turned and stalked out of the house without waiting to hear her agreement — which she did not give.

1775

CHAPTER THIRTEEN

As Boston emerged from winter's repressive embrace, and warmer, sunnier days appeared in fits and starts, Anna found herself enjoying a sense of hope. To be sure, political discord continued to fill the air, but owing to the watchful eye of the increasingly omnipresent army, the incidences of violence seemed to have waned to some degree. Ignoring the small part of her that was made uncomfortable by the military presence and clinging to her hope for peace, Anna had hummed happily to herself as she ticked a day off the calendar that morning. *March 5*, she thought, her eyes lingering on the date. It was exactly five years to the day since that unwarrantable business on King Street — the tragedy routinely referred to by many propagandists as "the massacre."

She did not want to think about that just at this moment, however. Not when she was feeling so especially cheerful. This was a warmer day than five years earlier, sunnier with not even the tiniest threat of snow. Even so, the downstairs fireplaces were stoked with toasty fires, and her uncle and Mr. Sprague were settled in front of the one in her uncle's study most of the afternoon, deeply engrossed in a chess match. The female Sprague covey had decamped for an extended visit with relatives in New York, leaving Mr. Sprague a temporary bachelor. Mrs. Garrett would be joining them later in the afternoon for supper, as would Mr. Hinton. It was to be a far less formal occasion than when they had last dined together, and Anna was expecting a pleasant time of it.

Despite her cheerfulness, she was restless and anxious. She had spent an embarrassing amount of time fussing over her dress and her hair. Then she had tinkered with the small vases of early blooming crocus she had placed around the parlor and dining room, and had arranged and re-arranged, fluffed, plucked and generally niggled over ever little detail of the house until the ridiculousness of her behavior dawned on her. Mrs. Cook had twice cast her from the kitchen when she made the mistake of wandering in and offering to help with food preparation, and now her uncle and Mr. Sprague were regarding her with knowing, side-long glances and a general air of amusement. Fond as she was of Selah Garrett, they knew that it was not for Mrs. Garrett's benefit that all of these pains were being taken.

It was something of a relief when the guests arrived and the ceremony that went with hosting a company of friends supplanted Anna's nervousness. Mrs. Garrett, who unfailingly seemed to know the right thing to say or the right gesture to make, had a calming effect, and Anna kept close to her, drawing on that aura. As always, Edward was the epitome of gentlemanly qualities and could not hide the fact that he was taken with Anna. For Anna, his attention was so flattering that it was almost intoxicating. But the unfamiliar sensation was unnerving as well.

Selah sensed that Anna was wrestling with internal questions. She carefully watched first Anna, and then Hinton. He was tremendously handsome, she had to admit, and was the sort of man whose attentions would be gratifying to any lady's pride. Certainly, she could see how Anna might be attracted to him. But did Anna fancy herself in love with him? Attraction was not love, and Selah suspected that Anna knew the difference.

Once the party settled down to their meal, considerable time was spent offering up heartfelt praise for Mrs. Cook's abilities, coupled with Mr. Sprague's ongoing attempt to steal her away from Wilton. Most of the meal was dominated by laughter and congenial conversation, but it was inevitable that the discussion eventually turned to politics. Edward Hinton's response to every query and comment betrayed his growing frustration with the situation, though none so much as when Mr. Sprague asked about the ongoing process of confiscating local militias' stockpiles of munitions.

"Disarming the militias has been a slow process, and not without its hazards," Hinton told them. "Many of our men sent out on these missions have met with some resistance — albeit feeble and disorganized."

Wilton frowned. "Surely there will be no real violence. These are merchants and farmers, after all."

"Thus far, the trouble has been limited to threats and the sporadic scuffle. There has been what some would refer to as 'saber rattling,' however, and muskets have been loaded on some occasions."

"The outlying areas of our colony continue to feel the threat of many dangers," Selah gently pointed out. "My late husband fought in the war against the French and Indians. He did so because it was clear that the king did not have enough soldiers to protect these vast colonies. We need to be able to protect ourselves. Surely the king and the Parliament can understand why the militias are reluctant to give up their weapons?"

"Though I see your point, these self-styled 'Sons of Liberty' should be brought to heel and this nonsense put to an end." Hinton's tone was severe and, hearing himself, he visibly curbed his passion.

"I recall your uncle saying that, as Englishmen, we are all 'sons of liberty,'" Anna told him. "He could not understand why much of the rhetoric was so inflammatory to many English ears when, in truth, the dissenters want those things that are considered every Englishman's right by law."

"It is beginning to appear that the dissenters want far more than that. However, their demands aside, my uncle plays dangerous semantic games."

"On the contrary. I always found that your uncle was a good example of the lawyer's precision in words."

"Is this the Mr. Christopher Hinton of whom you have often spoken?" her uncle asked.

"If Miss Somerset has told you much about him," Edward put in quickly, "you need to know that he is considered something of a black sheep by the family." It was said with a smile, yet everyone sensed that a part of Edward worried about the impression his uncle's words and actions might reflect on his family.

"Not to worry. Everything she has told me has been quite admirable."

"He is a remarkable man," Anna enthused. "I found him to be extraordinarily intelligent, and possessed of a fine wit. More than that, he is so very patient with Lady Sylvia whose own family neglects her terribly in my view."

"You have mentioned Lady Sylvia before," Sprague pointed out. "Is she a lady who demands great patience then?"

Anna considered the question. "Perhaps patience is not the correct word. She does require *understanding*, however, and one must be on their toes to keep up with her quick mind. Mr. Hinton is the perfect friend to her in that regard."

"Is Lady Sylvia very grand?" Selah asked.

"In many ways, yes, she is very grand. However, she is quick to tweak her nose at convention, and has little use for anyone with an unduly inflated view of themselves. Though she dresses herself in the appropriate guise, I'd say that titles and wealth do not seem to matter to her nearly so much as what lies beneath. Perhaps the silks and jewels are actually a kind of concealment from which she can observe those around her."

"Your Lady Sylvia sounds more and more like a person whose company I would enjoy," Sprague commented.

"Oh, you would! You would adore her, and I know she would adore you. All of you."

"Do you miss her?" Selah asked.

"Very much. And I miss her garden. I often wished I had the artist's gift so that I could paint some of the views and bring them here to you."

"Perhaps you will return to London to enjoy it again?" Edward suggested.

"Perhaps." Anna shrugged noncommittally. "I was very fond of one particular fountain because it was adorned with figures of mermaids and dolphins. I thought about it when we were making the crossing from London to Boston. On a moonless, starless night, when the ship seemed to be suspended in a kind of black void, I thought how lovely it would be if mermaids and myriad other fantastical sea creatures were cavorting all about us, just out of our line of sight. I imagined all sorts of creatures that came out only at night and were aware of ships crossing here and there but were intelligent enough to stay beyond the sight of anyone on board. Wouldn't that be lovely?" Her face was alight with the flight of fancy, and she looked to Edward, expecting similar enthusiasm.

But, in the way of men firmly rooted in concrete thought, Edward was struggling to imagine the unfathomable scenario she suggested. "I . . . um . . . well, yes, that would indeed be interesting."

Anna's smile froze, and a slight flush rose in her cheeks. Knowing she had revealed too much of her affinity for things that could be seen only with the mind, she lowered her eyes to stare at her plate.

Selah saw it all. To the sensible mind, there was every reason in the world why Anna should encourage Edward Hinton's attentions. He came from a good family and was inarguably a gentleman. Perhaps more importantly, he was a good man, a kind man, even an intelligent man. His intelligence was no match for Anna's quick mind, however, and he had no inner complement at all to her originality. The tragedy, in Selah's view, was that Anna seemed to feel the need to conform herself to Edward's ideal. "A good many men who make their lives on the sea would tell you that they have, in fact, seen mermaids," she ventured.

"Surely those men have been deluded by the appearance of a seal or dolphin or other such creature," Hinton countered soberly.

Sprague shrugged. "Perhaps. Or, perhaps it is simply that they availed themselves a bit too liberally of the grog." The comment triggered a ripple of laughter.

"I did not say that I believe that mermaids exist," Anna replied softly. "Only that I think it would be lovely if they did."

"Take heart, my dear," Selah told her. "Your lovely fiction may yet become fact. I do not believe that we know or have yet seen everything there is to be seen in heaven, on the earth, or in the sea. And, I feel certain that, in the creation of His universe, God would not have limited Himself to only what we hold to be logical or rational. It seems to me that the fantastic is an inherent part of God."

Sprague raised his glass in salute. "Well said, Mrs. Garrett!"

Supper was concluded without any further ruffling of feathers, and cordials and easy conversation finished out the evening. Throughout it all, Anna continued to be aware that Edward was not quite his usual self, as though uneasy in his own skin, and there was an occasional brittleness to his tone of voice. At the end of the evening she saw him to the door but held him up just before he departed. "Are you well?" she asked quietly. "You seem different today. Edgy. Is something amiss?"

"No," he said softly. "Or, perhaps yes. Every week that I've spent in Boston has further convinced me that all of this is headed toward disaster. I worry that the colonists are not considering the consequences of these acts of defiance. They take it too lightly. It troubles me, not least because I worry about what it could all mean for you and your uncle."

"Are you saying you are worried for our safety?"

He nodded. "I worry for the safety of us all, Miss Somerset."

*　　*　　*

The little clock on Martin Ainsworth's desk chimed four times. He counted each one, resisting all the while the temptation to go to the window yet again. If Charlotte saw him watching for her return, she would be cross, and he was loath to provoke her anger for it seemed that they were already teetering on the brink of something quite horrible. He knew something must be done, and that it must be done carefully. Charlotte's many angry outbursts over the course of the previous months had made him face that fact. Attempting to determine exactly what must be done, however, left him at a loss.

He looked at the portrait of Charlotte's mother above the fireplace. Charlotte had inherited her mother's cool beauty but none of her inner warmth. It deepened his sadness to think that his beloved wife would be disappointed in his failed attempt to raise their daughter well. "If only you had stayed with us," he told the portrait. "If you had, surely Charlotte would have learned your sweet nature."

Charlotte had ridden out for the afternoon with Lieutenant Chastain, a man Martin Ainsworth found particularly distasteful. It was not merely the officer's arrogance and condescension that offended Ainsworth but also the sense he had of Chastain's character. Whenever he attempted to broach the subject of his reservations about Chastain, she cut him off with either cold silence or a hasty departure from his presence. Martin Ainsworth could bear neither of those things. Tears clouded his vision until he could no longer see his wife's image, and his shoulders sagged under some invisible, unbearable weight.

Charlotte, who was happily making considerable progress in the achievement of her own goals, spared no thought for her father or his concerns. She had ridden out into the countryside with Chastain in a lovely little gig he had procured for the day, and she was working at providing gay, desirable company for the lieutenant. Watching how he handled the reins, she admired the elegant ease of his hands. She found herself watching his hands a great deal, for they were the only graceful thing about him. It was early March and still chilly for such an outing. Charlotte would not be deterred, however, and she huddled close to Chastain.

"You are cold," he observed. "Shall I turn back?"

S.D. BANKS

"Don't you dare! We've not had a chance to be together like this for the entire winter. The sunshine is marvelous. Spring has come early I think." The couple was quite scandalously alone, which did not overly concern her as she did not intend to be much longer in Boston.

They reached the destination he had planned, and he guided the carriage off into a field bordering an apple orchard. "Here we are." He helped her down from the carriage. "Have you ever seen such apple trees!"

"Yes," she laughed. "I live here. I have quite my fill of apple trees."

"Ah, yes. I suppose that was a foolish question. Things do seem to grow . . . *bigger* here."

"Though not better. I doubt for one moment that these apples are in any way superior to those in England."

Actually, they are, he thought, but had no intention of admitting it aloud. "You have such avowed preference for England. I wonder that you and your father remain here instead of transporting yourselves there."

"Well," she chirruped, perching prettily on a rock wall, "this is where my father has made his fortune, and he is somewhat reluctant to leave behind what is familiar to him."

"Understandable. What makes you think he will eventually change his mind?"

"Me," she laughed lightly. "I shall go and, because he cannot bear to be parted from me, he will follow." She dearly hoped he would not follow but thought the suggested scenario would sound more respectable to Chastain than what she actually planned. "When I am of age, I shall book passage on the first available ship for London. I have a substantial inheritance from my mother, so I can be quite independent in that regard."

He had not known of any such inheritance and failed to disguise his heightened interest when it was mentioned.

"My mother wanted me to have some control over my own future, so she left me quite a substantial sum, as did my grandparents on her side." She was pleased with the lie. It had taken her several hours one night, lying in bed and staring up at her bedroom ceiling, to think of a plausible story to explain the money she was amassing thanks to Teague's concerted efforts. She indifferently lifted one smooth shoulder. "I doubt I shall need to rely on that. I am, after all, my father's only child. Have I ever told you that I almost died when I was a child?" She barely waited for him to shake his head before continuing what was one of her favorite tales. "Yes, I did. I had a horribly high fever for days and days. Everyone was certain that I would die, but I did not. I believe the fact that he almost lost me made my father determined to hold onto me all the more tightly." A sweet, serene smile, convincing in its blithe performance flickered across her lips, to be quickly replaced by an attractive little moue and quick intake of breath. "Oh, but that was unseemly forward of me! You've allowed me to prattle

240

on about such a personal matter. Surely I have embarrassed you, and I do apologize! You must think me a product of the backwoods."

"Not at all," he assured her with good humor. "You were merely carried away with your thoughts."

"Yes. That's it." She frowned slightly, as though searching for her a lost thread of thought. "Now, I believe we were discussing London?"

"We were indeed." But Chastain was according only superficial attention to her wandering, inflated thoughts on London. His mind was spinning through the possibilities this pretty girl represented. He considered that her striking face and figure would make quite a favorable impression within his London social circle, and it was possible that the money she spoke of would enable him to purchase a captaincy at the very least. Given that she made no secret of her social ambitions, it was unlikely that she would balk at underwriting his career. How to determine the truth of her claims, though? Something would occur to him, he had no doubt. In the meantime, he found that the misery of his colonial post was being ameliorated. He had the mystery of the general's stolen property to occupy his duty hours and Charlotte Ainsworth's titillating company to entertain him at other times. From his viewpoint, therefore, things were definitely beginning to improve.

Twilight was overtaking the sky by the time Chastain returned Charlotte to her father's house. The afternoon had passed as a delightful flirtation punctuated with moments bordering on salaciousness, and the glow of that stimulation remained palpable as Martin Ainsworth watched his daughter being handed down from the carriage by the arrogant lieutenant. Seeing the familiarity Charlotte allowed the young man made Ainsworth cringe.

He stepped back from the window as she approached the door, and he was standing in the middle of his small study when she swept into the foyer. A flick of her eyes told him that she saw he was there, though she pretended otherwise. "Did you enjoy your outing?" he asked in a carefully neutral tone. The answer did not really matter to him, he already knew it well enough, but he was unwilling to let the relationship with Chastain go further without some conversation on the subject, and this seemed as good an opener as any. It was a terrible risk, but something must be done.

Her back was to him and she hesitated, hovering between responding and marching past as though he had not spoken. *Ah, well,* she thought, *perhaps this is the moment to finally make plain his irrelevance in my life.* Pasting a self-satisfied smile on her face, she slowly turned to address him. "Yes," she said, carefully folding her hands in front of her, "I enjoyed it very much." He had lost a great deal of weight over the past few weeks, she observed, making him appear even more timorous than was the norm.

"I am glad. Seeing you in such good spirits delights me, and I'm happy that you have formed a new friendship." He hesitated over his next words, choosing them carefully. "I wonder, though, if it is advisable for you to be seen keeping such intimate company with this man? After all, he will only be here as long as his regiment is here."

"If you are suggesting that my relationship with Lieutenant Chastain might hamper my chances of finding a husband among Boston's eligible sons, then you should not be concerned. I have no intention of marrying one of the unsophisticated fools who parade about this town as though they actually matter. I'll not be shackled to this horrid place or to a man who smells either of fish, hay, or the counting house." She sniffed in a manner intended to show that she included him in her disdain.

"That is disingenuous of you, Charlotte," he replied gently. "The men of this colony have worked hard as fishermen, farmers, and merchants. They have built this place into what it is, and have made their families comfortable in the process. You wear fine clothes, enjoy a full larder, and live in a prosperous home because of the time I spend in the counting house, as you phrased it."

"I may enjoy fine things by Boston's standards," she retorted loftily, "but not by London's standards, and it is those to which I aspire."

"And, you believe Chastain will help you reach your goal? You cannot be thinking of him as a possible husband!"

"I can. And, I am."

"Charlotte! We know almost nothing about him!"

"I know enough. He is sophisticated, has ambition to match my own, and is not the sort of man to be hampered by apprehension or timidity."

"And, you think that is enough?"

"I do."

"Oh, my dear daughter," he moaned, dolefully covering his face with his hands. "Can you truly be so foolish? I have seen his sort of man too often. He will dally with you and then return home to England without so much as a glance back."

"He will not."

"Has this man actually mentioned marriage? After such a short acquaintance?"

"Not directly, but there have been veiled suggestions."

Ainsworth shook his head. "If he is a gentleman, and if he were entertaining such thoughts, he would have spoken to me."

"I have made it plain to him that I follow my own wishes. What you will or won't allow is of no consequence."

"I remind you that I am your father. My wishes on such matters are of considerable consequence!"

"Only so far as any money you might settle on me. If I must, I shall manage without that."

"I've seen enough of him to know that this man is not the sort to marry simply for love — assuming anyone could arouse such a sentiment in him. He'll not do anything without my blessing. He will want the money."

"He will if he believes my income is not solely dependent on you."

"And, does he believe such a thing?"

"He does."

"Then you have lied to him. What a fine foundation to build a marriage upon!"

Deeming it preferable for him to think that she had lied to Chastain over revealing the money she had amassed by selling off Teague's stolen goods, she merely shrugged.

"I shall tell him the truth."

She narrowed her eyes. "You will do no such thing."

"If that is what it takes to keep you from setting yourself on the path of ruin, I most certainly shall." His tone was firm but, inwardly, he trembled in fear.

"You will only embarrass yourself," she insisted, her words clipped and supercilious. "I shall find a way around whatever you tell him, and you'll have accomplished nothing in the process. You old fool. You sniveling, pitiful, pathetic old man. Don't you know you lost this battle long ago?" She turned her back on him and started up the stairs. "I shall be leaving here soon," she called back over her shoulder. "Hopefully, it will be under Lieutenant Chastain's auspices, but I shall leave regardless." On the upper landing, she turned to look down on him, her hands folded complacently in front of her, a portrait of icy elegance. "It would be so much more pleasant for all concerned if you would gracefully accept that and keep your mouth shut."

For the first time in her life, Martin Ainsworth finally saw his daughter with a clear eye. He felt his blood begin to rush hotly, his pulse pounded in his ears, and every muscle in his body grew painfully taut. He mounted the stairs, taking each one with agonized deliberation, anger and despair tightening their grip on his heart and lungs with every step so that, by the time he reached the landing, he found it difficult to draw breath.

Charlotte did not wait for him to climb the stairs, choosing instead to continue on to her bedroom. She paused only because, once he had reached the top of the stairs, his breathing was so labored — so peculiar sounding — that she turned out of curiosity. He was leaning on the top newel, gasping for air and sweating profusely. Detachedly, she observed that his color had changed from the scarlet red of fury to a darker, bruised color. His hand clutched to his chest, he looked up at her in a silent, wretched plea, seemingly unable to form words with his white-rimmed lips.

He wavered slightly, tipping forward and back. Watching the teetering, she cocked her head, curious to see which way he would fall. But she moved not a muscle to help him.

*   *   *

Daniel stood in the middle of the room — *his room*, he had finally come to acknowledge — and turned a slow circle. It was a very small room, one of the two that comprised the apartments above his mother's store. As far as his mother was concerned, it had always been his. But for so long, he had only occasionally stayed there, and that was only grudgingly. As a boy, the places Teague took him, abandoned places, or caves, or, later, rooms like the one over Withers' tavern had seemed far more appealing. There was an excitement in the hint of danger that lurked about such places, a kind of romance to living the vagabond life and, more importantly, it was a way to lose himself. Sometime in recent years, though, that had begun to change. The change was so slow as to be imperceptible, yet somewhere along that brief timeline, finding himself had become more important than losing himself.

He pivoted like the hands on a clock, taking in the room's evolution. Originally, there was only a cot, a wash stand, pegs on the wall for his clothes, and a stool that was solid enough to allow him a place to sit while he pulled on his boots. Over time, the cot had become a small bed, and a table with an oil lamp was placed beside it. The bed had linens, a fine quilt, and even a pillow. A dressing mirror was added to the wash stand, and a chest of drawers held his clothes. A chair that had once belonged to old man Healey sat cozily by the small hearth, accompanied by a table that was ample enough to hold some of the books he occasionally borrowed from Dr. Warren. There was an over-sized rag rug on the floor, which was a luxury he had regarded as unnecessary but for which he was grateful.

A bit of color, ribbons used as a bookmark, caught his eye. Just the tips were visible — two pieces of ribbon, one cream and one rose-colored — peeking from between the pages of one of the books on the table. Hastily, he reached for the book and placed the ribbons between its pages so they could not be seen when the book was closed. It was senseless, he knew, to work so hard at keeping them hidden. But having to explain to his mother or anyone else who might happen to see them how he had come by them or why he kept them was something he particularly did not want to do. He closed the book and replaced it on the table.

He heard Drum enter the downstairs kitchen from the back door and picked up his haversack and hat, then loped down the stairs to join them. He and Drum were going to watch the Regulars unload some artillery pieces that had arrived with a recent wave of troops. Daniel felt a tad guilty; Drum believed the expedition was all about getting to see the guns.

In fact, Daniel would be there to count the guns, and whatever else was unloaded, and deliver those tallies to Dr. Warren.

The gathering of intelligence in Boston had become an elaborately inventive affair, and Drum unwittingly benefitted from much of Daniel's participation in the process. The day before, they had visited a chocolate shop, lingering long enough to enjoy more than one warm, bittersweet cup while Daniel eavesdropped on the conversations of the officers' wives who frequented the establishment. It was amazing to Daniel how much could be gleaned from the incautious gossip of women. Because Drum believed that chocolate was one of God's finer creations, he did not complain about spending most of the afternoon there. In Daniel's view, it was time well spent for he had come away with troubling hints about Gage's plans to arrest members of the Provincial Congress and to conduct a search-and-destroy mission that would encompass militia munitions depots at Lexington and Concord.

Dr. Warren was appreciative of the information Daniel relayed about Gage's purported plans, and was clearly troubled by the information. He had heard similar tales from other sources, and it all seemed to add up to something significant. Daniel felt that every time he delivered some bit of overheard gossip or details regarding the arrival of reinforcements and equipment, he was adding to Warren's burden. But Warren insisted that it was all important and urged Daniel to continue his observations. So, today it was artillery pieces. Drum would actually be somewhat useful in this case because he had learned to recognize the types and sizes of cannon far better than Daniel had done, and he was quite pleased to show off his knowledge by naming the guns for Daniel. Drum's fascination with the guns caused Daniel a pang of apprehension; he hoped Drum would never have to learn exactly what each piece of artillery could do to men or their homes.

*   *   *

When, after what seemed to Charlotte an unnecessarily protracted amount of time, Martin Ainsworth finally collapsed, he fell forward, face-first onto the landing. Charlotte's mouth twisted disapprovingly, for she considered that it would have been far more convenient if he had fallen the other way and tumbled down the stairs. Dispassionately, she watched her father as his body jerked in painful seizures, her mind weighing options. For the most part, his death would simplify her plans — though not, she reminded herself, if he died before everything was in place. With him alive, but ill, she would have access to money from his business as well as the household account. If he died, things might become far more complicated, and might cost her money she was loath to forego if it could be avoided.

And so, sighing heavily at the inconvenience, she had sent for someone to help her get him to his bed, sent for the physician, and acted the part of the concerned, doting daughter. That part she had enjoyed for, as always, she found pleasure in creating a convincing illusion and took great pride in her ability to deceive. Now, however, she was alone and burdened with the care of her helpless father. On the infrequent occasions when he awoke, he would lie still, staring at her, unable to speak. Whenever she approached the bed, his right hand would jerk spasmodically against the quilt as though he wanted to reach for her but could not make his muscles obey. Occasionally, for no reason that she could detect, one leg would begin to tremble so violently that the entire bed shook.

More often, he lapsed into long periods of death-like sleep during which he emitted a string of guttural gurgling noises that she found to be as disquieting as they were unpleasant. Worse, his bodily functions continued uncontrolled and, because of her desire to keep secret so much of what happened inside the house, she had long ago dismissed the maid and was forced to deal alone with the filth and effluvia. As she sat watching him sleep, her mind churned through scenarios and formulated plans.

Two weeks passed as Charlotte began to put her plans into play. Just before a visit from her father's business manager Milton Mickelson, Charlotte changed her father's nightshirt and bedclothes. But, as she knew it would, the reek of urine, feces, and an unwashed body continued to hang in the air. The window was open now, allowing in a flood of fresh air and enhancing the illusion that she attempted to keep her father and his room clean.

This was how she had been arranging for Mickelson's visits ever since her father's becoming bedridden, the result being that Mickelson dreaded his audiences with Martin Ainsworth. By now, she knew Mickelson would latch onto anything that would allow him to avoid the encounters. She had already convinced Mickelson that the myriad twitches and grunts Ainsworth demonstrated during Mickelson's visit were a way of communicating his wishes to her, and it would be easy enough to now convince Mickelson that, given his condition, visitors were a humiliation for her father that could be avoided if he would merely agree to accept direction through her. That accomplished, it would be a trifling matter to create a convincing string of directives instructing Mickelson to liquidate the contents of her father's warehouse.

Satisfied that all was in place, Charlotte left her father's room and prepared her own appearance for Mickelson's arrival. Fate had smiled upon her, she decided, and handed her the means by which she could have not only a life in London but also her father's money and the freedom to enjoy it all.

*　　*　　*

Drum regarded every moment he had spent working at the Ainsworth house to be a misery. He had promised himself more than once that whatever task he'd been given would be his last, and that he would tell Charlotte he could no longer work for her. Time and again, however, he would lose his nerve and meekly accept more work.

It wasn't just that being in Charlotte's presence was a reminder of his many shortcomings. Mostly, Charlotte left him alone, affording him only an icy regard. When he failed to perform a task to her liking, however, she would serve him with heated tongue lashings that left him stunned by their irrationality. It surprised him when, out of keeping with either of those constants, she approached him one afternoon in late March as he struggled to set to rights some stone pavers on the Ainsworth's garden path.

She was smiling and, though she clutched her shawl protectively about her, seemed full of warmth and friendliness. His shock was all the greater when she commented on the fact that he appeared to be the worse for the unusually warm spring sun, and invited him to step into the kitchen for something cool to drink. Motivated more by obedience than an actual desire for refreshment, Drum followed her around the house to the back stoop and, hat in hand, into the kitchen. He had never before been inside the Ainsworth house, and he shivered at the cold emptiness of the place.

Charlotte invited him to sit at the kitchen worktable while she fetched some cellar-chilled cider. Smiling, she sat across the table from him, two cups between them. "I'm so very thankful that Teague suggested I hire you." She took a tiny sip from her cup. "You've been helping out around here for — how long now?" She rolled her eyes toward the ceiling as though she expected to find the answer written there. "Why, it has been almost four years, hasn't it?" she noted with some amazement.

Drum nodded but said nothing. He was surprised that she knew how long he'd been working there. Taking a hearty draught of cider to hide his discomfort, he watched her over the rim, hoping for some explanation for her sudden interest in him. Despite Charlotte's ethereal beauty, he felt supremely uncomfortable in her presence. There was an unsettling undercurrent there that he could neither define nor trust. He knew Teague was in love with her and thought the strong attachment must surely be due to something aside from her beauty, though he could never quite see what that thing might be.

"It has been wonderful to have your help." Charlotte's words flowed quickly, breathlessly, as she struggled to strike a balance between her effort to curry his good sympathy and her desire to be done with the matter. "Such a Godsend, actually! With my father ill, I have to take care of so much on my own. I don't know how I would manage without your help."

The mention of her father brought to the forefront of Drum's mind something that occurred to him each time he came to the house. "I haven't seen Mr. Ainsworth in several weeks," he told her. "He used to stop and speak to me, but he never seems to leave the house anymore."

"He is bedridden," she replied curtly, "and does not see anyone." A flash of iciness appeared in her eyes before, just as quickly, her mask descended again as she returned to the purpose of her conversation with him. "Oh, Drum," she drawled, her voice suddenly weary, "It has been such a trial. I do not know how I would manage without friends like you and Teague." Her lower lip quivered ever so slightly.

Drum set his cup down and stared at it. She had never before referred to him as a friend, and he could feel a blush crawling up his neck into his face. It was not, however, a blush of pleasure, but of guilt. He had no desire to be considered her friend and, though he could not change his feelings on the matter, it made him feel ashamed to dislike someone so much.

Mistaking Drum's reddening cheeks as a sign that she was having the desired effect, Charlotte smiled and reached across the table to lightly place her hand over his. Suspecting that it would be regarded as bad manners for him to do so, Drum expended considerable effort to not flinch at her cool touch.

"I know I can rely on Teague, and on you," she said softly, "and that means the world to me. I have so few people in my life on whom I can rely. I especially value your friendship, Drum, because I feel that you are trustworthy. I am right in that, am I not?" She smiled triumphantly when Drum nodded. "Yes, I thought so. I've always told Teague he should appreciate that in you — that he should appreciate your loyalty and trustworthiness."

Drum frowned, unhappy with the suggestion that Teague needed Charlotte to tell him any such thing.

"I need to ask you something now, Drum," she told him, her voice growing low and conspiratorial. "I need to ask you to perform a task for me . . . for my father, actually. And, I need for you to keep it a secret between us. Can you understand that? Can you keep a secret for me?"

Drum was very good at keeping secrets, but he thought it odd that Charlotte would be asking such a thing of him. Not knowing how to respond, he simply shrugged.

Charlotte, mildly annoyed that her request had not met with quite the eager agreement she anticipated, shifted in her chair as she prepared to put forth her proposal. "My father is concerned that, with all the unrest and with the increasing number of troops in Boston, our home is not as secure as it once was. All these new men — these *soldiers* — are strangers, and he worries that they are not all good people. He sees them from his bedroom window, and they frighten him."

This Drum could understand. He'd heard plenty of complaints about the presence of the regulars from folks in Boston. He nodded his head.

"I've tried to reassure him, of course. I try to tell him that he need not concern himself, but he thinks me too trusting. His fear has grown until I believe that it is actually making his illness worse. Because I love him so very dearly, I've thought of a plan that seems to have eased his mind considerably. I cannot enact my plan without help, however." Her expression indicated that his was the help she sought.

Drum had begun to feel very sorry for Mr. Ainsworth. He thought how terrible it would be to be so helplessly ill and afraid. Charlotte's grip on his hand had tightened, pleading with him to help do he knew not what, but something that would ease her father's mind. It surprised and impressed Drum to learn that she was so devoted to her father. "I'll help you," he said, pleased to be able to do something good for a sick, powerless old man.

Charlotte's entire body relaxed. "Oh, thank goodness! I knew I could depend on you."

"What is it that you need me to do?"

"Well, my father owns a few things that are quite dear to him, mostly because they belonged to my mother, you understand, and it would devastate him if something were to happen to any of those things — if any of them were to be damaged or stolen."

Drum nodded. He thought of his marbles and the little box he kept with things that meant so much to him.

"Father wants them hidden away someplace where they will be secure . . . someplace where they are unlikely to be found. Do you know the shed that is at the back of the yard behind this house?"

"Yes, of course I do. I cleaned it out for you four months ago, remember?"

"Ah, yes. So you did! Well, I thought that you could remove the slatted floor and dig a deep pit underneath. I can put my father's little treasures in the pit, and then we could put the slats back into place. It seems to me to be the perfect solution."

Drum nodded. "I could do that."

"Here is the important part, Drum." She leaned close to him again, and spoke so softly that it was almost a whisper. "Absolutely no one must know what you are doing. You must not tell *anyone* — not even Teague, not even Daniel. You and I must be the only people in Boston who know about the hiding place."

"And Mr. Ainsworth."

"Yes, Drum. And my father. But no one else. It will be a secret between us. Otherwise, the wrong person might learn of it and it would no longer be a good hiding place. Do you understand?"

Drum did not see why he couldn't tell Daniel or Teague, but he nodded in understanding, nonetheless. It actually made him feel somewhat important to be the keeper of Mr. Ainsworth's secret, to be privy to something that not even Teague or Daniel knew.

The very next day, Drum started work on the secret hiding place. Charlotte insisted that he work inside the shed with the door closed most of the way so that no one would see what he was doing. He first pulled up the flooring slats, and stacked them neatly to one side, then began to dig. The hard-packed earth did not yield easily to his shovel, so the work was exhausting, and he did not like working inside the dark shed. She also insisted that he pile the dirt to one side of the pit so that it would be easier to refill when the time came. Because the piled dirt took up so much room, it made the inside of the shed a bit crowded, especially for a man of Drum's size, but he made the best of it. The difficulty of the job was further compounded by the fact that Charlotte wanted the pit to be wide and several feet deep, which he did not think was necessary for just a few little mementos. But she had insisted, and so he had complied. He worked diligently and now, a week later, the work was done.

Eager to collect his pay, Drum presented himself at the Ainsworth's back door as was their established routine. But even after knocking determinedly at the door, he could raise no response. Disappointed that he would have to go away empty-handed, Drum trudged around the corner of the house headed toward the front gate.

Half-way along the path, he was stopped by sounds of a disturbance coming from an open window on the upper floor of the house. It seemed odd to him that, despite the fact that someone was apparently at home, no one had responded to his knock. More sounds — breaking glass, the thud of something heavy hitting the floor, and what sounded like a strangled cry — tumbled down from the open window, convincing Drum that something was awry. Quickly, he back-tracked to the kitchen door and let himself into the house.

"Miss Ainsworth?" Drum closed the door behind him and listened for some response. The kitchen was empty and, though he strained to hear, there was only a vacant hush. "Miss Ainsworth?" He tried again, raising his voice so that it would reach out to anyone in the house. "Mr. Ainsworth?" There was only silence.

Drum cautiously made his way through a door that led from the kitchen into a narrow corridor that passed under the staircase in a straight line between the kitchen and the front door. Drum continued to call out, and continued to receive no response. Ever more wary, he edged along the corridor, stopping frequently to listen, anxiously peering into the empty parlor and study. It seemed he was utterly alone in the house, and yet, he was certain of what he had heard coming from that bedroom window. He stood in the foyer, staring speculatively up the stairs, uncertain of his next move, when a clock somewhere in the parlor chimed the hour. The sound startled him so much that he jumped.

"Miss Ainsworth?" He hoped she would appear at the top of the stairs, nothing awry, and save him from having to climb the stairs into the unknown. Instead, he heard the choked call of someone in distress drifting down from above stairs. His palms grew clammy, his heart pounded in his chest, and he desperately wanted to leave the house in search of someone else to deal with whatever was on that upper floor. That would take time, however, and he sensed an urgency in what he took to be a cry for help. He forced himself to mount the stairs, arriving on the upper landing to find himself confronted by two doors. The door to his left stood open on what he correctly surmised to be Charlotte's bedroom. He guessed that the door to his right, which was closed, led to a room overlooking the path on which he'd been standing when he heard the initial sounds of distress. All was quiet now, yet he knew what he had heard. Resignedly, he opened the door and stepped into Martin Ainsworth's bedroom.

* * *

"The butterflies on your bonnet are *alive!*" Anna was gaping at the adornment on Charlotte's hat, mortified by the realization that the butterflies pinned there were not well-executed artifice as she had at first thought but, in fact, real butterflies. One or two still struggled against their impalement, lovely iridescent wings flapping weakly as they tried in vain to escape.

"Why, yes, they are!" Charlotte touched her hand to the brim of the bonnet, seemingly delighted that someone had noticed her creation. "It required considerable effort to catch them. I had eight to begin with, but their wings fell apart when I tried to pin them to the hat, so I'm left with only six. They are lovely, aren't they? I could feel them flapping against the hat when I first put it on, which was bothering, but they settled soon enough. Certainly, I consider the final effect worth any inconvenience."

Anna was horrified beyond words. They were at a garden reception celebrating a parish wedding, and the day and the event had until this moment been quite lovely. Anna was surprised to find Charlotte in attendance. The new couple were not notable, making it the sort of event Charlotte would normally have disdained. Seeing how she was alight with pleasure in the company of the handful of regimental officers who were also, inexplicably, in attendance helped to explain her presence, however. She was standing before Anna now only because she'd been drawn to the little group, anchored by Lieutenant Barringer, engaged in conversation with Anna. Upon inserting herself into the group, the men's attention had shifted to Charlotte's charms, yet Anna had noticed only the butterflies among the silk flowers on her bonnet.

Watching the one pitiful butterfly that still survived use its waning strength to struggle against its deadly entrapment absorbed Anna's attention to the exclusion of all else. She felt deeply the insect's pain and terror and could think of nothing beyond her desire to free it, even if only to allow it to die a peaceful death. The compulsion pushed her forward a step, and she extended her hand toward Charlotte's bonnet. Before she could snatch away the pin that held the butterfly in place, however, she felt her elbow gripped by a firm hand that arrested her advance and steered her away from Charlotte and the others with whom she'd been conversing.

"Come along, Mouse."

"What the devil?" she spluttered, hearing Daniel's voice in her ear. "What are you doing?" She slapped at his hand where it held her elbow in a vise-like grip.

"Saving you from doing something you'd likely regret later." His words were clipped and he did not release her arm.

"I would not regret it," she snapped. "Let go of me! You don't even know what I was going to do."

"Yes, I do." Once he had dragged her well clear of the other guests, he stopped and turned her to face him. "You were going to snatch Miss Ainsworth's bonnet away because of the butterflies."

"I was not. I was going to unpin the one butterfly that is still alive," she huffed. "You do realize those are *real live* butterflies?"

"Yes, I realize it. She has done the same thing before, and I've told her how abhorrent I think it is."

"Who *does* something like that?" she cried. "What kind of person thinks something like that is acceptable?"

"Someone like Charlotte Ainsworth," he replied matter-of-factly. "I've told you she's a reprehensible . . . ." The appellation he wanted to apply seemed inappropriate for Anna's ears.

"Witch?"

"Something like that."

"Well, you should have let me unpin the poor creature. It would have at least made a point."

"All it would have accomplished would be to earn you a reputation as the girl who ravaged Charlotte Ainsworth's bonnet. Is that what you want?"

"No. But I don't want to let it go without some sort of censure! How can everyone smile and chat with her, pretending all the while that they don't notice her atrocity?"

"Because, it's what polite people do. Especially at weddings."

"Well, *bollocks!*" Frustrated, she folded her arms in front of her and glowered across the garden to where Charlotte still stood, smiling, ringed by three scarlet-coated officers. "I don't think it's right!"

"Neither do I, but there it is."

She could hear in his voice that he was trying not to laugh at her uncharacteristic use of an expletive. "What are you doing here, anyway?" she snapped angrily. "I doubt you even know the bride or groom. Besides, there must be a dozen regimental officers here. Not exactly your type of crowd, is it?"

"There are eight officers here. I counted. And, no, it isn't my type of crowd. But, as to what I'm doing here, I came looking for you."

"Well, you've found me — unfortunately. What do you want?"

"I've heard some news that I wanted to tell you before you heard it from someone else."

At that, she gave him her undivided attention. "What is it? What has happened?" she asked warily. "If you're wanting to soften the blow, I know it must be bad."

"I wouldn't call it 'bad,' exactly . . . or, not necessarily bad. It depends on your viewpoint and, I know from your viewpoint, it may seem bad."

"Just tell me, please."

He produced a folded piece of paper from his pocket. "I was with Dr. Warren earlier when he received some news from a friend in Virginia. The Virginia Convention met in Williamsburg a few days ago and voted to raise a force to defend themselves against further interference from the English."

"But that's absurd!" Anna laughed. "The Virginia Convention has no more official standing than the so-called Massachusetts Assembly your friends are operating from Cambridge!"

"Not in the eyes of Parliament, maybe. To the people who live here, however, the provincial assemblies are still their government. It will take more than a parliamentary act to undo that."

She sighed with exasperation but decided to let the point go. "Well, what exactly is it that the Virginia Convention is proposing?"

"They resolved to increase their militia by raising a cavalry or infantry company in every county."

"And do what? Stand up to General Gage's entire army should he decide to march it to Virginia? Does the Virginia Convention enjoy the notion of serving up so many lives for cannon fodder?"

"Of course not. And that's not the point."

"Then what is the point?"

"It's an act of defiance. It's a way of saying they are out of patience with petitions for reconciliation. It's as much a message to the Continental Congress as it is to London, I think."

"They can send messages to your Continental Congress all day long, and I fail to see how it matters," she asserted impatiently. "And I certainly fail to see how any of this can matter to us here in Massachusetts."

"It matters because these views are not limited to Virginia. There are folks in all of the colonies who feel the same way. This will spread. This will give them a rallying point." When she arched one skeptical eyebrow, he handed her the folded paper. "A man named Patrick Henry made a speech during the debate. Apparently, it was quite a powerful speech and moved a good many people — some of whom had previously been urging caution." He watched her unfold the paper and read a few lines, her brow creasing as the words sunk in. "Skip to the last few lines," he directed.

Anna's eyes skimmed down the page to the words reported there. She started to read them, stopped in mid-sentence and started again, aloud this time. *"Is life so dear, or peace so sweet, as to be purchased at the price of chains and slavery? Forbid it, Almighty God! I know not what course others may take; but as for me, give me liberty or give me death!"* She read it once again, silently this time, before folding the paper and handing it back to him. "I cannot deny the man's eloquence," she allowed, "though he seems a bit given to hyperbole. 'Chains and slavery'? Surely he does not suggest that the king holds us as an enslaved people!"

"If he did, he would not be alone in the argument."

"That's absurd!" she scoffed. "And what does Mr. Henry propose the Virginia colony do about all of the enslaved people on whose backs their colony has been built and is maintained?"

He looked away from her, his jaw tense. "It is a good question," he admitted, "for which I can offer no good response."

"So, the man is both a traitor and a hypocrite?"

"The man," Daniel replied sharply, "is persuasive in the extreme. His words have moved many listeners to take up the standard of rebellion, and it will spread. There are already some at the Continental Congress who are talking of rebellion — even of independency."

"The Adams cousins among them, I understand."

He nodded. "The Adams cousins among them. But they are not alone, and this may increase their numbers."

"Oh my," she breathed. "What can they be thinking?"

"Tell your uncle, Anna. This is serious, and there are contingencies for which he should plan. You must make him take this seriously. I know Mr. Sprague has tried, but you must make him understand. I don't want to see you, or your uncle, hurt by any fallout."

"Well, *bollocks*," she repeated.

*   *   *

When he walked into Martin Ainsworth's room, the first thing that hit Drum was the stench. Fetid beyond anything outside of a sewage-filled alley, the overpowering air was rank with the odor of human waste and sweat. The first gagging lungful drove him back a step before he could, through stinging eyes, focus on what he was seeing in the room. Soiled bedclothes were strewn in a jumbled cascade from the bed onto the floor, and the night table was overturned. Drum rounded the bed to find Martin Ainsworth on the floor, prone and still, among items he assumed had been on the night table. Shards of porcelain were everywhere, the remains of a basin and pitcher that had likely come from the washstand. It took Drum a moment to comprehend that Ainsworth must have tried to get out of bed, upsetting the night table and washstand in the process of his effort.

Had it not been for the fact that Ainsworth, dressed only in his night shirt, shivered in the cold air pouring across the open window sill, Drum might have mistaken him for dead. The hitherto plump little man was so frail and wasted as to be almost unrecognizable. His night shirt, which was caked with filth, had bunched itself around his thighs to expose skeletal blue-veined legs.

Fighting the nausea brought on by the stench, Drum bent to the old man. "Mr. Ainsworth? What has happened here? Do you need help?" The moment the words left his mouth, Drum realized that it was a stupid question, but it was all he could think of to say. "Here, now," he said, reaching down to gently turn Ainsworth onto his back. "Let's see what's to be done for you."

Ainsworth's eyes were open, and his mouth was moving as though to form words, but the only things that came out were choked gurgles and a stream of saliva. Drum was shocked and overcome with pity.

"Oh, no, Mr. Ainsworth! You poor soul. You poor, poor soul!" Moaning with dismay, bewildered, and somewhat frightened by the old man's plight, he rocked back on his heels and considered what he ought to do. Once again, his first thought was to find help, but this easy solution was quickly supplanted by a sense of urgency. He was not sure whether it was the right thing or not, but he knew what he *could* do and, that decision made, he acted without hesitation.

"I'm going to help you back into bed," Drum informed him, his voice unusually assertive.

Ignoring the odor and the filth on Ainsworth's night shirt, Drum carefully gathered the man into his arms and placed him gently on the bed. It occurred to him that it might be a good idea to tidy things up a bit, and he set about the job as best he could. He poked about in a cupboard until he located a clean night shirt, and this he exchanged for Ainsworth's filthy gown. Though he could do nothing about their soiled condition, he straightened the bedclothes and added a quilt he found draped over a trunk in the corner of the room, tucking Ainsworth in as he might a child.

Ainsworth stared at him through rheumy eyes the entire time he worked, which Drum found disconcerting.

As much to sooth himself as to reassure Ainsworth, he kept up a steady monologue, telling Ainsworth what he was doing as he tidied the room. "There, now," Drum said when he had done all he could. "Things are a little better now. It's the best I can manage anyway." Looking about the room, he realized that his effort had achieved little in terms of improving Ainsworth's situation. "No doubt Miss Ainsworth will make things better when she comes back," he added apologetically. "I don't know where she has gone, but surely she will return soon."

Drum was startled by the sudden appearance of fear and pleading in Ainsworth's eyes. The old man struggled again to form words and managed to stretch one bony hand out from under the quilt, reaching for Drum like a skeleton from the crypt. Drum understood that Ainsworth was afraid and that he wanted something from Drum, but what that was he could not fathom. "Can I fetch you some food, maybe? Or, some cider?"

Martin Ainsworth was beyond food or drink, however. His body was failing, and he knew it, for as a final, terrible injustice, his mind continued to function quite well. So full of sorrow that the weight of it threatened to crush him, Ainsworth looked up at Drum and knew he would never be able to communicate to the well-meaning young man that what he really needed was to be rescued from his own home, from his own daughter whom he had loved beyond life itself. Tears flowed down his cheeks, carrying with them the last traces of spirit to which he had clung. He closed his eyes, dismissing Drum, and tried to think no more.

Drum remained at the old man's side until he settled into a deep sleep, his rattling breath drifting in and out of his chest. Then, not knowing what else to do, he left the room, planning to return to the clean outdoor air to wait for Charlotte's return. He crossed the landing toward the stairs when something in Charlotte's room caught his eye. The sun's rays, slanting in through the window, were being caught by an object on top of her bureau, exploding into golden fractals and fantastic color. Though he knew it was wrong of him to do so, he could not resist getting a better look.

The item sat alone, displayed upon the bureau's top like some sacred religious artifact. Drum's eyes went wide with wonder at the beautiful thing, and he leaned down for a closer look. It was an egg-shaped box about double the size of a goose egg, seated on a small, three-legged stand. The egg was enameled in a brilliant, sapphire-blue and decorated with bands of gold filigree so delicate and intricate that it was difficult to imagine the work had been done with human hands. A tiny latch was worked into the filigree band that circled the egg's equator, and he dithered over whether or not he dared try to open it. Eventually, curiosity won out and, as carefully as could be managed with his meaty hands, he used one finger to lift the tiny gold clasp.

Despite his care, the egg toppled from its stand and rolled fitfully across the polished wood surface. Drum gasped, and thought his heart stopped until he safely caught the egg up in his two hands. He clutched it to his chest as though to keep it from escaping again. Once his equilibrium was restored, he cradled the egg in one hand and gently opened the latch. The top of the egg folded back to reveal a treasure within. Like an oyster shell, the inside of the lid was finished in mother-of-pearl. The bottom half of the ornament housed a tiny music box that clicked into action when the egg was opened, playing a sweet little tune and causing a single miniature pink porcelain rose to twirl on a tiny axle.

Drum drew a deep breath and held it. He had never in his life seen anything so exquisitely beautiful. Mesmerized, he stood staring down at the pale pink flower as he listened to the fragile-sounding music. The tiny gears clicked inside the mechanism as they spun and plucked and chimed out a tune he did not recognize but knew he would never forget. He could have stood there for hours watching and studying the wonderful little ornament, but after only a few minutes, the mechanism wound down bringing the delightful little show to an end. Not understanding that the device needed to be wound, Drum feared he had somehow broken it and, panicked, hastily returned it to its three-legged cradle. As he left the room, he cast one last look back at the egg, memorizing its every detail that he might be able to recall its beauty whenever he pleased.

He crossed the upper landing to the stairs and loped slowly down. His foot settled upon the final tread just as Charlotte came through the front door returning from the garden reception. Having spent the afternoon at the garden reception enjoying the attentions of several handsome officers, she was in high spirits — until she spied Drum. The fact that he'd been upstairs was perfectly plain to Charlotte, and she froze in place for a moment, hand on the still-open door, while she took the measure of his countenance. He seemed somewhat distressed, she thought, yet there was no accusation on his face, no sign that whatever he might have seen had aroused either alarm or suspicion in his artless brain. Gently she closed the door, and then moved to stand before him, her bearing full of disapproval that unsettled Drum.

"What are you doing in my house?" she demanded levelly. "You should not be here."

"I . . . I was looking for you," he stammered. "I've finished the hole and I wanted my pay. I knocked at the door, but you didn't answer."

"And, that dim little mind of yours told you it would be acceptable for you to simply let yourself in?"

Drum frowned. He hated being derided for his lack of intellect. He knew he was slow and did not need others to remind him of the fact. "I heard a noise," he replied defensively. "Someone called out. It sounded like someone was in trouble." The eyebrow she arched in response to this further unsettled him. "It sounded like your father. I thought he needed help."

"Indeed." She glanced up the stairs, apprehension replacing some of her anger. What had her father done to attract Drum's attention? "You saw my father?" She brushed past him and started up the stairs. "You should not have done that."

"I thought he needed help," Drum repeated huffily.

She wheeled on him, glaring down upon him with startling ferocity. "You should not *think*, Drum. It is not something you do well, and no good is likely ever to come of it."

"But he did need help. He had fallen, and there was a mess, and . . ." Drum searched about himself as though the rest of the words he wanted were scattered somewhere on the stairs.

Charlotte descended the stairs until she stood two steps above him and leaned her face so close to his that her hissing breath made him blink. "I shall take care of my father, you imbecile. You are not ever to come into this house again. Do you understand?"

Confused by her irrational anger, he could only nod in response.

"Good. Then please leave now."

"But . . . my money."

"Damn your eyes! You will get your money! I shall send it to you." But Drum did not move and she realized that it would be most expedient for her to simply give him what he wanted. "Wait here," she ordered and stormed up the stairs to her bedroom.

When she returned, he had not budged even an inch. She held out the money but dropped it before he could take it from her hand. Coins skittered down the steps onto the polished floor of the foyer, forcing Drum to take some trouble to retrieve them all.

"Now go," she commanded with an imperious wave of her hand. "And please do not return unless I send for you."

Drum crossed to the door and opened it but turned back to face her before leaving the house. "Don't send for me, Miss Ainsworth." His words were slow with precision. "I won't come back." He felt it was the boldest thing he had ever said in his life and, though the saying of it frightened him somewhat, replaying it in his mind put a smile on his face as he walked away from the house.

CHAPTER FOURTEEN

Privates Cudahy and Foster were growing weary of their association with Teague Bradley. Cudahy's involvement was the result of a desperate need to help his widowed mother and three younger sisters. He was an earnest young Dorchester lad who had joined the king's army because a recruiter had filled his head with visions of the money he would be able to send home to his needy family. However, the recruiter had failed to mention how much of Cudahy's meager army pay would be subject to stoppages to cover the cost of many of his daily necessities, substantially reducing his net pay. The unhappy situation made him open to any opportunity to pad his earnings. Foster's incentive to join in the criminal pursuit was less complex and far more mundane — he liked gambling and women, and needed more money to support those passions.

The young men's dissatisfaction with Teague stemmed from the fact that he consistently failed to distribute the fruits of their endeavors in a timely fashion, and when he did put money in their hands, the amount seemed to them to be far less than what was warranted by the risk they were taking. Though Cudahy and Foster had voiced their dissatisfaction in clear terms, little had changed. Not being men who would turn the other cheek when they felt themselves cheated, the privates decided to remedy the situation.

He was making money on his sales, they knew, and plenty of it, but what exactly he was doing with that money had required diligent shadowing before they hit upon the connection with the Ainsworth house. Clearly, the old man was serving as Teague's bank, and possibly providing other assistance, as well. Once that fact had been established, they resolved to spend every minute of their free time watching the house, waiting for an opportunity to launch their assault. They needed what was tantamount to an alignment of the stars — a moment when their free time coincided with one of Teague's journeys afield, and when the big man they presumed Ainsworth employed to do odd jobs was not about. It would be nothing, then, to wring the amassed money out of the elderly man.

The opportunity for which they waited finally presented itself late one afternoon and, inflated with bold resolve and a distorted sense of personal injustice, they presented themselves at the Ainsworth's front door with all the confidence of men who knew they would not — could not — be turned away. Cudahy, mindful of prying eyes, had counseled a rearward approach, but Foster argued convincingly that the small squads of soldiers deployed across Boston with the charge of confiscating rebel weapons and munitions provided an irreproachable cover story for their presence.

Charlotte, who did not know Cudahy or Foster and was unaware of their role in her improving fortunes, regarded the two redcoats with the same haughty disdain she would have afforded two steaming piles of manure. Her cool, steady appraisal momentarily took the soldiers aback for they had expected their appearance to elicit immediate fear and capitulation. "Yes? What do you want?" she demanded.

"We'd speak with your father, Miss," Foster replied. He stared down his nose at her, fixing her with his most withering gaze.

It had no effect. Charlotte stood her ground, unflinching. "My father is ill and does not see anyone," she snapped. "If you have business with him, you will need to—"

Foster did not wait for her to finish the sentence. Thrusting one substantial hand at the door, he pushed his way past her, Cudahy close on his heels. They stood in the narrow foyer, turning in circles as they took in their surroundings.

Charlotte opened the door wider, inviting them to reverse course. "What do you think you are doing?" she demanded. "I did not give you permission to enter this house, and you will leave at once!"

"What we are doing," Foster informed her, "is searching for weapons, and we don't need your permission for that. We have the king's order, and that's all we need."

"My father is no rebel and has no weapons for you to confiscate."

"We'll just need to verify that for ourselves, Missy." He sauntered toward the parlor door, eyes constantly roaming in search of hints that others might be in the house. Satisfied that they had cornered the girl alone, he turned on Charlotte. "Yes, we'll be needing to verify that for ourselves. Especially as we're particularly looking for muskets of the stolen variety." He grinned and leaned close enough that his foul breath assailed her nose. "Or, better yet, the money your friend Teague Bradley has made selling them."

Charlotte's heart jumped into her throat and a cold dread gripped her stomach. She was suddenly quite angry with Teague for not being present, despite the fact that she insisted he take a crate of muskets far out onto the frontier where they would fetch the highest price. "Don't be ridiculous," she snapped. "Mr. Bradley is not my friend, and I don't know anything about stolen muskets or money." Her eyes flicked to the pistols each man had shoved under his belt, then back to their hostile faces.

Foster's grin broadened. Though her voice was full of confidence, he had caught the spark of fear in her eyes. "Oh, I think you know a good deal about it, little Missy." He pulled the door out of her hand and closed it. "And I think you're going to tell us what you know and help us find what we're looking for because that's the only way you'll be rid of us." Taking her elbow in his rough grasp, he forced her into a chair in her father's study. "Your friend Teague has been holding out on us. We helped him procure some merchandise, and he hasn't paid us for our part in that venture. I believe he has broken faith with us, and we're here to claim our just desserts. I think your father is helping him somehow — holding the money for him, maybe. Helping him sell some of the items."

"That's absurd. My father has been bedridden for weeks."

"Well, that's interesting because we've seen Teague coming and going from here pretty regularly for quite some time now. If he's not dealing with your father, then he must be dealing with you."

Charlotte evinced an utterly convincing guise of incredulity. "I am nominally acquainted with Mr. Bradley," she sniffed. "He comes here from time to time because he helps me supervise our hired man, Mr. Fisackerly." She paused for a breath, struggling to maintain her composure and affronted countenance. "Mr. Fisackerly is somewhat simple-minded, you understand, and Mr. Bradley watches over him." She detected a flicker of doubt, a slight waver in their conviction, and pressed her case further. "Whatever scheme Mr. Bradley has involved you two gentlemen in has nothing to do with me or my father, I assure you." She laughed lightly, as though dismissing an amusing misunderstanding. "Surely, gentlemen, you cannot imagine that my father would welcome someone of Mr. Bradley's character into our home!"

This seemed logical to Cudahy, and he began to feel that they had made a mistake. Foster remained unconvinced, however, and he made no effort to hide that fact as he met her wide-eyed gaze. Her beauty, which had served her so well in other dealings with men, sounded an alarm bell in his brain. In Foster's somewhat distorted experience, beautiful women were self-absorbed, troublesome, and deceitful, and he suspected that this one was no exception. A slow, brown-toothed grin stretched his lips. "I'll still be wanting to speak with your father, Missy."

"I've told you, my father is—"

He lunged toward her, hissing, "I thought you understood that I don't care whether your father is bedridden or well enough to dance a jig! I'll speak with him." His hand gripped tightly on her arm, he wrenched her up out of the chair. "Up you go, now, and take me to him. If he's so poorly, then he's upstairs, I assume?"

She nodded reluctantly. Her mind was spinning furiously in search of a way to keep them from going upstairs. Unlikely though they may be to talk to anyone about the condition in which she kept her father, there were things in the upstairs rooms that would spell disaster for her plans should the two redcoats find them. No inspirations were forthcoming, however, leaving her with little choice but to allow Foster to force her up the stairs.

"You stay down here," he told Cudahy. "Look around. See what you can find." Then, shoving Charlotte ahead of him, he made for the stairs.

Standing on the upper landing, Foster glanced through the open door into Charlotte's bedroom before pushing her ahead of him toward the closed door of her father's room. He drew his pistol as she opened the door and then, shoving her ahead of him, he entered the room — and immediately wished he hadn't. The stench, which stung his eyes and nostrils, was so unbearable as to force Foster to pull a dirty handkerchief from his pocket to hold over his nose. It took only the most cursory inspection of the man on the bed to deduce that he would not be able to provide any useful information. Foster was not even certain that Ainsworth was alive. "This is how you care for your old papa, then?"

Charlotte sniffed in defiance of his reproach. "Considering that you are a thief and a discredit to your uniform, I believe you have no call to sit in judgment of me, Private Foster."

He stood over Ainsworth's bed, staring down at the withered, comatose form. "This old man isn't in any shape to be helping Teague. That just leaves you, Missy."

"Stop calling me that! I am Miss Ainsworth to you." She was fighting desperately to gain control of the situation and knew that she was failing. "I told you, I don't know about stolen weapons or anything else Teague Bradley might be doing. It seems to me that you should be having this discussion with him, not with me."

"I'm sure you'd like that, but from my point of view, the road through you will be an easier one. Are you going to tell me what I want to know? Are you going to tell me where you've hidden the money?"

"I can't tell you what I don't know," she insisted through gritted teeth.

"Have it your way, then."

Foster tore into her father's room like a berserker, tossing aside anything in his path, and searching every possible hiding place. Watching his unrestrained frenzy, Charlotte edged toward the door. The men were unlikely to find her hidden treasure, she reasoned, so the safest course seemed to be simply to get out of the house until they had gone. But Foster sensed her intent and stopped her with a violent fury that frightened her beyond anything she had ever experienced. He shunted her across the room and forced her onto a small wooden chair in one corner of the room.

"Move from there, Missy," he snarled, "and you will regret it."

Obediently, she sat in the chair watching him search the room, her mind awhirl with possible outcomes of the situation — none of which appealed to her. Mentally, she cursed Teague for bringing these two men into her life. She stared daggers at Foster's back as he rummaged through the room. The notion of invoking her friendship with Lieutenant Chastain occurred to her but was discarded for fear of measures Foster might take to ensure that she did not inform the officer of Foster and Cudahy's activities.

Once satisfied that nothing was hidden in the room, Foster glared at her and jerked his head toward the door. "Let's go," he growled. They stepped out of the room, and Foster drew several deep breaths to clear his lungs of the fetid bedroom air. "You should be hanged for that mess in there."

She flashed him a mincing look but said nothing as he nudged her along the landing toward her own bedroom. Foster paused at the top of the stairs. "Cudahy," he shouted down the stairs. "Have you found anything?"

"What?" Charlotte scoffed. "Are you afraid he might find something and simply abscond with it rather than alert you? No honor among your little band of thieves, then?"

"I'd hold that sharp tongue of yours if I were you, Missy." Cudahy appeared at the base of the stairs to report that he'd not yet found anything. "Check the cellar," Foster ordered. "Search it good. There has to be something here. Either some of the goods, or the money, or both. There has to be something." He thrust his hand roughly into Charlotte's back and shoved. "Go," he said, indicating the door to her bedroom. "In there."

"I say again, you're wasting your—"

"If you say anything else that doesn't start with 'I'll tell you where I've hidden the money,'" he threatened, "I will hit you in the mouth so hard that you won't be saying anything at all for a long while. Now, walk."

Charlotte stepped into the room ahead of Foster, and her eyes went immediately — as she expected his would — to the brilliant blue egg-shaped music box perched proudly on her bureau. She had kept the egg on private display to help satisfy her need to be surrounded by luxury, and she was unwilling even now to admit the folly of her vanity. Instead, she focused on formulating the explanation she would give when Foster recognized the item.

Contrary to her expectation, Foster did not immediately notice the glittering blue music box. He paused for a moment to take in the room, which was far more luxurious than Ainsworth's. Ultimately, however, none of the finery was enough to keep his attention away from the music box. Grinning in satisfaction, he crossed to the bureau in two broad paces, picked up the enamel box and waved it at her.

"So, you don't know anything about Teague's activities, huh? And, I suppose you don't know this came from a wagonload of the general's personal property?"

"Of course I don't. Yes, Mr. Bradley gave that to me. He did not mention where he had obtained it, and I did not ask." She tore her eyes away from where he bounced the egg in his hand in an unnervingly casual manner and met his even gaze. "He often gives me gifts. I believe he thinks to impress me."

Foster snorted. "Impress you? I think a man doesn't give a valuable little ornament like this to a lady unless he feels he has already made some progress in impressing her. A man reserves such baubles for those times when he feels he will get something in return. I'd say you and Teague are far more than you let on, Missy."

"You are being quite tedious, Private Foster." She sighed as though dealing with a difficult child. "And, if the ornament is as valuable as you say, should you perhaps stop tossing it in the air as though it were nothing more than an apple?"

Laughing, he replaced the egg on its stand. "Let's just have a look around to see what else your would-be suitor might have given you, shall we?" Abruptly, he jerked the top drawer free of the bureau, allowing it to crash to the floor and scattering its contents.

"Stop that!" Reflexively, she reached her hand toward his but quickly pulled back at the last moment. "Here," she said, her voice full of angry vehemence, as she moved toward the mahogany clothes press. She threw open the cupboard doors and knelt to the two drawers at the bottom. One of these she opened and, from the very back, withdrew a small, simple wooden box. With some reluctance, she handed the box up to him. "Here is everything he has given to me."

His face twisted with skepticism, Foster opened the box. It was lined with velvet and divided into several small compartments. Within each compartment, there nestled a piece of jewelry, several of which appeared to be costly. He selected a necklace and held it aloft admiringly. The piece was familiar to him for he had stolen it himself and was considerably piqued by Teague's insistence that he hand it over to be added to the common cache of goods. The pendant swinging before him on a delicate gold chain was a cameo of finest quality, and he watched it for several long seconds as he considered Charlotte's story.

"No." He slowly shook his head. "I don't think so. I don't think this is all. I think you have more, and I think you have the money. Teague doesn't have any other safe place to keep it. Now, where is it?"

She rose to her feet, glowering at him. "I don't—"

But she got no further. Foster grabbed her wrist and jerked her to him. "Where is it?" he demanded once again, his breath hot and foul in her face. He wrenched her arm around and tossed her to the floor, then stood over her, breathing hard, as she struggled to free herself from the tangle of her skirts. When she was almost to her feet, he struck the back of his hand across her face knocking her sideways onto the hearth.

Charlotte stayed down on her hands and knees. The stinging pain of the blow brought tears to her eyes and the brimstone glow of the banked fire swam in her vision. Time seemed momentarily to slow. She focused on the feeling of the smooth, warm hearth tiles under the palms of her hands and only distantly heard Foster ask again where she had hidden the money. With one hand, she swiped away the vision-obscuring tears, the film of soot her hands had acquired from the hearth tiles leaving dark streaks across her cheeks. The hearth tools — poker and shovel, blowing tube and tongs — came into focus.

"Behind the wash stand." Her voice was soft and her eyes never left the tools.

"What? I can't hear you."

"Behind the wash stand," she repeated more loudly. "In the wall. There's a hidden compartment."

Gratified that he was finally getting results and eager to possess his prize, Foster turned on his heel and stalked hurriedly to the wash stand. He knocked it aside, heedless of the shattering pitcher and basin. Charlotte rose to her feet and crossed trancelike toward him, her shoes crunching on the porcelain shards. He was running his hands along the wall, feverishly attempting to locate the edges of the purported compartment. "Where is it?" he demanded, barely glancing at her.

"Down low. Close to the floor." She watched him kneel and test the surface of the wall with his fingertips. It did not take long for him to find the seam that marked the edge of the door to the compartment. "You'll have to use your knife to pry it open," she lied. Unhesitatingly, he drew his knife and began to work at the seam, so completely absorbed in the task that he practically forgot Charlotte's presence. He did not see her, therefore, raise the fireplace poker from where she had concealed it among the folds of her skirt.

Charlotte struck the poker so hard against Foster's skull that the force of the blow reverberated painfully through her arms. And yet — and to her disappointment — it was not enough to kill him. He fell, slightly dazed, and lay on his back, staring up at her in surprise. Before he could gather his wits, she struck again. And again. Over and over until his face and scalp were a bloodied mess. Yet the stubborn man refused to die. Finally, she lowered the poker and stepped forward onto his neck, balancing with one hand against the wall so that the full force of her weight was bearing down on his throat. She felt the snap of his hyoid bone and then the crunch of cartilage giving way under her foot, heard the horrible high-pitched sound of his struggle for air. His body jerked violently, threatening to unbalance her, but she managed to keep her foot planted. Finally, she bounced up and down until his throat's entire structure collapsed and his last breath came gurgling forth.

Without pausing to survey the result of her efforts, Charlotte hurried out of the bedroom and peered down from the landing to assure herself that Cudahy was not close by. Hastily placing one of the small rugs under Foster's head so that there would be no trail of blood, she then dragged his body out onto the landing. While struggling to arrange him at the top of the stairs, she was startled to see her father staring at her from his bed. His bedroom door had been left ajar and, inexplicably, he seemed to have awakened. His head was turned on the pillow so that he stared out through the door, seemingly watching her every move.

Shaking off the eeriness of his staring gaze, she closed his door and went about the business of rolling Foster's body down the stairs. It was more difficult than she had anticipated because she could only get his limp form to fall a few steps at a time, and his arms and legs continually tangled in the spokes on the railing. Once his body finally came to rest at the base of the stairs, she sprinted back up to retrieve his pistol. Gun primed for firing, she hurried down the blood spattered stairs.

Feigning hysteria, she rushed down the hallway frantically calling for Cudahy, crying that something terrible had happened and beseeching him to come quickly. The young private emerged from the cellar just in time to collide with her as she rushed along the corridor. Charlotte was sobbing and tugging at his sleeve, describing some chain of events with such incoherence that he could just manage to make out that Foster had attacked her, they had struggled, and Foster had fallen down the stairs. Cudahy would have doubted her story had not the bruise on her face and cut lip from Foster's blow lent it credence.

He allowed her to lead him to Foster's body and stood staring in shocked disbelief at what remained of his friend. He cocked his head one way and then the other, frowning over some puzzle, and then knelt for a closer look at Foster's wounds. It occurred to Cudahy that the damage to Foster's face and throat seemed beyond what the fall might have produced, and he was on the verge of saying so when Charlotte fired the pistol. She was so close to him that there was no danger of missing her target, which was a spot just behind his ear. The ball entered Cudahy's head and burst it like a melon so quickly than the young man never for even a millisecond had to comprehend that he'd been shot. He fell in a dead heap on top of Foster before the sound of the shot had quit ringing in Charlotte's ears.

Charlotte dropped the pistol and backed into the parlor. She collapsed into a chair and sat considering the two corpses piled in her foyer. Her first reaction was to be furious with Teague for putting her in her current predicament and for not being there to help her deal with it. After some thought, however, she began to see how the situation might be used to further her aims and that Teague's presence would only have complicated things. He would be away long enough to enable her to dispose of the bodies in the manner she envisioned and to clean up all traces of the afternoon's events before he returned. Smiling with pleasure that things had once again turned, as they should, in her favor, she set to work.

CHAPTER FIFTEEN

Daniel was pushing his horse too hard, he knew, driven by the need to reach Concord ahead of the British Regulars. The warmer afternoons and chilly nights of mid-April produced heavy morning fog, and he cursed it now for slowing his progress. He did not think the troops had yet completed their march out of Boston, but was keenly aware that they were on their way as he calculated the miles he needed to cover and time it would take to reach Concord. Alone, he would surely move faster than the cumbersome regiments of Regulars, but he did not want to rest upon any sense of surety; the unexpected always happened. Certainly, he never expected to find himself in a furious race to reach Concord ahead of Gage's troops.

Four days earlier, it was learned that General Gage had received orders to arrest the participants in the Provincial Congress. Deciding to kill two birds with one stone, Gage formulated a plan to both destroy the munitions he knew the Provincial Congress had ordered stockpiled and to arrest Samuel Adams and John Hancock, whom he considered to be ringleaders of the dissidents. Secrets were difficult enough to keep in Boston, but the intelligence network Warren and Revere had built up rendered almost impossible Gage's attempt to keep his plans secret. As the days passed, the Patriots learned every detail of the plan — except for the critical points of precisely when the operation would be launched and where. A Committee of Observation, with Revere at its center, watched and listened for any change in the army's routine that might signal the beginning of Gage's mission, and that signal had come just the previous day.

The Patriots set about moving their arsenal, especially the large cache in Concord, and this was why Daniel needed to get there — not to help move the weapons, for he assumed that would have been accomplished already — but because Drum was in Concord. The influx of Regulars into Boston had given Drum his first close look at artillery, and he was captivated. The big guns, so stately and imposing as they sat on their frail-looking wooden limbers fascinated him, and the first time he actually witnessed one being fired, he was struck with an almost visceral thrill by its power, the spectacle of the explosion, and the rumbling vibration it set rippling through the ground. The cannon were the most exciting things he had ever seen, and he longed for an opportunity to get closer. Therefore, when word went out that strong backs were needed to help move the Concord munitions, which included some artillery pieces, he eagerly volunteered.

And now, the Regulars were on their way to Concord. Haunted by visions of the massacre on King Street five years earlier, Daniel feared the ramifications of any encounter between the Regulars and local militia. Select militia companies were directed to stand to twenty-four hour readiness, able to respond at a minute's notice, should the Regulars move against their towns. Given the unstable atmosphere, it seemed unlikely that these minutemen would quietly step aside and allow the Regulars to confiscate or destroy the Patriot arsenal. If there was to be a Concord massacre, Daniel did not want Drum in the middle of it.

Several hours earlier that evening, Warren had sent Revere and William Dawes over two different routes to Lexington, their mission being to quietly spread the alarm and warn Adams and Hancock that the Regulars were on the march. Dawes took a southerly route, across the Boston neck to swing up through Roxbury. Revere took the shorter route, ferried in a small boat across the Charles to where a horse awaited him on the Charlestown shore. Daniel had crossed with him, was at his side when he looked back to see two signal lanterns glowing from the tallest structure in Boston — the belfry of the Old North church. The assault would come from across the sea, then, not the land route across the neck.

Bidding Revere Godspeed, Daniel set out cross-country, not bothering to stick to roads when a more direct line was available. He thought it likely that Gage had sent out an advance screen to intercept anyone who might warn the local militias of the army's approach. Daniel constantly checked himself against blundering into that screen and hoped Revere and Dawes would do the same.

*   *   *

It was just past one o'clock in the morning, and Lieutenant Edward Hinton was cold, wet, tired, confused, and frustrated. The only discomfort that seemed to be missing was hunger, and he guessed that would arrive soon enough. After five years in the army, all of these irritations should have seemed nothing more than routine. But Edward Hinton was an optimist by nature, and optimists always thought that, with each disaster or defeat or crisis, lessons would be learned and improvements made so that "next time" things would run more smoothly. Slogging his way up the river bank in the dark and cold, he was finally beginning to accept that every "next time" was unlikely to be an improvement over its predecessor. He was reminded of the old adage that there was a right way, and an army way — and the two seldom were the same. At least, that seemed to be the underlying principle of this particular operation.

Given the darkness, unsure footing, and his lack of familiarity with the horse he'd been given, he had elected to walk the animal up the slippery bank. Aside from an odd dun coloring, there was nothing remarkable about the mare. She had a broad back and seemed steady enough, her ears flicking with alertness whenever he spoke, but he doubted that she was battle-trained and hoped it would not matter in this small campaign.

Swinging into the saddle, he scanned the upper ridge of the river bank looking for Major Pitcairn.

The scouts and light companies of several regiments had been peeled off and placed under the overall command of Major John Pitcairn with orders to advance toward Lexington ahead of the main column. Pitcairn, who was a practical-minded Scot and much-respected officer with the Royal Marines, had argued that, to end this little colonial rebellion required but one forceful campaign, one smart action, perhaps the burning of two or three towns and everything would be returned to normalcy. Edward hoped he was right and that this mission would prove to be the one smart action Pitcairn had envisioned. Painfully aware of his own lack of combat experience, Edward was heartened to know that the marine led them. Not that anyone expected there to be any actual fighting; this was a mission to destroy stockpiled weapons and to arrest Adams and Hancock.

The physical discomfort was only a miniscule part of Edward's irritation. More disturbing was the reality that, aside from occasional flashes of brilliance, words like "smoothly," "clockwork," and "efficient" were simply not in the army vocabulary and likely never would be. From the moment the operation had begun, it seemed that everything that could possibly go wrong had done so. Hoping to have the element of surprise on their side, the troops had begun their mission shortly before midnight, their officers constantly haranguing them to keep quiet. They had wrapped every bit of metal with rags and kept conversation to only what was necessary, but twenty-one companies of men generated a great deal of noise simply by *being*, so he suspected that their march to the river had not been as clandestine as hoped.

Once they reached the Back Bay, it took far longer than anyone had anticipated to load the men into the longboats. By the time the boats pushed off, the tides were against them, and the shallow shoals at the landing point meant that the men had to disembark and wade through hip-deep water to shore. Then, inexplicably, when all were assembled and prepared to move out, there was another delay while rations were handed out. Men stood in close order, stowing their newly-acquired rations, checking their muskets and powder, and waiting. They were a mixed-bag of light infantry and Grenadier companies stripped from several different regiments, not all of them familiar with each other.

Finally, the order came down the lines to advance. Lieutenant Colonel Smith, who had overall command of the operation, was taking an inordinate amount of time over every decision and the men, many of whom were not much impressed by Colonel Smith to begin with, grumbled quietly, earning sharp looks or hissed reprimands from their Sergeants. Inwardly, however, the Sergeants agreed with their men. Most would have preferred that Pitcairn be given the command. Had that been the case, many felt, there would have been far fewer delays and blunders. Hinton tended to agree with this consensus.

As the men formed into column and set off down the road toward Lexington, Edward edged his horse forward and took up a position close on Pitcairn's flank. Unlike many of the officers, Pitcairn preferred to ride at the head of the column where he could keep an eye on what lay ahead. Trying to see what Pitcairn was seeing, Edward squinted at the bit of road that stretched before them, silver-grey in the moonlight, and hoped he was interpreting the scene with at least a modicum of Pitcairn's insight.

The scouts and light companies had fanned out ahead of the column, some on the road, but most combing through the fields along the way in search of any threat. Everything was done with as much stealth as eight-hundred men encumbered with the accoutrements of soldiers on the march could manage. Edward guessed they had advanced only two miles into the countryside before Pitcairn reined his horse in and signaled the column to halt. The men stopped and seemed to hold their collective breath, allowing the air to fall still and silent. They strained to hear what Pitcairn seemed to hear, and then wished they had not. Bells. Every church bell within miles was pealing out a warning, their sound building and rolling out across the farms and fields to greet the Regulars. A faint glow on the distant horizon, then another, suggested that signal fires were being lit. Some of the men cursed softly under their breath. If they had ever enjoyed the element of surprise, it had been lost.

*   *   *

Daniel heard the first bells at around two o'clock in the morning. Lexington. The Lexington bells were sounding the alarm, which should mean that either Revere or Dawes, or both, had made it through. They would have warned Adams and Hancock, and he hoped both of those men had fled to safety. Daniel felt a small sense of relief, which surprised him, for he thought the sum of his anxiety sprung only from the fact that Drum was in Concord. The bulk of the tension was still there, however, pushing him to keep going as recklessly as he dared.

Twice he heard horses on the road ahead and wheeled his own mount quickly off into whatever cover was available. The first time, a group of travelers who, as far as he could tell, had nothing to do with the night's business, ambled past his hiding place. They were sleepy in their saddles and likely would hardly have noticed Daniel if he had stayed on the road. A mile or so later the sound of hooves on the road ahead sent him dodging for the woods, and this time, it was a group of Regulars who rode past. They advanced with caution, their voices low, giving Daniel the impression that they might have heard him as well. He held his breath and prayed his horse would not pick this moment to grow restive. When the threat had passed, he still did not feel comfortable going back to the road and, instead, opted to keep to a path through the woods.

The sound of the bells was spreading now, from town to town and village to village, and here and there a signal fire glowed bright against the night sky. If the alarm had reached Concord, would Drum keep himself somewhere safe? Daniel doubted it. Drum would follow the men he was with, and he was with men who were members of Concord's minute company. Whatever resistance they decided to throw in the face of the Regulars, Drum would be part of it.

Nearing Concord, Daniel began to encounter militiamen in ever-increasing numbers moving from villages and farms to pre-arranged assembly points. The assembly areas, hilltops for the most part, were spread along the distance between Lexington and Concord, good vantage points to observe the actions of the Regulars. Meeting the men in small groups, he had no good estimation of how many were assembling or from how far afield. If all of the militias within earshot of the tolling bells responded, there could be a force of several hundred gathered before long, but he wondered if it would be enough and if they would be in time. A force of even a thousand men would do little good if they did not arrive and deploy until after the redcoats had done their work and returned to Boston.

Dawn was still a distant promise when Daniel reached the edge of Concord. The hour was approaching only three o'clock. He was startled by a rider who, riding with an urgency to match Daniel's, suddenly exploded onto the road from a narrow lane running between fields. Frightened by the near collision, the horses whinnied in angry protest as their hooves slew across the packed dirt road. Daniel's horse reared repeatedly, and cursing both the animal and the unexpected company, Daniel tightened his grip on the reins.

"Sodding idiot!" The other rider, as disconcerted as Daniel, showered him with expletives while he worked to control his own startled mount. "Who the hell are you?" he demanded.

"I might ask you the same thing, you horse's arse! What call do you have bursting onto the road like that?" Daniel kept the man carefully in sight as his horse danced about in an erratic circle.

The other man, just managing to curb his own horse, squinted into the darkness swallowing the road behind Daniel. "Tell me who you are. Where have you come from?" he demanded. "Did you see any Regulars on the road?"

"I'll tell you nothing until you give me your name," Daniel snapped. "Otherwise, I'll be on my way and leave you to your own travels." He laid a hand on the pistol that sat secure in its saddle holster, but did not draw it.

The man seemed to consider him for a moment and then responded in a substantially more civil tone. "I am Dr. Samuel Prescott." He said no more and watched carefully for Daniel's reaction.

Daniel relaxed visibly. Prescott's name was familiar to him, though he had never met the man. "I apologize, Dr. Prescott. It has been a night of dangerous surprises. I thought perhaps you were one more. My name is Daniel Garrett, and I've come up from Boston."

Prescott chuckled. "A night of dangers, indeed. No one knows that better than I! I set out with the intent of helping two other men to warn the countryside that the Regulars were on the march, which would have been more than enough excitement for me. But then, hardly more than an hour ago, we found ourselves in the custody of a redcoat scouting party. Fortunately, they were not expecting to take prisoners, much less three of them, so they bungled the job of holding onto us. I was just trying to put as much distance between myself and them as I could, and to give warning to Concord."

"Then you'd best tell me the rest of your story while we ride. There's an entire column of redcoats coming up the road, and I'd sorely like to be in Concord before they arrive."

They rode at a pace that would allow Prescott to continue his narrative, but the highlight of his tale stopped Daniel in his tracks. "Revere was captured?" Stunned, he repeated what Prescott had said, hoping he had not heard correctly.

"He was," Prescott nodded. "Dawes, too."

"But the bells! Did he have time to warn Lexington? Adams and Hancock?"

"He did. Adams and Hancock are safe. The three of us, Revere, Dawes, and myself, met up after Revere left Lexington. Fools that we were, we let a bunch of lobster-backs surprise us. They took all three of us, but Dawes and I escaped. Dawes went back to Lexington, and I came on toward Concord."

Daniel swore softly under his breath as he nudged his horse forward again. His mind was in a whir. "What will happen to Revere? They won't shoot him, will they?"

Prescott shrugged. "I doubt it. As I said, they didn't quite seem to know what to do with us. And, if you know Revere, you know he could talk his way out of just about anything. By morning, he'll probably have made friends with them and convinced them to place orders with him for new silver tea services for their wives."

Daniel found it difficult to share Prescott's optimism and began to try to formulate a plan for going to Revere's rescue. Surely there would be time for him to retrieve Drum from Concord and then find a way to free Revere. But Prescott could not say exactly where Revere was taken. Finding him would be nigh onto impossible. Riddled with concern, he rode in silence the rest of the way into Concord.

*   *   *

Lieutenant Hinton took out his pocket watch to check the time. A quarter past four. He stowed the watch back in his weskit pocket and cast his eyes skyward. Moonlight served as their lantern for most of the march, but now the sky was beginning to show a lighter gray off to the east. It was about an hour before dawn, he reckoned, as he mentally recounted the interminable hours it had taken to march the troops up from the landing site near Cambridge. Pitcairn's smaller contingent of six light companies had outdistanced the main column by quite a bit and Edward suspected Pitcairn would earn a drubbing from Smith for moving too fast. Pitcairn did not seem worried by the prospect, however.

Word reached them that the alarm bells had prompted Smith to send a rider back to Boston to ask Gage for reinforcements, but Edward had stopped worrying about the alarm bells and signal fires some time ago. Pitcairn had scoffed at the notion that they need worry. Even if the rebels could assemble men in the hundreds, he argued, they would be millers and farmers armed with pitchforks and fowling pieces. For this column of Regulars, it would be like sweeping away a swarm of gnats. A nuisance, nothing more.

Lexington was not much farther, Edward knew. He had ridden there one afternoon a few weeks earlier, and recalled that the town was little more than a wide spot in the road, a cluster of houses and small buildings huddled about a common. And a church. With bells. He and his fellow officers had joked that the Massachusetts colony seemed to have a church for every five inhabitants, and he guessed that, starting with Lexington, all of them were now ringing their bells. He glanced at Pitcairn to see if he could detect any change in the man's demeanor, but he seemed as untroubled as ever.

Abruptly, Pitcairn signaled the column to a halt. Edward squinted at figures standing on a small rise across the road in the distance. A rose-tinged dawn was spreading into the sky now, pushing the darkness from east to west like an incoming tide and bathing the land with just enough light so that colors were distinguishable. Red. The figures on the road ahead wore red coats. The advance guard was waiting for them to catch up. Edward looked about him and realized that, just over that small rise lay Lexington.

Electing not to wait for Smith and the main column to join them, Pitcairn ordered the Sergeants to quietly chivvy the men into closer formation. Muskets were shouldered more purposefully, hats tamped down more securely onto their heads, and then they stepped out for the last few yards of the march into Lexington. Most of the men expected to find a deserted village, sleepy-eyed inhabitants having fled into the countryside at the sound of the alarm bell. Instead, Pitcairn and his companies marched into Lexington and swung onto the common only to see, lined up across Lexington Green in something akin to military order, a force of around eighty armed militiamen.

Pitcairn turned his lead companies from column into line, but then rode a few paces forward and called out to the militiamen. "You will surrender your arms and disperse," he shouted. The faintest shimmer of uncertainty rolled like a wave through the rebel lines, and then some sort of unspoken agreement was reached. The militia did not budge.

Edward could hardly believe his eyes. Did these foolish men actually think they could stop six companies of trained, professional British Regulars? And that did not even take into account the twenty companies of the main column that would doubtless be arriving shortly. He heard a few of the men make derisive remarks in low voices and could not blame them. The whole thing was like some ludicrous pantomime. Ludicrous or not, it would not do to merely march around Lexington and leave any sort of armed force at their backs. He heard Pitcairn ask one of the scouts if he knew the man who had command of the militia.

"Man named Parker," the scout replied. "John Parker. Locals call him 'captain' because he soldiered under Wolfe at Quebec, though he's really nothin' but a farmer."

Pitcairn nodded and looked to his lieutenant, who signaled the Sergeants to advance the line five paces. As always, Edward was awed by the unhesitating obedience of these troops to such an order. The limitations of muskets meant that battle lines had to advance to within sixty yards of the enemy if the volley was to be effective. It was not an easy thing to ask men to move closer to an armed opponent. Edward knew, however, that close-proximity was a double-edged sword. The closer the lines advanced toward an enemy, the more fearsome those red-coated soldiers appeared. Already, a sense of fear was rolling off the militiamen, palpable and unsettling. Perhaps if Pitcairn could push them just a bit, they would break and run. He advanced his line again.

They did not run, however. Afraid as they might have been, the militiamen stood their ground. Parker's voice drifted across to them, low and steady, undoubtedly trying to encourage his skittish militia. "Calm now, men. Stand firm. It's time to show them we're not of a mind to stand aside while they vandalize and destroy our property. Time to show them we've had our fill of them marching about our countryside like *they* own it."

Doubtless, Pitcairn was correct in his prediction that these would be farmers and millers, yet none of them were armed with pitchforks. A few of the men carried fowling pieces, but most held muskets with a soldierly air of authority. One man, Edward noticed, had only a pistol, but it was leveled at the Regulars as surely as if it were a cannon. Suddenly overcome by a sense of seriousness, a sense that there was more threat here than they had at first supposed, Edward shifted in his saddle. He thought of the fierce determination he had seen in some of the rebels, thought of Anna's friend Daniel who was clearly not a man easily deterred from his chosen course, and found himself studying more carefully the faces lined up across the green.

Pitcairn advanced his line another five paces, bringing them to within thirty yards of the militia, yet the rebels still did not give way. Exasperated by their foolish obstinacy and impatient with the waste of time, he barked out angrily, "Throw down your arms ye rebels! Disperse, damn ye! Disperse!"

Stand your ground," Edward heard Parker tell his men, his voice calm, assertive. "Don't fire unless fired upon, but if they mean to have a war, let it begin here."

Edward blinked and drew a short breath. So, he supposed, did every one of the Regulars. *If they mean to have a war.* Could Parker truly have uttered those words? Was such a thing on the minds of these militiamen — these farmers and millers and shopkeepers — standing nervously before them? Edward turned his head to see Pitcairn's reaction and, in that instant, the sound of a musket being fired cracked through the chilly air of the newborn sunrise, followed by a wisp of smoke drifting across the space between the two lines. Edward had heard no order to fire on either side, nor could he be certain from which side the shot had come. In the next moments, it mattered little. That one shot triggered a hail of fire from the line of Regulars.

The British line fired in unison, executing with practiced precision the firing drill that made them so effective in battle. Each individual musket might not be terribly accurate, but numbers of muskets fired simultaneously across an expanse of ground launched a massive sheet of deadly lead that could not miss. And the well-drilled British lines could keep up that lethal fire almost without pause if so inclined.

Startled, Edward's horse reared under him. By the time he had the panicked animal under control, the British companies had fired another volley. Fueled by the anger and hostility the troops had weathered during the long frustrating months of confinement in Boston, they were momentarily deafened to cease-fire commands from their officers. Their two volleys expended, the companies began a quick-paced advance through the scrim of powder smoke, bayonets fixed, apparently bent on running down the militiamen. He heard a scream and wheeled his horse to see a woman, clutching a small child, standing at the corner of one of the houses arrayed around the green. Her face was contorted with shock, and she shrieked in horror. He turned back to the advancing line and, along with

S . D . B A N K S

the other officers, fought to pull the line back into order. The militiamen
— those who were still on their feet — were trying to flee, and many of the
troops wanted to run them down. Tragedy had descended like a lightning
bolt into the tranquility of Lexington Green, and now there was chaos.
Another woman was running onto the green, screaming a man's name.
Uncomprehending, Edward watched her run, saw that she was putting
herself in the path of advancing troops, and moved his horse to protect her.
He sat, like a rock in the midst of a stream of red-coated men, shielding the
woman as she knelt over a fallen militiaman.

Along with the other officers, Edward barked at the troops to stop and
reform, his voice croaking with the strain. Finally, they began to respond
and fall back into formation. He looked around for Pitcairn just in time to
see the major coming back across the green, stormy-faced as he bore down
on his men. Somewhere behind him, Edward heard a drum beating out a
marching cadence. He wheeled the uneasy mare around as the head of the
main column came into view. Smith had finally caught up.

Once Pitcairn's companies were returned to order and reunited with
their regiments in the main column, a contingent of men were ordered to
fan out through Lexington, searching every house and haystack for their
quarry. Yet, as Edward had suspected would be the case the moment he
saw the militia deployed across the green, Adams and Hancock were
nowhere to be found. Doubtless they had bolted at the sound of the first
alarm, impossible now to find in the wide expanse of unfamiliar
countryside.

To compound the frustration of having one part of their mission
thwarted, the officers were dealing with the reality that, by now, Concord
would certainly know they were coming and would likely have moved any
stockpiled munitions. Perhaps worse, there was the uneasy feeling among
the officers that they had given the rebels another weapon for their
propaganda arsenal. Two militiamen were killed outright, five more were
certain to eventually die of their wounds, and numerous others were
seriously wounded. Recalling the sensationalized accounts of events like
the debacle in front of the Custom House years earlier, Edward's mind was
already conjuring the sort of story that would be spun from this mess.

By the time the column advanced down the road toward Concord, the
sun was fully above the horizon. Men, tired of the strain of picking their
way along dark, unfamiliar roads, were glad of the light and of the warm
rays that hit their backs, driving away the last of the pre-dawn chill. Pitcairn
once again rode at the head of the column, Smith at the rear.

"Have you noticed it?" Pitcairn asked Edward when they had ridden
some distance away from Lexington. Without actually turning his head, he
managed to indicate the crest of a hill a short distance off to the side.

Edward, as surreptitiously as possible, looked sideways toward the hill. "We have an audience," he replied.

"Aye, we do," Pitcairn agreed.

"Do you want to do anything about them?"

Pitcairn shrugged. "What's to do? As long as they do not engage us or attempt to hinder our progress, let them watch."

And, watch they did. From just about every hill or open spot of high ground, left and right along the road, clusters of grim-faced militiamen watched the column snake its way along the road toward Concord. None showed any inclination to challenge the column, but their presence was unnerving, nonetheless. Scouts probed warily ahead, fanning out along and across the road, their focus sharply tuned to any sign of potential ambush or further massing of militia. The cavalier attitude that had permeated the column before the encounter at Lexington had now been replaced by a watchful disquiet that stretched the miles from Lexington to Concord.

Eventually and without incident, the column drew within sight of the unimportant little town. Surveying the cluster of houses, shops, and other small buildings so similar to Lexington, Pitcairn was relieved to see no assembled militia. "Hinton," he called, gesturing for Edward to join him. "You've been here on a previous occasion?"

"Yes, Sir. It is much as you can see from here. There's a river beyond the town that essentially bounds it on that far side." He swept his hand in a north to south arc along Concord's far perimeter.

"Bridges?"

Edward nodded. "Yes, Sir. Two. One there, to the north." He pointed out the direction. "And a second there, to the south."

Another junior officer had handed Pitcairn a hand-drawn map, to which he directed his attention. "And this?" He pointed to a mark on the map across the river to the northwest. "This is Barrett's farm?"

"Yes, Sir. He's the commander of the local militia. Most of their supplies are stored at his farm."

"Let us hope that's still the case," Pitcairn said. He tilted his face to the sun, gauging the time. Almost seven o'clock now, he guessed. "We have orders to wait for Colonel Smith."

Edward knew better than to reply. He doubted it was necessary, anyway. The irritation of Pitcairn and the rest of the officers at Smith's slow progress was quite apparent without putting it into words. They sat in silence, listening to the sound of their internal clocks tick off the long minutes while they waited for Smith to appear. Once the colonel drew into sight, Edward was struck by the thought that the poor horse struggling to carry Smith's immense weight could probably not have moved faster even if the colonel was so disposed. Edward coughed smartly to cover the laughter that gurgled up in his throat.

"Here, now." Smith pompously rode into the midst of the assembled officers. "What do we know of this little hamlet, Major?" He pursed his lips and nodded as though absorbed by his own sagacious thoughts while he listened to Pitcairn's briefing. "Very good," he said when the recitation was complete. "Captain Pole. You will take three light companies out to secure the south bridge. We do not want any unexpected guests arriving via that route." He frowned, suddenly unable to recall what deployment he had next intended.

"You might perhaps want to refer to this, Sir," Pitcairn suggested, offering the map.

Smith frowned at him, and irritably snatched the map from his hand. He held the map out in front of him, mouth tightened thoughtfully as he considered the lines on the paper. Grunting, he turned slightly in the saddle in search of one of his other captains. "Ah, there you are, Parsons. Gather up seven companies, if you please, and take them out to the other bridge — the . . .," he referred to the map, "North Bridge." He chuckled at the name. "These colonials are somewhat lacking in imagination, are they not?" The officers managed a small show of polite laughter. "Seven companies will likely be far more than necessary, but after that little melee in Lexington, I am inclined to err on the side of caution."

It seemed to Edward that Smith had persisted firmly on the side of caution ever since they set out from Boston, but he carefully kept his expression unreadable.

"Once you have secured the bridge," Smith continued, "you will leave three companies under the command of Captain Laurie. You, yourself, will take the remaining four companies across the bridge to search Barrett's farm." He waved the map at Pitcairn. "Your information concurs with that of General Gage's spies, Major, so I've every reason to believe that we will find what we seek hidden somewhere on those premises."

Not bloody likely, Edward thought. *These militiamen may not be much in a fight, but they're damned well smart enough to hide their supplies when they've known for hours that we were coming.*

"In the meantime," Smith added, folding the map with an air of finality, "the Grenadier companies will search the town proper. I would not put it past this rabble to hide a powder cask under a cradle." He handed the map back to Pitcairn. "Put a torch to anything you find. I want every bit of powder, every flint, and every musket destroyed. Leave them nothing with which to continue this absurd resistance."

*　　　*　　　*

Daniel had set out with the intent to ride into Concord, collect Drum, and return to Boston along a route that would give the advancing Regulars a wide berth. With one thing and another, however, his plan had begun to unravel almost the moment he arrived in Concord. Now, not only did he find himself standing on Punkatasset Hill at the rear of the Concord militia, musket on his shoulder, but Drum was here, too. He had wanted to take Drum out of the path of danger, but Drum was having none of it. More obstinate than Daniel had ever seen him, Drum refused to be rescued and insisted that he be allowed to stand with the militiamen.

"I hope they'll be all right." Drum's voice was fretful.

Daniel glanced to the side. Drum was fidgeting nervously, giving Daniel hope that he might yet choose to stay out of the fight — if there was one. Daniel would not leave now, though he hoped Drum would choose to go off into the woods and wait until it — whatever "it" was going to be — was over. "You hope *who* will be all right?" It would be like Drum to be worried about a litter of puppies he had befriended in some barn.

"The guns." He and Daniel were standing to the rear of the assembled militia, and he was peering over the heads of the men in front of him, anxiously trying to see what was happening in Concord. "The big ones. The cannon." He turned his attention to Daniel, looking at him as though he thought him witless. "Colonel Barrett said we might as well leave them there, but I think we should have hidden them. I think the redcoats will steal them."

If the redcoats found the cannon, Daniel thought, they were much more likely to destroy them. To the Regular army, the three twenty-four pounders would not be worth the immense effort it would take to transport them back to Boston. He decided it might be best to keep this assessment to himself, however. Drum had practically formed a personal relationship with the guns, and Daniel doubted he would stand still if they were to be molested in any way. "The guns are tough," he replied simply. "Tougher than us. We're the ones you should be worried about."

"Why?" Drum was looking at him, blinking in bafflement, and it was all Daniel could do to keep from slapping him on the side of the head.

At the thought, his eyes went to Drum's hat. It was a battered tri-corn that Drum had obtained from heaven only knew where, and it sat atop a head that poked out like a lightning rod above the rest of the men. Daniel was taller than most of them, but Drum towered over him. "Never mind," Daniel sighed. "If anyone starts shooting, though, try to keep your head down. Understand?"

Drum nodded and stared straight ahead. He seemed to be concentrating on Daniel's words, mentally adding them to the list of instructions Barrett had already given him. Watching him from the corner of his eye, Daniel swore lightly under his breath, causing the man in front of him to turn around and glower at him. He glowered back until the man turned away. "Do you even know how to fire that musket?" he hissed at Drum.

"Of course I do. I've fired one before. But Colonel Barrett showed me how to load it faster." He was clearly proud of this fact, so Daniel let it go, lapsing into a grudging silence.

"I still don't see why we had to leave the cannon in Concord," Drum grumbled a few seconds later. Overhearing him, two of the militiamen began to snicker.

"Would you stop worrying about those damned guns?" Daniel exclaimed in exasperation while, at the same time, firing a quelling look in the direction of the amused militiamen. "The cannon are too heavy to be moved without leaving tracks a blind man could follow," he snapped. "How do you suggest that they could have been hidden?"

Drum had no answer to this. Certainly, he had racked his brain trying to come up with something when Barrett had ordered the guns left where they sat. He shrugged.

"No? Then stop talking about the damned guns, all right?" They lapsed into an uneasy silence. Drum was not happy with him, he knew, but there was nothing he could do about it now. He looked around at the assembled militia, studying their faces for some sign that his concern was misplaced. All the men were grim-faced, their eyes boring ahead, minds plainly on the mystery of what lay ahead.

The militiamen were a sight; that was for certain. Attired in the brown work clothes and round hats they wore to work the fields, tend their shops, or man a forge, they could not have presented a more haphazardly slapdash picture if it had been by design. There were five full companies ranged across the hilltop, two from Concord and one each from Acton, Bedford, and Lincoln. At the sound of the warning bells, the men had left their homes and shops to hurriedly assemble here, with little notion of what might be asked of them before the day was through.

Colonel Barrett, commander of the Concord militia, had taken charge of the small force. Aside from the fact that he was incongruously dressed in his old coat, flapped hat, and leather apron, there was nothing remarkable in Barrett's appearance. A miller by trade, Barrett was of average height and build, and possessed of the same lean, weathered face that was characteristic of most of his neighbors. It was a shrewd face, however, and his eyes were clear and sharp. It was his force of personality that made him a man other men looked to for leadership.

Barrett had seen the companies of Regulars cross the bridge and knew they would search his farm. Barrett smiled to himself. They could search all they wanted. There was no longer anything there for them to find. A show of defiance must be made, nonetheless, a statement that the colonists were disinclined to stand aside and let the Regulars ransack and abuse with impunity. He called his companies to attention and marched them to a ridge three-hundred yards west of the North Bridge. Daniel had to admit that the maneuver could not begin to rival the smart, precise maneuvers he had seen the Regulars execute, but it was performed with a creditable level of efficiency, nonetheless. Barrett shook the companies out into battle lines, and ordered them to load their muskets. Then they waited. If there was to be a fight, it would have to be started by the Regulars.

*   *   *

Colonel Smith was growing impatient. As the hour neared nine o'clock, the Grenadiers had spent almost two hours ransacking Concord with nothing of consequence to show for their efforts. His men were showing the strain of the long, overnight march and were increasingly impatient with the intractable local population. Smith, equally fatigued and impatient, wanted nothing more than to complete the mission so that the army could return to Boston. But he dearly wanted to do so with triumphant news of having destroyed considerable quantities of rebel munitions, and as the morning ticked by, it appeared less and less likely that such would be the case. His spirits were lifted by the sight of a young corporal hurrying toward where he sat in a make-shift command post under a towering elm tree. Smith motioned for an aide to intercept the young soldier and learn what he had to say, then waited, fingers drumming on his camp desk for the information to be relayed to him.

The aide returned, his stride exaggerated as he tried to cover the ground quickly without appearing to hurry indecorously. "They have found something, Sir," he reported as he snapped to attention in front of the Colonel. "Three twenty-four pounders hidden in an outbuilding down behind the livery." He knew Smith would welcome the news and hoped some of the resulting glow would somehow burnish him as though he had actually been part of the discovery.

"Well done!" Smith exclaimed, drawing a pleased smile from his aide. He looked about for someone to send to investigate the find, and his eyes landed on Hinton. He remembered the young man as having been with Pitcairn most of the day yet could not recall his name. "You there. Lieutenant. My apologies — your name?"

"Hinton, Sir. Edward Hinton."

"Very good. Go with the corporal and verify the find, please. Then tell them to spike the guns and burn the limbers." He acknowledged Hinton's salute and watched the lieutenant march briskly down the slope toward the waiting corporal. "Three cannon. That is a considerable find, I believe," he proudly announced to his staff. Most of them did not agree but wisely held their tongues. Barrels of powder, muskets, and shot would have been a far greater prize, and yet those stores had eluded their search. "Though, I daresay we would be safe enough leaving the guns in the hand of the militia. If they tried to fire them, I feel certain they would do more damage to themselves than we could ever inflict. Save us a good deal of trouble, it would!" He laughed riotously at the idea, and checked to see that every man had appreciated his jest. It did not escape him that their laughter was tight and strained. "So, then," he said, clearing his throat. He smoothed the front of his weskit and tugged at the lapels of his jacket as though he thought they might actually close over his barrel of a stomach. "Perhaps even more will be found at Barrett's farm. They have powder and shot. I am sure of it. It will be found at the farm." He drummed his fingers and looked off into the distance. Which way had Hinton gone? "Once Parsons brings his men back," he assured them, "we can consider our mission accomplished and depart this uncivilized backwoods and return to Boston." He chuckled at the joke that formed in his head. "I suppose that is tantamount to leaving one uncivilized place for another. Yet all things are relative, are they not?"

The corporal led Edward to the guns. The three cannon sat lined up in a neat row like cows in a byre, a quantity of hay piled off to one side where it had been moved to reveal them. The guns, which were of unknown provenance, were old and their reliability doubtful, but Edward suspected that those small points would be omitted from Smith's official report.

"The Colonel wants them spiked," he told the Sergeant in charge of the men who had found the guns. "Then burn the carriages."

"If we spike them, what's the point of destroying the limbers?" The Sergeant, who had probably been commanding men when Edward was still in the nursery, made no effort to hide his disdain for the Colonel's young errand boy.

"It's what Smith ordered," Edward snapped. He was exhausted, as were all of the men, though in hearing his own voice, he immediately regretted his tone. "Just do it," he said more evenly. "Roll them outside and burn them."

The Sergeant nodded his understanding and half-heartedly returned the young lieutenant's salute. Edward, too tired to take offense, walked out of the shed and slowly made his way back to Smith. The Grenadiers watched him go, then turned questioning faces to their Sergeant, whose orders were the only orders they cared about. "Find something to spike them with," he grudgingly told them. "But we are not hauling the goddamned things outside. Put a torch to them where they sit. If we burn the whole bloody barn down, so be it."

CHAPTER SIXTEEN

Militia from four more towns had arrived and joined the assembled men on Punkatasset Hill, swelling Barrett's ranks to over four-hundred men. Not trusting the Regulars to keep their distance, Daniel had watched them closely all morning. Appearances were that they intended only to secure access to the bridge while Captain Parsons took his men to search Barrett's farm, and to that end, Captain Laurie had sent two companies across to the west side of the bridge where they took up a defensive position at the base of the hill. The remaining company stayed on the town side of the bridge. And there they all waited, militia at the top of the hill, Regulars at the bottom, watching lest the other side show signs of going on the offensive.

There was some grumbling among the militiamen, and even among their officers, that the time for waiting and watching was at an end. Gage had his grip around the Massachusetts Colony and would continue to squeeze ever more tightly until complete subjugation was achieved. Barrett, who was arguing for caution, stood toe-to-toe in heated argument with another militia officer. "It's time we take action," the officer insisted. "And I don't mean no boycotts or petitions, either. They started out telling us who we could trade with and how, then they emptied our pockets without so much as a by-your-leave. Now they're confiscating our personal property. I'm telling you, Barrett, we need to stand up to them! It comes down to this: They are English. We are American. They need to go back to England and leave us in peace."

"It isn't that simple," Barrett growled. "We can't—"

But he got no further. "Look there!" one of the militia lieutenants, Joseph Hosmer, called. He pointed to where a dark column of smoke was rising above Concord. Fear that the Regulars were burning the town sent a ripple of alarm through the militia ranks. Hosmer was not merely alarmed, however, he was furious — and not just over the actions of the Regulars. A young, passionate man, Hosmer was tired of the dithering and out of patience with what he perceived as Concord's indecisive, overly cautious leadership. He spoke in a loud voice that rang out across the hill, "I've heard the British boast that they could march through our country, laying waste to our hamlets and villages, and we'd not oppose them." He paused, looking at the faces of the men around him. "And I begin to think it is true." Dramatically pointing to the rising column of smoke, he added, "Will you let them burn the town down?"

"Oh, dear God," Daniel murmured under his breath.

Hosmer's words had fanned in the militiamen their smoldering urge to fight. With a nod of silent agreement, the officers returned to their units. In a confident, unflagging voice, Barrett ordered the companies back into column and marched them down toward the North Bridge. They had no drummer, but a young fifer managed a spritely rendition of *The White Cockade*.

Drum was thrilled. He grinned at Daniel, and then gave his whole attention to what lay ahead, oblivious to Daniel's scowl of concern. Drum had often watched the militia drill on Boston Common, wishing that he could join them. Though he knew he was supposed to spurn the presence of the Regulars, he could not resist watching them drill, awestruck at the perfection and efficiency with which they executed each maneuver, longing for the opportunity to be part of something so glorious. And now he was.

The militia marched directly toward the two regiments Captain Laurie had sent across the river to hold the far side of the bridge. Uncertain of what the militia intended, the young lieutenant in charge of those two regiments, a man named Kelly, ordered his men to fall back onto the bridge, where they re-deployed into a defensive line. And waited.

Around them the countryside spread out into gently undulating green hills, luxuriant and fragrant with spring. The water flowing under the bridge was calm, almost without a ripple, and a hawk carved out long, slow circles high in the sky, its distant call the only sound in the air.

Barrett urged his men to remain calm, but every militiaman marching down the hill felt the charge of excitement in their fingers, coupled with the gut-churning ogre of fear in their stomachs. Mouths were suddenly dry, palms clammy, and more than one man was kept in line with his companions only by the dread of what would be thought of him if he followed his instinct, dropped his musket and ran back up the hill and as far away as his legs would take him from the intimidating line of redcoats waiting on the bridge.

The militia had closed to less than seventy yards from the redcoats when, unaccountably, a shot rang out that was closely followed by a volley of fire from the Regulars. A militia captain was killed outright, and one or two men hobbled, but the militia did not waver in their advance. Following one of the principles learned during his service in the war against the French and Indians, Barrett sternly ordered his men to wait to return fire. Until they had closed to fifty yards, their muskets would have little impact and he did not want to waste the round of ammunition. As they neared that critical mark, Barrett prepared the men to deploy into lines.

Daniel knew that, once they had moved into lines, the front two lines should fire first, then fall back and allow the men behind to step forward to replace them. The men who had fallen back would hurriedly reload their muskets and prepare for firing when they, once again, cycled to the front lines. This process allowed the line to keep up an almost continuous barrage of musket fire. It was efficient, effective, and a drill the British Regulars could perform in their sleep.

But the militiamen were not professional soldiers. They spent their days working on their farms and in their shops, on their fishing boats or at their sundry trades, not practicing battle drill. He was not surprised, therefore, when a somewhat less-organized result was achieved when Barrett ordered them into line.

Professional though they may not be, however, the militiamen did not hesitate when ordered to fire. With their first volley, they disabled four of the eight British officers, killed three rankers, and wounded nine more. The stunned British Regulars, their discipline essentially lost when their officers went down, fled.

Drum was stunned as well. From where he stood in the militia ranks, he could clearly see the dead and wounded where they lay, their wine-red blood spreading in the dirt around their bodies. This had not been part of his glorious vision, and he was stupefied.

Daniel hollered at him to move and, receiving no response, grabbed a fistful of Drum's shirt. "Come with me, Drum," he ordered. "Don't look at them now. You have to come with me." He dragged Drum to the rear line. "Re-load your musket now." He was hurriedly reloading his own weapon while trying to keep Drum steady.

"I don't think I ... I ....." Drum's voice trailed off as he looked toward the fallen men on the bridge.

"It doesn't matter," Daniel told him steadily. "Just load the musket. You don't have to fire again. I'll fire mine, then take yours and fire it. Can you do that?" He was practically nose-to-nose with Drum, determined to hold his attention away from the dead and wounded. "It's alright, Drum. I'll do the shooting. But can you keep the guns loaded for me?"

Drum swallowed so hard Daniel could see his Adam's apple bob, yet he managed to nod, his face earnest, if distressed. "Yes," he said, his voice rasping in his dry throat. "Yes, I'll keep them loaded."

"Good." Daniel clapped him on the shoulder reassuringly. "Then we'll be fine. Just stay with me, understand? Stay right behind me and keep reloading the guns."

On the bridge, Captain Laurie attempted to restore order to the ruptured companies of Regulars. He shouted for Kelly's men to form up so that they could return fire while they inched backward. Gradually, they regained some of their composure and managed to make it off the bridge where they took up positions behind the cover of a stone wall.

*   *   *

Back in Concord, Edward was in the process of completing another errand for Colonel Smith when he heard the sound of volley fire coming from the direction of the North Bridge. He hastened back to the elm tree in time to see Smith laboring to climb into the saddle. His aides were scrambling for their mounts, and officers were barking commands to their lieutenants. Edward found his horse and Major Pitcairn at almost the same moment. "What is happening?" he asked.

"Not sure," Pitcairn replied curtly. His mouth was set in a thin line, his eyes focused on the road leading to the bridge. "It sounds as if the foolish rebels decided to put up a fight. Smith is taking two Grenadier companies out to the bridge. The rest of us need to be ready to return to Boston as soon as this business is settled." He looked now at Edward. "Hinton," he said, blinking as though he only just realized to whom he was speaking.

"Sir?"

"Shadow Smith's contingent, would you? Find out what is happening at the bridge, and then report back to me, aye?"

"Yes, Sir." Edward wheeled the mare around and spurred her down the road after the Grenadier companies. The light companies of the Fourth were at the bridge, and it rankled that he had been kept from joining them by Smith's insistence on using him as an errand boy. He hoped he would not be too late.

The Grenadiers were on a fast march, Smith at their rear, but needed no prodding from the colonel or any other officer. The sound of musket fire was enough. After being cooped up for so long in Boston, if there was a fight nearby, they were eager to be part of it. Edward could smell the skirmish even before it came into view. A pungent haze of powder smoke clung to the air around the bridge, partially obscuring the men on the far side. The firing was less organized now, with nothing save for sporadic cracks of sound. Given the relative positions of the combatants, any musket fire essentially was now a waste of ammunition.

The Grenadiers reached the bridge to the relief of Laurie's men. Like hunting dogs unleashed, they charged through the wisps of powder smoke that clung to the air across the bridge, driving the militia back up Punkatasset Hill. There, in command of the high ground, the militia turned to face them, causing the outnumbered Grenadier companies to wisely fall back to the bridge.

Edward dismounted and walked toward the bridge in search of his company Sergeant. Before he could find him, he encountered the men detailed to remove the three fallen soldiers from the bridge. Edward was mortified to see that all three were privates from the Fourth. He abandoned his attempt to find the Sergeant and, instead, walked to where the Grenadier companies stood ready to cover Parsons' men once they made their way back to the bridge. There was no conversation and little movement as they waited, and a good ten minutes ticked by before Parsons and his men finally returned from their fruitless raid on Barrett's farm. On Smith's order, the Grenadiers advanced to protect the four companies, but it was not necessary. The militia allowed them to pass unmolested.

Edward hurried back to Pitcairn to report all he had seen. "Colonel Smith is bringing the column back to Concord," he finished, "and wants to depart for Boston without delay. He considers our mission complete."

Pitcairn nodded gravely and turned his horse toward the waiting companies. Edward would have liked to follow the major, but no such order or invitation had been issued, so he returned to his own regiment. Concord, its roads having been churned throughout the morning by the movement of the British troops, was hazed over by a cloud of choking dust, and the plume of smoke generated by the burning gun carriages continued to smudge the sky. Hogsheads of flour and other stores were scattered, and many of the homes and buildings vandalized. Edward supposed that Smith was correct when he decreed their job done, though it was difficult to see how all of this was worth the cost.

The sense of relief among the men was palpable as they set out on the road, back the way they had come from Boston. It was close to the noon hour, so the sun stood almost directly overhead tormenting them with a heat that was unusual for April. Extreme fatigue was beginning to set in, coupled with a general feeling of dissatisfaction with the way the whole operation had played out.

Edward saluted Pitcairn as his company filed past. The major returned the salute, though he seemed hardly aware of the column as it paraded by, his attention being fixed on the rear-most companies he would command. These men would guard the column's rear, and his only concern for the moment was that they be alert and fully prepared should the bothersome militia take it into their heads to pursue the column.

For the first mile or so of the march, there was only scattered firing from militia who had concealed themselves in the woods. They were too far from the road to be more than a nuisance to the column, and flankers who were deployed on both sides of the column kept it that way. Edward began to relax slightly. If the militia intended any further harassment, he thought it would likely come in Lexington, and that was several more miles down the road.

But he was wrong. The column made it only as far as the turn at Meriam's Corner, which put them on the road back to Lexington, when the first major assault came from the militia. The road crossed a substantial creek there, and the bridge was narrow. The flankers were forced to drop back to the road to cross with the main column, which allowed the militiamen to get within striking distance. With lethal effect, they closed on the road, firing on the British Regulars as they funneled across the bridge. As the flash and dull crack of musket fire erupted all around them, some of the troops began to break their line, darting to either side of the road in search of cover.

Officers bellowed at the light companies to form their lines and prepare to return fire; drummers took up the command and beat out the call to battle line. Steeling their nerves, the men complied, forming into two firing lines that would provide thin cover until the rest of the column had cleared the bridge.

Edward moved to a commanding position beside his unit and raised his sword. He had done this on a parade ground numerous times, but never in actual combat, and his parched throat was constricted with tension. Sitting ramrod straight in the saddle, looking to every man there as if he harbored nothing but absolute self-assurance, he ordered them to load and make ready. His blade quivered imperceptibly as he held it aloft for a few disciplined beats. And then, he sharply lowered the sword.

He knew the instantaneous response would be the deafening roar of an entire line of muskets firing in unison, yet he flinched at the sound, nonetheless. Each muzzle emitted a burst of flame and acrid, eye-stinging smoke shrouded the line and obscured the view. These soldiers did not need to see what was beyond that grey pall, however. With habit conditioned into them by hours of drill, the front line stepped neatly back to allow the rear line to take their place.

Edward felt a frisson of power as he watched the almost perfect execution of this oft-repeated drill, and he raised his sword to repeat the process. The unrelenting barrage of musket fire shredded bark and leaves as it tore into the tree line. He prepared the men for a third volley, but there was no point. The rebels had vanished into the woods as abruptly as they had appeared. If not for the number of dead and wounded men scattered throughout the column, he might have thought the whole thing a mere apparition — that there had never been any rebels there at all.

Quickly, with little conversation, the column collected the fallen, regained their order, and began marching again, slowed now by the wounded and by energy-sapping heat and fatigue.

Edward assumed that the rebels in the woods were the same ones who had stood up to Laurie's men on the North Bridge. Though the column was spread thinly along the road, Smith's twenty-one companies far outnumbered that handful of militia. They would be fools to attack the column directly, he reasoned, and relaxed in the assumption that the rebels would feel their point made and disperse.

As before, his assumption was short-lived. Less than an hour later, the column reached another choke point in the road, a place where it crooked sharply north and then east again to avoid marshy ground latticed with streams. With the untenable ground at their backs, the column had once again to turn and fend off a militia attack. This assault was even fiercer than the last, and plainly involved far more militiamen than had been assembled on Punkatasset Hill. The British column fired several volleys, which managed to keep the rebels at bay. But, this time, the rebels did not hastily vanish into the woods. Instead, they stood their ground, managing to wound and even kill a number of the British troops.

"Fix bayonets! Fix bayonets!" An officer from another company raced by, screaming the order. "Charge them! Run the rebels down!"

Edward had only a moment to mentally process the command before his attention was diverted by a wave of shouting that rolled across the field from somewhere off to his right. Farther up the road, where the order to charge the rebels had already been delivered, troops were breaking formation and pouring out across the open ground, all of their pent-up anger and frustration apparent in their shrieks and battle cries.

Following suit, Edward raised his sword and bellowed out an order that sent his company hurtling across the open field, screaming like berserkers after the devil himself. He went with them, spurring the mare forward toward the rebel's exploding muskets. The animal was walleyed with terror but did as he asked and barreled forward into noise and chaos every instinct told it to avoid.

Despite the speed with which everything was happening, a part of Edward's mind seemed to slow down so that he could take in odd details. The sound of the mare's hooves kicking up clods of dirt; the animal's breath heavy in its chest; the colors of the early spring grasses peppered with wildflowers — all of these things lodged themselves in his mind. He caught glimpses here and there of men jerked backwards by the impact of a well-placed shot. One or two fell in the boneless way of men dead before they hit the ground. Others writhed on the ground in pain, while a few staggered to their feet to continue the assault.

A musket ball ripped through his sleeve. He cursed and, absurdly, tried to locate the man who had fired it, but there were too many militiamen and, despite their lack of uniform, they all seemed to look alike. Worse still, the tans, browns, and dark greens of their leather and homespun blended so well with the surrounding vegetation that they were difficult to pick out without standing still and giving his eyes a moment to focus. But remaining in one place, especially on horseback, would make him an easy target, so he pushed forward.

The militiamen were retreating toward a thick line of trees seventy or more yards distant that ran almost parallel to the road. They were not in the complete panicked confusion he might have expected. It was a disorganized retreat, certainly, yet most of the men seemed to have enough of their wits about them to turn and fire from time to time, reloading as they ran. A few had rifles. Those men would stop, turn, kneel, take careful aim, and fire. Far more accurate than the muskets, the rifles could pick out particular targets with alarming precision. And they were picking their targets carefully — officers. Edward thought of the rent in his sleeve and, face tightened with concentration, he altered his course toward one of the riflemen.

The rifleman at first did not see him coming. Oblivious to the impending danger, the man had planted himself and was firing, reloading, and choosing another target with mechanical efficacy. Sword drawn, Edward barreled toward him, pushing his mare as hard as he dared on the uneven ground. In seconds that seemed minutes, he was within one stride of the rifleman who, too late, finally realized his danger. The rifleman twisted where he knelt on the ground and attempted to fire, but Edward was on him too quickly.

Edward's straight-bladed sword was ill-suited to a slashing, cavalry-style attack, forcing him to stab rather than slash. The end result was essentially the same, if less cleanly executed — the sword pierced the man's throat — but the mare's momentum was carrying Edward forward too quickly, and he had to release the sword before he could withdraw it. He jerked his horse around, afraid that the man would manage yet to fire his weapon, but there was no danger. The rifleman lay on the ground, bright blood spurting from his neck, eyes staring uncomprehendingly into the sky. His mouth gaped open, and his entire body twitched slightly for the few seconds of life he had yet to bleed out. Edward leaned down from the saddle and grasped the sword. It came away easily enough and, without looking back, he steered the mare toward his company.

The fleeing militiamen had made it to the trees before the British troops could catch them. With the trees for cover, they turned and blasted away at the soldiers who, in consequence, were reluctant to continue their pursuit. There was no need. The drums were sounding retreat, officers barking orders to return to the road and re-form into ranks. Edward rode behind his men, watching them gather up their wounded comrades, scanning the ground for any who might have been overlooked. Men had already been detailed to scour the field for the dead.

And, Edward noted despondently, there were several of those. More than they could afford to lose.

The column was moving more slowly than ever, for the futile dash across the field had sapped a considerable amount of the little energy the men had left. They were running out of water, had no rations, and now had the additional burden of caring for the wounded. Edward's head was spinning. They'd encountered so many rebels, spread over such a wide area — far more than had assembled back on Punkatasset Hill. How many were out there?

A messenger rode hastily toward him on his way to take information back to Pitcairn. Edward pulled his horse to the side of the road and watched him come. The messenger, one of Smith's aides, rode with the urgency of a man pursued by demons. He scarcely paused long enough to deliver his message, and his horse danced nervously as he talked. "Keep your company formed up, Sir," the messenger told him. "March them as fast as you can."

"What is happening?"

The messenger jerked his head in the general direction of the trees. "The scouts report militia assembled along the road all the way back to Charlestown. Thousands of them. Colonel Smith wants us to keep moving."

Edward nodded dully, and then weakly returned the corporal's salute as the young man rode away. There was no other way to go, nothing else to do but keep pushing forward. They were marching through a gauntlet of rebel militia, and nothing could be done but get through it as best they could manage. Edward stood in his stirrups and bellowed for the company Sergeant. "Push them, O'Donnell" he ordered, trying not to sound as frantic as he felt. "Move the men more quickly. As fast as they can march. And, be sure their muskets are kept loaded. We expect more trouble."

O'Donnell's face said quite plainly that Edward was wasting time and breath telling him something he had already surmised. "The men can only move as fast as the companies ahead of us, *Sir.*" The statement was made with a trace of hostility, pointing out the obvious to a younger, less-experienced — but senior — officer. "Though we'll do our best, Sir," he added quickly. He saluted and returned to the column, barking at the men as he walked.

The rebels kept up a relentless hail of harassing fire from every opportune position along the road. Edward could see them now, on every hill and clearing, and darting like deer among the trees in wooded areas. From what he was able to make out, the scouts had not exaggerated the rebel numbers; there had to be two thousand or more. His men had seen, too, and had come to the same conclusion. A sense of unease was spreading through the ranks that could easily lead to panic if not quelled. He rode close to the lines, offering encouragement and trying to set an example of composure while, at the same time, keeping one eye on the massing militia.

Just west of Lexington, they had to pass a broad, boulder-strewn pasture. Edward remembered it from the trip to Concord as an eerie place, reminiscent of an ancient graveyard. When he looked upon it now, it was not so much eerie as terrifying. There were so many rocks, brushy stands, and trees. Too much cover and concealment close to the road, too many places for a man to hide with a musket or rifle. Every nerve in his body knew the firing would come — it was just a matter of when.

He did not have to wait long. The first volley came the moment the head of the column reached a rocky, brush-covered hill on the far end of the pasture. It was an overpowering volley fired by an enormous mass of militia, and it was effective. A number of troops were killed, and even more wounded — including Colonel Smith. A musket ball to the thigh knocked him clean out of his saddle. Men who saw him fall were torn between the urge to panicked flight and the desire to stand and fight and, so, they did neither. They simply froze in place, the worst thing they could have done. Like a dam in a stream, they blocked the road and caused the column to begin to pile up behind them. Unable to move or find cover, the troops became easy targets for the militia's muskets.

Edward struggled to keep his men under control. Their best chance, he knew, was to be had by staying together and covering each other as much as possible. He had no idea why the column had stopped and was on the verge of sending O'Donnell to find out when Pitcairn raced by, cursing a blue streak.

"Come with me, Hinton," Pitcairn snarled as he galloped by. "I may have need of you."

Edward could not imagine what use of him Pitcairn had in mind, but if whatever it was would get the column moving again and out of this narrow kill zone, he would do it in a heartbeat. Leaving O'Donnell in charge of the company, he rode after Pitcairn. The major was bellowing at men to clear out of his way, practically running over one or two who did not move quickly enough. They reached the head of the column to find Smith down and being tended to by one of his aides.

"Bloody hell!" Pitcairn roared. "Get him out of the road! And get this bloody column moving!" He had dismounted, and was physically shoving men in the direction he wanted them to move, cursing every musket ball that whizzed past his head. "You," he said, pointing at Hinton. "Detail two men to get the Colonel to a wagon. Get these damned men organized and get the wounded moved to where they won't hold up the column! If we stay here, we're sitting targets."

Without thought, Edward was off his horse and coordinating the effort to clear the wounded out of the way. He suspected that Pitcairn was at the point of simply leaving them on the side of the road if that was what it took to get the column moving, and he did everything in his power to keep that from happening. He surrendered his horse to the purpose of helping to more quickly move the wounded.

Pitcairn had assumed command and dispatched a company to move up the hill and drive the militia away. Then he turned on the men at the head of the column. "Get your sorry arses moving! And, by God, if you stop and block this column again, I'll shoot you myself and leave your worthless carcasses where they fall!"

With Pitcairn driving them, the column marched forward. He continually dispatched skirmishers out to push the militiamen back away from the column, though the relief these quick forays provided was minimal. Again and again the column was set upon by the militiamen, and casualties were mounting. Edward was sent to monitor the column, pass Pitcairn's instructions and situation reports to the officers of the various units, and generally cajole, badger, or bludgeon as necessary. To survive, they had to keep moving, and the men's instincts were telling them to do the opposite — to stop and seek cover where they could find it.

They struggled past Fiske Hill and just to the edge of Lexington, when the hardest blow fell. Taking heavy fire, Pitcairn's horse was struck and reared, throwing Pitcairn and injuring him badly enough that he could not continue to lead the column. With so many senior officers wounded, the column began to fragment into units under the leadership of individual officers, most of them low-ranking and having no combat experience.

Fatigue, compounded by the overwhelming number of wounded, slowed the column to a crawl, ammunition was running out, and water supplies had begun to run dry a mile back. All order was disintegrating and, with it, any hope that they could continue to fight as a unit — as they must if any of them were to make it back to Boston.

Edward, believing in Pitcairn's assertion that they must keep moving, joined a handful of officers who were fighting valiantly to maintain some semblance of control. They were achieving little, however. In desperation, he made his way back along the column in search of his own regiment. The Fourth, like the other light companies, was exhausted to the point of collapse by their protracted flanking duties, and they looked up at him with faces that seemed beyond the ability to register any emotion. Except for their Sergeant. O'Donnell stood as Edward approached, his face red with fury and frustration.

It was exactly what Edward had hoped for. "Come with me," he said. "We can get out of this yet, but I need your help."

Without a word, O'Donnell picked up his musket and followed Edward to the front of the column. He looked about him as he stalked along, glaring into silence the men who were making their complaints heard, wordlessly threatening those who looked about to run. He had a notion of what Edward might be about and, to that purpose, gathered up two additional Sergeants from other regiments as he passed.

The men, Irishmen like himself who met whatever life gave them with a firm chin and squared shoulders, needed no explanations. They fell in behind O'Donnell and followed Edward to the front of the column. When they arrived, it was plain to the Sergeants that Lieutenant Hinton, along with another lieutenant and two ensigns who were even younger and less experienced, were all that stood between the crumbling troops and complete defeat. If their lives had not been in danger, they would have found it highly amusing.

Edward addressed O'Donnell. "We have to get these men into order," he pointed out. "We need them to form up if they are to be able to defend themselves. If they break and run — if it becomes every man for himself out here — none are likely to survive.

"I can see that, Sir," O'Donnell replied. He looked to where the other lieutenant stood face-to-face with a man who was screaming back as loudly as he was being screamed at. "Though you're going about it the wrong way, I'd say."

Edward spread his hands in a gesture of surrender. "That is why I need you. What would you suggest?" He pointed to the stormy-faced troops who, at this moment, seemed more bent on killing their own officers than on standing against the militia.

O'Donnell held out his own musket, looking meaningfully from its lethal bayonet to Edward. "Can you get yourself one of these, do you think, Sir?"

It was a simple matter to find an abandoned musket and affix its bayonet, and then Edward and the three Sergeants marched to the front of the column to face the mutinous men. The Sergeants at his back infused Edward with fierce confidence and, with a murderous eye, he stared the men into silence. "I order you to form up into a double-file column without further delay. You will prepare your muskets for firing, and you will advance or stand and fire at my command." He saw from the corner of his eye that the other three officers had picked up muskets and joined him. "If any man among you steps out of line, you will die on the spot."

For one blessed moment, he thought he had succeeded, that the men were going to do as ordered. And then, one of the men reached forward with surprising quickness, grasped the musket away from a startled ensign and smashed the gun's butt into the young man's face. Reflexively, Edward swung his own musket into the back of the assailant's head, knocking him to the ground.

Another man feinted toward Edward, but O'Donnell caught him square in the face with a blow from his massive fist. O'Donnell spat in the dirt near where the man lay writhing in the agony of a broken nose and loosened teeth. "If you've that much energy left in you," he told the man, "you'd best be using it to fight your way out of here, you pig turd." He raked his angry gaze across the other men, most of whom seemed considerably less confrontational than a few seconds earlier. "My fist's tired now," he told them, his tone easy. "So, if any of the rest of you maggots feel the need to be quarrelsome, I'll be forced to use my blade."

None of the men were of a mind to continue their challenge. Possible death at the hands of the militia seemed a much better gamble than certain death on a bayonet blade wielded by one of the Sergeants. They wilted like sails left without wind. With these men quelled, the others began to settle back. Officers up and down the column retook control of their ranks, and the troops hunkered down, prepared to fight their way into Lexington. If they could get into Lexington, occupy its buildings, perhaps they could regroup and devise a way out of this debacle. It was a thin hope, yet it was the only one they had for the moment.

There was only a short distance left to go, but they were taking such heavy fire that every foot gained seemed a mile. At some point, Edward realized, they were going to have to admit defeat. White flags would have to be waved, weapons surrendered. For an odd moment, his mind wrestled with the protocol and politics of the thing. Would the militia accept their surrender? *Could* they surrender? Strictly speaking, they were not at war. How would it all play out? More to the point, how would the news be received in London? *Dear, God,* he thought. *A British army forced to surrender to a country militia.* He felt sick.

Salvation, heralded by distant cannon fire and drum cadences, came down the road from Lexington in the form of a fresh brigade under the command of Brigadier the Right Honorable Hugh Earl Percy, second Duke of Northumberland. The brigade could have been under the command of Jack the Candle Maker for all Edward and the rest of the men cared. When they looked up to see the reinforcements coming, many cheered, some wept. Percy's brigade enveloped Smith's exhausted, dehydrated men in a protective cocoon.

"Your men have thirty minutes in which to recuperate," Percy told the officers once they had all reached Lexington. He looked regretfully at the ranks of men, beaten down by the more than twenty hours they had been on the march with no rest and little to eat or drink. "It is all I can give them. Tell them to get food and water, restock their ammunition, and rest as they can. The wounded will be cared for and prepared to move. We dare not linger longer. Thirty minutes, gentlemen. Not a minute longer."

S.D. BANKS

CHAPTER SEVENTEEN

For Daniel and Drum, the afternoon had been comprised of spurts of fast-paced overland travel occasionally broken by pauses to join militiamen in harassing the redcoat line. After the Regulars had left Concord, Daniel collected Drum and their horses, and set out with the purpose of getting Drum safely back to Boston. He chose a route that ran through the woods and hills parallel with the road, though far enough away to avoid being seen by the British troops. Here and there along the way, he caught glimpses of the redcoat column on the road, and could hear the almost constant report of musket fire. Despite his sense of responsibility for Drum's safety, he occasionally felt the tug of something he could not define to help the militia and could not, therefore, resist stopping to add his musket to their effort.

The first time, he left Drum and the horses safely out of harm's way while he made his way down to an overlook near the bridge at Meriam's Corner. The bridge, which formed an effective choke point, was a well-chosen place to stage an ambush, and the militia gave the redcoats far more of a beating than he would have thought possible. The militia lost some of their own men, however, and Daniel lingered a bit after the redcoats had marched on, walking the ground along with the men of the Concord militia in search of their wounded and dead friends. Thankfully, there were very few. He found, too, patches of blood-soaked ground where he knew wounded redcoats had fallen. They had been carried away by their comrades, but some of the men had lost muskets, cartridge boxes, and bags of musket balls in the process. These he collected.

He stood, surveying the field, when a woman raced from the trees and dropped to her knees in the tall grass. He crossed to her, and saw that she was weeping over the body of a fallen rifleman. "Can I help you, ma'am?" He swallowed hard. A woman's tears were difficult. He would rather look at the dead man's face than at her tear-stained one. "Can I help you move him, maybe? I have a horse . . ." The right words escaped him as he felt unequal to this challenge, inept at offering something useful to the woman.

She was shaking her head, drying her eyes on the hem of her apron. "No, but thank you," she replied softly. "My brother is coming. We came out just behind the militia wanting to see . . . well, wanting to see what happened. But not *this*." She seemed baffled by it all, as though it had not occurred to her that the militia's actions might result in someone's death.

"Is this . . . was this your husband, then?"

She nodded and fought back a fresh wave of tears. "His name is Henry. My brother told him he should stay out of this. But Henry said it was important. He said he couldn't sit behind his locked door and let others fight for his rights and his land, not if he was capable of fighting himself."

"He was certainly capable," Daniel told her. "I saw him with that rifle. He was more than capable."

She smiled thinly. "Yes, he was quite proud of that." She touched the rifle where it lay on the ground, running her fingers lightly along the barrel.

"He was right, I believe," Daniel told her after a long silence. "It is important. And what he did was important. It will matter." He hoped that was true or, at least, hoped she believed it was.

The woman nodded but did not look at him. "Will you be fighting? If this goes on — will you be in it?"

"Yes." He stared toward the road. The dust stirred by the passing redcoats had settled. "Yes, I expect so." He met her brown, tear-filled eyes, sorrowful as a calf's. "And, I do think it will go on."

She nodded again and, pursing her lips together, picked up the rifle and seemed to consider for a moment. Daniel had the horrible thought that she might be planning to join the fight herself. *Where the hell is her brother?* he wondered anxiously.

She stood, staring at him, clutching the rifle to her as though it were an infant. Finally, she seemed to make up her mind about something. "Here," she said, thrusting the rifle toward him. "You should have this."

Daniel backed up a step. "No, thank you, ma'am. That's very generous of you, but I couldn't possibly—"

"I believe Henry would have wanted you to have it. He treasured this rifle, and he would have wanted it to keep fighting even if he couldn't. He thought this fight was important, and he would want the rifle to be part of it." She held the gun out again, her face set in firm resolve.

Daniel was shaking his head. He stopped himself from asking if she was daft. "I just can't, ma'am." It was the most outlandish thing he'd ever heard and, being around Teague and Drum, he had heard some pretty outlandish things. "Besides, if I took it, you'd probably regret parting from it before long. Maybe you should wait a bit. Then, if you still feel this way, give it to someone you know better. Your brother maybe?"

She shook her head. "My brother wouldn't know what to do with it. I've the feeling that you will put it to good use. Please, Sir, take it. You asked if there is anything you can do for me. Well, this is it. This is what you can do for me." She shoved the rifle into Daniel's arms, then knelt and searched the ground about her husband's body for ammunition. She was putting this into Daniel's hands when her brother emerged from the trees leading a mule. "Go now," she told Daniel, pushing him gently as she looked over her shoulder. "My brother's coming and I don't want to have to explain to him why I gave you the gun."

"I thank you for the rifle, then," he said, not knowing what else he could say. "I'll do all I can to be worthy of the gift."

The woman nodded, then shooed him away. He jogged back to where he had left Drum, awkward under his burden of newly acquired weapons. Drum dropped his jaw when he saw the guns, which bristled from Daniel's person every which way.

He watched Daniel stow one of the muskets and the rifle on his own horse. "Where'd you get those?" he asked when Daniel handed him the two remaining muskets to carry.

"The muskets were dropped by some careless redcoats. The rifle is a long story."

"We've got time," Drum pointed out as he rolled the muskets in his blanket and lashed them behind his saddle.

"Not really. The redcoats are moving. My guess is the militia will attack them at the next choke point along the road, and I want to be there." Drum was scowling at him, perfectly aware that Daniel simply did not want to tell him the story. "I'll tell you about it when we get back to Boston," he assured Drum. "It's just that it's . . . complicated."

"Did you steal it?"

Daniel jerked his head up. "No," he said firmly. "I did not. Why would you think that?"

"Just checking." Drum shrugged. He put one big foot in a stirrup and swung easily up into the saddle.

Daniel stared at him. "Checking?" he repeated.

"Yep." Drum clucked his horse into a slow walk. "Just checking."

Muttering to himself about the conundrum that was Drum, Daniel climbed into the saddle and spurred his horse forward. They picked their way along for a mile or so until, once again, they could hear the whip-crack sound of musket fire and the shouts of officers trying to salvage order from chaos. Adjuring him to remain behind with the horses, Daniel left Drum in the safety of a dense coppice and made his way toward the sound. He carried two muskets, but left the rifle behind. He had fired a rifle only one time and did not want to risk his life to an unfamiliar weapon. The rifle, for all of its beautiful distance and accuracy, would have to wait until he had time to become accustomed to it.

The outcome of this ambush, and the next, was even more devastating to the British column than the first. Outnumbered and without benefit of defensible ground, the Regulars had, essentially, been engaged in a running battle since leaving Concord. They were a very different show now, their drums and fifes silenced, their brilliant red coats dark with sweat, their haggard faces caked with dust. Many of the men staggered, barely able to stay on their feet, and there were so many wounded that he could smell the blood in the air. He almost felt sorry for them.

Everything changed at Lexington, however. Just when the militiamen thought they had forced the Regulars to give up, reinforcements arrived in great enough numbers to swing the advantage over to the Regulars. Between Lexington and Charlestown, things were likely to be quite different, Daniel knew. He returned to the horses. "Unpack those muskets," he told Drum, indicating the two tied behind Drum's saddle. "We're likely to need them."

They shadowed the road eastward, eventually falling in behind a militia company from Danvers as they angled south toward Menotomy. The militia had covered the sixteen miles from Danvers to Menotomy in only four hours and had to be tired, Daniel knew, though he heard no complaints among them. The talk was all for the news they had heard of events at Lexington and on the bridge near Concord, and they were full of determination to add their effort to that already expended by other militia units to ensure the British understanding that colonists were no longer of a mind to allow such actions to go unanswered.

The village of Menotomy stood at a crossroads, a good place for the assembled militia companies to make one final statement before the British could cross back to Boston. As Daniel and Drum rode into the village, it appeared that it would be a statement the British were not likely to forget. Over thirty militia companies had spread themselves throughout the village, taking up positions behind every fence and rock wall, in the windows of every possible house and building, and every bit of ground that might offer cover. Many of the villagers had fled, yet a number remained behind, determined to aid the fight.

"Take the horses and follow the road toward Boston," Daniel told Drum, handing him his horse's reins. "Go a couple of miles or so until you find a good place to pull off the road and hide. I'll catch up with you when things are finished here." He was unwrapping one of the extra muskets and several of the cartridge boxes.

But Drum was shaking his head. "I want to stay with you."

"Drum, it isn't safe." Daniel's voice was weary and edged with impatience. "There's going to be a fight. Probably worse than back at the bridge. Please take the horses and go."

Tenaciously, Drum continued to shake his head. "I know there's going to be a fight. I want to help. I will be better than I was back at the bridge. Even if I can only load the guns for you, I want to help." He saw that Daniel was becoming angry and spoke quickly to forestall the words he suspected were coming. "You don't always have to protect me, Daniel." His tone was even, almost matter-of-fact. "I know you think you have to look after me, but I'm a man, too. I have to do things sometimes."

"But not this."

"Yes, this. I want to help. I *need* to help if I can."

Daniel studied him for a protracted moment, weighing all of his thoughts against each other. "All right," he said finally. "Keep your head down, though, will you?"

"You keep telling me that," Drum said as he dismounted and began to collect the remaining musket and the cartridge boxes.

"And I always have the feeling that you don't listen." Daniel stopped Drum as he reached for the rifle. "Leave it with the horses. I don't yet know how to use it properly, and it'll be safe here."

But in a gesture that was becoming too familiar for Daniel's taste, Drum shook his head. "I'll keep it safe," he insisted. "It's valuable. I'll look after it." He slung the shoulder strap across his body so that the rifle hung at his back.

"Well, I have to admit, it gives you a certain air of authority," Daniel grinned.

Liking the notion of that, Drum shifted the rifle slightly so that it would achieve — to his mind — maximum effect. His stomach rumbled loudly, and he clamped his hand over it trying to quiet the noise. They'd not eaten since before dawn, and it was now nearly half-past four o'clock in the afternoon. Drum was keenly feeling the privation.

Staying with the Danvers men seemed as good a place to be as any, so Daniel and Drum lined up with them behind a wall surrounding one of the village houses. Daniel had one musket primed and at the ready. Drum had charge of the others and was diligently arranging them, checking his supply of powder and balls, carefully setting in his mind the order in which he would need to do things to keep Daniel supplied with loaded muskets.

A tall, lanky man ambled up, sized up the spot Daniel had chosen for himself and, shrugging, settled in beside Daniel and Drum. The man got awkwardly to his knees, but did not stay long in that position. With a muttered oath, he rested his musket on the wall and settled into a sitting position. "My old knees can't take much kneeling anymore," he explained to Daniel. He began to massage one knee. "I'll be sixty years old next year, though my joints seem to think it'll be more like ninety." He laughed at that. "Tried every sort of liniment, I have, yet none seem to do much more than make me smell like everything but a man. Some even made my ol' dog shy away!" He laughed again.

"Willow bark tea," Drum said without looking up from the business of consolidating all of Daniel's salvaged powder cartridges into two cartridge boxes. "Mrs. Garrett says willow bark tea helps sore joints."

Daniel looked at him in surprise. "Mrs. Garrett? My *mother* Mrs. Garrett?"

"Yes." The tone in Daniel's voice made him look up from his task.

"And, when did she tell you this?" As far as Daniel could recall, his mother had never told *him* anything about willow bark tea and, unaccountably, it annoyed him that Drum seemed to know little details about his mother, of which he himself was ignorant.

Drum shrugged and returned his attention to the cartridge boxes. "I heard her," he said. "One time when I was at her shop with you. An old lady who was there to buy a hat was telling your mother how bad her hands hurt sometimes, and your mother told her about the tea." Now he looked at the man who had complained about his knees. "Mrs. Garrett is very nice." He said it as though it was the most important quality any person could possess. "And she knows a lot of things, too. If she says the tea might help, I think it will."

"I'll have to give it a try." He looked at Daniel and Drum as if seeing them anew. "Russell," he said, introducing himself. "Jason Russell."

"Nice to meet you, Mr. Russell. I'm Daniel Garrett, and this is Drum. Drummond Fisackerly."

A voice rang out from across the road, interrupting any further conversation. "Jason, is that you behind that wall? You get your ornery old hide out of there and come with me! Those redcoats will be here any minute, and you have no business trying to tangle with them."

"The Devil's teeth! What does that old man want?" Russell was struggling to his knees so he could peer over the wall. "What do you want, Cutter?" He glanced toward Daniel. "That's old Ammi Cutter," he said. "Lives across the road there. And," he raised his voice so that Cutter could hear, "just because he stumbled into a stray supply wagon and wounded redcoat officer earlier today, thinks he knows all about the redcoats."

Cutter, who was considerably older even than Mr. Russell, was advancing toward them with the jerky gait of a stringed-marionette. A musket, which probably weighed as much as Cutter, was propped on one shoulder. "We didn't just stumble onto it," he growled, "we captured them. Wagon and man, both. That's where I got this," he added, slapping his palm against the musket. "You old fool," he said when he reached the wall. He pointed one bony finger at Russell and stood waiting for him to get to his feet. "What do you think you're doing out here?"

"This is my house," Russell said, jerking his head toward the house behind them. "An Englishman's home is his castle, and it's his right to defend his castle."

Cutter spat a stream of tobacco juice into the road. "That's all well and good," he said, "but I'm not sure the redcoats think you're an Englishman, and I *know* they don't have any interest in your rights. Most of Menotomy has already lit out, and you need to do the same. Leave it to the militias to do the fighting. You never done anything like this. You're like to get yourself shot!"

Hearing the old man's tone, Drum rose to Russell's defense. "It doesn't matter if he never did it before. Sometimes men have to do things they never did before. That's just the way it is."

Looking sideways at Drum, Daniel cursed under his breath as he got to his feet and introduced himself to Cutter more to forestall an argument than out of politeness.

Russell was not sidetracked. "The boy's right." He clapped Drum on the shoulder approvingly, which made Drum glow with pride. "Right now, it doesn't matter what I've done before. This is my home. Right now, I need to help defend my home."

"You old fool." Cutter spat again. It truly seemed to escape him that Russell was at least a decade younger than himself. "Then I'd better stick around to watch your back." He climbed over the wall, demonstrating a sprightliness that surprised Daniel, and stood beside Russell, looking his friend up and down. "You'll do, I guess."

They all sank down behind the wall and settled themselves in to wait. Drum's stomach growled, his hunger becoming more difficult to ignore. "You know what else Mrs. Garrett is really good at? She makes wonderful venison stew." His voice was wistful, his mind lingering over the remembered taste and aroma of Selah's stew. Daniel, hungry himself and in no mood to be reminded of the fact, glowered at him, but Drum merely frowned back. "Well, she does," he insisted adamantly.

Russell dug into a haversack he had tossed nearby. "Here you go, Mr. Fisackerly." He offered Drum two rock-hard biscuits. Drum accepted them gratefully, munching away at the biscuits and washing them down with water. They were a poor substitute for venison stew, but they filled the hole in his belly sufficiently to keep it quiet for a while.

Daniel studied Russell and Cutter. One was inexperienced and unable to move quickly, the other so wiry that Daniel suspected the musket would knock him backwards the first time it discharged. "Lord, help us," he prayed softly. They watched and waited, listening for the tell-tale sounds of troops on the move. Daniel heard only insects buzzing in the tall grass, however, and the light breeze rippling the trees. The sun was high and bright in the afternoon sky, but not too hot. There were some high clouds far in the distance, a feathering of virga extending beneath them. Under other circumstances, it would be perfect for napping, he thought.

Shaking himself out of that reverie, he replayed the morning's events in his mind, picturing all he had seen and heard, looking for scraps of memory that might prove useful. His mind's eye saw again the column of redcoats as they approached the crossing at Meriam's Corner, their drummers tapping out a brisk cadence, regimental colors stirring lightly, sun bright on buckles, officer's gorgets, and bayonets. He recalled the moment when the flankers had to pull back onto the road so that they could cross the bridge with the column, and his eyes went wide. Flankers. "Shite!" he cried, visibly startling the other three men.

"What in creation's the matter with you, boy?" Cutter asked, annoyed.

"Flankers." Daniel slid back and looked urgently up and down the length of the wall. "The redcoats will have sent out flankers. We shouldn't be this close to the road. They'll get behind us!"

Cutter spat off into the grass, pausing a moment to admire the distance he had managed to achieve. "Foster already thought of that," he said, speaking of the lieutenant in charge of the Danvers militia. "He doesn't think it's a concern. He's more interested in being close enough to take some good shots at the column."

"But—"

At that moment, the discussion became immaterial. The sound of musket fire splintered the peaceful afternoon, and militiamen began to fall. Daniel turned toward the sound of the firing, shoving Drum down closer to the ground as he did so. A full company of British light infantry was sweeping across the fields to the rear of Russell's house like the leading edge of a wildfire. They had the militia pinned against the wall and were picking them off so easily it might have been mere target practice.

"The house!" Lieutenant Foster's voice boomed across the field. "Take cover in the house!"

Many of the men had not needed Foster's order to tell them where their best hope lay and had already started running for the house. Few were making it. Russell and Cutter had managed to get as far as a woodpile, and seemed unwilling for the moment to try to go any further. Daniel considered jumping to the far side of the wall but a quick glance toward the road revealed the senselessness of that plan, for the British column had come into view. They would soon be trapped between the company to their rear and the column advancing down the road.

"We have to get to the house," he told Drum. "It's our only chance." Drum was nodding and, keeping as low to the ground as he could manage, began gathering up the extra muskets and slinging cartridge boxes around his neck. Daniel picked up two muskets and one cartridge box Drum had left on the ground. "Stay close behind me and keep moving!" They ran toward the house, erratically changing direction like rabbits escaping a fox.

Daniel and Drum toppled through the front door of Jason Russell's house just behind two other men and ahead of five more. Foster was already there with a handful of men. They were attempting to take up firing positions at the windows, but the British fusillade was hindering them. If a militiaman got close enough to a window to return fire, he would fall victim to a musket ball before he managed to fire even one shot. Another group of men burst through the door. Daniel turned in time to see Jason Russell fall dead on his own doorstep, two redcoat musket balls having found him.

Pulling Drum with him, Daniel climbed the stairs to the second floor and, keeping low, made his way to a back window. Other men had followed them up the stairs and, soon, they had guns positioned in every upstairs window. Not wanting to waste any of the precious musket balls or powder, Daniel chose his targets carefully. He was a better than average marksman, but even the best shot in the colonies could only do so much with the highly-inaccurate muskets. He and the militiamen hit many of their targets, yet many more got through and, before long, the redcoats were storming the house, bayonets fixed.

Daniel fired one last round, heard glass break downstairs, and saw a militiaman launching himself from the broken window out into the yard, only to be shot by three different soldiers at once. A second man followed from another window, and was shot in the leg. He fell, but then managed to get to his feet and stumble away, musket balls singing past him until he was out of range. Knowing that they needed to go to the aid of the men on the first floor, Daniel took stock of the eight men who had come up the stairs with him. There were only four other men still alive, and one of those was injured too badly to continue the fight.

Two of the men rose from where they'd endeavored to make the wounded man comfortable and walked toward Daniel. He recognized them as two of the Danvers militiamen he had met earlier, Peter and Martin Wendell. They were brothers, a year apart in age, but so much alike in appearance they could be mistaken for twins. "It's our pa," Peter Wendell said. "He's shot through the leg."

"There's too few of us to make much difference." Martin Wendell's voice cracked with emotion. "But Pa says he thinks we need to try." Openly despairing, he glanced to where his father sat propped against a wall, his leg wrapped in a bandage devised from strips of Peter's shirt.

"I agree with your father," the third man replied. He had introduced himself earlier by the unlikely name of Ezra Dibble. A burly man, accustomed to being the largest man in any group, Ezra had been giving Drum — who towered over him — a speculative look ever since he first laid eyes on him.

"Not that that it'd do us much good to try to surrender," Peter added. "I saw a man try to yield a few minutes ago and the redcoats shot him on the spot."

"Damned redcoats," Ezra growled.

"We're not going to surrender." Daniel's tone conveyed a good deal more certitude than he felt. "Unless we can find another way out, we'll have to fight our way to the front door." That option, he did not relish. Not with a wounded man in tow. He looked around for possibilities, and found few. "Go up," he told Drum, pointing to the ceiling above them. Check the attic. See if there's another way out. Maybe there's a window that opens onto the roof. We'll do what we can do to help the men still downstairs." He watched Drum go, then followed Ezra and the two Wendells to the top of the stairs. A quick look was all they needed to see that the situation below was already hopeless.

Redcoats poured through the front door into a salvo of fire from the militiamen packed into the lower floor. Many fell, only to be replaced by more coming in right behind them. The militiamen realized too late that they had made a mistake by firing as individuals in disorderly fashion. Each man could not reload before three or four redcoats had come through the door. In seconds, they were overrun and the fighting had become hand-to-hand. Most of the militiamen had knives, and one or two had axes, but they were no match for bayonets wielded by men trained in the skill. Daniel and the three militiamen fired from the stairs, injuring two redcoats and killing one outright. Now they had the attention of other soldiers, who advanced toward the stairs.

Using his second musket, Daniel shot point blank in the face the first soldier who attempted the stairs. As the redcoat fell backward, Daniel managed to wrench the musket from his hands. It was not loaded, but it was fitted with a bayonet and Daniel used it to defend himself as he climbed back to the top of the stairs. The staircase was only wide enough to accommodate one man at a time so that, from their position at the second floor opening, Daniel and the militiamen could fire down on the advancing redcoats, picking them off one at a time. They could keep the soldiers at bay only so long as their ammunition supply held, however, and Daniel knew that was rapidly dwindling.

He was dimly aware of Drum's returning to them, but could not hear what was said as he pulled Ezra away for some purpose. Daniel heard a loud crash, which he took to be the sound of something heavy being overturned. There was no time to turn to see what they were about, for keeping the redcoats pinned down on the stairs demanded his full attention. He, Peter, and Martin were firing and reloading as quickly as they could manage. Peter's effort was hampered by the fact that his anxiety made him fumble-fingered to the point that he was dropping musket balls more often than he was able to ram them down the barrel of his gun. Daniel was preparing for the inevitability of their being overrun when he felt a nudge at his side.

"Move out of the way! Now!" Ezra bellowed.

Daniel and the two Wendell brothers rolled to the side just as Ezra and Drum shoved an enormous, overturned cupboard into the opening at the top of the stairs. It lodged there, creating an effective blockade.

"That won't hold them for long," Daniel observed.

But Drum was shaking his head. "Doesn't matter," he said. "I found a way out."

They gathered up the wounded elder Wendell and followed Drum up into the attic. As it turned out, Drum had not actually found a way out so much as he had created one. Using an axe, he had bullied a hole through the roof. Daniel peered up at the patch of blue sky that was visible through the hole. It was big enough to accommodate Drum's shoulders, so he knew the rest of the men would fit. Drum went up first so he could help haul the wounded man up.

"What about the redcoats outside?" Peter asked.

"We'll deal with that when we get up there. We're on the back side of the house; most of them are around front. Maybe they won't notice us. Keep low, though." The risk was real, and he was not certain what they would do once they were on the roof, yet it seemed a better gamble than staying where they were and facing the redcoats who would be breaking through their make-shift barricade at any moment.

One after another, they clambered out onto the roof and belly-crawled across the rough wooden shingles to the edge along the back of the house. No redcoats were visible in the yard or fields below. So far, luck was on their side. Proceeding on the hope that, if he could not see redcoats, no redcoats could see him, Daniel inched right up to the very edge and peered over. Glass fragments glittered on the ground below, and he could hear the sound of continued fighting rolling out of the house from the shattered window. But still, not a soldier in sight. He surveyed the back of the house looking for some place to get a foothold, something that might enable them to climb to the ground, but found nothing useful. Jumping the two stories to the ground might have been a possibility were it not for the wounded man.

The clock was ticking in his head. How long would it take the redcoats to clear the stairway and figure out where their quarry had gone? Not long, he reasoned. Certainly not long enough for him to spend much more time hunting for an easy way off the roof. He got to his feet and, stooping low, awkwardly crossed to the side of the house nearest the orchard. He paused there, watching the trees for any tell-tale flash of red, but the orchard seemed to be deserted. Dropping to his belly, he warily stuck his head out over the eaves. Still no redcoats and, almost as fortunately, a way down off the roof presented itself in the form of a closet-sized protuberance jutting from the first floor as if Russell had stuck a privy on the side of the house. Though Daniel doubted the small addition was what it resembled, its roof ridge was just the right height for them to drop to from the second floor roof.

Daniel assembled Drum and the other men and, shouldering one of the muskets, slid off the roof, hung for a second on the edge of the eave, and then dropped lightly to the lower roof. Ezra followed him, landing with considerably less lightness of foot and considerably more noise. They were on the verge of signaling Drum to lower the wounded man into their waiting hands when a half-dozen redcoats trotted by just below them. Daniel and the militiaman dropped where they stood, pressing themselves as flat as possible against the shingles. If they were spotted, they were as good as dead.

But the redcoats kept going. They rounded the back corner of the house, temporarily out of sight, and then came into view again as they moved in the opposite direction away from the house. Hastily, Daniel motioned to Drum who, lying flat, his head and shoulders at the edge of the roof, his feet and legs anchored by the combined weight and strength of the Wendell brothers, lowered the wounded militiaman down until Daniel and Ezra could grab him and ease him the rest of the way.

The fact that they all made it down off the roof and across the open ground to the cover of the orchard without being seen by the redcoats was almost enough to make Daniel believe in miracles. The Wendell brothers wanted only to get their father away from Menotomy and, hopefully, into a physician's care. Daniel watched them set out through the orchard, laboriously carrying their father. "They'll never make it like that," he told Drum. Go after them and tell them where to find our horses." It pained him to give up the two horses but thought it might make the difference between life and death for Mr. Wendell, so he swallowed his reluctance and let them go.

Ezra Dibble elected to remain with Daniel and Drum, at least for a bit. Most of his militia had either been killed or captured during the fight at the Russell house, but he knew some had to still be alive, and he hoped to find them. The three men set out together, leapfrogging between trees, walls, abandoned wagons and anything else they could use as cover. They had each retained a musket, and Drum still had the rifle slung across his back, but they had no ammunition, so enemy encounters were something to avoid. Once Dibble located a pocket of men he recognized, he peeled off to join them, wishing Daniel and Drum good fortune in what remained of the day.

Daniel realized that the army was moving through Menotomy with the same devastating zeal they had shown at the Russell house. The once peaceful, lovely village was now a ravaged array of houses and buildings with shattered windows and walls riddled by musket fire. Every field, orchard, and building was host to a fight. Roads were littered with every sort of obstruction, from abandoned carts and wagons to the wounded and dead. Swords or bayonets clashed and muskets fired on all sides, and so many men were dying that Daniel lost count. The redcoats were searching every house for snipers or hidden militiamen, and putting nearly every man they found to the sword, militia or not. Houses, barns, and shops were being ransacked and looted. Any civilians foolish enough to stay behind were harshly displaced and sometimes murdered. It was chaotic horror.

As they traversed the garden behind a house, they saw two children and a woman with an infant in her arms being rousted from the house. The children were crying and clinging to their mother, the mother was crying and pleading with the redcoats who, it appeared, intended to put her house to the torch. None of their tears were having any effect.

"Shite." Daniel, watching from the cover of a piled-stone fence, cursed vehemently. Every emotion and mental process was at war within him as he grappled with the conflict between wanting to help the woman and wanting to keep Drum safe. Not to mention the fact that he had no ammunition, no weapon other than his dirk and the bayonet affixed to the end of his appropriated musket.

He evaluated the scene before him; in no way did it come out in his favor. One lone redcoat had charge of the woman and the children, but the others inside the house were within earshot, particularly if the redcoat fired his musket. "They've burned other houses and left the families unharmed, likely they'll do the same here." He hoped he was giving Drum more assurance than he felt himself.

Drum was scowling. "The little ones are afraid. Why do the redcoats have to scare the children? They're not going to trouble them."

"I don't know," Daniel replied, though, he felt he did know. Frustration, anger, fear, the desire for revenge — all the things those soldiers had to be feeling after the day's events would coalesce into something that would be blindly irrational and indiscriminant in its manifestation.

The woman's voice changed in timbre, becoming more shrill, more insistent, but the redcoat was paying her no heed. She reached out for him, grabbing his arm and tugging so hard that she pulled him off-balance. The soldier rounded on her, slapping her twice, knocking her to the ground. Her son, who could not have been more than about eight years old, rushed to her defense, latching onto the soldier's leg and clamping his teeth firmly into the man's thigh. The soldier wailed in pain, then hit the boy repeatedly in an effort to free himself. The woman was coming at the soldier now, and he struck her with the butt of his musket. She fell again, blood pouring from her nose and mouth.

"Bloody hell." Things had spiraled too far out of control for Daniel to abide and so, weapons or no, he had to act. "Wait here," he told Drum as he rose from his hiding place. The musket in one hand, his dirk in the other, he sprinted toward the scuffle, hoping the soldier was distracted enough that he would not see his approach.

Daniel covered the distance fast, and did not slow his pace before throwing himself into the unsuspecting soldier, flattening the redcoat to the ground under the full weight of his body. The soldier hardly knew what had happened. Daniel's dirk slid easily through the man's throat just above his sweat-stained stock, silencing him before he could cry out for help. Without waiting for the redcoat to bleed out, Daniel sprang to his feet, gathered the youngest child up in his arms and was reaching for the older boy's hand when Drum brushed past him.

"Run!" Drum told the woman as he scooped up her son and started for the rock wall.

"But, our home!" The woman was hysterical, turning in circles, not sure what to do or where to go next.

"It's gone," Daniel insisted urgently. "There's nothing to be done for it now. If you want your children safe, do as the man says!" He grasped her elbow and pulled her toward the fence.

Without looking back, they raced across the yard. Daniel lifted the children over the wall while Drum helped their mother. Only when they were safely hidden behind the wall did they look back toward the house. Flames were visible through the kitchen door, and smoke was beginning to curl from the windows on the lower floor. The woman sobbed loudly. Between her tears and horrified expression, and the damage done by the musket butt, her face was an appalling mess.

"We cannot stay here long," Daniel said. "The redcoats will finish their business and start looking for their mate soon enough." He looked at the woman, offering her a touch of contrition. "I'm afraid they may think you did that," he said, indicating the dead soldier in the yard. She stared at him, and clutched the infant more tightly to her breast. "Do you know where your husband is?"

She shook her head and choked back her sobs. "I haven't seen him since the lobster-backs arrived."

Daniel decided not to voice his feeling that the man was most likely dead. "Is there someone else? Someone you could go to for help? Not here in Menotomy — some other place. You need to get away from here."

She shook her head. "I need to find Benjamin. That's my husband. I need to stay here until I find him . . . or his body. There are several families here who I know would hide us until the redcoats have passed."

Daniel wanted to argue but knew it would be useless. "We'll see you into the woods, then." His tone was colored with his disapproval of her choice. "We'll find a good hiding place for you and you should stay there until the redcoats have all gone."

With a wistful glance at her children, she nodded her understanding. "We'll manage it."

"Good." He and Drum each picked up a child and, after checking once more to be sure they'd not be seen, they struck out across a hay field in the direction of a dense line of woodland. Daniel expected at any moment to hear the crack of musket fire, but it never came.

They made it safely to the trees and began to search for a suitable hiding place. It turned out that they were not alone. As they pushed through the thicket of undergrowth, a voice called out to them. It was barely more than a whisper, calling the woman's name, and drew them to a sheltered place underneath an outcropping of rocks that was partially hidden by the low-hanging branches of two aged chestnut trees. It appeared a number of Menotomy's citizens had gathered to wait out the red-coated plague that had descended on their town. Knowing she would not be alone, Daniel felt better about leaving the woman and her children. He and Drum turned once again toward Boston.

"I thought I told you to stay behind the wall." Daniel afforded Drum his most severe look. They were walking just within the fringe of the woods, in sight of the road but within easy access to cover if it became necessary.

"You needed help." Drum met his gaze with the directness of a man who feels he has done the right thing.

Daniel opened his mouth to disagree, but was stopped short by something ahead of them in the woods. He'd caught a glimpse of scarlet, just a flash, as likely to be a bird as it was likely to be a soldier. He stopped nonetheless, pulling Drum down beside him. They crouched, and listened, eyes straining toward the spot where the bright flash of color had appeared and then, just as quickly, disappeared. Until they could identify it, they dared not continue along in the woods, and veering out into the open was just as risky.

"Likely a flanking company clearing the woods of militia," Daniel said quietly. He looked back over his shoulder, running his eyes along the road back into the village. There was no one in sight, but a cloud of dust hovered in the air beyond a bend in the road, and he could hear, faintly, the sounds of boots pounding the dirt and metal clinking against metal that heralded the approach of an army. "The column is moving again. We can't stay here." He signaled Drum to follow him, and they slipped deep into the woods.

They were running as fast as the thicket would allow, but were brought to a sudden halt by the sound of shouts and muskets being fired in orderly volleys. "The flankers must have found what they were looking for," Daniel said.

"We should try to help the militiamen."

"I agree, but we can't do them much good without ammunition." So weary he found it difficult to think, he scrubbed his hand across his face. "Let's go," he said finally. "We'll figure it out when we see what's afoot."

Moving quickly but carefully, they made their way through the trees toward the sound of musket fire. The din led them to a place where the trees gave way to open field. Rocks cleared from the field by some farmer were stacked to one side forming a low wall between the tree line and the field. A partially completed barn loomed up less than fifty yards across the cleared area. Its upper loft was still in skeletal phase, and there was no roof, yet it commanded a perfect view of one stretch of the main road where it curved past the far side. A handful of militia snipers who had set up there hoping to ambush the column as it moved past, were finding themselves under fire from the five British flankers who had taken up position behind the stone wall.

To Daniel, it seemed an odd arrangement with both sides using up a good deal of ammunition to little effect. Then, he saw the reason for the deployment of muskets at the stone wall. These five men were providing diversion and cover for four others who were circling the barn in an effort to get in behind the militiamen. Once the redcoats got into position, the militiamen would be surrounded and have no chance of escape. He turned his attention to the men at the wall. Five against two was not particularly good odds, but he and Drum did have surprise on their side. The British were unaware of their presence, giving their whole attention to keeping the militiamen in the barn engaged.

"If we're going to help those men in the barn, we will have to kill the soldiers," he told Drum. "And do it quickly. There are too many of them for just the two of us. If we get tangled up in a fight, we'll be the ones dead. Do you understand?" He watched Drum struggle to swallow that difficult instruction. "We can go around," Daniel told him. "We can move on and they'll never know we were here."

But Drum shook his head. "I want to help them," he said, indicating the men trapped in the barn. "The redcoats killed too many people already today."

"Right, then." Daniel handed Drum the bayonet-equipped musket and drew his dirk. "We get as close as we dare. On my signal, we hit them." He outlined what he envisioned might work, the series of killing strokes they might make, and felt a pang of misgiving when Drum blanched. "We have to get them all before they have time to turn on us."

Drum nodded again, and swiped his sleeve across his sweating forehead. His hand was quivering but he seemed determined.

Once they made their move, they were on top of the Regulars before any of them knew what was happening. Daniel sliced his dirk neatly through the throat of the first man and, before the soldier could hit the ground, snatched his musket away. He fired it into the face of the next man, and then used the bayonet on the third. Three men dead in only a few seconds, he thought in a detached part of his mind. But there was no time to survey his handiwork. He whirled around to see how Drum was managing.

As Daniel had instructed him to do, Drum had driven his bayonet through the back of the first soldier's neck. He'd planned to withdraw it and turn it on the second soldier, but the blade did not come free as easily as he'd expected. The momentary delay had given his second target time to turn on him. The soldier had not yet reloaded his musket after his last volley. The bayonet was affixed, however, and this he thrust toward Drum with the full force of his weight. More from reflex than design, Drum threw his arm up to block the progress of the bayonet. The blade skimmed across his forearm, but was deflected from doing any lethal damage. Before the soldier could try again, Drum grasped the musket from the man's hands and smashed the butt squarely into his face. Nose broken, teeth shattered, the man fell back crying out in agony.

"Kill him!" Daniel growled. "Use the bayonet before he recovers!" When Drum did not move, Daniel pushed past him and, without hesitation, stabbed his bayonet into the fallen soldier's throat.

"You didn't have to do that!" Drum cried. "He was too hurt to fight any more."

"He had a broken nose and some of his teeth were knocked out. Once he got over the shock, he'd still be able to fire a musket," Daniel snapped. He was breathing hard and his heart pounded in his chest. Adrenaline was pumping through his body, pushing him to feverishness. "He could have shot us before we'd gone ten steps. He could have called out to the others — warned them that we are here!"

Drum nodded. He understood, but still did not like it. His arm was bleeding profusely, soaking the sleeve of his shirt and jacket, though he did not seem to notice. Daniel ripped enough fabric from the hem of his shirt to use as a bandage, tying it firmly around his sullen friend's arm.

There was shouting from the barn, and a new round of musket fire. Instinctively, Drum and Daniel both ducked. None of the musket balls came their way, however. With the men at the wall no longer pinning them down, the militiamen had seen and were able to fire on the flankers who had circled the barn in an effort to get in behind them.

Daniel took a cartridge box from one of the dead soldiers and handed it to Drum. "Get off in those trees," he said pointing to a place away from the clearing. "Hide yourself and stay put. And, this time, do as I say. Understand?" He watched Drum slip off into the trees before setting about the business of arming himself. Searching among the dead soldiers, he gathered cartridges and musket balls, taking time to load two of the muskets. None of the dead men was an officer and, yet, he found a battered sword lying near the body of one. This he buckled about his waist before crossing the clearing toward the barn. Once there, he flattened himself against the wall and waited.

It was clear now that the militiamen inside the barn were outnumbered. Likely, they were running low on ammunition, Daniel knew. They continued their defense a bit longer and then, quite suddenly, burst from the barn and sprinted toward the trees. Daniel heard the British officer in charge of the flanker company order his men to give chase.

In pursuit of the fleeing militiamen, the redcoats streamed around the ends of the barn in two groups. To his right, a group of five men passed, fanning out into the trees as though on a turkey hunt — and far less likely to catch one of the militiamen than a turkey, Daniel thought. The second group, two enlisted men and a lieutenant came around the corner on his left. The three men were moving more carefully than the first group, on guard lest they be fired upon from some hidden position. They circled to a spot directly in front of Daniel and only about twenty yards away. There they stood, their backs to him, scanning the trees that surrounded the clearing. Daniel held his breath.

The three men stood without moving for several long seconds before one of them glanced back over his shoulder. At first, Daniel thought the glance might have been fleeting enough that the man did not see him. But then, as recognition of the threat registered in the man's brain, something about his posture began to change. He turned, raising his musket as he did so, and fired at the same moment that Daniel pulled the trigger on one of his two loaded muskets. The ball from the soldier's musket plowed through the upper sleeve of Daniel's jacket, carving a painful furrow in his skin. Daniel's aim was luckier. The musket ball ripped into the soldier's chest, throwing him backwards.

At almost the same moment, the second soldier turned and began to level his musket. But Daniel had not waited to raise his second musket and he fired before the soldier could even draw bead on him. The soldier fell beside his comrade, his musket discharging wildly into the air as he fell. Only the lieutenant remained, and he had no musket.

Drawing his sword, the officer advanced on Daniel with ferocious speed. His uniform was filthy with sweat and dirt and blood, and his face was black with powder stains and dust. There was wildness in his eyes, a blood-curdling hatred for the rebel who had just killed two of his men. He would barely have been recognizable to his own kin, so it was no wonder that it took Daniel a few beats to recognize him. It was Edward Hinton.

If Hinton recognized Daniel, he gave no sign of it. It seemed that he saw before him only one of the rebels who had, ever since they'd left Concord, harassed and hounded and made life for him and his men into a living hell. He had seen too many men killed and wounded, and had endured too many brutal ambushes that day to feel any inclination toward mercy or understanding. He simply wanted the rebel before him dead, and had drawn his sword and advanced unwaveringly toward Daniel with that singular purpose.

Having no alternative, Daniel drew the shabby old blade he had taken from one of the dead soldiers at the wall. It felt heavy in his hand, awkward, and he shifted it uneasily in his palm as he tried to get the feel of it. There was little time for such preparations, however. Hinton was on him, swinging his first blow the moment he was within reach. It would have been a killing blow if Daniel had not managed to duck. As it was, the blade lodged momentarily in the wooden wall behind him, giving him a moment's grace to dodge away.

But he stumbled. What he had intended to be a graceful movement out of the trap between Hinton's blade and the wall of the barn, became a clumsy, stumbling effort to simply stay on his feet. He regained his balance and turned just in time to parry Hinton's next thrust, this one aimed at Daniel's heart. Hinton did not linger on the deflection. With speed that astonished Daniel, he struck again and again, driving Daniel back a step with every blow. Daniel could do nothing more than try to parry each blow. He missed once, and Hinton's blade sliced into his waist, opening a long, painful cut. Daniel suspected it was bad but pushed away the worry and pain to focus on keeping Hinton's blade from scoring again. It was the best he could do; Hinton was giving him no time in which to launch his own attack.

Finally, Hinton's exhaustion came to Daniel's aid. Hinton faltered, missed a beat in the rhythm he had established. The fractional moment gave Daniel an opening, which he exploited as best he could. He ducked away from Hinton again, forcing him to change direction so that the sun would be in his face. It amounted to only a small nuisance for Hinton, but Daniel was willing to take whatever advantage he could find. Hinton came at him again but the fatigue in his arms was beginning to tell and he was slower than he'd been.

Holding the sword two-handed, Daniel rounded on Hinton with an inelegant backhanded slash of his battered blade. Hoping for an end to the encounter, he put all of his strength and momentum into the stroke. But Hinton parried. The force of the blades striking together sent a shock through Daniel's hand and up his arm, threatening to oblige the muscles and tendons to relax their grip on the sword. By sheer force of will, he held on, kept his hand fisted tightly on the sword's grip. He pressed against Hinton's blade, effectively locking men and swords into a perilous embrace, the smell of sweat and blood and rage fecund between them.

Employing a strength Daniel had not suspected he possessed, Hinton shoved him. Daniel stumbled backwards, scrambling to rebalance himself and his sword even as Hinton came on the attack. When the lunge came, all Daniel could manage was a clumsy parry that only barely succeeded in deflecting Hinton's blade away from his gullet. The tip of the blade nicked Daniel's jaw in passing, opening a thin, painful cut. He felt blood trickle down his neck and was enraged by the satisfied smile that glinted in Hinton's eyes. The lieutenant believed Daniel to be already defeated and, Daniel knew, if things continued on their present course, he would be correct.

Desperate, Daniel looked for an opportunity to change the pace and nature of the fight, to bring it onto the sort of field that was more familiar to him. Planting his feet and refusing to be moved, he parried blow after blow. He watched Hinton's sword with only a part of his mind, allowing the more active, calculating part to focus on the same things he would watch had it been a fist fight. His reactions to Hinton's blade were a matter of defensive reflex only. It was Hinton's core that held his sharpest focus. The way Hinton's body moved — what he was doing with his arms, what direction his shoulders tilted, and where he planted his feet — all of these things became of far more importance to him for these where the things that determined which direction the sword would take. He watched carefully, waiting for the opportunity he knew would come if he were patient.

Sweat was pouring from Hinton's brow and had soaked his uniform through. His breathing was labored and there was a slight quiver of fatigue in his legs. And yet, he continued to come at Daniel like a fiend. One blow, and then another, came so quickly and with such power, that Daniel was forced to give a step or two. He felt the back of his leg brush against something and knew he had stupidly allowed himself to be cornered. And then, without him knowing how it had happened, his sword flew from his hand and, in the same split second where he thought himself dead, the opportunity for which he had waited appeared.

It was Hinton's eyes and a barely perceptible shift in the tilt of his shoulder as he tightened the muscles to deliver his killing blow that betrayed him. Daniel knew which way the blow would come, and he dodged it. He ducked to one side, twisting slightly as he did so, and the blade missed his neck. The guard slammed painfully into his shoulder, but he did not care. A bruise he could survive. From his slightly crouched position, he drove up into Hinton's breastbone with his shoulder, forcing the breath from his lungs and shoving him backwards. Before Hinton could recover, Daniel clasped his hands into a double fist, which he brought up with all his might into Hinton's groin, following quickly with a forceful elbow to the reeling man's stomach. Gasping for breath and dizzy with pain, Hinton could only stagger in shock as Daniel's fist came at him again and again, pounding every vulnerable part of his body until he could no longer stand. Hinton landed on his back, arms and legs flailed out to his sides. Daniel stomped one heavy boot down onto Hinton's wrist, grinding muscle and tendon mercilessly until Hinton released his grip on the sword.

Daniel picked up the weapon and held it two-handed, point down above Hinton's throat. "You bloody bastard," he said, his voice rasping in his parched throat. His chest was heaving with tortured breath, sweat stung his eyes, and he could taste blood in his mouth, but none of it mattered. All he could really feel was how much he wanted to kill the man sprawled helpless on the ground below him. "You goddamned bloody bastard!"

Hinton's mouth was moving as though he wanted to speak, but he had neither breath nor strength to form words.

"Don't bother," Daniel snarled. "I've no interest in whatever it is you're trying to say." He raised the sword, preparing to drive it through Hinton's throat.

But he did not strike. The blade hovered there, uncertain and confounded by the unwelcome thought that had just popped into Daniel's mind. Anna. Her face had appeared, unbidden, and the vision stopped him cold. However much cause he might think he had to kill this man who was her friend — perhaps even more than a friend — Daniel knew he would never be able to face her with what he had done. Worse, he feared she might never forgive him. Painful and inconvenient as it was, he knew that price was not worth the pleasure he would take at that moment in ending Hinton's life.

"Shite!" He followed that expletive with a string of worse ones, every one that came to his mind, as a matter of fact. But still the sword hovered over Hinton's throat. Arguments raged in his brain, and the muscles in his arms and hands began to shudder with their struggle against his will — against his conscience. *Damn her, anyway*, he thought. He raised the blade again, preparing to make that killing thrust. Instead, screaming with fury, he tossed the sword with all his remaining strength. It went spinning off into the brush, glinting in the sunlight as it flew.

He stared down at Hinton for several long seconds. The man almost looked as if he might die without any further assistance from Daniel. *Won't happen*, Daniel thought. *I've already used up all my luck today.* "Go back to Boston, you bastard," he snarled, filling each word with venom. "You are done here. Go back to London. Every bloody one of you. Go home and leave us in peace." He thrust Hinton away from him and stalked away.

Daniel clasped his hand to the wound in his side, grimacing at the new surge of pain that erupted from his touch. It was bleeding profusely, and had soaked the entire side of his shirt and the hip of his trousers. "I need something to bind this," he told Drum.

"I can tear a strip from this." He was walking toward Daniel, the reins of two horses in one hand, a discarded battle flag in the other.

"Appropriate, I suppose." Daniel took the flag, which was a long piece of white linen, hand-lettered with a taunt to the British, and tore away a long, thin strip. He tied it tightly about his waist to curb the bleeding. "Where'd you find those horses?" He spat blood out of his mouth and wiped his sleeve across his face.

"They were just milling about, eating grass," Drum said. "I'm pretty sure their owners are dead, so this isn't really stealing, is it?"

Daniel decided not to point out that, technically, the horses were owned by the British army so that they were, in fact, stealing. "At this moment," he said, accepting the reins Drum was holding out for him, "I don't particularly care." They walked toward the road, passing the place where Hinton's sword had landed. Drum bent to pick it up.

"Leave it," Daniel barked.

"But it's valuable, isn't it?"

"Not to me. Leave it."

He climbed into the saddle. Every part of his body was hurting and he knew it would only get worse over the next several hours. Something to look forward to, he thought, then checked himself as he realized that there were a number of men lying dead between Menotomy and Concord who would gladly trade fates with him. "Let's get back to Boston."

"Isn't that Miss Anna's redcoat?" Drum asked, jerking his chin to where Hinton lay sprawled on the ground.

Daniel practically growled at him. "Would you stop calling him that?"

"Well, I can't ever remember his name."

"Hinton," Daniel snapped. "Lieutenant Edward bloody Hinton."

CHAPTER EIGHTEEN

It was early evening when they finally made their way back to Selah's shop. Daniel was struggling to remain upright in the saddle and his insistence that he was not badly injured was met with a doubtful look from Drum. Exhausted, they stumbled through Selah's back door and collapsed into two of the small chairs with a level of commotion that brought Selah hurrying down the stairs. Her eyes went immediately to Daniel and the massive amount of blood staining his clothes.

"Dear Lord," she gasped, crossing to him.

"The blood's not all mine," Daniel quickly assured her, managing a weak smile as he leaned back to allow her to inspect him.

"Obviously," she snapped. "Else you'd be dead. Are you injured as well, Drum?" She glanced at Drum who, feeling the cut on his arm unworthy of attention, shook his head. "Help yourself to some cider, then," she told him. "And there's bread and cheese if you're hungry." She helped Daniel out of what was left of his shirt, cringing visibly at the myriad cuts and bruises scattered across his torso. Her attention moved methodically from wound to wound, gauging the severity of each with a light touch and practiced eye. "Should I ask what you've been up to this time?"

"Might as well," Daniel replied. "I imagine everyone in Boston will know within the hour, if they don't already." He hissed through his teeth when she pulled the strip of linen away from the slash in his side. "I think we may have started a war."

Selah stared at him.

"The Regulars and militia exchanged shots on a bridge outside of Concord. Everything went to hell after that. A running fight followed the Regulars all the way back to Charlestown. They lost scores of men. There won't be any whitewashing or stepping around this one."

"My God." She could hardly grasp what he was telling her. "Who fired first?"

"I honestly don't know. I was there, and even I cannot say for certain. I'm not sure it matters at this point, anyway." He looked at her horrified face. "It wasn't *me*, if that's what you're thinking!"

"Don't be absurd." In fact, a part of her had wondered. "Here, now." She wiped her hands on her apron. "Can you stand?" He tried, but was so unstable that Drum had to come to his aid. Between them, they were able to help Daniel up onto the table. Selah swung the ever-simmering kettle nearer the fire, set a pail of water on to boil, and darted about the room lighting additional lamps and gathering anything she thought might be useful in treating Daniel's wounds. "Drum, do you have enough left in you to go and fetch Miss Somerset?" When he nodded, she looked pleased. "Good. Go and ask her if she can come help me."

Daniel jerked around so suddenly that it ignited another wave of pain. "Why?"

"Because I need her help," Selah snapped.

"You've been patching me up since I learned to walk," he protested, "and never needed anyone's help before."

"Yes, well, you've never come home with anything quite like this before," she replied with a pointed look in the direction of the deep, bloody slash.

"Why her? If you need help, can't Drum do it?"

Drum's eyes widened with alarm at the idea and he took two steps toward the door. Daniel closed his eyes and leaned back as he surrendered to the prospect of having to face Anna. The motion ignited a new stab of pain and his breathing shallowed.

"Ask Miss Somerset to bring some of her little packets of herbs, Drum," she instructed. "She had yarrow and calendula, I believe, and arnica." Drum was frowning over the names. "Never mind. Just ask her to bring all of them. And some of the fine silk thread, if she would spare it. I've used all of mine and haven't been able to get more. And, do please make haste?"

Drum went as instructed, and once he'd talked with Anna, did not need to urge her to hurry. The moment he told her that Daniel was injured, and what Selah had asked of her, she flew about her room assembling a basket. She snatched up her cloak and, as she was dashing out the door, told Mrs. Cook to tell her uncle not to wait supper. By the time Drum returned with Anna, Selah had managed to clean away some of the dust, grime, and dried blood, but he was a sight, nonetheless.

"Dear Lord," Anna breathed when she took in his battered body.

"That is apparently the greeting of the day," he retorted sourly.

"Probably because you look like you may at any moment need a prayer for your departing soul," Selah snapped. "Come in, Miss Somerset."

"Please call me Anna." She closed the door behind her and crossed to where Selah was assembling needles and scissors, cotton lint, and myriad other items on the table beside Daniel. "I've brought the things you asked for," she said. "How can I help you?" She stared at Daniel, hardly believing what she saw. He was a bruised, bloodied shambles. Worse, it appeared that, beneath the powder burns, his face was unnaturally pale. It alarmed her, and she looked away quickly. Illogical though it may be, it seemed bad form to let an injured man know how terrible he looked.

"What?" Daniel jibed. "Aren't you going to chastise me? Or, mock me for being so foolish as to allow myself to get wounded?" There was a definite note of challenge in his voice, which went a considerable distance toward dispelling the sympathy she was feeling.

"Hush now," Selah hissed. "You're causing us all a good deal of trouble. You can at least manage some civility." She gestured toward a long apron hanging on the back of the door. "You'll be needing that," she told Anna.

Grudgingly, Daniel kept quiet and watched as Selah poured a good measure of whisky onto the wound. He drew a sharp hissing breath between his teeth and blinked to clear his watering eyes. It crossed his mind that she might be deliberately making the process as painful as possible, but decided against voicing that opinion.

Selah threaded one of her long needles with some of Anna's silk thread, then dropped the needle and thread into a small cup of whisky. "Baptizing them Scots?" Anna asked, smiling.

"Aye, weel," Selah replied in a lilting but highly-exaggerated Scottish accent, "ye canna be too careful, now, can ye?"

"Have you been drinking that whisky?" Daniel asked.

"I'll have you know, that was a very good imitation of your Grandfather Garrett." She fished the needle and thread out of the whisky. "Anna, move that lamp closer and, if you'll stand just here and use your fingers to press this end of the wound closed like so?" She demonstrated what she wanted, causing Daniel to wriggle with discomfort. "I'll start sewing from the other end." She made the first stab through his flesh with the needle, and there was a minor disturbance as Drum, fearing he would be ill, retreated out the back door. Selah pulled the needle through and tugged the first stitch tight. "Hold still, please, Daniel," she said evenly when he flinched.

"That's a tall order when you're stabbing a needle somewhere that was already hurting something fierce." He was trying to keep his tone light, but Anna heard the ragged fringe of pain in his voice. She sympathized with Drum's flight. The sight of the needle passing through Daniel's flesh was causing her stomach to quiver slightly and a sheen of perspiration appeared on her face.

Selah laughed softly at Daniel's complaint. "Your grandfather would have poured black powder in the wound and set it afire, then slapped you on the back and told you to get on your feet." She was pushing the needle in and out, drawing the silk thread through the skin along the edges of the wound as she talked. "He'd have considered this little more than a scratch." Her hand hovered in place and she looked up at Anna. "There's a bit too much blood here. I can hardly see what I'm doing. Could you wipe that away for me?" She nodded toward some strips of linen she had laid aside for the purpose.

Anna carefully dabbed the excess blood away, clinching her teeth every time she felt Daniel recoil. When she had done, Anna shifted her attention from the stitch Selah was tying off and completed a quick inventory of his many other wounds. There was a small gash across his chest, and one along his jaw, neither of which looked particularly serious, and an impressive bruise spread across one shoulder like an enormous purple flower. His forehead bore a sizeable, red-purple lump, the area around one eye was dark and engorged with blood, and his lower lip was cut and swollen.

"You look as though you fought your way through the entire British army."

"Pretty much feels like I did, too."

Someone was pounding on the shop door. Selah cast a frown toward the sound. "The shop is always closed at this hour. Who could that be?" The pounding demanded attention, however.

Daniel stopped her as she rose and started toward the door. "If it's the redcoats. . . .." His mouth was dry, and talking was difficult. He swallowed. "I don't know what will happen now. If they decide to hunt down those involved in today's battle . . . I just don't know. Some of them will have recognized me."

"Wonderful." Selah made no effort to hide her annoyance. "I really could just about slap you, Daniel." She rinsed her hands quickly and peered out through the divider curtain. "Oh, rot," she said. "It's Mrs. Winters. I assume she's looking to pick up her order. It may be after hours, but she particularly wanted it today, so I doubt she will give up and go away." Selah snatched up a towel and dried her hands as she made for the front of the shop. "Stay here. And, do not get off this table, Daniel." She looked anxiously from one face to the other. "And keep quiet. I've no idea who can be trusted with what information now."

"One would think my mother has experience with clandestine doings," he chuckled. Anna did not respond, however, and he watched her for several long seconds. She stood by the table, head bowed, eyes fixed on his discarded shirt. She had grasped it in both fists and was wadding and twisting it as though she thought she could thus remove the blood stains. He sighed resignedly. "Out with it, Mouse. I know you want to give me a tongue lashing, so get it done." In fact, it was the last thing he wanted, but he knew that to plead for kindness or sympathy would break him.

"I am numb, Daniel. I don't even know what to say." But then, she looked again at his blood-soaked shirt and rage welled up inside her so quickly that it surprised even her. "What were you thinking?" She kept her voice to a whisper, yet the force of it was the same as if she shouted. "What could any of you have been thinking? Have you all lost what little sense you had?"

Daniel frowned. "I thought you were numb and didn't know what to say?"

"Don't do that!" she snapped. "Don't you dare try to make light of this. Picking a fight with the *British army*! You must be out of your mind!"

"I'd say it was they who picked the fight when they decided to march into our towns and confiscate our property."

"Your *property*? A few guns are worth this?" She raised her fist, shaking the bloodied shirt in his face. "Look at this! Look at this, Daniel! How can your blood be worth a few guns? Who knows how many men lost their lives today. Was it worth it? Was making a point worth all of those lives?"

"Yes. I believe it was."

"Well I doubt the women who lost husbands and sons, or the children who lost fathers would agree with you."

Her voice was ragged with emotion, and it struck deep in his heart. "Not all. But many would."

"You are an impossible man!"

He caught the shirt she threw at him and absently folded it as he considered his next words. "You always seem to be cross with me these days." There was an element of sadness in his voice, which he attempted to disguise. "More so than usual, that is. I begin to think you just don't like me, Mouse." His mouth quirked up at one corner, just the hint of an uncertain smile.

"You know very well that I am cross with you because you and your friends are tearing my home apart. I want peace. I want things to return to the way they were!" She was angry and frustrated, and fighting the tears that would betray both.

"That is what we wanted — a return to the way things were, a return to a time when our trade was unrestricted and we were left to govern ourselves."

"Don't turn this into a political lecture. I am not in the mood."

"But the king and Parliament decided to meddle, and to take from us without asking," he went on, ignoring her. "We still want peace, but we also want the freedom to get on with our lives as we see fit."

Sighing, she let her hands fall weakly by her side. "I just want things to go back to the way they were."

"Oh, Mouse," he said gently. "Can you not see that it was an illusion? It was a bubble we were living in; a bubble destined to burst sooner or later."

She considered him for a drawn-out moment. "I heard Mr. Franklin speak. While I was in London — I heard him speak twice. And, I read accounts of his other speeches. He always seemed so level-headed, his views so carefully thought out. He seemed so sensible. I hoped, with men like him at the helm, a compromise would be found. I thought—"

"You thought we could get back inside that bubble?"

"If it was a bubble then, yes, that's what I thought."

He shook his head, which was a mistake. He could feel a throb of pain with each beat of his heart, and the room was swimming unsteadily. Shaking his head had made it worse. He blinked his eyes, trying to clear his focus. "We've outgrown what we were. There could be no going back."

"Then, what am I to do?" She swung her cape over her shoulders and raised the hood, opened the door preparing to leave. "And, you are wrong." She had hesitated before saying it, standing uncertainly on the threshold. "I do like you. Very much. That is part of the problem."

He saw that she was intent on leaving. "Wait!" he slid off the table and knew immediately that he should not have attempted to stand. He felt as if all the blood dropped from his head to his feet and the room, which had not been too steady to begin with, spun out of focus and into darkness. His head hit the floor with a solid thwack, but he was oblivious to the pain.

The next thing he knew, he was waking up with a head that ached as though he had drunk half the whisky in Boston the night before. He peered carefully through the narrow slits to which he had managed to open his eyes and saw his mother's fuzzy outline.

"She has gone," Selah told him. "Anna has gone, if that's who you are looking for. She helped me get you up off the floor and asked me to tell you for her that you are an idiot. I'm not certain whether she was referring merely to your idiotic attempt to stand up, or something else."

He closed his eyes and, muttering, turned his face away from her. "Bloody hell."

"Indeed," Selah agreed.

*   *   *

As the sun rose on the morning after the events at Lexington and Concord, Boston found itself under siege — surrounded by an ever-increasingly large militia army. To the infuriated rebels, the British army was a disease that, if it could not be eradicated, needed to be contained lest it spread throughout the colonies. Local militias from all of the New England colonies had answered the call and marched through the night to join the encirclement of Boston. They were a disorganized lot, but armed, and full of determination to keep the British confined within the city. On the other hand, frightened Loyalists all over the countryside were flocking to Boston in search of safety.

Anna made her way slowly to her uncle's study. Mr. Sprague was with him, she knew, and she hoped his old friend would have a leavening effect on Wilton's dark mood. "It is intolerable!" she heard her uncle say as she quietly opened the door. "They will force Gage to declare martial law. We will all be made to suffer for this insolence!"

"That does not appear to be his intent," Sprague replied evenly. "He has persuaded the town leadership to hand over all of their weapons in exchange for a promise that any rebel or sympathizer who wants to leave Boston will be allowed to do so."

"*Allowed* to do so? They should be thrown out! Or, better, they should be given a taste of their own medicine and ridden out of town on rails!" His face was red with a fury Anna had never before seen in him. "Damned ungrateful murderous fools! I've heard that they killed almost a hundred British troops yesterday, and wounded twice that number! That cannot be forgiven!"

"I do not think they expect to be forgiven," Sprague pointed out. "I think they had made up their minds before that first shot was fired that the talking was over."

"Fools." Wilton filled the word with all of the revulsion and uncomprehending astonishment he felt.

"You must look at it from their perspective."

"I cannot. It is simply beyond me."

Sprague sighed and tried another tack. "These men have petitioned the king in respectful and appropriate fashion, John. They have attempted to make their voices heard in all manner available to free Englishmen. The king has responded with threats and bullying."

"He is a king. It is his prerogative to ignore insolent rabble. They are fortunate that he did not hang them outright when they first raised their obnoxious heads."

"We are not the French. Our king rules at the pleasure of his subjects. I should not have to remind you of that."

Wilton glared at him but did not respond.

"Now this has happened, and the 'insolent rabble,' as you call them, are not of a kind to continue to go, hats in their hands, to beg for crumbs. These men are not accustomed to wearing a yoke. They want to determine their own course, and will fight to gain that ability."

"Then they are bigger fools than I thought." Wilton eyed his friend suspiciously. "I did not think you a fool."

"The king has shown that he does not consider us worthy of the same consideration he extends to his English subjects. I find myself doubting that such a man is deserving of my service, of my loyalty. Kings govern with the approval of their subjects, and I cannot say that this king has my approval."

"Because it is expedient for you to say so?"

"No," Sprague snapped. "Because it is the only reasonable conclusion, the only *rational* conclusion I can reach."

He watched the set of Wilton's shoulders for some sign of his friend's thoughts. But Wilton stood, hands clasped behind his back, staring out the window as though he were the only person in the room. When the silence continued, Sprague gathered his hat and cloak. "You saw what happened after that terrible business in front of the Custom House five years ago. You saw how news of the event played out in the court of public opinion. This will be far worse, John. The fight is no longer merely about mundane things like taxes. It has gone far beyond that. We will all be forced to choose among our loyalties, to decide which loyalties transcend all others." He placed his hat on his head and swirled his cape onto his shoulders. "Be certain that you choose carefully."

Wilton turned on his heel. "Have these rebels managed to sunder even our friendship, William? Has it come to that?"

"Not for my part. Pray it does not become a matter that is beyond our control."

When Sprague had gone, Wilton settled wearily into his favorite chair by the fire. Anna crossed the room, her footsteps silent on the woven rug. She pulled the small footstool into position and sat at her uncle's knee, worry creasing her brow. "I am sorry, uncle." She took his hand in hers, clasping it gently in the comforting embrace of her warm fingers. "I am so sorry to see you hurt."

"Ah, Anna my dear." He leaned forward and stroked a wisp of hair away from her face with his free hand then settled back and stared without seeing into the fire. "It seems that so many of the things I was heretofore certain of are now being called into question. It makes me wonder if the learning and experiences of my lifetime were all for naught."

"Of course that's not the case. Perhaps it's like your library. When you acquire a new book, you add it to those already on the shelf. You don't throw away all of the old ones."

"When did you become such a philosopher?" Chuckling, he reached out and lightly touched his fingertips to her cheek. Anna smiled, and laid her head upon his knee. He sat stroking her hair, recalling all the times she had sat like this as a very small child. In those instances, it was she who needed to be comforted. His melancholy deepened. "That business on the Lexington road yesterday," he said, a thought having occurred to him out of nowhere. "Do you know if Mrs. Garrett's son was involved?"

The poker in her hand hesitated for just an instant before finishing the job of pushing the last piece of wood back onto the grate. "Daniel?"

"Does Mrs. Garrett have more than one son?"

She wondered if it was obvious that she was stalling. "No." She tapped the poker on a log, testing to see that it would not fall off the grate again. "She does not. And, yes, he was involved." She regained her seat on the footstool and delayed meeting his eye by fussing over the arrangement of her skirts. When she looked up, she saw that he was watching her closely.

She drew a steadying breath. "Actually, he was quite involved. And he was rather seriously wounded."

"Oh?"

She nodded. "And, you should know that I went to help Mrs. Garrett tend his wounds."

"Is that where you dashed off to last evening?"

"Yes. I should have told you where I was going. I am sorry."

"Did you not tell me because you thought that I might prevent you going? Or, was it because you thought I might not approve?"

"Honestly, I didn't give it that much thought at the time. I received the message that I was needed and I went." She realized it sounded very impetuous and even somewhat irresponsible.

Wilton nodded as he turned this bit of information over in his mind. "I believe I would have done the same," he said at last. "If William Sprague needs my assistance fifteen minutes from now, I shall go without giving a moment's thought to the disagreement we just had." He sighed resignedly. "I don't suppose I can expect you to be less to your friends. But I would ask that you take great care. As of yesterday, I believe our city became a much more dangerous place."

"I shall be careful." Anna lowered her head and rested her cheek on his knee and they sat in companionable silence for several minutes.

"Anna." The grave tone in her uncle's voice when he broke the silence compelled her to look up. "You do understand that the Rubicon has been crossed? Those men who have set themselves in open rebellion against our king — they may face the gallows. All of them."

Nodding her understanding, she swallowed the lump that formed in her throat. "Yes," she said softly. "I know." She laid her head on his knee again, her face to the fire's warmth, and blinked away tears.

*　　*　　*

Liquidating her father's assets took more time than Charlotte had anticipated. On the other hand, creating the impression that her father had left Boston for a healthier southern climate had proved far easier and less necessary than anticipated. A comment dropped here and there provided sufficient explanation, especially considering that non-loyalist households were evacuating Boston in droves. Most folks were too caught up in that process to even notice Martin Ainsworth's absence.

It was the fourteenth day of May, and the cold had long since surrendered to the warmth of spring. Yet, she pulled her wrapper more tightly about her shoulders for the house was unusually quiet, as though nothing lived within its walls, and the emptiness made her shiver. She studied her mother's portrait where it hung over the fireplace, cocking her head, comparing the image on the canvas with the image she saw every time she looked in the mirror. Charlotte stepped closer to the portrait, narrowing her eyes to sharpen their vision. Her father had once commented that Charlotte and her mother were like two variations on the same set of features — one winter, and one summer — and Charlotte decided he was right. Her mother's sunny beauty lacked the cool aloofness Charlotte worked so hard to maintain. *Her face shows no guile*, Charlotte thought. *I believe she must have lacked ambition.* "It would certainly explain why she settled for marriage to Martin Ainsworth," she added aloud.

The thought reminded her that she had one more task to complete that day, and she sighed wearily at the prospect. It seemed there was always one more thing to be done, one more chore to be completed before she could rest, and she found the cycle exhausting. She smoothed her skirt and patted down a hair she believed to be out of place, then stepped out of the parlor, carefully closing the double doors behind her.

Her course set, Charlotte trudged up the stairs. It seemed like work to lift her foot at each riser, though not because she had any trepidation over what she was about to do. It was the burdensome aspect of the thing she dreaded — the time and effort it would require — not the thing itself that made her sigh as she climbed the stairs. Her father, such a weight around her neck for so long, seemed yet determined to continue in that role, and it angered her afresh to think of it now. She marched across the landing and into his room, resigned to what she was about, yet full of irritation that it was necessary.

She stood over her father's bed, staring down at the grey, skeletal shell he had become. "Why did you not die?" she asked. "You should have done weeks ago, but here you linger. Never mind, though," she amended. "You have given me the time I needed to make my arrangements." She sighed heavily, and allowed herself to be momentarily distracted by a stray thread she noticed hanging from the edge of her sleeve. The dress was her plainest wool, unattractive but serviceable when there was work to be done.

"Your usefulness has ended," she told him, explaining what she was about to do. "And I need to be gone soon." Perfunctorily, she slipped the pillow from beneath his head, fluffed it, and pressed it down firmly across his face. Several long seconds elapsed before there was some sign that his body had registered the oxygen deprivation, and even then his frail, atrophied muscles could manage only the most insignificant of struggles. It was over quickly and quietly, and Charlotte congratulated herself on having no blood to scrub from floors and walls as had been the case after the encounter with Cudahy and Foster. There was still the matter of his body to be disposed of, but that would be as simple as wrapping his bedclothes around him and dragging him down to the final resting place she had arranged for him. *Yes*, she thought, *it has all played out quite satisfactorily.*

CHAPTER NINETEEN

Daniel dared rest his wounds at Selah's home for only a few days before insisting that Drum help him slip out of Boston and across the river to Cambridge. He wanted to learn what was happening, and precious little information was making its way to him in Boston. Once Daniel arrived at Joseph Warren's headquarters, the doctor inspected his wounds and, pronouncing Selah's ministrations satisfactory, insisted that Daniel remain in Cambridge for a few more days of rest. It took little persuading, for it was clear that much was afoot, and Daniel wanted to be a part of it. Within only hours, however, a part of him was regretting the decision to remain in Cambridge for even a few hours. There was indeed much to do, but almost all of it seemed to require lengthy debate, with which he had little patience.

He was beginning to feel that rule by committee — any committee, made up of any men, for any purpose — was not necessarily the most efficient way to achieve an end goal. He had watched the Sons of Liberty bicker among themselves and splinter into uncontrollable factions, and had watched the clock tick while their successor, the Committee of Correspondence, moved at a snail's pace to reach a consensus regarding what information should be disseminated and to whom. Despite the organizational problems and occasional differences of opinion between members, however, things had progressed, convincing Daniel that the process was actually more effective than the sum of its parts. Now, after months of watching the Massachusetts Provincial Congress' Committee of Safety vacillate between bold, preemptive actions against the Regulars, and their desire not to appear too aggressive, his doubts were renewed.

The Committee of Safety had evolved out of the colony's determination to resist the Massachusetts Government Act. All across the colony, municipalities launched organized efforts to keep the king's courts from sitting. In a pleasant departure from what had occurred in other instances, and despite the fact that townspeople who faced down the judges were usually armed, there was no violence associated with the court closings. In Daniel's view, that was progress, as was the movement to local government chosen by town meetings. The local governments were amazingly effective at handling local issues and organizing their own constituents, but less so when it came to presenting a united response to things that threatened the entire colony. And so, the Committee of Safety, with Dr. Warren as its head, was formed.

A small distraction from routine Committee business had come with the news that, on the tenth of May, a mere four days past, John Adams had proposed that the Continental Congress declare the colonies free, sovereign and independent states. It was an astonishing proposal, and one that was quickly rejected by the majority of the delegates who continued to argue that ways be found to achieve reconciliation on equitable terms. But, for the Committee of Safety and many in Boston, the notion that such a reconciliation was still possible seemed laughable. "Bring those dunderheads from Philadelphia here," one member groused. "Let them see for themselves what their lives will be like if we back down. Let them see for themselves the oppressions that will surely spread to their own colonies!"

But such matters were not the province of the Committee. For these men, the primary issue for debate, and one that was trying Joseph Warren's patience even more than it was trying Daniel's, regarded Boston's geography and the best way to go about containing the Regulars. To most members of the Committee, the events at Lexington and Concord had made this of paramount importance. The siege was effective so far, but maintaining that siege was becoming onerous. No one wanted to maintain a stalemate.

There was a map of Boston spread across Warren's desk, pointed to and consulted so often that Daniel was surprised that the ink had not been worn off the page. The map showed Boston proudly perched upon a peninsula that jutted into the harbor that was its lifeblood. The peninsula was connected to the mainland by only a very thin neck of land, which would have made it a nicely defensible position were it not for the proximity of Dorchester Hill to one side of the neck, and the three hills of Charlestown Peninsula.

These high points on either side of the city offered the perfect locations at which to implant artillery for the purpose of bombarding the city if it became necessary. This fact was so obvious to everyone that Warren and the others were astonished that General Gage had not already taken control of the hills and emplaced his own artillery. It was what Warren would have done — if he'd had artillery. Benedict Arnold, along with Ethan Allen and his Green Mountain boys, had set out weeks earlier to capture the munitions stored at Fort Ticonderoga, but they had not yet returned. Therefore, Warren was still without artillery and, so, had turned his attention to Noddle Island, which sat just east of Boston and was currently populated with a considerable presence of livestock and, reportedly, stores belonging to the British navy.

For a number of years, several livestock owners had grazed their stock on the island, and had often sold the livestock to the British army and navy. After Lexington and Concord, however, pressure from the Committee of Safety and outright threats from other quarters had forced the livestock owners to quit selling to the British. But the livestock was still there, and the British had warehoused some supplies there, so foraging parties from both the army and the navy were common. After endless debate that made Daniel want to pound his head against the wall from listening to it, the

Committee of Safety finally decided to launch an expedition to remove from the island the livestock and other provisions that might benefit the Regulars, and to perhaps capture some of the munitions for their own use.

Despite his lingering wounds, Daniel was determined to be part of the mission, which was being planned for two weeks hence on May 27. Surely, he reasoned, he would be sufficiently healed by then to go out and round up a bunch of sheep and cattle. In the meantime, however, he felt himself to be in everyone's way and, so, asked Drum to help him return to Boston. Rather than risk compromising his mother by returning to his own room, he elected to take a room at Withers' tavern, rest his wounds, and keep out of sight until time for the raid.

*   *   *

Lieutenant Richard Chastain refolded the note the orderly had just delivered. A few weeks earlier, he would have been pleased to be told that Charlotte Ainsworth was waiting to speak with him. Though some jibes and off-color comments would be in order, in truth, such a visit bolstered a man's stock among his companions. There was little Richard Chastain enjoyed more than the sensation of creating envy among his fellows, especially considering that it so rarely happened. Since the debacle on the road between Lexington and Concord, however, everything was so turned on its head that he doubted anyone would notice the girl's visit. In fact, given that all of the officers suddenly found themselves burdened with additional imperatives, the visit was somewhat inconvenient.

He would not send her away, however. He had prodded in subtle ways for some proof that Charlotte's purported fortune was genuine, and she — in equally subtle fashion — had demonstrated that it was so. That she was willing to invest that fortune in the career of a promising young officer if he could return the favor by providing her with a life in London had also been made clear. Tempting as the arrangement might be, it was still merely only a suggestion. Things had not progressed to the point of any actual exchange of promises and, despite the temptation, Chastain temporized. Marriage had never held much appeal and there had not been enough time with Charlotte to allow him to warm to the notion.

She'd been put in the small sitting room at the front of the house the officers had commandeered for their use. It was a shabby room with sparse, utilitarian furnishings, and Chastain at first felt ashamed to have to receive her there. But he decided the austere setting gave him an aura of toughness — the hardy soldier enduring the rigors of a primitive post. He straightened his posture and entered the room with the demeanor of a man who has been called away from pressing matters.

She smiled warmly. "I apologize. I would not have called on you in such unbecoming manner and at such an incommodious time if I did not think my errand justified the intrusion."

"Nonsense. Of course I'm delighted to see you. We have little in our lives that is pleasant these days, so I welcome such a lovely interruption."

Charlotte smiled, pleased that he had not failed to say the right thing. "I shall not waste your time, and will come directly to the reason for my visit," she said. "You have mentioned on more than one occasion how dearly you would like to solve the mystery of the theft of some of General Gage's personal belongings?"

"Yes." His tone was guarded, and he watched her face carefully.

"Well, I believe I have some information that might be useful to you. I believe I know who is responsible and, more than that, I believe I know where you might find some of the missing items." When he looked skeptical, she added, "Most particularly, I can arrange for a specific item you mentioned to be placed directly into your hands."

"And, what might that item be?"

"A blue, egg-shaped music box."

Chastain's brows shot nearly to his hairline. "Indeed?"

"Yes. I thought I recalled you saying that an item like that was among the stolen property. That, and a cameo broach, correct?" She smiled, gratified, when he nodded. "I wanted to tell you because I know that returning the general's belongings to him would not only be personally satisfying to you, but would likely help your career. Is that not so?"

"Yes. Of course it is. But . . . are you saying that you know where these items are to be found?"

"I am saying that I know for certain where those particular items are, and I have a good idea where you might find the rest."

"And, you know this how?"

"Because someone gave me one of the items as a gift. He has been attempting to win my affections for some time now and I believe he thought this would further that goal. I did not let on that I knew where he had obtained them. I accepted the gift, and now have come here."

"How do you know he didn't merely purchase the items from the real thief?"

"Because he has something of a checkered past. He's just the sort who would do something like this. It is why I have repeatedly rebuffed his advances."

"I see. The man is a friend, then?"

She sniffed disdainfully. "More like an acquaintance."

"I gather that there is a price for this information?"

"But naturally. And, I would have thought that would not surprise you."

"It does not," he confirmed. "What is the price?"

"I have two conditions for assisting you." She leaned forward slightly in her chair, indicating that she was about to impart some confidence. "First, it is imperative that no one ever know my part in this. I'm terrified of the men involved and what they might do to exact revenge. You must give me your most solemn vow that you will never divulge to a soul that I was the source of your information."

Chastain nodded. "I give you my most solemn vow that no one will ever know." It was an easy promise to make for his preference was that Gage believe that Chastain had rooted out the culprits through his own intelligent deductions and sleuthing. "And, the second condition? Though, I believe I know what that is."

She smiled and lowered her lashes demurely. "I appreciate that you understand me so well. I believe I understand you equally well." Her grey eyes opened wide and met his in a frank, silent agreement. "It is what will make us good partners." His slow smile encouraged her to continue. "Good then. Because we understand one another, I'll not need to waste your time by playing the coquette and dealing in subtleties. What I want is marriage, as soon as possible, and immediate conveyance to London. If this tedious business regarding our harbor means that I cannot take ship from here, I would ask for arrangements to be made for me to travel to one of the southern colonies and, from there, passage on the first available ship."

Once again, his eyebrows betrayed his surprise. The demand for betrothal he had expected, but the expectation of immediacy he had not. He surveyed her narrowly. "And, why the urgency?"

"I am not carrying another man's child if that is your veiled suggestion," she snapped. "If you like, we can wait some months before consummating our union."

He barked with sharp laughter. "You do have brass, speaking so unabashedly of such things!"

"As I said, I see no point in wasting time with bandying or pretense."

"Indeed." He considered her suggestion for a few moments. "What you ask will be difficult though not impossible to arrange. If I am to seek favors, I do feel I have a right to know the reason for all the haste."

"I've told you, I am terrified of retribution should it be learned that I betrayed the perpetrator of the thefts."

"And, I have given my word that no one will learn of your involvement. What else?"

"Very well. If my father becomes aware of our plan, he will try to block it. He cannot prevent our marriage but he could cause trouble — especially if he makes it plain to your superiors that he does not approve. He is away for a time, visiting friends in the south while he recovers his health. I want to have the deed done before he returns."

Chastain felt uncomfortable with the notion that Ainsworth would not approve of him marrying his daughter but brushed principle aside in favor of Charlotte's money. "And, is there a third reason?"

"Myriad small reasons though none of consequence to you."

He arose and slowly circled the room, mulling her words as he paced. "You are quite certain about this? About the music box and the necklace?" he asked after a time. "There is no mistaking the items?"

Charlotte laughed lightly. "One would think that you are reluctant to strike this bargain with me, Lieutenant Chastain. Certainly, there could be no mistaking a music box or cameo as distinctive as those in question. But if it will help settle your mind," she reached into her reticule and drew out a cameo pendant on a gold chain and held it out to him. "Here is the pendant. See what you think."

Chastain accepted the necklace and knew after one glance it was the piece they sought. He had seen it around Mrs. Gage's neck on more than one occasion. "And the music box?"

"I shall surrender that when some progress has been made toward meeting my conditions. However, I shall tell you where I think you might find other goods stolen from your supplies."

"And the name of the person you believe responsible? Your admirer?"

"I shall give you that as well, when you give me your word that we shall be married and you will send me away from Boston, and on to London as soon as it can be arranged."

"I give you my word."

"I am glad." Her face beaming with pleasure, she stood and offered her cape to him. "The man's name is Daniel Garrett," she said as he placed the cloak around her shoulders. "And, I believe it very likely that he has been hiding the stolen property at his family's abandoned farm outside of Boston."

*   *   *

Daniel wanted to stretch out on the cot, but it was too short for any sort of comfort so he gave up and moved to the floor. It was only nominally harder than the cot, and at least he could straighten his legs. He had to move gingerly for, even though the running fight on the road from Concord to Lexington had been weeks ago, too many parts of him were still hurting. The wound in his side was healing, but slowly, and it needed attention from time to time. Selah wanted him to stay in his space over her shop but he continued to fear personal retribution from the army and did not want his mother mixed up in his trouble.

The siege had pushed Gage to send for reinforcements. The army's tendency to forbearance had ended, and it worried him. He needed a place where he could keep out of sight until he was in better shape, so he appealed to his old acquaintance Withers for a room above his tavern. Because Daniel had hoped never to have to return there, that in and of itself would have been enough to send him into a state of gloom. But his battered body and the memory Anna's anger made it all that much worse.

And Drum, who would not leave his friend's side as long as he was in need of care, moped about, looking at Daniel with an expression he could not quite decipher. Lying on his back, Daniel closed his eyes for a few minutes. He could not relax, however, for the feeling of Drum looking watching him. "You don't have to stay with me, Drum," he said without opening his eyes. "You've been hovering for four weeks. I'm fine. I can look after myself now."

"I don't have any other place to be at the moment," Drum said simply.

"Well, then, I wish you'd quit looking at me like that. It's bad enough to have Mouse be cross with me. She seems to think me personally responsible for what happened at Lexington and Concord, but you were there. You know better, so quit looking at me as though you're blaming me."

"I don't blame you. I just don't see why all those people had to die."

"Nobody wanted this fight, Drum. Not on either side of it. But it happened. It has been a long time coming, and maybe that's why things got as bad as they did. I don't know." He sighed wearily and scrubbed his hand across his face. "The truth is, we've picked a fight with the biggest bully on the street and, when you pick a fight with someone like that, you'd better be ready to hit hard or you will lose. You of all people know that well enough." He sighed in exasperation when Drum looked unconvinced. "All right, then." He raised himself up on one elbow, wincing at the pain the movement caused in his side. "Do you remember Hal Waters?"

Drum nodded somberly. Waters had reigned as the meanest, toughest young man in Boston for a time. He and his band of thugs would pick one of the streets or alleys leading out of the rope yards and declare ownership. When one of the young boys who worked in the ropewalks happened along, they would demand payment of the unfortunate boy's wages in return for being allowed to pass. Most of the boys would pay, and then be far more careful about allowing themselves to be caught alone again.

When Waters and his bunch cornered Drum, however, he refused to pay. The money was all he had to live on and he thought, wrongly, that if he explained that fact, Waters would let him go. Or, settle for just part of the money. Waters had not been so agreeable, however. He and his gang pounced on Drum. Pushed to it, Drum had fought back. But there were eight of them. They beat him nearly senseless, and then took his money.

The next day, Daniel and Teague sought out the Waters gang. They never told Drum what happened at that meeting, but Hal Waters disappeared for quite a long while and, when he emerged again, it was with an arm that did not function normally and a considerably tamer disposition. His gang dispersed and the boys who worked at the rope yards were able to hold onto their hard-earned wages.

"With some bullies you have to hit hard to make your point," Daniel repeated.

"But that doesn't mean you have to like it."

"No, it doesn't. And no normal person does like it. Do you think I enjoyed any of what happened at Lexington and Concord?"

Drum shook his head vehemently. Such a thought had never crossed his mind. "But I feel bad that *you* have to do it."

Daniel laughed at that. "Sometimes, Drum, I think it's the only thing I'm particularly good at. And, if that's the case, maybe it's what I was put here to do."

"It isn't the only thing you're good at," Drum corrected. "And I also don't think Miss Anna believes that what happened is your fault. Not entirely, anyway. I think she's just scared. I was scared. And I'm scared you'll have to fight again."

"I think that's fairly likely, Drum. You needn't be scared, though. I'll be fine. And, if you talk to Mouse, maybe you should tell her not to be scared, either."

"It might be better if you tell her."

"I don't think she's interested in hearing from me," Daniel sighed. "I'm certainly not interested in listening to another lecture from her. So, I think I'll just keep my distance for a time."

But his time for recovering had run out. A squad of redcoats, led by Lieutenant Richard Chastain, had just entered the tavern and, despite protests from Withers, were on their way up the stairs to Daniel's room.

*   *   *

After Lexington and Concord, Edward Hinton had waited as long as he could bear, hoping his bruises and other visible injuries would heal before he had to face Anna. But the damage to his psyche cried out for the comfort of John Wilton's house and the palliative effect of being in Anna's company and so, ignoring the faint discoloration that remained of his bruises and disguising his limp as best he could, he worked up the courage to call on her.

Now that he was there, however, he decided that he had made a mistake. He was filled with dread that she or her uncle might ask about the events of that day, and that they would hear his voice catch when he tried to put on a brave face and recount the events in sufficiently sketchy detail as to make it all suitable for their hearing. But neither of them asked for details and, though he could see the cloud of concern on Anna's face when she beheld the lingering evidence of his injuries, she kept any thoughts beyond basic commiseration to herself and the conversation remained light.

After only a few minutes in Anna's company, he felt better. The room was comfortable and pleasant, and so far removed from garrison life that he could easily imagine himself transplanted to a whole other country. One of the windows was propped slightly open, allowing in the sound of an occasional horse or carriage in the road, along with the heavy fragrance of lilacs. Homey sounds and aromas drifted out from the kitchen where Mrs. Cook was baking pies. He could understand why Anna had missed it so much.

But there were lilacs in England, too, he would have liked to remind her, and there were roses in a lush, fragrant profusion that could not be matched by any garden in Boston. He knew, however, that the real challenge would be to convince her that she could replicate in England a home like this one, with its comfortable parlor, homey aromas, and piles of books, and, in the same moment, knew that it was far more than those physical things that bound her to this place.

"How is Lieutenant Barringer faring?" she asked, jolting him from his contemplation. "Is he quite recovered from his mishap with the unruly mule?" Several days before the army crossed the river for their march on Lexington and Concord, a mule had stepped on Barringer's foot. Several bones were broken but, after the fact, the circumstances of the accident had seemed so entertaining to Hinton that he had recounted the incident to Anna.

"Yes," Hinton assured her. "He is recovering nicely. I would say that, sadly, he still uses a walking stick – though he seems to feel it lends him a certain air, so I don't believe he considers it an unhappy outcome at all."

She laughed lightly. "Poor Mr. Barringer. You were horrid, you know, to find so much amusement in your friend's misfortune."

"Oh, now. Don't be overly hard on me, Miss Somerset. You chastised me, but I could tell you were fighting hard against giving into your own laughter. Barringer has enjoyed a good deal of cosseting from the ladies, so don't feel too sorry for him."

"He's an irresistible package — an appealing young man, dashing in his uniform, and injured, to boot. Of course he's drawing the ladies like flies to honey!"

Wilton cleared his throat disapprovingly. "I fear too many of our Boston ladies are overly dazzled by scarlet coats and gold braid."

"It isn't just Boston ladies, uncle. When I was in London, I heard more than one father lament the loss of his daughter's heart to a handsome officer."

"I hope you are not concerned, Mr. Wilton. I wager your niece is far too sensible to fall into such a trap." He was smiling, yet there was the hint of question in his eyes when he looked at Anna.

"You would win that wager, Mr. Hinton," she laughed. "My eye might be momentarily distracted but it will take far more than a splendid uniform to hold my attention. I can appreciate style, but I'm far more interested in substance."

"Ah!" Wilton cried. "I have done something right in my efforts to bring you up, then."

"You have done many things right in that regard, uncle."

Edward thought he would give a great deal to be on the receiving end of a warm smile such as she bestowed upon her uncle. "Unhappily for the regiment, we've lost several men to the affectionate arms of local ladies," he said. "On the other hand, Boston has lost a few of its lovelier flowers to our officers. Even that stick of a man Chastain has found a wife, I hear."

"Indeed? And who would be so blind?"

"Anna! Such a thing to say!" Wilton shook his head disapprovingly.

"It is only the truth, uncle. If you'd spent weeks getting to know him as I did, I assure you that you would be just as harsh in your judgment. He's quite a horrid man, I believe. Now, who is the foolish girl?"

"I'm trying to recall her name. Let's see . . . a Miss Charlotte Wainright, I believe. No, no. Ainsworth. Charlotte Ainsworth. That's it."

Anna nearly dropped her tea cup. "Charlotte Ainsworth?"

"Yes, I believe that is the name I heard." He leaned back in his chair, suddenly wary. Anna was clearly shocked by this bit of gossip, and he could not fathom the reason. He looked from her to Wilton, but there was no help on that front. "Why?" he asked. "Is something amiss?"

Daniel had shared with her his reservations regarding Teague's relationship with Charlotte, and had given her the impression that nothing seemed likely to sunder them. "No. Not amiss. It's just that . . . well . . .," she seemed to be having trouble making sense of what she had just heard. "I understood that she had set her heart on someone else. It seems rather sudden. I doubt her father considered the other young man to be suitable — perhaps he encouraged the arrangement."

"I'm afraid I wouldn't know. I only have the news second or third-hand. From what I hear, Chastain has been pulling strings to arrange for them to be married quickly, and he intends to send her to his family in London."

"Well, that *is* interesting." She drummed her fingers thoughtfully on the tea table.

Wilton was watching his niece carefully. "I did not think you and Miss Ainsworth had more than a passing acquaintance, Anna."

"We don't. But a friend of mine . . . well, actually, a friend of a friend." She shook her head dismissively. "It doesn't matter. What other tidbits can you share, Mr. Hinton? Garrison gossip is generally far more interesting than the usual nattering about who was seen dancing one too many dances with whom, or how Mrs. So-and-so has retaliated against Mrs. Such-and-such for some perceived insult."

"Ah, well," he responded soberly, "I'm afraid that we are suffering under a general effort to stem the flow of gossip out of the garrison. It's suspected that too many loose tongues contributed mightily to our recent calamities at Lexington and Concord."

"I'm afraid I don't follow."

"What he's trying to say, my dear Anna," Wilton clarified, "is that the rebels were well warned of the army's intentions before even they left Boston, and it enabled them to launch their treacherous and treasonous resistance!"

"I fear that was, indeed, one of the many things that went against us that day." His thoughts returning to the sad place he had hoped by coming here to leave, Hinton picked up his spoon and absently stirred it about in the remainder of his tea.

Wilton, on the other hand, was brought back to his outrage. Blind to the discomfort he was causing either his niece or Hinton, he launched into his oft-repeated litany, inveighing against his fellow colonists for their outrageous and inexcusable behavior. Edward listened with only cursory attention. Most of his mind was on Anna. He watched her carefully, trying to decipher the varied expressions that flitted across her face as she listened to her uncle talk.

Edward had wondered for some time, and the question now came to him afresh, whether or not Daniel Garrett had told her of their encounter near Menotomy. If she knew about the fight — knew that each of her friends was responsible for most of the damage sustained by the other that day — she gave no indication of that knowledge. On the other hand, she did seem to know more than her uncle about the details of that horrible day, and he suspected her emotions were conflicted for more reason that just her friend's involvement. Clearly, her spirits were sinking lower and lower as her uncle talked, and Hinton desperately wished they could be alone so he could hear her thoughts. It startled him when, as though he could read Hinton's mind, Wilton excused himself and went into another room.

Edward waited for her to speak first, but she did not. She was sitting quite still, hands folded in her lap, the picture of calm. He knew her well enough by now to know that there was nothing approaching calmness inside her, however. "You've said little," he ventured quietly. "I would like to know your thoughts."

"I don't think you would like to hear my thoughts at all."

Her words were clipped and ill-tempered, and it took him aback. "I . . . well, yes, I would. Something is troubling you and—"

"*Troubling* me? Have you seen your own face in a mirror? Have you seen how you wince when you stand? My friends are in tatters and you ask if something is *troubling* me?" Her hands, no longer relaxed, had formed into tight fists.

"That isn't . . . you misunderstand me," he stammered. "I simply want to know what you are thinking."

"What I am thinking is that it is disgraceful that blood must be shed and lives must be ruined because a bunch of fat-headed men cannot bring themselves to compromise! Tea? Taxes? Who will be allowed to trade what with whom? Are those things really worth a man's *life*?"

"I think there is a good deal more to it—"

"Oh, yes. I know there is more to it," she interrupted, springing to her feet and pacing back and forth in front of him. "I've heard the various *principles* ground into sausage every place from a London salon to right here in my uncle's house. It seems to me that men are very fond of hanging onto to principle and forgetting about the things that really matter."

"I think," he offered softly, "it is because those principles have such a strong bearing on what really matters.

"My uncle believes in the king's wisdom. If he is so wise, why is this the best he can do?" She waved her hand to encompass the whole of the situation. "Why did he have to push and push until, men being what they are, someone was bound to push back?"

"You are speaking of the king, Miss Somerset." It had come out with a good deal more sternness than he intended, and he immediately regretted it.

Anna stared at him. "Are you going to accuse me of treason, now? Are you going to shoot *me*?"

"Of course not. Please sit down. It was not my intention to upset you." He saw her hesitation, and was relieved when she dropped into her chair, albeit rather huffily. "It was not my intention to upset you," he repeated. "And, if my being here is causing you distress, I shall leave immediately."

"No," she said, withering under the realization of her harshness. "And, I apologize."

"No need. I do understand." He considered his next move for a moment before daring to shift his chair closer to hers in the hope that their proximity to each other might bring the discussion down to a more personal level. "You are perfectly correct to say that bloodshed is a terrible business. A part of me longs to share with you just how terrible because I feel as though doing so might somehow shrive me of the horror I experienced on that road back from Concord. But I cannot do that."

For the first time, she saw in him the terrible emotional price he had paid for his participation in the fight, and regretted the bitter words she had spoken earlier. "You can talk to me about it, you know," she offered softly. "If you'd like . . . if it will help."

He shook his head. "No. Such things are not for your ears. But I do need you to know that I wish none of it had happened. I wish with all my heart that, as you suggested, both sides in this argument could bring themselves to a peaceful resolution. That didn't happen, however, and this is where we are now. It cannot be undone."

"The situation will get worse, won't it?"

He nodded solemnly. "I'm afraid it will. I wish that were not so but I can see little chance of it being otherwise. Despite what is said of him, General Gage has done everything in his power to prevent the situation from coming to this point. He's a good man, Miss Somerset. A good man who wanted peace every bit as much as you do." He lowered his voice and hoped he would not regret the confidence he was about to share. "Yet peace has eluded him and London has lost faith in his tactics. It is for no one else's ears at this point, but three generals — each one far more willing to do whatever is necessary to bring the colonies to heel — have arrived."

"Gage is being replaced?"

"Not immediately. The official line is that these three are to be his subordinates. No one is deceived, however. It's clear that London expects them to exercise a firmer hand and succeed where General Gage has failed."

"Then, things can indeed only get worse."

"I believe so."

Without stopping to consider her action, Anna reached out and took his hand. "Then, I shall worry for you and will keep you in my prayers."

"I am more concerned that you will continue to consider me a friend."

"Of course I shall. You will ever be dear to me."

The warmth of her smile convinced him that she meant what she said, and he was on the verge of telling her just how dear she was to him when they were interrupted by urgent pounding at the front door.

Anna reached the door as her uncle was stepping out of his study on the opposite side of the foyer. She opened it, and was nearly bowled over by a distraught Selah Garrett. Selah rushed directly to John Wilton and clutched both of his hands in hers. Everything about her suggested that she had run all the way up the hill from her shop to the house.

"Why, Mrs. Garrett! Whatever—"

She did not wait for him to finish his question. "Oh, Mr. Wilton. I've come to beg your assistance," she sobbed. "Daniel has been arrested! A troop of redcoats found him and hauled him away. Drum was there and came for me. He says they hit Daniel and—"

Wilton stopped her and directed her attention to Edward Hinton, who stood awkwardly in the parlor, watching them. "Perhaps we should go into my study and speak confidentially," Wilton suggested.

But Selah was in no mood to be discreet. She broke away from Wilton and stormed toward Edward like a hurricane coming ashore. "Did you do this?" she demanded. "Did you tell them lies about my son so that they would take him away?"

Edward gaped at her, momentarily at a loss for words. "I assure you, Mrs. Garrett," he insisted when his equilibrium returned, "I know nothing about this." His eyes darted to Anna. "I promise you, I do not know what this is about."

Wilton intervened to rescue the lieutenant from Selah's wrath. "Come," he urged her. "Sit down and tell us what has happened."

Selah continued to dart accusatory looks in Edward's direction while allowing herself to be steered into the nearest chair. "They say that he has been stealing from the army," she said, gasping for breath between words. "And worse, they say he has murdered two soldiers."

"*What?*" Anna went from relatively calm confusion to outrage so fast that it made all of them turn to look at her. "That is preposterous! Daniel has not been stealing anything. I know that as sure as we are sitting here. And he certainly would not murder anyone! Who would make such a ridiculous claim against him?"

"They say they have evidence that he is responsible for the thefts of supplies, and for the theft of General Gage's personal belongings. I don't know what that evidence might be."

"And, what is the murder accusation based upon?" Wilton asked.

Selah looked up him in wide-eyed horror. "They say the bodies of two soldiers were found buried in a shallow grave at our old farm."

"Oh, dear God," Anna said, slowly sinking into a chair. She was thinking hard, trying to reconcile what she was being told with what she knew of Daniel. "It can't be," she insisted, shaking her head. "There has to be some other explanation." She looked at Edward. "He did not do this. I tell you, it simply is not true."

Selah said, "I came to you, Mr. Wilton, because I did not know where else to turn. I don't know what to do!"

Wilton pulled a chair near to hers and sat down. He leaned very close and placed his hands over hers. "I am glad you came," he said. "We will sort this out. Can you tell us anything else about these accusations? Has he been formally charged? Do you know exactly who is holding him or where?"

She shook her head. "No. Drum didn't know or, if he did, he couldn't recall it. He was there when they arrested Daniel, and he was very upset and frightened when he found me. All he said was that the soldiers had burst into Daniel's room and hit him several times — I assume to prevent his resisting. Then, they bound his hands, told him why he was being taken, and hauled him away. You know the mood of the army, Mr. Wilton. You know they are in no frame of mind to treat with any degree of fairness someone they think has murdered two of their own." A new rush of tears flowed down her face. "I fear we will be lucky if he isn't hanged by this time tomorrow."

"That will not happen," Hinton informed her firmly. He was gathering his hat and cloak as he spoke. "I will go and see what I can learn. I shall send word, or bring it myself." He touched Anna lightly on the arm as he left, but could offer no further reassurance.

*   *   *

Daniel stood as Anna entered his cell, which was nothing more than the cellar of a conscripted house, and managed an insouciant smile. "I won't bother to say that you should not be here." He gestured toward a battered three-legged stool in one corner, offering her the only seat in the cell aside from his cot. It was quintessentially Anna, he thought, that she showed no distaste, but accepted the seat as though he had offered her a finely-upholstered chair. "I don't know which surprises me more," he said. "The fact that you have come, when you were so angry with me the last time we spoke, or that they would allow you to see me."

"Of course I came. I would have come sooner had it not taken three entire days to discover where you were being held and secure permission to see you. My anger with you did not change our friendship. And, as to the other, having an uncle who is a well-known Loyalist sometimes has its advantages."

"Advantages to me as well. I believe I have your uncle and Mr. Sprague to thank for the fact that the accusations against me are being given careful scrutiny, and I do thank them for that." He grinned. "When the redcoats took me, I fully expected them to drag me to the nearest tree for hanging."

"If that was supposed to be humorous, it failed." She studied his face, frowning over the new injuries that had not been there when last she'd seen him. A dark stain decorating his shirt indicated that the wound in his side had set to bleeding again. "Are you all right?" She nodded toward the stain. "Your mother says you have asked that she not visit you. Can't you at least allow her to come and dress your wound?"

"It has been seen to," he told her dismissively. "I believe your uncle is responsible for that as well. I don't want her to see me in this place." He perched on the edge of his cot and studied her as closely as she was studying him. There was a question in her mind, he could tell, and it pained him. Could she believe he might be guilty? "I did not do this," he said. "What they have accused me of — I did not do it."

"I know." She waited for him to say something more, but no words were forthcoming. "You know who probably did, however." His blank expression irritated her. "Why will you not give Teague up to them? You must know that he is responsible for this."

"No, I don't know. Not for certain."

"Don't you?"

Shaking his head, he looked away from her, and his knuckles whitened under the strain of his grip on the edge of the cot. "I cannot believe he would do this. Despite all, I refuse to believe he would murder two men, or that he would allow me to hang for it."

His eyes seemed to focus on some small spot on the floor, but it was apparent to Anna that they were, instead, focused on some distant point in his mind. She allowed the silence to stretch between them, allowed him to form his thoughts into words. He was struggling, she saw, wrestling with the things that writhed through his mind and gut with devastating effect.

"He was born in a brothel," he said at last. "Teague. He was born in a brothel." When she did not respond, he looked up and forced himself to meet her even gaze. "I don't think he ever told anyone but me. He did not know who his father was, and his mother was a — well, you must be able to guess what she was." Daniel lowered his eyes again and swallowed hard against the lump of emotion that threatened to choke him. "He was born in that place and spent his first few years being exposed to everything in life except goodness. Then, when he was just old enough to understand what was happening, a man bought an hour of time with him, and *that* Teague knew he could not bear, so he ran. He ran away to live on the streets and I'm not sure he has ever really stopped running."

Daniel slowly raised his eyes, full of apology for telling her something so sordid, so unbefitting her ears. The shock he'd expected to see was not there. Instead, he saw only compassion. So, he continued his tale. "I chose to live as I did. I chose unwisely, but I did choose. For him, though, there was no choice — no parents, no home — nothing. He has never known anything but street life, and he has been abused and beaten down at every turn all of his life."

"He could have chosen another path," she pointed out gently. "He could have pulled himself out of that gutter."

Daniel shook his head. "The thing is, I don't believe he has ever known how. Perhaps if the right person had come along. Perhaps if there had been someone to shine a light on that other path. That's what I had that he did not."

"If he'd been open to it, it would have come. Your mother tried to take him under her wing. I saw that often enough, and saw him reject her. You've tried to be that light for him, and he has resisted at every turn."

He lowered his eyes and his shoulders sagged under the weight of her words. "I cannot," he said softly. "I cannot give him to them. I cannot be the catalyst for his final ruin."

"He, himself, has been that catalyst. He brought his final ruin on himself by his actions. And, I don't accept your claim that he has known no goodness in his life. For as long as I remember, whenever he got into trouble he could not manage, you helped him. Others have helped him, too, and perhaps they should not have. Perhaps we should all have stood back and let him reap the rewards of his own actions."

"I don't expect you to understand," Daniel said quietly. "His world is too far removed from the one you've known. You can't understand what it's like or the things you have to do to survive."

She opened her mouth to say that others like Teague had managed – through a willingness to do hard, honest work – to drag themselves up out of that world. She suspected that Daniel's emotions were not in a place to hear those words, however, and held her tongue. Before she left, Anna made one last plea. "You owe it to your mother and all of us who care about you to defend yourself from these charges. If you allow yourself to be hanged, you will cause us unendurable pain. And, for that, I shall not forgive you, Daniel Garrett."

Anna walked home in silence beside her uncle. He had escorted her to the place where Daniel was being held and, despite some misgivings, agreed to wait for her while she went in alone to visit him. It was late afternoon, though one would not have known without a clock for the sky was a dense, dull grey that stubbornly refused to allow any glimpse of the sun. It was a perfect reflection of her mood, Anna thought.

Drum followed a few paces behind, head bowed in misery. Daniel had asked him to watch over Anna but he would have followed her regardless simply because, right now, he needed someone to whom he could cling. Though it was unclear to Drum whether or not he and Teague were still friends, he wished Teague was there now.

S.D. Banks

Chapter Twenty

By Daniel's reckoning, it was May 28. He had expected on this day to be part of a raiding party intent on removing livestock from Noddle Island, not confined to a make-shift cell, wondering if Richard Chastain would find a way to beat him to death or lynch him before he could face trial. A week had passed since Anna's visit and, though he was reluctant for her to see him in this place, in this position or condition, a part of him wished she would come again. He sat as he always did, with his back propped against the door. It was not the most comfortable choice — though, it could be argued that there were *no* comfortable choices — but it was the one place in the cellar from which he could hear conversation among the guards. As best he could tell, he was the sole prisoner, which made the presence of two guards excessive, in his view. But then, they did believe that he had murdered two of their own. Perhaps that explained their diligence.

Initially, he'd thought it explained Chastain's fervor. Upon bursting into Daniel's room, Chastain's men had moved quickly to subdue Daniel. Once they had him firmly in hand, Chastain had signaled one of the privates who, using the butt of his musket, had hit Daniel first in the gut, and then in the head. The blow to his stomach had doubled him over, retching, and had set the saber cut in his side to bleeding again. He had barely managed to stop Drum from attempting to protect him as the redcoats dragged him out of Withers' tavern.

Chastain was in no hurry to get him to the place where he was to be incarcerated. What Chastain wanted far more than he wanted the man who had murdered two redcoats was to recover General Gage's personal property. He was convinced that Daniel knew where it was, and was determined to get that information out of him as expeditiously as possible. To that end, he had directed a systematic and brutal beating that barely left Daniel time to breathe, let alone respond to the questions being put to him. Because he would never sully his own hands with such work, Chastain had chosen a particularly burly young private with a fondness for fist fighting to administer the blows.

Withers had emerged from the tavern and sauntered over to where Chastain stood. "What's this all about, then?" The brutish man stopped beating on Daniel long enough to give Withers an appraising look.

"Off with you, old man. You've no business here," Chastain ordered.

But Withers merely spat in the dirt at his feet. "That lad there's a friend of mine," he said. "A friend to all of us, matter of fact." In subtle warning, he had gestured toward the men who were pouring out of the tavern. "We'd like to know what he's done to deserve this."

Chastain had cast a circumspect eye toward the cluster of spectators. Not wanting to have to deal with them, he had said in a voice loud enough for all to hear, "This man murdered two members of my regiment. This is the king's business. Now, move on." He looked down at Withers. "All of you."

"I don't think so."

Chastain, completely taken aback, had blinked at the old man. "What did you say?"

"I said, we won't be going nowhere. There are many disreputable things that Daniel Garrett is, but a murderer ain't one of 'em." He spat again, several inches closer to Chastain's polished boot.

Chastain had stepped back, and was on the verge of ordering his men to take Withers into custody along with Daniel, when one of his men called his attention to the fact that the crowd of spectators had swelled to include, not just the men from the tavern, but fishermen, shipwrights, dockworkers, warehousemen, and any number of others who had no love for the Regulars. Mindful of the many times such incidents had deteriorated into a matter of regret for whatever officer was involved, Chastain had backed down. The redcoats hauled Daniel to their ersatz jail where, though Chastain could continue to rough Daniel up a bit, there would be limits for most of the Regulars were men who followed a code of honor that was quite foreign to Richard Chastain.

That was how it all had started. Since then, he had languished in this place where Chastain could visit him at his leisure to pose more questions about Gage's stolen property. But on this day, late in the evening, when the guards were relaxed from their supper and enjoying their card game, Daniel could hear their conversation. And, what he heard made it the best day of his captivity save for the day Anna had come to see him.

The guards were not happy, it seemed, because the day before, the hated rebels had handed some of their compatriots yet another humiliation. Having got wind of a militia raid on Noddle Island, General Gage had sent a small contingent of marines out to deal with the situation. The marines were using a schooner named the *Diana*, onto which they had mounted four six-pounder cannon and two lighter swivel guns, and should have had an easy time of the matter.

During the ensuing fight between the militiamen and the marines, however, the *Diana* was forced aground. After nightfall, the militiamen boarded the schooner, took possession of the guns, and then burned the boat — all to the chagrin of the British garrison watching from the far bank. Daniel leaned his head back against the door and laughed out loud. Dr. Warren now had his cannon. Not long range guns, to be certain, but guns that, if mounted on either the Heights or on the hills of Charlestown, were capable of causing the Regulars a good deal of trouble.

And, there was more. After the previous night's humiliation, the British had sent a larger sloop, the *Britannia,* out to do the job the marines on the

Diana had failed to do. However, the militiamen had greeted them with cannon fire, managing to disable the *Britannia* so that it became disabled and had to be towed to safety. Yes, Daniel thought, it was a good day.

*   *   *

Teague could feel the west sun on his back, warming him against spring's final chilly days that stubbornly clung to the Pennsylvania hills. He'd been away from Boston since early April, nearly two months, riding down through New York and into the mountains. He'd not gone as far as Charlotte had told him to go and, in fact, had turned his horse toward home a good three weeks earlier than planned. Charlotte had insisted that he take the muskets all the way out to Lake Erie where he would get the best price for them. But Teague was tired of riding, and — though he hated to admit it even to himself — tired of doing Charlotte's bidding. It seemed that her schemes increasingly demanded his absence from Boston and it was beginning to eat away at him. Ever since Daniel had told him about Charlotte and Chastain, Teague had not been able to shake the fragment of a suspicion that Daniel was telling the truth.

No doubt visions of prancing about London, the wife of an army captain, have been bouncing around that otherwise empty little head of yours ever since you met him. Teague could not shake from his memory the accusation Daniel had leveled at Charlotte. It had angered Teague at the time, and he had allowed himself to be talked out of believing it because he did not want to believe it. But there was that lingering, nagging splinter of doubt. It seemed to bore into his back like a knife between his shoulder blades and was becoming increasingly difficult to ignore. He vowed to determine for himself the legitimacy of Daniel's accusations, even if it meant spying on the woman he loved.

*   *   *

For a little more than three weeks, ever since the redcoats had taken Daniel away, Drum stopped by the Wilton house at least twice a day. He would not knock at the door but, instead, would loiter, watching and waiting. Occasionally, Anna spotted him and stepped outside to chat. His opening question was always the same — was she doing well? The next question was equally predictable — did she think the soldiers would allow him to visit Daniel? The answers were always "yes" and "no" in that order. Because she was struggling with her own emotions and concern, it took some time before she came to comprehend that what he really wanted was to be with someone who understood how worried he was and who would offer comfort.

Finally, one afternoon she sat down on the back steps ostensibly to enjoy the warm, brilliant June day, and invited him to join her. "I'd be glad of your company, Drum," she said, indicating the place beside her on the step. "If you don't need to be some other place right now?"

Drum shook his head and eased himself onto the wooden step beside her. "Why have the redcoats kept Daniel locked up for so long?"

"I don't know," she sighed. "Mr. Sprague thinks it's because they don't have enough solid evidence against him to hang him without starting a riot. My uncle believes it is just that they are too busy right now to bother with him."

"It doesn't seem right that they can keep him locked up like that for so long."

Better locked up than hanged, she thought. "I agree, Drum. It doesn't seem right. But there it is."

They sat in silence for a time until Drum noticed a chickadee flitting busily about the yard. He launched into a protracted discourse on the characteristics of chickadees, followed by a monologue on the relative merits of finches. Anna hardly heard a word, but let him talk.

Abruptly, he launched off onto a new tangent. "Things have become a terrible mess, haven't they?"

"Yes, Drum," she sighed. "They have indeed. Lately there have been moments when I wish I'd stayed in London. And, I certainly never thought I'd feel that way. It passes, though. All in all, I'd still rather be here."

"Was London nice? Did you like it very much there?"

"Yes, it is nice. I liked some of it. A great deal of it, actually, but it wasn't home. I particularly miss some of the people I met there, and I miss the music and the art." She sighed at the memory. "Oh, Drum. I saw paintings so exquisitely beautiful that they brought tears to my eyes."

"I saw something beautiful like that once."

"Did you?" She was only half-listening.

"Yes." His gloom deepened.

"What was it?" she asked, picking up on his marked sadness. "If it was beautiful, why does it make you sad?"

He shrugged. "There were other things that made me sad, not the beautiful thing."

"What was it?"

"If I tell you, you can't tell anyone. I don't want anyone to be angry at me."

"All right," she said slowly. "I won't tell anyone. What did you see?"

He thought for a moment, uncertain of how to describe what he had seen. "An egg," he said finally.

"An egg?" It was not what she'd expected. She imagined him accidentally upsetting a bird's nest and was struggling to figure out why he thought anyone would be angry with him for it.

"Yes. A blue egg."

"Like a robin's egg? Robin's eggs can be very pretty." It would be like Drum to be moved to tears by a robin's egg.

"No. It wasn't a bird's egg. It wasn't a real egg at all. It was a box shaped like an egg. It was painted a shiny color of blue I've never seen before and it had pretty gold decorations on it."

Anna became quite still. Something tripped in her memory and, hardly daring to breathe, she waited for him to say more.

"The top of the egg opened and there was a flower inside. And, the egg played music when you opened it. I felt like I could stand there looking at it forever, but I wasn't supposed to be there and I was afraid I would get in trouble. You won't tell anyone what I did, will you?"

"No, Drum," she said carefully. "I won't tell anyone if that's what you want. But where was this egg when you saw it? Did Daniel have it?" She held her breath.

Drum shook his head. "No. I wish it was his, because then I could see it anytime I want."

"Who did the egg belong to?"

"Miss Ainsworth."

Anna's jaw dropped and she stared at him. "Charlotte Ainsworth?"

"Yes. I finished digging the hole for her — the hole in the floor of the shed where her father is going to hide his valuable things from the redcoats. I wasn't supposed to tell anyone that," he added sheepishly.

"Never mind. It doesn't matter now. Go on."

"I wanted to get the money she was supposed to pay me for digging the hole and not wait for it. I knocked at the door, but no one answered. Then I heard her father call out like he needed help. I let myself in and went upstairs to see her father. I thought maybe he fell or something." His words became rushed as though he felt the need to explain before Anna got angry with him for doing something he was not supposed to do. "Miss Ainsworth wasn't there. I went up to her father's bedroom and he was in a terrible state. I helped him back into bed. I didn't know what else to do."

Anna frowned in confusion. "Was the egg in Mr. Ainsworth's bedroom?"

"No. It was in her bedroom — Miss Ainsworth's. I saw it after I left Mr. Ainsworth. And, I couldn't help it — the egg was so beautiful, and I never saw anything like it before. I just had to take a closer look. I know I shouldn't have, but it was so beautiful."

"It's all right, Drum." She laid her hand reassuringly on his arm. "I understand. I believe I'd have felt the same way. You're not in trouble. I am very curious about the egg, though." Wanting to verify whether Drum's egg was the stolen item for which Lieutenant Chastain searched, she tried to think of details Edward had given about Margaret Gage's music box. "How big was it?"

"Like this." He held his hands up in pantomime of holding the egg. "Much bigger than a bird's egg, and heavier. I picked it up, so I know." He flushed red and stared down at his feet. "I accidentally dropped it, Miss Anna. It didn't break, but I accidentally dropped it! I know Miss Ainsworth would be angry if she knew. She was angry that I'd been upstairs to see her father."

"Was she? How did she know you'd seen him?"

"She came home when I was coming down the stairs. I tried to explain why, but she was screaming terrible things at me, so I left."

"I'm glad you did," Anna murmured. "So, you didn't tell her you'd seen the egg?"

He shook his head hard and widened his eyes. "I think she would have set the constable on me."

"I doubt that. Though she would likely have been quite upset." Her mind whirred through possible explanations, testing then discarding one after another. "Drum, the music box you describe sounds very much like one that was stolen — very much like one of the things they are saying Daniel stole. And, they are saying that he killed the two soldiers because they found him out."

"But he didn't steal it. Do you think Miss Ainsworth did?"

"Certainly not. But I do think it likely that Teague did, and that he gave it to her as a gift. If she has the egg, she might have other things, and her possession of those things might be enough to convince the army that Daniel did not steal them. If they believe Daniel didn't commit the thefts, maybe they will believe that he had no real motive for the murders. They will need to discover who gave her the egg, though." She jumped to her feet. "Will you come with me to speak to my uncle? We must tell him what you saw. He will go to the Provost Marshal and insist that they investigate further."

Drum looked horrified. "But then Miss Ainsworth will know! If she knows I did something bad, she might tell them to arrest me. Please, Miss Anna! I don't want to get into trouble!"

"You won't get into trouble, Drum. I'll think of some way to keep you out of it. But, don't you see? We must tell someone. This could convince them that Daniel isn't the thief they are looking for. And, if he isn't the thief, he probably isn't their murderer, either. At the very least, it might plant the seed of doubt."

Drum considered it for several long seconds before consenting. "Even if I get in trouble, they won't hang me just for dropping the egg, I don't think. It didn't break after all."

"No, Drum, they won't hang you for any of it. I doubt very much that you will be in trouble at all."

"And, it will help Daniel?"

"Yes," she nodded. "I believe it will."

That settled it for him, and he followed Anna into her uncle's study where, with some prompting from Anna, he repeated his story to Wilton. When the tale was done, he held his breath in fear of the lambasting he expected to take for his transgression. Wilton did not castigate him, however. Instead, he sat thoughtfully ruminating on what he'd been told.

"Chastain's men found a stolen ring belonging to Mrs. Gage near the place where the two murdered soldiers were hidden," Anna said by way of closing argument. "Because of that, they believe the theft and the murders are somehow connected. If we can produce doubt about the thefts, perhaps they will take another look at the murders."

"It is a compelling line of reasoning, of course," he said thoughtfully. "Though, playing devil's advocate, I have to point out that Mr. Garrett could just as easily be the one who gave the music box to Miss Ainsworth."

"But he didn't! He wouldn't have." She pulled up a chair and sat so that she could look him in the eye. "Mr. Garrett despises Miss Ainsworth. He wants nothing to do with her. He told me so himself!"

Wilton pursed his lips and studied his niece's face. He was aware, perhaps more so than Anna herself, that she was over-fond of Daniel Garrett. And, he himself had a certain liking for the young man. But he also appreciated that the men who would not want *something* from a girl like Charlotte Ainsworth would be few and far between.

"Please, uncle," she begged. "We must at least try. We must try for Mrs. Garrett's sake if for no other reason." She knew it was an unfair card to play, but she could not resist doing so.

Wilton raised his eyebrows. "If I help you with this, it will not be for the sake of either Mrs. Garrett or her son, my dear. I shall help because it is important to you and because I believe in justice."

"But, you *will* help?"

He sighed heavily. "Yes. I shall help." He fished his hunter-case watch out of his vest pocket and checked the time. "It's too late to go this evening. I shall go with you first thing tomorrow to see the Provost Marshal. Will that suffice?"

Though Anna would have preferred that they go immediately, she nodded her head in agreement. Tomorrow it would have to be.

But, despite the zeal she and John Wilton put into the effort, they never found out how useful Drum's information might be. The army was engaged in an explosion of activity and mobilization. Wilton and Anna had difficulty finding anyone who would speak with them, and the young officer they finally pinned down barely took the time even to accept Wilton's hastily written note requesting a meeting with the Provost Marshal. The man had tossed it on his desk and offered vague assurances that it would be passed along to the appropriate official. He had dealt with them distractedly, his mind plainly on weightier matters. Because, after weeks of receiving reinforcements, General Gage had finally decided to clear the occupying militia from Breed's Hill.

*　　*　　*

Fearful and impatient, Anna felt that they could not wait for the Provost to act on Drum's information about Charlotte's possession of the egg. If Edward Hinton's gossip was accurate, Charlotte could leave for London at any moment. Furthermore, it occurred to Anna that Charlotte might not be cooperative, or that she might lie about the circumstances under which the egg came to be in her possession. Anna did not know her well, but what little she did know about Charlotte Ainsworth was enough to make it fairly certain that she could not be trusted. That Teague was somehow involved Anna had no doubt. The question of how much he had involved Charlotte in his crimes made her mind dizzy with guesses, however. It could be that he had simply made a gift of the egg in an effort to woo her. If that were the case, he might have given her other items as well, and the discovery of those items and the story they had to tell might lead to an explanation of how two dead redcoats had ended up shallowly buried at the old Garrett farm.

And so, she settled upon what was admittedly the most outrageous of all the outrageous schemes she'd ever concocted. She decided to search the Ainsworth house to see what useful evidence might be found there. The plan defied all sense or logic, but she was convinced that such radical action would be necessary to accomplish her goal. Questioning Drum more closely about the pit he had dug in the Ainsworth shed persuaded Anna that the shed was a good place to start her search. If that should yield nothing useful, then she'd have to wait for an opportune moment to slip in and search the house. That moment might not present itself anytime soon, so she dearly hoped the evidence she sought would be hidden in the shed.

She waited until almost midnight. Her uncle's household was fast asleep and she knew most of Boston would be as well, including the Ainsworth household. She assembled a costume comprised of a pair of breeches she had purchased from the shoemaker's son for far more than they were worth, an old shirt, and a tattered old jacket. To conceal her neck and face, she added a scarf and, stuffing her hair under a stocking cap, she set out. She had no illusions that her clothing would disguise her gender from anyone who gave her more than the most cursory of glances, but it was far more serviceable than skirts and petticoats for climbing fences and rooting around in garden sheds.

There was a significant distance between her uncle's house and the Ainsworth house, and covering it took all the longer because, in her effort to move undetected, she took a particularly circuitous route. Gage had declared martial law in Boston on June 12, four days earlier, and patrols bent on keeping folks in their houses at night were frequent. She stayed away from the Common and its army encampment, and followed a small lane that ran parallel with Beacon Street down toward Cornhill and Newberry Streets. It felt odd, and somewhat enjoyable to be out at such a late hour. The night air was pleasant, the clear sky boasted a bright full moon and, with the exception of the night-loving animal population, she seemed at first to have the streets to herself.

At Newberry Street, she followed alleys and lanes that would take her roughly south toward Windmill Point. Once, a small group of inebriated men, one of them complaining loudly that he needed to piss, stumbled by. Their approach was so noisy that she'd had plenty of time to find a good hiding place and went unnoticed. Less than a block later, she darted back into the shadows when she caught sight of a pair of redcoats on patrol. They came toward her at a leisurely pace and, though she felt they had looked directly at her, passed by without seeing her. Relieved, she doubled back to the narrow lane just off Bennet Street where the Ainsworth house stood, more impressive than the rest, at the middle of the lane.

She approached the house along a back alley and let herself into the yard through the tall wooden gate. Just inside the gate, she stood perfectly still and held her breath, listening. A dog barked somewhere in the distance, and crickets chirped away in the darkness. She heard the faint ruffle and flap of an owl's wings, but the bird remained invisible to her as it hunted somewhere in the sky above. Soft, occasional murmurs emanated from the coop where the Ainsworth's chickens slept safe in their roost. A light breeze gently stirred the trees and shrubs, wafting the overpoweringly strong scents of lilac and honeysuckle through the air. From the house, however, there was nothing, so she relaxed and steeled herself for the business at hand.

From a cloudless sky, the bright moon cast the yard in a wash of blue and grey tones with everything clearly visible, though lacking in any sort of natural color. She could pick out the kitchen garden; it's neatly mounded rows and plant stakes ghostly as a burial ground in the moonlight. And, on the far side of the garden, a large shed with double-doors took up an entire corner of the yard, squarely upright, its roof and shingle siding in excellent repair. Drum's handiwork, Anna knew. An enormous stack of firewood formed up along one side of the structure, well-sheltered under a jutting overhang.

Keeping to the shadows along the fence, she made her way across the yard toward the shed. Twice she stumbled over unseen objects, and she painfully barked her shin on the edge of an upended produce crate at one point, but all was managed with very little noise. She reached her objective and stood before the large double-doors contemplating the lock dangling below the hasp. Drum had not mentioned there being a lock. It was an unexpected obstacle that would require some improvisation.

She jumped back as a rat skittered across her feet and watched it dart off toward the kitchen garden, passing the splitting stump on its way. An axe lying on the stump caught her eye. Anna smiled. She picked up the tool and bounced it lightly against her palm, testing its weight in her hands. It would be awkward, she thought, though not impossible. Struggling somewhat with the weight, she worked the thin splitting edge in between the latch and the wood of the door. Once it was tightly wedged, she grabbed the handle and pulled as hard as she could. The latch did not budge. She tried again and again with similar results until, more from frustration than any notion that it would work, she grasped the handle and, bracing her feet up against the door, pulled outwards with all her weight. The latch broke free, and the axe and Anna both tumbled roughly — and noisily — to the ground.

Anna held her breath and watched the house for some sign that she had roused someone inside, but no candle was lit, no face appeared at any window. She got to her feet, dusted herself off, and pulled the doors open. The smell that roiled out from inside the shed stung her eyes and forced her back a step. Manure, presumably to be spread on the garden, was piled in one corner. Why it was piled *inside* the shed Anna could not imagine, but there it was, filling the small confines with horrendously foul fumes.

Wrapping her scarf around her mouth and nose against the smell, she propped the doors wide open to let in the moonlight and let out the horrible fumes, and allowed a moment for her eyes to acclimate to the shed's dim interior. A small workbench was along one wall, and various tools stood in a rack close to the doors. Wide planks were laid to form a floor, but Anna knew from Drum's description that they also concealed a hiding place underneath. She dragged several of the center planks out of the way, took a trowel down from a peg on the wall, and began to dig.

Drum had told her that the hole he'd dug was quite deep, but Anna hoped something might be found within the shallower layers. This was not the case. After digging several small holes almost a foot deep, she had uncovered nothing but more dirt. Sighing resignedly, she took up a shovel and began a more serious excavation. Having recently been dug out, the dirt was quite soft and the removal of it went surprisingly quickly. Nevertheless, her palms became painfully raw, forcing her to stop at one point and wrap them with strips of cloth torn from the hem of her shirt. She set to work again and steadily made good progress. Her shoulders were aching, but she dared not stop. She guessed there were only a few hours before dawn, and she had no idea how much farther she would have to dig.

At times, she thought she detected a new odor — something akin to a dead animal and even more foul than the manure. She hesitated, wondering if perhaps the Ainsworths had used this place to bury an animal. She had never seen Charlotte with a pet, and doubted that she kept one. Was she doing all of this only to find herself with the buried carcass of a lap dog? She thought it far more likely that a dead animal was buried in the hole to dissuade anyone from digging deep enough to find the valuables hidden there. Wrapping her scarf more tightly across her face, she toiled on.

*　　*　　*

The stranglehold in which the loose confederation of militia units held Boston had stretched on for nearly two months. Joseph Warren had only just managed to keep the militiamen together and organized enough that they were able to contain the British in Boston. During those two months, the Patriot camps deteriorated into disease-ridden squalor, and the troops cooped up in Boston became a restless, irritable lot eager to be out in the countryside, and more eager to take out their frustrations on some rebels. It was a stalemate, occasionally enlivened by a bit of skirmishing, but a stalemate, nonetheless.

General Gage's officers had no more patience for stalemates.

"I wish to argue once again, Sirs, for permission to unleash such a bombardment from my ships as will level the entirety of this wretched city."

Edward Hinton had watched Admiral Graves' face as he made the suggestion, hoping to see some sign that the admiral was being ironic. There was no such suggestion, as there had not been on the previous occasions when Graves had put forth this same proposal over the several weeks since the business at Lexington and Concord. The notion of such an action appalled Edward, and he was relieved every time General Gage dismissed the suggestion with much the same bearing and expression of a parent rebuffing a nagging child.

Hinton did not care for Graves. At age sixty-two, the dour admiral represented the worst of the navy in the American colonies, Hinton thought. Granted, Graves was charged with the almost impossible mission of protecting and enforcing trade laws the length of the entire colonial coast with a tiny fleet of only twenty-six ships. But his arrogant sense of superiority over his counterpart army officers, which he made no effort to conceal, was insufferable. Furthermore, his disdain for the colonists, contempt for local authorities — even those appointed by the Crown — insensitivity to local customs and issues, and use of press gangs to help fill gaps in his ships' crews had served to further fuel antagonism on the part of the colonists and, thus, made Gage's job all the more difficult.

Infinitely patient, Gage suffered Graves because he had to, just as he was suffering the presence of and continual jockeying for dominance between his three new generals. Gage had asked London for reinforcements, and reinforcements had arrived — along with three new generals to lead them. Gage remained ostensibly in command, but the fact that London had sent Generals Burgoyne, Howe, and Clinton to assist him communicated quite clearly London's waning confidence in Gage.

Hinton was forced to endure the intolerably long, uncomfortably contentious planning meeting because, against his will, he'd been transferred to General Howe's staff as an aide-de-camp. The position was supposed to be a feather in Hinton's cap, but he detested it. Duty as personal secretary and valet was not what he'd had in mind when he took up his commission. His dislike of the position was somewhat ameliorated by Howe's character, but it was a bitter pill, nonetheless.

Aged forty-six, Howe was regarded as an experienced, gifted commander. Clinton and Burgoyne viewed him with some skepticism, however, because of his opposition in Parliament to the Intolerable Acts and stated reluctance to serve against the Americans. But, because his king had asked it of him, Howe was here in Boston, prepared to do his duty, and that was something to which Hinton could connect. Throughout the day's difficult war council, Howe had listened to the views of other officers, and then had offered his own opinion regarding the best way to approach the problem of securing the Dorchester and Charlestown peninsulas. It was done without Burgoyne's flamboyance, Clinton's insufferable ego, or the admiral's overweening obduracy.

In the end, General Gage ordered a plan that, to the particular chagrin of Burgoyne and Clinton, was most closely akin to what Howe had proposed. The operation was to be executed quickly and in such a fashion that it would be over before the rebel militias had time to mount any sort of defense and, to that end, preparations were to be cloaked in secrecy. On the statement of that last point, Hinton had to suppress a snort of derision. Nothing could be kept secret in Boston, least of all military plans. If Lexington and Concord had taught them nothing else, he thought it might have taught them that one lesson.

Gage dismissed them with the final order that the operation was to be launched on Sunday, June 18.

CHAPTER TWENTY-ONE

Charlotte waved to Richard Chastain one last time before softly closing the door. He had suggested leaving through the back way, but Charlotte doubted any of the neighbors were up at this hour to see him stealing out of her house and, besides, she and Chastain were to be married at the end of the following week so, what did it matter if someone saw him? She smiled to herself, pleased that all of her careful planning was coming to fruition, and quietly snicked the lock into place. Why she was taking care to do things quietly she could not say. There was no one in the house except for her, no one to hear her close the door on her lover, no one to be aware of her padding about the dark house in her night shift as she checked all of the doors and windows to see that they were securely latched.

There was a time when she would not have bothered with all of the locks and bolts, but the visit from Cudahy and Foster had set her nerves on edge so that she needed the feeling of extra security at night. She liked having Chastain there in the evenings for that reason, among other things. Having convinced Chastain that her father had conveniently removed himself to another colony for a time, she often considered allowing him to stay all night but decided that would be flaunting it a bit too freely.

She felt, as she always did after his nocturnal visits, as though she were literally glowing. Her blood seemed to thrum warmly under her skin and the most delicate of places still tingled from his not always gentle touch. Not that they'd actually had intercourse. Chastain had taken her up on her offer to abstain for some time after their marriage to ensure that she was not already inconveniently pregnant. She'd laughed at his openness regarding his lack of trust for she did not trust him, either. Not completely. Each of them knowing exactly where they stood in that regard made them good partners, it seemed. And, because she understood him so well, she had on this night given him the money he would need to buy a captaincy. After all, he had made good on his promise to arrange their marriage, and had pursued the lead she'd given him regarding Gage's stolen property without bringing her name into it.

She laughed aloud now, thinking how excited he'd been when he told her of his own cleverness in following the clue she had provided to find — not merely evidence that the stolen property was nearly in his grasp — but the murdered remains of two privates everyone had assumed were deserters! He was being praised no end for his cunning and, when he so easily apprehended Daniel, his stock rose that much further. They'd not yet persuaded Daniel to tell them where the rest of the stolen property could be found, but that would come. If not, seeing the bastard hang for the murders would have to suffice.

None of that was what had Charlotte floating now, however. Abstaining from actual intercourse did not mean Chastain had to go entirely without pleasure, and Charlotte was learning to take her pleasure as well. He taught her how to perform acts on him that she never could have imagined, and pushed her to allow him to take her in ways that would not damage her presumed virginity, but gave him great satisfaction, nonetheless. The menu of possibilities seemed to expand every night, some of which were more enjoyable to Charlotte than others, but all of which she found exciting.

She had not bothered to bring the candle from her bedside table. With so few furnishings remained to present obstacles, the house was easily navigated even in darkness. Humming a little tune to herself — the tune from the blue music box, she realized — she moved from room to room, routinely checking the latch on each window. In the kitchen, she tried the door first, and then the window that looked out over the kitchen garden and yard at the back of the house. She tested the latch and tugged on the window to be sure it would not open, glancing out through the wavy glass at the familiar, moonlit scene as she did so. She turned her back on the window, took two steps, and froze.

Slowly, she returned to the window and peered out, dipping her head this way and that in an attempt to look between the bubbles and ripples scattered through the imperfect glass. The shed doors were standing wide open, and should not have been. Because she checked them every afternoon, she knew they were closed — and locked — earlier.

Anna's shovel struck something. What it was, she could not tell for it was far too dark down in the narrow pit she had managed to excavate. Awkward in the confining space, she knelt down and tried to identify the object by touch, but came up with nothing conclusive. It was not rigid like a wooden box, and because the stench of death had become almost overpowering, she thought she might have unearthed whatever animal was buried there. But she could feel cloth, and a great deal of it, and doubted that such would have been wasted on the burial of an animal.

She climbed out of the hole and rooted around the workbench until she turned up a candle. Not daring to try to light it where the light might be seen from the house, she slid back down into the pit and dug about in her pocket for her uncle's small brass tinderbox. She had never been particularly good at striking a flame with the small steel and flint implements in the box, and being down in a dark hole, breathing nauseating odors, and trying to keep the piece of candle balanced until she could light it did not make matters easier. Finally, she managed to ignite the wick. She cradled the candle, protecting the flame until it matured, and then held it close enough to the ground to see what she had unearthed. And, immediately wished she had not done so.

The force of her shovel and extra effort of digging and tugging with her hands had torn away the layers of protecting cloth to reveal a somewhat decomposed, though quite unmistakable, human hand, presumably attached to a body yet to be uncovered. Despite herself, Anna cried out and, dropping the candle, scrambled out of the hole.

Charlotte had hastily grabbed up her cloak and slipped her feet into the clogs she kept near the back door. Quietly, she unlocked and opened the door, then closed it again when another idea struck her. She hurried through the house to the parlor, jerked open a drawer in one of the few remaining tables there, and withdrew a pistol. It was Private Cudahy's pistol – or perhaps Foster's. She couldn't remember which, and it really didn't matter one way or the other, she thought as she shoved the weapon into the pocket of her cloak. She raced again to the back door and let herself out quietly, pausing on the step a moment to see if anything moved before starting across the yard toward the shed.

She walked hurriedly, slowing her approach only as she drew near enough to hear the sound of someone shuffling about in the dirt. There was too little noise, she decided, for there to be more than one trespasser, and the thought emboldened her. Carefully, she drew the pistol from her cloak and primed it for firing, then changed her plan when she spotted the axe lying discarded by the shed door. Why risk arousing the neighbors by discharging a pistol when a silent alternative was at hand?

Without a sound, she picked up the axe and stepped through the open door of the shed just in time to see the candle flicker out and be startled by Anna's choked scream as she came scooting backwards out of the hole, colliding with Charlotte's legs in the process. Charlotte stepped back to keep from being knocked over, allowing Anna just enough time to rotate around and recognize Charlotte standing over her. Anna was still sitting in the dirt, arms braced against the ground behind her, and her mouth fell open as she gaped up at Charlotte.

Charlotte was no less surprised when she recognized Anna. "You! You little *bitch*! I will *not* let you undo everything I've worked so hard for!"

Anna's mind had not quite put everything together, and all she could manage was some stuttering nonsense about the body she had unearthed. It surprised her when, instead of evincing astonishment, Charlotte simply smiled. The smile, which had sprung from the realization that Anna had done Charlotte the favor of digging much of her own grave, spread so slowly across her lips that it gave Anna time to register that there was something far more wrong here than what she had originally supposed. She scuttled backwards along the ground, trying to stand as she moved, but

Charlotte was wasting no time. Raising the axe as high above Anna as the low-ceilinged shed would allow, she swung it downward with all the force she could manage.

Charlotte had never in her life wielded an axe. It looked easy enough, but she was not prepared for the weight of it, had not braced herself against the effect the momentum of that weight would have on her. As the axe went forward in its arc down toward Anna's head, it pulled Charlotte just slightly off balance. It was not much, but it was enough to alter the axe head's trajectory so that, instead of landing a blow that would have cleaved Anna's skull in two, the flat of the blade grazed the side of her head while the slicing edge dug into her shoulder. The cut went deep, though not as deep as it would have had the blade not been stopped by the leg of the wooden workbench behind Anna.

The pain made Anna's head swim. She reached out blindly and grasped the handle, holding it to keep Charlotte from using it again. Dizzy and clumsy, Anna managed to stand just as Charlotte wrenched the axe free and swung again. Anna ducked under the swing and drove her uninjured shoulder into Charlotte's midsection, forcing her backward toward her father's makeshift grave. Charlotte stumbled over the shovel Anna had left on the ground before her last descent into the hole and, cursing furiously all the while, tumbled into the open pit.

Staggering under the pain of the wound in her shoulder, head spinning, Anna made for the door. She cleared the door, and could just see the moon above her, smell the clear honeysuckle-scented air again, when the shot rang out and her leg buckled beneath her. Charlotte had managed to get to her feet in the pit and, bracing the pistol had tried to aim at Anna's head. But the shot went low and caught her in the thigh, instead. As Charlotte climbed out of the hole, she did not take her eyes away from where Anna clawed at the ground as she tried to flee.

When Charlotte reached her, she grasped Anna by one ankle and dragged her back into the shed. "That is my father you uncovered," she said, leaning down to hiss directly into Anna's dirty, bloodied face. "It is a pity you did not know him better because you will be spending a very long time in his company." She picked up the shovel and struck it hard against Anna's head, knocking her unconscious. Then, she set her foot upon Anna's throat, preparing to crush it as she had Private Foster's.

But the sound of a man's voice pulled her up short.

"Charlotte?" Teague's voice, low but insistent, made itself heard.

"*Bloody hell!*" Angrily, she looked down at Anna's still form and made some quick decisions. "You'll die from your wounds soon enough anyway," she whispered as she used one foot to shove Anna toward the pit. Watching as Anna's body, limp as a rag doll slid over the edge she added, "I believe you are dead already." Smiling, she snatched up the pistol and tucked it back in her pocket, then ducked out of the shed just in time to see Teague approaching. It appeared that he had come from inside the house.

She closed the shed doors behind her, cursing softly over the fact that Anna had broken the latch. "What the devil are you doing here?" Praying the doors would remain closed, she turned and walked toward him.

"Me? What the devil are you doing out here?" He looked about the yard, truly baffled by her presence. "I thought I heard a shot."

"We've been having trouble with stray dogs and such getting into the shed and wreaking havoc. I thought I heard one and came out to shoo it away." She walked quickly toward the house.

"Dogs?" He looked back toward the shed uncertainly.

"Yes, dogs," she hissed. "Now come along. I'm getting chilled."

"You shot at a dog? With what? Did you hit it?"

"With this." She pulled the pistol out of her pocket and handed it to him. "And, no, I didn't shoot at a dog. I actually shot at a rat that startled me, but I missed."

He was turning the pistol over in his hands studying it. "Where did you get this?"

"My father left it with me when he went south. I suppose I should have you teach me how to use it," she laughed lightly. "Apparently aiming is a more complicated matter than I supposed." She marched toward the house, leaving him no choice but to follow.

Once they were safely inside the kitchen, Charlotte discarded her cloak and clogs, making him gasp at the realization that she wore only her night shift. "Christ, Charlotte. You're filthy! What happened?" he asked as she lit an oil lamp.

She waved him away with a flick of her hand and reached for the pitcher of water and basin. "When the rat startled me, I stumbled on something and fell, that's all. It's just a little dirt. I'll be fine." As though performing some ritual, she poured water into the basin and dipped her hands in, raising and lowering them so that the water ran down her arms and back into the basin, carrying dirt and Anna's blood with it. The water was cold, and prickled her skin to gooseflesh. "What are you doing back so soon?" She picked up the soap and began lathering her hands and forearms. "You weren't supposed to be back for several weeks, yet."

"You sound disappointed that I've come back early."

"Not disappointed," she lied. "Merely baffled. Did something go awry? Were you not able to sell the muskets?" Her hands stilled, waiting for his response.

"I sold them."

"You could not possibly have gone all the way to the frontier and back in such a short amount of time."

"No, I didn't. I found a buyer for them without having to go so far."

Charlotte rinsed the soap from her hands and arms before responding. "I thought," she said as she picked up a small towel and, drying her hands, turned to face him, "that we agreed you would go all the way to the borderlands so we could get the best price."

"The price I got is sufficient." He gestured toward her dirty shift. "What possessed you to go out in the middle of the night like this?"

"I already told you, I thought I was driving away—"

"Yes, I know — a dog. That's madness, Charlotte! What if it had been a dangerous animal? Or, worse, what if it had been a man?"

"Well, it wasn't." She tossed the towel aside. "So, could we please get back to discussing the money you collected for the muskets?"

"There's your bloody money," he snapped, tossing her a small leather pouch.

Greedily, she opened it, her eyes going wide when she saw the contents. "Oh, Teague! This is wonderful!" The bag was full of silver coins, and she poured several out into her palm. "You did get a good price!" She looked up at him, her eyes glittering with pleasure.

"You seem a lot happier to see the money than you were to see me."

"Oh, for heaven's sake, Teague! Of course I'm glad to see you. How do you expect me to react when you startle me by turning up so suddenly? You seemed to appear out of nowhere." She put her hands on her hips. "You're lucky I had already fired the pistol. Startling me like that — I might easily have shot you by mistake!" It occurred to her that such a chain of events would have actually been quite convenient, and wondered if there were some way she could yet arrange such a scene. But he had the pistol. Besides, she'd already learned that her marksmanship skills left much to be desired, and merely wounding him would not help her situation at all.

"Yes, I suppose you might have." He held the pistol closer to the lamp, examining it carefully. "This is a nice piece," he said. "Where did you say you got it?"

"It's my father's. He left it here when he went to the Carolinas with his friends. He went so suddenly, I find he left several things here he probably would have taken with him had he been able to plan more carefully."

"Including you? Surely he wishes he had taken you."

"So he says in his letters." She smiled tightly. Something in Teague's behavior was sounding alarms in her mind.

"I'm surprised he left you here. He has always been so attached to you, and he seemed to rely on your care."

"He didn't want to leave me, but it was necessary for me to be here to deal with loose ends. I shall join him soon enough."

His eyes narrowed. "Will you, now. And, how does that fit with our plan to be together?"

She shifted uneasily. "It actually fits quite well. With him away, we can be married without worrying about his interference. He can hardly object if he isn't here, can he?"

"So, you do expect us to be married?"

"Of course I do. Isn't that what we've been planning all this time?" She straightened with indignation. "Or, have you been trifling with me?"

"You know I have not," he replied evenly. "It would suit me if we could make arrangements to be married tomorrow. No doubt you have some reason why we cannot?"

Something had made him distrustful, she knew, but what that was she could not fathom. She'd assumed that he had only just returned to Boston, but began to wonder. "No reason aside from the fact that there are certain conventions to consider. You are suddenly impetuous!" she laughed.

"We've been planning this for several years now. I don't consider that to be impetuous. And, given that we knew from the start that your father would never give his consent, I can't see how you could be concerned about any conventions."

"Not concerned," she sighed. "It was meant to be humorous. You are so very serious this evening, Teague!" She stepped closer to him and took his hand.

"It isn't evening. Dawn will break in little more than an hour."

"Very well, then." Her voice lost its admonishing tone and became warm and silky. "You are being very serious this morning."

"It was a long road, and I'm exhausted. I'll be less serious after I've rested, perhaps."

"Of course you are exhausted. And I've offered you nothing." Tugging his hand, she made to lead him toward the parlor. "Come and sit with me a while. Tell me about your journey. I assume you have only just returned?"

"Yes, I've only just returned. I came directly here, but I think that was a mistake. Startling you was not my intent."

"No, it wasn't a mistake. I'm glad you came to me."

"I should go before the sun comes up."

It was the very thing she did not want. She needed to keep him close to her and ignorant until she could devise a way to be rid of him. "If we are to be married within days, you hardly need worry about my reputation," she told him lightly.

When he said nothing, she adopted a new tack. She began to quiver imperceptibly and her eyes filled with tears. "Oh, Teague. I am glad you have come back. Truly I am. And, I'm sorry if I did not appear to be so. Being alone for so long has strained my nerves almost to breaking. Please stay with me tonight." She slipped her arms around him and buried her face in his chest. "I've tried to keep a brave face, but I just cannot. Please, let's be together tonight." The words were almost whispered and were heavy with suggestion.

He basked in the warmth of her body against him and could not resist enjoying the feel of her lithe form through the thin fabric of her shift. When she tilted her head up to receive his kiss, he thought there could never be anything so warm and full of promise. Every nerve, every sinew of his body ached to accept her invitation. But then, he buried his face in her hair — that cloud of pale silk — and his blood went cold. The smell there was faint, but unmistakable. It was the musky smell that, even when brought on by pleasure, never failed to take him back to the unhappy place of his origin. And, this time, the pleasure that had produced that scent was not his own.

"I have to go, Charlotte," he said, his voice ragged and rasping with misery. He pushed away from her. "I have to go."

Before she could object or plead or cajole, he was gone.

*　　*　　*

Anna could not see. The unmistakable smell of death enveloped her and, had it not been for the horrible pain, she would have assumed herself to be the source of that sickening stench. But, as she understood it, there was not supposed to be pain after death, so she held out hope. She gingerly touched her face, carefully feeling the area around her eyes. One side of her face was covered in some sticky substance, but that did not explain why she could not see. She tried to focus her mind, to understand her circumstances, but could not call the picture into focus. Her head throbbed unbearably, her left arm was consumed by a searing sharp pain, and the temptation to retreat back into sleep to escape all of that pain was overwhelming. But some tiny part of her mind told her that she was in danger if she stayed, and so she attempted to move.

Fighting through the pain, she rolled on to her side and, using her good arm, tried to ease herself up to her knees. Immediately, the stench and dizzying pain reached into her stomach, and she vomited. Gagging and gasping, she leaned her weight on her good hand and felt what should have been dirt beneath her, but was not. Images flooded her mind — a hand, a body, a grave — and along with them, the abrupt reminder of where she was. Pain be damned, she had to move. She had to get out of that place.

Using the hand on her uninjured side to push against the walls of the pit, she struggled to her feet — and immediately went back down. The pain from the pistol shot had been temporarily lost amongst the rest, but the moment she tried to stand on it, the leg reminded her. The ball from Charlotte's pistol had ripped into her right calf, and the wound protested mightily against her attempt to test it. There was no choice, however. Gritting her teeth, she struggled to her feet once more and, with a slow, agonizing combination of clawing with one hand and pushing with her good leg, she climbed free.

She allowed herself to lie there for several minutes, panting and hoping the pain would subside at least a little, but it was not to be. Her sight seemed to be improving somewhat, however. Gradually, she began to understand that her lack of eyesight was mostly due to the fact that the shed doors were closed. Thin streaks of pale light shone here and there, and she guessed that the sun must be rising. Stoically accepting the pain as the price of her freedom and safety, she worked her way along the ground toward the work bench. There, she pulled herself to a standing position. Immediately, the little slivers of daylight began to spin and she vomited again.

Using the shovel as an improvised crutch, she hobbled toward the doors. Blessedly, it took no more than a gentle shove to push one open wide enough for her to squeeze through. Dawn was only just stretching its pale, pastel-hued light into the sky, though even that was too much. The soft light stabbed into her eyes with excruciatingly dizzying effect, and she had to fight the urge to wretch yet again. Like someone half-drowned, she gulped lungfuls of fresh air. Each deep breath provoked a new wave of pain, but ridding herself of the shed's stench was worth it. Her ability to see had improved only nominally. Aside from the pain inflicted on her eyes by light, she found that everything was an indistinct blur, a kaleidoscope of wavy shadows and highlights as though she was viewing her surroundings through thick bottle glass.

All in all, she would have preferred to simply lie down where she was and hope someone who was not Charlotte would appear to help her. Even her foggy mind knew the fallacy of that desire, however. Fighting the pain and constant nausea, she made her way along the fence until she located the gate, and then out into the alley. The full weight of her disorientation occurred to her then. She could not remember which direction to turn, or even how to get home once she found her way out of the alley. The immediate imperative being her need to get as far away from Charlotte as possible, however, she simply chose a path and set out.

Though it seemed far longer to Anna, she staggered along the alley for less than a quarter of an hour without finding an outlet. She had lost her crutch somewhere along the way, and was growing progressively weaker with each stumbling step. The sensation of pain seemed less overwhelming, but it was being replaced by a peculiar numbness. Her own heartbeat was loud in her ears, almost to the exclusion of any other sound. The reality around her had become a nightmarish distortion that confounded and confused her at every turn. She leaned against a wall, panting, and realized she was being attacked by yet another fetid smell. It was not the reek of death this time but a somewhat familiar stench borne on salty air. The fens. That fragment of her mind that seemed yet able to function identified it as the fens — the tidal flats where sewage and river and salty sea water mingled. The marshland was not actually nearby, but the sea breezes were carrying the stench inland, and telling her that she was going the wrong way.

Had she possessed the strength, Anna would have sat where she was and cried, for the thought of doubling back along the path on which she had come was overwhelming. What she needed, she thought, was rest. But what if Charlotte discovered she had escaped and decided to pursue her? Using the wooden structure for support, she slid along the wall until it gave way to fence slats, and along the fence until she found a gate. The gate opened easily, and she tumbled through onto the ground, and then used her good leg to nudge the gate closed behind her.

Lying flat on her back, she turned her head to one side, praying that she was within sight of the house and help. All she saw, however, was a low fence surrounding a small animal enclosure that stood between her and the house. Unless one of the house's occupants ventured outside and walked to where she rested, she would not be found. But she could not think about it now. She would worry about getting help after she'd rested, she decided. Sighing at the relief it gave her, she closed her eyes against the light, and drifted away to unconsciousness.

*   *   *

Drum was frantic and afraid, and did not know what to do. Therefore, he decided on the same course of action he invariably took in such situations — he would talk to Daniel. His distress had begun early that morning when Mr. Wilton had visited Mr. Sprague. Though Drum did not immediately know the reason for the visit, he saw Wilton arrive, and could tell that Anna's uncle was in an agitated state. After the two men conferred for a few minutes in Mr. Sprague's study, Drum was summoned. Apparently repeating what he had just told Mr. Sprague, Anna's uncle explained that Anna had gone missing.

Putting together the evidence left behind, Wilton deduced that she had slipped out of the house sometime in the night wearing he could not say what, for the maid had accounted for all of his niece's clothing. She had not returned and Wilton had been unable to locate her. His visit to the constable was fruitless, and the man had angered him with some vague suggestion about elopements and other romantic adventures of young girls. Wilton had sputtered over the preposterousness of the suggestion but, not wanting to discard any possibility, had visited Lieutenant Hinton. Though he expressed genuine concern for Anna, Hinton had seemed distracted and could give Wilton only a few minutes of his time. Finally, unable to think of other options, Wilton had come to his friend for suggestions.

Though he did not voice it, Sprague's first thought was of Daniel. But that young man was still a prisoner of the redcoats, and could not possibly be involved in any sort of escapade. That left Sprague without any helpful suggestions — until he thought of Drum. Knowing that Drum was probably familiar with those people and places in Anna's life that she did not share with her uncle, Sprague suggested that they ask for his help.

Drum was more than willing to help. In fact, he stood listening to Mr. Wilton's recitation of what he knew and what he had already done in terms of searching for Anna, and wished the man would come to the end of it so that he could begin his own search. What neither man fully understood was that, while Drum did have knowledge that might be useful, he was not capable of sorting through and analyzing what he knew in a way that might yield fruitful conclusions. And, because he did not know what was useful and what wasn't, he could not provide them with the information they sought. Numb with worry over Anna's safety, he could only stand there nodding his head until, feeling compelled to some action, he announced that he would find her, turned on his heel, and marched briskly out of the house.

Because Drum dealt best with methodical tasks, he tended to reduce every challenge as much as possible to that form. So, not knowing any other way to go about searching for Anna, he started at the waterfront and diligently worked his way up and down every street and lane in Boston until he had covered them all. When the search did not yield results, he could not think what to do next, which led to his decision to talk to Daniel.

It was late afternoon when Drum presented himself at the door of the house the army had commandeered for use as a detention barracks. There was no guard at the front door, so he let himself in, surprising the two young men on duty. They were eating their supper, and Drum's abrupt intrusion startled them to their feet. Grabbing hats and muskets, they lurched across the room and into Drum's path.

"Hey there," one of them demanded, putting out a hand to stop Drum's progress. He was particularly short, and very young, but full of confidence when he drew himself up in an ineffective effort to match Drum's impressive size. "What do you think you're doing coming in here? Civilians are not allowed without a letter from the Provost Marshal."

Drum frowned, looking from one man to the other. "I need to see Daniel."

"As I said, civilians are not allowed without permission," the short soldier insisted. "No one can see prisoners without the approval of the Marshal or an officer. Do you have that permission?" He glanced at Drum's hands to reassure himself that no official-looking piece of paper was being offered.

"No. But I just need to talk to him for a moment. It won't take long." To Drum's mind, it seemed a perfectly reasonable request and, as it would not place any inconveniencing demand on either of the soldiers, he saw no reason why they should not acquiesce.

The second soldier, who was even younger than the first and suffered from a serious case of razor burn, stepped forward to bolster his colleague's position. "It doesn't matter," the red-faced young man told him. "You can't see the prisoner. Now, you need to turn around and take yourself out of here."

Drum decided that he had not explained his situation well enough. "It's important."

"It can't be any more important than the fact that my food is getting cold," Red Face groused. "Now, off with you."

"But I need to see Daniel." Drum was becoming frustrated and had a sense that valuable time was being wasted.

"What's the matter with you? Can't you understand what we're saying?" Red Face poked at Drum with the barrel of his musket. "Are you weak minded?"

Drum's face flushed with self-consciousness. "Sometimes I can't figure things out, and I need Daniel's help. I need his help now. It's important."

"Enough of that, now," the short man growled. "Take yourself out of here, or we'll lock you up along with your friend."

Though Drum could not understand the recalcitrance of the soldiers, he could understand that getting locked up would be a bad turn of events on many different levels. "I don't want to be locked up," he huffed. "I just want to talk to Daniel." He grasped the musket barrel and jerked the weapon out of Red Face's hands.

Red Face grew redder and gaped in disbelief. Drum seemed to have no intention of turning the weapon on them and, in fact, was dangling the musket down by his legs. The soldiers were taking no chances, however. Simultaneously, they stepped back a pace and Shorty leveled his musket at Drum. Red Face had recovered his wits quickly enough to realize that being disarmed in such fashion, and by a civilian, was likely to bring down a world of trouble and ridicule on his head, so he decided to do something about it. Drawing back his fist, he put all of his strength into swinging at Drum's jaw. The momentum of the attempted blow pulled him in between his fellow soldier and Drum, meaning that Shorty could not fire his musket without risk to Red Face. Shorty bellowed at Red Face for his foolishness, but it was too late.

Drum did not like to fight but had been in enough of them to know how to handle himself when the occasion demanded. Furthermore, he was out of patience with the soldiers' unreasonable obstinacy and was in no mood to waste any more time dealing with them. He dodged the punch, and retaliated with a solid punch of his own to Red Face's midsection, quickly followed by a blow to the man's face that broke his nose and sent him lurching backward.

The turn of events caught Shorty by surprise, and caused him to delay his own response for one critical moment too long. Because it happened to be in his hands, Drum swung the musket upward. There was a loud thwack as it made contact with the side of Shorty's head, and the redcoat crumpled to the floor like a puppet that has had its strings cut. This seemed a very expedient and satisfactory outcome to Drum, so he swung the musket at Red Face's head, and was pleased when he achieved the same result.

Drum stormed through the lower level of the house, then the upper story, in search of Daniel. Finally, he tried the cellar door. It was locked, and he was too agitated to think to look for a key. "Daniel? Are you there?" he called, pounding on the door. Without waiting for an answer, he charged into the door shoulder-first, splintering it from its hinges. In the dim light of a single candle, he saw Daniel sitting on the edge of a cot, blinking up at him in amazement. "I need to talk to you," Drum announced.

"Drum?" Too shocked to move at first, Daniel looked from Drum to the splintered door and back again. "How did you . . . . Never mind. Let's go." Gathering himself, he led Drum down the corridor — only to come to an abrupt halt when he came upon the two redcoats bloodied and sprawled on the floor. "Oh shite. What have you done?"

Drum stood beside Daniel, looking down at the soldiers. "I needed to talk to you," he explained sulkily. "And, they wouldn't let me."

Daniel swore a few choice oaths, and moved to examine the unconscious men. "Are they dead?"

"I don't think so." Drum's brow wrinkled with uncertainty. "I wasn't trying to kill them. But Daniel, I need—"

"No, they're still breathing." Satisfied that the men were merely unconscious, he returned his attention to Drum. "At least the redcoats won't come after you for murder. What the hell were you thinking?"

Drum was beginning to tremble with frustration. "I needed to talk to you," he repeated again, hoping finally to make himself understood. "I think something bad has happened to Miss Anna, and I don't know what to do."

"What do you mean? What has happened to her?"

"No one can find her. Her uncle came to see Mr. Sprague this morning and said she left the house sometime last night, but she never came back. He can't find her, and I told them I would find her, but I can't." He spoke in a rush, becoming more breathless and hurried with each word. "I've hunted everywhere and I don't know where else to look. I'm so afraid something bad has happened to her, Daniel! I can't think and—"

"All right, Drum. It will be all right. We'll figure it out." He maintained a calm exterior for Drum's sake, but his insides were roiling with worry. "We can't stay here and wait for more redcoats to show up, though. Let's get away from here and then we'll figure out what to do. Yes?" He laid his hand on Drum's shoulder and looked him square in the eye, reassuring him.

Once he sensed that his friend was steadier, he patted him on the arm and busied himself about preparing for their flight. "Find his musket," he instructed Drum, pointing to where Red Face lay, his head resting against the wall as though he'd sat down for a quick nap. "And take his cartridge box. I'll get this one." He bent over Shorty and loosened the belt holding his cartridge box. Blood was running freely from the soldier's obviously broken nose. "Poor bugger. You'll be feeling that for a while." Daniel almost felt sorry for him. Almost. Once he had the cartridge box in hand, he rolled Shorty over onto his stomach to ensure that the poor fellow would not drown in his own blood, then snatched up his musket.

"Got them?"

Drum held up the musket and cartridge box in response.

"Good." He jerked his head toward the back of the house. "Let's go out the back way, shall we?" They moved quickly toward the door. Daniel peeked out of all the rear-facing windows checking for guards, but there were none. "Once we're out the door, we'll need to move quickly. Straight into that little lane across the way, then duck into the first place we can get out of sight. Ready?" When Drum nodded, Daniel opened the door and the two of them sprinted across the road and into the shadows without anyone catching so much as a glimpse of them.

Once they were well clear and Daniel felt reasonably safe, he hopped a low fence and, with Drum close on his heels, slipped inside a hay-filled goat shed. He took the musket and cartridge box from Drum, and sat him down on a bale of hay. "Now," he said, sitting opposite him, "tell me again about the trouble Mouse has got herself into this time."

CHAPTER TWENTY-TWO

Charlotte wished there was more room in her heart for the hatred she was feeling toward Anna at this moment. But her heart — indeed, every organ she could name — was already so full of hate that not even the tiniest bit more could be added. And Teague. Teague was part of her trouble as well, though Charlotte could not quite bring herself to hate him. He had become an inconvenience, a hindrance to her plans and obstacle to her happiness, but she did not hate him. She would need to dispose of him, nonetheless. First she had to find Anna and *finish* disposing of her, however, hopefully before Anna could tell anyone what she had seen in the shed.

The sun had risen that morning to reveal that the girl Charlotte thought well dead only a few hours earlier, had up and left — and was nowhere to be found. The first order of business was to put the dirt back in the hole Anna had excavated. Charlotte could not risk someone stumbling upon her father's grave and so that took primary importance. When she first buried her father, the chore had not been accompanied by the stomach-turning stench. This time, the job was almost unbearable, and she added it to her list of grievances against Anna. She hastily refilled the hole and put the flooring slats back in place sufficiently to prevent discovery.

Now she turned her attention to finding Anna. She started with the alley because it seemed the most likely place the troublesome little pest would have gone. Charlotte disliked the alley. She guessed she'd been in it two or three times at most in her entire life. Little more than a narrow passage between the yards and buildings on either side, it served as a conduit for runoff rainwater and a corridor for the ragmen and junk collectors and other less-desirables who plied their trades with household servants along its way. It was constantly damp, full of rank smells and, owing to the high fences most households had erected around their yards, somewhat dark even on the sunniest days.

Assuming that Anna would have headed back toward her uncle's house, Charlotte explored that path, searching every possible hiding place she could find. If she could not see through fences, she carefully opened gates to peer into yards. She dearly hoped none of the neighbors caught her poking around, for she was not sure how she would explain her actions should it become necessary. But diligent as her search was, it yielded nothing.

She doubled back and repeated the process in the opposite direction, though with less enthusiasm because there was no logical reason that Anna would have come this way. Her heart began to sink with the realization that Anna may have reached home and told her tale to John Wilton. A group of young boys came toward her, their voices loud as they engaged in a boisterous game involving knocking a bladder ball along the ground between them with sticks. Charlotte, promptly deciding it was time to abandon her search, tugged the hood of her cloak down over her face and ducked quickly back through her own gate before she could be spotted. But it would not have mattered. Far more interested in their game, they would have paid her no more heed than if she'd been any of the random boxes or other obstacles scattered here and there along the alley.

The boys continued on their way, laughing and shouting good-natured derision at anyone who missed the ball when his turn came to take a swing. A discarded shovel tripped one of the boys, who cursed roundly. Another boy, laughing at his friend's misfortune, picked up the shovel with the intent of carrying it off. It was well made, probably expensive, and he couldn't understand why anyone would have abandoned such a fine tool. His friends argued him out of his plan, however, pointing out that the owner would surely return for it. With a shrug, the boy tossed the shovel away, hardly noticing as it clattered along the cobbles before coming to rest in the center of the alley.

Farther along, when the game's intensity had been recaptured, one of the boys was shoved against a wooden wall. His shirt snagged on a nail, and a scrap of cloth was torn away. He wailed a protest against the boy he thought had pushed him, complaining of the boxing his ears were going to take when his mother saw the damage to his shirt. And on it went, until the group of boys reached the end of the alley, and left it to its former empty silence.

*   *   *

Drum finished his tale, repeating everything Mr. Wilton and Mr. Sprague had told him, and recounting all of the places he had looked for Anna. But he was getting restless. He felt they were spending too much time talking when they should be out looking for her. He'd expected that Daniel would immediately know where they should look but, so far, Daniel was not proving to be much help.

"Just tell me again what she has been doing lately," Daniel urged. Drum had stayed at Anna's side as much as possible in recent weeks, of that Daniel was aware. Knowing how Anna's mind worked and how she launched upon adventures, he thought there had to be something amongst the things she had said to Drum that might prove useful. "Tell me what she has been talking about."

"All she has talked about for three days is trying to get someone to listen to my story about the egg." He had told Daniel about her excitement when he shared the secret regarding the blue egg. "She was just sure it would prove that Teague has been doing the stealing. She said if they believed he'd been doing the stealing, they might believe he had killed those men. She called it 'evidence,' and said we needed to find more of it."

"Wait. Say that again. You didn't tell me that part before."

Drum shrugged. "I didn't think it was important. What does it have to do with where she might have gone?"

"Possibly, quite a lot. Now, tell me again. What was she saying to you about getting more evidence."

"Well, she thought Teague might have given Miss Ainsworth some of the other things he had stolen. Other things besides the egg, I mean. Miss Anna wanted the redcoats to go and talk to Miss Ainsworth, but they wouldn't listen to us and Miss Anna was afraid Miss Ainsworth would leave before the redcoats got around to going to see her."

"Why did she think Miss Ainsworth might leave?"

"Because Miss Anna's redcoat — I mean, that lieutenant — the one who calls on her all the time?"

"Yes, I know who you mean," Daniel assured him irritably.

"Well, he told Miss Anna that Miss Ainsworth was supposed to marry some other officer and go off to England."

Daniel sat bolt upright. "Are you certain about that?"

Drum nodded. "But what does this have to do with—"

"Is there anything else, Drum? Anything else you talked about that doesn't seem important to you? Anything about Miss Ainsworth?"

"Well, I did tell Miss Anna about the hole Miss Ainsworth paid me to dig."

"A hole?"

He nodded. "A big hole. Under the floor of Mr. Ainsworth's shed. It was supposed to be a secret. Miss Ainsworth made me promise not even to tell you or Teague. She said it was because her father wanted to hide his important things from the redcoats. But he went away with some friends so he could get well, so I don't think he ever—"

"Never mind," Daniel said, getting quickly to his feet. "I believe I know where we need to start looking for Miss Anna. No doubt, she thought she would find the evidence she was looking for buried in that hole, so that's where we need to start. In the Ainsworth's shed."

*   *   *

Anna had not returned to her uncle's house. Charlotte was happy to have finally confirmed that fact, though she was irritated that it had taken so long to do so. After her labors in the shed that morning, she'd had to clean up and make herself presentable so that she could appear in public. Then, she'd walked briskly to John Wilton's house and planted herself in a spot suitable for watching the house without being seen. Once she felt confident that no one was at home except for the cook and the maid, she dared to present herself at the door to inquire whether she might call on Miss Somerset.

Doubting that the maid would know who she was, Charlotte had given a false name.   The effort was rewarded with the information that Miss Somerset was not at home and, no, the maid did not know where she could be found.   Furthermore, the few bits of information Charlotte was able to wheedle out of the girl convinced Charlotte that Anna's foray into the Ainsworth's shed had been a secret from her uncle, and that the household was distraught because Anna's whereabouts was unknown.

All of that had taken far more time than Charlotte would have liked. She still had Teague to deal with, and myriad other details that needed addressing before her marriage and departure from Boston.   Once again, she railed inwardly at Anna for causing so much trouble.   But worst of all, she still did not have Anna in hand, and time was running out.   Even if she found the little menace, she was not certain of her next move.   That bridge would be crossed when necessary.   For now, the primary imperative was finding her.   She walked slowly, turning the matter over in her mind, and felt almost divinely inspired when it occurred to her that Mrs. Garrett's shop was closer to the Ainsworth house than was the Wilton house.   It seemed unlikely that Anna would have gone there, but not impossible. Putting more purpose in her step, Charlotte set a course for Healey's Millinery.

*   *   *

Using many of the same little-traveled lanes and back alleys Anna had followed, Daniel and Drum made their way across Boston to the Ainsworth house without being seen by anyone who would know enough to question the fact that Daniel was roaming about, a free man.   As they neared the house, Daniel chose an approach that offered as much concealment as possible.   He had no idea who might be in the house, and felt fairly confident that none of the possibilities would offer him a friendly welcome. The house had all the earmarks of emptiness but, nonetheless, Daniel decided to send Drum up to knock at the door.   If someone answered, Drum was to claim that he had left his hat in the shed the last time he'd been there, and ask permission to go and retrieve it.

No one answered when he knocked at the front or back door, however. Cautiously, Daniel scouted the entire perimeter of the house, peering in windows, listening for the sound of voices, and finding nothing.   Quietly, he tried the handle on the back door, and found it locked.   If their search of the shed yielded no clues, he would find a way into the house, but decided to leave it for the time being.   Waving Drum to follow, he crossed the yard to the shed.   He stood staring at the closed doors, half-afraid to open them.

"I wonder who broke the latch?" Drum asked.

"What?" Daniel was studying the ground in front of the doors and had not noticed the dangling metal latch.

"I put a new latch on for Miss Ainsworth when I was working on the hole. She particularly asked me for one with a lock. It was a new latch, and now it's broken."

"I don't know who broke it," Daniel said, "but it will make our job easier." He stepped around the patch of ground that had aroused his interest and pulled the doors open. They were immediately assailed by a stench so powerful that it drove Daniel several paces backward. "Damnation!" He buried his nose and mouth in the crook of his elbow. "What the hell *is* that?"

Drum tugged the collar of his jacket up over his nose. "I don't know. It wasn't like that before."

Reluctantly, they peered into the dark shed. The initial shock was subsiding but the effect of the foul air was still powerful enough to cause Daniel to take out his handkerchief and tie it so it covered his mouth and nose. Drum copied the tactic, but did not think it was really helping all that much. His eyes were beginning to water. "There," he said, pointing to the pile of manure in the corner. "That must be what's causing the smell. Why would the Ainsworth's store manure *inside* the shed?"

"I don't know. And I don't think that's all we're smelling. I think there's something else here." He kicked at the boards that seemed to have been hastily arranged to form a floor. The ground underneath them had not been smoothed so that the planks were uneven. "Did you do this?"

Drum shook his head. "Last time I was here, there was just a big empty hole with all the dirt piled around it. That's how Miss Ainsworth wanted me to leave it."

Daniel shifted a few of the planks out of the way and squatted down to examine the ground. Nothing was as smooth or hard-packed as it should have been, and one area was particularly raised as though most of the dirt had been piled there at some point. He stood, brushing loose soil from his hands, and looked around the shed. "Looks like some of the small tools are missing." He indicated the empty pegs above the workbench.

"Yes," Drum agreed. "And there used to be two shovels, not just one." He picked up the axe, which was left propped against the workbench, and examined the blade. "I always kept this clean." His tone was disapproving. "Someone has made a mess of it. And, it's a good axe, too!"

Daniel took the axe from him and stepped out into the early evening light to look at it more carefully. Dirt was thickly crusted on the blade's cutting edge. "It looks like the blade was wet when it was set down in the dirt." Returning to the shed, he returned the axe to the place where they'd found it and, in the process, spotted a cut in the leg of the workbench. The wood around the cut was weathered. But inside the cut, the wood was still raw. "This hasn't been here long," he said, probing at the splintered nick with his finger.

Drum was once more growing restless with the sense of wasted time and, besides, he dearly wanted to get out of the shed and away from the horrendous odor. "But Miss Anna isn't here," he pointed out. "We need to look somewhere else. Do you think she could be in the house?"

"I doubt it," Daniel said. "Though we may check just to be sure." His attention was on the floor of the shed. Something was buried there, and he doubted it was Mr. Ainsworth's valuables. "Let's go back out in the yard," he said. "There's something I want to look at more closely."

He returned to the patch of ground that had caught his eye on the way into the shed. Kneeling, he leaned down and peered closely at what he'd at first thought was wet soil, a place that looked as if someone had spilled a bit of water from the pail on their way from the well. But it was not wet he discovered when he touched it. Instead, the darkened area seemed to be the result of staining. It looked very much like ground on which a wounded animal had lain. The thought made him shiver.

Casting his net wider, he began to study the surrounding ground, looking at it from every angle until patterns began to emerge. The well-trodden paths between the shed and the house, or between the shed and the kitchen garden were easy enough to pick out. What he sought, though, was the unusual, and it took several minutes for that to present itself. "Here!" He jumped up, startling Drum, and walked briskly to another place in the dirt that had caught his eye. "Look here. You can see where someone walked here, but the steps are irregular and there is something mixed in among them. Long straight marks here and here. Do you see?"

Drum nodded. He had no idea what it meant, though he could indeed see the trail when Daniel pointed it out to him. There were places where the dirt was soft enough to register a foot print, and the print that was part of this trail was small. He walked along behind Daniel as he followed the indefinite signs that seemed to mark an uneven progress away from the shed. When they came to the gate, even Drum could not overlook the smudge on the gatepost. He turned a worried, questioning look upon Daniel, who shrugged. It could be blood, but it could be other things as well.

They stepped out into the alley and Drum instinctively turned in the direction that would have taken them uphill toward John Wilton's house. Daniel stopped him, pointing in the opposite direction toward something lying across the drainage culvert that formed the alley's spine. A shovel. "You said there's a shovel missing from the shed?"

Drum nodded, and followed Daniel along the alley.

Daniel reached the shovel first and snatched it up for Drum to inspect. "Does it look familiar?"

Drum had only to glance at it before nodding his head. He recognized it; he'd held it in his hands often enough. "Though," he added forlornly, "these stains weren't on it before."

That the stains on the shovel's handle were blood, Daniel had no doubt. How they had come to be there, he could only guess. As to his next move, that was a guess as well. He anxiously looked around the alley, pacing one direction and then the other, searching for another clue. But there was nothing. He widened the circle of his search, and then twice had to widen it further before his diligence paid off. A bit of light-colored cloth that had snagged on the back wall of what appeared to be a goat shed caught his attention like a signal flag. Daniel pounced on it hopefully, and was disappointed when he could not identify it as having come from something belonging to Anna.

He pulled the piece of fabric free of the nail it had caught on and stuffed it in his pocket. There were a lot of nails sticking out of the wall, he noticed, studding it like barnacles on a ship's hull. He would not have noticed any of it had the piece of cloth not attracted his attention, for the sun was beginning to set, casting long purple shadows that obscured much. He was on the verge of moving their search farther up the alley when Drum, standing a few paces away, caught his eye. The way Drum was standing — so still, his head cocked to one side as though he was trying to solve a puzzle — made Daniel hesitate.

"What is it?" He walked toward where Drum stood staring as though he was afraid to verbalize what he was seeing. Instead, he raised his hand and pointed at something on the wall. In the shadows, it was invisible from Daniel's previous position. Here beside Drum, however, he could make out a dark stain on the rough, unfinished wood.

"It looks a lot like blood," Drum observed glumly.

There was a large blotch, and then a trail of stains that spread like haphazard brush strokes along the wall. The two of them followed the trail, slowly at first, then more hurriedly. It came to an end at the gate where there was a distinct handprint on the gatepost, and more blood on the latch, which was unlocked. The gate was closed, though not tightly enough to engage the latch. Daniel pushed on the gate, but it would only open a few inches — not even wide enough to see what was blocking it. Handing his musket off to Drum, he pulled himself up on the high fence and peered over, swore mightily and, telling Drum to stay put for a moment, heaved himself up to the top of the fence to drop lightly down into the yard on the other side.

Drum could hear Daniel's voice coming from the other side of the gate. He could not make out the words, but the tone was alarming. Finally, after what seemed a very long time, Daniel pulled the gate open from the inside. Drum stepped through and gasped at the sight of Anna's body on the ground, so battered and bloodied he hardly recognized her. She lay limp, eyes closed, her skin ashen as a dove's feathers. He stood there, not knowing what to think or do, a look of abject horror on his face.

"She's alive, Drum," Daniel said reassuringly. "But only just. We've got to get her some help, and quickly." He had tried to determine the extent of her wounds but there was so much blood that he could not manage a good assessment.

"Who did this to her?" Drum asked.

"I don't know for sure." There was a sick feeling in the pit of his stomach. *Could Teague have done this?* "We'll figure that out later. We need to get help for her."

"Should we take her to Dr. Warren?"

"No. I thought of that, but he's up in Cambridge. I can't think of another doctor close by. Let's take her to my mother. She'll know what to do for her until we can find a doctor."

"Shouldn't we take her to Mr. Wilton?"

"My mother's place is closer. Besides," he added as he gathered Anna into his arms. "If an escaped accused murderer shows up on his doorstep with his half-dead niece, he might not wait for explanations before he does something rash."

"I can carry her," Drum offered.

But Daniel shook his head. "I want to." When he lifted her, Anna's head fell back to expose her soft white throat and the fragile pulse that flickered there. He had the uncanny sense that the fluttering pulse would escape, like a butterfly, carrying her life with it, so he shifted her in his arms until her head rested on his shoulder. They moved quickly through the fading light, recklessly ignoring any possibility of watchful eyes.

"Come along, Mouse," Daniel said softly, his lips close to her ear. "We'll get you help, and you'll be fine. Just hang on, please?" He kept up the constant stream of cajoling, pleading, urging — whatever he could think of to keep talking to her. Whether or not she could hear him was irrelevant; it seemed important to keep talking. He was more afraid than he could recall ever having been, and talking to her was the only thing that was holding him together.

*　　*　　*

Charlotte was in sight of Selah's Kilby Street shop when Teague caught up with her. Had she seen him approaching, she would have ducked into a convenient doorway to avoid him, but he had come from behind, as though he'd been stalking her for some time. Before she knew he was there, he caught her by the arm and fell into step beside her.

"What are you up to?" he asked through gritted teeth. To any passerby, it appeared that they were walking together quite congenially, but Teague was in fact gripping her with uncomfortable firmness and leading her, against her will, in the direction he wanted her to go.

"I am completing errands," she replied stiffly. "Though, I fail to see why I am under obligation to account to you for my actions." She tried in vain to pull her arm free from his grasp.

Teague steered her across the road and down a narrow lane that passed between buildings three shops away from Selah's. The lane emerged onto a narrow road that was hardly more than a cart path paralleling Kilby Street. The isolation worried her and she glanced up and down the dark lane in search of someone to summon if help became necessary. The lane was deserted, however, except for two men at the far end, too far away to be useful.

"Where are you taking me?"

"To your father's house. We need to talk."

As he turned her southward, Charlotte glanced back in the direction of the two men but immediately discarded them as a possible source of rescue. Resignedly, she fell into step beside Teague, her mind busily calculating. Teague's unexpected appearance would require quick alteration to her plans. "You are being tedious," she said. "There's no need for your rough handling of me. I'm perfectly willing to have you accompany me back to my father's house."

"Are you?"

"Of course!" She laughed brightly. "Why ever would I not be? Really, I can't understand what has changed in you."

"A great deal," he growled. "An enormous dose of reality, bolstered by all I learned in the few hours I've been back in Boston."

"I cannot imagine what you refer to," she sniffed. "I'm confident we will be able to straighten everything out, however. Now, do please let go of my arm. You will leave a bruise."

"You'll be lucky if that's all I leave before we're done."

"How ominous you sound." She managed a light tone while, in fact, was made uneasy by his words. "Whatever you think you have *learned* it clearly is not truth for I assure you nothing has transpired that should cause you so much distress. I've our money all tucked safely away, and—"

He interrupted her with laughter. "I am entertained to hear you refer to it as *our* money."

"Well, of course it's our money. Am I to assume that something has given you other ideas? I don't suppose you intend to take it all for yourself, do you?" She coupled her indignation with what she considered a convincing amount of innocence.

Without responding, Teague kept walking, pulling her along with ever increasing urgency.

"Teague! Stop this foolishness! Tell me what has upset you."

"I will. But not here. Keep quiet until we get to the house. I don't want to listen to you anymore."

"Well, if you are unwilling to listen to me, I fail to see how I can defend myself against any false—"

"Enough." He gave her arm a rough jerk, shaking her into silence. "I said keep quiet. And walk."

Through surreptitious glances and stolen sidelong looks, she watched Teague, gauging his mood, weighing his state of mind. That he was angry was perfectly plain. What was less certain was whether or not he still fancied himself in love with her. That, she knew, was the best hope she had for managing him or, at least for buying the time she needed to deal with him.

*   *   *

By the time he arrived at the back door to his mother's shop, Daniel's arms were beginning to ache under the burden of carrying Anna. Small though she was, her dead weight was becoming too much for him. Yet, he would not relinquish her to Drum. All of the downstairs lamps were extinguished for the night, the windows dark. They made a noisy business of entering through the back door, bringing Selah hurrying down the stairs clutching a wrapper tightly about her with one hand, and wearing a fearful expression on her face.

Selah was on the verge of exclaiming over Daniel's unexplained freedom when she laid eyes on the bundle in his arms. "Dear Lord," she breathed, and swept across the room toward them.

"I'm sorry," Daniel said. "She needs help badly, and this was the closest place."

"Never mind." Selah waved away his explanations and pointed toward the stairs. "Take her up to your room. The bed has been made up with clean linens."

She followed them up the narrow stairs and, as soon as Daniel had laid Anna upon the mattress, shooed him out of the way so that she could take a quick inventory of Anna's condition. *So much blood,* she thought as she peeled back layers of blood-soaked clothing. *Too much blood.* "We need a doctor," she told them. Her wide eyes and expression of alarm banished any notions Daniel might have had about arguing the point. "Dr. Hawkins is closest. You go, Drum. Hawkins is a Loyalist, so it may be better if Daniel doesn't go to him."

"Go," Daniel told Drum. "If you hurry, you can be there in ten minutes. Keep out of sight as much as possible. We don't know whether or not the two guards have come 'round and told the rest of the redcoats what happened. They may be out looking for you as well as me."

"After you bring Dr. Hawkins here," Selah told Drum, "go to Mr. Wilton. Tell him what has happened and bring him here." They heard

Drum's heavy footfalls as he clamored down the wooded stairs, and Selah turned her attention back to Anna. "Go down and swing the kettle over the fire, Daniel. It should still be warm and won't take long to boil. Fill that big copper pot with water, too, and set it to heat. When the kettle boils, bring it and a pan and some of the clean linen strips I use whenever you need mending. Hurry now!"

Daniel did as instructed, working as quickly as he could, trying to keep at bay his worries over Drum's safety and Anna's survival. But it wasn't easy. *I should have gone and let Drum stay here.* He set the water to boil and located the box of rolled linen strips. Though she had not asked for them, he grabbed up the pouch of needles his mother always used for suturing his wounds, and the herbs she most often used on him. It was wishful thinking, he knew. Anna was beyond these things.

The kettle had not yet boiled, so he dashed up the stairs with the linen strips and other supplies, but pulled up short the moment he stepped into the room. His mother had undressed Anna down to her undergarments, revealing the frailness of her body and full horror of her injuries.

"Stop gaping," Selah barked, quickly drawing the sheet up to hide Anna's semi-nude body. She took the boxes from Daniel's hand and laid them on the bedside table. "Go back for the hot water."

Daniel nodded, but did not move and did not take his eyes away from Anna.

Selah saw him swallow hard against the lump that was forming in his throat. "Daniel," she said more gently. "Go and fetch the hot water."

Struggling against all that had rooted him to that spot, he turned and scuttled back down the stairs. It seemed that no kettle in existence had ever taken as long to boil as the one he sat watching in his mother's kitchen. When, finally, he could hear the tell-tale gurgle of water roiling inside the copper container, he snatched up a rag to wrap around the hot handle and lifted the kettle off its hook. In his other hand, he picked up the pan Selah had requested, and sprinted up the stairs.

Without a word, Selah took the kettle and pan from him. He watched her pour part of the water out into the pan and set the kettle aside. She had torn some of the clean linen strips into pieces and these she dipped in the hot water before using them to clean away the blood and grime that caked Anna's face and body. She rinsed the rag frequently, turning the water first pink and then dark brown. "Empty that," she told Daniel, nodding toward the pan.

Daniel opened the window and, without checking to see whether or not anyone was on the street below, tossed the fouled water away. He put the pan back in its place and refilled it for Selah, then stepped back to watch her continue the process of bathing Anna. If Anna felt any of it, or was aware of their presence, she gave no sign. His thoughts drifted again to

Drum. *Where is he? Why is it taking so long? What if the redcoats have arrested him?* A part of him insisted that he go after Drum. But he could not move, could not take his eyes away from Anna.

His mother's voice intruded on his thoughts, and he realized that she'd been trying to get his attention for some moments. Quickly dashing his sleeve across his face, he responded to her. "I apologize," he said, his voice oddly distant in his own ears. "My thoughts were elsewhere. What did you say?"

She crossed the room to stand in front of him, blocking his view of Anna. "I said that you need to go," she told him. "You cannot be here when either Dr. Hawkins or Mr. Wilton arrive."

"I don't care if they turn me in."

"No? Well, I do."

"It may go easier on Drum if I turn myself over to them, explain what happened and how Drum's mind works."

"I am not so certain," she said. "At any rate, I'm unwilling to risk the possibility that they might not give you the chance to explain anything. Please go, Daniel. Please get as far away from here as you can." Her voice was ragged with heartbreak.

Slowly, he nodded. "I'll go," he agreed. "I'll find Dr. Warren. He'll know what I should do."

"Good, then. Take some food and whatever else you might need, but do it quickly. Drum should be here any moment with Dr. Hawkins."

He turned and took two steps toward the door but checked up. Without looking at her, he reached out and grasped her hand, too tightly at first, then let his grip relax slightly. "I am sorry," he said simply. When she did not respond, he turned his face back to her, meeting her eyes. "For everything. For being such a poor example of a son. Mostly, for wasting so much time." He looked down at her hand, pale and graceful in his harder, calloused one. "I've spent so many years being angry. I was angry because father died, and angry because you moved us here, and—"

She cut him off with the tips of her fingers against his lips. "It doesn't matter now, my son. I've always known, and it doesn't matter. Just keep yourself safe. Do that for me, please?"

He forced a grin. "I'll do my best," he told her. "But you know how trouble just seems to find me."

"Yes, I know," she laughed, thinking it might choke her. "You are so much like your father. Please, whatever trouble finds you, come back home — and come back home in one piece. Yes?"

He nodded, and was gone.

*   *   *

Darkness had made a complete descent by the time Charlotte and Teague reached the Ainsworth house. Teague strode past her into the parlor, leaving her to unhurriedly remove her cloak and hang it on a peg by the door. Displaying absolute imperturbability, she smoothed her hair as she entered the room, and calmly took up a taper to light the oil lamps. Teague stood in the middle of the room, fidgeting impatiently as he watched, yet making no effort to hurry her.

"You could do something about the fire," she pointed out. "There's a chill in the air, I think."

He glowered at her but, reluctantly, hefted the curfew away from the front of the banked fire and then used the blowing tube to bring it back to life.

"Shall I make us some tea?" She finished lighting the lamps and blew gently on the taper to extinguish it.

"I don't want any damned tea!"

"Suit yourself." With an indifferent shrug, she seated herself on the best of the chairs in the room. She plucked at the folds of her skirt, lifting and resettling them until everything was as she wanted, and gracefully laid her hands in her lap. "Now," she said, clearing her throat and raising her face to, at last, give him her undivided attention, "What is it that has you in such a stir?"

"I understand that you are to be married soon," he snarled, angrily thrusting the poker back into its rack to one side of the hearth.

"Well, yes," she laughed. "Of course I'm to be married soon! To you. Or, so I believed." There was a slight note of question in her last words.

"Is that what you believe? Because, I've been hearing a far different story." He was beginning to pace, pausing now and then to shoot dagger-eyed stares at her. "What I hear is that you are planning to marry Chastain."

"Am I?" She laughed again, and demonstrated marked surprise. "And, who has told you this tale?"

"Apparently, it's known in a number of the shops. Some of the redcoats have talked about it."

"Have gossiped about it, you mean. I did not think you one to listen to gossip."

"I believe it's more than that."

"Do you indeed? I'm not certain which I find more offensive. That my private life has apparently become a subject of distorted gossip is quite disturbing. To know that the man who professes love for me would listen to and believe such nonsense is beyond disturbing."

"I listened," he hissed, "because the source of the information is Chastain, himself."

"If that's true, then Lieutenant Chastain is indulging in falsehoods. He wants there to be an understanding between us, but that does not make it a fact."

"Why would he want it to be true unless you'd given him some reason? I told you to stay away from him."

"And I told you that keeping company with Lieutenant Chastain is useful. He shares information with me that matters to us."

Teague snorted derisively. "What sort of information could he be whispering in your ear that would matter to me?"

"For one thing," she retorted imperiously, "he has shared confidences regarding the status of his investigation into the theft of General Gage's property. I would think that would matter to you a great deal."

"What has he shared with you on that score?" He stopped pacing and narrowed his eyes at her.

Charlotte shrugged and feigned interest in the lace on her sleeve. "It's of little consequence now. He believes they have found their culprit."

"Which brings me to the day's second revelation. Did you know that Daniel has been locked up? That they think he killed two redcoats and is probably responsible for the thefts?"

"Yes. I'm aware of that. Plainly, he did not commit the thefts, though that is small stuff when held against the murder charge. I'd say his innocence regarding the thefts is irrelevant."

"I suppose your friend Chastain has told you why they believe Daniel committed the murders?"

"He has. But it wasn't necessary. It's known that the bodies were found at his family's abandoned farm."

"Daniel didn't murder those men."

"No?" She leaned back in her chair, laughing. "All of the evidence would indicate otherwise."

"He did not murder them, and you know it."

"I know no such thing. What I do know, besides the location of the bodies, is that Daniel Garrett is fully capable of having killed them. You cannot tell me you don't agree with that."

"He may be capable, but he's not a murderer."

"He hates the Regulars." She waved her hand dismissively. "Everyone knows that well enough. And, I understand that he was seen leaving the property at about the time the two men went missing."

"It's his family's property. He has a right to be out there."

"Yes, he does. As you and I both know, however, he rarely does go there. You once used that to your advantage, if memory serves."

Teague shifted his shoulders uncomfortably under the onerous memory of Daniel's anger over his use of the farmhouse to hide stolen munitions. He remembered, too, that the use of the Garrett house was her suggestion. "Daniel did not kill them," he snarled.

"Very well, then, believe what you want. I understand that Mr. Sprague and Mr. Wilton have gone to great lengths to delay proceedings and ensure a fair trial so, if you are correct in your belief, you should have nothing to concern you." A hint of disappointment crept into her voice despite her effort to keep it hidden. "At any rate, I see no point in arguing about it. And, I see no reason why you should be cross with me over the matter."

"Don't you?"

"This is becoming tedious, Teague. I feel as though I am in the witness box being cross-examined by some dreadful lawyer! I do wish you would stop it and talk to me with the civility that has been our custom."

"You would let him hang for something he did not do, wouldn't you?" He said it quietly, sadly almost.

"Honestly Teague. It's becoming impossible to follow your conversation. To what are you now referring? Daniel, I assume? If so, I'd remind you that I've no control over his fate."

He stood still, staring at her for several moments, and then, as though he had reached some decision, crossed to the sideboard and picked up the decanter of port. It surprised him that Martin Ainsworth had not taken the excellent — and, undoubtedly, expensive — port with him. But, considering it his first stroke of good luck for the day, Teague pulled the stopper from the decanter and poured a generous measure of the dark liquid into a glass. He held it up to admire the effect of the light passing through the cut glass and ruby-colored wine. Finally, he took a long, deep swallow before turning back to face Charlotte. With slowness born of reluctance, he drew the pistol from his belt and laid it on the table in front of her. "This is the pistol you gave me last night. Where did you get it?"

"I told you, my father—"

"No more about your father!" He slammed the glass of port down beside the pistol, splashing the wine across the dark wood of the tabletop. "You did not get this from your father!"

"I did."

"Christ, Charlotte!" Roughly, he moved a spindle-backed chair to a position opposite her and dropped wearily onto the hard wooden seat. He reached out and dragged the glass of port across the table toward him, trailing blood-red port along its path. "The two Regulars who were killed were my inside men — my partners. Their names were Cudahy and Foster." He waited for a reaction from her, but she sat still, her expression absolutely unreadable as she watched him. "Mostly, they helped me steal munitions, though they helped with other jobs as well. A few months back, we committed a fine bit of highway robbery that netted, among other things, a matched pair of pistols. They were particularly fine weapons, and Cudahy and Foster decided to take them as their share of our booty. The pistols were unmistakable in that they both had a set of initials carved at the base of the handle." He turned the pistol around so that the butt-end faced her and pointed to where a small set of initials was carved under the handle's curve. "I recognized it the moment you handed it to me."

She shrugged. "I fail to see what any of this has to do with me. For all I know, my father purchased the pistol from one of them."

"No, Charlotte, he didn't. You know he didn't, and I know he didn't, and I want you to tell me how this came to be in your possession. I want you to tell me what happened."

If anything he had said concerned her, she did not show it, but sat in silence, still as death, watching him.

Her placidity enraged him. "Tell me what I want to know!" He sprang from his chair and, grasping the arms of the chair in which she sat, leaned down and bellowed in her face. "Tell me!" His face was almost as dark red as the port. Veins stood out in his neck and forehead, and he trembled with the desire to strike her.

Not even an eyelash fluttered as she responded. "Very well," she said, her voice soft and emotionless. "Sit down. I shall tell you what you want to know."

He hung there for a moment, blinking in surprise at her response, and then regained his seat.

She waited until he was settled, and watched as he took another swallow of the port. One corner of her mouth lifted in the suggestion of a smile, the only outward indication that she was at all engaged in their conversation. "They came here," she stated flatly. "Your partners. They came here looking for you. Or, more precisely, they came here looking for the money you cheated them of."

Teague waved away her scorn. He glanced at the fire, expecting to see that it had grown too large, for the room seemed suddenly over-warm. There was nothing unusual about the fire, however. "Go on," he urged. "They came here looking for the money. Did they find it?"

"No, obviously not. But they made themselves horribly unpleasant in the process of looking." She eyed him narrowly. "Are you unwell? You look as though you've been dipped in candlewax and are beginning to melt."

"I'm fine." He tugged at his collar, which seemed unusually tight. "It's warm in here is all. Now, go on."

"Yes, well — as I said, they were exceedingly rough and disagreeable. There were moments when I feared for my safety. I was quite angry with you for putting me in that position, you know."

"I never expected them to come here," he said, annoyed with himself for feeling that he needed to apologize. "I didn't know they were aware I had any connection to you or this house." His stomach was beginning to complain, and he tried to recall what he'd eaten earlier in the day that might be disagreeing with him. "Why didn't you tell me they'd been here?"

"Because, they did not get away with anything, so troubling you with the matter seemed unnecessary."

"I'd say it was extremely necessary!" He scrubbed his shirtsleeve across his face and loosened his collar. "Didn't it occur to you that I might need to know they had become a problem?"

"No. Because they had not become a problem. I dealt with them."

A tightness was forming in him, constricting his chest so that he began to have difficulty breathing. "Dealt with them how?" The words were spoken with some effort as he struggled against the nausea that was beginning to overtake him. When she did not answer, he looked up to see her smiling at him. It was a peculiarly satisfied smile that made his skin crawl. "Dealt with them how?" he repeated hoarsely.

"I killed them," she said with a delicate lift of one shoulder. "They were trying to take away my money. They would have destroyed everything — ruined everything — so I killed them. Just as I killed my father, and just as I shall kill *anyone* who threatens my plans." She rose to her feet and stood, head cocked to one side, looking down at him. "Daniel threatened to become a problem. One way or another, the redcoats will solve that problem for me."

Teague tried to stand, but was quickly overwhelmed by intense nausea and dizziness. "Charlotte?" He looked up at her, and was unsettled to see before him multiple manifestations of her. The entire room, which seemed to have become unbearably hot and devoid of oxygen, was spinning. Slowly, Teague turned his gaze to the glass of port on the table. Firelight hit the facets on the glass and the dregs of red liquid inside, and fractured into a brilliant array that hurt his eyes. He blinked, and tried again to fix it in his sight, but the glass slid in and out of focus as though he were viewing it through a seaman's spyglass. "What have you done?"

The question was imbued with an unbearable measure of pain and betrayal, yet it did not cause even the slightest twinge in her heart. "The arsenic was purchased long ago," she told him, "when I first formed the notion to be rid of my father. Then I learned that arsenic murders could, in some cases, be detected, and had to abandon the scheme. I must say, when you so inconsiderately decided to return to Boston early, I was quite glad I still had it on hand. Because you always avail yourself of my father's good port, I knew exactly how to get the arsenic into you."

Teague blinked the pistol into focus. It was not loaded, he knew, but his instinct was to reach for it anyway. Anticipating him, Charlotte slid the pistol across the table away from his reach. She picked up the glass and gathered the decanter, and emptied the remaining port into the fireplace. The logs hissed as the liquid hit them and, fueled by the alcohol, some of the flames leapt momentarily. She held the decanter aloft and seemed to consider its value for a moment before, with a shrug, throwing it and the glass into the fire as well. The glass shattered and fell, glittering in the ashes. "The threat of detection no longer matters, you see," she said, wiping her hands and returning to him, "because it will likely be weeks before anyone finds your body. And even in the unlikely event that your death is somehow connected to me — though I doubt anyone would actually care enough to pursue the matter — I shall be far beyond the reach of Boston authorities."

She leaned down so that she could take a close look at his face. "Oh, you are *quite* ill, aren't you? I believe you must feel wretched, though I must warn you that it will get much worse before it is all done. It's a shame you didn't drink more. The end would have come so much more quickly and your suffering reduced accordingly."

Once again, Teague's attempt to stand was in vain. He immediately collapsed on the floor in front of her, reaching out a beseeching hand. Charlotte stepped back, quickly snatching her skirts out of his reach. "Charlotte . . . why?" he groaned. "I only wanted my half of the money."

"Your half?" She laughed. "Do you honestly think I would part with even one coin?" She thought for a moment, and amended her statement. "Though, you should know that I did give a portion of it to Lieutenant Chastain, who will soon be Captain Chastain thanks to your sacrifice. You were correct, Teague. He and I are to be married, and then I'll be leaving for Philadelphia to take ship for London. It is all so exciting!"

She walked toward the front door and took her cloak down from the peg on the wall. "But because that maddening little Somerset girl had to stick her nose into my affairs, I shall need to go and deal with her, first. I cannot risk her telling anyone what she saw here." Sweeping her cloak around her shoulders, she walked back to where he was using the chair as a crutch that he might pull himself up off the floor. "I'd be rid of her already if you hadn't interfered." Angrily, she kicked the chair away so that Teague crumpled back onto the floor.

Charlotte hardly noticed. Her thoughts seemed to be drifting to Anna. "She may be dead already," she mused. "That eventuality certainly appeared to be eminent, at any rate." Scowling, she looked down at Teague. "If you hadn't been so bent on manhandling me, you'd have seen them. Daniel and that idiot Drum. Lord only knows how Daniel got away from the Regulars, but that will surely be remedied soon enough. He was carrying the wretched Somerset girl to Mrs. Garrett's shop. She looked like a rag doll," Charlotte laughed, "which is pretty much what she has *always* looked like, in my view!"

Sighing wearily, Charlotte redirected her attention to Teague. "I cannot leave her fate to chance, however." Inspiration seemed to strike suddenly, and she bent down to retrieve the knife she knew he kept hidden in his boot. "This may be useful. Considering how much you've always disliked her, I'd think you would be pleased to know, Teague, that it may be your knife that kills the little bitch." She picked up the pistol, and rummaged in a desk drawer for ammunition before making her way again to the front door.

"I would like to stay with you to see the arsenic run its course but, as I'm sure you can understand, this business with Miss Somerset is quite pressing." She walked toward the door, turning back to him just before leaving. "And, do, please, have the good grace to die before I return. I've had quite enough of cleaning up blood, and I'd prefer not to have to finish you in some inconvenient manner."

Teague watched the door close behind Charlotte. His first thought was that he was a dead man. His second thought was, *but not yet*. Survival might be unlikely, yet he seized onto the slim hope that he could buy some time. Fighting the pain that was gripping his gut, he struggled to his hands and knees, jammed his fingers down his throat, and vomited. Over and over again until nothing would come up, he gagged himself in an effort to purge from his stomach as much of the poison as possible. When his stomach was empty, he struggled to the kitchen and drank water, waited a minute, and made himself vomit again. Finally, he dosed himself first with salt water, and then vinegar, both of which came up with little prompting from him.

Once he arrived at the point where he doubted much could be gained by further purging, he leaned against the table, panting and trying to steady his wobbly legs. The band of excruciating pain continued its hold on his gut, and dizziness and nausea came and went with disconcerting frequency but, by force of will, he could stay on his feet, and he could move, and that was all he needed at the moment. Fighting through the misery that seemed to course through his body like his own blood, he stumbled out of the house and into the darkened street. The household at the end of the street kept a stable, and to that he headed. All things considered, he doubted very seriously that a charge of horse stealing was going to matter to him one way or the other.

*   *   *

Charlotte did not realize that she had missed Daniel's departure from his mother's shop by mere minutes. She hid in the shadows behind the shop, hood pulled low to hide her fair hair, watching and waiting, thinking, planning. It appeared that one lamp was lit in the kitchen. Otherwise, the lower floor was dark. An upstairs window showed more illumination, and Charlotte thought it likely that Anna was there. The question was, how much had she been able to relate regarding the events in the Ainsworth's shed? If Anna had not yet been able to inform on her, then it was imperative that no time be wasted before ensuring that it did not happen at all.

She stepped out into the moonlight and moved stealthily toward the door but had to change her course when she heard the sound of someone approaching from the lane behind her. She ducked into the shadow of an outbuilding and watched as Drum and Dr. Hawkins passed by without seeing her. From the bit of conversation she heard exchanged between them, she gathered that they were much delayed in reaching the house. She could not know the difficulty Drum had encountered in his attempt to convince Dr. Hawkins to leave his warm bed and accompany him to Selah's home. Charlotte only knew that she was grateful for whatever had postponed the doctor's ability to attend to Anna.

Drum and the doctor entered the house without knocking at the door and, seconds later, the glow of a hand-held lamp rose up the stairs. Charlotte took that as her opportunity. Her feet were quick and light as she darted up the steps to the back door, cautiously let herself inside, and dashed through the kitchen into the darkened shop beyond. Her heart was pounding, but not in an unpleasant way. There was thrill to be had in the suspense of the moment, and she absorbed it as though it were an aphrodisiac.

Slowly, pausing over each footfall, she made her way up the stairs that climbed from the shop to the upper floor. Near the top, where the building's two staircases intersected at a landing, she stopped to listen. The sound of voices — Selah's and the doctor's — drifted down to her, though nothing that sounded like Anna's voice. Perhaps the little nuisance was yet unconscious. At any rate, there was nothing to be done while both the doctor and Selah were in attendance. Charlotte would have to bide her time.

CHAPTER TWENTY-THREE

Even Edward Hinton would have been surprised by the rapidity with which details of Gage's planned assault on the Dorchester and Charlestown peninsulas had reached the Committee of Safety's headquarters in Cambridge. When Daniel arrived there, it was to find the place in such a frenzy of activity that almost no one seemed to notice his sudden appearance among them. He'd been at the headquarters prior to his arrest and, at that time, the occupation of Cambridge and vicinity was accomplished by a disorganized mélange of militias, predominately from Massachusetts and Israel Putnam's men from Connecticut. Since then, others had arrived.

Colonel John Stark had brought twelve-hundred men from New Hampshire, and Nathanael Greene had come from Rhode Island with roughly one thousand men. At the direction of the Committee of Safety, the ad hoc assemblage of militias had shaken out into something resembling regimental order under the over-all leadership of Artemus Ward. But there was still a critical lack of organization and too many bickering officers, resulting in a less-than efficient response to the news that Gage intended to take control of the two peninsulas.

Daniel located Dr. Warren at the Harvard University house the Committee of Safety had occupied as its headquarters. A general hubbub pervaded as messengers bustled in and out of the doors setting off new levels of frenzy with each wave of communication. Daniel was largely ignored and left to seek out Warren on his own. He found the doctor seated at a table, scratching out various communications as fast as his quill would move. Without looking up, Warren handed each of his hastily written missives off to one of the numerous messengers standing at the ready. Hat in hand, Daniel stood to one side, biding his time as he waited for an opportune moment to interrupt.

When Warren finally did spot him, he paused in his frenzy of work and, blinking in surprise, greeted Daniel. "I assume the lobster-backs did not set you free?"

Daniel shook his head. "No, Sir. I'm a fugitive. How I came to be one is complicated, and I came to you for advice on what I should do next. But my story will take a while in the telling, and I can see that this is not the time."

Warren waved his quill through the air, brushing away Daniel's reticence. "There may not be another time," he said soberly. "But whatever your tale, I suspect any advice I might give on the subject will soon be of an entirely different character than what it might have been earlier today. Gage is planning to take the Charlestown and Dorchester peninsulas two days hence. We can't cover every hill around Boston, so I'm sending a force out to dig in on Bunker's Hill and a second to reinforce one of the hills on Dorchester Neck. We're focusing on Charlestown in the hope that we can divert Gage's attention from Dorchester. So, I suggest we put your tale aside and focus on the crisis at hand. I'm glad you are here, Daniel. I've no doubt we can put you to good use."

*   *   *

Waiting on the dark stairway, it seemed to Charlotte that the doctor was spending far more time with Anna than could possibly be necessary. She waited impatiently until she heard the doctor announce that he had done all he could. He was collecting his belongings as he issued instructions to Selah regarding Anna's care, and Charlotte was able to pick out the all-important words, "if she wakes up." *If she wakes up.* Charlotte felt relief flood through her. Anna was yet unconscious and, therefore, could not have revealed anything of what had happened to her.

With only darkness for cover, Charlotte pressed back against the wall as Selah and Dr. Hawkins crossed the landing above her on their way down to the kitchen. Neither of them ventured even a glance toward the place where Charlotte waited. She listened to their footsteps as they descended, and it was in that moment that Charlotte hit upon a method of dealing with Selah. It was a simple plan, one with which she had dabbled before in regard to her father and, therefore, she felt comfortable bringing into play at this critical moment.

Silently, she moved to the stair just below the landing, careful to remain out of view. When Selah returned to Anna, Charlotte would hear her ascending the other staircase clearly enough and would have only to wait for Selah to reach the top of the stairs before stepping out onto the landing and, taking Selah by surprise, giving her a good, hard shove back down the stairs. If the fall did not kill Selah, then Charlotte knew well enough how to dispatch her in a manner that would fit the picture of an accident. Charlotte felt very pleased that such a happily-fortuitous circumstance had presented itself for her use.

She heard the door close on the doctor's departure, followed by sounds of the kettle arm being swung from the fire and water being poured into a pan. Once again, it all seemed to take an interminable amount of time, and her patience was waning. When, at last, she heard Selah begin her ascent up the stairs, Charlotte breathlessly poised herself for her planned strike. A frisson of excitement pulsed through her, anticipation of the rush of pleasure she had first felt at the climactic moment of Foster's killing. As Selah neared the top of the stairs, Charlotte began to experience a visceral arousal that, with particular urgency, demanded satisfaction.

But then, someone was pounding at the kitchen door, and Selah turned back down the stairs before Charlotte could have her moment. Cursing inwardly, she took deep breaths as her body struggled to adjust from complete readiness to a more relaxed state. She heard the door open, and Selah's voice raised in surprise. And then, incredibly, she heard Teague's voice, and a whole new panic took her in its grip.

*   *   *

At Warren's suggestion, Daniel fell in with the thousand or so men, pulled from three regiments, which William Prescott was leading out to fortify Bunker's Hill. The hills of Charlestown Peninsula — Morton's Hill, Breed's Hill, and Bunker's Hill — belonged to three farmers, from whom each hill took its name. It was a lovely, peaceful place, predominately used for grazing livestock. But with hordes of hungry militiamen nearby, not to mention the British army just across the river in Boston, the farmers had not grazed any livestock on the land for a good long while, and the grass had grown to waist-high. Daniel wondered how the farmers would feel about what was soon to happen to their land. Prescott's small force was accompanied by Colonel Richard Gridley, an artillerist and engineer, the cannon taken from the *Diana* during the raid on Noddle Island, and several wagons loaded down with entrenching tools. None of it boded well for the three farmers' property.

Prescott was nearing fifty-years old, which, in Daniel's view, seemed an age when one ought not to be out chasing across the countryside in the middle of the night. After only a short time in the Colonel's company, however, Daniel had to revise his opinion. Prescott was an energetic man, with a commanding presence. Like so many of the militia officers, Prescott had cut his teeth on service in the war against the French and Indians, earning both a reputation for solid leadership and the respect of his men.

There was another officer present who, like Prescott, held admirable credentials and the respect of his men. Israel Putnam had a good ten years on Prescott, and matched him in energy. Irascible, colorful, and irritatingly outspoken, Putnam had also served during the French and Indian war. Daniel had heard that Putnam was once captured by the Mohawk and was only saved from being burned alive by the timely outbreak of a torrential thunderstorm and the intervention of a French officer. After spending some time in the old man's company, Daniel was convinced that what had really saved him was that the Mohawk decided it would be a greater punishment to the white men if they set this irritating man free.

Once Prescott's small force reached Breed's Hill, they realized that, in their haste to get there, no one had bothered to formulate a plan regarding what should be done when they arrived. The three officers and several of their subordinates began a discussion that picked up antagonistic momentum as it progressed. Daniel sighed, and found a reasonably comfortable place to settle himself while yet another committee decided their next step forward.

The dispute centered on the best location for the redoubt. Despite the fact that their orders were to fortify Bunker's Hill, Putnam argued forcefully for siting it on Breed's Hill, instead. Breed's Hill, he argued, was a mere five-hundred yards from the Charles River, meaning that any gun emplacements there would be more threatening to Boston and its harbor — including the Royal Navy. Additionally, he argued, the location would be more likely to achieve the strategic goal of drawing the Regulars away from Dorchester Heights.

Gridley and Prescott were determined to follow their orders and site the redoubt on Bunker's Hill. Aside from being the higher ground, it was a smaller area to defend. Breed's Hill, they argued, placed their main force too far from supplies and reinforcements that might come from the Neck, and made them vulnerable to being cut off by any troops Gage might land to their rear. But Putnam had the greater force of personality and it was decided that the redoubt would be built on Breed's Hill.

*   *   *

While Daniel was listening to the three officers argue, Drum was making his way across Boston to Mr. Wilton's house. Upon arriving at his destination, it took Drum several long seconds to work up the courage to knock on Mr. Wilton's door. He expected that Mr. Wilton would have retired for the evening, and was thus surprised when, not only did Wilton answer the door quite promptly, but he was fully-dressed when he did so.

"I've not been able to sleep," Wilton explained as he showed Drum into his study. "I've been sitting here, mad with worry and trying to think what to do."

"We found her," Drum blurted out. "Daniel helped me, and we found her."

"But where is she?"

"We left her at Mrs. Garrett's because Miss Anna was hurt bad and Daniel thought it would be better."

Wilton was already gathering for his hat and coat. "Hurt? What do you mean? Where did you find her?" He paused, Drum's words finally sinking in. "And, how did Mr. Garrett help you? Has he been released?"

"Well, no." Drum flushed. "They didn't release him. I guess I did."

Wilton could tell that Drum's story was far more complex than he wanted to take time with at the moment. "Never mind. Let's go." He bustled Drum out the door and they set off in the direction of Selah's shop.

*   *   *

Selah could not have been more surprised to see Teague Bradley standing on her doorstep. She stared at him, speechless and uncertain, for Daniel had told her of his possible involvement in Anna's injuries. He looked so haggard and ill, however, that compassion won out and she invited him in. The moment the lamplight hit his face, she began to cast about for a place to let him lie down and a way to fetch Dr. Hawkins back.

"You needn't bother," Teague insisted. "There's naught he can do for me, I think."

"What has happened, Teague?"

He bent double as another wave of cramps convulsed his stomach. The attacks had plagued him all the way across Boston, even forcing him to climb down from his horse several times. A patrol of Regulars passed him once while he was in the throes of dry heaves. They had laughed and moved on, dismissing him as a drunk. It was a relief, for he was in neither mood nor condition to be questioned by them. "She has poisoned me," he said. "Charlotte. Miss Ainsworth. She has poisoned me."

*   *   *

Daniel heard someone mark the fact that midnight had just passed. It was a new day. June 17. Somehow, he suspected he was going to remember it as a pivotal day in his life, a day when everything changed. He did not know whether that change would be good, or bad. *What if she dies?* June 17, 1775. He hoped it would not be the final date on her tombstone, or on his own.

He watched Richard Gridley plot out a redoubt on the summit of Breed's Hill. Once it was done, the men set aside their muskets and picked up shovels and pickaxes. Construction had finally begun. They had arrived on the hill at around ten o'clock in the evening. The officers had taken over two hours to debate the matter and, now, the redoubt needed to be completed by dawn's first light, a seemingly impossible task.

The redoubt was essentially an oblong box, with its longest sides facing north and south. On the side facing Charlestown, a triangular-shaped protuberance jutted from the wall at one point so that defenders could harass attackers with musket fire from more angles. The walls were predominately earth, about six feet high. In the back wall of the redoubt, facing up toward Bunker's Hill, was a narrow opening designed to serve as the sole entry or exit to the redoubt. In a touch of irony, the meager fortification would be augmented by the British cannon removed from the *Diana* during the raid on Noddle Island.

The backbreaking work was done in darkness, with no pauses for rest and not enough water to drink. Almost every man there knew their orders were to fortify Bunker's Hill, and the change of location seemed senseless to them. Some attempted to sow seeds of insurrection by suggesting that they were being sacrificed either to some treachery or to a need for martyrs to fuel the propaganda of rebellion.

Inwardly, Daniel agreed that the site was not the best choice, though he also felt confident that there was nothing more than a difference of opinion involved. He urged the grumblers around him to think sensibly. "It does no good talking like that," he told one man. "This is what we've been handed, and neither you nor I can change it. If a thing is beyond your control, you'd do better to spend your time figuring out how to make the best of it."

Such statements were enough to quiet most complainants, but one or two needed more persuasion. "Who are you, boy?" one particularly cantankerous man named Hue demanded. "You ain't with this regiment." Hue sized Daniel up through one squinted eye. Are you Massachusetts militia? One of them New Hampshire boys?"

"Neither," Daniel said. "I'm not militia."

"Then, what you doin' here?"

"The same thing you are," Daniel shrugged. "But on my own accord."

"Humph. If you're not one of us, you oughtn't be telling us what we should and shouldn't do or say."

"All right, then. I won't tell you. I'm going to build this redoubt, though. Then I'm going to pick up my musket and stand here and try to keep the redcoats from taking this hill away from us. If you don't want my help, I'll move on down the line. I'm sure I'll find someone who won't mind another pair of hands to help build this thing, and I'm damn sure I'll find someone who won't care whether I'm militia or not so long as I'm willing to cover his back in a fight."

"Leave him be, Hue," another militiaman urged. "Get on back to work and leave him be."

But Hue was not ready to give it up just yet. "Don't know that I'd want some snot-nosed, untrained boy on my flank during a fight," he groused.

"The *boy* may be untrained, but he's hell in a fight." Another man stepped forward and it took Daniel a moment to recall where he'd seen him before. "Ezra Dibble," the man said, nodding toward Daniel. "We were at Menotomy together. Briefly, anyway."

The fight in the house at Menotomy came flooding back into Daniel's memory as he greeted Dibble. "How are you, Sir?"

"Recovered well enough."

"You?"

"Likewise."

"How did that big fellow who was with you come through it? Drum I think his name was."

"That's right. Drum. He made it home in one piece."

"I liked him," Dibble said. "Is he here with you?"

Daniel shook his head. *Thank God*, he thought. "No, he's not here."

Dibble turned to Hue. "I wouldn't be alive if it weren't for this young man. I'd listen to him if I were you. He may not have our training, but his instincts in a fight are nothing short of amazing."

398

The praise surprised Daniel. He did not remember anything particularly astonishing he had done that day — aside from staying alive. Grudgingly, Hue picked up his shovel and set to work, though not without a parting look that told Daniel he would be in Hue's sights for the duration.

*   *   *

On hearing Teague's statement to Selah, Charlotte knew that she needed to act quickly if she hoped to salvage any of her cherished future plans. A quick peek around the corner persuaded her that it was unlikely that, from their position in the kitchen, either Selah or Teague would see her cross the landing. Bundling her skirts to keep them from rustling, she quickly tiptoed across the landing and into the room where Anna lay unconscious.

The fire was stoked up so that it cast its warmth and flickering light across the small room, and oil lamps burned brightly on the bedside table and a small table positioned by a chair to one side of the hearth. She crossed directly to the bed and stood looking down at the pathetic, battered little thing to which Anna was reduced. In Anna's current condition, she held about as much appeal as a piece of rotted fruit, and Charlotte felt quite glad that this would be Daniel's last memory of her. Wondering just how deeply unconscious Anna was, Charlotte took out the pistol and used the barrel to poke firmly at a dark patch on one of Anna's bandages. The dark patch spread as blood flowed more freely, but Anna did not flinch.

Charlotte laid the pistol down on the bedside table, accidentally jostling the tea cup Selah had left behind, and weighed her options. Her original plan had been to hold a pillow over Anna's face and smother her, and then return the pillow to its proper place. It would be assumed that Anna had died as a result of her injuries and might slow the process of any investigation leading back to Charlotte. However, Teague's arrival, and the fact that he had revealed so much to Selah, had complicated the plan. They would have to be dealt with, and quickly. Staging accidents was no longer an option. The best she could hope for was to make it look as though Teague was responsible for the deaths. And, that put her in mind of Teague's knife.

Downstairs, Selah stared at Teague, so shocked by his statement that she could formulate no response. "Miss Ainsworth has *poisoned* you?" Numerous questions sprang to mind but they all seemed far less important than trying to determine what could be done for him. "Dr. Hawkins has only just left here," she reached for her cloak, but hesitated, casting a quick look up the stairs. "Miss Somerset is here," she explained. "She is in a very bad way and I cannot leave her. Drum will be here soon, though, and I can send him to bring Dr. Hawkins back."

"No. I don't think he can help me. It's arsenic, you see." His face felt clammy, and he wiped his sleeve across his forehead. "That isn't why I came. Not for your help. I came to talk to Daniel, to warn him. I wanted to try to help Miss Somerset. I wanted to do it to try to make things right with Daniel."

"I don't understand any of this." Between Teague's condition and her need to return to Anna, Selah was frantic. "But surely it can wait until we get help for you." She dipped a cloth in some cool water and began to bathe his face.

He reached out and grabbed her wrist. "No! You have to understand. Charlotte is out of her mind, I think. She has killed people, and she has hurt Miss Somerset. And she wants to hurt Daniel."

Selah momentarily shut off her concern for Anna and focused on what he was saying. "Who has she killed?" She knelt before him and blotted his face with the cool cloth while he talked.

"The two redcoats," he said. "The two they think Daniel murdered. I didn't know about it. I came to tell Daniel that. I'd never have let him be taken. I need him to know that." He was pleading, almost tearfully, and the effort of it was draining him. Another convulsion overtook him and, once it had subsided, he continued his attempt to say the things he had come there to say. "She killed her father, too. And, when she left the house, she said she was going to stop Miss Somerset from ruining her plans. Anna discovered something, though what it was, I don't know. Charlotte took my knife and I believe she intends to use it on Anna."

Selah rose slowly to her feet considering all he had said. "Anna is safe upstairs," she told him. "Drum and Mr. Wilton will be here soon. We can keep her safe from Miss Ainsworth. But we need to get help for you, too. There may yet be something the doctor can do."

He shook his head. "What about Daniel? Where is he? Charlotte said she saw him coming here earlier."

"He isn't here now. They brought Anna to me and then I sent Daniel away. I was afraid the redcoats might come here looking for him when they found he'd escaped."

Teague's heart sank. The one thing he had wanted to do before he died was to be sure things were right between himself and Daniel, and now that could not happen. "Do you know where he has gone?" he asked weakly. "Did he go back to the room over Withers' tavern?"

"No. He was—" Something rattled in the room upstairs. The cup and saucer she'd left on the table beside Anna's bed? "Oh, thank the Lord! Anna might be waking up. I'll hurry right back, but I must go."

Teague watched her dash up the stairs and disappear into the bedroom. Less than two minutes passed, during which he was considering the floor, and how appealing it would be to stretch out on it in front of the fire, when he heard the pistol shot.

*　　　*　　　*

"Mr. Fisackerly. I do wish you would show a bit more alacrity!" John Wilton wanted to reach his niece as quickly as possible, and he was growing impatient with Drum's insistence on staying away from major thoroughfares. "Why on earth do you keep leading me down these winding alleys? I'm certain we would arrive there more quickly if we follow a more direct route!"

"I have to stay away from the Regulars," Drum told him. "On account of they may be angry with me for hitting two of them and letting Daniel out of jail."

"You hit two soldiers?"

Drum nodded. "I didn't kill them, but I knocked them out good. I needed to talk to Daniel, and they wouldn't let me," he huffed indignantly. "The men who were guarding him, I mean. And, one of them poked his musket at me. I didn't mean any harm. They wouldn't listen to me, though, and they wouldn't let me see Daniel!"

Amazingly, Wilton felt he was forming a fair idea of what had occurred. Certainly, it explained Drum's choice of route, and the fact that he hid himself in the shadows whenever they crossed paths with the Regulars. And, that had happened often. Aside from the usual patrols, the streets were thick with entire units on the march tonight, all of them headed up toward the river.

"I see," Wilton said. "Though I feel we do need to make better time. Perhaps we can take at least a somewhat more direct route. If we are stopped, I feel I shall be able to explain our presence on the street to the satisfaction of any patrols, and I promise to keep you out of their hands. Would you be comfortable with that?"

Drum thought on it. He did want to reach Selah's place quickly. Miss Anna had looked quite bad when he left her. "Yes, we could do that," he agreed, nodding.

They set off once more, now keeping to main streets and lanes. At every juncture, they would peer ahead, listening. If there was any indication that Regulars were approaching, they would drop back into the shadows and wait for the threat to pass. Their progress was still slower than Wilton would have liked but, agreeing that any encounters with redcoats could be even costlier in terms of time, he did not complain.

*   *   *

Selah had entered the room full of hope that she would find Anna had awakened. Instead, she found Charlotte Ainsworth standing beside the bed with a knife in one hand, poised to strike. Had Selah been prepared for such an exigency, she might have responded better. As it was, all she managed was a strangled sound of protest, which served the purpose of giving Charlotte time to neutralize the threat that Selah might have been. Without a second of thought, Charlotte dropped the knife, snatched up the pistol in a two-handed grip, and fired. Considering that she had not taken time to aim, it was surprising that she managed to hit Selah at all. She found it quite gratifying, then, when the shot knocked Selah backward. Dazed, Selah groaned and clutched her hand to the place above her waist where a dark stain was oozing into the fabric of her dress.

Charlotte spun about searching for the discarded knife, ending up on her hands and knees searching under the bed. When she finally had it once more in hand and was prepared to use it on Anna, it was too late. Teague was coming through the door, and the look on his face left her with no doubt that any feelings he'd once had for her were gone.

As much as his weakened state would allow, Teague lunged toward her. He had hoped to knock the knife from her hand, but she was quick. She dodged out of his way and made for the door. Selah, struggling to get up from the floor, saw what was happening and, grasping Daniel's little reading table by a leg, slung it into Charlotte's path. The books flew across the room, and the oil lamp crashed to the floor, extinguishing the flame and dashing oil along the floor in front of the door. It seemed a small contribution to the struggle, but it did the job. The overturned table tripped Charlotte up enough that Teague could catch her.

Her back was to him as he drew her into an unrelenting bear hug. He held her there, fast against him, the effort requiring all of his strength. Charlotte struggled against his embrace, kicking and wildly lashing about with the knife. Executing their odd dance, they caromed about the room, bumping into things and leaving a trail of upheaval in their wake. Realizing that she could not wrestle her way free of him, Charlotte turned the knife inward and, struggling against the awkward angle, drove it into the back of one of his hands. Teague yelped and momentarily relaxed his grip on her, giving her enough room to break free of his embrace, but he caught her by the arm and wheeled her back to him.

They were face to face now, and Charlotte hissed and spit at him like a cornered snake. Teague backed her toward the wall with the intent of pinning her against it. She stumbled against the bedside table, upsetting it enough that the oil lamp tipped to the floor. He heard the lamp crash, and then was stunned into motionlessness by what he saw. The lamp had spilled its contents on the back of Charlotte's skirts and, instead of being extinguished in the fall, the small flame had ignited the spilled oil.

In the instant that Teague was realizing the danger, Charlotte was realizing only opportunity. Momentarily oblivious to her own peril, she took advantage of Teague's hesitation and plunged the knife into his gut. She left it there, and stepped back, staring at the blood that covered her hand. And then, terror dawned. The back of her skirt was in flames and, panicked, Charlotte began to tear at her skirt hoping to rid herself of the flaming fabric. But her frenzied effort was of no use. The flames had spread too quickly. She stretched out a beseeching hand toward Teague, but he was on his knees, clutching the knife she had plunged into his stomach.

Screaming, she backed toward the door, but the flames on her skirt ignited the lamp oil that had spilled there, and the eruption drove her back toward the center of the room. Her hair caught next, and then, in an instant, she was nothing more than a pillar of flame, wailing as the inferno burned away her beauty, peeled away the layers of her life. When she was all but dead, she dropped to the floor directly in front of the hearth, burning like some giant, stinking piece of brimstone spat from the edge of hell. It had all taken only seconds, yet to Teague, who could only watch in horror, it seemed far longer.

His instinct for self-preservation kicking in, Teague took stock. The room was in flames, Selah was dazed and hardly able to move, and Anna was unconscious. Having no idea how to extricate the three of them, he would easily have lain down and let the fire do its worst. He reminded himself that he had come to make amends with Daniel, however, and letting Selah and Anna die here would not accomplish that goal.

Grasping the bedframe, he managed to get to his feet. He scooped his arms underneath Anna, but her limp weight was too much for him. He could not lift her, nor could he remain standing while he continued with the struggle. The room was filling with heat and smoke, making the air above bed level impossible to breathe. Before long, the killing air would be low enough to reach Anna. Teague knew he could not lift her from the bed, nor could he carry her. He might, however, be able to buy her some time while he worked out a solution. He grabbed the bedclothes and tugged until he had pulled Anna to the edge of the bed, and then tugged one last time to unceremoniously dump her onto the floor. It was no way to treat someone so badly injured, he knew, but, if he could not get her out of this room, her injuries were going to prove irrelevant.

He could see that Selah was attempting to move, though she was in so much pain, so dazed and muddled in her thoughts, that she seemed as likely to go toward the fire as away from it. Selah, he believed he could help. Teague rolled up one side of the rag rug and partly slid, partly heaved it onto the line of fire that blocked his path to the door and to Selah. The rug smothered the fire and created a small break in the flames, which he could crawl through without setting his own clothes ablaze.

When he reached her, he found that Selah was conscious, though the wound at her side had bled enough to completely soak the waist and bodice of her dress. Blood flowed down the back of her neck from a wound to her scalp. "Mrs. Garrett?" He touched her face, snapping her attention to him. "We have to go," he told her. "Can you move?"

"I don't know," she replied vaguely. "I think so. But I'm so dizzy."

The fire crackled ominously behind him as it gained strength. Even through the smoke, he could pick out the stench of Charlotte's charred flesh and it threatened to gag him. "Never mind," he said. "I'll help you. But we can't stand up. We need to crawl. Can you try that?"

She nodded. "But Anna!"

"I'll come back for her." He hoped it wasn't a lie.

She allowed herself to be led by him and they made their way toward the door. By the time they had cleared the threshold and collapsed on the landing, they were both spent. Teague had no more strength to help Selah down the stairs, and he doubted that she could make it by herself. He lay on his back, the pain of failure heavier upon him than the pain of the poison eating at his insides, sorrow for the lost opportunity to make amends to Daniel more overwhelming even than sorrow over the lifeblood that was pouring from the stab wound in his gut.

From their approach at the back of the building, Drum and Wilton could not see the fire in the upstairs bedroom. But the moment they stepped into the kitchen, the crisis became obvious. Both men immediately made for the stairs, but Wilton pulled Drum back. He caught up a strip of linen Selah had left on the kitchen table and doused it in a bucket of water. "Here," he said, handing the strip to Drum. "Wrap this around your nose and mouth. It may help." He prepared a similar mask for himself, and then picked up the bucket and poured some of the water over himself, the remainder over Drum. A shrug was the best response he could offer Drum's questioning look. He didn't know if having wet clothes would help protect them from the fire, but it couldn't hurt. And then, they wasted no more time in getting themselves up the stairs.

They came upon Teague and Selah heaped together on the landing. Teague was slumped on the floor, his back against the wall.. "Where is Anna?" Wilton demanded. Teague opened his eyes and struggled to focus on the face in front of him.

Drum was kneeling beside Selah. She was on her stomach, and she moaned when Drum rolled her over. He called her name and asked where Anna was, but her only response was to moan.

"God in heaven!" Wilton cried, alarmed by the blood soaking her dress. "She has been shot! Get her downstairs and out of the building, Mr. Fisackerly. I'll find Anna."

"Drum, no," Teauge said. "You need to get Anna. I couldn't carry her, and he probably won't be able to, either. She's still in there." He raised his hand to gesture weakly toward the room. "She's on the floor by the bed."

They looked at the room in dismay. Almost the entire room was consumed in flame. From where they stood, they could not see the bed clearly, and it seemed doubtful that anyone in the room could yet be alive. Without further thought, Drum shifted Selah to Wilton's hands.

"Stay low, Drum," Teague said. "On the ground if you can. It's the only way you have a chance to make it out of there."

Raising his arm to shield his face, Drum dove into the room and was lost to Wilton's sight.

*　　*　　*

The militiamen finished the redoubt in the pre-dawn hours, reclaimed their muskets and, to a man, sank down to the ground, exhausted. Daniel, back propped against the walls they had labored so hard to build, closed his eyes though he did not expect to sleep. Hue surprised him by sitting on one side of him, and Ezra Dibble settled in on the other. But the respite did not last long. In the early light of day, Prescott was able to see what had gone unnoticed the night before — that their position on Breed's Hill left the redoubt vulnerable to being flanked on both sides.

Hastily, he rousted groups of men and put them to work building a protective breastwork at a right angle from the back wall of the redoubt northeast down the hill to a track that paralleled the shore. Two-hundred yards from where the breastwork ended, they constructed a barricade of fence rails thickly-packed with hay and mud. The gap between these two defensive positions was covered only by three v-shaped barricades made of rail fencing. It was a weak defense, but there was little to be done about it, just as there was no time to shore up their right flank. With its single opening and this new wall extending from its one side, the redoubt now loosely resembled an ink well, with the newly-constructed breastwork standing in for its quill pen.

The men were anxious about what they would face once Gage decided to come and take their hill, and they dealt with the nerves the way men so often did, by talking about every triviality that had nothing to do with the business at hand, trading insults, or sitting in silent contemplation. They'd had no sleep, nothing to eat, and more rum than water to drink, and more than one man audibly lamented that state of affairs.

Ammunition, and precious little of it, was distributed. "Once the fighting starts," Daniel said, "We'll need someone to keep us supplied with ammunition. Has anyone taken care of that?"

Hue and Dibble shrugged in unison. "I doubt it," Hue told him. "I don't think they've had time to think of anything but getting us up here to build this damn wall."

They'd have had time, Daniel thought, *if they hadn't wasted so much of it arguing.* "Is there anyone among you who would be more use keeping us in ammunition than he would be manning a musket?"

The two militiamen seemed to give this some thought before Dibble replied, "I think I know just the man."

"Find him," Daniel said. "Tell him to locate the nearest munitions wagon and scout the fastest route between it and us. It'll be his job to ensure we don't run out of ammunition. If you think he's the sort to drag his heels, tell him it'll be his hide if he doesn't keep us firing."

"Won't need to threaten him," Dibble assured them. "Youngster named Sam Everett. He's young and eager, but I doubt the trueness of his aim when the fear sets in for real. He'll carry ammunition for us, though." He disappeared in search of Sam Everett.

"Do you think Gage'll wait until tomorrow to launch his assault?" Hue asked. "That's when I heard he planned it for, and the Regulars ain't exactly light on their feet when it comes to changing plans."

Before Daniel could respond, they heard a distant boom closely followed by the whistle of a cannon ball sailing past. It exploded into the ground some distance short of the redoubt. "I'd say he isn't going to wait," Daniel replied wryly.

Cautiously, they poked their heads up high enough to see down the hill to where three Royal Navy ships rode at anchor in the Charles River. A thin trail of smoke from one of them, the twenty-gun HMS *Lively*, betrayed it as the ship that had fired upon them. In seconds, a belch of fire, followed by more smoke, heralded the launch of another cannon ball. Hue and Daniel, and everyone else who had poked their heads above the redoubt, quickly ducked and curled themselves as tightly against the protective wall as they could manage.

"Bloody hell! They're going to bombard us!" Hue cried. An attack from sea had not been part of his mental image of how the day would play out. He cursed again when round after round slammed into the ground in front of the redoubt or, occasionally, hit the redoubt itself.

"Once they've figured out the right elevations for those guns, they'll start pounding us for real," Daniel guessed.

"Bloody hell! Seems downright unethical to me." Hue seemed genuinely offended. "Or, at the very least, it ain't very sporting of them. What're we supposed to do in the face of that?"

"Nothing," Daniel replied as a ball crashed into the breastwork. "Keep our heads down, keep the redoubt repaired as best we can, and wait until they send something we can shoot at, I suppose."

"Bloody hell!"

*   *   *

If Drum had been able to think about it, he would have known he was terrified. But the heat and smoke, even the noise of the fire devouring everything in the room engaged his senses so completely that there was no room left for such thoughts. The moment he entered the room, he was staggered by the heat, and wanted to race across the room as quickly as his long legs would carry him. But, as Teague had warned, the heat forced him to the floor where he had to grope his way along toward the bed.

He found Anna lying quite still in a puddle of bedclothes on the floor. Not certain that she was still alive, he pulled the bedclothes tight about her and tied the loose ends together like a shroud. Then, picking up the neat bundle, he took one deep breath, half-stood, and bolted toward the door, crossing the room in five long strides. He had to lay Anna down on the landing for a moment because a loose end of her impromptu wrapping had caught fire and needed to be extinguished. Teague had disappeared, he noticed, and assumed Mr. Wilton had come back for him. Still, he did not check to see if Anna was alive, but gathered her into his arms once more and carried her down the stairs.

Wilton met him, guiding him to the place where he had left Selah and Teague. They heard a bell begin to toll in the distance. Someone had seen the fire and sounded the alarm; help would be coming soon. Drum lowered Anna to the ground and sank down beside her. He unwrapped the wet cloth from his face and took a moment to notice how dirty it had become before casting it aside. He was afraid to look to where Wilton leaned over Anna, afraid that he might see in Wilton's face the thing he dreaded.

Wilton seemed to sense Drum's fear. "She is alive, Mr. Fisackerly," he said quietly. Sitting on the ground, he pulled Anna into his lap and cradled her close to him. "Thanks to you, she is alive."

CHAPTER TWENTY-FOUR

Edward Hinton, along with the rest of the British garrison in Boston, was jolted awake at around five-o'clock on the morning of June 17 by the sound of the HMS *Lively* opening fire on the newly-constructed redoubt atop Breed's Hill. One after another, British officers tumbled from their quarters to train spyglasses upon Charlestown Peninsula in search of the reason for the *Lively*'s sudden interest. They were shocked to see that Breed's Hill, which was bare the night before, was now a fortified rebel stronghold. Few gave voice to their amazement, but all were astonished at the feat of constructing the redoubt over the course of only one night.

General Howe knew that this move by the rebels demanded a revision to Gage's plan for taking the hill. There could be no delaying until the next day; they would have to act immediately. And so, he did not wait for the summons he knew would be coming soon from Gage. With Edward in his wake, he strode toward Gage's war room, adding finishing touches to his dress as he walked. Clinton was already there, ignoring Gage's request that he wait for the others to arrive before launching his argument for a revised battle plan.

"Land troops on the Neck," Clinton was urging, if not demanding, as Howe entered the room. "Cut off the redoubt." He pointed to where a large circle was drawn around the newly fortified area at the center of the map. The Charlestown Peninsula was an odd, pork chop shape, with Charlestown located on the wide end almost directly across from Boston. At the narrow, opposite end, it was connected to the mainland and Cambridge via a slender neck. "If we cut off the Neck, we isolate the rebels on their little hilltop. We cut them off from their headquarters in Cambridge, and from supplies or reinforcements. We also block their one avenue of retreat."

Gage waved his hand for silence and acknowledged Howe's arrival. Nothing more was said during the brief time they had to wait for Burgoyne, and then General Gage repeated for the benefit of all ears the plan Clinton had been espousing. "And, before we engage in further discussion on the merits of this plan," Gage added, "I must tell you that I am opposed to it on the grounds that it will place our forces between the rebels in the hilltop redoubt and the rebels still at their headquarters in Cambridge. I believe that is a recipe for disaster."

Howe stepped forward, laid his hat on the edge of the table, and leaned over the map before them. "Then, may I suggest, Sir, that we consider another approach? The simplest solution to any problem is often the best and, it seems to me, the simplest solution to this problem is a straightforward, frontal attack." He ran his finger along the depiction of the hillside on Gage's map. If the Peninsula was a clock face with the redoubt on Breed's Hill at its center, Bunker Hill would have resided at roughly ten o'clock, Morton's Hill at two o'clock, and the town of Charlestown somewhere between four and five o'clock. "The terrain is open, and of easy ascent and, in short, would be easily carried."

When Gage nodded his agreement, Clinton said nothing. Edward could read the resentment plainly enough on his face. It was no secret that Clinton considered his experience superior to that of Gage — or any of the other generals, for that matter. Every time Gage rebuffed one of his opinions, Clinton would grouse to anyone who was willing to listen that it was because of Gage's own insecurity and jealousy. Edward knew that Clinton's constant whining did nothing to enhance his image among the men and, in fact, had quite the opposite effect.

Because he outranked both Clinton and Burgoyne, Howe was given command of the operation. He issued orders for the first wave of the assault to be ready to launch at high tide, shortly after noon. Ten light companies, ten Grenadier companies, and battalions from the Fifth and Thirty-Eighth Regiments of Foot would depart from Long Wharf. The rest of the Grenadier and light companies, along with battalions from the Fifty-Second and Forty-Third Foot regiments would depart from the North Battery. Over fifteen-hundred men would make up that first wave, to be closely followed by Major Pitcairn's marines in the second.

Because he had developed such a high level of respect for the major during the running scrape between Lexington and Concord, Edward would have preferred to accompany Pitcairn. Instead, he would be landing with Howe at Morton's Point. Howe had picked Morton's Point because it was far enough from the rebels' redoubt to allow the men to land, disembark, and assemble for their assault without rebel musket balls flying about their heads. It seemed a prudent consideration, though it also meant that a great deal of time was lost while they waited for the high tide that was necessary to make landing at that particular site, and there was a sense among many of the men that every hour of delay was another hour the rebels could spend preparing for the assault.

*   *   *

Hours later, Lieutenant Richard Chastain sat with his regiment along the boardwalk at Long Wharf waiting for his turn to be stuffed into one of the longboats that would ferry him across to Charlestown Peninsula. As he understood it, they were now waiting for the tide to be right. Or, perhaps they were waiting for the clouds to move in front of the sun, or for the generals to get their wigs on just so. He would not have been surprised to hear that it was any of those, for it was a morning of inexplicable waiting. They were ordered to carry full kit, which had meant taking time to assemble it all, and then waiting while it was inspected. They had waited for bread to be baked and distributed, for extra cartridges to be issued, and myriad other details to be seen to, all of which seemed to many of the men a waste of time, considering that they were only going across a river and up a hill.

Chastain had mixed feelings about this little sortie. Inarguably, a battle was one of the best places for a soldier to garner attention, accolades, and possibly even advancement. That is, if the soldier managed to come through said battle alive. Richard Chastain's goal on entering the army had been to secure, with as little actual effort on his part as possible, a livelihood and a certain status in society. Things had gone relatively well in that regard. Thus far, all of his postings were reasonably tolerable, and he had managed to manipulate his position so as to completely avoid the dirty business of combat.

When the Thirty-Eighth was ordered to the American colonies, he had experienced a pang of concern that his fortunes might be taking an unwanted turn but consoled himself that the business would likely be finished quickly. Furthermore, as had turned out to be the case with this particular one, colonial postings frequently offered unique opportunities for catching the eye of senior officers and landing agreeable staff positions. He had caught General Gage's eye through an extraordinary set of circumstances, which would not likely have occurred any other place, and he had little doubt that a staff position was in the offing.

But for now, he sat under the hot June sun, wrestling with doubt upon concern upon — well, it had to be admitted — *fear*. Lieutenant Richard Chastain was about to go into battle and, whether it was over quickly, as most suggested it would be, or not, the risks would be many. He knew his nervousness was making him twitchy and, to hide his nervous symptoms, he began to fuss with the arrangement of his clothing, adjust his accoutrement, and scowl over the dust that had accumulated on his polished boots and fawn-colored breeches. It would have mortified him to know that all of his posturing was only serving to demonstrate his nervousness to the men around him.

Edward Hinton hurried by, earnestly and efficiently carrying out whatever directive Howe had given him. It was not the first time Chastain had seen Hinton pass, and he pretended not to have seen him at all. Chastain, who thoroughly resented the fact that Hinton had managed to land on a general's staff, refused to make eye contact with the younger man, and directed dagger-sharp looks at Hinton's back each time the lieutenant passed by. Chastain's pique momentarily distracted him from his mounting fears, and he turned his mind to ruminating on the unfairness of his life.

*   *   *

In Daniel's opinion, the beginning of the redcoat assault was something to look forward to, if for no other reason than because it would mean a halt to the shelling the men in the redoubt had suffered all morning. Earlier in the morning, the *Lively* had cast off from its moorings and relocated to a spot off Morton's Point that afforded the gunners a better line of fire at the redoubt. His Majesty's other ships in the area, the *Glasgow*, the *Symmetry*, and the *Spitfire*, came abreast of the peninsula and added their cannon to the barrage. Shells screamed through the sky, sometimes passing close over their heads, sometimes scudding into the ground in front of them, but occasionally hitting the redoubt itself. Additional work had continued on the fortification throughout the morning and, each time spotters glimpsed spouts of fire flaring from any of the ships' guns, they would call out and every man would drop his tools and fall to the ground until the shells had done their worst. Then, it was back to work until the next barrage.

Looking around the redoubt, Daniel wondered how these men could possibly fight. They had not eaten or slept for over twenty-four hours, and had not had enough water to drink. And some were deserting. Tempers were beginning to flare over the fact that no replacements were sent up, no more weapons or ammunition. He knew Prescott had dispatched a request back to Artemus Ward in Cambridge but, so far, only two-hundred men from John Stark's New Hampshire militia had arrived. Everything seemed to be happening with agonizing sluggishness, and it took considerable willpower for him to keep to his place instead of going to Cambridge and dragging back as many men as he could lay hands on.

"What does that mean, d'ye suppose?" Hue, who had popped his head up for a look after the most recent barrage of shelling, nudged Daniel.

"What is it?" Daniel asked, swinging up onto his knees and then standing just tall enough to peek over the redoubt. The sun's brightness shining off the water momentarily blinded him, and he blinked to clear his vision.

"That flag. The blue one on that ship there in the middle. They only just ran it up. What does a blue flag mean?"

Daniel opened his mouth to say he had no idea, and then he spotted the longboats. There seemed to be hundreds of them, though he knew his anxiety was likely inflating the numbers. Tamping down his nerves, he forced himself to carefully count the number of boats so that he could react with his mind, not his fear. Twenty-eight, he counted, and each one was full of redcoats. "I believe it means the attack has begun," he told Hue.

*   *   *

Seated beside General Howe in the stern of a longboat, Hinton looked up at the sun, and then checked his pocket watch to confirm his estimate. It was only minutes after one o'clock. They had pushed away from the wharf at high tide, exactly in keeping with Howe's timetable. Edward chose to view it as a good sign. A cannon ball, and then another, screamed over their heads. Reflexively, everyone in the boat ducked despite knowing that it was friendly fire, the beginning of the barrage from the cannon behind them on Copp's Hill that would cover their crossing. Furthermore, the artillery fire from Copp's Hill and from the warships would serve to keep the rebels pinned down behind their barricades until Howe's force was ready to engage. The thought made the scream of missiles overhead more tolerable.

The longboats carried the cream of the troops garrisoned in Boston. An odd fact, Edward considered, in the face of the low regard Gage and his three generals had for the rebels. Indeed, during the meeting in the war room, reference to *fighting* the rebels on Breed's Hill had pointedly been abjured in favor of stating that the rebels were to be *cleared* from the hill. This operation was to be a cakewalk. The rebels may have forced Gage to meet them at a place of their choosing, but that was the only part of the drama they authored.

He looked at the faces of the men in the longboat. Plenty of nerves here; that was clear enough. But plenty of determination as well, for this would be their redemption — and, perhaps even a measure of revenge — for the humiliations of Lexington and Concord. This time, the rebels would be facing superior numbers in a conventional fight, the sort of straightforward assault at which these troops were perhaps the best in the world. This was their kind of fight. This was the kind of fight at which they were experienced, and for which they trained in a way no other army on earth trained. This would be their day.

Please, God, Edward prayed, *let it be so.*

$$* \quad * \quad *$$

Lieutenant Chastain was experiencing an odd bit of misplaced panic for a man who was on the verge of going into battle. Because he had never learned to swim, he hated small boats, and it seemed to him that he'd been required to spend far too much time in them for a man who had deliberately chosen the army over the navy. He added that fact to his mental list of his life's particular injustices. In addition to the panic that was brought on by acute fear that the boat might capsize at any moment, he was feeling seasick. That particular affliction he had never before suffered, and it seemed damned inconvenient to be suffering it now. He knew everyone else in the boat believed his incommodiousness to be brought on by fear, and that knowledge appalled him. Wiping his mouth on the back of his sleeve, he glowered at every man who dared to make eye contact and, inviting the enmity of the coxswain, bellowed for the rowers to pull harder. It was an order the seamen enjoyed ignoring.

When the boat finally, *finally*, thudded into the soft mud of the shore line, Chastain piled out of the boat and scrambled to firm soil faster than any man. Not that any of them were scrambling all that quickly. Between the weight of their Brown Bess muskets, fully-loaded packs, and other accoutrement, each man carried over fifty pounds of kit — most of which needed to be carried in such a way as to keep it dry. Landing was a cumbersome bit of business, and more than one man was happy not to have rebel musket or artillery fire complicating the process. No man was more happy than Richard Chastain, however.

All around him, Sergeants were barking orders, chivvying the men into well-ordered files. It was done with amazing efficiency, he observed. Nothing like having a snarling sergeant on one's tail to instill a sense of urgency in a man. Chastain happily stood back and let the sergeants do their work with no input from him. It was yet another thing he liked about sergeants; they knew even better than himself what needed to be done and how to go about doing it, and that fact relieved him of the burden of having to be engaged in the process. He much preferred looking like a lieutenant — or, soon, a captain — than actually having to do the work of one.

When they'd pushed off from Long Wharf, someone had pointed out the crowds of onlookers that were beginning to assemble all along Boston's shore, and he knew the spectatorship would expand to encompass every available rooftop and hilltop before it was all done. It was a well-known and common perversity of battlefields in close proximity to populated areas that gawkers would turn out, each for their own reason, to watch the unfolding drama. Self-conscious, as though he felt himself on stage, he straightened his posture and checked to see that nothing was amiss with his uniform.

More than a score of barges, each loaded to almost over-crowding with scarlet-coated Regulars, had crossed the sparkling water from Boston to the Charlestown Peninsula, and he had no doubt it was a stirring sight worthy of even the finest martial pageant staged upon the Thames during the golden years of Elizabeth I's reign. Each barge represented a bright splash of red, white, and blue, punctuated by the sun's gleam off of every bit of metal. The polished brass field-pieces in the lead barges glimmered as if made from gold, and pennants and regimental flags fluttered on the breeze. It filled him with pride to be part of the spectacle that must surely be puffing out the chests of every Loyalist within sight. It was too bad, he thought, that the king was not here to witness the pageant. And now, the empty barges were returning to Boston to pick up yet more men.

*   *   *

Standing at his post slightly behind General Howe, Edward Hinton continued to be amazed by the general's composed, almost casual demeanor as he went about the business of directing preparations for the assault. Though, privately, Edward did not agree with the assessment, he knew that almost everyone believed that the rebels would turn and run as soon as the regiments began their ascent, and he wondered if this belief was what informed the general's calm.

Once assembled on the shore, the troops had shaken out into battle order with efficient professionalism and then marched across Morton's Hill. Over fifteen-hundred men now stood waiting in the pitiless June sun while Howe issued final instructions to the officer corps. Upon seeing the alterations Prescott had made to his redoubt since earlier that morning, Howe decided upon a slight adjustment to his own plan of attack. He sent for his reserve troops, and also dispatched four companies of light infantry with instructions to dig in at an appropriate flanking position. Then, while they waited for the reserves to arrive, they all sat where they stood and ate their mid-day meal.

*   *   *

From within the redoubt on top of Breed's Hill, Prescott and the other militia officers watched the British actions with curiosity. "What the devil are they doing?" someone asked. In deploying the four companies of light infantry, Howe had signaled his intention to launch a frontal assault on the redoubt. He had more than enough men to do the job, it seemed, and the reason for the hesitation was wholly unclear to those in the redoubt.

"I've no idea," Prescott replied, his mind considering possibilities. "But, if it affords us more time, I'll take it."

The hastily-added barricade that ran from the north side of the redoubt was still being completed, and shoring-up of the redoubt itself was an ongoing process. Unlike Howe, Prescott had no staff, no lines of communications beyond shouted direction or what message a runner could carry and faithfully repeat. As a result, commands were frequently misinterpreted or misunderstood, causing the overall picture Prescott had in his mind to be executed imperfectly. Neither Prescott nor his militia officers had more than a vague notion of what they needed to do or how they needed to do it, and they were all exhausted and dealing with exhausted men. Men were deserting in greater numbers than reinforcements were arriving. No food, water, or additional munitions had yet arrived. Prescott was happy to grab onto any suggestion of good luck.

Aside from Howe's apparent lack of haste to get on with the business of attacking the redoubt, the highlight of Prescott's morning had come less than an hour before, when John Stark arrived with rest of his New Hampshire regiment. They had taken up position along the rail fence, thus strengthening the weakest point of the fortification. Colonel John Stark was the stern-faced, forthright, no-nonsense son of a Scottish immigrant. Tall and lean, with sharp-edged features that suggested a Viking or two in his heritage, he was a physically striking man. At age twenty-four, he'd been taken prisoner by the Abenaki during a small skirmish and, having managed to impress them with his skills and knowledge of the wilderness, was allowed to live among them for nearly a year.

Now, as Colonel of the New Hampshire militia, Stark was one of William Prescott's most valuable assets. Quickly surmising that it was vital that his men not, in their anxiousness, fire too soon, Stark paced out forty yards from the fence line where he drove a series of stakes into the ground parallel with the fence. "See those stakes?" he asked his men when he rejoined them behind the fence. "Not one of you better fire before the redcoats cross that line. Not one of you better fire before I damn well tell you to! Understood?"

Another valuable asset to Prescott, and to the Provincial Congress, Committee of Safety, and the rebel army as a whole, was Joseph Warren. Though he was advised by those around him to remain in Cambridge, he had, upon being informed of the British landing, immediately set out to join Prescott's army. Because the original plan was to fortify Bunker Hill, that was where Warren first went. When he arrived there, he was immediately met by Israel Putnam, who offered to relinquish command to Warren, a newly-commissioned Major General.

But Warren demurred. "My commission has not yet been officially delivered," Warren said. "I shall fight among the regular troops." And then he realized that things were not as expected. "There's no redoubt?" he asked, looking at the meager entrenchments around the hill.

"No, Sir," Putnam replied. "We elected to fortify Breed's Hill instead." He gave no further explanation for the deviation from what had been ordered, and Warren did not linger to seek one. In seconds, he was on his horse, turning the mount toward the lower hill.

"Wait!" A man Warren did not recognize stepped forward and took hold of the horse's mane. "You best get down off that horse, Sir. You'll be quite the target up there. The Regulars are just that close." The man spat in the dust. "Either that, or one of them cannon balls will get you. Took a man's head clean off his shoulders earlier this morning," he informed Warren in a tone that implied awe that such a thing was possible.

"Thank you," Warren said, dismounting. "I'll be walking, then." Gripping his musket, he set out down the hill, moving at a quick lope toward the redoubt.

A murmur of surprise and approval made its way through the men in the redoubt when Warren arrived there. He was respected and well-liked, and his arrival gave their spirits a much-needed lift. Daniel, on the other hand, was less happy to see his mentor. If something were to happen to Joseph Warren here today, Daniel wondered who could possible pick up his weighty mantle. By the look on Prescott's face, Daniel suspected that the same thoughts were passing through the Colonel's mind as well. But whatever reservations he might have had about Warren's being there, Prescott quickly offered to turn over his command.

As before, Warren demurred. "I have no command here. I've not yet received my commission," he said sincerely. "I shall be privileged to fight alongside these men, Colonel Prescott, and privileged to fight under your command." With that, he took his place among the men lined up along the redoubt.

*   *   *

William Howe finished his mid-day meal. Edward had tried to eat but did not share the general's insouciance and so had managed only a few bites. The reserves had arrived, and Howe performed yet another reassessment of his situation. He had received reports that, despite the considerable distance, rebel snipers positioned among the Charlestown rooftops were successfully harassing his troops deployed to the left flank. The fleet's assistance in dealing with the nuisance was requested, and Admiral Graves responded enthusiastically.

As far as the British knew, the town was all but abandoned hours earlier, making the response to the snipers an easy choice. The ships were ordered to lob super-heated cannon balls onto Charlestown, the Copp's Hill battery was ordered to hit the town with combustible cannon balls or carcasses, and a small landing party ventured ashore to put the buildings nearest the water to the torch. The blanket of incendiaries took effect with startling swiftness, enveloping the town in flames within minutes.

The second decision to emerge from Howe's reassessment regarded the focus of the newer part of the fortification to the east, erected since dawn, Howe reasoned that it would be the weakest part of the fortification. "This section," he pointed to the barricade extending from the redoubt, "has only been in place a few hours, at most. There has been no time to solidify its defenses."

Howe straightened, folded his hands behind his back, and peered over the heads of his officers as they bent to look at the map. "The right wing assault should have no trouble taking that section of the fortification, allowing the light-infantry companies advancing along the beach to overrun the stone wall and then sweep in behind the rebels positioned at the rail fence." He gave them time to locate the place he had indicated. "At the same time, the Grenadier companies, the Fifth and the Fifty-Second regiments will advance on the fence."

Following the track Howe's mind was taking, the officers were starting to nod in agreement. A few rebels strung out along a rail fence would be nothing in the face of Grenadiers and two regiments. Coupled with the advance, to be led by Colonel Pigot, on the Charlestown-side of the redoubt, not one of them could see how the operation could be anything less than a quick success. And, that was if the rebels put up any resistance. Save for a few who, like Hinton, harbored private concerns, none of them thought it likely that the militia would stand and fight. So certain were they of this fact that Howe instructed them not to stop to fire as they made their advance. The bayonet, he insisted, would be sufficient to the task.

Final preparations were made, and the men were lined up, ready to begin their assault. Once again, Hinton marveled at Howe's calm as he addressed the troops, praising them for good soldiers, and stating his belief that they would conduct themselves as Englishmen. It was a rousing speech, Hinton thought, and a shame that it was unlikely that it was being heard by all fifteen-hundred men assembled at the foot of the hill. Finally, Howe wound up with a dramatic flourish the like of which Hinton would not have thought him capable.

The general reached down and scooped up a conveniently situated musket, brandished it, and impassionedly cried out, "I promise you, I'll not ask you to go one step further than I myself am willing to go!"

The order to advance was given. Drums beat the order out to the ears of the farthest ranks, flags were raised, and the two twelve-pounder cannon Howe had deployed on Morton's Hill fired their opening volley at the redoubt. Up and down the ranks, grim-faced men who knew their business better than just about any troops in the world began the ascent up Breed's Hill.

*   *   *

When the cannon fire erupted from Morton's Hill, all of the men in the redoubt instinctively ducked their heads. All except for Israel Putnam, that is. Putnam, who had only just arrived with a final handful of reinforcements he had scavenged from a quick trip to Cambridge, cursed a blue streak at the blaggards who had dared to startle his horse. He waved his musket threateningly in the general direction of the artillery, and then joined Prescott at the center of the redoubt. Prescott had only about one-hundred and fifty men still in the redoubt, with two-hundred or so strung along the breastwork. A mere four-hundred men were deployed behind the rail fence and stone wall to the rebels' left. He knew there were probably this many men, if not more, behind him on Bunker Hill, men who were unwilling to come down to defend the more exposed position. But there was nothing to be done about that. With a little under a thousand men, he was resolved to stand up to what appeared to be about two-thousand British Regulars.

Together, Prescott and Putnam watched the Regulars begin their advance up the hill. "Good luck to you, Sir," Prescott said, bowing.

"And, to you as well, Sir," Putnam replied gruffly as he returned the bow.

The two officers separated, and Putnam climbed back on his horse to return to Bunker Hill, there to order further entrenchments, to rally men, and funnel any reinforcements down to Breed's Hill. It would be up to him to sort out the chaos that Prescott expected would engulf the entire peninsula before it was all done.

Before he rode off, Putnam bellowed a final bit of advice to the men in the redoubt. "Don't fire until you see the whites of their eyes," Daniel heard him say. "And then fire low."

Daniel, who had never before heard the advice, did not realize that all of the rebel officers were telling their men essentially the same thing. It was instruction given on battlefields the world over, and these officers had learned the lesson during the war against the French and Indians. Muskets had a very limited range and were notoriously inaccurate, and following this rule of thumb helped mitigate those two shortcomings.

But Putnam did not stop with that bit of advice. "Aim first for the officers," he growled. "Take down as many as you can as early as you can. The beast does not function well without its brains."

And, Daniel thought, it *was* a beast. There could be no more apt name for the mass of men advancing up the slope toward the redoubt, a solid, undulating wave of red and white that approached with precision and determination, their bayonets glistening wickedly in the sun. On they came, marching through the tall grass, driving insects and the odd rabbit before them, stirring a cloud of dust that served to make them appear all the more other-worldly. Their drummers beat out an incessant, intimidating tattoo; their artillery relentlessly pounded the sky. Through the din, Daniel could hear the rhythmic clink of metal on metal as every weapon, belt buckle, and odd bit of metal took up the cadence of those drums. He could hear their boots pounding the ground. It was a terrifying spectacle that defied the men in the redoubt to stand in the face of it.

And, Daniel *was* terrified. His hands had grown clammy, his heart pounded in his chest, and his bowels would have betrayed him had they not already been empty. He was afraid to stay, afraid to run and, finally, afraid that the fear would paralyze him and he would die without ever firing a shot. Never had he doubted himself to such a degree, never had he dug so deep to find a shred of strength. And, he could feel the same fear in the men around him. He looked right, and then left, up and down the line, frantically uncertain that he was equal to what was being asked of him.

By chance, his roving eyes landed upon Dr. Warren. Standing among the militiamen, musket at the ready, Warren had taken a moment to cast one last look at the men around him. They were an untrained, untested, ragtag lot — farmers and merchants and fishermen, for the most part — but he believed in them with his entire heart, with every fiber of his being. He had told Daniel that more than once. These men, and men like them all over the colony, were what made continued subjugation to a king untenable. They had grown too far beyond that. Warren briefly made eye contact with Daniel, and smiled. Daniel, with his rough edges, survivor's instincts, and courage was the epitome of these men.

Meeting Warren's brief gaze, Daniel blinked, and then found enough of a smile within himself to return what he saw as Warren's benediction. It was a fleeting moment, so much so that he could not be certain it had even happened. In that moment, Daniel imagined that he had seen his own father standing behind Warren. He shook off the odd sense and turned his attention back to the advancing redcoats. His heart had slowed, and his stomach had calmed. He was still afraid, but now he could contain it, tuck it away where it would not interfere with what he had to do.

In front of the New Hampshire militiamen, the redcoats crossed the stake line. One row, then two. Their faces became discernible, then buckles and insignia on their uniforms, and then even their buttons. Men resisted the desperate urge to pull triggers until, all along the breastwork and then the redoubt, the order was given. "Fire!" Daniel fired his musket and, without waiting for the smoke to clear, reached behind him to where Sam Everett waited to exchange loaded muskets for the ones Daniel, Ezra, and Hue had just fired. Taking a fraction of a second to locate a target, Daniel fired again. Sam was still reloading the first three muskets, so Daniel began reloading his own. He'd practiced this, simply because he knew the redcoats practiced it, and had it down to a process of only a few seconds. He fired again, and then accepted one of Sam's loaded muskets for a quick fourth volley.

As men up and down the rebel line struggled to reload their muskets, the smoke cleared to reveal that, along the entirety of their line, the redcoat advance had stalled. To Daniel's surprise, it appeared that almost a quarter of Howe's light infantry vanguard were on the ground, dead or wounded. Daniel was stunned, as were the Regulars. They wavered in place for a long, uncertain moment before, first as individuals, then in pairs or threes, and then in whole groups, the Regulars began to fall back. The impulse to retreat became contagious and, before long, Howe's entire force was retreating back down the hill.

Some of the men in the redoubt and along the breastwork, those who were not too stunned to move or speak, cheered. But Prescott and Stark moved hurriedly along the line, quieting, congratulating, calming — and preparing the men for the next assault, which they did not doubt was to come.

*   *   *

Hinton suspected that the shocked expression on General Howe's face was a mirror for his own. Of all the possible outcomes he had considered, the retreat of this army was not one of them. Howe did not waste time ruminating on the situation, however. Within fifteen minutes, his officers had achieved order and reformed the decimated lines. They would advance again, Howe insisted, though this time they would not spread themselves along the entirety of the rebel defense. This time, he folded his light infantry into line with the Grenadiers on the right where, supported again by the Fifty-Second and Fifth Regiments, they would focus their assault on the rail fence. On the left, Pigot's forces would be on their own against the redoubt.

Resolutely, they advanced up the hill again, albeit a bit slower this time, Hinton noticed. Rank upon rank they marched, their lines wavering occasionally — as they had done on the first ascent — when one section met with a low wall or fence that had to be climbed. Having already been trampled, the tall grass was less of a hindrance, but the numerous rabbit holes and rocks still made for uneven footing. Hinton found it difficult to watch where he trod while also attending the larger panorama of the operation. His eyes darted between the advancing lines and the ground at his feet, and he stumbled only occasionally.

Howe's forces formed an absolute juggernaut, Hinton thought. That first stalled effort could only be attributed to a singular coincidence of small factors that surely, *surely*, could not be repeated. This time, they would overrun the rebels in their dirt fort and behind their puny walls and fences. He had to believe that, or he could not have made himself climb that hill again. On the one hand, it seemed that they were moving with unbearable slowness; on the other, that they were approaching with lightning speed that line of demarcation between the safe ground and the killing ground that lay within the range of the rebel muskets.

To say he was afraid did not begin to describe the absolute terror that held his heart and entrails in its unrelenting grip. He had no doubt that there was no man on this hillside who was less afraid, however, and so he held his head up and marched on. For all he knew, the real glue that held the British army together was not loyalty to the king, but fear. Perhaps the glue was loyalty to the men who marched on either side of each man because of the fear that united them. Whatever the elusive element was, he counted on it to keep him and those around him alive.

* * *

For Lieutenant Chastain, who had barely endured the first advance, the second advance was beyond the pale. But his terror was replaced by anger. He was angry with General Howe for his foolishness in conceiving this horrid plan. Why could they not have sat snug in their Boston barracks and simply set Graves' ships to shelling the rebels into obliteration? Admittedly, most of the rebels would have turned-tail and run, but General Gage would have had his hill without the loss of so many of his own men. Additionally, Chastain was angry at the cowardly, ungentlemanly rebels who were clearly targeting officers. In Chastain's view, he would have been within rights to refuse to make this second ascent. And, he intended to do something in that regard before a lucky shot from some derelict's musket found his chest. With his pedigree, intellect, and ambition, it would have been a sin for Richard Chastain's life to be lost in pursuit of such a small matter as the ownership of some colonial hilltop, and it was to that point that he'd been giving his full focus.

Not that it was an easy matter to focus on anything but the physical difficulties of ascending the hill. Besides the impediments presented by the terrain, the June heat was yet another obstacle to men in wool jackets carrying full packs. In many cases, their uniforms had become so soaked through with sweat that the scarlet dye was beginning to bleed onto their buff-colored breeches. And yet, to Chastain's amazement, they pushed on. He could not comprehend why men would endure such conditions. He felt the same way about the rebels behind their walls and fences and in the redoubt. In the end, they could not possibly win any fight against this army. Why would they persevere in the face of such odds? He did not understand what drove any of these men, and had no intention of throwing himself away on whatever rubbish notions were involved.

They had worked their way up the hill until they were within steps of the line that marked the killing ground. Here and there on in the grass lay the bodies of the men who had fallen, dead or wounded, during the first assault. Most were clearly beyond help, while others were attempting to drag themselves back down the hill. Some cried out for help, or for water, or for their mothers. Chastain felt himself recoil from them, tried not to look at them. And then, the bodies on the ground were no longer scattered, but lay in a thick line one on top of another. The moment they crossed this demarcation, the rebel lines exploded in a blaze of musket fire. It was the moment for which Chastain had waited. He held his saber aloft, bellowing at his men to advance, giving the best imitation of a brave and bold officer that he could manage. All the while, he was stalling, gradually falling behind the line of advancing troops.

The rebels were reloading and firing as fast as they could, presenting the Regulars with an unrelenting barrage of musket fire. A wreath of smoke was forming around the hilltop. The few lines of Regulars that managed to get close enough, tried to return fire, but they were too few. Suddenly, the sound of two small cannon roared and cannon balls exploded out of the smoke to rake Howe's right flank. The Grenadiers on that flank began to sustain staggering losses. And yet, they pushed on.

All around him, Chastain saw the lines of men enduring the ceaseless musket fire while they struggled through the tall grass or paused to clamber over a fence. The irregular pace meant that rearward lines sometimes collided with forward lines. The assault was disintegrating into confusion, and Chastain knew his opportunity had come. He glanced about to assure himself that he was not being directly observed, and then performed a theatrical fall that was designed to imply that he'd been shot. Dramatically, he dragged himself along the ground. Had someone stopped to help him, his ruse would have been discovered. But no one was going to stop to assist Richard Chastain. For once, his lack of popularity worked in his favor.

He dragged himself along on his stomach until he reached a place where men had fallen in a heap during the first assault. The corpses were all horrendously bloodied and disfigured by their wounds and, seeing them so closely, Chastain tasted bile in his throat. He steeled himself, however, for the thing that had to be done in the name of self-preservation. The ground around the corpses was blood-soaked and slightly muddy, and he wriggled into that mire, making himself as much a part of the pile as possible. Closing his eyes against the unpleasantness, he rubbed his hand in the blood on one of the bodies, and this he smeared liberally on his face, neck, and the front of his uniform.

Chastain had just about finished settling in when he was startled to realize that he recognized the face of one of the corpses. He could not put a name with the young man's face, but it was a familiar face that stared blankly — accusingly? — at him, and so he reached out and shoved the man's corpse off of the pile. And then, he hid his face in the crook of his own arm and lay quite still, quite safe, as the battle raged all around him.

*　　*　　*

Hinton saw General Howe pause slightly ahead of him on the slope of the hill for the briefest of seconds to take stock, musket in one hand, saber in the other. The rebels were slamming them with musket fire of unbelievable intensity. Line after line was advancing on the fence, which should have been the weakest point in their defenses, only to be mowed down like grass under the scythe. On his right, his Grenadiers were all but obliterated, while Pigot's forces, on his left, were being driven into retreat.

Hinton felt that Howe's thoughts must surely echo what was going through his own mind. *How could this be happening? How could it be that this army could not fight themselves into close enough proximity to drive home a bayonet charge? How could it be that this army was being forced into retreat by a handful of colonial rebels?* For, retreat they must. He could see that, and he knew Howe could see it as well. But the general never got the chance to order a retreat. Abruptly, the demolished ranks broke and ran yet again.

This time, Howe did not seem so much angry as frustrated. He looked back up the hillside, which was littered with the dead and wounded, and inwardly cursed every foul oath he could command. Outwardly, he was silent, apparently weighing his options. And, those options were few. It was suggested that they go back to the boats and attempt a landing behind the rebel defenses. Even had it been practical, however, the tides were not favorable to such a plan. Many of his officers were begging him not to try another assault, but he felt he had no choice. This was his plan, and he'd be damned before he'd see it fail.

And so, General Howe ordered his officers to re-form their lines, but to keep them at ease. In the interim, and though it pained him to have to do so, he sent to General Clinton for the reinforcements he knew were standing by at the wharf in Boston.

*   *   *

Among the rebels on the hilltop, the redcoats' retreat was cause for another round of subdued celebration. And, when Howe kept his troops at ease, the rebels dared to hope that they had won the day. But all too soon, the reinforcements Howe had requested began to arrive and they knew there would be another assault. Daniel checked his cartridge box and realized he had almost nothing left. "You'd better scrounge up some more ammunition, Sam."

The boy shook his head. "There isn't any more. Just what I have here. When I went for another supply last time, there was almost none left."

Daniel cursed, though — as he told himself in unsympathetic language — he should have guessed this was coming. There had not been that much ammunition to begin with. During the assaults, the defenders had not fired in the orderly volleys of soldiers, but in the fear-driven frenzy of men who felt they had to fire as fast as they could or lose their lives. To keep up the unrelenting stream of fire that had twice repulsed the redcoats' attack, the men were firing and reloading as fast as they were able. For many of the men, that amounted to four or more shots each minute. Now there was so little powder left, that Daniel saw Prescott break open a few unused artillery cartridges so the men could avail themselves of that powder.

"I'm sorry, Sir," Sam said weakly. It seemed as though he was fearful of having let down the three men who had entrusted him with something so important.

"It isn't your fault," Daniel assured him. "You did a good job here. We'd never have lasted this long without you." Sam perked up a bit, especially when Ezra and Hue added their agreement to what Daniel had said. But Daniel knew what was coming. With so little ammunition, they would never hold back another assault. And, he knew what would come then. He had seen the redcoats at work with their terrifying steel bayonets. Ezra and Hue knew as well.

"You need to get gone from here," Hue told the boy. He knew others were leaving, and he could not say that he blamed them.

Sam looked from Hue and Ezra to Daniel. "What about you? Shouldn't you leave, too?"

Daniel laughed. "We probably should," he agreed. He nodded at Ezra and Hue. "And, I certainly won't fault you two if you want to live to fight another day. But I think I'm supposed to be here. Don't know why I feel that way, but I do. So, I think I'll stay."

"And, what makes you think this is any more your fight than ours?" Ezra asked indignantly. "We'll be staying, too. But you." He slapped Sam on the shoulder. "I promised your mother I'd get you home in one piece, so I want you to go on now."

Sam shook his head, however. He wanted to run. In fact, he wanted to be far away from this hill as fast as he could get there. But he shook his head. "This is my fight, too," he said stubbornly.

Ezra and Hue puffed themselves up, ready to demand that Sam run, but Daniel held them back. He recognized that stubborn pride all too well. "You can stay," he said. "You can stay and cover our backs." The first moment he had arrived on the hilltop, Daniel had felt the loss of Teague's friendship, had felt an inner sadness that the person he'd always counted on to cover his back in a fight was no longer with him. Sam could not fill those shoes, but Daniel made the offer, nonetheless. "We'll need someone to do that. Can you do it? Watch our backs to make sure no one surprises us from behind?" He waited for the earnest nod of the head. "Good then. I feel much better."

In fact, he felt worse, for he was certain he had just ensured that the boy would not make it home to his mother as Ezra had promised. *Hell*, he thought as he turned his back on Sam and the others to pretend an interest in what the Regulars were doing at that moment. *For all I know, he wouldn't be able to get away to safety, anyway.* They'd seen the smoke from Charlestown, and knew the Neck was taking heavy artillery fire. There may be no safe place to which Sam could run, and no way to get there in any event.

All at once, Daniel's pretended interest became quite real. Down by the river, the redcoat drummers were beating out a cadence, ordering the men to formation. The Regulars were coming again and, this time, they had over four hundred fresh troops.

*   *   *

Hinton was as frustrated and exhausted as any man making the climb up that blasted hillside for the third time. But this time, he had a renewed sense of urgency, a prevailing belief in the probability of their success on this attempt. Aside from the fresh troops, Howe had decided to vary his tactics again, but in ways that held more sense to the men who would have to execute them. This time, heavy packs and all superfluous equipment would be left behind. Troops would be moving light and fast, and they would be doing so in columns rather than spread out in firing lines. A column offered fewer targets for the enemy to hit, and made for a more organized progress along the difficult ground. Once they were close enough to the enemy lines, they would deploy and return fire but, until then, the impact of enemy fire on their advance would be considerably mitigated.

Additionally, he focused his assault on the breastwork and supported it with strategically-placed artillery. *This time*, Hinton thought, *we will succeed.* For, succeed, he knew they must. To do otherwise would be to create a situation with ramifications far beyond failure to take one hill away from the rebels. *We will succeed.* It became his mantra as they advanced through the smoke that clung like fog to the hillside, through grass that was now trampled into insignificance, but also streaked with the blood of the wounded and dead. And, the hillside was littered with bodies in such numbers that the advancing troops could not help but step on some of them. It was a terrible, sickening feeling, to put one's foot down and know it was the body of one's comrade beneath that foot. There were wounded among the troops advancing up the hill, as well. More than one wore a bandage or sling, more than one wore blood on face and uniform.

*   *   *

Daniel watched the columns advance in narrow, endless files of men that snaked down the hill as far as he could see. It occurred to him that it didn't matter if the redcoats presented them with fewer targets. With so little ammunition, they would have to choose their targets more carefully, anyway. But, muskets being the wildly inaccurate things they were, aiming at a single target and actually hitting that target were two very different things.

Once the head of each column drew within musket range, the rebels began firing. Though fewer men were falling now, whenever one did, the man in file behind him would quickly move up into the vacated position, and the column kept advancing. "If we were all crack marksmen," Ezra observed, "and could take a man down with every shot—"

Daniel finished the sentence for him. "We'd still run out of ammunition before they run out of men."

They watched as the columns marched within range and then deployed into firing lines, one behind the other, several rows deep. Once they had formed, the Regulars became an efficient bit of clockwork. The first row would kneel and, in conjunction with the row immediately to their rear, would fire a volley. With amazing speed and precision, those two lines would drop to the back and begin the process of reloading their muskets while the two lines that had replaced them fired. Daniel had watched them practice this drill time and again on Boston Common, and had admitted to being impressed by the beauty of it, though he could not see what value it would have in actual combat. Now he saw the value, and was even more impressed with the beauty of it.

The Regulars were pounding the militiamen with deadly volleys, every bit as unrelenting as was visited upon them during their ascents up the hill.

Of more concern, however, was the fact that they were also advancing. With almost every volley, the lines advanced a step or two closer to the rebel defenses. The rebels were returning fire with equal ferocity, dropping redcoats with astonishing frequency. Daniel knew it would not be enough, however — not unless the Regulars broke rank and ran again. And, they showed no sign of any such inclination.

Up until now, there were few rebel casualties. But as the defenders stood up so that they could pick their targets more carefully, they began to lose men first by ones and twos, and then in larger numbers. Ezra stood up, raised his musket to draw bead on one of the redcoats, and was knocked backward into the dirt at Sam's feet by a musket ball striking his chest. Dibble looked up at Sam and was about to assure the boy that it was only a small wound when he was taken by a fit of coughing. He managed to complain that it hurt to cough, and then noticed the blood in his mouth. Dibble just had time to curse the redcoat who'd shot him before succumbing to the wound. Death had taken Ezra Dibble so fast that neither Daniel nor Hue had seen him go.

Sam had seen, however. With the fierceness peculiar to young boys, he swiped his sleeve across his eyes and nose, and then set about trying to find something for Hue and Daniel to load into their muskets when the balls ran out. Some men were already using nails and other small bits of metal. Soon, they'd be reduced to throwing rocks. The range of Sam's search was necessarily limited by the fact that, the farther one got from the walls of the redoubt, the more dangerous it became. He saw two men taken down as they tried to help an injured friend to the rear where he might receive medical attention. He knew it meant the redcoats were now practically on top of them, but continued with the business of gathering up objects that could be fired from a musket.

The fighting all along the rebel defenses had taken on an intensity that, within its scale, was the equal of just about anything the British army had ever faced. Every inch of ground the British advanced was dearly bought, and that expensive ground was slick with blood and littered with fallen men. There were bodies that showed no visible trauma, and next to them could be a dismembered body, or a disemboweled body, or simply a body so bloodied as to be unrecognizable. The men who were still on their feet had taken on layers of sweat and dust and blood until they were almost as unrecognizable as the corpses at their feet.

Daniel could see their faces now as they fought their way closer. Their eyes, wide and white against bloodied, powder-burned faces, were almost feral, and their mouths were set in snarling rictus that was as much terror as it was determination. They were at the wall now, dying in unthinkable numbers, surging forward into the storm of musket fire the rebels unleashed in one last, desperate volley. The redcoat line hesitated for a fraction of a second, wavering between continuing the fight and breaking to run again. It was palpable, that hesitation, and Daniel held his breath as he waited for the balance to tip one way or the other.

It tipped against the rebels. There were enough men among those weary, decimated redcoat lines who were determined not to accept defeat, enough to give impetus toward continuing the assault, enough to storm forward over the walls and fences and breastwork, pulling the rest in their wake. Daniel saw them rise up and surge over the wall of the redoubt like storm surge overwhelming the rocks on a beach. Even as they were discharging their muskets one last time, the redcoats were leveling their lethal bayonets, preparing to give vent to all the day's miseries.

Daniel and Hue, like the rest of the rebel defenders, had already spent their last ammunition. Now, there was nothing to do but pick up anything available that might be used to help defend oneself. Few of the rebels had bayonets, even fewer carried swords or sabers. Many had knives or clubs to hand, but little else. Nothing that was the match for bayonets wielded by professional soldiers with killing as their only object.

"Go!" Daniel shouted, pushing Sam ahead of him. "Run! Get out of the redoubt! Get up to Bunker Hill!" He watched Sam stumble in front of him, then regain his feet and began to make his way toward the opening in the redoubt wall. There was only one way out, and Daniel now realized that it made the redoubt a trap. "Go with him," Daniel said to Hue. "If the gap is blocked, find a place to get him over the wall!" He waited for Hue to nod his understanding. "Get him out safe, Hue."

"What about you? Come with us!"

Daniel shook his head. "I'll be behind you. I want him to get out of here alive. I'll cover your retreat."

Hue did not like the arrangement, but there was no time to argue. The redcoats were over the wall. He heard Prescott yelling for his men to retreat, but there was no need for the order. Those who could break free were already running toward the gap in the redoubt. Just as he turned to follow Sam, Hue saw a redcoat bear down on Daniel, bayonet at the ready. "Behind you!" Hue yelled. But he did not linger to watch the outcome. Grabbing Sam's collar, he pulled the boy toward the gap in the redoubt.

*   *   *

Richard Chastain had not expected this third assault. He had expected Howe to admit defeat, and then to request that he be permitted to collect his dead and wounded. Chastain had planned to allow himself to be found, dazed and bloodied, but adamant that the orderlies attend to those more needy than himself. Once attention had gone elsewhere, he would simply melt back into his regiment where he would manage to convincingly take part in commiserations over the outcome of the day's endeavors.

But there *was* a third assault, which Chastain resented if only because it meant that much more time he had to endure hiding under a pile of corpses. The columns of troops had marched past him without a glance in his direction, and had apparently managed to form ranks somewhere within the killing ground and return the rebel fire. That much he could tell by the orderly volleys and the sound of barked commands. It had gone on and on, and then there was an infinitesimal lull during which he expected the troops to break ranks and run again. That had not happened. Instead, there was a great roar, the sound of men shrieking as though their lives depended upon it. It was, he guessed, he sound of men breeching a defense. It seemed impossible, and yet, when he raised his head enough to see up the hill, that was exactly what was happening. Howe's and Pigot's forces were overrunning the length of the rebel defenses.

Chastain hastily revised his plan and, struggling to his feet in a manner he thought befitted a man temporarily knocked out of the fight, he limped up the hill to join the last of the troops to pour into the redoubt.

*   *   *

Running along the leading-edge of the churning, death-filled surf that was the massive redcoat advance, Daniel followed Hue and Sam, protecting their retreat as best he could. Some of the redcoats had made it into the redoubt ahead of the larger mass, and were engaged here and there with militiamen, fighting with a passion that could only find resolution in death. These small battles slowed their progress, especially because neither Hue nor Daniel could bring themselves to simply run past without offering help where they could. Hue had only his empty musket left, and Daniel had nothing but his knife, so they improvised as they ran.

Swinging the butt of his musket against a redcoat's head, Hue stopped one man who was on the verge of driving his bayonet through a militiaman's chest. Sam looked back, wide-eyed with terror, and Daniel bellowed at him to keep going. The redcoat Hue had struck on the head dropped his musket, which Daniel scooped up as he ran by. Immediately, he found it necessary to turn the bayonet against a redcoat who was rushing toward Hue and Sam. With all the force he could muster, Daniel drove the bayonet into the redcoat's gut, and then found to his surprise that he could not pull it free. Cursing, he left it behind and moved on.

They were close to the gap in the wall of the redoubt, but so were too many of the other militiamen. The storm surge of redcoats had filled the redoubt much more quickly than Daniel had anticipated, bringing chaos and bloodlust along with it and the redoubt, which had protected them all day, became a charnel house as a lethal bottleneck formed at the single exit. Fleeing militiamen and pursuing redcoats alike were piling up and, unable to move forward, were fighting where they stood. Black powder smoke hung thick in the air, choking them and obscuring their vision to the point that it was difficult to tell friend from foe. And still more redcoats streamed into the redoubt.

"Forget the gap! Go for the wall!" Daniel shouted at Hue, waving his arms wildly in that direction. "We'll lift him over! Go! Go! Go!" He was shoving them forward, imploring them to greater speed. He stumbled over a tall, metal hat that had fallen with its grenadier owner, and lurched sideways into a red-coated officer who was poised to put one of the militiamen to the sword, knocking him off-balance as well. The officer rounded on Daniel, cursing, and raised his sword to strike at this new target. Daniel grabbed up the abandoned grenadier's helmet and used it to parry the blade, and then ducked under the officer's arm and threw himself shoulder-first into the man's ribs. He could hear and feel the ribs cracking under the force of the impact, and heard the officer cry out in pain, but did not linger to take it further. Twenty paces ahead, he could see Hue embroiled in a fight he was certain to lose.

*   *   *

Richard Chastain was admittedly not the last redcoat over the wall into the redoubt, but any man behind him was likely hobbled by injury or hampered by some other physical burden. Chastain picked his way along so methodically that anyone watching from afar would likely have thought him a man out for a stroll and concerned lest his boots become untidy. When it came time to scale the wall, he did so with exaggerated caution, keeping himself as safe from harm as it was humanly possible to do while in the midst of a battle. But when he crested the wall, the scene he witnessed before him was enough to shock his indifference and momentarily still his mechanistic heart.

The British troops had poured into the redoubt in staggering numbers, their red uniforms displacing the militiamen's brown and tan. Powder smoke, black and foul in the nostrils, drifted in long fingers that alternately hid or parted to reveal the legions of dead and dying. The annihilation was complete, the slaughter incomprehensible. Chastain thought this must surely be akin to standing at the gates of hell, a hell into which he knew he had now to descend.

*   *   *

Daniel raced toward Hue and Sam, ducking flailing arms and every sort of swinging weapon like a man running through a field of windmills. The redcoat, who had his back to Daniel, had Hue in a chokehold. Hue's arms were thrashing outwards, his feet kicking in a wild, futile effort to work himself free. Trying to reach the struggling man, Daniel felt he was running in deep sand. Drawing his dirk as he ran, Daniel could not recall ever trying to run so fast, and yet seeming to go so slow. Finally, in seconds that seemed like hours, Daniel reached them. Hardly slowing his momentum, he swept down with his knife in one fluid movement that sliced through muscle and tendon just above the back of the redcoat's knee. As the lamed soldier fell, Daniel swept up with the knife and cut through the strap that would free the soldier's musket. Before the redcoat had hit the ground, Daniel had the musket in his hands. Still moving toward Sam, he swiped the knife across his breeches to clean the blade of blood and returned it to its sheath.

Hue, hands clutching at his throat as though to assure himself that his head was still attached to his body, nodded his thanks to Daniel and raced alongside him toward where Sam stood, wide-eyed with terror.

"I told you to keep going," Daniel barked, roughly taking Sam by the arm and leading him toward the wall. They had reached the wall of the redoubt and, looking at it now, it seemed to Daniel that it had grown twenty feet taller. Hue shared this distorted view. "We can get Sam up," he said. "Then I'll give you a leg up."

"And, what about you?"

Daniel shook his head. "You go with Sam. See he gets home."

"You don't think I'll leave you behind."

"I want to stay. I saw a friend who needs my help." During their headlong rush across the redoubt, he had spotted Dr. Warren near the gap, frantically directing the retreat while simultaneously trying to help fight back the redcoat advance. "I'll be fine," he assured Hue. "But Sam won't if you don't stay with him." They lifted Sam up onto the wall, and then Hue paused to shake Daniel's hand before allowing himself to be boosted up.

Without watching to see that they got safely down to the other side, Daniel turned and searched through the melee for Dr. Warren. He could not find Warren, but a grenadier was charging toward him, bayonet first. Daniel leveled the musket he had taken from Hue's attacker and fired — but nothing happened. Whether the musket was not loaded or had misfired did not matter. Pulling the trigger had not stopped the grenadier. Having no other option, Daniel braced the musket for a bayonet charge of his own. The men came together like two jousting knights. But it was an uneven joust. The grenadier's training gave him the edge and, though Daniel was able to dodge the bayonet, his musket was easily knocked from his hands. The grenadier wasted no time in renewing his attack. Daniel was scrambling to recover his weapon, trying to stay out of the grenadier's reach, when a musket discharged from somewhere behind him. The shot caught the grenadier in the gut and he crumpled to the ground where he sat, looking up at Daniel as though perplexed by what had just happened. Daniel, who could not determine who had fired the shot, was equally perplexed. He left the grenadier to his fate, and continued his search for Warren.

When he finally spotted his friend, Warren was near the gap, urging a final group of militiamen through. Daniel saw something else as well, and that sighting made his blood run cold.

*   *   *

Chastain made his way across the redoubt, avoiding all confrontations except those that involved using his cherished sword to finish off wounded, disabled rebels. In all his years of mastering the art of the beautiful weapon, he had never yet experienced the particular sensation of driving it through a man. His first thrust was clumsy, and he almost forgot the final twist that was necessary to cleanly withdraw the blade against the sucking force of the wound. But, with practice, he found that he was becoming quite good at it, and imagined how dashing he must look as he smoothly served up each killing thrust.

Save for the sound of bayonets and sabers, men screaming in rage or pain, the hill had become oddly quiet. After the day-long din of artillery and musket fire, it was eerie, almost unnerving, but quiet had descended almost as abruptly as the noise of battle had begun so many hours earlier. There was no more artillery or ordered musket fire lest the British troops who had swarmed onto the summit of Breed's Hill become victims of their own guns.

Chastain slowed as he approached the place where struggling men had massed, some trying to escape, others trying to prevent that escape. The horrible, acrid smoke stung his eyes, and now the overpowering smell of blood threatened to make him wretch. The need to be quit of the redoubt suddenly overwhelmed him. He pivoted where he stood, searching for the best way out. That was when he spotted Joseph Warren near the frenzied mass of fighting at the gap in the wall, delaying his own escape while he urged his men on to safety.

He recognized Warren at once. The doctor was a well-known person in Boston, and had paid more than one visit to General Gage to negotiate on some point or other. Chastain stopped in his tracks for a moment to regard the man most of his fellow officers considered the bane of their existence. Warren's fine coat and elegant silk waistcoat were a marked contrast to the clothes worn by the men around him, Chastain noticed. He might have found much to admire in the way Warren dressed and in the refined manner of his bearing had he not been overcome with a wave of resentment that this colonial doctor seemed to embody the flawlessness and level of accomplishment that eluded him. Bostonians adopted an almost reverential tone when they spoke of Warren, and even many of the British officers admitted to the man's eloquence, his reputation as a forward-thinking doctor, and his skillful leadership.

Chastain drew his pistol slowly. He pretended to himself that it was a matter of prolonging the pleasure of the moment, but in the tiny part of his heart that was still capable of holding forth the truth, he knew it was fear. If he moved too quickly, Warren's attention might be drawn and he did not want to feel the doctor's eyes on him, did not want to remember the look in them when Warren realized his own death was imminent. It was so much easier, Chastain felt, to shoot a man in the back.

* * *

Daniel saw Warren gathering up the last of the survivors into something resembling an organized retreat. A handful of men ran through the gap, and Warren turned to follow. But, unnoticed by the doctor, a solitary British officer had worked his way to within a few paces of him and seemed to hesitate there. Initially, Daniel thought the officer meant to take Warren prisoner and started running toward them intent on spoiling the officer's plan. But then he saw who the officer was, saw him draw his pistol, and knew Richard Chastain was a man whose intent would be far more deadly.

Chastain was drawing the pistol slowly. Daniel ran harder, and screamed for Warren to turn around, to see, to run . . . to do *something*. But Warren could not hear, and did not turn.

Warren's back was to Chastain when the lieutenant pulled the trigger, so he had no notion what was coming. Daniel, however, felt as though he could actually see the ball leave the pistol and travel the short distance to Joseph Warren's head. He knew what was coming, but felt no less shock at the sight of the lead ball tearing into Warren's skull. The effect on bone and tissue was devastating, and killed Warren almost instantly. Daniel was within ten paces of Warren when he fell, and kept running straight for Chastain even as he saw Warren's limp body crumple to the ground.

Daniel crashed shoulder-first into Chastain with so much force that both men were lifted off their feet. Chastain landed on his back with Daniel on top of him, and felt the breath rush from his body. Three different sensations traveled through his mind with head-spinning rapidity. First, there was confusion. He had no idea how he had gone so quickly from standing on his feet with a smoking pistol in his hand, to flat on his back with no breath in his lungs. Surprise came in the next fraction of a second as he recognized Daniel, who he believed to be safely locked away. The man who was supposed to be Chastain's ticket into General Gage's good graces was sitting astride his chest, one hand clutching at Chastain's throat. Finally, everything in Chastain's mind — indeed, in his whole body — gave way to only fear, for Daniel was holding a knife and there was no sign of hesitation as he prepared to use it.

Richard Chastain knew death had come. He had no strength with which to fend it off and no breath with which to cry out. At the last second, even his body betrayed him by discharging his bowels in a sluice of foul excrement that soaked through his perfect buff-colored breeches to betray his fear to the world.

All of the rage Daniel felt over Warren's death was released into the thrust of his dirk into Chastain's gullet. That done, Daniel was utterly spent. He meticulously cleaned the blood from the dirk by wiping the blade back and forth across Chastain's scarlet coat. And then, the tide of violence swirling around him momentarily forgotten, he rose to his feet. His chest heaved with the effort of each ragged breath as he stood looking down at Chastain. His stomach knotted and lurched and, had there been anything in his stomach to give up, he would have vomited.

Thinking that he might carry Warren's body from the redoubt, he turned and started toward the place where he had seen his friend fall. But he took only a single step. Edward Hinton stood before him, less than thirty paces away, musket leveled at Daniel's chest. Reacting instinctively, Daniel tensed for a fight and reached for a weapon with which to defend himself, only to find himself wanting. He had no musket or pistol, and Chastain's sword was beyond his reach and of little use against a man who was armed with a musket, as was his dirk. He considered charging Hinton, but that seemed as foolhardy as the urge to run was unrealistic. All of these options were weighed and discarded within the fraction of a second. Ultimately, he did the only thing he could; he relaxed, straightened his spine, and looked Hinton in the eye as he waited for the shot to come.

Hinton did not make him wait long before he squared his shot and fired. Daniel saw the muzzle flash, saw the smoke envelope Hinton, and heard the crack of the musket firing. He flinched and grabbed his chest, certain that he'd been shot but was perhaps too mortally wounded to feel anything. His hands came away dry, however. There was no blood, no wound. Incredibly, Edward Hinton had missed. It seemed incomprehensible to Daniel that Hinton could have missed at such close range, and he wondered if it was done deliberately. But, because Hinton was methodically reloading the musket, Daniel chose not to question his good luck any further. He turned and bolted through the gap where he was swallowed up by John Stark's New Hampshire men who had stayed to cover the last of the retreating defenders.

Expecting the British to pursue them, the surviving militiamen straggled up Bunker Hill, and then across the Neck. But there was no pursuit. Like them, the Regulars were spent. Like them, the Regulars had endured more than anyone would have believed possible for a human to endure.

CHAPTER TWENTY-FIVE

It had taken Daniel hours after the battle ended to slip past the British Regulars and work his way back across the river into Boston. The safer thing would have been to steer a course as far away from Boston as he could get, but he had pretty much decided that choosing the safe course was simply not in his blood. Skulking and darting from concealment to concealment, he had picked his way through the streets to his mother's shop, only to find it gutted by fire. Fearing that his mother and Anna had perished in the fire, his insides felt about the way the burned out building looked until a neighbor recognized him and told him that his mother and others who were in the building were taken to the home of Mr. John Wilton. It was good news, and bad —his mother and Anna were alive and being cared for, but it could prove difficult for him to see them.

He was here now, standing outside John Wilton's house, facing the moment, and full of uncertainty regarding how he should proceed. Perhaps he should just leave, he thought. Perhaps it should be enough that he knew they were alive. But it wasn't enough. Doubting that Wilton would want in his house someone who had just taken up arms against the king's army, Daniel considered sneaking in through an upstairs window. But that seemed unfair and a show of disrespect to a man he held in high regard. So, stiffening his spine, he climbed the steps to the kitchen door and knocked. He had expected Mrs. Cook, or perhaps the maid, to answer, and was taken aback when Wilton himself appeared instead.

"I've no right to ask, Sir," Daniel said softly, "and will certainly understand if you turn me away, but I'd like to see my mother if you would allow it. I'll not stay long."

Wilton blinked. "What an extraordinary thing to say!" He opened the door and held it, indicating that Daniel should enter. "Mr. Fisackerly has told me of your part in finding my Anna and getting her as quickly as possible into helpful hands. I do not believe she would be alive if not for your actions. You are welcome in my home, Sir."

Daniel fidgeted uncomfortably. "I think Drum — Mr. Fisackerly — may have overstated my importance in the matter," he said modestly.

But Wilton waved away his humble protest. "None of that, now. Once you were set free, you could have bolted to safety and left Anna's fate to the rest of us. That is what many would have done in your position, but you did not. Furthermore, I believe it was your considerable capacity for solving such problems that enabled you to find her in such timely fashion." He peered over the top of his glasses at Daniel. "No, Mr. Garrett. I'll not accept your modest protestations, and I'll insist that you receive my gratitude without further discussion."

Wilton's earnestness, which bordered on severity, would have been comical under other circumstances, Daniel thought. He did not laugh, but bowed instead.

"Good then," Wilton said. "I'll take you up to see your mother. She's doing quite well, by the way. I don't know how much Mr. Fisackerly has already told you."

"I'm afraid I haven't yet spoken with him. I hoped he would be here."

"Ah, I see. Forgive me. Of course, there was no way for you to know. He is with Mr. Bradley. That young man was in grave condition, but would not allow us to bring him here, insisting on going to a place of his choosing. Mr. Fisackerly took him and, I assume, is with him still. I hope you will know where they are to be found as he left no direction or address."

"Yes, I can guess where they are," Daniel said. "But how did Mr. Bradley come to be involved?"

Wilton briefly sketched out all that Selah had told him. "You see, then, that Mr. Bradley is at least partly responsible for the fact that neither your mother nor Anna perished in the fire."

Daniel nodded. "You say Teague is in a bad way?"

"Yes. The doctor could do little for him."

Daniel's heart tightened with cold dread. "I'll go to him as soon as I've seen my mother and Miss Somerset."

"Yes. Very good. I wonder if you might want to at least wash your face before you see your mother? Even she might not recognize you under such a grimy mask."

It was said with a touch of humor but, on seeing his own reflection in the polished surface of Mrs. Cook's pewter, he had to admit to some truth in the statement. He was a sight, his face caked in dirt, powder burns, and blood. "Yes, I believe a wash might be in order," he agreed.

He dunked his entire head into the wash bucket. Then, using strong soap, he scrubbed his hair, face, and neck. He finger-combed his hair and retied it in a neat queue at the back of his neck. These things done, he nodded to Wilton, who led him up the stairs to the bedroom in which his mother was resting.

She appeared to be asleep when he entered the room, but opened her eyes and smiled at him when he approached the bed. "I'm glad you have come," she said, her voice weak. "We heard about the battle, and I knew you would have been there. I'm relieved to see you well and whole."

He moved a small chair from the corner of the room to a place nearer to the bed and sat. "I came because I was worried about you and Miss Somerset," he said, taking her hand in his. "I'm sorry that it didn't occur to me that you might be worried, too. When I left you yesterday — was it only yesterday? — yes, it was. When I left you yesterday, it was with the determination to be less of a trial to you. I think I'm not off to such a good start."

She laughed, and then grimaced. "If you want to be less of a trial to me at this moment, Daniel, please do not make me laugh! Dr. Hawkins thinks I have a cracked rib, and I find that even breathing deeply is excruciating. Heaven help me if I have to cough or sneeze!"

"How did you come to have a cracked rib?"

"Miss Ainsworth took umbrage to the fact that I interrupted her attempt to murder Miss Somerset, and shot me. Very discourteous of her, I think, but then, I never did like that girl."

Daniel smiled at her jest, but was not deceived by her light tone. "She might have killed you," he said. "She might have killed both of you. I should have been there to protect you instead of running off to save my own skin."

"Nonsense. You did as I asked — though, I did not have it in mind that you would run from the redcoats in Boston straight into a battle against them." She shot him a sharp look from the corner of her eye. "At any rate, it does not do to sit around discussing should-haves. We all do the best we can at any given moment. That's all anyone *can* do. So, no more blaming yourself or I shall be cross with you." She watched him struggle with the retort he wanted to make and then discard it in favor of pleasing her. "Dr. Hawkins says I have luck either in strong bones, or Miss Ainsworth's poor marksmanship. He believes the ball from the pistol went through the fleshy part of my lower arm, and was further hindered by my stays so that, by the time it impacted on my rib, it did little real damage. Quite a journey. The rib is cracked and quite painful, and I bled a great deal, but I shall mend soon enough. I suppose I might have suffered worse."

"Then, I'm thankful for your hard bones and Miss Ainsworth's lack of experience with pistols."

"Have you seen Teague?" She ventured the question carefully.

He shook his head. "I didn't even know of his involvement until I spoke with Mr. Wilton downstairs. I am glad to know he isn't responsible for hurting Miss Somerset. Perhaps it would be well if you told me everything that happened from the beginning."

She told him, watching his face carefully as she recounted the string of horrors the night had been. When she had done, he buried his face in his hands and said nothing. "Teague tried to help us," she said gently. "He did help us, in fact. It was his whole reason for being there. He asked me to tell you — in case he was not able to tell you himself — that he wanted to try to make amends. He wanted me to tell you that you were right about everything, and that he was sorry." Daniel looked at her, but still did not speak. "You will go and see him, won't you?" she asked.

"Yes. Of course I'll go. But I need to first see Miss Somerset."

Selah nodded. "I believe she hasn't yet awakened, but Dr. Hawkins insists there is every reason to hope that she will recover. She had a bad time of it, but she's strong. You know that about her."

"Yes. I know that about her." He squeezed Selah's hand, and then raised it to his lips, kissing it gently. "I know that about you as well," he added.

Wilton showed Daniel to Anna's room, and surprised him by leaving them alone. There were tiny roses printed on the bed hangings and coverlet — pink roses — and he wondered why he noticed such a small thing at this moment. He eased himself onto a chair that was already pulled beside the bed and surveyed her face. She did not appear to be any better, but neither did she appear to be worse, and he decided to be content with that. He leaned his elbows on his knees, wondering what to say for, despite the fact that she could not hear him, he felt compelled to talk to her.

"I'm sorry, Mouse," he began slowly. "I'm sorry for what you've suffered while attempting to help me. And, I thank you for it. But, honestly Mouse, if you ever again do something so recklessly foolish, I shall throttle you!" He thought for a moment that she had smiled in response, but it was not so. "I can't stay here with you as long as I'd like. Teague is likely dying, and I need to go to him. I know you'd understand that, but it pains me, nonetheless."

Despite the fact that she could not see him, he ducked his head, hiding the tears that were beginning to fill his eyes. He'd never been one for tears, and it irritated him no end that, lately, he seemed to be shedding them so often. "You must wake up," he insisted. "You must get better!" He picked up her limp hand and cradled it in his hands, studying the image of the two hands entwined, committing it to memory.

He rose abruptly and fled the room — fled all that unwelcome emotion. Wilton and Mrs. Cook seemed to be waiting for him downstairs in the kitchen, which was not his preference. He would have liked to be able to escape without being seen. "I thank you," he told Wilton, fighting to keep his voice steady. "I thank you for looking after my mother, and for allowing me to see her and Miss Somerset."

"As I said, you are welcome in my home."

Daniel nodded and excused himself, barely pausing to accept and thank Mrs. Cook for the sack of food and provisions she handed to him as he went out the door.

*　　*　　*

Exhaustion was fully upon Daniel by the time he reached Withers' public house. He had crossed Boston as quickly as possible, not bothering to keep to back alleys and not pausing to answer anyone who attempted to speak to him. Thoughts had tumbled through his mind ever since hearing his mother's account of what had happened to Teague and what he had done. It seemed to Daniel that he must say something significant to his dying friend, give him something to take with him in his heart when he went wherever men such as Teague went when they departed the world. But he could not think of a single thing that was appropriate or equal to the moment.

Withers looked up, plainly surprised, when Daniel entered the tavern. The last time the old man had seen him, Daniel was being led away, surrounded by redcoats who seemed unlikely to allow him to live past dawn of the next day. And yet, here he was, battered but alive enough, and Withers knew without asking the reason Daniel had come. He jerked his head toward the stairs. "He's up there," he said, attempting a gruff tone. "He won't let anyone do naught for him, though."

Daniel nodded his thanks, and took the stairs two at a time as he climbed to the upper floor. Not knowing exactly what to expect, he opened the door slowly. He saw Drum first, sitting near Teague's cot, head down and shoulders slumped in defeat. And then he saw Teague. It seemed to Daniel that he had seen more than his share of men hovering on the thin line between life and death, and yet it did not prepare him for the waxy pallor of his friend's skin, the red-rimmed, sunken eyes, and the sense that Teague had been battered by some terrible thing.

Drum looked up, and slowly rose to his feet when he saw Daniel. Relief was plain on his face, and he offered Daniel his chair as though he was passing along some dreadful burden. Daniel did not sit immediately, but stepped forward to embrace Drum, which he had never before done. "Thank you, Drum," he said quietly. Drum looked at him, embarrassed and confused, but Daniel just smiled reassuringly. *It's all right. We'll talk later.*

"You came," Teague said, his voice rasping and soft. "I hoped you would."

"Of course I did. I'd have been here sooner if I could have. What's this foolishness about not wanting to stay at Mr. Wilton's place? There are people to look after you there."

"Not much point," Teague said.

"You don't know that."

"I do. I saw the look on Hawkins' face when he looked me over, and I can feel the poison eating away at my insides. She poisoned me, you know? Charlotte. She put arsenic in the port. Her father's port. I always like that stuff. Damn, Daniel!"

"Let me take you to Mr. Wilton's. Let me ask Dr. Hawkins to take another look at you." He knew there was no point, but desperation had replaced rational sense.

"No. I'm a dead man already. I'd rather be here where I'm comfortable."

Daniel nodded. He still would have preferred to make the effort, but he understood. His shoulders sagged in resignation, and he sat in the chair Drum had vacated. "Then, I'm glad I got here in time to thank you," he said. "You saved them. My mother wanted me to give you her thanks, too."

"Your mother is a good woman. I've always thought that, though I wouldn't have admitted to it. I was a dolt to reject her efforts to take me under her wing when we were boys." He was suddenly overcome with a cough that sounded as if his lungs were tearing apart. "Sorry," he said, wiping his mouth with one trembling hand. "I think the fire did its worst to me."

"You shouldn't be talking so much."

But Teague just shook his head. "It's what I waited around for. I needed to tell you how sorry I am about the things I said and the things I did."

"It doesn't matter now."

"It matters to me. It matters that we part as friends. That matters very much to me, Daniel." Another cough, and blood appeared on his lips.

Daniel tried not to look at the blood. It chilled his heart to see it, but there was no need to let Teague know that. "We are friends," he said. "Just because we quarreled . . . we were always friends."

"Thank you for that. And, I wanted to tell you that you were right. You were right about Charlotte. If I'd listened to you, I wouldn't be lying here like this."

"It's not your fault. You're not the first man to have a pretty girl twist you around until you no longer recognize yourself. And, anyway, I just thought she was going to break your heart. I never thought any of this would happen. Even I didn't see the madness in her — and it must surely have been madness. I don't think anyone did. Maybe not even her father."

"She was planning to marry that sodding son-of-a-sow Chastain."

Daniel laughed. "Well, if she were still alive, it would be to meet disappointment. Chastain didn't make it down off the hill today."

"Did you kill him?"

"I did."

"Well, that's the best news I've had all day. The lousy son-of-a-sow." He gave Daniel a sideways look. There was far more to say than the time he guessed he had left would allow. "I'd never have let them hang you, you know. I didn't know you'd been taken, or what had really happened until yesterday. But even if I hadn't known you were innocent, I'd have got you free somehow."

"I know you would. Drum did a fine enough job of it, though." He looked over his shoulder to where Drum was hovering in a far corner of the room. "Somewhere in Boston there are two redcoats with headaches the size of whales, and likely a particular enmity for Drum." That made Teague laugh, which made him cough, but Daniel guessed the laughter might be worth the price to him.

"And you thought I was the one who would get him into serious trouble," Teague reminded him.

Daniel shrugged. Teague seemed to be having difficulty keeping his eyes open, as though sleep was determined to overcome him. "Should we let you rest now?"

"No." He fought to open his eyes, but was obviously unable to focus on Daniel's face. "There's plenty of time for rest. I need to tell you a few more things."

"You don't need—"

"Shut up, Daniel, and listen. I've told Drum I don't want to be buried in one of those tidy burial grounds with the stones all lined up like teeth. Bury me out near that creek where we used to go fishing. Will you do that for me?"

"Of course we will."

"Also, I told Drum where to find the money and some of the stolen things. Charlotte thought she was very clever, but I got the better of her on that one." He chuckled, and coughed. "I gave her some gold a few weeks back. She thought I had gone, but I circled back and snuck into the house. I watched her put the gold away in a special hiding place. Yesterday, while she was away from the house, I went by and cleaned it all out – the gold and all the rest of the money. I told Drum where I hid it. Go with him to retrieve it. I think you'll know best what to do with all of it."

This bit of news surprised Daniel, and he did not quite know how to respond. "We'll take care of it," he said vaguely. "You should quit talking so much and rest."

Teague shook his head. "Tell me about the battle. I should have been there. I should have been there to have your back like always used to be."

"That would have been nice," Daniel agreed. "Of the two of us, you were always the better fighter."

"But you were always the better man." His eyes were closed now, but he raised one hand, gesturing for Daniel to talk.

Moment by moment, starting with the point where he found Dr. Warren at his desk in Cambridge, Daniel took him through the events of the previous evening and early morning. When he reached the point in the story where they lost Dr. Warren, he realized that he had lost Teague as well. But he did not stop talking. He finished the entire story, lingering particularly on Chastain's demise. "It was a bloody bad time," he finished up sadly. "And it would have been good to have had you there, watching my back like always."

S. D. BANKS

CHAPTER TWENTY-SIX

Even after their eviction from the Charlestown peninsula, the assembled colonial militias continued to besiege Boston. Gage's army and the Loyalists who had fled to Boston for safety were contained within the confines of the city, and an uneasy stalemate persisted. Just as the militiamen sought to keep the army bottled up in Boston, the Regulars strove to keep rebels out. The situation served to make it difficult for Daniel, who was staying in the militia camp near Cambridge, to come and go as freely as he liked. Almost a week lapsed, therefore, before Daniel and Drum could slip past the pickets and make their way to the Wilton house.

Anna was comfortably arranged on a chaise in her uncle's parlor, her wounded leg elevated on pillows, a blanket across her lap, and tea on the table at her elbow. It would have been a tranquil scene, Daniel thought, were it not for the dark bruises on her face and arms, and the large bandage around her head. Nevertheless, she was doing remarkably well all things considered. She was reading, or seemed to be, but looked up immediately when he entered the room.

"You've been expecting me," he charged. He set aside the canvas bag he was carrying and crossed the room to her.

"I have. Mrs. Cook told me you'd arrived and were visiting with your mother." She closed the book on her lap and folded her hands on top of it, the picture of placidity. "I suppose you're here to chastise me for being foolish."

"And reckless," he added, taking a chair near her. "But I've already rebuked you for that, though you may not remember it as you were asleep at the time."

One corner of her mouth lifted, but she managed to repress the remainder of the smile. "Ah," she said, setting her book aside like a warrior putting aside her shield. "It's good that's done with, then."

"I do want to thank you, however. Reckless and foolish though it may have been, I know you did it with the intention of helping me and, for that, I thank you." He leaned forward to more closely inspect the damage to her face. "All in all, I suppose simply thanking you isn't enough, but it's the best I can do for now."

"Never mind. I'm certain I'll be able to devise a way for you to show your gratitude at some time in the future."

"No doubt," he replied drolly. He pointed at the hump under the blanket where her leg was elevated. "Now you know what it's like to be shot, Mouse, perhaps you'll be more understanding if ever I am in the same circumstance?"

"Are you planning to be shot soon?"

"Not planning on it. All things considered, however, it does seem a strong possibility."

She regarded him for several moments. "You're going out to join up with Mr. Washington's so-called army, aren't you?"

"He's a general now, you know. Not just 'Mr.' Washington." He smiled at her pretended disdain. "The Continental Congress has given him overall command of what will, hopefully, become the Continental Army. And, yes, I was weighing the possibility of joining them."

Her hands formed into tense fists that clutched at the blanket. When she realized what she was doing, she hastily released the handfuls of fabric and smoothed away the wrinkles she had made. "I received your message about Teague," she said without looking at him. "I am sorry he's gone."

He took a breath to respond, but hung there, thoughts suspended in mid-air, while he composed himself. Finally, he said, "Teague thought he had betrayed me. He thought he had let me down. But, if that's true, then I let him down as well. A better friend would not have given up on him as I did. A better friend would have seen and understood why he was choosing that path. I was too caught up in other things — too busy to give him the attention of a friend."

"You make it sound like he was a child caught in some mischief. He was lying and stealing, Daniel. I don't think you can hold yourself responsible for his choice to become a criminal."

"He was stealing from the Regulars," Daniel laughed. "As of a few days ago, I think that made him a Patriot."

She narrowed her eyes at him. "Are we going to quarrel over politics now?"

"No. We are not. But talking about Teague's escapades reminds me that I brought something to you." He retrieved the canvas bag and laid it beside the chaise, reached inside, and withdrew a large blue egg, beautifully filigreed in gold.

Anna gasped. "Mrs. Gage's music box?" She reached out to take the egg from him. "Drum was right. It is beautiful." Carefully, she opened the latch and set the music box to playing. "Where did you get it?"

"Teague told me where to find it. Charlotte had it, along with the other things in that bag." He watched her reach into the bag and pull out the assorted pieces of jewelry, sterling toiletry set, and other small items. "As best I can tell, all of them likely belong to either Mrs. Gage or the general himself. I thought you could give them to your uncle. I'm sure he can find a way to see that they are returned to the Gages without involving me."

"Of course. And, soon I hope. Beautiful as these things are, I'd rather not have them here to remind me of all the horror attached to them."

"That's done, then." As he sat looking at her, he felt the threat of the same unwelcome wave of emotion that had overcome him when he visited her the day after the battle. Thankfully, she'd been asleep then. But she was wide awake now, and there would be no hiding it from her. "I've stayed too long, Mouse," he said, rising abruptly. "I came to satisfy myself that my mother is well and that you'll live, and now I must go."

"Wait, Daniel. Please? Stay and talk to me. Tell me what happened. Tell me about the battle?"

He looked at her uncertainly. "It might be better if I don't."

"Why? Because you think I should not hear? Or, because the telling of it would hurt too much?"

"Both, I think."

"Then only tell me bits of it. The parts that hurt can wait, but it might help to talk about it some. You know me, Daniel. I've never been a delicate thing. You know that my sensibilities are not so easily offended by the hearing of such things."

He nodded and sat down again, slowly this time, uncertain whether it was the right thing to do. He leaned forward, forearms on his knees, hands folded and head lowered as though in prayer. She was right; he did want to tell her what had happened on that hill. But though it would ease his soul, he was reluctant to trouble her as he knew the hearing of it all would do.

"It's all right," she said softly. "Just start at the beginning."

And, he did. At first, his words came in fits and starts as he sifted through all that was in his mind to try to find the things he could share. But, as he talked, his voice so soft it was audible only to her, all of it began to pour out. He talked of the fear and the pain, of the heroics he had seen as well as the shameful things.

"Colonel Prescott was brilliant," he said. "But Putnam, in whom we had so much confidence, did not bring his forces from Bunker Hill down to Breed's Hill to reinforce us. I don't know that it would have made any difference, but it is being remarked upon. Our artillery was . . . well, I can't even begin to explain how pathetic it was. Worst of all, Artemus Ward sat in Cambridge and did nothing to reinforce us, sent no food, water or ammunition . . . nothing. I harbor a good deal of anger toward that man and doubt I shall forgive him anytime soon."

He told her about the horrible devastation to the British lines as they tried to climb the hill once, then twice; how they lost numbers so staggering it seemed unfathomable that they would try again. But they did. And then he told her about the terror of realizing the ammunition had run out, of seeing those red coats pouring into the redoubt, killing militiamen with a vigor borne of their own pain and grief and frustration. He told her about losing Warren and, daring to raise his eyes to meet hers, told her what he had done to Chastain. Struggling mightily against the dredged up emotion, he told her about losing Ezra Dibble and so many others whose names he did not know but whose loss he mourned, nonetheless.

But he did not tell her about the encounter with Hinton. He had made it a practice not to discuss Hinton with her, and especially not their conflicts, because he was afraid it would suggest that she choose sides — and he was afraid of which side she would choose.

Mrs. Cook came into the room, quietly closing the door behind her. "I am sorry," she whispered, "but I thought you should know the lieutenant is here." Neither Anna nor Daniel had to ask which lieutenant she meant. "Your uncle is entertaining him."

"I should go," Daniel said, hastily getting to his feet.

"You needn't." Anna held out her hand to stop him. "I can have Mrs. Cook tell him I'm not up to seeing him today."

But Daniel shook his head. "I've stayed too long already. Your uncle is being very generous in allowing me to visit so freely. I wouldn't want to impose on that generosity, and I certainly don't want to put him in an awkward position with the redcoats." He started toward the door, but stopped midway, turning to grin at her. "Happy birthday, Mouse."

"What?" Her mind was on formulating some way to make him stay a bit longer, so she did not at first understand what he'd said.

"Your birthday. It was only a few days ago, wasn't it?"

"Yes, as a matter of fact, it was. My nineteenth. How odd that you'd remember. You remembered once before — when I was in London. I assumed someone had told you, though I couldn't imagine who. Did your mother say something about it?"

"I can never forget your birthday," he snorted. "You made a point of insisting that I wish you a happy birthday on the event each year when we were children. Do you remember?"

"Oh, dear," she sighed. "I had forgotten until you just reminded me." She stared at him, a deep frown appearing on her brow. "I've often been an insufferable and difficult friend to you, haven't I?"

He took a step back toward her, and opened his mouth to deny the charge and, further, to confess his heart. But his notion of his unsuitability for her took hold and he told her instead, "You were. Quite insufferable and difficult. You've always been worth the effort, however." Forcing himself into an insouciant grin, he bowed and started once again toward the door.

"Take care, Daniel." It was such a ridiculous thing to say, but it was all she *could* say. It was said in a tone of voice that made him pause, though. When he looked back at her, she said, "The threads of our lives have become entangled in quite the Gordian Knot, haven't they?"

"Yes, I suppose they have."

"Lieutenant Hinton's uncle once – quite presciently, as it turns out – said to me that duty and honor, loyalty, friendship, and even family all can become a Gordian Knot in our lives, and that one must choose carefully the sword they will use to pick apart that knot."

Daniel watched her expression and considered her words. "And, what sword would you choose?"

"A sword of heart and conscience, I believe."

"That is two swords."

"Not in my view," she replied. "For me, my heart and my conscience are quite inextricably linked."

Daniel grinned, for it was exactly what he was counting on. "I must go, Mouse. I'll take care. And, I won't be far away."

*   *   *

Edward did not accept the chair she offered, choosing instead to stand with his back to her, looking out the window. They had exchanged pleasantries — rather stiffly he thought — and he had assured himself that she was mending satisfactorily. Now he stood, looking at the view from her uncle's window, searching for his next words. He caught a glimpse of Daniel and Drum slipping away from the house, and inwardly bristled. Further, and for the first time, he realized he could just see the hills of the Charlestown Peninsula from here. *That bloody hill!* Anger, which had plagued him since returning to Boston, regained its hold on him.

"It is inexcusable, really. I believe we were overly confident." He swallowed hard against the knot of bitterness gripping his throat. "We lost so many. Estimates are forty-five percent lost. London will never stand for that. And, a disproportionate number were officers." He turned to look at her. "We lost Major Pitcairn. He was one of the finest officers in the entire army, and he is gone!"

"I am sorry," she said. "I know it's a personal blow to you as well."

"Are you sorry?"

The sharpness of his tone startled her. "I beg your pardon?"

"Are you sorry we lost so many men?"

"Of course I am! What a preposterous thing to ask!"

"I heard one of the generals say that, if the British army as a whole were to enjoy five more such victories, the king would have no army left." His mouth twisted with irony. "And, the rebels are crowing that they would gladly sell us more real estate at the same price."

"They are not all crowing."

"Aren't they?"

"No. They lost many as well."

"Not enough, in my view," he snapped. "Besides, they would have to lose a hundred or more men to every one of ours before they would begin to suffer as we do! They know how difficult it will be for us to replace every man we lose."

"What a horrible thing to say! Someone suffers over every life lost or destroyed! What difference does it make whether the man was wearing a red coat or a brown one? What difference does it make whether he was an officer, or not? If he was someone's husband or son or father — what difference does it make? You speak as if those men were nothing more than pawns on a chess board!"

"I did not intend it that way, and I apologize for upsetting you. Of course each of the lives lost is a tragedy." He turned away from the window and looked across the room toward her. "I saw Mr. Garrett leaving here just now." He had blurted it out quite suddenly, and regretted the fact immediately, for it had not been his plan to mention it.

"He is a friend," she said simply, "and, his mother is staying with us." It was an explanation, not an apology for Daniel's visit.

"Friend or no, under the circumstances, do you think it is appropriate to entertain him?"

She tried to make out his shadowed face, silhouetted against the window behind him. It was far easier to see the dazzling day outside the window, and she felt her eyes drawn away from the shadows and toward the brilliant blue sky beyond. "His mother is staying here while she recovers. It would seem far less appropriate to deny her the company of her son."

He studied her, his face full of a question he was reluctant to put into words. "You will continue as friends?"

She shrugged. "I cannot imagine otherwise."

"I suspect he imagines otherwise." He'd said it bitterly, and almost under his breath.

"I'm afraid you have lost me," she replied baldly. "Are you suggesting that Mr. Garrett would forsake my friendship?"

"I am suggesting that Mr. Garrett would like to be far more than just a friend."

She gaped at him. "If you think that, then you have observed very little regarding the nature of my relationship with him."

"On the contrary. I have observed a great deal in that regard."

Anna felt her face flush. "Have you? Mrs. Garrett says that I am fueled by dreams, while her son is fueled by fire. It seems an observation that is quite on point, and likely explains why he and I cannot seem to agree on the best way even to cross the street."

Hinton's thoughts returned to the battle. "Sometimes, dreams and fire are a powerful combination," he said bitterly. "If we learned nothing more from our *victory*, it should be that."

Anna looked at him, blinking in surprise at the comment, not certain how to respond. "What fuels you?"

"Duty, I suppose."

"Yes, I believe that's accurate. It's an admirable quality."

"But there are other qualities you find more admirable?"

"Not necessarily," she shrugged. "One cannot say that any one personal quality is necessarily more admirable than another. Perhaps it depends upon one's orbit. I think in your world, to be driven by duty would be of paramount importance. On the other hand, in my little world, love and loyalty transcend just about everything else."

"I had believed our worlds to be one and the same."

She looked at him for several drawn-out moments, weighing the response that had sprung immediately to mind. "A week ago," she said carefully, "I would have agreed with you. And yet, I realize that I knew five years ago — practically the moment I arrived in London, really — that they are not the same at all. I have hoped I was wrong, but admit now that our worlds are, indeed, irreconcilably different."

"Then, perhaps it is time for me to go." He picked up his hat, and not without a certain amount of anger.

"I am sorry, Lieutenant Hinton. Truly, I am."

He hesitated as though he might respond, but said nothing. Instead, he bowed to her and took his leave. As the door closed, Anna was surprised to find that she was not sorry to see him go.

*   *   *

Drum was waiting outside the back door for Daniel. Mrs. Cook had given him some corn fritters, so the waiting was certainly not something he minded. It was a fine June day, sunny and clear and full of summer-day promise. When Daniel emerged, Drum stood up and handed him the corn fritter he'd saved for him.

"Thanks." Daniel bit into the fritter and started walking away from the house.

"I think I saw that redcoat going into the house," Drum said, falling into step beside Daniel.

"You did. But you needn't sound so concerned. I didn't encounter him."

"I wasn't concerned about you. Is he here to see Miss Anna?"

"I'm sure he is."

"That's what concerns me."

"Why?"

"What if he asks her to marry him?"

Daniel hesitated slightly before responding. "She won't marry him."

"Are you sure about that?"

"As sure as I can be about anything she does."

"But, what if she does? Is that what you want?"

"It doesn't matter what I want. If she feels he's the right man for her, then she should marry him, I suppose. But she won't."

"But I thought you—"

Daniel stopped abruptly and turned to face him. "Drop it, Drum. I do not want to talk about Miss Anna right now, understand?"

"But—"

"*Do you understand?*"

Drum pursed his lips and frowned at Daniel. "Yes," he replied finally.

"Good." Daniel turned on his heel and started walking again, the muscle in his jaw clenching visibly.

Drum walked about ten paces before the compulsion overtook him. "But you don't want her to go away to England, do you?"

"No."

"And, you don't want her to marry that redcoat lieutenant, do you?"

"No."

"But did you tell her that?"

"No." Daniel was practically growling at him.

"Why not? Teague said if you didn't tell her you love her, she might marry him, instead, and that would be bad."

"Dammit, Drum!" Flushed with anger, Daniel whirled on him. *How did they know?* he wondered. *Was it that obvious?* He glared at Drum's earnest face. "At the risk of being disrespectful to Teague's memory, I'd like to point out that he was perhaps not the best person to be dispensing advice regarding women."

"But—"

"Enough, Drum! Let. It. Go!" Daniel sighed and, looking up the street while he gathered his thoughts, forced his posture to relax. He did not like to be sharp with Drum, and regretted his tone. "Do I want her to marry him? No. I don't. But it isn't up to me, is it? And, as far as telling her how I feel," his voice cracked slightly, "I just can't. I have nothing to offer her right now. I cannot give her what the Edward Hintons of the world can give her. Please understand that and let it go. Please?"

Drum was not certain he understood, but he nodded nonetheless. He and Daniel started walking again, and Drum waited a while before asking, "What will you do now?"

"I'm of a mind to collect that rifle the woman gave me on that hillside near Concord and find someone who can teach me to use it properly. Maybe someone in General Washington's new army can help. I don't know yet if I'm going to join them, but I was planning to go out to Cambridge to see what sort of man Washington is. Beyond that, I really don't have much of a plan."

"I want to come with you."

Daniel stopped walking and turned to face him. "I don't think that's a good idea, Drum."

"You never think it's a good idea, but I always end up following you anyway, so I don't see why you try to make me stay behind."

Daniel opened his mouth to respond but, seeing Drum's point, closed it again.

"I want to go with you," Drum repeated. "I don't have to stay if I don't like it, but I at least want to go with you and find out. I want to make up my own mind about it."

"Very well, then," Daniel sighed. He turned, clapping Drum on the back as he did so, and set off once more up the street. "Let's go see what we think of General Washington, shall we?"

Indeed, people all over the colonies were waiting to see what General Washington was made of. Like them, Daniel could not have guessed how long the years or how many the miles it would take for the question to be fully answered. Nor could he know the part he, Drum, and Anna would play, the many paths they would have to travel, or how it would further test their loyalties, and bonds of friendship and affection. They, like the rest of the colonies, were soon to discover.

ABOUT THE AUTHOR

S. D. Banks lives and works in Austin, Texas. She holds a Bachelor of Arts in history from Texas State University, where she also studied writing. Banks is a member of the Writers' League of Texas. You may contact her at: sdbanks60@icloud.com.

With Gratitude

No words can fully express my gratitude to my personal support group, all of whom contributed to the tough job of keeping me going whenever my confidence or my muse failed to show up for the day.

I particularly want to thank my husband, Lee, who gives me time and space in which to write, and who puts up with my tendency to choose vacation destinations based on their historical significance. Also, my sister-in-law, Karen Huston, who has taken every opportunity over the years to ask, "When are you going to write a book?" until I finally sat down and actually did it.

Anita Mosel, Denise Mitchell, Amber Yates, Michele Barker, and Christine Hodges have been very generous with their time, selflessly serving as critics and proof-readers whenever asked. Any typos in this book are there only because human eyes miss things, not because we didn't try to catch them all.

Linda Nickell is an unflagging cheerleader and possessor of an unbelievable network of friends, which can be mined for information on such diverse topics as swords, poison, and viable suturing materials.

Finally, I'd like to thank Beth Watkins. Beth offered her considerable copy editing talents to help me identify my worst writing tendencies, and maintained her enthusiasm even as she waded through my unwieldy manuscript. Any flaws in the copy editing of this book are not Beth's fault, by the way, but are probably the result of my own stubbornness.

Made in the USA
Charleston, SC
18 August 2016